KENNETH ROBERTS

Rabble in Arms

DOWN EAST BOOKS

CAMDEN, MAINE

To Booth Tarkington,
without whose generous guidance
the Chronicles of Arundel would
still be unwritten

Copyright © 1933, 1947 by Kenneth Roberts. All rights reserved.
Published by arrangement with Doubleday, a division of
Bantam Doubleday Dell publishing Group, Inc.
ISBN 0-89272-386-6
Cover illustration: *Benedict Arnold and Men*, oil on canvas,
by N. C. Wyeth. Hood Museum of Art, Dartmouth College,
Hanover, N.H. Gift of Kenneth Roberts.
Map by Kathy Bray.
Color separation: Roxmont Graphics
Printed and bound at Capital City Press, Inc., Montpelier, Vt.

2   4   6   8   9   7   5   3   1

Down East Books, Camden, Maine

LIBRARY OF CONGRESS CATALOGING-IN-PUBLICATION DATA
Roberts, Kenneth Lewis, 1885–1957.
    Rabble in arms / Kenneth Roberts.
    p.   cm.
    ISBN 0-89272-386-6 (pbk.)
        1. United States--History--Revolution, 1775–1783--Fiction.
    2. Arnold, Benedict, 1774–1801--Fiction.   I. Title.
    PS3535.0176R33   1996
    813'.52--dc20   96-19617
                                                              CIP

"I despise my Countrymen. I wish I could say I was not born in America. I once gloried in it but am now ashamed of it. The Rascally Stupidity which prevails, the Insults and Neglects which the army have met with, Beggars all description. It must go no farther. They can endure it no longer. I am in Rags, have lain in the Rain on the Ground for 40 hours past, & only a Junk of fresh Beef & that without Salt to dine on this day, rec'd no pay since last December, & all this for my Cowardly Countrymen who flinch at the very time when their exertions are wanted, & hold their Purse Strings as tho they would Damn the World, rather than part with a Dollar to their Army."

—*Colonel Ebenezer Huntington to his brother, 1780.*

"Benedict Arnold's country and the world owe him more than they will ever liquidate; and his defection can never obliterate the solid services and the ample abuse which preceded it."

—Rev. J. F. Schroeder; *Life and Times of Washington.*

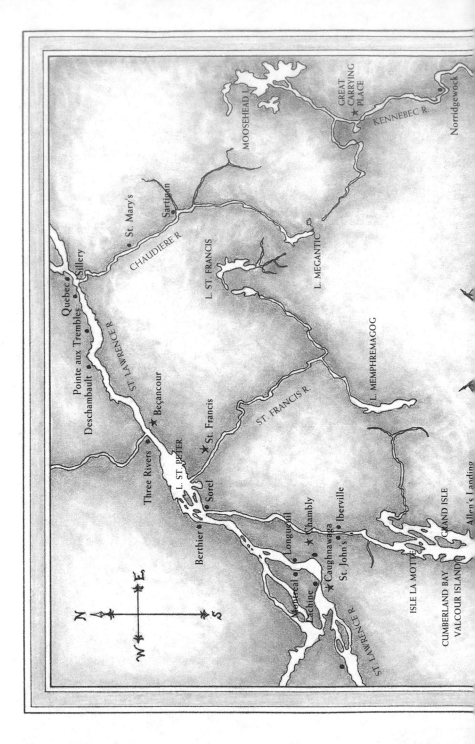

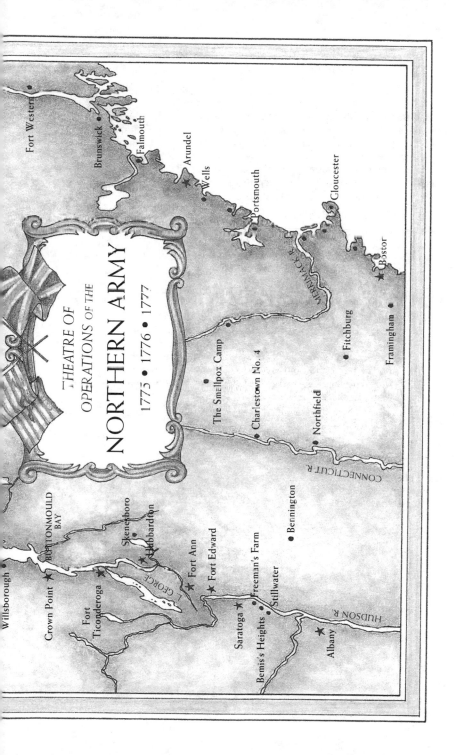

THEATRE OF
OPERATIONS OF THE

NORTHERN ARMY

1775 • 1776 • 1777

Fort Western

Brunswick
Falmouth
Arundel
Wells
Portsmouth
Gloucester
Boston

MERRIMACK R.

Fitchburg
Framingham

The Smallpox Camp
Charlestown No. 4
Northfield

CONNECTICUT R.

Willsborough
Crown Point
BUTTONMOULD BAY
Skenesboro
Hubbardton
Fort Ticonderoga
L. GEORGE
Fort Ann
Fort Edward
Bennington
Saratoga
Freeman's Farm
Stillwater
Bemis's Heights
Albany

HUDSON R.

"*We are starving*, and unless something very efficacious for the supply of the army is done very speedily, we must disband or turn *freebooters*—an evil of almost as much magnitude as the first. You have much influence with members of Congress. I entreat you to make them sensible of the risk to which they are exposing their country, and of the double risk to which they expose themselves; for it begins to be a prevailing sentiment, both in the army and in the country, that a party among them has been bribed to drive things into confusion."

—*General St. Clair to Joseph Reed, 1780.*

"*I see nothing before us but accumulating distress. We have been half our time without provisions and are like to continue so. We have no Magazines nor money to form them. And in a little time we shall have no Men, if we had Money to pay them. We have lived upon expedients until we can live no longer. In a word, the history of the War is a history of false hopes and temporary devices, instead of system and economy.*"

—*George Washington to Cadwalader, 1780.*

"Arnold displayed more real military genius and inspiration than all the generals put together, on both sides, engaged in the war, with the most undaunted personal courage."

—*Charles Knight; History of England,* Vol. I, p. 430.

"A rabble in arms, flushed with success and insolence."

> —*General Burgoyne to Lord Rochfort*
> *describing American troops before*
> *Boston.*

I

It was Cap Huff who said that no business or profession, not even the managing of a distillery, can provide the profusion of delights to be encountered in a good war. I have not found it so; and for my part I want no more of such delights as the powder-blackened faces of the men who died beside us aboard the row-galleys on Lake Champlain, the painted masks of the greasy Indians that laid us by the heels, and the dreadful labors we endured before we stopped the British. Unfortunately I have others to consider; and it is for their sakes that I recall the burdens of those nightmare days.

In the beginning I must say that this is no book for those who swear by old wives' fables, holding all Americans brave, all Englishmen honorable and all Frenchmen gallant. It cannot please such innocents as are convinced that men in public office always set the nation's welfare above their own, nor those who think all soldiers patriots. It will disappoint the credulous who cherish the delusion that patriotism burns high in every breast in the hour of a country's peril. In it there is scant fare for romantics who wish to hear how courage and ability bring greater recognition than mediocrity and bluster, how virtue always triumphs, and how cowards meet a fitting retribution. Those who crave such poppycock must turn to fairy tales for undeveloped minds; for I am obliged to deal with facts and write what I conceive to be the truth.

. . . My father's letter was delivered to me in our London lodgings, early on a March evening in 1776. When the letter arrived, my brother Nathaniel and I were on the point of setting out for Ranelagh, the occasion being a special entertainment at that resort of fashion because of somebody's birthday: the Queen's, it may have been, or that of one of the King's innumerable royal relatives in Germany.

We had learned that upon such anniversaries it was usual for the King himself to visit Ranelagh, and that on this account dukes and generals and statesmen who wished to be seen in the train of royalty would be there, making a show that brought women off the street, shopkeepers hunting for new mistresses, shopkeepers' wives looking for adventure, and young bucks out to make themselves disagreeable to as many people as possible.

We had never been to Ranelagh, Nathaniel and I; and Nathaniel was eager to go, not only because he might see famous folk, but because he could write familiarly about the place to his college classmates in Boston.

When, therefore, Nathaniel caught sight of the name "Capt. Asa Merrill" written above the red seal on the letter's back, he said, "Put it by, Peter, until we get to Ranelagh. We'll never be there if you wait to translate it now!"

He was impetuous, my brother was: airy and a trifle English in his speech from attending Harvard College, where he had associated with Boylstons, Doanes and other codfish aristocrats. It was like him to speak of translating my father's letter: a little disrespectful, certainly; yet not far from the truth; for my father was a bad speller, able to spell almost any word in several fashions, all of them wrong.

I thrust the letter into my pocket, letting Nathaniel have his way, which I may have done too often for his own good.

The truth was that a large part of my thoughts revolved around Nathaniel—not only because he was my mother's favorite and because he had always looked to me for help and guidance during his younger days, but because I saw in him the instrument by means of which our family might, through its shipping interests, become a power in the Province of Maine, just as had the Hancocks and the Derbys and the Bowditches in Massachusetts, and the Palmers in Connecticut.

He was not cut out for a mariner, to my way of thinking, having an aversion to loneliness and a leaning toward the society of his equals. There is as much of one, on a long cruise, as there is little of the other; and I knew from observation that if he were forced to be a seaman against his will, he would not be the first in that situation to take to the bottle.

This very sociability of his, however, fitted in with my purpose; for men as well as women took to him immediately; and what was more important, he wore well, which is not often the case with those who seem companionable at first sight. Consequently I could ask no better agent for the handling of our freights in some likely port—Canton, say, or Malaga, where fortunes may be made quickly by a shipowner working in conjunction with an agent who has no other interests to serve. It was for this reason that I had interceded with my father to send Nathaniel to Harvard; and now that he had received a proper education, topping it off with a course under me in carrying and disposing of cargoes, I had high hopes for him and the future. My father had a knack for getting stout brigs built, and I knew how to sail them: we had our own shipyard in Arundel—and so, if Nathaniel expressed a wish to do a thing, I humored him, after the fashion of an older brother who has built fond dreams around a younger.

We walked over to the muddy Strand; then off up the river to the gardens and rotunda of Ranelagh.

It was well we walked; for by the time we had covered two-thirds of the mile that separated those winter pleasure-grounds from the central portion of London, the coaches of the pleasure-seekers were so wedged together in the roadway that their occupants, we thought, would be hours in reaching their destination.

. . . I might say here that people have spoken to me, often, as though it were astonishing for two Americans to be in London at a time when we were at war with England; but their wonderment is due only to their lack of understanding.

England considered herself not at war, but almost at peace with her American colonies, and merely annoyed and disgusted by the rebellious hypocrites with which New England, according to the belief of most Englishmen, was entirely populated.

Why it was that the English regarded us as hypocrites for refusing to submit to their tyranny, I have never exactly understood; but that was the fact of it. We were rebellious, praying hypocrites; and that belief, I fear, will never be allowed to die in stubborn Albion.

At all events, England reasoned that hypocrites would succumb more readily to force than to justice; and while she stabbed at the rebels with one hand, she held out an olive branch with the other; and on all sides there was constant expectation that the olive branch would be gratefully accepted—either through poverty or timidity.

London was sprinkled with Americans—a thousand of them, maybe: wealthy and influential persons who had come to England to escape lawless English-haters in America. I had avoided them, my feelings being what they were; for I wanted no arguments with any man until my father's specie was safely home; but I'm bound to say they were fine people except as regards their admiration for England.

There were even Englishmen who sympathized with our rebels, as I well knew from repeated readings of Dr. Price's book on Civil Liberty —a book that had come to seem as valuable to me as the other small volumes I carried on all my voyages: the Bible, *Tristram Shandy*, *Don Quixote*, *Roderick Random* and *Gulliver's Travels*: books which, if read with care and fully digested, will give a man more learning than he can get from a score of colleges put together.

Dr. Price's book had recently been published in London, and had been widely read by the English, though it maintained that England could commit no greater folly than to seek to keep our liberty from us. Consequently even a rebellious American could live peaceably in England, provided he was judicious in his speech, and kept his mouth shut when tempted to speak impulsively—which, after all, is a requisite of peace everywhere.

. . . The English are easily satisfied with their own belongings, I have found, and still more easily amused by matters amusing to no one else; so I was prepared to be disappointed in the Ranelagh rotunda, which every Londoner considers more magnificent than anything in Egypt or Greece. But when I found myself under that great inverted bowl and looking up into it, I was amazed and full of admiration. Its airy space was so enormous that the throng of finely dressed folk who strolled slowly about its floor had the dwarfed look of ants moving aimlessly on the bottom of a vast round box. The roof was supported by a tremendous eight-sided column, hollow. Within the column a bright fire flamed and danced, so that the place had warmth.

All around the room were arcades, a table set in each one; and above the arcades were boxes, similarly equipped with tables. At one side of the main entrance was an elevated platform, and over it a sounding board; and on the platform was an orchestra of fifty pieces, all playing away for dear life. The place was filled with the gay and stirring sound, though there was nothing happening save hundreds of people walking slowly around and around, ignoring each other.

It had cost us a guinea to get into this pleasure resort, which seemed to me enough to pay for a night's entertainment; but Nathaniel, who had little regard for money, never having had to earn much of it, was of a different mind.

As we stood at the entrance, staring about us, Nathaniel plucked at my sleeve and pointed to an arcade-box done out in red brocade.

"The royal box!" he exclaimed.

He dragged me across the circular floor, walked boldly to the box beside the royal enclosure and made as though to enter. A lackey jumped up in it, his nose in the air, and said, "Resarved for Lard Jarge Germain."

Nathaniel swung me into the adjoining box, and almost before I knew what had happened he had pushed me into a chair at its table and dropped into a seat across from me.

A waiter came in and stared at us angrily. But Nathaniel, who was skilled at aping the English, turned to him and said haughtily, "What is it, my man?"

On this the waiter became ill at ease, and mumbled that the box was reserved.

Nathaniel seemed pained. "I won't be spoken to in such a way!" He appealed to me. "Do you suppose the clown doesn't know who I am? Throw five shillings on the floor for him, Sir Peter! Not another farthing, mind! And have him bring us a bit of ham, eh, Sir Peter? And a quart of rack punch, by Ged!"

The waiter, at once obsequious, took the five shillings I tossed him and darted from the box with such alacrity that he tripped over the curtains.

"Look here!" I told Nathaniel. "You'll get us into trouble if you call me Sir Peter; and we can't be spending like a couple of dukes."

Nathaniel smiled at me affectionately. "The ham's a shilling a plate, and the punch seven shillings a quart. Only two dollars, Peter, for sitting in a box beside the box that's next to the box where sat the King of England, and having an experience your grandchildren will be bragging about a hundred years from now!"

What he said was probably true; for a king is a king, even though weak in the head. Therefore I made no further protest and we listened to the orchestra and watched the throngs parading slowly around and around, like a school of pollock following one another's tails in and out of a cove in the Arundel River, each one goggle-eyed with brainlessness.

How the paraders could imagine they were taking pleasure was beyond me; for the entire gathering had the air of despising everything and everyone. Yet for Nathaniel and myself it was as exciting as a play at Drury Lane; and as the evening went on it became more so.

Our platter of ham arrived, and the bowl of rack punch; and the thinness of the slices of ham was something remarkable—something that proved the carver a master craftsman, both with knife and niggardliness. As soon as Nathaniel saw the ham before him, he examined it with an air of incredulity; then said, "Peter, where's Father's letter?"

As I felt in my pocket for it, I was conscious of a perfume so sweet and so arresting that I looked up suddenly, as if the scent of violets that filled the air had been a hand laid upon me to gain my attention. My eyes went beyond Nathaniel, and encountered, standing before the adjoining box, which we had been told was Germain's, a lady in a dress of pink brocade, and a tall, languid gentleman in black.

The lady was beautifully slender and rounded. A pink turban bound her head, and from under it two half moons of golden hair curved down, lying tight upon her cheeks and concealing her ears. Her eyes were blue, the blue of a summer sea in the morning; and beneath her eyes was a dust of freckles that made her look too young and innocent to be in such a place as this.

Beautiful as she was, her companion was equally striking. He was all in black satin: black coat, black knee breeches, black vest and stockings and shoes; but he wore a white wig; and at his throat was a cascade of white lace. In this white frame was set a placid, olive-tinted face: a face that seemed to slumber, because of the way in which its eyelids drooped. There was no look of weariness to him, despite those drooping lids: merely a sort of quiet relaxation: a kind of suspended animation.

Even as Nathaniel took the letter from me, I heard the girl in pink speaking to the lackey in the next box. I couldn't hear the words; but her voice was soft; and when the answer came, she turned a little doubtfully in our direction.

It was then that Nathaniel, having opened the letter, picked up a paper-thin slice of ham and held it before his face, so that he appeared to be reading the letter through it. Since the orchestra ceased playing at that moment, his words must have been clearly heard by the lady and her escort.

"Dated from Arundel in the Province of Maine," Nathaniel announced. "My dear sons:—I hope while you are in England you will go to Ranelagh and learn how to cut one ham into slices so thin there'll be a slice for every man in the army."

I reached over and took the letter from him none too gently. He winked at me and whisked the slice of ham into his mouth. The lady's escort raised a sleepy eyelid at my sudden movement; but the lady herself stared frankly, as if fascinated by what Nathaniel had said.

I looked at the letter, and saw Nathaniel had been joking. The words that met my eyes were not about ham, but were ominous, and so not difficult to read, despite my father's dreadful spelling:

The winter finds us well, and still something to eat and it is the hoap of your mother and me that these Fue lines find you the saim. I have a change of hart about your staing in England until the rebellion should be over, as it now appeers God knows when that will be. Thare is talk on all sides that America must be a sepperate country by itself. Those who are suspecktit of wishing to come to a peaceabil arranjement with England are in danger of losing thare property, thare hoams and thare verry lives. Thare are some who suspeckt us because you still remane in England. Tharefour if you can come saif home with the speshie, I would say come. I will leave it to Peter's judgement. God knows we need the speshie. Thare is no money to be had anywhere, only paper money not worth mutch. Everyboddy is pore except those who become ritch out of our distress, and thare is no money to provide our army with powder or unaforms or pay. The British burnt Falmouth, leaving near 2000 women and children without rooves, cloathes or food for the winter whitch was a hard one. Steven Nason is hoam from Quebeck, where Nathaniel Lord was killt, and 18 men from Arundel captivatit by the British, among them Noah Cluff, who workt in our shipyard. Steven says the men not killt or captivatit will go on fiting, even if they fite with nothing but axes. . . .

II

I STARED at my father's small handwriting, straight and regular, but somewhat trembly. The orchestra was playing again, a rollicking air that the young bucks liked to sing—*The World Turned Upside Down*. I seemed to smell the lilacs that flank our front door in Arundel and to hear the babble of my sisters, as I so often heard it when they were young, playing with their dolls in the crotches of the gnarled apple tree beside the kitchen. Dimly I heard Nathaniel singing beneath his breath:

> *What happy golden days were those*
> *When I was in my prime!*
> *The lasses took delight in me,*
> *I was so neat and fine;*
> *I roved about from fair to fair,*
> *Likewise from town to town,*
> *Until I married me a wife*
> *And the world turned upside down.*

Phrases came out from the letter, striking into the back of my eyes, so that they ached a little. ". . . still something to eat . . . losing their property, their homes and their very lives . . . some who suspect us because you . . . the British burned Falmouth . . . the men not killed will go on fighting. . . ."

Nathaniel stopped his humming and looked at me anxiously. "What's the matter? It's not bad news, is it?"

Before I could answer, a figure loomed close beside us. It was the white-wigged man in black, and he bowed to us profoundly, as though we were personages.

"You forgive this intrusion, I hope," he said to me. His voice was almost a whisper, and he raised his eyelids with difficulty, as if they were weighted. "My niece, a countrywoman of yours—"

He stopped, so that it was easy to see he was by nature a silent man. Behind him the girl in pink gazed indifferently at the throng of people who moved slowly before us, circling and circling the arcaded hall in time to the strumming of the orchestra.

"So she's American!" I exclaimed. Nathaniel craned around the edge of the box to see her better.

The man in black bowed and gave us a sleepy smile. "We could not avoid hearing when you read your letter through the ham. My niece, Marie, she said you were Americans and might permit us to share your box."

Our reply made it plain we would feel privileged to have their company; whereupon he turned and beckoned to his niece. She came to us with a pretty air of being modestly confused by the lack of ceremony in such a meeting, and with her came a sharp, penetrating fragrance of violets that seemed, like a single glass of fine wine, to stimulate and sharpen all my senses.

"You're most obliging to permit this intrusion," she said, taking the chair we offered her. "Your kindness—I said to my uncle you'd be kind, being Americans—we had asked for a box near the King; but they're occupied, all of them."

"Well," I said, "what's your loss is our gain!" I thought guiltily of the manner in which Nathaniel had forced his way into the box, which might readily belong to these very people; and I attempted to atone by making a flowery speech. "Indeed, ma'am, there's only one trouble with having you in this box. If the King sets eyes on you, he'll want to steal you into his own: then we shall be bereft."

She had a way of lifting blue eyes and staring hard into a man's face: then smiling suddenly, a sweet, tremulous smile. This she did to me when I had finished my blundering speech and sat there, feeling hot and foolish. Yet, oddly, at her smile there flashed into me a little doubt that she was as young and innocent as she appeared. From the first day I went to sea my father had told me again and again: "Be sure you see what you look at, whether it's clouds or a lee shore or a man's face: there's nothing so useful to a sea captain." So I looked at her carefully. It seemed to me there were hints about her mouth that might emphasize themselves into hard lines upon occasion; and that her blue eyes were amazingly cool in their scrutiny of Nathaniel and me.

"What good fortune!" she said. "What pleasure to meet with Americans in such a nest of—such a nest of——" She looked helplessly at us, seemingly at a loss.

Thinking to test her sympathies, I suggested "Lobster-backs," an epithet New Englanders had applied to the English for many years.

She seemed prettily shocked, and looked at me roguishly. "Such a word!" Then she accepted it. "In such a nest of lobster-backs: yes! I feared when we came here a few days since, that I would be the only

American in the entire country. My uncle, you see, is Canadian: Mr. Leonard."

Mr. Leonard bowed to us and smiled. Already we had come to take his silence for granted, just as did his niece, who was quick to supply the words he seemed to find such difficulty in saying.

She nodded brightly at him, explaining him to us as she might have explained a bit of jewelry, unable to speak for itself. "A true Canadian, disgusted with the actions of these terrible English."

Her own name, she added, was more formidable than her uncle's. "It's French, and you may find it troublesome. Marie de Sabrevois. You must say it, please." I did so, and found nothing difficult about it.

"But," she told us, "I'm not at all French, in spite of my name. I'm entirely American—entirely. When you read a portion of your letter through the ham—and that was droll—I heard your home is in the Province of Maine."

"Arundel," I said.

"Yes: I do not know that place." She mispronounced it prettily. "You know Albany, perhaps? Or Poughkeepsie and New York?"

We shook our heads.

"That's where I have lived," she told us. "In all those places. Also a very little in Quebec, with my father. He was a fur merchant, my father was. A great fur merchant." She sighed. "He is dead: killed by the English. That's why I am here in England—to settle his affairs." She lowered her voice and leaned across the table to me, an appealing picture. "I'm sure it's the same with you as with me. You're eager to go home and be away from these terrible people—these terrible English!"

"Yes," I said.

Nathaniel coughed delicately behind his hand, an affectation he had acquired at Harvard. "You'll find worse places to be than here; worse people, too." He made it plain he thought I had received enough of the lady's attention, and wished some for himself. "We can't go home, anyway. We sold our ship."

Marie de Sabrevois looked at him curiously. "Your ship? You own a ship?"

"It was my father's," he told her. "Peter was captain and I was supercargo. We'd been to South America and the Spanish ports, and when we reached England we had a letter from my father saying that fighting had broken out; that we should sell the ship as well as the cargo, so his investment might be safe from seizure. Now we must stay until the war's over, and that won't be long."

"What makes you think so?" I asked, remembering my father's letter.

Nathaniel smiled. "What's the use of going over that again? Our country's got no money to fight England with, and no generals, and not many men."

"You don't know what we've got," I told him. "One thing we haven't got is a lot of rake-hells and nincompoops to direct our affairs."

Nathaniel turned to Mademoiselle de Sabrevois. "You see how it is. Peter thinks all English aristocrats must be rake-hells or nincompoops."

"Don't misquote me," I said. "I don't think they *must* be; but I think most of them *are*. I can prove it by Dr. Price's book."

Nathaniel laughed. "Your book! You can prove almost anything out of your book!"

"Yes," I said, "I can. Almost anything. No matter what bad thing I say about England, it can be proved out of *Roderick Random* or Dr. Price."

I drew Dr. Price's thin book from my side pocket, where I always carried it in case an Englishman took it into his head to force offensive misstatements on me. Since Price himself was English, I could quote from him without being condemned myself.

"Listen," I told Nathaniel. "Price says this: 'An abandoned venality, the inseparable companion of dissipation and extravagance, has poisoned the springs of public virtue among us.' That's the opinion of one wise Englishman: that his country has been brought to the brink of ruin by dissipation and extravagance."

"The trouble with Price, probably," Nathaniel said carelessly, "was that his dinner wasn't resting well when he wrote his book."

I looked at Marie de Sabrevois. Her face was blank, as if she were unaware of our argument, but I knew she had missed none of it. I could see she had heard worse things than I could ever say to Nathaniel, so I spoke to him sharply. "Before you discredit a man like Price, just bear in mind that every great man in England has a mistress or two. They brag of it. The country's sprinkled with illegitimate noblemen and generals, and they even brag of *that*. What's more, if there's a decent woman in polite society, you'd never suspect it after listening to the conversation of any of your London rakes."

I had it in mind to speak even more frankly; but then I saw Mademoiselle de Sabrevois staring over the top of her feather fan at a group of ladies and gentlemen who had detached themselves from the ever-circling crowd and were advancing to the box beside us.

The leader of the group was tall, with a white, contented face that had a sort of sheep-look to it. He was as tall, almost, as the silent Mr. Leonard; and he switched himself gently from side to side as he walked, which increased the self-satisfaction of his manner. He wore a white wig, and a suit of pale blue satin, and there was a showy ribbon of blue watered silk across his breast.

Clinging to his arm was a short, plump lady, young and vivacious, who took quick, tripping steps. She stared adoringly into the sheep-face of her escort, gabbling all the while in a way that did nothing to alter his blandness. She hopped up into the box like a gorgeous little tropical bird, casting a quick glance in our direction, as did some of the others in the party.

On that I looked at Marie de Sabrevois, and found her face hidden behind her fan—a singular thing, I thought, since I had never known a beautiful woman to shrink from the scrutiny of strange men.

"Do you know who that is?" I asked.

She seemed almost angry at my question. "How should I know who it is?" she retorted sharply. "We've been in England only a few days, my uncle and I!" Then she smiled and was sweet again, adding, "But I'd like to know."

It seems to me my dislike of Marie de Sabrevois crystallized at that moment. Her swift changes from coolness to caressing warmth made me uncomfortable inside: I found her gushes of sweetness almost as re-voltingly cloying as the pink-frosted cake I stole from our pantry as a boy and ate in the haymow, to the detriment of the hay. I trust my feelings sprang not wholly from vanity, though it is true that I perceived her to be a woman who never in this world could possess any interest whatever in so outspoken and plain a young man as myself.

"Well," I said, "the next box is Lord Germain's, we were told. There's no doubt the tall man in blue is Lord Germain. It's he who has charge of sending troops to America, and I understand has something to say in planning what they shall do, once they're there."

Above the music of the orchestra we could hear the gabbling of the new arrivals. "Stop your teasing, Peggy!" a man's voice said. "I'll wager you'll be eaten by lions or chased by savages if you persist in going to that wilderness. Stay in London where you'll be safe."

"Shafe!" a woman cried. Her speech was slurred, as if from liquor, and I knew it was the tropical bird. "Shafe! You know nothing about it, Mel! 'Tisn't a wilderness: it's like a regatta on the Thames! I shaw it all on the map. Jack showed it to me. After you leave Quebec, you come to lakes, beautiful lakes, and then to Hush'n River; and before you know it, you're in New York. Ain't you, my lord?"

I looked at Nathaniel, to make sure he heard. "Listen to that!" I said. "Just a pleasure jaunt from Quebec to New York!"

An arrogant voice cut in: that of the man who had been called "my lord," and certainly, therefore, the voice of Germain. "She's quite right,

Mevil. If she wants to join Burgoyne, I'll be the first to say yes. The rebels won't bother her! They'll run like sheep when they see the regulars. You heard what Jack said about them: they're beggars—rabble! Officered by shoemakers: butchers: barbers!"

Incredulous laughter greeted his words.

"'Pon my soul, it's true!" Germain went on. "Not one of their officers, not even the best of 'em, but could be bought for a dollar a day! Peg'll be as safe over there—safer—than she'd be strolling in Hyde Park. Don't let me hear any further talk about its not being safe!"

Nathaniel eyed me drolly. "I don't believe it!" he declared. "Officers from our section, they wouldn't sell out for less than a dollar and a half a day!"

I looked at him. "That doesn't strike me as funny. I can tell you something much more amusing."

"Indeed!" Nathaniel said in his most indulgent Harvard manner.

"Yes, indeed! The gentleman you just heard—the gentleman who has charge of the war against our people—the gentleman who thinks we'll run like sheep and can all be bought—fifteen years ago there wasn't a man in England who didn't consider him a coward and a traitor! He was court-martialed for disobeying orders at the Battle of Minden, and was adjudged unfit to serve the King in any military capacity whatever. So now they let him make war against America!"

"Oh well," Nathaniel said lightly, "it goes to prove the English know how to take a joke, after all."

We were silent, the four of us. Not only was I angry at Germain, but I was worried by Nathaniel, with his apparent liking for the English—worried by the thought that some day his careless words might be misinterpreted, and bring trouble on him and others.

At the moment, however, what he said brought him no trouble at all, but something quite different. Marie de Sabrevois gave him a sidelong look: as her eyes caught his, she smiled entrancingly. The effect was immediate. Nathaniel's air of carelessness disappeared: his glance returned hers warmly. Nay, he seemed to need to memorize every soft curve and faint freckle of her pretty face. Then, when she turned toward me, he watched her as though his very life depended on missing no syllable of what she said.

"Did you hear them speak of Burgoyne—of the one they called Jack?" she asked me. "We've heard about him and his army, and it does not amuse us. Have you heard about it yet?"

"No."

"I think it must be true, what Germain was saying," she murmured, lifting sad eyes to mine. "The troops under Burgoyne are the best and bravest in the entire British army, and with them are going the most skillful officers. Our poor Americans will be able to do nothing against them. There'll even be Hessian troops with Burgoyne: great fighters."

"Hessians! Do you mean Germans?"

She nodded. "Under a general as fine as Frederick the Great, I'm told. And they say Indians will fight with him too: five thousand of them! It means the end of the war, you shall see! I mean, I'm afraid that's what it means."

The thought of so powerful and deadly an army howling and roaring down on our small towns and our defenseless people gave me a shivery feeling along my spine. But I sought not to believe such a thing possible. "Five thousand Indians!" I cried. "Why, there aren't that many anywhere in the east! They'd have to use western Indians! They wouldn't dare! That means"—I hesitated, thinking of the black forests that rise up from the opposite bank of our river in Arundel, and of my mother and my three sisters in the very shadow of the pointed pines— "that means we've got to go home."

"Home?" Nathaniel asked. "But Father said we were to stay."

"Not in this last letter," I said brusquely, and was sorry I had spoken; for Nathaniel was immediately indiscreet.

"Ah! So he wants us to come home," he said. "I suppose you're planning to take the first ship we can get?"

Marie de Sabrevois leaned over the table, enveloping us in a wave of violet perfume from her laces. "Splendid!" she whispered, and there seemed to be admiration in her eyes. "Splendid! If you and your brother can go safely, it's your duty to do so." Again she glanced up at Nathaniel; and his eyes clung to her. "Perhaps I haven't told you, but my uncle is returning to America in a few days. He will return safely: safely. If I thought otherwise, I wouldn't let him go. If you should wish to go by his ship, he could arrange it easily, I'm sure. It would be a privilege for him to have the company of such pleasant gentlemen."

Mr. Leonard bowed without speaking.

"What ship is that?" I asked. "What makes it safe?"

"A French ship," she said quickly. "One of the French ships that carry French officers to America. They're saying in Paris that Congress will commission any Frenchman who owns a sword and uniform—especially those with titles who can find nothing to do in France; so they've begun to hurry over, each one expecting to be placed in command of the entire American army. These gentlemen consider themselves too important to risk traveling by vessels that aren't quite, quite safe."

Never once, while Marie de Sabrevois was speaking, did Nathaniel take his eyes from her. When she had finished, he cleared his throat and said huskily: "Shall you go with your uncle?"

She looked up at him slowly, and as slowly looked away again—a glance that must, I was sure, have set the blood to pounding in his throat. "No," she said. "No. I cannot go back yet. Not yet. I have property in France that must be settled. My poor father has died." She sighed pathetically. "And so my uncle must return without me; for I have a ward—a little friend—a young girl, at school in—in Canada. It was this army of Burgoyne's that changed all our plans. While I attend to my property here, my uncle must return to my little ward and take her to a safe place before soldiers lay waste the country." She raised her eyes to Nathaniel's again, a sweet and candid glance.

I had a thought that schools in Canada, for the most part, were convent schools, and that the little ward of which the lady spoke was, in all likelihood, a Papist. That being so, the lady herself might even be a Papist; and to me the thought of Nathaniel entangled with a Papist was repellent.

For one thing, we have suffered from French Papists in our Province of Maine, and a man who follows after one of them is thought to be lost to his family and friends, and as good as damned. For another thing, I had already seen Nathaniel and the lady exchange soft speeches beneath their breaths—speeches in which, I told myself, a meeting might have been arranged. Nathaniel had often proved himself quick-witted, and certainly the lady had found him pleasing; and I had come to know that two such people can, in a few whispered words, lay plans enough to wreck a dozen lives.

I may say that I have prejudices; nevertheless I hope that I have always kept an open mind; and suddenly I saw that this chance meeting was a stroke of good fortune. If Mr. Leonard had a ship that was to sail soon, my brother and I were precisely in need of such a means of transportation. More, Mr. Leonard looked to be a man as resourceful and trustworthy as he was silent; and Marie de Sabrevois would not be upon his ship.

Impulsively I pushed back my chair from the table, bowed, and held out my hand to Mr. Leonard. "We're indebted," I said. "Indebted for the chance to go with you. When is it you sail for America?"

III

W<small>E WERE</small> driven in state to our lodgings by these new acquaintances of ours; and it was settled, when they left us, that Mr. Leonard would come for us, four mornings hence, and that we would set off together on our homeward travels.

As their coach clattered away toward the dim lights of the Strand, leaving behind it the heady perfume of violets, it seemed to me that Nathaniel's sigh was almost ecstatic. He was silent, too, climbing the stairs to our rooms; and this was unlike Nathaniel, who had something gay to say, usually, of everyone we met.

At length, knowing that the cleaner the break between Nathaniel and his enchantress, the sooner he would recover from his tender thoughts, I spoke my mind about her. "At Drury Lane the other night," I reminded him, "you had no patience with the actresses who played the parts of Goneril and Regan. They were unreal, you said. No woman of position, you maintained, could be so hard."

"Did I?" Nathaniel said indifferently.

I strove to speak mildly. "Nathaniel, you know I have your own good at heart, always; and I only say this for your own good. There was something about the lady we met tonight——"

The glance he shot at me was scornful. I hesitated, fumbling for words.

"So she put you in mind of Goneril and Regan?" he asked, with exaggerated politeness.

"If I'm not mistaken," I said, "she has much in common with them."

Nathaniel studied a picture on the wall, and laughed; and I thought best to ignore his manner of doing it.

"There's something behind that girl's face," I persisted. "For all her softness and sweetness, I'll warrant she's hard and bitter underneath."

Nathaniel softly whistled *The World Turned Upside Down* to show his lack of interest in my opinion. When I would have said more, he stopped me with an airy wave of his hand. "Never mind, Peter. Never mind. I liked her."

I saw, then, that he believed me to be jealous of him, and that whatever I might say would only nourish that belief. I felt myself burdened by a singular discomfort; for I longed to express myself more forcefully about Marie de Sabrevois; yet was unwilling to do so for fear the very expressing might cause a breach between Nathaniel and me.

My discomfort became even greater on the following evening. During the afternoon Nathaniel had left me at my father's agents and strolled off on private business of his own. I returned to our lodgings, expecting to find him there; but our rooms were empty. He might, I thought, have met a friend and dined with him. Later I told myself, though with some misgivings, that he must have gone on, after dinner, to a play. But as midnight passed, and then one o'clock, my misgivings became almost a panic. I visualized him beaten by footpads; run through by one of the young English bucks who were as free with their swords and their tempers as they were with their morals and other people's money I saw him, in my mind's eye, trampled into the mud of the turbulent, roaring Strand, or floating in the filthy waters of the Thames.

I must have fallen asleep around two. An hour later I wakened to see Nathaniel undoing his stock before the mirror, as unconcerned as though just back from an afternoon stroll in Hyde Park.

I lay for a while and watched him. I seemed to see, about his face, a little heaviness that was new to me. From time to time, as he laid off his garments in the candlelight, he smiled the fixed and foolish smile with which one contemplates, when alone, a pleasure more agreeable than amusing. Even before I caught from him a faint, elusive perfume of violets, I knew he had been with Marie de Sabrevois.

I coughed to let him know I was awake; but the only sign he gave of hearing me was to compose his face at once, as though his happy memories were sacred to himself alone. Seeing that he had no intention of saying anything, I asked him mildly whether he had enjoyed his evening. Nathaniel, rapt, at that moment, in examining in the mirror an imaginary something on his cheek, nodded and mumbled, and I took his mumble for assent.

"I suppose," I said, still good-naturedly, "I suppose you wouldn't want to tell me about it."

Nathaniel looked at me briefly over his shoulder and as briefly answered, "No."

The next night I took him to a play; but two nights later, the night before we were to depart, Nathaniel again escaped me while I superintended the packing of our specie, and again he disappeared. This time I knew with whom he was engaged; and I was in a ferment, but not at all surprised, when he was absent on this private business until four in the morning. He was flushed when he came back: a little excited; but beyond what showed in his face, he kept his feelings to himself. Not a word would he say to me.

My only feeling was one of thankfulness: thankfulness that we were leaving; for if ever I had seen a woman who seemed to me as dangerous as she was fascinating, it was Marie de Sabrevois.

o   o   o

. . . I was glad indeed when, a few hours later, our breakfast eaten and our belongings packed, there was a noisy whipcracking and clattering outside our lodgings. Here at last, I said to myself, was Mr. Leonard, bringing the means of escape from the blue-eyed girl who, in four short days, had made herself so ominous a part of our lives.

When I threw up the sash to look down into the street, my gladness was abruptly tempered; for two conveyances stood before our door. One was a dark green post chaise which must, of course, be Mr. Leonard's; but behind it stood an empty sedan chair that had a fluffy and feminine look about it.

It was no surprise, therefore, when Nathaniel, uttering a muffled exclamation, turned from the window and ran from the room, and when I saw, close beside the placid, olive-tinted visage of Mr. Leonard at the window of the chaise, the pretty face of Marie de Sabrevois.

When the hustle and bustle of our departure was mostly over, and the driver and postilion had lashed our heavy boxes to the rack, she emerged from the chaise, a dainty perfumed figure in blue velvet and brown fur, and bade us farewell then and there, kissing her uncle affectionately and looking up at us pathetically from under the fur that fringed her blue velvet bonnet. Her good-byes to me were cordial enough; but there was more than cordiality in the way her little hand lingered in Nathaniel's, and her eyes clung to his.

"I wish you all good fortune," she said, including both of us in her glance, though I knew she spoke for Nathaniel's ears alone. "We shall meet again. I feel it. No doubt you'll go bravely off to Canada to struggle against Burgoyne's army, and it might be we'll encounter each other on the road. I must make sure my little ward is taken to friends in Albany or New York if there should be need, and there are not many roads from Canada to Albany." She smiled at both of us, as innocent and trustful as a kitten.

"But won't your uncle see to that?" I asked.

She shrugged her shoulders. "I hope so, but Ellen is an innocent! You cannot imagine what an innocent she is! She was taken by the Indians when she was little, and so she is learning to live all over again. She is like a wild creature, and I fear she will not make the journey

unless I'm there to make it with her. Her teachers, too, will be reluctant
to let her go without me, for fear she might come to some harm."

"You're as kind as you are beautiful!" Nathaniel said huskily.

She touched his sleeve lightly. "No, no! There's nothing kind about
picking up a waif in the street and seeing she's properly clothed and
educated."

The glances that passed between them seemed to me revolting. "We
must be going," I told Nathaniel.

"See," she said, ignoring me and drawing an envelope from her velvet
muff, "I've written a letter that perhaps you'll carry with you, in case
you go to Canada." She handed it to Nathaniel, who took it fumblingly
and stared at her like a fool. Then she added: "It's a small world, and
it might readily happen you could do a kindness for Ellen, somehow or
somewhere. Some day I might even be in St. John's myself—or across
the river from it. I have—I have property there. And you must pass
through St. John's to reach Albany."

"You'll be in St. John's!" Nathaniel whispered.

Her eyes caressed him. "I'm delaying your departure," she said softly,
"so you must see me to my chair." Her blue eyes slid toward me, almost maliciously.

On that I clambered, growling, into the chaise and settled myself
beside Mr. Leonard, expecting to find him annoyed at the delay. Yet
he was not. "A fine young man, your brother," he whispered faintly,
as if half asleep.

"Yes," I said; but what I thought was that Nathaniel needed a good
rope-ending to rid his mind of foolish matters, like his admiration for
the English and this parting softness for a Frenchified lady like Marie
de Sabrevois.

The sedan chair swayed past, a white handkerchief fluttering at the
window. A moment later Nathaniel climbed in with us, somewhat too
unconcerned and matter-of-fact; and with him came the heavy odor
of violets. Mr. Leonard tapped his stick against the front of the chaise,
the driver cracked his whip smartly, and we lurched toward West-
minster Bridge and the Dover road.

. . . Three days later, in the harbor of Boulogne, we boarded the privately owned ship-rigged sloop-of-war *Beau Soleil*—a fast vessel with
a great cabin equipped to house six passengers in separate berths—
though the word "great" could be applied to it only as a sort of French
politeness.

Already there were two Frenchmen aboard, Captain Gallette and
Captain La Flamme, bound for America to obtain the highest possible

rank under the gentleman they called Vasington. They had taken the
best berths for themselves, so that we tucked ourselves in where we
could.

That evening a third Frenchman unexpectedly arrived—a colonel, a
most courteous and highly bred gentleman. Distinction and affability
seemed clearly stamped all over him; and we were nearly a week, such
was his surface polish, in seeing the meannesses and arrogance and
selfishness that lay beneath that cultured exterior. He had enough
names and titles to equip the officers of an entire regiment, some of
them being Chevalier Mathieu Alexis Roche-Fermoy. He had three
swords and a whole trunkful of uniforms; and the best berth, of
course, was conceded to be his, as by an act of God. Consequently there
was no berth for Captain La Flamme save the poorest of all, which,
we were at once made aware, was galling to the pride of a French gentleman. In fact, he said openly that Nathaniel and I, being Americans,
were without birth or breeding or military ability, and so entitled to no
precedence whatever. He wished, in short, to have one of our berths.

When we did not see fit to accede to his demands, he took it for
granted that we could not be so ill-bred as to take offense at the remarks he had made about us. He turned polite and amiable again, so
that we found it impossible not to be friendly with him; and in no time
at all we were joining him in a glass of wine and helping him write a
letter to Congress—a letter in which he spoke highly of himself and
demanded the rank of brigadier general in the American army.

We found all these Frenchmen pleasant to be with, though it seemed
to me they spent a large part of their time in speaking of their honor
and breeding, and at the same time boasting of their amours and planning how to take advantage of somebody—preferably an American.

Yet we became even intimate during our long voyage, nor could it
have well been otherwise, considering the smallness of the great cabin,
in which we ate our meals and played piquet, and tried to be deaf to
the petulant outbursts of the Frenchmen when we caught them pressing their advantages too closely, which they were prone to do.

There was a dreadful sameness to our food, and to our games as
well; for though we played to help the Frenchmen pass the time, their
object seemed to be to inconvenience us to the utmost, and to ruin us
if possible, whether by fair means or foul. Thus there was a deal of
talk in the cabin; more than a little bickering, and a vast amount of
bragging from our companions, who were scornful of bragging not done
by themselves. Indeed, they were scornful of all the faults of others,
even when those same faults were also their own, and usually in a
higher degree.

But I should not imply that the entire ship's company of passengers thus became intimate, bickered, bragged and played cards: Mr. Leonard seemed to stand outside, like a spectator at a play, looking on sleepily and with interest, but never taking the stage himself.

A more reticent man I never met than Mr. Leonard appeared to be at this stage of my acquaintance with him. He was polite, monosyllabic, benevolent-looking and miraculously self-effacing—so much in the background that one actually forgot his presence.

There are silent people about whom one puzzles and speculates, but the silent Mr. Leonard was not of that sort. He made his shadowiness so inconsequential that he was disregarded: when he did speak, we were mildly surprised to be reminded that he indeed possessed a voice; and as his infrequent use of it was always upon the most insignificant of occasions, nobody bothered, so far as I recall, to make the slightest response.

In a word, we forgot him, even while he was in our company; he seemed to be a piece of luggage that one had somewhere about, through habit, and not because one had any use for it.

I cannot say as much for the Frenchmen, for all their acts seemed designed to prevent us from forgetting them, and at last this even became the case with the captain of the vessel, who had set his course for Newport, but was more in danger, according to my reckoning, of running us into the Bay of Fundy. Like the other Frenchmen, he was polite when we protested mildly; but he believed nothing we said until at length, on our twenty-ninth day at sea, we sighted land—a lone rock about the size of a whale's back, and far, far beyond it the loom of the main.

The captain hunted on his chart for a similar rock near Newport, but couldn't find one, and for a good reason. The rock was Boon Island, which lies north-northeast of the Isles of Shoals, not far from Arundel. Since this showed the captain to be a hundred and thirty-six miles off his course, he was not only willing but eager to have me take the wheel and run the *Beau Soleil* for a port I knew well—that of Old York in Maine: a snug harbor with a narrow curving entrance, as if specially created for pirates and smugglers.

It was off York that the war, which, for all we had seen of it, might have been on another planet, suddenly came close.

We were running in fast on a southwest breeze when we sighted a longboat wallowing toward shore. An oar was upended in it for a mast; and on the mast was a sail made from two jackets, the oar being pushed through the sleeves. We ran past her, and saw she held nine men, five of them flat on the bottom and in no condition to take an interest in us. Of the other four, three were bailing weakly, using their shirts as sponges.

The helmsman was a man with arms that were all over the boat, like the feelers of an octopus—clutching a steering-oar, trimming his makeshift sail, pulling the faces of his half-dead crew from the bilge-water. They were badly off from thirst, their lips black and the tongues of two so swollen that they protruded. The helmsman seemed hardly to notice us as I brought the *Beau Soleil* into the wind to leeward of him and backed her fore-topsail—though I found this to be his habit: to pay small attention, seemingly, to his immediate surroundings because of his interest in the sky, which he watched unceasingly.

Since the men in the boat were unable to move, Nathaniel went down and fastened ropes to them, and we pulled them aboard.

Their cheeks were cracked from exposure to the sun and the salt water, and their voices like the croaks of crows.

We greased their faces and gave them wet cloths to suck. The helmsman was David Hawley, a Connecticut privateer captain from Bridgeport, who had been captured in March by the British frigate *Bellona* and carried to Halifax and imprisoned. He had escaped with eight members of his crew and had been a week at sea, in which time he estimated they had rowed and sailed five hundred miles.

When we asked him whether he would go privateering again, he scanned the sky carefully and felt tenderly of the back of his neck—not because it pained him, but because this, too, was one of his habits. "No," he said. "No. I'm done with privateering. I'm cured. 'Tisn't enough to destroy their property. It's *them* that matters." He sucked at his wet cloth and smiled at us grimly. "It'll take some little time," he added, "to pay 'em back for the way they treated us at Halifax."

We arranged with the captain of the *Beau Soleil* to carry all nine of them to Newport in return for Hawley's pilotage, and knew, somehow, that in one short hour we had made a better friend in Hawley than we had made among all our French companions in a month.

Our one regret, as we prepared to go ashore in York, was that we had not become better acquainted with our silent companion, Mr. Leonard; but when we began to speak of this to him, he surprised us by saying in his unnoticeable way that he would like to accompany Nathaniel and me as far as Arundel. When we made sounds of acquiescence, he at once resumed his silent blandness—became again little more than the shadow of a man.

We, thinking ourselves happy to have him with us, promptly forgot him in the bustle of departure, and were almost perplexed to find him beside us in the coach. In this forgetfulness he seemed to encourage us, so that we came to treat him as an unconsidered trifle—one which the winds of chance had blown across our paths.

IV

It was early May when our heavily laden coach lumbered from the forest between York and Wells to skirt the long marshes and the tumbled sand dunes that showed us we were nearly home at last.

Nowhere is spring so vivid and refreshing as on the coast of Maine in May. The dunes are brilliant green and gold against the smooth blue ribbon of the ocean; and up from the marshes drift the sweet odors of young grass and newly-turned earth. Maples, shamed by their long nakedness, blush a little; while willows, wakening from their winter's sleep, clothe themselves in a fragrant gauze of green. Over everything there seems to hang a web of song woven by the blackbirds, robins, bobolinks and plovers that nest along the marshland.

I am impatient for home, always, when I reach that strip of sea and marsh and ragged dunes; and on this occasion there was such activity along the road that I was doubly impatient; close, even, to leaping from our clumsy coach and running the remainder of the way.

Carts, loaded with provisions and livestock, creaked southward along that dusty thoroughfare—carts bound, our driver said, for Boston to feed the army. Between the carts were knots of men with muskets, packs on their backs and kettles tied to their belts with string—shoeless, some of them; disreputably clad, and all moving south.

In Wells, where the inland road branches off from the sea road, there was a sizeable gathering of men and women before Littlefield's Tavern, listening to a behemoth of a man who stood on the steps bellowing at them. His face was round and red: his garb a loose smock of dirty brown cloth, with a high pointed hood that gave him a look of a person from another world. The smock was belted at his waist, and below it were Indian leggins ending in moccasins the size of a punt.

From time to time he hesitated in his bellowing to rub his face with a hand like a bundle of sausages. Whenever this happened, a man who sat near by, dressed similarly, made a quiet remark, at which his hulking companion coughed portentously and resumed his bawling.

I recognized the quiet one as Steven Nason, who owned all the land at the mouth of our river, and maintained a tavern and garrison house

behind the dunes across from Cape Arundel—a tavern which for food
and cleanliness was the equal of any I knew.

Unable to pass because of the crowd, we sat and listened to the
bellower. "Look here, now!" he roared. "We got eleven men agreed to
go back to Canada, but that ain't enough! We got to have twenty!
What's the matter with you, anyway? You're rebels, all of you, just the
same as me and Steven! If the British ain't drove out of Canada, they'll
come down here and hang every damned rebel there is, and that means
the whole kit and caboodle of you! Ain't it better to go off on a nice
long trip, that you'll get paid for making, and have a pretty uniform
to wear, and free rum, and learn to talk French? Ain't it better than
getting hung? I hope to die if it ain't!"

In the midst of his noisy discourse, his eye fastened on mine. He
hesitated, rubbed his forehead with vast hands as if to clear his mind
of cobwebs: then pushed toward us through his audience.

He thrust his head and shoulders in at the open window of the coach,
darting his eyes from our faces to the packages at our feet. "Where
you from, brother? What's your name? Where you live, and what's your
father do?" His breath was so redolent of rum that a whole distillery
seemed to be crowding into the coach with us.

Before I could answer, his head and shoulders were withdrawn from
the window even more suddenly than they had been inserted. Beyond
him I saw Steven Nason, his hand still clutching the bawler's shoulder.
"Cap," Nason said, "you got to be more careful around here! I know
these people. They're from Arundel."

"Where they been?" Cap demanded belligerently.

Nason ignored him, gave a glance to sleepy-looking Mr. Leonard,
and shook hands with Nathaniel and me. "I'm glad you're back," he
said. "We need people like you. These people around here, they won't
fight unless you guarantee 'em half a dozen cows bounty, and sometimes not even then." He smiled at us apologetically. "It's made Cap
Huff kind of fretty. He's peaceable enough when he's marching or
fighting."

He eyed Cap benevolently and added, "Or when he's drunk. Once
you get to know him better, these little ways of his won't mean a thing
to you! Not a thing!"

He stepped back, motioned our driver onward, and said, "We'll be
over to see you later!"

So the last five miles of our travels were thoughtful ones, and we
were happy indeed when our coach rolled along the edge of the pla-
teau that lies above the marshy, winding valley of the Arundel River,

and we caught once more the smell of oak chips and marsh mud that
rises from the shipyards at the river's edge.

From the look on Mr. Leonard's face, when we bumped to a stop
before our front gate and the door flew open to reveal my sister Jane,
saucer-eyed with amazement, I could see he had expected no such
house as ours.

That's the way of it with Englishmen and Frenchmen, I've found,
to say nothing of people from Virginia, New York and Boston. They
think we're savages in our Province of Maine, living in log huts with
dirt floors, dipping our fingers into one iron pot at meal-time, and talking a strange and unrecognizable language; whereas the truth is that
most of us learn our English out of the Bible through being made to
read it aloud when young; and we live about as well as anyone anywhere—some poorly, and some in style, but for the most part sensibly
and quietly.

. . . It is for the sake of folk who know nothing of us that I tell here a
few things about the howling wilderness in which Maine men live.
Half the wars that are made would never be fought if those who have
the directing of affairs, like George Germain, should know the truth
about the people and the country where the fighting must be done.

Our Province of Maine is larger than all of England; it has fine har-
bors, rivers and mountains; exhaustless rich forests, and a wealth of
game. Our people are willing and enduring—friendly when treated
properly, but the very devil when put upon and their rights disregarded: as much so as Virginians, though garrulous Virginians have
talked the world into thinking bravery is almost exclusively restricted
to Virginia—along with chivalry, honor, hospitality and other virtues
that Virginians imply are non-existent elsewhere, especially in New
England. But Maine men can fight, too, if properly led; for it was
mostly men from Maine who sailed to Louisburg, in 1745, and took
that granite fortress from the French—as handsome a piece of fighting
as any soldiers ever did anywhere.

Nor are our towns to be sneezed at. Falmouth was as beautiful as
any seaport I know before the British Captain Mowat sailed up to its
unprotected and undefended wharves and set the place ablaze. It's
true our towns are poor, because of the wars our people fought for
England against the French and Indians for so many years; and there's
a deal of rum drinking in them, and over-much prying from behind
curtains at the doings of others. We don't have the palaces and churches
and statues that dot the English countryside. But neither do we have
the trulls and rakes, footpads, debtors' prisons and diseases with which

England is peppered; so all in all I think our towns are better than most.

Our home in Arundel stands a mile and a half from the sea, at the double curve in the river, where my great-great-grandfather settled when he removed from Ipswich because of being deprived of his vote by that enlightened community as punishment for harboring a Quaker.

It's a square house of two stories, painted red, with three gables protruding from each side of the four-sided roof. Perched on the top is a cupola with windows on all four sides, from which my father can look down into the shipyard behind the house and shout at any shirking adze-man or carpenter. From this vantage-point, too, he can train his glass on the mouth of the river, and know what vessels are making port, and how they are progressing with their loading and unloading as they lie at anchor beyond the bar.

Our river is small so small that we build our vessels parallel to its channel and slide them in sideways. Yet it's large enough to accommodate a brig of two hundred tons, which is as big as a man needs, no matter to what part of the world he wishes to sail. I can stand on one bank and shoot a duck as she rises from under the opposite bank; and in the spring of the year, after the salmon have stopped running, I can cast a line entirely across the stream, as the tide turns upward, and take sea-run trout from their feeding-places under the edge of the foam that comes slipping along the shore, fresh from the ocean; so, in more ways than one, the very smallness of our river is an advantage.

Our house is large, as are the houses of most Maine shipbuilders. Upstairs and down the rooms are plastered; and painted on the plaster are imaginary scenes, done by one of the Germans who travel periodically through our section, coming from the German settlements on the Kennebec—scenes showing merchant brigs breaking bulk in the lee of ruined castles, and scantily clad people performing on musical instruments in the front yards of Greek temples. Over the mantels in the dining-room and the front room is woodwork carved with jackknives by two of the best workers in our shipyard; while over the dining-room mantel is a painting of my mother, done the year after she and my father were married, by John Smybert—excellently done, too, although my mother thinks there is something wrong with the mouth.

We have nothing so elegant as Benjamin Pickman's Salem house, which has a codfish carved on every stair-rise in the front hall; but our silver is good, part of it made by Paul Revere, and our feather beds can't be beat anywhere, unless there's some place where goose feathers are softer than in Arundel.

Under the house is a dry cellar, stored with crocks of mince meat

made from properly cooked bear and venison haunches—which is to
say scarcely cooked at all—mixed with French brandy and chopped
apples from the tree that shades our kitchen windows: also smoked
goose breasts, hams, smoked eels, dried apples, dried corn, salted codfish, pickled tinker mackerel, bags of onions and potatoes, racks of
squashes, jars of brandied peaches, barrels of corned beef, cucumbers
in brine, tubs of pigeon, plover and partridge breasts packed in melted
fat, so they can be eaten when fresh meat is scarce in the winter.

. . . It was my middle sister Jane who saw us first; and she screamed
fit to wake the dead. It brought my mother from the kitchen, my father up from the shipyard, and Judith and Susanah down from the
bedrooms. There was warmth in their welcome, and more; but there
was a cautiousness about them that was strange to me.

Instead of hurrying us into the front room, as they always did when
I returned from a voyage, they stood in a row, looking at us, as though
expecting an answer to a question they feared to ask.

"They treated you well in England?" my father inquired, after all
the family had shaken hands with Mr. Leonard and had our explanation of the convenience he had been to us.

"It was wonderful!" Nathaniel exclaimed. "It was an education, the
time we spent there."

My father continued to stare at me.

"They treated us well enough," I admitted, "but the only good thing
I have to say of 'em is that they're careful in money matters. The government's a pack of blundering fools! If our ships and trade are going
to be regulated by corrupt incompetents three thousand miles away,
we might as well take to cobbling shoes."

My father smiled sourly. "We didn't know," he said. "We didn't
know! We had a letter from Nathaniel, speaking highly of the English.
It got around. Somebody saw it—somebody opened it. It's easy to be
misunderstood these days. Some of the best folks are Loyalists: some of
the finest: but mostly they keep their mouths shut. We didn't know—
we didn't know——"

Nathaniel laughed. "No great harm in seeing the good side of the
English, I guess."

"Well," my father said, studying him, "outside of having all your
property seized and being driven up to Halifax to live, there's no great
harm in it, unless somebody takes it into his head to tar and feather
you." He shot a quick glance at Mr. Leonard, whose eyes were almost
hidden by their heavy lids. Mr. Leonard concealed whatever lack of

interest he may have felt in our personal affairs by coughing pleasantly and making my father a polite bow.

"Don't fret about Nathaniel," I told my father. "He's only being contrary, as he was taught at Harvard."

My father sighed. "Let's go into the front room," he said, "where we can all sit down and have a thimbleful of something to better days."

V

My mother sat on the sofa, with Nathaniel's hand in hers; and my father made small talk with Mr. Leonard, while my sisters mixed flip: Judith holding the pitcher of beer and stirring, Susanah adding the rum and the sugar, and Jane holding above it the red-hot poker from the kitchen stove, so to plunge it, hissing and rumbling, into the mixture.

"Look here," I said to my father, when we had sampled the flip, "we saw Steven Nason in Wells. He said he'd be over later. In case there's anything we ought to know before he comes, you'd better let us hear it."

My father's eyes strayed from me to Mr. Leonard, who rose to his feet at once. "Perhaps I may go to my room," he said. "I am not as young as I once was; and this journey——"

We protested; but he was firm, in his smiling, silent way; and so my mother showed him to his room—the southeast room, facing down river. That was our best room, the walls painted with hunting scenes by a German painter from Dresden on the Kennebec. He must have been colorblind; for he painted a yellow sky on the hunting scenes; but we liked the yellow sky, all of us, and the room was called the yellow room, which shows that one can become accustomed to anything, no matter how strange it may be.

"It's just as well," my father said, when Mr. Leonard was gone. "Let him get rested up. He's all right, of course, being such a helpful friend of yours; but we'll all feel more comfortable with him out of sight and sound. You get in the habit of being careful after what's happened."

"Happened where?" Nathaniel asked.

My father drank his flip, went to the window and looked both up and down the road: then resumed his seat. "I don't know whether you heard what happened to the Bostonians that sympathized with England when the English left Boston six weeks ago."

"We've heard nothing," I said. "Nothing."

"They had to crowd aboard sloops and schooners and pinks," my father said, "men, women and children—thousands of 'em—not a stitch of extra clothes or a mite of food or furniture or anything—and put to sea that way. Taken to Halifax, they were, and pushed ashore to live as best they could; and every last scrap of their property in Boston seized by our folks. Every last scrap!"

We stared at him.

"Over at York," he went on, "Judge Sayward, Judge of Probate, talked too much. You ought to do things according to Constitutional forms, he said: not go against law and order the way our folks were doing. They mobbed him—manhandled him! He can't go out of his house. He isn't allowed to leave town. Folks won't speak to him. Folks won't speak to his family. He just sits and shakes for fear they'll mob him again."

"You mean he wasn't allowed to say what he thought?" Nathaniel demanded.

My father smiled grimly. "Why, no! He was allowed to say what he thought, but he was encouraged not to keep on saying it."

Nathaniel looked incredulous. "I'll be damned if I'd let——"

"They got close to home when they came after Adam McCulloch," my father interrupted. All of us knew Adam McCulloch. He was another shipbuilder who lived almost within spitting distance of us. "Adam thought we could never whip such a powerful nation as England, and he said so. So the mob came down here and stood in front of his house."

My mother held Nathaniel's hand against her breast. "We could see them from the window," she whispered.

"What did they do?" Nathaniel asked.

"Not much," my father said. "They stood there and made a noise like a gale growling in the rigging of a ship. Then the leaders pounded on the front door and talked to Adam. He had to crawl. He had to crawl in writing. He had to apologize to all friends of America. He had to ask humbly for forgiveness—promise never to do it again—generally squirm around on his belly."

"But," Nathaniel protested, "you used to think there was nothing so foolish as for us to try to fight England."

My father ignored him. "Dr. Alden over in Biddeford sent lumber to Boston to be sold to the British troops for barracks. Cap'n John Stackpole carried it down. A mob from Biddeford, Saco and Arundel called on 'em. Alden and Stackpole had to get down on their knees and ask the mob's pardon. Down on their knees!"

"But——" Nathaniel said.

"There's no 'but' about it, son! You remember Dr. Ebenezer Rice, who lived in the village? He thought the rebellion could never succeed. He thought everyone who took part in it would be hung. Well, he's gone."

"Gone where?" I asked.

My father shook his head. "Nobody knows. Some say he went to live in the woods, where he can't hear about the war. Some say he was——" My father stopped; then cleared his throat and repeated, "Nobody knows. It's considered dangerous to talk about it, even."

Nathaniel raised his eyebrows. "You said somebody opened one of my letters. Who did it? How could anyone open a letter?"

"You've been away a long time," my father said. "Too long. When you're away too long, you lose the feel of your own people, just as you lose the feel of a ship when you're too long ashore.

"Same with us that live in big houses and have servants. We only talk with others like ourselves, who have comfortable homes and plenty to eat. We forget what poorer people think, and it's next to impossible to make ourselves think the way they do. You've been away so long you've forgot how some people feel about England. There never was anything like it! They're all a-boil inside. They won't have the English back! They just won't have 'em back! They say England wants to run this country the way a man runs a mill: wants to use it for nothing but making money for the owner: regards the people in it as no better than mill-stones, to be worn smooth for England and then thrown into the creek."

"It's the truth," I said. "The English think we're just rabble! They call us that—rabble! I've heard 'em!"

"What's that got to do with my letter?" Nathaniel persisted.

"Why," my father explained patiently, "those that hate England feel everyone's got to think the way they do. Everyone's *got* to. They're watching all the time to make sure nobody thinks different. Knowing I had two sons in England, they watched me. They watched your mother and your sisters, too. When they couldn't find out what they wanted to know, they opened letters."

He took his spectacles from his pocket and perched them on his nose: reached into a compartment of his desk to draw out a soiled square of paper.

"Here," he said. "They opened this one, and right away they read this that Nathaniel wrote:

"There's no place like London, with its fine theatres and palaces, and soldiers parading in the park. It's a city that makes you feel at home. Peter and I went down to Salisbury and saw where Great-great-grandfather Merrill lived before he went to Ipswich a hundred and fifty years ago. We found Merrills living there still—relatives. Long ago their name was DeMerle. They were Huguenots who came from Auvergne—

Place de Dembis—at the time of the Massacre of St. Bartholomew. One of them, Sir Peter, was a captain in the English army, and was knighted in 1634."

My father folded the letter and looked at Nathaniel over his spectacles.

"What's wrong with that!" Nathaniel demanded indignantly. "Damn 'em! Who gave 'em the right to open my letters!"

"Right or not, they opened this one," my father said. "Then they called me before the Committee of Safety and questioned me."

"About what?" Nathaniel asked.

"About you and Peter."

"What did they want to know?"

"Whether you were well disposed to the cause of Liberty, after being in England and finding there was no place like London."

"Liberty!" Nathaniel exclaimed. He laughed. "Where's the liberty in having your letters opened! It's almost enough, I should think, to make you want never to see this place again!"

My mother cried, "Oh, Nathaniel!"

My father shook his head. "No! I've lived here all my life. It's part of me. It's in my blood. This land we're on was granted to your great-grandfather Peter Merrill by the town of Arundel for killing an Indian. My roots are in it. I can't leave it. The smell of the sea and marshes and meadows is sweeter here than anywhere else in the world."

My sister Susanah put her handkerchief to her lips and went suddenly from the room.

"What did you tell the Committee?" I asked, feeling choked myself.

"I told 'em," my father said slowly, "that you were well disposed. They didn't believe me. They—well—the men on these committees aren't the sort of people you'd expect to find running things. So we've been watched—all of us. We have trouble buying necessities. Shopkeepers don't like to sell to folks under suspicion: they might be suspected themselves. Some of 'em will, but only if we accept Congress money at par, when they make change for us, even though it's worth less than the paper it's printed on. We can't complain, because if we did, it would mean we were spreading reports about the currency; and instead of being ruined gradually, we'd be ruined quick. Talking against the currency's worse than having sons in England."

The room was silent except for the soft sound my mother's hand made against Nathaniel's.

My father hesitated: his next words seemed irrelevant. "There's been a drought. The crops last year were terrible, on account of so many men being away in the army. Theodore Lyman speculated in corn last fall, and now he's selling it at two dollars a bushel to those in the village."

Theodore had been clerk in the store of Waldo Emerson, a rich man and a kind one, but dead almost three years.

"That's robbery," I protested.

"We have to pay three dollars," my father said. "He'll only sell to us secretly, and only if we pay him in hard money. Theodore's smart."

"We'll see about that!" I said. "We'll see about that! I'll step over to call on Lyman after supper."

My father shook his head. "Don't do it! Lyman's a rich man. In a few months he'll be richer, because he's marrying Waldo Emerson's daughter."

"What do you mean?" I asked. "Waldo Emerson only had one daughter. She's a baby."

"Not quite," my mother said. "She'll be fourteen years old some time this year."

"Keep away from Lyman," my father said. "He does favors for the Sons of Liberty. We're under suspicion; and people under suspicion don't have any rights. Folks can assault us or blackmail us or slander us, and we have no standing in the law courts. We can't buy land or sell it, or make a deed of gift, or make a will, even, while we're under suspicion."

I looked at Nathaniel, feeling as though the veins in my neck would burst the fastenings of my muslin neckcloth. Nathaniel stared moodily at his knuckles. I knew the best way to handle him was to let him alone, so I waited for him to speak first; but I told myself that if he said the wrong thing, I'd wait no longer.

Twilight was on us, and from the meadows came the sweet piping of baby frogs—a plaintive chorus that seemed to hold us, speechless, in a spell. The spell was broken by a violent thumping on the front door.

"That must be Nason," I told Nathaniel. "If you can't make up your mind, get upstairs. I'll talk to him. I'll—I'll tell him you're sick."

"What do you think I am!" Nathaniel exclaimed. "My mind's made up."

VI

$\mathbf{M}$Y SISTER Susanah opened the door while my mother and my sister Judith slipped away to the rear of the house. A moment later Steven Nason stood in the doorway, and over his shoulder I saw the round red face of Cap Huff—the hulking man who had bellowed at the crowd in Wells, and pried into our coach. Their brown smocks had been replaced by coats of dark green cloth.

Nason was a big man, though not as wide as his companion. He looked slow and a little thick-witted, like many of our Arundel seafaring people, who move and think as quickly as anyone if the need arises. There was nothing slow about his eyes, however. They moved from our clothes to our faces and back again, and missed nothing in the moving.

My father bustled around, lighting the whale-oil lamps. "Come in, Steven," he said. "How's your wife? I guess she's glad to have you back from Quebec."

Nason smiled and came into the room. Behind him his clumsy ox of a companion edged sideways through the door, as if fearful of wedging himself there.

"Yes, come in," I said, anxious to get in the first blow if there were blows to be struck. "What's this they've been doing to my father?"

"Your father?" Nason asked. He stared at me as if puzzled, while Cap Huff hopefully eyed the pitcher of flip.

My father stood up, his face gray. "It means nothing to Steven, Peter. He's just back from Quebec."

"I guess I can make it mean something to him."

"Now, Peter!" he protested. "First thing you know you'll be in trouble yourself."

Cap Huff cleared his throat noisily. "That thing on the table looks something like a pitcher." His eyes became more protuberant. "Ain't it maybe a pitcher?"

Nathaniel jumped up and gave each of them a tumbler of flip, and when he had refilled our own glasses, Cap Huff held out his glass to be filled again.

"Now," I said, "I want to tell you about my father. These damned midwives here——"

"By God, that's right!" Cap Huff bawled, surprisingly. "That's what they are! Half of 'em don't care whether we win or not, as long as they can go on making a dollar! That's all they think of! Money!"

"Cap," Nason said, "I'll thank you to put a curb on your tongue. Those from this town that went up Dead River and down the Chaudière with us weren't midwives, and there's plenty more like 'em. Just bear that in mind."

"I think your friend's right," I told Nason. "Theodore Lyman's been charging my father three dollars specie for a bushel of corn. Why suspect my father of being a public enemy when there's bastards like Theodore Lyman running loose?"

Nason stared at the ceiling. "He's a Patriot. He's planted a row of elms to celebrate the Battle of Bunker Hill."

"He's a hell of a Patriot!" I said.

Cap Huff hitched his chair forward, and his voice was hoarsely eager. "Three dollars? He charges three dollars for a bushel of corn? Whereabouts does he live?"

Nason eyed him suspiciously, but spoke to me. "I heard about your father. It was too bad, but it appears to me it was his own fault. If he hadn't thought the war was going to be over soon, or if you hadn't thought so, you'd have come home before this, wouldn't you? And if he thought the war was going to be over soon, he didn't think it was because we were going to win it, did he?"

"Well——" I said, and stopped. Nason had it right, and there was nothing I could say.

"Such opinions don't bother me," Nason said. "I wouldn't think we could ever whip the English, either, if I didn't know they'd blunder into trouble sooner or later. But people in Arundel don't look at it like that."

"Not anywhere they don't," Cap Huff growled.

"It's pretty serious business," Nason went on. "If we get whipped, we're rebels, and rebels pretty often have their last words with the hangman; so those in charge of things aren't going to let anybody even talk about being whipped. If they do any hanging they've got to hang us all, because we're all going to hang together. Everybody's got to be a Patriot or get out. There's some sense in it, too. If it came to hanging, and there were Loyalists still living everywhere, the Loyalists would probably help to hang everyone else, wouldn't they?"

Cap Huff wagged his head. "You got to meet a few Tories before you know how people feel about 'em. Why, over around Albany there's so many of 'em that they go prowling through the woods, skinning Patriots and making saddlebags out of the skins to sell in New York. That's why we ain't going back to Quebec by way of Albany. Winooski River and St. John's: that's the route we got to take, on account of those damned Loyalists or Tories or whatever you want to call 'em."

"But my father's no Loyalist!" I told them. "Why, he's no more of a Loyalist than I am."

The two men were silent, staring into their empty tumblers. Nathaniel looked in the pitcher and laughed: then went to the dining-room and took the rum bottle from the sideboard.

I knew what was on their minds, so I added hastily, "I've been aching to get home and fight the British ever since I heard Burgoyne was going to use Hessians and Indians against us."

Nason and his huge companion stared at me, their mouths wide open.

Nathaniel added a tot of rum to all our tumblers. "I'm with Peter," he said. "I'll go wherever Peter goes. That ought to settle my father's case."

What he said made me feel better than any amount of rum. For months I had fretted over his perverse admiration for the British, and then been in a stew for fear he might become infatuated with Marie de Sabrevois; and finally I had worried myself sick at what might happen to my father and mother and sisters if he persisted in his determination to be what he called logical about everything. Now he had committed himself; and my relief was such that I could have forgiven even Theodore Lyman.

"There you are," I said to Nason, who was peering into my face as though he doubted his own senses. "If anyone in this family's a Loyalist, you're one too."

"Burgoyne!" Nason whispered. "Burgoyne! And he'll use Hessians!"

"And Indians. Five thousand Indians. God knows where he'll get that many, but they say he's got 'em!"

Cap Huff got up and moved his great arms backward and forward, as if his coat bound him. "Did you say Burgoyle or Burgloyd? Who in God's name is Burgloyd?"

"Burgoyne," I repeated. "He was a general at Bunker Hill. He writes plays and poetry. They say in England he's an illegitimate son of Lord Bingley, but that's not so."

"How do you know it ain't?" Cap demanded hoarsely. "All the Englishmen we've seen so far, they've all acted as if they was illegitimate sons—not Bingley's, of course, but *somebody's*. And you know what the Bible says about——"

Nason's voice cut sharply into Cap's. "Hold your tongue! You're in a decent house!"

"What if I am!" Cap muttered. "Ain't the Bible a decent book? And ain't it the truth, what I say about Englishmen? Ain't it the simple truth?"

Nason ignored him and took me by the lapel of my coat. "Five thousand Indians! How could Burgoyne—where could Burgoyne—who told you so?"

"All England knows it. He was supposed to sail for Quebec soon after we sailed from France. Part of his troops, we heard, would sail with him, the rest to follow through the month, and in May."

"Troops?" Nason said. "You mean regulars?"

"Five thousand regulars was what we heard. Five thousand regulars and three thousand Hessians."

"And they're going to Quebec?"

"Yes," I said. "That's why I felt we had to get home quick. They figure on landing in Quebec and marching down the Hudson to join Howe. Everybody in England seems to know about it. The idea is to split the colonies in two—cut off New England from the rest of the country, and then smash the rebellion by smashing New England. If they're going to turn western Indians loose on these settlements, there's got to be something done about it, hasn't there?"

A silence fell on us—a silence so profound that the shrill sweet piping of the baby frogs grew and grew until it seemed to come not only from out-of-doors, but from the cornices of the room in which we sat: even from the fireplace, and from the chairs and sofa and pictures.

Nason looked up at Huff, a wry smile on his lips. "We'll waste no more time. We'll set off tomorrow with what men we've got. Send Doc Means back to Wells to tell the rest of the men to be at Littlefield's Tavern at noon tomorrow, ready to march."

"By God, Stevie," Cap Huff said, his voice rumbling like thunder, "not even Arnold could stop that number of men with what he's got!"

"Arnold?" I asked.

"General Arnold," Nason said. "The one we serve under: the one that got us to Quebec safe. There isn't another man in the world could have done it. He was wounded when we stormed the city. If he hadn't been—if he hadn't been——"

"If he hadn't been," Cap Huff declared, "we'd be sitting on top of that damned big rock this minute, swigging cider and brandy."

"How many men has he got?" I asked.

Nason's laugh was one of exasperation. "We've had a little trouble getting men. That's why Cap and I came home—to get twenty scouts. When we left Quebec, the end of March, Arnold had two hundred and eighty-six effectives. That's the kind of general Arnold is! Two hundred and eighty-six men, and he had the British bottled up in Quebec!"

"Bottled up!" Cap Huff echoed. "Bottled up and scared to death! Had the strongest city in the world surrounded, by God, with two hundred and eighty-six men! Surrounded and damned near starved, and the garrison afraid to take off their breeches when they went to bed, ever since January, for fear Arnold would climb over the wall with his two hundred and eighty-six men and club 'em to death with icicles!"

"That's about right," Nason agreed. "He's a great man—a great man! There isn't anything he can't do! If they'll send him enough men and let him alone, he'll take Quebec this spring just like this!" He tossed off the remainder of his rum and rose to his feet to tap Cap Huff on the chest. "I want word taken back to Wells that we're marching in the morning. Tell Doc Means. Have him start right away."

"What about us?" I asked Nason.

He looked blank, seeming to have forgotten our conversation. "Well, what about you?"

"Aren't you going to take us with you for the army?"

Nason scratched his chin as if in doubt. "This is for scout duty. A man has to be handy with an axe. He has to know how to shoot."

"Nathaniel and I worked in the shipyard when we were boys," I reminded him. "We can lay a tree on a peg, both of us. I can trim a beam with an adze so you'd think it was planed. As for shooting, I'll go out with you tomorrow morning, and if I can't fill a hogshead with plover in fifteen minutes, I'll eat the hogshead."

Nason nodded slowly. "I guess maybe you can. I forgot, seeing you in good clothes, you'd been brought up around here. To tell you the truth, though, you probably wouldn't get any pay. Cap and I haven't had any for three months."

"Well, if you can get along, we probably can," I told him.

Nason seemed uncomfortable. "There's one more thing. It's important, and you'll have to swear not to tell. When you hear it, you may not want to go; but whether you go or not, you've got to keep quiet about it, or you might get us shot. It's against the law."

"Well, what is it?"

"You swear, both of you?" He looked from Nathaniel to me.

We said we did.

"Well," he said, "smallpox is bad in Canada. Bad! It's hard to dodge. Nearly everybody gets it. There's no use taking men to Canada for scout duty unless they've had the smallpox. They'd be busier dying than scouting. All that go with us must take smallpox by inoculation."

"Where must we take it?"

Cap Huff cleared his throat importantly. "I got my own doctor with me. He'll fix you in a jiffy."

Nathaniel came to stand close beside me. "You mean we'd take the smallpox right here: right in this room?"

"You'd just get inoculated with scrapings from a mild case," Nason said. "Doc Means took some nice scrapings. You won't break out for a week."

"Break out?" Nathaniel asked. "Will we have scars on us?"

Cap Huff helped himself from the rum bottle. "Listen, I'd ruther have this kind of smallpox than one flea, and everybody's got to have fleas sometime. You've had 'em, ain't you?"

He went to the outer door, opened it, and, to our astonishment—for we hadn't suspected that our two guests had been accompanied by a third guest who waited outside—we heard him speaking to someone.

Immediately there walked in a man as mild-looking and helpless-appearing as I had ever seen. He was certainly sixty years old, and maybe even seventy. His hair was white and his face a fresh pink, in spite of its thinness; and perhaps because his eyes were a faded blue, there was an air of childish innocence about him: a trustful, useless look. He was, I thought, somewhat insecure on his feet: he seemed to waver a little in his walk. The fact is, my own youthful vanity in my strength and agility led me to feel a certain compassion for his feebleness. Since that time I have found that there were few who were not similarly affected by Doc Means; but the truth is that he was about as feeble as a young wildcat.

It was not Doc Means's feebleness, however, that upon our first meeting impressed us most poignantly and instantly. It was his smell. With his entrance the room was filled with an acrid, penetrating odor that made the eyes water.

Nason and Huff, apparently inured, seemed not aware of anything unusual; but Nathaniel, unprepared, uttered a muffled sound of surprise and protest, opened a window wide and remained near it.

For a moment I didn't myself attribute the odor to its true source, and was puzzled. "What's that smell?" I asked.

"What smell?" Cap Huff wanted to know. He turned his head from side to side, sniffing. "Everything smells all right to me."

"Maybe," Nason said, "it's Doc's asafoetida bag."

"Yes, I guess that's it," Cap agreed. "I remember I used to smell it some when I first got to know him. If you can learn to stand it at all, the more you get to know him, the more you get over it." He looked at us patronizingly. "Doc has to wear an asafoetida bag around his neck on account of his health. It ain't nothing to worry about, so just roll up your sleeves."

We did so, and Doc Means wavered forward to stare placidly at our upper arms with weak blue eyes. With a trembling hand he dusted at my biceps, as if to free them of a non-existent web: then turned to Nathaniel.

I considered him careless as well as helpless; for in the dusting, he scratched me, which was not pleasing, since his fingernails were less clean than some I had seen. In my own mind I set him down as a doddering old fool and wondered how Nason could seem to set store by him. Indeed, I thought the man little better than half-witted; for when he had fumbled at Nathaniel's arm, he appeared to forget about us and stood staring at the rum bottle out of eyes that seemed half blind.

"Pour yourself a glass of rum if you like," I said.

He shook his head and spoke in a flat, weak voice. "I don't touch it, hardly ever. What kind is it?"

He picked up the bottle and smelled of it, looking at it inquiringly. Then, as if the more readily to smell it, he poured a glass half full. "What kind is it?" he asked again. "I seldom touch it." With that he lifted the glass and the rum vanished. He set down the glass, shaking his head. "Not any more," he said in a faint voice. "It don't have a good effect on me—likely to make me eat too much."

He looked at Nason meekly. "Cap says you want me to be off for Wells." He turned and moved toward the door, walking with that wavering gait which was not a limp, and suggested decrepitude, not lameness.

"Here," I said, "why doesn't he give us the smallpox?"

"You got it," Nason said. "What's the matter with your eyes?"

I looked at my arm. There was a red welt across it. On Nathaniel's there was a similar welt. Thereupon I stared hard at Doc Means and wondered if I had made a mistake about him.

Doc Means blinked at us. "Good-bye, all," he said in a whispering voice. He opened the door and went out droopingly.

. . . Nason watched him go: then turned to us. "There's just one more thing: your requirements. Living isn't any too easy in Canada, and you'll need the requirements: yes, and some old clothes to have the smallpox in. Repeat the requirements, Cap."

Cap looked up at the ceiling with eyes a little crossed and made his recitation in a high, artificial tone. "Each man enlisting for scout duty expected to serve for period three years an required equip self an be constantly provided with good firearm ramrod worm priming-wire brush bayonet scabbard belt cutting-sword tomahawk or hatchet a pouch containing cartridge box that'll hold at least fifteen rounds hundred buck-shot jackknife tow for wadding six flints one pound powder forty leaden balls to fit firearm knapsack blanket canteen or wooden bottle capacity one quart provisions for three days."

He lowered his eyes and spoke naturally. "Get yourself a tow-cloth coat same as we had on. You can drop things down inside it—things like chickens or wine bottles. Mine's outside. It's kind of ripe, but it'll do for your womenfolks to get a pattern off of. You get the brown color into it by putting it to boil with brown ears of corn."

"All right," I said. "We'll be ready, but it's got to be understood, before we go, that there's to be no more talk in this town about my father or any other member of my family being a Loyalist."

"I'll send Cap to see somebody," Nason said.

"Yes," Cap agreed hoarsely, "there's a few people I ought to see. Maybe I'll have to start a little later than you, Steven, but I can catch up in no time." The two of them eyed us solemnly as they moved toward the door; and their minds, I could see, were already on other matters.

The door closed behind them: then opened again, and the moist red face of Cap Huff re-appeared. He spoke in a whisper so harsh it set the fire-irons to vibrating. "I'll tend to Theodore Lyman for you! Where'd you say he lived?"

VII

By six o'clock the following morning our new belongings were laid out on the front steps in the brilliant sunlight, so we could see what we had and what we lacked.

Early as the hour was, our unnoticeable, quiet guest, Mr. Leonard, had departed, saying no more than that he had a mind to see something of the country, and might not soon return, and that if he did not return, he would write to us; but the truth is that as Nathaniel and I looked over what Nason had called our requirements, we had already forgotten the existence of this shadowy companion of ours.

My mother and sisters sat on the iron benches beside the door, sewing at our tow-cloth smocks, and between thrusts of their needles doubtfully eyeing our piles of clothes. My father stood by the front gate, whisking flies from our bay mare Bessie with a willow shoot; while Zelph and Pristine, our two Negro servants, bobbed in and out of the house and kept up a meaningless conversation as if to ease the silence that hung about us.

I call them servants; but in reality they were slaves, Zelph having been bought in Wells for fifty-three dollars to keep me from falling in the river when I was young, and Pristine having been picked up for forty dollars to help my sisters around the house and make a wife for Zelph.

Even they were silent at last, and in the stillness the singing of the bobolinks, as they sank fluttering onto the flat land at the bend in the river, seemed almost to pierce our ears with a metallic shrillness.

When I looked up at the two Negroes, standing together on the top step, I saw they were staring down the road that curves at our front gate, and stretches straight away toward the ocean.

I turned to look. At the crest of the rise in the road, where it cuts through the tall pines that have sprung up in this section since the Indian troubles ended, I saw a straggling knot of people, men and women, with Steven Nason striding along at their head. The men had muskets over their shoulders.

"Hurry up," I told my mother. "Here they come." I gathered my belongings in a pile, so to stuff them into my blanket and knapsack.

"Put all of it in the chaise," my mother said. "We'll take it as far as Wells for you."

"No," I said. "We've got to carry it. I want people to see us carrying it."

My mother nodded and smiled brightly: then bent her head over the smock as though she found trouble in seeing where to thrust her needle.

"Let Pristine finish that," I urged her.

"No," she said. "No! I want to do it myself!"

The little company came up to our front gate with a gabbling of voices and a clatter of accouterments. I recognized Thomas Bickford, who had gone to school with Nathaniel and was regarded as a paragon by all the mothers in Arundel, because he was tall and handsome and polite beyond all reason, even to persons his own age, and so should have been hated by all young men, but was not. He had wished to go to Harvard with my brother, so that he could be a minister; but his oldest brother Eliakim would not hear of it, and made him go to sea instead. Also I recognized Thomas Dorman, a cousin of Tom Bickford; and Paul Durrell, whose father and mother had been captured by Indians when they were young. The others I did not recognize; but all of them had womenfolk with them—sisters, possibly, or cousins, with a mother or two thrown in for good measure—in addition to a sprinkling of fathers and small brothers.

Nason opened the gate and came into the yard. His wife was with him, carrying his canteen and powder horn over her arm and clinging to him by a finger hooked through one of the loops of his belt. She was a thin, dark girl, no bigger than a ten-year-old boy. She wore sea boots and breeches, like a man, and a blue handkerchief bound around her head in place of a hat, with almost nothing to show she was a woman except the smallness of her waist and a string of glittering brownish beads around her throat. Yet I knew that for all her size, she was a seaman and a good one, able to navigate better than most masters who sail out of our river.

"Almost ready?" Nason asked.

His wife smiled at my mother and sisters and came to look at our piles of clothes. "They've got too much, Steven," she said at once.

"Weed it out," he told her.

She went down on her knees on the bottom step, and reached among our clothes with both hands, tossing a shower of stockings, shirts and other odds and ends into the front hall between Zelph and Pristine.

"They'll need those things, Phoebe!" my mother protested.

"You'd be surprised what you don't need if you haven't got it," Phoebe said.

"But there's others that might need 'em," my father ventured.

"That's right," Phoebe agreed cheerfully, "only it's better to be able to carry what you've got than to throw away what you need because you've made yourself sick trying to lug what you don't need."

Nason cast a sharp eye over the piles that Phoebe had left untouched. "Roll 'em up and come ahead."

"Can't we put all those things in the chaise for a few miles?" my mother asked.

"Of course," Nason said. "Throw 'em in."

I took my smock from my mother and struggled into it, then strapped on my knapsack and blanket. "I've got to carry 'em," I said again. "I don't want any misunderstanding in this town about where we're going." I gave Nathaniel his tow-cloth garment and helped him with the rest of his things.

"Get in the chaise," I told my mother. "We can't keep these men waiting."

My mother looked at Phoebe. "You'd like to ride with us, wouldn't you?"

Phoebe shook her head. "The time's too short, I guess I'll walk."

"It's too short!" my mother cried a little wildly. "It's too short! I won't ride! I'm going to walk with the boys."

"It's seven miles by the road," my father said. "You'll tucker yourself."

"I'm going to walk!" my mother repeated. "Jane, get my shawl!"

We followed Nason out of the gate. My father began to shout for Zelph. "Zelph! Come here and take Bessie! I'm going to walk, too!"

We left him shouting. The little crowd disentangled itself from before our gate and straggled around the bend in the road. My mother walked between Nathaniel and me. My father, overtaking us, plodded silently at my right. My sister Jane had Nathaniel by the arm, and skipped a little as she walked beside him. Judith and Susanah attached themselves to Tom Bickford, staring over their shoulders at us so that we perpetually dodged their lagging heels.

As we went through the village, we were as far removed in appearance from anything martial as a lot of Spanish fisherwomen plodding up a beach. I looked at Nathaniel and caught him eyeing me sidewise, a bitter smile on his flushed, perspiring face. Something told me he was thinking, as was I, of the British regiments we had seen parading before the King in St. James's Park, drums beating and bands playing, flags waving above them, and the sun glittering on the regular ranks of bayonets and on the brass buttons that flashed like sparks against their red coats.

A few people came out of the stores and the sawmill to watch us go by, but none of them did anything, barring Sammy Hill, the village idiot, who pointed at us and made uncouth sounds: then pretended to shoot himself and fell down in simulated death throes.

We crossed the river and mounted the hill beyond. As we trudged off to the southward through the deep woods, a meditative silence settled on most of us—a silence that may have been caused by a sudden dark foreboding of what lay before us.

My unaccustomed knapsack and the truck with which I was hung weighed heavily on me; and the others, I suspected, were in no better case, for there began to be complaints among them concerning their dryness: hoarse suggestions as to the quality of toddy to be had at Pike's Tavern and the large size of the beer mugs at Storer's Tavern.

Nason turned and eyed them coldly. "There'll be no lally-gagging for liquor till we reach Littlefield's Ordinary," he announced. "The sooner you get there, the sooner you'll get it, and the sooner we'll get started on the road to St. John's."

In the moment the last words fell from his lips I had a picture in my mind of how Marie de Sabrevois had stood with Nathaniel before our London lodgings, her hand resting on his sleeve and her blue eyes raised to his, telling him that some day she might be in St. John's. I looked over at him quickly: caught his furtive glance across my mother's head; and then I remembered another thing. It was immediately after Cap Huff had spoken of going to Canada by way of the Winooski River and St. John's that Nathaniel had agreed to go to the war with me. I called myself a fool to have such thoughts—such petty and ungenerous thoughts; but still they buzzed within my brain like the flies that followed us to light again and again and yet again on nose or cheek or neck.

The post-rider came up behind us, clopping westward for Portsmouth, his saddlebags and elbows a-flop as though he aimed in time to rise and fly. He made what he conceived to be an Indian whooping, howling dolefully and breaking the howls by slapping a hand briskly against his open mouth. "Ice was late going out of the lakes," he shouted. "Six regiments got through to St. John's a week ago!"

He flopped onward, leaving me agape at his mention of St. John's at the very moment when the name of that distant town had come to fill my wandering mind with odd fancies about my brother.

When we passed the first log huts of Wells, the talkativeness came back to the women who walked beside us. My sisters gabbled to Tom

Bickford. My mother reminded us of this and that: to air our blankets, lest the moisture cling in them and chill us into sleeplessness at night: to keep our feet dry: to read the Bible regularly and give thanks to Providence for all blessings: to drop wild cherries in our canteens against the flux.

She was interrupted by a suppressed exclamation from my father, who stared unbelievingly over his shoulder. When we turned to look, we saw our bay mare Bessie drawing close. From the chaise peered the anxious black face of Zelph, our Negro servant. He wore an ancient suit of badly tanned moose skin, fuzzy and brownish, so that he had the look of a small brown bear with a bad case of the mange. What was more remarkable than his garb, however, was the fact that beside him lay a pack and musket.

My father spoke to him severely. "Zelph, where you think you're going, and where'd you get that musket?"

"Cap'n Asa, sir," Zelph said, "that musket was giu to me by Cap'n Steven Nason's friend, Cap'n Huff. I'm goin' to war, along with Cap'n Peter." The mare Bessie breathed heavily, sniffing at my father's shoulder and wrinkling her upper lip pleasurably.

My father dropped back to walk beside Zelph. "Zelph," I heard him say, "I don't believe you're cut out for a soldier. It appears to me you'd do better to stay right in Arundel where you can take care of Pristine and the girls—and where we can take care of you." He shook his head sadly. "Nobody'll ever know, Zelph, how hard it is to make you work!"

"Cap'n Asa," Zelph said, leaning forward in his seat to speak confidentially, "Cap'n Huff said that was the nice thing about a war: there ain't any regular work to do—only wear a uniform and walk around a lot, and camp out. Cap'n Huff, he said I'd make a real good soldier. He said I was twice as good a soldier, right now, as any of them York troops that went to Quebec."

Steven Nason, hearing the talking, had come back to investigate; and at these words of Zelph's, he spoke to him even more abruptly than had my father. "Did Cap Huff ask you to join the army?"

Zelph made a dignified reply. "Cap'n Nason, Cap'n Huff never said a word to me, only come along after you set out, an ast was there anything to eat in the house. I brung him a punkin pie, Cap'n Nason, an he et it all." Zelph made two turkey-like motions with his head to give us an idea of the rapidity with which Cap had demolished the pie. "Nen he ast who made that pie, an I said I made it."

"Then what?" Nason asked.

"Nen he breathed sort of loud and kind," Zelph said, "so's I told him about being scairt somebody'd think I was an Englishman, an I ast him how much a man had to pay to get into the army."

"You were scared of being taken for an Englishman!" Nason exclaimed. He stared from Zelph to my father and back again.

Zelph nodded. "I was lissenin' yesdy," he told Nason frankly. "I was lissenin' outside the winder when you was in the house talkin'. I wouldn't choose to be mistooken for a Englishman, Cap'n Nason, nor for a Tory, on account of how they're hated around here." To my father he added, "I wouldn't be no good around here no more, Cap'n Asa, not till the war's over, on account of never knowin' when I might be mistooken for an Englishman. Meks my hand tremmle, jest thinkin' 'bout it, Cap'n Asa, so's I'd drop dishes—bus' 'em all over the place! In the army, they won't be no dishes to drop."

My father and Nason eyed Zelph distrustfully; but it was Nason's wife, Phoebe, who settled the matter. She had come back to walk with her husband, and now she nudged him warningly. "Steven, don't fly in the face of Providence! This boy knows how to make rabbit stew and fish chowder! There'll be times when a good fish chowder'll be more help to you than all the powder and generals and sharpshooters in the world." She laughed and added, "When anybody thinks war consists of a lot of nice walks, it's high time he completed his education."

Nason nodded grimly; so Zelph, grinning happily at the vacation in store for him, slapped Bessie on the rump with the ends of the reins and clumped past our little column to escape the crowd of townsfolk who stood at the Wells crossroads, watching our approach.

In spite of the poverty of the town and its people, the place had a gala air, for two red blankets hung from upstairs windows of Littlefield's Ordinary; and farmers, flushed and noisy with rum, stood in the doorway, shouting encouragements at the militia company drawn up across the road.

Some of the militiamen wore no shoes; but they might have looked worse; for all of them had muskets, and they wore red handkerchiefs around their necks to provide a flavor of uniformity. Also there was a man thumping on a drum, and a number of women and children and old men standing around with food on bark trays and in milk pails; and in front of the crowd was a barrel of beer on a wooden horse.

Sitting on the steps of the ordinary was Doc Means, fumbling helplessly with a number of clumsy parcels, each one thrust into the leg of a woolen stocking for protection. He was tucking the bundles into his brown smock, only to remove them and poke them in elsewhere, as if hopeful of so disposing them that they would interfere neither with his comfort nor his appearance. The odor of his asafoetida bag was powerful—so powerful that it rose piercingly above the scent of dust, crushed grass, unwashed bodies and stale beer.

While we stacked our muskets and packs and made free with the beer, Nason had a word with Doc Means. "Doc," he said, "we've got a long trip ahead of us. You'll never make it with any such load as you've got there."

"Those things might come in pretty handy," Doc said mildly. "They don't weigh as much as one goose, and I'd hate to say how far I could carry a goose, if I wanted to use it when I got where I was going."

"Maybe we could divide 'em up, if you're set on taking 'em."

"No," Doc Means said. "No. I couldn't spare none of 'em. When you want one of 'em, you're like to want it quick." Baffled, he removed the bundles from his smock; and to watch him was like watching a magician remove from a hat more things than the hat could possibly hold. Plaintively he added, "If only they was as soft as a goose—even as soft as a frozen goose—I wouldn't have no trouble."

Phoebe Nason sat on the step beside him, looking, with her kerchiefed head and her sea boots, like a sympathetic boy. She swept Doc's parcels into a pile beside her. "What are they, Doc? Asafoetida bags?"

Doc's glance wandered over the shouting, milling crowd; then returned to the brown beads at Phoebe's throat. He shook his head. "I don't recommend asafoetida bags. The reason I wear one myself is because it gives me more room in case I get in a crowd. Crowds ain't good for my rest, and rest is the most important thing you can get. People don't bother you if you wear an asafoetida bag—not unless they're real used to you."

Phoebe nodded thoughtfully. "I didn't know, from the smell around here, but what you were trying to carry enough asafoetida bags for the whole army. What is it you've got in these bundles?"

Doc pawed at them. "Medical supplies and my medical liberry. This here's my Culpeper's Herbal. It tells how to make medicine out of any kind of plants or leaves. This here's my book by Tryon, that tells how to cure yourself by not eating nothing. This here's my Almanac. It tells what's the most favorable time to do things and take things. This here's my Venesection Mannekin and my trigger-lancet, and my hazel wand for finding minerals and water. And this here's my Digby's Sympathetic Powder."

Phoebe picked up the bundle that held the Almanac; stared at it, back and front; then eyed Doc Means doubtfully. "What does your Almanac say about today?"

Doc took it from her and dropped it carefully into his smock. "Today? It says today is the most favorable day there is for embarking on any enterprise."

Phoebe fingered her brown beads and squinted at the sky through one of them. Then she pounced on another bundle and had it out of its protecting stocking before Doc could prevent her. "Digby's Sympathetic Powder!" she said. "I never heard of it. What's it for?"

Doc would have taken back the bundle, but Phoebe moved it beyond his reach and unknotted the string that bound it. "What's it for, Doc?"

Doc sighed. "It's the greatest remedy there is. It's good for everything. There ain't anything, hardly, that it won't cure. It's so powerful that if you got stuck with a bayonet, I could cure you by rubbing the bayonet with Digby's Sympathetic Powder."

"Did you say you could do it by rubbing the bayonet?"

Doc nodded, and the watery blue eyes that he raised to Phoebe's were as innocent as those of a new-born babe surfeited with milk.

Phoebe had the bundle open by now. Nason and I, peering over her shoulder, saw it held a yellowish powder. Before Doc could stop her, she placed a pinch of it on her tongue. While she tasted it, she stared pensively at Doc; and Doc's eye again roamed over the noisy throng that pressed around the beer barrel.

Strangely, then, Phoebe laughed. "Here! I'll show you what to do!" She replaced the Digby's Sympathetic Powder in its wrappings, took the Almanac from Doc's smock, and neatly knotted together the stockings that held the two. Then she pushed one of the bundles under the belt of his smock, so that the two of them hung snugly against his back, a little below the level of his belt. "There! Do the same with the other two, and you'll find 'em no harder to carry than that goose you spoke of."

Doc rose waveringly to his feet to paw delightedly behind him. Phoebe went to Nason and hooked her finger in his belt. "Well, Steven, the sooner you start, the sooner you'll get back." Together they went to the man with the drum, who had drunk so much beer that he had trouble finding his drumsticks.

The drum rolled twice in such a way that a thickness came into my upper chest—a thickness like wool, that seemed to keep the air from passing into me. The crowd fell silent, except for a drunken man inside the ordinary, who kept bawling that even though a lobster pot should be coopered around his head and shoulders, he could whip King George without half trying; and the faces around me grew vacant, as is the habit of New Englanders when their feelings are in danger of becoming noticeable.

"Get your packs on," Nason said. His voice had a flat sound, as if he spoke from the depths of a heavy fog. I saw him press Phoebe's shoulder, and heard him clear his throat. "We'll go alone from here," he added. "No stragglers—neither women nor boys. We've got to go fast —and alone."

My father helped me with my blanket-cord, and I saw my mother go around behind Nathaniel and fumble with the straps of his knapsack, but to no good purpose, since tears filled her eyes and splattered on her dress. The militia company lined up raggedly and presented arms.

"Come along," Nason said.

My feet weighed a ton; I could do nothing but stare at my mother: see nothing but the slender streaks of moisture her tears had left on her gray dress. Doc Means wavered past me, looking as though half the town of Wells were fastened to his aged back. I saw my father pat my mother's arm and heard his comforting words, loud in the hush that had fallen on that crossroads gathering: "—no worse than a voyage to Cadiz, and not near as long."

A moment later, without knowing what had happened, or how, I had my hand on Nathaniel's shoulder and we were going rapidly around the first bend in the narrow mountain road, headed north.

VIII

Oᴜʀ route lay through the New Hampshire town of Rumford, now called Concord, though its early name will always be remembered because Benjamin Thompson lived there, but could not stomach our cause, so went to live in England and became Count Rumford, a celebrated man of science. From Rumford we would bear to the northwestward along the forest trails: first up the Merrimac a little way: then over to the Connecticut and up it to the trail that leads to the Winooski River, which flows into Lake Champlain about midway of its eastern shore.

It was just beyond Rumford that Cap Huff caught up with us.

He was riding a dappled gray mare which, in spite of being large, looked almost shrunken because of the way Cap towered over her and bulged out on either side. He had a huge bundle lashed to the pommel of his saddle, and another to the cantle, so that he could not swing himself down when he reached us, but seized the mare by the ears and fell to the ground with a clatter.

"So it's you, is it?" Nason said. "Where'd you get that horse?"

"Look here, Stevie!" Cap complained. "No matter what I have, you look at it as if I'd got it in some underhand way. That horse was a gift!" His round red face exuded righteousness.

"A gift? Who was it given to, and when?"

"To me!" Cap said firmly. "You remember that Theodore Lyman—the one that planted the elms and charged Pete Merrill's father three dollars for——"

"Certainly I remember him! What's he got to do with it?"

"That's what I'm trying to tell you," Cap said impatiently. "That horse was a gift from Theodore Lyman, and so were these other odds and ends." He pointed to the pack on the pommel and avoided Nason's eye.

"So Theodore Lyman made you a lot of presents, did he?" Nason said. "That's something new for Theodore."

Cap stared up at the cloudless sky. "Looks a little like rain, don't it?"

"What kind of presents did he give you?" Nason persisted.

Cap closed his eyes, held up a huge hand and ticked off items on his outspread fingers: "Ten gallons rum, twenty pounds powder, five frypans, ten pounds glass beads, one gross awls, three dozen pocket knives, one hundred fish hooks, thirty papers needles, ten gallons rum."

"You counted the rum once before," Nason said.

Cap sighed at Nason's obtuseness. "Yes. He gave it to me twice— the second time because I kind of hinted. That makes twenty altogether."

"Now look here," Nason protested, "I want you to be careful! We're liable to get into trouble if you let people give you things this way. What in God's name did you want to take that horse for!"

"Stevie," Cap said earnestly, "there's nothin' like a horse for trading purposes. You give me a horse, and I'll guarantee to swap it for anything in reason. If there ain't nothin' to swap it for, I can eat it. Yes, and for every man that's got into trouble over borrowing a horse, there's a thousand good men have died for lack of one."

There were times, during the next two weeks, when it seemed to me there might be something in what Cap said.

It was on the following morning that Nathaniel began to complain of having smallpox symptoms—a headache and a pain under his arm. I went looking for Doc Means and found him at the head of our little column, staggering along at Nason's elbow—and that was one of the most singular of the many singular things about Doc Means. Old as he was, and half dead with fatigue as he always seemed to be, he somehow contrived to keep abreast of the leaders—and that, too, in spite of the bundles stored about his person.

Not only could he travel as fast as anyone, but seemingly he could travel longer. He was given to shambling off the path to hunt for moose tracks, for which he had almost a passion; and when he came stumbling and lurching back, his stumblings and lurchings carried him past the rest of us and up to the head of the column again.

No matter how early I unrolled myself from my blanket in the morning, Doc Means was puttering about the camp, searching with watery blue eyes for traces of animals that might have been near us during the night, or poking feebly at the fire—though the very feebleness of his poking seemed to set it to roaring unaccountably. And at night, too, if I waked and sat up for a smell of the weather, there would be Doc, peering around the fire into the darkness, or fumbling with one of the leaves, roots or berries he was perpetually pocketing during the day's march.

When I told him about Nathaniel, he came shuffling back with me, and looked Nathaniel up and down. "So you got the symptoms, have you?" Doc asked helplessly.

Nathaniel nodded and gulped, nor could I blame him; for smallpox is a cruel disease, threatening its victims not only with death, but with disability, blindness, pain, disfigurement and social ostracism. It was true we had deliberately taken it mildly, to protect ourselves from catching it naturally in all its severity; but for all we knew, the mildness might, through some unforeseen accident, become violent.

All the men of our little company gathered around us with serious faces—expecting, no doubt, to see heroic remedies applied to Nathaniel. Doc stared from Nathaniel to them and back again so ineffectually that I had misgivings as to what our fate might be in the hands of such a doctor.

"I'm glad you got it," Doc said. "You couldn't have picked out a better day to be took sick—not unless you picked tomorrow. According to the Almanac, the next few days are the best days of the year to get anything in." He moved closer to Nathaniel and scrutinized his eyes. "Where's that pain under your arm, and how much of a pain is it?"

Nathaniel felt of his right side. "It's sharp. Sharp."

Doc shook his head. "You ain't got it! You was scratched on the left arm. If you had a pain, there's where it would be: under your left arm: not under your right. That's the way with most of these inoculated cases: they ain't sick at all, only because of being scairt, or because a doctor makes 'em sick."

Cap Huff stopped him when he started to hobble away. "If he ain't got the symptoms, he ain't far from having 'em. If I was you, Doc, I'd give him a few pukes."

Doc Means shook his head. "I don't take any stock in 'em. Anybody that wants to take a puke can take one; but there ain't no reason for doing so: not as I know of."

There was some murmuring among the men; for it was common knowledge that those who inoculated themselves with smallpox were supposed to physic themselves heavily, both up and down. As for Cap, he became noisy at once. "No reason? No reason? Nobody never heard of a doctor that set up a smallpox hospital without puking his classes when inoculated! Ain't there a reason for it? Answer me that!"

"That's so the classes won't forget they're sick," Doc Means said. "How's a doctor going to make a living if his patients ain't aware of being sick? If you ain't aware of being sick, you ain't going to bother with a doctor, are you?" He sighed. "The trouble with a puke," he added feebly, "is that it makes you feel sicker than what you are. What I say is, if you don't feel sick, you ain't sick." He turned suddenly to Nathaniel. "How's your side? How's your headache?"

"Headache?" Nathaniel asked. He seemed surprised. "Headache?

Why, it's not as bad as it was." He kneaded his side sheepishly. "Neither's the pain. I guess maybe they're gone."

"That's right," Doc said. "You'd still have 'em if you'd tooken a few pukes." He went tottering off; and in spite of Cap's grumbling, we found ourselves heartened by Doc's stubborn refusal to physic us.

In another day, however, Nathaniel's symptoms came on in earnest, and those of some of the other men as well. Doc professed himself delighted at the symptoms and at once halted and fumbled in his smock until he found what he called his dowsing rod. It was a Y-shaped branch, and he held it by its two arms, gripping it tightly, its stem pointed straight upward. Holding it thus, he shambled aimlessly hither and yon, a living embodiment, it seemed to me, of futility and delusion. Suddenly the rod jerked violently downward, on which Doc threw it from him and angrily examined the welts on the palms of his hands.

"Some folks think there ain't nothing in this dowsing rod business," he said, "and every time I get me a mess of blisters finding water for 'em, I swear I'll let the whole damned world go thirsty rather than use a rod to help a pack of unbelievers!"

He marked a spot with his heel. "Dig here," he said. "There's a big spring about three feet underground."

We did as he ordered, and unearthed a spring of ice-cold water; so there was more in Doc's dowsing rod than met the eye.

Nason sent Cap pelting back toward Rumford on his gray mare to buy or borrow a fresh cow; and the rest of us pitched our camp and went to work. In an hour's time we had chopped trees for a three-sided cabin, long enough to hold bed-places for all of us, and open on the front. It had a bark roof that overhung the open side by four feet, so that we could have protection from the weather and yet be warmed by the fires that burned before it.

"There!" Doc Means said benevolently when the work was finished. "Anybody'd be altogether too dirty for my gizzard that didn't think this was a terrible nice place to have the smallpox in." To me he added, soothingly, "You and your brother got your inoculation the same day as those in Wells, so the whole company ought to be bustin' out pustulin' before tomorrow night."

When Cap Huff returned, early the next morning, dragging a protesting black and white cow at the end of a halter, the symptoms had set in on all of us, and we were a silent and thoughtful crew. My head felt as though a peck of potatoes had been stuffed into my skull; and my muscles ached as though Cap's cow had slept on me for a week.

Cap staked the cow near the spring: then stood before our cabin and stared at us, his thumbs hooked in his belt and his huge hands slapping

his barrel of a stomach. Doc Means stumbled out from behind the camp
and stood beside Cap, contemplating us with moist blue eyes.

"You want to go to work on that cow," Cap told Doc. "She's fresh,
and she ain't afraid to let go of her milk. I had mebbe a quart this
morning, with some rum in it, but it's kind of wore off." He smacked
his lips. "You better feed these boys right away, because I'd ought to
have a little more before I start off to the westward. Half milk and
half rum makes a nice drink."

Nason came from behind the cabin and looked hard at Cap. "You're
going to the westward?" he asked. "What's the matter with staying
right here?"

Cap's fingers tapped the front of his tow-cloth smock. "Stevie, I got
a lot of trading to do, off to the westward." He glanced over his shoulder and added, in a lower tone, "I picked up a few things in Rumford."

"I told you to get a cow," Nason said. "I don't recall asking you to
pick up anything else."

"Stevie," Cap said patiently, "we're fighting a war. When you're fighting a war, you're entitled to be helped. If folks ain't eager to help, or
don't know how, then they ought to be kind of helped to help." He
stared at Nason defiantly and added, "We've got to find some way of
getting from Allen's Landing to St. John's, ain't we—nearly the whole
length of Lake Champlain?"

"Certainly," Nason said.

"All right!" Cap retorted triumphantly. "Allen's Landing ain't nothing but a little woodchuck-hole of a place, and if we was forced to borrow boats there, or anything else, we might get into trouble, on account
of having no other place to go until our borrowing was completed.
Rumford's a big town, though, Stevie—a rich place, with twenty roads
running out of it. I wouldn't want to see a nicer town to borrow things
in, on account of nobody knowing which way you went. What's more,
we don't ever have to go back to Rumford again."

Seeing that Nason continued to eye him with disapproval, Cap affected a bluff and hearty manner, slapping Doc's back and jovially ordering him to milk the cow for the nourishment of his patients.

Doc Means blinked at him and shook his head. "No," he said, "they
ain't got no appetite."

"No appetite!" Cap bellowed. "Well, why don't you do something
about it? They'll starve if they don't eat!"

Again Doc shook his head. "I ain't found it so. They don't need nothing, only a cup of warm milk now and then, with maybe a pinch of
Digby's Sympathetic Powder in it."

Cap was aghast. "Warm milk! That's no drink for 'em! Why, they'd die of weakness!"

"Why would they?" Doc asked. "Don't a bear lie in a tree for four months, not eating nothing? You show me a bear that ever starved to death in the winter, and I'll eat the whole of him, hair and claws included."

Cap looked incredulous. "You got to do *something* for 'em! You got to bleed 'em, anyway. Every last one of these men, they ought to have about three pints of blood drawed out of 'em."

"Who said so?" Doc asked.

Cap was indignant. "Who said so? Why, all the doctors say so!"

Doc sighed. "Yes, they do. That's right. That's why I ain't going to do it."

Cap stared at him. "That's a hell of a reason, that is!"

"It's the best reason in the world," Doc said. "The doctor you want to foller is the one that thinks different from the rest of 'em. Look at these doctors all around everywhere. Look at these surgeons we got in the army. Do you know how they got to be doctors?"

"Certainly," Cap said. "Certainly. They got to be doctors by doctorin'."

"Nothing of the sort!" Doc cried. "They got to be doctors by holding a doctor's horse and sweeping out his office! Most of 'em never even saw a childbirth and wouldn't want to. They couldn't even help a weasel be delivered! Doctors! Look at the best doctors we got in the army—Levi Wheaton and John Morgan and William Shippen—there ain't no better army doctors than those fellers. They're regular doctors, and everybody says they're fine ones. Do you know how they treat sick folks?"

"Listen," Cap said, "I ast you a civil question, and I expect a civil reply."

"By Grapes!" Doc said. "You talk like a doctor! You don't know, so I'll tell you! According to them, all diseases are inflammatory, and to get rid of the disease you got to get rid of the inflammation. So when they find a sick man, they bleed him first and then feed him tartrate of antimony, epsom salts and calomel. They don't leave nothing inside the feller—no blood, no food, no courage, no nothing! They ain't as sensible as what a dog is!"

Cap made an effort to speak, but Doc silenced him with a gesture. "If I bled you right now, and then gave you a dose of tartrate of antimony and calomel, d'you know what you'd feel like? You'd be sick abed for three days! You'd be sicker than these here smallpox patients."

"I s'pose," Cap said contemptuously, "I s'pose you consider yourself qualified——"

Doc interrupted him. "Now when a dog's sick, he crawls under the barn and stays there, don't he? He don't bleed himself and fill himself up with all kinds of gurry guaranteed to rip his insides to pieces. He lays there and sleeps, and don't eat nothing; and when he comes out, he's cured. If you was sick, that's the kind of medicine I'd give you, too —let you sleep, and not give you nothing to eat. There's some sense to treatment like that."

"I s'pose," Cap sneered, "I s'pose there ain't no doctor that knows so much as you! I s'pose you know better'n all of 'em."

"No," Doc said. "Some of 'em have a little sense. There's a feller down in Virginia—Dr. Siccary. He says the best food there is for anyone is tomatoes. He says if you can eat enough tomatoes, you won't never die. That feller Siccary, he sounds all right. Then there's Benjamin Franklin's doctor, Thomas Tryon, over in——"

Cap became violent. "Tomatoes? Love apples? Why, they're rank poison! Any doctor'll tell you that!"

I saw fit to put in a word. "It's true that most doctors say they're poison, but those of us who've sailed to Spain know it's not so. The Spaniards use tomatoes on everything they cook, nearly, and every Arundel mariner that's sailed there has tomatoes planted in his garden, and has 'em made into ketchup for winter use."

"They're poison!" Cap insisted. "Any damned fool knows love apples is pure poison!" He eyed Doc craftily. "If doctors ain't no good, and all their ideas is so wrong, what you want to carry a medical liberry around with you for?"

"So to find out what the best doctors recommend, and then do different," Doc said.

Enraged at Doc's stubbornness, Cap would, I think, have taken our treatment into his own hands if Nason had not interfered and ordered him away to the westward, reminding him that the citizens of Rumford might be on his trail. So Cap loaded his supplies on the back of his gray mare, frequently pausing to drink copiously from a kettle in which he had mixed two quarts of rum and a quart of warm milk; and we all felt more at peace when he hoisted himself clumsily into the saddle and went lurching off toward Lake Champlain, hoarsely bawling a French song.

Due, perhaps, to the thimbleful of Digby's Sympathetic Powder that Doc had put in our milk, we were able to be on our feet and move around on the following day.

Nason set rabbit snares in the lowland at the foot of the hill, so that we might have fresh meat when our illness was over; and twice a day he drilled us—in the morning in the English fashion; and in the afternoon in the Indian fashion. In the first we formed straight ranks and held in our stomachs, very military, shouldering oak saplings in place of muskets. In the second we learned how to break from single file into double and shelter ourselves behind trees, facing outward, so that no enemy could take us in the rear.

For the most part we lay and listened to Doc Means, who gave us repeated assurances of how healthy he proposed to keep the lot of us after we should reach Canada, provided we kept away from regular doctors and went without food occasionally—a piece of advice to which even he, in after days, sometimes referred sardonically.

He took pleasure in quoting to us from his medical library and calling attention to some of the drawbacks connected with the remedies that had come to his notice.

He had learned by heart, out of his books, a cure for everything on earth that anybody could name, from warts to fright; and the only one with which he seemed to find no fault was the fright cure.

Unlike many of the panaceas of the day, Doc's fright remedy was easily compounded. There was, he told us, an infallible means to prevent being struck by lightning, and also a cure for those who have been struck; but since for the preventive he lacked the skin of a seal, we would have to take our chances during thunderstorms. There were many wart cures, he said, but the one recommended by the most enlightened doctors was to hunt for a shooting star, and then, as soon as possible after seeing one, to pour vinegar on a door-hinge, which isn't easy to find in the depths of the woods.

The fear remedy, however, was not so difficult. Its chief ingredients, according to Doc, were gunpowder and pepper, mixed with rum, and flavored with Digby's Sympathetic Powder. We had the gunpowder and the rum, while Doc had the Sympathetic Powder. We could, he said, get along without the pepper, and even without the gunpowder too; for it was the Sympathetic Powder and the rum that were the two necessary ingredients. The gunpowder and the pepper, he assured us, only made the remedy more lasting in its effects.

"It stands to reason," Doc said, "that the farther you can keep away from doctors, the healthier you'll be. Look at what these doctors call for in their most expensive medicines—snake skins, slow worms, red coral, ambergris, gold leaf, Venice treacle, vipers, oil of stones, rape of storax, camel's hay, the bellies of skinks——"

"You mean skunks, don't you?" Nason asked.

"No," Doc said, "I mean skinks."

Nason was skeptical. "What's a skink?"

"How would I know?" Doc asked. "How would anyone know? There ain't none in New England, and there ain't no camel's hay, neither. What I say is, these doctors that tell you to use skinks' bellies and camel's hay in medicines, they don't know what they're talking about, and a feller that don't know what he's talking about ain't worth listening to. He ain't no good, and he wa'n't never no good, and he won't never *be* no good."

Unconventional as were Doc's medical beliefs, he really was an expert with a saw and knife, and able to take off a leg or an arm before, almost, the patient could scream. But to my mind the most singular of his powers was the ability to rub a sprain or a rheumatic joint in such a way that the pain, in no time at all, was relieved; and this ability or gift, he declared, was due to the fact that he was a Seventh Son, so that his touch was a guarantee of good fortune.

Since his childhood, he said, persons contemplating matrimony, sea voyages or hunting trips had come for miles to touch him, knowing they would be fortunate because of the touch. It was this gift, he said, that had led him to join the army; for so many had gone to fight, and so many were afraid of being hanged if they guessed wrongly which side they should take in the Rebellion, and so many were in danger of losing all their small savings through the increasing worthlessness of the currency, that his house was overrun, day and night, with people possessed to touch him for good luck.

They came from as far away as Falmouth and York, he said, arriving at his house at two and three o'clock in the morning, or at dawn or supper-time or any time at all, and pounding on the door until he allowed himself to be touched. Then, as like as not, he would have to provide them with food or rum; and all this touching and feeding people had come to be so tiring and annoying to him that he thought going to war would let him lead a quieter life and get more sleep.

Whatever it was that gave him his singular power, it did us more of a service than all his fright remedies and wart eradicators; for it cured Joseph Marie Verrieul and made him our friend, which turned out to be a matter of importance to me.

. . . As Doc had predicted, our symptoms vanished in two days, and for the next week we fared sumptuously on fish chowders made of trout, milk and hard bread, and on messes of greens that Zelph was indefatigable in gathering. On the seventh day we were hard put to it, even, to find a pustule, which proved to be fortunate; for toward sundown of that chilly gray day we heard a raucous voice singing a French song about rolling a ball.

"Behind our house there is a pond," the song ran, "Roll on, my ball, roll on: Three beautiful ducks are bathing themselves in it: Roll, roll, my rolling ball: Roll on, my ball, roll on."

"There's Cap!" Nason said.

It was indeed Cap and his gray mare; but he was not riding the mare: he was leading her; and on her back, slung across the saddle like a sack of meal, was the body of a man.

"Come get him!" Cap shouted.

"Has he had the smallpox?" Nason called.

Cap stopped the horse, put his hand on the man's shoulder and roared at him, "Hey! have you had the smallpox?"

The man just hung there.

Cap shouted again and shook him; crouched beside him and examined his face; then announced, "He's got a pit under his ear and two on his forehead."

"Go ahead and get him," Nason told us.

We took him off the horse and laid him beside the fire. He was young, about Nathaniel's age, but painfully thin. His eyes were sunken, and his cheeks had fallen in, so there was something about his head that put me in mind of a bird's skull. Yet his face, under the grime and tear-streaks on it, was smoothly brown, and his eyebrows were thin and arched, so that even in his pitiful condition he had a look of distinction.

Cap was puzzled by him. "Picked him up in the woods," he told us. "There he was, all alone, a thousand miles from nowhere, just lying beside the path like he was dead." He shook his head, adding: "No food; no blanket; not even any money."

"How do you know he didn't have any money?" Nason asked.

Cap looked hurt and tapped Doc's shoulder. "What's the matter with him?"

"I'd say he was starved," Doc said. "Starved and tuckered." Almost hopefully he added, "Maybe I'll find something else the matter with him when there ain't so many folks around, and I get a chance to look at him."

Tom Bickford pointed to the young man's knees. The breeches over them were torn; and under the holes the skin was raw. We saw, then, that his palms were raw as well.

"Well, now," Doc said, "that boy must have been anxious to get somewhere! He's been crawling!"

He knelt stiffly to fumble at the boy's legs. "Ankle. Sprained." He pawed at him again: then sank back on his heels to look up at us. "Both ankles! Both ankles sprained."

We poured rum and milk into him, and peeled off his Indian leggins and moccasins, while Doc began to feel, knead, and poke the two sprained ankles. When he groaned, we gave him more rum and milk. Doc worked on, pulling at his heels and twisting his toes; and in half an hour the boy was sitting up, taking all the rabbit stew we would give him: clamoring for more, too, and filling out under our eyes.

His name, he said, was Verrieul—Joseph Marie Verrieul, and he had been in the army on Dorchester Heights. When the British left Boston, his regiment and nine others had marched for New York. By the time he reached New London, he was, as he put it, very much beat out. Consequently he signed aboard a privateer brig that sailed from New London on the night of his arrival.

"A privateer!" Cap Huff protested. "What about your regiment?"

Verrieul smiled up at Cap so artlessly that Cap looked abashed. That was Verrieul's way—to smile happily and confidingly at everyone, whether friend or enemy; nor was his smile something put on for the moment, to attain his ends. He was perpetually happy within: eager and full of enthusiasm: ready for anything, like an amiable dog; and it seemed impossible to be with him, or to look at him, even, without feeling toward him as one would feel toward a friendly puppy.

"But I tell you I was beat out—very much beat out," he told Cap. "I was doing nothing in the army: nothing! Merely sitting and freezing, and of no use to anyone. On a privateer, I thought, I would be active, alert! Better that, I think, than to hide in the woods, like many in my regiment. What do you think?"

Cap growled noncommittally and gave him more rum and milk.

He was so unfortunate, Verrieul continued, as to encounter bad weather, and water poured through the deck-seams of the brig, both day and night. For nearly two weeks he was unable to dry his clothes or obtain warm food, and was greatly troubled with gurry sores. They sighted no prizes, and to make things worse, the mate knocked him down and kicked him. When, consequently, the brig put into Boston two weeks ago, he was overcome by a depression that filled him with a desire to visit his friend Dr. Wheelock for consolation and advice.

"And did you visit him?" Nason wanted to know.

"Visit him?" Verrieul asked. "How could I arrive at Hanover, considering what happened to me?" He moved the ankle on which Doc Means wasn't working. "I was proceeding alone along the path to Hanover, happy at my approaching reunion with the Revrint Doctor, when I stepped on an insecure stone and suffered a wrench in one ankle.

The path was rough; so when I went on, I fell often, and at length I wrenched the other also." He drew a deep breath. "Then I was indeed unhappy, not only for myself, but because of the pain it would cause the Revrint Doctor if he learned I had died like this: crawling in the forest; of no use in the world. He would have been sad to think that after he had labored so industriously to give me learning and usefulness, all his efforts had come to nothing through one small misstep of mine."

Cap spoke carelessly. "If I was you, I wouldn't lose no sleep worrying about how this Doctor, or anybody else for that matter, might take sick on account of fretting about me. People down our way, they got troubles of their own, and they spend all their time griping about themselves. What leads you to think this Doctor might lie awake nights, wringing his hands over your whereabouts? Did you owe him some money, maybe?"

Cap, I saw, was being facetious after his own manner, partly in relief at Verrieul's recovery, and partly to keep the boy's tongue wagging.

Verrieul seemed a little hurt by Cap's words. "You must understand that my case was unusual. From the manner in which you shower kindnesses on me, I can see you find me pleasing; and that was even more the case with the Revrint Doctor. For three years there was no pupil regarded with as much warmth by the Revrint Doctor as was unworthy Joseph Verrieul."

"You don't say!" Cap remarked. "Well, well! Maybe that's a compliment for the Doctor, and maybe it ain't! Who is this Revrint Doctor, if we might make so bold as to ask?"

Verrieul was incredulous. "The Revrint Dr. Wheelock? You don't know him? Truly, I thought he knew everybody in the world! He writes letters to all neighborhoods—to General Washington and great sachems everywhere."

"His letters to me must have got lost," Cap said. "Where's he live and what's he do?"

"He is president of the seminary in Hanover! You have heard of it: the Indian school? We call it Dartmouth College."

"Indian school?" Cap asked quickly. "You're an Indian?"

"No, no!" Verrieul said. "I am an American, descended from French people. My father was lieutenant colonel, living in Sillery. Now he is dead. I was at school in France for two years: then I am discovered by the Revrint Dr. Wheelock! A fine man! A man with a large, warm heart, wholly confident of my future. He paid the cost of my studies in the seminary, out of his own pocket; because, you see, I have nothing myself."

He smiled his confiding, engaging smile; and Cap, staring at him, opened his mouth to say something, but didn't say it.

"You met Indians at this Indian school?" Nason asked.

Verrieul laughed. "*Met* them! They're my brothers! Lewis Vincent from Caughnawaga, and Joe Gill, the son of the sachem of St. Francis: they are brothers to me. It was I who went with Kendal to Caughnawaga as an interpreter when he founded the school. Kendal and James Deane and I, we are much loved in Caughnawaga."

Nason spoke to him rapidly in a language that had a peculiar click and catch beneath and between the words.

"Indeed, yes!" Verrieul exclaimed. "It was the first I learned—Abenaki. Now I speak many, including Chippeway. All the western nations speak Chippeway. I learned it when I traveled with James Deane to the westward."

The name James Deane meant nothing to any of us; but Verrieul quickly enlightened us. "He studied at Dartmouth also. He lived among the Oneidas from boyhood, placed there by his father, a minister, for the purpose of becoming a missionary. His family is a great family. He has an uncle, Silas Deane: a great man. James Deane speaks Iroquois better than the Iroquois themselves. There is nothing at all—nothing—that the Oneidas would not do for James Deane. I have traveled with him. It was he who taught me to speak the Iroquois language better than most.

"Then I am good at Huron—very good. Of course, there is little difference. They are about alike, Huron and Iroquois speech. Lewis Vincent is a Huron. Maybe you have heard of Payne's Tavern in Hanover?"

We stared at him, fascinated by the activity of his mind and his talent of speaking highly of himself without giving offense.

"It was Payne's Tavern," he told us, "that caused the battle last year between the Revrint Dr. Wheelock and the townspeople, and the battle had its beginning because Lewis Vincent and unworthy Joseph Verrieul were unfortunately affected by liquor obtained there."

"You mean you got drunk with this Huron?" Cap asked.

Verrieul made a slight movement with one hand, a gesture expressive of a faint distaste. "Observers said that Lewis and I temporarily lacked our usual good judgment," he admitted. "If the Revrint Doctor had not loved me greatly, I think it would have gone hard with Lewis, because he danced naked in the halls of the college, very noisy. It was I who went to the Revrint Doctor and explained such lack of discernment; and because of my explanation, he placed the blame on Payne and his tavern." There was an angelic look on Verrieul's thin brown face. "So that will show you how I am situated with Lewis Vincent.

Lewis Vincent has made me his brother. I have learned from him to speak nicely in Huron. I have made orations in the tongue. Last year I made an oration to Lewis Vincent on the wickedness of drinking—an oration so powerful that Lewis wept and for over three days refused to think, even, of liquor."

Doc Means, who had been gently kneading Verrieul's ankles, sat back on his heels. "Move your feet," he told the boy. "See how they feel."

"Why," Verrieul said, "there's no pain in them: only some stiffness!"

Doc Means puttered about him, making him comfortable; so the rest of us took our bowls and spoons and sat before the long fire in the dusk to eat our rabbit stew.

For the first time, then, Cap Huff mentioned his trip to the westward. "Stevie," he said uneasily, "how long before we can move? Something's happened up north. The lake-shore's thick with deserters, hiding in the brush and saying nothing to nobody."

Nason stared at him, frowning. "Deserters? Deserters from where?"

"There's no telling. You can't catch 'em. They act as if all hell was after 'em."

Nason's reply was both short and sudden. "We'll move tomorrow. We'll burn the clothes and the cabin after breakfast, and then we'll wash up and go." He looked doubtfully at Verrieul, who was lying back, his eyes closed, a thin seraph in the firelight. "You'll have to put this young man on your horse and carry him to the first settlement, so he can have help until he's able to start for Hanover."

"There's nothing to hinder him making his own way," Doc Means said. "I'll have him walking by morning."

At the weary weakness of Doc's voice, Verrieul sat up to stare solicitously at him. Then he smiled fondly. "I'm in no hurry to return to Hanover. I've taken a notion to go along with you for a time. It might be I could be useful."

It was apparent to all of us that he could indeed be useful; but how useful he was to be, we couldn't dream. Nor had we even a slight suspicion that our meeting with Joseph Marie Verrieul was the last piece of good fortune that was to come our way for many a long day.

IX

At ALLEN'S LANDING, where the Winooski River flows into Lake Champlain, there was little besides a sawmill and a gristmill, and a store run by one of the Allens that are almost as plentiful in the Hampshire grants as Starks in New Hampshire. Here we took possession of two canoes for which Cap, during his absence from our smallpox camp, had arranged to trade his horse and frying pans. They were ancient relics, the bark gone in patches and the pitch over their seams black and broken with age, so that they looked about as seaworthy as corncribs.

Nason and Verrieul, however, commended Cap for acquiring them. They were North canoes, Verrieul said, made by Indians far to the northwest, beyond Lake Superior; so they must have been brought here and abandoned by traders. To me they seemed unwieldy and too large; but Verrieul said No: they were snug and tidy, easy to handle by comparison with Master canoes, which are forty feet long, manned by fourteen paddlers: yet they were heavy enough for lake travel, unlike the twenty-foot half-canoes to which eastern pork-eaters like ourselves are accustomed. They were nine paces long, and two paces wide, accommodating eleven men—a lookout in the bow, a steersman standing in the stern, six middlemen with paddles on the three thwarts amidships, and three passengers.

Following Verrieul's instructions, we peeled bark from yellow birches and laid it over the rents in these dilapidated hulks, stitching it in place with *wattape*—the fine roots of red spruces; after which Nason and Verrieul daubed the seams with hot pitch. It was like a miracle to see these bargains of Cap's changed, almost in a moment, from ragged wrecks into trim and glistening craft.

They were discouraging to handle; for with six men sitting high on the thwarts, they were so skittish that we needed practice if we didn't want to end our days on the bottom of Lake Champlain. We were trying to get it when Cap bawled to us from the shore that a fleet of bateaux, loaded with supplies, had passed north the day before.

"There ain't enough supplies here to feed a sick pee-wit!" Cap shouted. "We better catch up with those bateaux, Stevie, and find some

food before the troops get ahead of us! You know how soldiers are,
Stevie: never thinking of nothing but food!"

He bellowed and complained until Nason beached the canoes and
ordered us to get our packs aboard and set off after the supply-boats.

To remedy their skittishness we lashed blocks to the bottom of the
canoes and stepped a mast in each—a mast with a single yard, so we
could lie in the bottom of the canoe and sail ourselves.

When Cap stowed himself in the after part of our canoe, between
Verrieul and Nathaniel, who tended the tacks of our rude sail while
I handled the steering paddle, he was in a bitter humor; for the suddenness of our departure had cut him short in some of his trading
ventures. He had been forced, he said, to exchange the choicest of his
supplies for a bundle of paper money corded up like old love letters,
hundreds of dollars worth of it. It was all the fault of Congress, he said.
Congress had taken a hand in financial matters, and printed money
whenever anyone needed some, which was about as sensible as a man
promising to marry every girl he saw. In such a case, he said, the girls
soon got to know that his promises didn't mean anything, and he
couldn't even get a howdy-do out of them, let alone anything more
comforting; and that was the way with Congress money. People knew
it didn't mean anything, and in no time at all they would refuse to sell
even a squash pie for less than two thousand dollars in Congress money.

Nason, who had taken Tom Bickford to handle the steering oar of
his canoe, shouted to us to get along. "Keep going," he told us, "till dark,
or till your seams open up."

We slid out into the lake, set a course between the point of Grand
Isle and the high shores of Valcour Island, and were off on our long
journey to the northward—a journey that we hoped, as do all those who
go off to war, would bring us nothing but comradeship and gay adventure, and perhaps a little glory.

When Cap had indiscreetly aired his opinions of the financial abilities
of Congress, he questioned Verrieul in a hoarse and angry voice concerning the Indians who might be used against us by the English—
provided we had heard correctly in London from Marie de Sabrevois.

"You want to listen to this, Cap'n Peter," he told me, while Verrieul
pondered. "You never can tell when information about these red
weasels might come in handy." Cap was profane, and put no curb on
his tongue where Indians were concerned when he was with me;
though in Nason's presence he sometimes contented himself with looking contemptuous when red men were mentioned.

"Weasels?" Verrieul asked. "Which ones do you call weasels?"

"All of 'em!" Cap said. "They're all a lot of dirty, thieving, red weasels! Cut your throat quick as a wink, and can't hold their liquor!"

"How about your friend Natanis of whom I've heard you speak?"
Verrieul asked. "How many throats has *he* cut?"

Cap was indignant. "Don't get the wrong idea about Natanis. He's
a friend. He's different, Natanis is. Stevie saved his life once. We've
all kind of helped each other a few times."

"But dirty, eh?"

"I told you he was different," Cap said. "He really ain't an Indian,
except for having an Indian father and mother and a red hide. He don't
even drink, the poor iggorollamus: he don't understand nothing about
pleasure at all!"

Verrieul nodded thoughtfully. "Yes, that's a strange thing about Indians. We find them peculiar because, although they are called savage,
they are often as civilized as white men, and sometimes more so."

"Like hell they are!" Cap said. "How are they?"

"Because," Verrieul said, "in every Indian nation, even the worst,
there are many good men, and more honest ones, and even some that
are merciful toward their enemies, which is against all common sense.
White men, being civilized and not at all savage, avoid common sense
as much as possible; but all Indians, whether good or bad, are taught
to have a high regard for common sense. Those that are merciful, therefore, are merciful in spite of their teachings; whereas white men, who
are forever taught to be merciful, are often the opposite."

Cap scratched his head. "I don't see no sense to what you say! Why
is it against common sense to be merciful to an enemy?"

"Look," Verrieul said. "We're making war against the English. We
make war against them in order to kill them, do we not?"

"For sure we do!"

"That's why Indians fight, too," Verrieul said. "To kill their enemies.
They can't understand it, many of them, when they're asked to go out
and kill enemies, and are then told it's cruel to kill them when the
opportunity presents. The way to kill enemies is not to be merciful to
them, they say, but to kill them."

"They're a lot of dirty, underhanded red stinks," Cap said.

"There's another thing," Verrieul explained. "The nations change a
good deal. It depends on the Manitousiou—*m'téoulin*—or whatever a
nation calls the man whose words it finds most acceptable. Sorcerer,
maybe, you'd call him; or maybe magician. Shaman, the western nations say. The nations are almost like trading companies: under good
men they're better than under bad men. And as the years pass, they
learn how to do things better. Even the Montagnais have learned to
make leggins that don't fall apart in a gale. I guess we were pretty bad

three hundred years ago. I guess we were dirty, and superstitious, too, maybe; cruel, even. The Revrint Dr. Wheelock told me that when the Holy Catholic Church tortured people, it thought up worse tortures than any Indian ever imagined. Catholics have changed, the Revrint Wheelock said, and so have Indians. They're better than they were a hundred and fifty years ago—better than when the Jesuit fathers first lived among them."

"Just a lot of red stinks!" Cap insisted.

"One thing I quickly learned when I traveled with James Deane," Verrieul said, "was that if you live with Hurons, you're sure they're the kindest people on earth, and Iroquois the most terrible; whereas if you live with Iroquois, you feel that no man ever had truer friends than the Iroquois, and that Hurons are wild beasts."

"Buzzards!" Cap remarked. "Red buzzards!"

"Well," Verrieul said, "if they're buzzards, how do you account for the white children who have been captured by Indian nations, and liked them so well they refused to go back to live with white men again?"

"Listen!" Cap said. "When a man gets used to buzzards, he ain't going to where there's buzzards he ain't used to, is he? He likes the buzzards he's got used to now better than the buzzards he used to be used to, don't he? Don't it stand to reason? You answer me that!"

"Now I have become confused," Verrieul said. "But in spite of what you say, Captain Huff—or maybe not in spite of it—I don't know which —James Deane is no buzzard. It is true, though, that after he had spent some years with the Oneidas, it was with great difficulty he was persuaded to come to Hanover with the Revrint Dr. Wheelock. The sachem of St. Francis, Joseph Gill: he was a white captive, and so was his wife. He's a wise man—no buzzard at all; but he wouldn't go back to live with white people, nor his wife either; by no means! In Dartmouth there are three from Caughnawaga, all grandchildren of white captives who would never go back among white people—the grandson of Mr. Stacy from Ipswich, the grandson of Mr. Tarbull from Groton, and the grandson of Eunice Williams from Deerfield."

Cap Huff tapped me on the knee. "You don't want to take too much stock in what he says, Cap'n Peter." He eyed Verrieul indignantly. "You're like all the rest of these friends of the Indians! Ask 'em something straightforward and honest about the red weasels, and they tell you everything but what you want to know. All I want to know is which of these red buzzards we'll have to fight; all I get is a lot of yap about white men that want to be Irryquartz or Onudders!"

That was Cap Huff's way when the talk turned on Indians. He would ask for information about them; but it seemed impossible for him to believe anything he heard, or even to listen to the information for which he asked. It was plain that Verrieul would have answered Cap's questions as well as he could if Cap had let him; but the more Verrieul tried, the louder Cap grumbled, so that Verrieul finally had to give it up.

. . . Thanks to our blanket sails and a fair wind, we camped that night on Isle La Motte, near the Canadian end of the lake, not only to rest our cramped muscles, but also to pitch our canoes once more; for the constant movement of these large canoes cracks off the pitch, so that they must be re-pitched each day.

We were eager to get forward. Our pork was gone; there wasn't enough corn meal among all of us to nourish a chickadee, and the fish Zelph cooked for us were watery and tasteless. So we were restless and up with the false dawn, and afloat soon after, hastening north between rocky shores that drew constantly closer together, and watching for the supply-boats of which Cap had learned.

So intently did we peer ahead into the faint mists that rose from the surface of this narrowing lake that without knowing how it happened, or when, we saw the lake was a lake no longer, but a broad brown river that swept us along between banks as flat as those behind us had been steep and rocky. We had come to Canada at last.

The river was the Richelieu, though Verrieul said it was also known as the Iroquois, because it was the pathway followed by the Iroquois in the old days when they went north to wage war on the Montagnais.

This river, Verrieul said, ran straight north and emptied into the St. Lawrence at Sorel, the town at the end of the tremendous wide place known as Lake St. Peter, and that was how we would go: through St. John's, a matter of thirty miles from Lake Champlain: then on twice as far again to Sorel, through water a little broken: then down the St. Lawrence to Quebec.

X

Whenever Cap Huff spoke of Quebec, which he often did, he smacked his lips. "It ain't much to look at," he told us, "but after we've reported to Arnold, we'll scout out around Sillery." He lowered his voice to a hoarse whisper. "There's a place out in Sillery that's got brandy in the cellar that'll surprise you! Take maybe a third of a bottle, and for three days afterward you won't remember none of the worst things you ever done. That's the nice thing about it!"

But the closer we came to Canada, the more silent Nathaniel grew. His increasing quiet, I felt, was somehow due to Marie de Sabrevois; to something she had said to him in London, or something in the letter she had given him—the letter Nathaniel had never mentioned to me. I became almost certain of this when I heard him asking Cap Huff how long we would stay in St. John's.

"Stay?" Cap asked. "We'll stay long enough to get some food. We'll buy us a couple of young pigs, maybe, and a barrel of that cider with brandy in it." His answer seemed comforting to Nathaniel, and I made up my mind to keep my eye on him in St. John's.

We were halfway between the lake and St. John's when we caught sight of the bateaux we were pursuing. They were abreast of a long, low island in the river—an island overgrown with alders. This low island, Verrieul said, was Isle aux Noix—a gloomy place, almost a swamp, but used for military camps by French armies and Indian war parties since time out of mind. We were to know it better soon; and even now there was a singular thing about it that caught our attention.

There were open fields on the island, and a white house with eaves that curved upward as if warped in the damp air of the place. The singular thing of which I speak lay in the actions of the people working in the fields. As soon as we came in sight, they ran like frightened rabbits, and vanished; so that the whole island, as we passed, might have been deserted.

Cap Huff scratched his head. "By Godfrey," he said, "that don't look right! These Frenchmen up here in Canada, they like us. Leastways, they always have. It was them as learned me my French songs, and

how to drink cider with brandy in it! What's got into 'em, I'd like to
know?"

He was aggrieved as we drew up toward the hindmost bateau—a
sort of scow with a swivel gun mounted bow and stern; and the greeting we received was not calculated to calm him. A man in the stern
pointed his swivel at Cap's stomach.

"Where you from and where you going?" he shouted. "What's your
business?"

I ran off to larboard to let Cap talk to him. "Detachment of scouts
for General Arnold," Cap roared. "Going to Quebec! What you want
to be so damned military about?"

The man in the stern swung his swivel gun to one side and jerked
his head by way of inviting us to come closer.

"Where you been?" he asked, as I laid the canoe alongside him. "You
been in jail or something?"

"We been coming over the trail from Maine," Cap said.

"You must 'a' denned up somewhere if you ain't heard the news,"
the man said. "You ain't going to see Quebec this trip." Grimly he added,
"Nor any other trip, neither, the way things look now."

"You mean they licked Arnold?" Cap asked.

"Arnold? No, not Arnold! They ain't got around to *him,* yet! Arnold
left Quebec when Wooster came down there to take command, in
April. There wasn't any room for Arnold after Wooster showed up, the
damned old woman, so Arnold went back to Montreal and took command there." He stared at us balefully, muttering "damned old woman"
under his breath.

"Who's a damned old woman?" Cap demanded.

"Wooster! He's out now. They threw him out. He was an old
woman. General Thomas tooken his place."

"Thomas!" Cap growled. "Thomas! I never heard of him! Where do
they get all these generals I never heard of! They must grow 'em on
bushes! Why didn't they leave Arnold where he was? There wasn't nobody as good as Arnold!"

The scow-man slapped his swivel gun. "There ain't nobody knows
why anybody does anything up in this stink-hole! If ever there was a
pack of fart-wits running things, it's here and now! Congressmen running an army! Hell!" He spat furiously in the river.

"Say, brother," Cap said, "you better be careful how you talk about
Congress! There's a law against it!"

The man laughed bitterly. "Wait till you been up here a few hours
before you start telling me how to talk about Congress! Wait till you
begin to look around for food! That's my job, carrying food! We carry

in half enough to feed them that's here. Just half enough! There ain't money to buy more! Congress ain't got none! No money and no brains, neither—sending men up here without giving 'em no way to keep alive! And more men to come, too: four regiments! Four more regiments, under Sullivan, due to leave Albany any day; due to come up here and holler for food that nobody ain't got!"

Nason's canoe, with Doc Means riding in the high curved bow, came up astern. Tom Bickford swung her alongside; and the middlemen laid their paddles across our gunwale to keep the bark sides from chafing.

Cap Huff emitted an indignant bellow. "No food, he says, Stevie! No food, by God, and we can't go to Quebec! This is a hell of a war!"

Nason seemed to ponder the words, and the rest of us were silent, contemplating the dark forests through which this broad stream relentlessly hurried us.

It was the man at the swivel gun who broke the silence. "I should say it *was* a hell of a war, thanks to your damned New Englanders!"

We transferred our attention from the forests to him. He fingered his gun and spoke defensively. "That's what it was: your damned New Englanders! Three weeks ago they sat outside of Quebec, pinching their pennies and stealing each other's food, same as ever. Then, by God, Carleton opened the gate and popped out at 'em; and the New Englanders, they're running yet! Left their guns and camp kettles: left all their ammunition and medicines: left the food in the kettles, even, so's they could run their heads off! Some of 'em ran all the way around Montreal, so Arnold wouldn't catch 'em; and some of 'em ran through the woods, all the way back to New England! You'll find some of 'em up around Lake Superior, still running, prob'ly! Look at these folks on shore, the way they act! They won't have nothing to do with us, since your damned New Englanders started running!"

Cap rubbed his face as if to clear it of insects. "You're a liar! If they did any running, they did it because the Yorkers started it! Where you from? New York?"

The man laughed derisively. "New York? Not me! I'm from a *real* place! I'm from Pennsylvania."

"All right, brother," Cap said. "When you're talking to us, don't be so damned noisy about New Englanders, because that's what we are. We don't like noisy people, and when anybody gets noisy with us, he gets so much noise back that he's most generally deef the rest of his life. You talk like you owned this country, but we know better. We been up in this Quebec country before: with Arnold. If we'd had half enough food then, we'd 'a' been well fed! Nothing to eat for a month but squirrel-hair and rock-tripe! None of our folks did any running, brother! A few, maybe; but none to speak of. If there's been any done since, I'll bet you a bottle of rum to an eel skin it was started by Yorkers, headed by Lieutenant Colonel Donald Campbell of the New York line!"

"Say," the Pennsylvanian admitted, "come to think of it, it *was* Campbell they were all cussing!"

Nason shouted at his middlemen. They dug in their paddles with such force that the water sucked and swirled. As Tom Bickford swung the craft into mid-stream with his steering-paddle, Nason spoke quietly to Cap Huff. "Drive your men! If we can't reach Quebec, we've got to leave the river at St. John's and get somewhere—and get there quick!"

XI

Sᴛ. ᴊᴏʜɴ's is a sort of seaport in the middle of nowhere; for vessels can sail to it from Champlain; but beyond it there are falls and quick water, difficult for even canoes to pass. Montreal lies to the west, Sorel and the broad St. Lawrence to the north, and Albany to the south, so it is well situated for a prosperous trading town. Ordinarily it looks pleasant enough, with its broad fortified enclosure containing barracks and a shipyard and various small buildings on the westward bank, and a winding road along the river, with farms and a large house or two fronting on it; and on the eastern side a ridge of high land with more farms and an imposing manor house.

But when we ran our canoes toward the landing on that cold May afternoon, St. John's might recently have suffered from a plague and an earthquake combined.

There was a half-finished skeleton of a vessel in a shipyard—a brig or schooner—and not a soul near it. The whole place looked dead. Shutters covered the windows of such houses as we could see, and boards were nailed across the fronts of warehouses and barracks, as if they had been gutted by a hurricane and hastily repaired.

The road that paralleled the landing was littered with rubbish. Amid the rubbish, around small fires, sat groups of men so dejected in appearance that they might have been beggars out of London slums.

They were thin, unshaven, half clothed. Some had bundles of muddy cloth tied around their feet in place of shoes: some wore coats with gaping seams through which the linings hung: their breeches were torn and draggled: some were coatless, and in ragged shirts as dingy as the gray clouds that drifted from the eastward.

As we stared at them, two men a little better dressed walked to the landing from the nearest warehouse. Their clothes were travesties on uniforms: but uniforms they must have been; for though the men were swordless, they wore officers' gorgets.

"Where's the provision-boats?" one asked.

"An hour behind," Nason said.

"How much this time, and what is it you're carrying?"

Nason shook his head. "We aren't with 'em."

"Not *with* 'em! Then you got to keep away from here! Orders are, no more men received in this section unless provided with rations! That's what's been holding Sullivan and Wayne in Albany, damn it, and here you come, contrary to orders! My God! There's two hundred and eighty smallpox cases—soldiers they call themselves—lying in huts here with nothing to put in their stomachs! I say you can't come ashore!"

Nason studied the cheerless town. "We'll feed ourselves," he said at length. "We——"

"Feed yourselves!" the officer cried. "What with! What're you going to eat in place of food? This army's supposed to be getting six tons of pork a day, and we're getting less than two!"

"We've got to get through to Arnold," Nason said. "He sent me back to Maine from Quebec on purpose to get these men to do scout duty."

The officer's face changed a little. "Scout duty? It's a pity you couldn't have been here sooner, to do some scouting on a few of the rats Arnold's got under him!"

Nason cleared his throat and spoke softly. "Rats? Who would that be?"

"That would be Bedel and Butterfield, just to name two of 'em!" the officer said. "You don't mean to say you haven't heard what happened at the Cedars!"

"Look here," Nason said, "I'm going to take these men through to Arnold! Do we come ashore here, or do we have to land back a piece and dodge around you?"

The officer spat. "Well, everything's in a mess, anyway, and I guess you won't make it much worse. Come ahead."

Drawing our canoes from the water, we overturned them to make shelters for our muskets and packs, while the two officers stood watching us. Nason placed guards over our baggage: then turned to the officers. "What's this about the Cedars? Was it because of something that happened at Quebec?"

One of them walked away: the other looked mutinous. Then the man in motion turned and came back to us, his face as red as an Indian blanket. When he spoke, there was venom in his voice. "A mess! A dirty damned mess!" When he saw all of us silent, watching him, he spoke more calmly.

"Quebec! No, it wasn't because of Quebec! The Cedars was worse than Quebec, some ways, if anything *could* be worse! You know where the Cedars is?"

Nason shook his head.

"It's thirty miles above Montreal, at a bend in the St. Lawrence. Before Arnold came up from Quebec, Colonel Moses Hazen was in charge at Montreal. You know Hazen?"

Again Nason shook his head.

"Hazen lives across the river, in Iberville," the officer explained. "You can see his house: the big one over there, on the high land." The house he meant was an imposing place, with small houses of retainers scattered along the ridge near it.

"Oh yes," the officer said, "he's got quite a place: quite a place! Farmers; and nuns to teach the farmers' children, and everything! He owns a mill here, and a tavern at Chambly, and sells rum that ain't fit for nothing but poisoning Indians. Quite a feller!"

When I smiled at his bitterness, he was offended. "Some damned fool made him an American officer; but if you ask *me*, I think he's neither flesh nor fowl nor good red herring. He changed sides once so he wouldn't lose his property, and if you ask me, he's ready to do it again. Anyway, it was Hazen that ordered four hundred of our men up to the Cedars, so's nobody could come down the river and attack Montreal. He put Colonel Bedel in charge of 'em. Timothy Bedel. Hazen likes him, and if you ask *me*, that accounts for everything." He stared at us defiantly.

"Well, sir," he went on, "there was some English and Indians up the river, and two weeks ago they *did* come down. Forty regulars and two-three hundred Indians there were, against Bedel's four hundred; and Bedel in a fort with two twelve-pounders. Bedel got word they was coming, and just drifted off to Montreal! Ran away, by God!"

"Anybody shot him yet?" Cap Huff asked.

"Listen," the officer said. "Bedel left a major in command of the Cedars. Butterfield. Major Butterfield. The British and the Indians, they came down the river and the British major sent word to the fort. 'Kindly surrender,' he says, 'as we got business elsewhere, and no time to waste on this annoying place.'"

Cap Huff laughed hoarsely.

The officer fixed him with an angry stare. "You can laugh, but that's what Butterfield did! Yes sir: that's what he did! He surrendered! Never fired a gun! Had four hundred men and a fort, and he surrendered to two hundred and fifty! Every last one of the four hundred was took prisoner! The Indians stripped 'em and killed a few. Sculped 'em! Chopped 'em up the way you would a halibut! They say the men were crazy at Butterfield—wanted to kill him."

Nason clucked, as a man does when he learns of a friend's misfortune.

"That must have tickled Arnold," Cap Huff said.

The officer shrugged his shoulders. "God knows! It was only last week this happened. No word's come through yet. We heard the British warned Arnold not to attack 'em, or they'd turn the prisoners over to the Indians and let every last one of 'em be butchered; but maybe 'tain't true."

We stood there silently beneath the heavy gray skies of Canada; behind us, squatted over their miserable fires, the dejected soldiers who waited for the scant supplies so parsimoniously provided for a hungry and frightened army. If this was war, I thought to myself—this muck of hunger, distrust, disease, raggedness, cowardice—it was different from all my imaginings: so different that a little was already more than enough for me.

I looked at Nathaniel. He was fingering his pocket and staring across the river to the small farm houses here and there along the ridge. There was something in his mind, I could see, besides the war: something important enough to veil the darkness of the prospect before us; and what that something was, I was sure I knew.

At length Nason laughed, but his laugh had a false and hollow sound. "We'll soon know what happened. We'll soon know! We've got to have food to get us to Montreal, and when we've got it——"

The officer interrupted him. "You might get it across the river in Iberville, from one of the French farmers, but only if you've got hard money. Since the retreat from Quebec, the French won't touch Congress money. They've turned against us, the lousy frog-eaters! That's why we're in such a hell of a mess! There ain't a cent's worth of hard money in sight anywhere, and none of us can buy anything. When Greaton's men went up to Montreal from Sorel the other day, to help Arnold, the only thing they could get to eat was thirty loaves of bread the Commissioners bought for 'em out of their own pockets."

"I've got a little hard money," Nathaniel said. "I think I can go across the river to those farms, yonder, and pick up enough corn meal to get this detachment to Montreal."

There was relief in Nason's voice. "Good! I won't forget it! Buy what you can and get back here with it as soon as possible. You'd better take Verrieul to do the talking."

"He won't need Verrieul," I said. "I'll go with him. I've got some hard money, too, and I can speak a little French: enough to get food."

That was how Nathaniel and I happened to cross the Richelieu together, and set off up the slope toward the small farms on the high land. We may have looked fraternal enough, being similar in height and appearance; but there was little brotherly love in the way Nathaniel pressed his lips tight together and stared straight ahead. When we were out of sight of the canoes, he spoke with what might have been indifference. "There's no need of our staying together. We'll probably get more if we go separately."

"Now look here," I said, "we have no time to waste. I know what's in your mind. When you got into the chaise in London, that woman with the French name gave you a letter to carry with you to Canada. Do you think I didn't take note of that, Nathaniel, or have forgotten it?"

Nathaniel's color heightened. "Well, what of it?"

"This," I said. "I think your mind's on that letter now, more than on your duty. To be frank about it, Nathaniel, I'm afraid that if I don't come with you, you may go out of your way to deliver that letter. As matters stand, I *am* with you, and our business is to get through to Montreal as quick as we can."

"I know our business as well as you do," he said. "I admit I've got a letter to deliver. It's one she wrote that little ward of hers she spoke of. It's a matter for you not to interfere in, I take it."

"You take it wrong," I said "Why is it you've fingered that letter in your pocket so much? Why is it that for days you've heard little that was said to you? Why is it you've been all along more bent on getting to St. John's than on getting to Quebec?"

His voice was testy. "What's wrong in such a note? A note of affection from a kind woman to a young girl! 'Tisn't a wickedness, is it?"

"We're wasting time," I reminded him. "This country's British, even if we *are* in it. My mind's made up: if anybody wants to know where you've been in this town, and who you've seen, I propose to be able to tell him."

Nathaniel faced me. "What is it you're hinting at?"

"I'm hinting at nothing. You saw, in Arundel, how much trouble can spring from next to nothing nowadays. Well, I want no more trouble of that sort. If you want to present your letter, hurry up about it, because I'm going with you."

Nathaniel's glance filled me with discomfort; for it seemed to me to hold contempt as well as anger. But at last, seeing that his displeasure had no effect on my stubbornness, he fumbled in his pocket and drew out a crumpled envelope addressed:

> *Ellen Phipps,*
> *Château de St. Auge,*
> *Iberville contre St. Jean.*

Along the ridge opposite the St. John's fort there were, in addition to Hazen's house, a number of small farm houses, but only one that might be called a château—and if it was indeed a château, then Hazen's big house, not far distant, was a royal palace. It was an affair of rough boards daubed with whitewash, capped with a roof of hand-split shingles. Its eaves, like those of most Canadian farm houses, curved upward as if warped by the heat and the moisture of this flat country.

We turned our steps toward it, whereupon another of my London suspicions was confirmed; for cut in the wood above the entrance was a cross. When I thumped on the door, it was opened by a spectacled nun who looked at us with a face as blank as a shuttered window.

"Hold up the letter for her to see," I told Nathaniel, "but don't let her have it."

He held it up, and I said, "*Est-elle ici?*"

The nun adjusted her spectacles and stared at the envelope: then, with a movement so quick that Nathaniel almost fell backward, she snatched at it. Nathaniel put it behind him, whereupon the nun sourly said, "*Entrez!*"

She left us in a room that had high-colored pictures of saints on the walls, and was furnished with four stiff chairs covered with horsehair. We waited in silence, not looking at each other, until, at length, another older woman, with an even more expressionless face, came silently into the room, and with her a girl no older than my sister Jane.

The woman, I thought, affected a nunnish air without being a nun; for her gray gown clung to her figure, but was fastened ostentatiously at the waist with a common leather strap, as if she advertised her sanctity. The girl with her seemed half a nun herself; for her dress was severe and simple, made from a rough gray material, better fitted for potato-sacking than for wearing. At her throat and wrists were bands of black, which gave her garb the look of a uniform, and not a gay uniform either.

In spite of the dullness of her garments, she had the cheeriest look of any girl I had ever seen. Her hair was dark brown—so dark as to seem almost black; and it curled in tight little curls around her forehead and ears and the nape of her neck, a cap of crinkly, glistening, chestnut-colored fleece. I was filled with curiosity, the moment I saw her, to know whether the ringlets were soft, or whether they would be harsh to the touch; and I think my curiosity was not unusual; for when the lady had looked at us almost sleepily, she said, "Sit down, Ellen"; and as she did so she passed her hand gently over the girl's tight mass of brown curls. Ellen sat down at once, prim and obedient, and looked up at us out of brown eyes so bright that they seemed to gleam as does the brown brass of my sextant when I look across it at the sun.

The lady regarded us. "You have a letter for Ellen? I am Madame St. Auge. I will take it, please."

Nathaniel gave her the envelope. When she had glanced at the name on it, she turned it over and looked thoughtfully at the seal; then fingered the square of paper dreamily.

"Yes," she said. "The writing is that of a dear friend. From where do you bring this letter?"

"From London," Nathaniel said. He coughed. "We were in London until the end of March. She—I met her——"

He coughed again.

Madame St. Auge's eyes darted from his face to mine, and fell again to the letter.

"Yes," she said, "yes." She broke the seal and gave the contents one swift glance. She smoothed the letter on her knee, then, and made a cooing sound. I could see there were only a few lines on the page, written large, so that much of the paper was wasted. "A sweet note," she murmured to Ellen. "Like herself; sweet, my dear!" Then she read it aloud.

"My darling Ellen; I send you my love by a kind gentleman who may see you before I do. I shall come to you as soon as I return. Pray assure the good Madame St. Auge that all goes well here, but that I long to see you once more, never again to leave you. To Monsieur Montgolfier I send my respects, and to you eight thousand kisses. The gentleman who brings this to you will, I am sure, assist you in any possible way, if the opportunity should arise."

Nathaniel looked at me reproachfully, and I could not meet his eye. I was ashamed of the curious broodings that had been mine concerning him and Mademoiselle de Sabrevois and the letter; and I wanted to tell him I was sorry, and to ask his pardon; but I suppose I have always had a stiffness, both in mind and manner, that makes such matters awkward for me.

At all events, I sat saying nothing; and then, abruptly, I began to think again about this letter. The surface of it was simple, kind and sweet; but there were three words in it that all at once repeated themselves to me, and gave me odd thoughts. "Eight thousand kisses."

Then, too, why was this harmless letter so brief? The woman who wrote it professed a deep affection for her ward, and had few opportunities to communicate with her. I thought so much love might have been more copious in expression: more ample of news.

And those eight thousand kisses? Lovers, mothers, tender women writing to children, send a thousand kisses, or ten thousand kisses; they do not send two thousand or six thousand or eight thousand, though I could admit the possibility that here and there five thousand might be sent. Eight thousand was a number that was somehow wrong.

However, seeing that Nathaniel was fumbling for words, I thought it wise to say a few myself. I said them somewhat at random, but not altogether. During our voyage, my musings had occupied themselves a little with the quiet figure that had been our companion for a time; and just at this moment I recalled rather sharply that we had first encountered that figure in Marie de Sabrevois's company. An impulse decided me to mention him.

"Well," I said to Madame St. Auge, "it was a pleasure to meet the lady, and her uncle, also. It was due to Mr. Leonard that we were able to leave England when we did. I hoped he might arrive here before us, even."

"Leonard?" she asked. "Leonard?" Then she smiled. "Ah, Lanaudiere!" The word was no sooner out of her mouth than her face seemed to stiffen. "Your English names!" she protested. "They're difficult for us! I do not know that name you spoke! I do not know that gentleman! We have no knowledge of him."

Here, at least, was something—not much, but a sign, perhaps: an indication. I fixed the name in my mind: Lanaudiere. It was possible that a Lanaudiere might somehow be connected with Marie de Sabrevois, and in no praiseworthy manner. At all events, Madame St. Auge had made a slip. That was clear from the volubility of her protests. She was frightened, too, at having made it; but I knew I could gain nothing by letting her see I had noticed her mistake.

"Too bad," I said, "too bad! If you should ever meet Mr. Leonard, please to tell him we inquired for him. And now about that letter: as she says, of course, we'd be happy to assist this young lady in any possible way; but we're in the army and not our own masters."

"Ah, yes," she said slowly. "You are a part of that poor army. Yes, yes! I understand! It is something we know little about, this terrible war. We hear sad tales: sad tales! These poor Americans! Without food and without medicines! I hope they can return safely to their homes and those who love them."

Nathaniel found his voice at last. "She said in her letter," he interrupted, "that she'd come here when she returned. Do you know when that'll be?"

Madame St. Auge shook her head.

Nathaniel's face was scarlet. I could see he was sorely tried at the need of speaking before me; but there was no way around it. "I'd like to leave a message for her," he said. "Could I write a message for her?"

I'd already risen. "There's no time, Nathaniel! We're supposed to be getting food. We can't be all day finding a sack of meal!"

He turned on me with a sort of desperation. "There's nothing to keep you here! I'm not a child, to be told what to do and what not to do! You can get corn meal without me, can't you?"

"You need corn meal?" Madame St. Auge asked.

"Enough to get seventeen men to Montreal," I told her. "We ate our last this morning. I could pay you in hard money."

"Yes, yes!" she said. "Of course I will spare one sack. It is high, now: fourteen dollars. But for you I will spare it. First I will get paper for your brother, and then the sack shall be brought."

"Fourteen dollars hard money for one sack of corn!" I exclaimed.

"Yes," she said sadly. "*C'est la guerre!*"

She bustled from the room, leaving Ellen looking up at the two of us—and pretty sights we must have been: Nathaniel, so absent that he stared through her as if she were a shadow; and I frowning because of the outrageous price of the corn meal.

Madame St. Auge bustled back with the paper and ink for Nathaniel: then ran from the room again. Nathaniel drew the chair vacated by Madame St. Auge into the farthest corner of the small room. Kneeling before it, he used the seat as a desk, ignoring us but, I was sure, hating us for being near him.

As for Ellen, she said nothing, but continued to stare at me out of eyes that seemed to have a golden fire burning deep within. It was foolish, I thought, to cause her embarrassment because we were disturbed; so I put the corn out of my mind and sat on the floor near her chair. "I have a sister," I told her. "She's your age, but her hair is black and straight."

"How nice!" she said. "If I had straight hair, then it wouldn't tangle, and there'd be no need to cut it off, like this." She bent her head and shook it, so that her curls danced. They seemed to have a look of softness, but there was no way of being sure. "I have a brother, too," she added. "An Indian."

I looked at her hard, but she seemed serious. I was at a loss how to reply.

"His name is Joseph," she went on. "Two months ago he came to visit me. He brought me a young fawn, a basket of cranberries, and a lump of maple sugar bigger than my head. Madame St. Auge would not allow me to speak with him until he had washed his face. It was painted black around the eyes and mouth, and red elsewhere. It was different from the way he used to paint himself, but not better, I think."

Nathaniel looked impatiently over his shoulder, at which she widened her eyes at me, and made a slight mouth, as if she regretted disturbing him.

"He's not really your brother," I protested. "How could you have an Indian for a brother!"

"Yes, he is really my brother. His name is Phipps, like mine. Joseph Phipps. What is strange about my brother becoming an Indian, any more than for a Frenchman to become a Canadian?"

She looked at me inquiringly, so I admitted there was something in what she said. She nodded, and her curls bobbed. "We were captured at the same time, Joseph and I, and my mother too—all of us, at the siege of Fort William Henry, where my father was killed. He was an officer of the English army. My mother was sold to a French gentleman in Quebec. He was kind, so he gave the Indians a little more than they asked, and I was thrown in for good measure. I was small, three years old, only; and so not worth much. Joseph was never sold. He remained in St. Francis and became an Indian. He has done well at it. When he came to see me, he had forty brooches in his shirt, and ten bracelets on each arm: also a robe of black squirrel skins."

I thought she might be laughing at me: yet her eyes held nothing save a sort of kindness, as though she talked for the purpose of keeping me amused.

"Where is your mother?" I asked.

She fingered her gray dress, pleating it carefully. "She died. That was how it happened I was placed in a convent in Montreal by my dear aunt. It was the same convent which she had attended, as a young lady. The nuns were sweet to me: very kind: like mothers, almost."

There was something heart-wrenching about the manner in which she tried to conceal her feelings by creasing that coarse gray cloth.

I cleared my throat. "So you enjoyed being in the convent?"

"Oh yes! It was pleasant. Of course, it's an opportunity, being allowed to come with Madame St. Auge to work among these poor habitants of Iberville. I'm grateful that my dear aunt learned about it and so made it possible for me to come here. But I miss the sisters in Montreal. It was my only home, the convent. It's possible to be homesick for even a convent, if you have no other home."

She glanced at me, as if to see whether I understood, and I felt a warm stirring in my chest, as though a vein had somehow opened and closed again.

Now where, I wondered, would Marie de Sabrevois have learned that Hazen, a landowner in this far-off place, had decided to employ nuns to teach the children of the farmers on his estate?

"I don't understand," I said. "Your father was an Englishman, and your mother, too, I gather. Yet your aunt is American."

Ellen smiled. "She would not be pleased to hear you say that! She is the sister of the gentleman—the French officer—who bought me from the

Indians. He died, also, last year; and when he died, my dear aunt took me from the convent and sent me here to Madame St. Auge."

"So she's French," I said, "and her brother died last year. Did her father die last year, too?"

Ellen shook her head. "Only her brother, whom she loved greatly."

Here was something else to think about! Certainly when we had met Marie de Sabrevois in the rotunda of Ranelagh, she had told us she was American. So, too, had the reticent Mr. Leonard. I distinctly remembered hearing him call her "a countrywoman of yours." And she had spoken, too, of the death of her father. I tried to recall whether she had told us when he died. It seemed to me she had either said or implied he had died within the year. I was sure she had said he was a fur merchant, and that she was in England to settle his affairs. That lady, I was positive, would have let no grass grow under her feet when it came to settling an estate in which she had an interest. I looked hard at Ellen Phipps and wondered how much she had in common with this aunt of hers—this aunt who had been so free with misstatements. If I was any hand at reading character, she had nothing in common with her, but I had heard that one could never tell about a woman.

"Why did your aunt take you from the convent to send you here?" I asked her.

She raised her eyes and started to speak. Then the golden light in them dimmed and wavered like a candleflame blown by the wind, and she was silent.

I knew what had happened. My words had sent a wave of homesickness over her—truly a pathetic homesickness, considering that its origin was a barren convent smelling, no doubt, of plaster and candles and dyed cloth! I knew, too, that she was no more like Marie de Sabrevois than a yacht is like a prison hulk.

I was filled with compassion for this lonely girl, and with anger at those with whom her lot was cast—a half-savage brother so senseless as to stick his shirt full of brooches; an aunt willing to push a motherless child about, from pillar to post; and a goat-faced duenna who welcomed the opportunity to charge hungry men fourteen hard dollars for a sack of corn meal.

Nathaniel, I saw, had finished his letter and was folding it; so I got to my feet, wondering what I could say to this girl with the brown curls. Seemingly she expected me to say nothing; for she was looking down at her coarse gray dress and carefully flattening the crease so recently made.

Outside there was a scuffling, which proved to be Madame St. Auge and the spectacled nun dragging a full meal sack between them. I counted out the fourteen dollars, and then shouldered the sack. My hat, I found, was still on the floor; but Ellen brought it to me and put it on my head.

"Be careful your hat doesn't drop in the mud," she said. "I hope you'll have a pleasant journey to Montreal."

Because of the bulky burden on my left shoulder, I could see nothing of her; but I had the feeling that she nodded cheerfully; and certainly a faint fragrance came to me from her brown curls.

I would have liked to say something kind to her; but I could think of nothing; and I well knew I was a grotesque spectacle, with my hat askew and a flour sack weighing me down—too grotesque for her to care whether I spoke or not. Therefore I felt only relief when Nathaniel pushed me before him through the doorway, and we stood beneath the dull Canadian sky once more.

XII

St. john's had been bad enough; but when we had plodded from dawn to noon across the plains of Canada on roads made mostly of logs, crossed the broad St. Lawrence at Longueuil and tramped the muddy streets of Montreal hunting our headquarters in the Château Ramezay, we knew St. John's had been nothing.

It was not so much the look of Montreal that made us hate the place, as it was the feel of it, and the gloom of the Americans we met wherever we turned. The city was a rich one, with fine residences and a wealth of warehouses; but its people had sour faces that grew sourer at sight of us. Some spat as they passed. Others were contemptuous, and their mutterings venomous, so that Cap Huff bubbled profanity beneath his breath, as if there were a fire under him, and he a kettle filled with simmering soup.

On every street were American soldiers, recognizable as such because they had bayonets in scabbards, or dented kettles banging against their hips, or the tattered remnants of blankets over their shoulders—though I'd have taken them for beggars if Nason hadn't stopped a few for questioning.

They were the raggedest men I had ever seen anywhere, and I have seen plenty of ragged ones, especially in Spanish ports, where the beggars wear clothes that must have been old when Columbus was a boy.

Most of them were shoeless and stockingless, and their breeches little more than dirty rags and ribbons. Their coats were good for nothing except to conceal the gaping holes in their shirts, or, in the case of those without shirts, to hide part of their nakedness. They were emaciated, too, with sores on their faces and legs; and their dull eyes were dejected. They started at small sounds, staring furtively over their shoulders, so that a person who looked at them too long became depressed himself.

They were hunting food, they always told Nason; and when he asked where their companies were, they said their enlistments had expired and they were trying to get home—though most of them, I think, were lying. When we went on, they slunk away, peering into alleys and up at windows like hungry cats.

When at last we reached the Château Ramezay, a low, solid, steep-roofed building behind a tall iron fence and iron gates, we found more of these scarecrow soldiers. They sprawled in the open field across from headquarters like heaps of rags, as dead men lie after a battle, or sat on the curbstone, staring at nothing with lack-lustre eyes. Some held up kettles to passersby, hoping for food.

At the gates of the château were two real soldiers, sentries in blue uniforms faced with red; and on either side of the double doors were two more. They looked out of place, somehow, like bright patches on an ancient mainsail.

"Stack your arms," Nason told us, "and keep tight hold of what flour you've got left. Cap and I, we'll go in and report. You're not to move till we come out." To me he said, "You'd better come in with us. If the general's there, I guess he'll want to hear what you've got to say."

We went past the sentries into a long stone hallway hung with Indian robes: some made of pieced-together wolf skins, and some of raccoon, with a few beaver and two or three squirrel robes, one black, the most valuable that Indians make.

On one side of the hallway was a large room in which sat half a dozen men, business men seemingly, waiting for someone. They eyed us as we came in; then went back to glowering at the floor or fondling their chins. In the room across the corridor was a young man in a plain blue uniform, as serious and busy as a dog burying a bone. He may have been nineteen years old, but he had the ponderous gravity of an English butler contemplating the insignificance of all mankind. He came out to us, carrying papers in his hand, and walking with cool deliberation, the picture of importance.

"You'll have to wait outside," he said, speaking with a southern accent. "The general's given orders that if there's food for distribution to unattached soldiers, the word'll be announced at sundown." He dropped his head to peer at us, and there was a movement of the muscles over his jaws, which gave him a determined air.

Cap Huff coughed portentously and whispered hoarsely to Nason, "Tell the major we ain't hungry."

The young man looked severe. "Not major. Captain. Captain Wilkinson: aide to General Arnold."

Nason nodded. "If the general can spare a minute, we'd like to see him, Captain. Nason's my name. I've got scouts for him—and some information. I guess he'd better have the information right away. I guess I'd say something to him about it, if I was you."

Captain Wilkinson stared at us, his jaw muscles throbbing. As he stared, a closed doorway at the end of the hallway banged open. "I can't promise, Doctor," a voice said. It wasn't loud, but it was high-pitched, with a sort of suppressed shrillness to it as though it could cut like a knife, if unleashed, through stone walls.

An officer popped from the open doorway, wheeling to look back into the room, as if impatient at the slowness of the man for whom he waited. Even before Nason told me, I knew he was General Arnold.

"I can't promise," Arnold said again in that high-pitched, suppressed voice, "but if you say they'll die unless they have medicines, we'll get medicines somehow! They're our men and they'll be looked after, even if I have to pull every drugstore in Montreal to pieces!"

He was stocky, and had tremendous broad shoulders. At first sight he seemed short, but he had a way of standing, poised a little forward, his head thrown back and his chest rounded out, that made him appear to tower head and shoulders above the man who followed him out of the door—a slender, worried-looking man about the same height as Arnold.

The general took the slender man by the arm and turned him toward us. "You understand the situation," he said in that strange penetrating voice. "We're destitute: we're paupers; but if there's medicine to be had, I'll get it for you. You'll hear from me before noon tomorrow. I'll come to the hospital myself!"

He gave Wilkinson a brusque nod. "I'm to see Dr. Senter tomorrow. Hospital. Eleven o'clock."

He clapped the slight young man on the shoulder, then looked in at the room where the half dozen business men sat. "What's all this?" he demanded, as if exasperated. "Captain Wilkinson, couldn't these gentlemen have been attended to? You know I promised to inspect the waterfront before dark—promised the Commissioners."

Captain Wilkinson stepped close to him to murmur a military secret. Arnold whirled to look at us; then nodded abruptly and turned back to the roomful of men. "Gentlemen," he said, "tell your business to my aide, Captain Wilkinson! I can't spare a moment from my duties till two o'clock tomorrow morning." To Nason he said: "Come back here!" He hurried down the hallway, limping a little.

We followed him into a low-ceiled room and stood in a row before his desk. I had the impression of being surrounded by a sea of documents. On the desk were piles of letters and papers, each batch held down by a horseshoe. On other tables around the room, and in corners, were other stacks weighted with horseshoes. Fastened to each horseshoe was a label to tell what was beneath it, all neat as pie. The walls were bare, except for a hand-made map.

For a moment Arnold, standing beside the desk, seemed to forget us.

He lifted one of the horseshoes, picked up a letter, examined it with a look of distaste; then replaced it carefully, dropped the horseshoe on it and threw back his head to stare at Nason.

"Well," he said harshly, "you've been long enough! I trust the results have justified your little vacation!" He came to stand close before Cap Huff, who was restless beneath his scrutiny. "It's Saved From Captivity!" Arnold said politely. "I can see you've not been starved on your trip, Saved From Captivity."

Cap Huff said nothing: merely shuffled his feet; and it was plain to be seen that his admiration for this handsome, swarthy general was such that he was speechless before him. It was evident, too, that Arnold took pleasure in Cap's embarrassment; for he pursed his lips to conceal a smile; and in the pursing his face seemed to lift, lengthen and become less swarthy.

He turned to me and looked me up and down; and if he was trying to discomfit me, he wasn't successful because of my London practice in seeming unconscious of the supercilious stares of Englishmen. "Don't tell me," he said to Nason, "don't tell me this is the sole result of two months' holiday!"

Nason shook his head. "No sir; but if it was we might have done worse. This here's Cap'n Peter Merrill of Arundel. He sailed from England the last of March, and he's got information. Anyway it was information to us."

"Captain? Captain of what?"

"Brig *Orestes*," I said. "Of Arundel. One hundred eighty-eight tons."

"What were you doing in England?"

"The war overtook us. My father sent orders to sell the vessel."

Arnold glanced from me to Nason. I saw Nason nod. "All right," Arnold said. "That's all right! You enlisted with Nason, did you?"

"Three years," Nason said.

"Why, that's all right!" Arnold repeated. "I can use you. What kind of a rig on your brig?"

"Jackass."

"That's what I sailed. I find they handle better than a full rig. What's your information?"

I repeated, as clearly and briefly as I could, what I had heard in London about Burgoyne's army; about the Hessians and Indians.

While I talked, Arnold watched me with pale eyes that expanded and contracted, like those of a cat watching a bird.

"Let's see about this," he said, when I had finished. "General Thomas thought his troops were stampeded by only two regiments from Halifax, but they may have come from England. They may have been the first of Burgoyne's army! Yes sir: what you say may be possible, in spite of the part about the Indians. That part's not true. There aren't five thousand Indians to be had for fighting, not by anyone, anywhere. But the rest of it might be possible."

"There's no doubt about it," I said. "I heard Germain tell a lady she could join Burgoyne in Canada."

"What lady was that?" Arnold asked.

"I don't know, sir. A lady they called Peg—a friend of Burgoyne's. A lady who'd heard you could row from Quebec to New York as easy as attending a regatta on the Thames."

Arnold nodded. "That's right! That's the way they talk! It's what they'd do, too: send Burgoyne to command a Canadian army. He's a cavalryman. Put him in these forests and he'd be like a hen in the middle of the St. Lawrence. That's the British of it: they always do the wrong thing first."

"Yes sir," I said, happy to find his opinion coinciding with my own.

The general stared at us. His mind, I could see, was miles away. Then he darted his head forward, his lips compressed so that his face looked round and puffy. "How'd you come? When were you in St. John's?"

"This morning," Nason said. "We got there last night and came on this morning."

"Who was there? Had General Sullivan come through? Did you see the new regiments? Wayne's and Irvine's regiments?"

"They hadn't got there," Nason said. "A man on a provision-boat said they'd just left Albany. There wasn't anybody in St. John's but two lieutenants and nearly three hundred cases of smallpox."

Arnold laughed abruptly. "A smallpox garrison! I might have known it! If we could fill our haversacks and cartridge boxes with smallpox, we could whip the world!"

"There was a vessel on the stocks in St. John's," I said. "A third finished. Maybe seventy tons."

Arnold nodded absently. Behind his pale eyes I could almost see his mind leaping about, examining from every side the information we had brought. Meanwhile we stood before him, waiting; stood until Cap Huff gasped twice, then sneezed explosively. At this Arnold became conscious of us once more.

"That's good!" he said. "You've done well! Nason, you've done well! How many men have you brought?"

"Seventeen," Nason said. In a low voice he added, "They've all had smallpox."

Arnold seemed not to hear. He scratched a few lines on a sheet of paper. "Here's your billeting order. I've got to go! I've got things to do—inspection—meet the Commissioners—write reports—write General Schuyler—write General Washington—write Congress—make lists. I'll tell you what you do: come back here at midnight. No: at one o'clock in the morning. Bring three or four of your best men. I'll put 'em to work. Have you got anything to eat?"

Nason's reply was dubious. "Enough for supper, I guess."

"Good!" Arnold said. "There's nothing but dried peas to be had around here. When you run out of food, I can get dried peas for you. They're not so bad when you make rubbaboo out of 'em. I'll give you the order tonight." He herded us to the door. "If I'm a little abrupt, you'll have to overlook it. A million things to do, and no time for doing them. Everything that's done, I have to do myself. There's nobody to obey orders."

He paused, and added, "Burgoyne, eh? Hessians and Indians, eh? Well, we'll see about that!"

He left us, hurrying down the hall and shouting for Wilkinson. A moment later he tore open the front door and leaped down the steps; and the restless quiet that ensued reminded me of that aboard a vessel when a squall has passed over it, leaving it safe but shaken.

XIII

I<small>T WAS</small> almost two o'clock when Captain Wilkinson came out from headquarters and found the seven of us sitting around a fire we had kindled on the opposite sidewalk, the night being overcast and as black as the inside of a stove, and therefore cold. The general, he informed us, was now able to see us. When he had given us the message, he moved his jawbones so that a pulse seemed to throb slowly and angrily in the lower part of his face. "Don't you know," he added, "you oughtn't to light a fire close to headquarters like this?"

Cap Huff heaved himself to his feet. "Why not?"

Captain Wilkinson was patronizing. "Why not? Why, because it's not military. It's not dignified."

Cap Huff seemed to mull over this explanation; and at length he appeared to find reason in it—which surprised me; for to me it seemed no explanation at all. Nonetheless, Cap said, in as mealy a voice as I ever heard, "Well, it ain't, now you speak of it. It certainly ain't dignified! I dunno what we could 'a' been thinkin' of!"

On that Captain Wilkinson turned away with a satisfied air, and we followed him into headquarters. As we went, I thought to myself that no matter how military Captain Wilkinson might be, he was no woodsman, since he walked with his toes turned out, and with gingerly deliberateness, as though he trod on ostrich eggs.

The general was writing when we crowded into his office and paraded before his desk. The four men we had brought, according to orders, were Nathaniel, Verrieul, Tom Bickford and Doc Means; and in that dim office, lighted only by the four candles on Arnold's paper-strewn desk, the seven of us, in our shapeless tow-cloth smocks, had small appearance of soldierliness or ability. Yet this general, in his bright uniform of blue and buff, seemed to find nothing strange in our appearance; for he looked up at us as if we gave him actual pleasure. "Well, well!" he said, "I haven't smelled an asafoetida bag since I worked for the Lathrops in New Haven. Who's wearing it?"

Cap Huff pushed Doc Means forward. "This is Doc Means. He's more useful than he smells."

"You're a doctor?" Arnold asked.

Doc wavered and looked helpless. "Well," he said, "I wouldn't like to say I was a regular doctor—not from what I know about some of 'em."

Arnold laughed. "We won't go into that! I've sold drugs myself!" To Nason he said impatiently: "Who are the others?"

Nason spoke proudly. "This here's Nathaniel Merrill, brother to Cap'n Peter. He went to Harvard College, and can talk like an Englishman so you wouldn't know the difference. He's been supercargo with Cap'n Peter. Next to him's Tom Bickford of Arundel. He'll catch fish where there aren't any, and track deer across solid rock. He wanted to go to Harvard and be a minister, but his family sent him to sea."

"Seaman or officer?" Arnold asked.

Tommy smiled his polite smile. "I can navigate, sir, but I never had a vessel of my own. First mate, I was."

Arnold's eyes glittered in the candlelight, and he hitched forward in his chair to look at Verrieul. "And what does this young man do? Anything unusual?"

"Well, you might say so," Nason admitted. "His name's Joseph Marie Verrieul, and he went to Dartmouth College. He speaks French, Iroquois, Abenaki and Chippeway, and can make orations in all of 'em."

"Not Dartmouth College!" Arnold protested. "Why, it was only ten years ago that I contributed the profits of a sea-venture toward the establishment of that institution! Surely such an investment can't be showing a return!" He laughed silently; and in the wavering glow his rounded face took on a lean, satirical look. He was pleased with Nason's men: no doubt of that; and I certainly would have counted myself fortunate if, in an hour of need, I could have had them on any vessel of mine.

"All right," Arnold said. "You're scouts, all of you. I sent Nason to Arundel to get good scouts, and I believe he's got 'em. I've heard a lot, up here, from Pennsylvanians and Virginians and Jerseymen, about what cowards New Englanders are: how they're no good—not to be depended on. Personally, being one myself, I don't hold with their ideas."

He eyed us from under arched brows. Cap Huff cleared his throat with the sound of a brig rubbing barnacles from a wharf.

"Yes," Arnold went on. "They say you New Englanders are cowards —ignorant bumpkins who never do as you're told; and I must admit I come across a few answering to that description—a few! I'm just back from clearing up a mess two of 'em made! Bedel and Butterfield!"

The very thought threw him into a passion. He hissed contemptuously, leaped to his feet to glare at us; then threw himself into his chair once more.

"Heart-breaking poltroonery! Shameful! By God, I can't believe it yet! Two weeks thrown away, trying to salvage four hundred soldiers, surrendered by those two capons—those two she-rabbits!" He thumped the desk and seemed about to burst with rage.

Surprisingly, he laughed. "Well, fortunes of war! That's done—all a part of the mess behind us! What I started to say is this: I've had enough to do with New Englanders to know they're all right, taking 'em by and large—all right! If you men do scout duty, you'll work under my orders, and I expect those orders to be obeyed. If anyone feels he can't obey orders, he shouldn't hesitate to say so. There's plenty that *can't* in this army! Probably there's no help for it, only I don't want any of 'em! I'd rather have 'em attached to Hazen, who has trouble obeying orders himself!"

He seemed to be listening for a reply. I was glad when Nason said quietly: "You don't need to send these men to Hazen, General! I've been watching 'em. They're all right."

From the manner in which Cap Huff heaved himself about, he had something to say. He prefaced his words with an explosive cough. "Hazen? Colonel Hazen? Seems like I heard that name before! Who was it lied to Schuyler about what he'd find in Canada when he started up to take Montreal? Wasn't that Hazen?"

Arnold's face was dark, and the name seemed to irk him. "Hazen!" he growled. "Yes, that was Hazen—always a thorn in the flesh! Always the starting-point of trouble and disaster! It seems as if there can't ever be an army without a Hazen in it!"

Jumping up from his desk, he went to stand beside the rough map on the wall. The broad St. Lawrence swept diagonally across it; Quebec in the upper right-hand corner, and in the lower left the monstrous divergence of river channels around the high land of Montreal. Half-way between the two was the broad oval of Lake St. Peter, with the Richelieu River extending straight downward from the western end to merge with Lake Champlain.

"You don't know it yet," he told us, "but scout duty'll bring you strange orders. Your orders'll be between you and me. What you hear from me is our business—yours and mine: nobody else's! There'll be times when you'll be supposed to know what's going on; but if you try to find out what's going on in Canada, you're going to hear wild tales. You want to be careful what you believe. Don't believe too much. I don't like to see people misled; so if you're still of a mind to serve under me, I'll supply you with your first batch of information, just to make sure you start to stock the right goods."

He ran his finger along the line of the St. Lawrence, from Quebec down to the edge of the map, west of Montreal. "That's a roadway, the St. Lawrence is: the roadway between the English and the Indians. If we have to get out of the road, the Indians can join the English when they please and where they please, and raise hell with our people."

He turned to face us. "We're in a mess! We're in as bad a mess as ever was! There's such a mess here, and in Sorel and St. John's, and up and down the river, that no man can comprehend it all. We've got an army, thanks to General Washington; but thanks to Congress it's got nothing to eat, nothing to wear, nothing to put in its guns. There never was an army as sick as this army. It's rotten with smallpox. Half the men are inoculating themselves; and those that don't inoculate themselves are catching it from those that do. We've got no money. We've got no officers worth their salt."

He reached over and slapped a pile of letters on his desk. "Here's letters from forty officers, begging leave to resign their commissions and go home! Forty officers! Forty puling nanny-goats! We've got Commissioners from Congress here, trying to help us win the war—Commissioners with no money and no knowledge of war! There's one good thing about 'em—they know enough not to try to get help from France! At least they can see the danger in *that!* They told Walker that rather than call in the assistance of France, they'd come to a reconciliation with England on any terms. They're fine gentlemen; but a mule knows more about discipline and the need of it! They encourage suggestions and letter-writing, these Commissioners do! Letter-writing! They think you can fight a war with letters!

"If a lieutenant doesn't like a captain's orders, he's free to write the Commissioners and tell 'em about it; and the Commissioners generally write the captain and tell him not to do it again. If a captain or a major or a colonel doesn't like my orders, he writes the Commissioners and complains, and the Commissioners ask me to explain the matter to them so they can write home and explain it to their wives, maybe, or maybe to Congress. Smallpox is a curse to this army, God knows; but it's less of a curse than the Commissioners of Congress! We're handsomely supplied with Commissioners, but not at all with contractors, commissaries or quartermasters. Not one of these have we got! I do duty for all!

"So there you are: no food, no blankets, no shoes, no tents, no medicines, no surgical instruments, no nails, no powder, no bullets, no pay, no credit, no reputation; and above all, no discipline. That was Wooster's fault! He let 'em get out of control before Quebec—no more fitted to command men than a dressmaker!"

He muttered under his breath, and I caught the word "midwife." He shrugged his shoulders and snapped his fingers, as if to snap Wooster out of his life. "After Wooster came the panic, and then the Commissioners. And now the bulk of the army's at Sorel—tattered, hungry, frightened, sick, helpless, headless!

"General Thomas came to replace Wooster, but he no sooner started to take hold at Sorel than he came down with smallpox. The Commissioners brought along one of their damned foreign generals—Baron, he calls himself: Baron De Woedtke; but he's too busy tippling to bother with such a small matter as discipline!

"Men whose time has expired are going home. They won't stay to help us. They've had a bellyful of war and sickness, hunger and disappointments. They wouldn't stay if you told them the British might destroy us next week!

"As for the Canadians, the weaker we get, the more insolent they grow. Two months ago they were our dear friends. Today they'd cut our throats if they could! And on top of everything, you tell us the British have sent thousands of their own troops against us, and other thousands of Hessians as well: as fine an army as ever left England! It may not be true, but probably it is! Thousands of the best-trained, best-armed soldiers in the world, and we with nothing to oppose 'em but a starved and naked rabble! That's how badly off we are! Can you men stay here and keep up your courage? Can you do as you're told under such circumstances?"

Cap Huff cleared his throat with a sound of ripping canvas. "In case anybody thinks he can't," Cap said, "Doc Means's got a sure cure for fear: pepper and gunpowder, mixed with molasses and maybe some rum."

"You got to have a touch of Digby's Sympathetic Powder in it," Doc Means reminded him in a low voice.

Arnold nodded. "There's another side to the picture. General Sullivan's coming up from Albany with four regiments—good regiments: none better, General Schuyler writes me. Properly handled, four healthy regiments can hold the St. Lawrence against all the ministerial troops that England can send against us. It's got to be done! We've got to block communication between the English and the Indians to the west.

"If they turn loose the Indians on us, God only knows what'll happen! Four fighting regiments, properly officered, could hang on here all summer! Hang on till winter! It can be done! Then when Carleton has to move back on account of the ice, we can take the city!

"Lee could do it! I asked Congress to put Lee in command up here;

but he was the best man for the place, so of course Congress sent him elsewhere!

"Well, it can still be done! I can do it myself! Give me the men and the money for supplies, and I'll guarantee to do it!"

There was a rasping quality to Arnold's voice that sent shivers along my spine; and I was sure that he spoke the truth: that given half a chance, he would somehow find a way to bring victory out of ruin.

He went back to his desk and settled himself in his chair. "But if we had forty fighting regiments, and they shouldn't be properly handled—if they should be commanded by officers of mean abilities, no education and little experience, they'd do us no good. Such officers cannot understand the precautions necessary to successful defense. We'd have to retreat! We'd have to give up everything General Montgomery won for us, and leave the gate open for our enemies to attack from the north!

"What would happen to all of us if we had to retreat, God only knows: yet it's something we have to prepare for. With no money, no food, no ammunition, I've got to seize enough supplies from the people of this city to get us safe home, in case the worst comes to the worst. I've got to seize supplies and give personal receipts for them!" He laughed harshly. "My accounts'll be in a tangle for the next thousand years; but it's got to be done! That's as much as I can tell you; and if you don't like the sound of it, go down to Sorel and join Hazen! I want no man unless he's willing. And I want no schoolgirls, unable to hear the truth without flinching!"

He looked up at Nason suddenly. "What's that you say?"

Nason seemed to have the solidity of a rock as he stood rigidly before the desk, staring down into Arnold's glittering eyes. "Nothing, I didn't say anything. But I'd like to have that order for peas right now."

XIV

Yₒᵤ came as a scout, but you're a ship man," Arnold told me, "and I've got a ship man's job for you. You're to go back to St. John's, number the timbers of that vessel on the stocks, and take her to pieces. Then send the timbers to Crown Point."

Instantly I began to wonder about Nathaniel: whether it would be better to have him with me in St. John's where I could keep him under my eye, or whether he'd be better off elsewhere, far removed from Ellen Phipps and other reminders of Marie de Sabrevois.

I might have saved myself the trouble of wondering; for Arnold had his own plans for all of us. "Take Bickford with you," he said, "and if you need more workmen, requisition any stray soldiers that can't account for themselves. If they don't want to work, handle 'em as you would on shipboard. If anybody tries to make trouble for you, squirm out of it the best you can. I'll leave the details to you; but whatever happens, get that vessel to Crown Point. Here's your authority."

He reached for a sheet of paper and drove his pen across it. The window was palely flushed with a Canadian dawn, and in that light his swarthy face was haggard; but the pen scratched on as briskly as though he were fresh from sleep.

While I read my orders, he instructed Nathaniel and Verrieul to get Canadian clothes for themselves and set off on foot down the St. Lawrence to find out whether any troop-ships had arrived from England and where they were: in the next breath he told Cap Huff and Doc Means to report to Major Scott and help him requisition supplies to be used in case of a retreat.

To Nason he said: "Get your men settled, and see me here at nine o'clock in the morning. Your friend Natanis ought to be back from Caughnawaga by then; and I'll have something to keep both of you busy." He winked at Nason, a most unmilitary wink. "Take 'em away! I've got work to do."

He picked up his pen, flipped a horseshoe from a pile of correspondence, and before we were through the door the quill was scratching across a sheet of paper as though we had been a momentary diversion from more serious business.

. . . That was how Tom Bickford and I found ourselves tramping south beside the shallow rapids of the Richelieu, bound again for the dreary settlement we had left two days before.

There was no change in St. John's, but it seemed to me less gloomy than when I had first seen it. I knew why, too. It was associated with Ellen Phipps and her coarse gray dress. How often a strange town, contemptible at first sight, will be made to seem downright pleasant by the knowledge that one interesting acquaintance lives there!

We found two provision barges tied up at the landing; and the same dilapidated lieutenants who had met us were overseeing the unloading of boxes, sacks and barrels. They jumped when I spoke to them; and one said "My God! I thought you were De Woedtke! What you want?"

I reminded him of our previous arrival in canoes, and showed him the order Arnold had given me. After reading it, he stared at me curiously. "Ain't you the man that owned to having some hard money?"

When I said I was, he took me by the elbow and moved me away from the soldiers who were dumping the provisions ashore. "What you need," he said confidentially, "is a pail of beer and a slab of ham, pan-broiled about ten minutes."

I was lost to know what he was driving at, but since it was an inexpensive way to obtain his good will, the four of us went around to the back door of a disheveled tavern with boards nailed across its windows. In the far bowels of the tavern, when we entered, we heard a strange rumbling, punctuated with noisy hiccups, almost like distant war-whoops. The lieutenant, whose name was Hersom, made signs at an angry-looking Frenchwoman; and she, having accepted four shillings from me, bit each one suspiciously; then drew four pails of beer, and threw four slices of ham in a skillet—slices about the thickness of a hatch-cover, and about as juicy.

The rumbling came clearer to our ears, and proved to be a voice speaking partly in English and partly in German, and never ceasing, apparently, except when its owner paused to drink or to hiccup.

"That's De Woedtke," Hersom said. "Somebody in Sorel sent him down here yesterday, with an aide-de-camp, so to have everything ready for Sullivan." He raised an eyebrow at me. "Heard about that? Sullivan's coming tomorrow. He'll be at Isle La Motte tonight. Here tomorrow. Four regiments!"

De Woedtke's voice rumbled on and on, exploding now and again into a racking hiccup.

"Yes, that's him," Hersom said, "telling his aide-de-camp how Frederick the Great used to do it. Got kicked out of Frederick the Great's army, he did, on account of telling Fred about the death of a pet nephew. He's in command of us. Trained under Frederick the Great, he says he was. I don't know anything about this Frederick the Great; but if De Woedtke's a sample of those he trained, he never trained nobody to do nothing but talk and drink! Anyway, De Woedtke's a general. Congress made him a general. Prob'ly he began to tell Congress about himself, and they made him a general to shut him up. If you want to do things right, you'd better report to him and tell him you're planning to take the vessel to pieces."

"Suppose," I said, "he told me not to do it?"

"Then you couldn't," Hersom said. "And you needn't worry about his not wanting you to. Our generals are all the same! Not a damned one of 'em wants anybody to do one damned thing any other general wants!"

I chewed my ham and remembered how Arnold had spoken of those in Canada who found it impossible to obey orders. "In that case," I told Hersom, "I never heard of De Woedtke! I've got to get that vessel to pieces and loaded onto barges."

"I just thought I'd tell you," Hersom said.

When we had finished our ham, Hersom brought us black paint, and by nightfall we had numbered every timber on the half-finished vessel.

. . . We slept beneath her keel, the night being foggy, but not enough to trouble us; and on the following morning, after we had drawn sour beef from Hersom for breakfast—beef that looked and tasted like anchor-rope ripened in the mud of Liverpool Harbor—we went hunting assistants.

Out beyond the shipyard we found six men sitting around a fire. Their breeches were worse than dilapidated, and they had sailcloth wrapped around their lower legs and feet. Only one of them had a tied queue; it was tied with a snake skin. They looked bristly and dirty, as if they had lived in caves for years, but I'd seen worse.

"Where you men going?" I asked.

They sat silent, peering stupidly at a kettle on the fire.

"All right," I said. "Since you're going nowhere, just hurry up with that kettle. Then step over to the shipyard and give us a hand dismantling a vessel."

One of the men turned a hostile eye upon me. "Not us, brother. You got the wrong men! We're York troops. Our time's up. We're going home."

"Before you go," I said, "I'll get you to help me out with this vessel.

General Arnold wants it shipped to Crown Point, where it'll be some protection to the people down York way."

"To hell with General Arnold," the same man said calmly. "We don't give a damn what he or any other general wants."

I contemplated reaching down and getting him by the collar, so to haul him up where I could take a swing at his ear: then it occurred to me that these men were, after all, able to account for themselves, whereas Arnold had said to use men who couldn't.

"Shall we start on 'em, Cap'n Peter?" Tom Bickford asked.

"No," I said. "We don't want trouble if we can avoid it." I made another appeal to the York troopers. "Here, this I'm asking you to do is to help your country. Seems as if you'd do that without urging."

"To hell with it," the spokesman said. "All we been hearing since we left York is some old woman with a sword and a cocked hat saying, 'Now, my brave men, forward for your country!' We ain't such fools as we look. Don't you suppose we knew he didn't give a damn about anything except getting promoted? We never got no food or powder or pay, excepting paper money that wa'n't good for nothing but wadding. We never got decent treatment when we took sick. What's more, we ain't never had no officers that knew what they was talking about —just a pack of he-schoolma'ams, squabbling over which one got into the army first. To hell with all of 'em!"

"Look here," I said, "we can knock that vessel to pieces in no time. There'll be free beer all round, and I'll get you a ride to Crown Point on the barge."

"Beer!" the spokesman said. "How much beer?"

The others, too, looked interested. "A quarter barrel a day?" one asked.

"Yes."

" 'Tain't enough," he said instantly. But I saw that this was merely a hopeful form of speech, and that my point was carried, whereupon I ventured to speak more decisively in order to make a good impression at the outset.

"Listen to this," I said. "You'll get a quarter barrel, and drink it after work. What's more, you'll toe the mark and do as I say, or you'll have your teeth knocked out through your ears."

They grumbled as they ate their kettleful of stew; but when it was gone they followed us to the shipyard peaceably enough. Indeed, after they had started on the demolition of the skeleton vessel, and had worked up a sweat, they became even amiable, so that I think one of their troubles had been an insufficiency of work, which is enough to make any man discontented with his lot.

❋   ❋   ❋

. . . At mid-morning we heard shouting on the outskirts of town. A man ran past us, bawling; and boys, barefooted, appeared from nowhere, with dogs capering and barking alongside, to run yelling after the man.

The whole settlement seemed to ooze women and girls and Canadian Frenchmen in bob-tailed summer jackets and battered stove-pipe hats, all with long queues hanging down their backs, and with the customary half-sour, half-doltish look that seemed peculiar to them. On the Iberville side, too, people emerged from farm houses and moved in knots along the Richelieu.

The river banks, in a moment's time, were lined with people; and above their babbling and shouting we heard from upstream the sound of drums and fifes.

Two canoes slid into sight, gliding over the Richelieu's brown surface. They were paddled by Indians, and in each sat six complacent soldiers in fine blue uniforms with white facings, white belts crossed over their chests, white vests, white breeches. Their muskets slanted outward, three to a side, all shipshape and military looking.

As the canoes slipped along between the crowds at the water's edge, there arose a ragged, welcoming cheer that spread and solidified until the soldiers in blue and white seemed to float on a river of cheering. Behind the first two canoes came another two; then two more, each with six soldiers in it; then a lumbering great bateau, packed solidly with soldiers in blue and white. Bayoneted muskets stood upright between their knees; and to my eager eyes those glittering rows of bayonets were a silver crop that soon would ripen into golden victory.

The ringleader of the ragged York troopers, balanced on a plank high in air, unenthusiastically identified the newcomers for us. "Sullivan's brigade!" he said, and spat copiously through the vessel's ribs.

A second bateau, filled with men in blue and white, followed the first, and close behind the second was a third. The men in them laughed and stamped their feet, and in time to the stamping they shouted, "QueBEC! QueBEC! QueBEC-BEC-BEC!" From the next bateau came the rattle of drums; and blue-and-white-clad fifers shrilled into *Yankee Doodle.*

Above me one of the York troopers yelled horribly and waved his torn hat. Unexpectedly the ringleader capered on his plank, and in a cracked voice bellowed, "Sullivan! Sullivan!" In a moment all six were shouting, hurrooing, and dropping one by one from their perches.

The ringleader glared at me furiously and bawled, "By God, we'll

show 'em!" He turned and ran like a madman toward the river; and
Tom Bickford and I ran after him.

Bateau after bateau came downstream between banks so packed with
people that the whole of Canada seemed to have crowded into St.
John's; and the unending welcoming clamor was sweeter, even, than
the rolling of the drums. These Canadian French folk, clapping their
hands and leaping for joy, were the same ones who had despised and
spurned us when we were weak and hungry; so it was clear that they
would join us fast enough if they thought we could whip the English.

When the bateaux laden with men in blue and white—Anthony
Wayne's regiment—had passed, the river was alive with bateaux bearing soldiers dressed in dark blue with red facings. These were Pennsylvania troops—the First Pennsylvania; and jostling along behind them
came bateaux filled with men in brown and buff; with more in gray
trimmed with blue, every man's musket tipped with a bayonet. Their
uniforms were handsome and new, and each soldier's hair was clubbed
and neatly tied. Even their women, who came last of all in the bateaux
that carried the baggage, were decked out in bright colors and stylish
sunbonnets; and though they were noisy, like most camp women, they
were none of them drunk, not that I could see.

Nowhere—not in St. James's Park even—had I seen regiments better
equipped or more soldierly. When they clambered ashore, they formed
ranks like veterans and went swinging off to the old British barracks
as if they owned Canada; and I, watching them, was filled with pride
and confidence.

Over two hundred bateaux were packed along the banks of the
Richelieu when this beautiful new brigade was all ashore; and not only
were there thousands of men, gay in their regimentals, but the waterfront was ablaze with sentry fires; and between the fires were piles of
stores under guard—cannon, ammunition, provisions: everything that
had hitherto been lacking for the success and well-being of our people
in Canada.

There was only one unpleasant aspect to the business: I found myself wishing that Nathaniel could be with me to see these fine regiments; and it dawned on me that I would never have had such a wish
unless, deep in my heart, there still remained dark doubts about him.
I told myself that he was safe, since a task had been set for him by
Arnold, and he had gone uncomplainingly off on it with Verrieul; and
then, remembering how Nason had told Arnold that we were all right,
I still felt doubts, and kicked myself for feeling them.

. . . The six York troopers came back to work when the new regiments had landed, though I had expected never to lay eyes on them again; and they were excited over what they had seen.

"By gravy," the ringleader announced, "if we'd had equipment like that, we'd 'a' tooken Quebec to pieces and throwed it in the river!"

"That's what these men ought to do," I said. "I don't believe you'd find better troops than these anywhere, not even in England."

"They ain't no better'n we were!" he protested. Then his eyes dropped to his frayed and stained remnants of breeches, untied at the knees; his hand fumbled at the growth of whiskers that made his face haggard and fearsome. Later, when I called him and one of his companions to go with me to get the quarter barrel of beer, they had scraped the bristles from their cheeks, tied their breeches, and their hair was combed and clubbed. They seemed to stand straighter, too, and to have less the look of being whipped.

The change in their appearance was a miracle, almost. I began to feel that war was not so bad; that it might be over before we knew it, so that Nathaniel and I could be starting back for Arundel before summer set in. It would be pleasant, I thought, to sit in the stuffed chair beside the table in our sitting-room in Arundel, wearing my blue coat, cameo pin and a ruffled shirt, and to speak modestly to callers about the great things we had done in Canada.

So nearly over did our troubles seem that I began to lay great plans for the future, as do all soldiers far from home. I'd build a new brig, I decided—a snow, perhaps: three hundred tons, with a master's cabin the width of the stern, and a 24-pound traversing piece so we could fight off pirates on the China coast, and I'd carry Tom Bickford with me as first mate. . . .

Not even the change of wind that brought rain that night, together with clouds of mosquitoes and black flies and midges, could dampen our optimism.

I have no means to tell how terrible those stinging insects of Canada were. In moist weather, when the wind was right, they blanketed the low land all up and down the Richelieu as fog-particles blanket the sea. Their faint shrill wings made an unending singing around us. The midges stung like hot needles; mosquitoes lanced us perpetually; but worst of all were the black flies, which crawled beneath our hat bands or behind our ears, their bites unfelt but so villainous that blood ran down from the punctures they made. Then the bites swelled, and we saw men with eyes closed from the poison of those damnable insects, necks puffed up like squashes, ears standing out like diseased growths.

Thanks to the hoods of our smocks, and to lying in the smoke of a smudge, we came through the night without being eaten alive. The morning was only half over when a squad of men in blue and white came swinging down the river road. At their head was a young lieutenant who halted them smartly abreast of us; then came up to eye us doubtfully.

"Who's in charge here?" he asked.

I told him I was.

"Well, General Sullivan wants to know what's being done with these ship timbers."

"They're being dismantled on orders. Orders of General Arnold."

"Well, General Sullivan's in command here. He wants it stopped."

"I take my orders from General Arnold," I told him.

"You'll have to talk to General Sullivan," the lieutenant said.

Seeing there was nothing to do but go, I told Tom Bickford to stay where he was, come hell or high water. Then I went splashing back with the lieutenant and his squad of men.

. . . Headquarters, in the square stone building of a mill owner, was in a turmoil, smelling of steamy wet clothes, and seething with people waiting to see General Sullivan. Officers blundered through the rooms as if half out of their wits, all of them mud-spattered and swollen with insect bites.

For five hours I stood on one foot and then on the other in the hallway before the general was able to take notice of me; and in that time I heard a world of cursing from impatient young officers over the dreadful conditions that existed everywhere. From them I learned that these new regiments would waste no time in hastening forward to make themselves masters of Quebec; nor could I help hearing that General Thomas, commanding all the forces in Canada, was lying blind and raving in Chambly, dying of smallpox, so that it was only a matter of hours before General Sullivan must succeed to the position.

When at last I was taken before him, I found him tall and florid, with tufts of hair sticking out in front of his ears, so that he looked like a good-natured lynx. From the set of his lips I judged him to be stubborn; and it was written all over him that he was determined to be well liked, even though he had to kick people into liking him. He was plainly elated, too, by the importance of the position in which he now found himself.

"Who's this?" he asked, mopping his sweaty red face. "What's the trouble here?"

The lieutenant spoke for me. "This was the man in charge of those ship timbers, General."

"Ah yes!" the general said. "I remember it now. Well, sir: what's your idea, interfering with ship timbers that we might make into a finished vessel and use for our own purposes?"

I liked nothing about him—neither his enormous self-satisfaction, his genial condescension, nor his catlike face; but since he was a general and I without any military rank whatever, I had to be more than civil. "Sir," I said, "I'm a scout under General Arnold. I'm a sea captain, so General Arnold gave me orders to get the timbers to Crown Point where they could be used in case of a retreat."

"A retreat!" the general cried. "In case of a retreat! Don't you people talk about anything but retreat, for God's sake? There's to be no retreat before an enemy no person has seen!" He laughed, pretending to a joviality that his eyes denied.

"My orders——" I began; but he banged his desk.

"I cancel 'em! No ship timbers leave here until I know whether we need 'em or not! That's why I'm here—to rectify the blunders that have been made—recover the ground our former troops so shamefully lost! I don't want the word 'retreat' mentioned in this army!"

I knew enough about discipline to keep my mouth shut; and when the general had mopped his face once more, he beamed on me as though we had a joke in common. "Here," he continued, "I take it you're regularly on scout duty, aren't you? Well, I'll put you to doing something more useful than stealing ships! Go around this section and find out what the Canadians are saying about us: how they feel. That's valuable! That's what we ought to know! Tell General De Woedtke what you learn, and he'll tell me." He coughed importantly. "That's all. You can go."

I saluted and went out, feeling as though I had been kicked. Once outside, I stole a glance at the lieutenant to see whether he considered the general's orders as foolish as they seemed to me. Apparently he didn't, and had no further interest in me or my affairs, so I saluted him as punctiliously as I had saluted the general, and made myself scarce.

We had more beer that night, Tom Bickford and I and the York troopers; and by the time it was half gone we agreed that Sullivan's orders applied to no one but myself, and that the others were free to do what Arnold wanted done.

"He ain't got no control over us!" the ringleader of the York troopers said virtuously. "You let him get a dozen rods out of town on the road to Sorel, and we'll have these timbers aboard a bateau before you can kiss a duck!"

As to investigating the feelings of the French, I already knew how they felt, and so did everyone else with any sense. And I knew there was no need to tell that drunken sot De Woedtke anything, because he wouldn't remember whether I had or not. The thing for me to do was to keep out of sight as much as possible, so that I might not be subject to discipline, or to more of Sullivan's orders.

Thus the matter was arranged to everyone's satisfaction: even to mine; for as I gave Tom Bickford beer-money against the days to come, I thought, as I had thought several times before, that my new orders, foolish though they were, would at least give me an opportunity to see whether there was anything I could do for Ellen Phipps.

XV

It was one thing, I found, to contemplate seeing Ellen Phipps, but another thing to do it; for I was no sooner in a canoe, headed across the river to Iberville and the Château de St. Auge, than I realized I could never talk with Ellen until I had provided Madame St. Auge with a reason for my presence.

I walked slowly up the hillslope from the river, then back to the river again, trying to think what to say, and at the same time trying to look as though I knew what I was doing. The more I walked, the more uncomfortable and like a fool I felt; and so, in desperation, I went boldly up to the door and pounded on it, trusting to something I had learned in storms at sea: that no matter what a captain may beforehand plan to do, he will surprise himself by behaving differently and more effectively when the emergency is actually upon him.

The same spectacled nun answered my knock; and when I asked for Ellen Phipps, she slammed the door in my face. I stood there, perspiring and grimly determined that nothing now would keep me from seeing the girl, even though I stood on the doorstep for a week. Almost immediately, however, the door opened again and Madame St. Auge stood there, her eyes slipping and roaming, from my face to my feet, off into space, and back to my clothes again.

"You asked to see Ellen?"

"Yes," I said. An idea popped into my head. "About her brother."

"About her brother? Tell me what it is, please, and I will tell it to her."

"Your pardon," I said. "I must tell her myself."

Madame St. Auge folded her hands over the heavy leather strap that belted her gray gown, and silently contemplated my shoes. At length she raised expressionless eyes. "I am sorry. It is not possible. You will have to tell me."

"Not possible! You mean she's ill? What is it you mean?"

"She is not here. She has gone away."

The woman's behavior puzzled me, and I only half believed her. "Where's she gone? When did she go? How did she go?"

Madame St. Auge's reply was both calm and cold. "You will excuse if I do not answer your questions. It is not our custom to reveal such information without excellent reason."

"But there'd be no harm, now, in saying when she'll be back, would there?"

"When she'll be back? When she'll be back?" Madame St. Auge's voice seemed to me unnecessarily loud, almost as if she wanted it to carry across the Richelieu and into General Sullivan's headquarters.

At the thought I glanced over my shoulder. Within a few paces of me, just turning from the path as if to go around to the rear of the château, was Marie de Sabrevois.

I knew her at once, even in her dress of sober blue and her little sunbonnet of gray silk, quite different from the billowing pink gown in which I had first seen her; but what was more remarkable was that she recognized me as well, notwithstanding my tow-cloth smock.

In spite of the dislike for her that had grown and grown in me since our London meeting, I was pleased at the sight of a familiar face in this dreary settlement; and my pleasure increased when she came to me with an exclamation of surprise. "To think," she cried, "of meeting in St. John's, of all places! Now how does it happen you're here?"

"It just happens. I was ordered to come here, and so I came."

"You were ordered to come here to this house?" she asked, studying me with a singular intentness.

"No," I said. "I was ordered to come to St. John's. Having come here, it occurred to me—I had some time to spare—I thought that Ellen——"

Her fixed stare made me uncomfortable.

Madame St. Auge said coldly, "He has a message for Ellen. A message about her brother."

"Indeed!" Marie de Sabrevois exclaimed. "Someone sends you to her with a message about her brother? Who?"

The eyes of both women probed at me; and I felt the more uncomfortable. I had put myself in a false position, which prevented the ordinary processes of conversation that might have taken place between Mademoiselle de Sabrevois and myself, wherein I would have inquired about her voyage, and told her of Nathaniel's and mine. And being in that false position of my own contriving, I stood conscious of a tensity between these women and myself, and wondered how it had come about that I seemed to be a liar. Nevertheless I perceived that I had lied: not to them, but to myself when I persuaded myself that my errand to Ellen was in the hope that I might be of service to her. I wanted to see her again, and that was the whole truth about what brought me.

Yet I wondered also about another thing, and that was why the mere mention of a message about Ellen's brother made these two rigid with some unguessable suspicion of me.

I hastened to clear myself of that suspicion. "Madame St. Auge is mistaken. I didn't say I had a message to Ellen from her brother or about her brother. I only said I wished to talk to her about her brother, which is true, because my wish was to talk with her about anything whatever."

At that Mademoiselle de Sabrevois gave me a shrewd look, and smiled as though we were the best of friends. To Madame St. Auge she said: "But we have many things to talk over, this gentleman and I— more important things than Ellen's brother; and a doorstep's no place for such conversation!"

She nodded to me gaily. "Come, we'll walk here on this quiet road. It's pleasanter than the dark house." She was right; for the country was fresh and green in the warm June sun after the rain of the day before. There was a smell of young grass and moist earth all around us, and the tremulous, halting songs of innumerable robins.

Marie de Sabrevois slipped her hand beneath my arm and looked up at me from under the brim of her sunbonnet.

"Now you must tell me everything!" Her voice was prettily commanding. "When you arrived, and for what! I'm dying to know!"

"Lord!" I said. "There's nothing interesting to be got out of me. Anyway, you must have had it all from Nathaniel."

She eyed me with that same watchful intentness I had seen before.

"You had a letter from him, didn't you?" I asked. "I saw him write it."

She nodded. "Of course. Yes, of course I had his letter. A friendly one, it was. It was thoughtful of him to write. You must tell him how much we appreciate his kindness, Madame St. Auge and I."

Up to now I had thought that Marie de Sabrevois, perceiving that I disliked her, had naturally mirrored my dislike. But when she spoke of Nathaniel's letter as "friendly," I knew she considered me a dolt. "Friendly!" I said to myself. "Friendly," for God's sake! If I knew Nathaniel at all, his letter smelled of scorched paper from the fiery words he had put in it. Still, if she thought me a dolt, let her continue to think so.

"After all," I reminded her, "there was no need of his carrying your message to Ellen Phipps. You might as well have brought it yourself. You were here almost as soon as we were."

"But there was no way of telling! I might have arrived here a year from now instead of day before yesterday. It was only luck that my affairs were so soon settled."

"You got here day before yesterday? You must have seen General Sullivan's brigade come in."

She raised her eyebrows. "I saw soldiers. It's hard for me to tell one from the other."

"You haven't seen many of our men, then. You must have come by way of Quebec."

She nodded, almost absently. "Yes. It's not difficult. With a little money, a person does as he likes. And it saved me a difficult journey. I was glad not to be obliged to travel by way of Albany and all the way up the lake to reach my darling Ellen."

"And Burgoyne's troops," I asked. "Did you see them? Have they arrived yet?"

"Heavens above!" she cried. "How should I know! I had a thousand things to do in the city without racing about looking for troops! There were soldiers, of course, as there always are in Quebec: but mercy knows whose they were!"

"Well now," I said, "it was a pity you didn't remember that your country's at war with England. Not many Americans have the good fortune to pass through Quebec these days; and it's too bad that those who do shouldn't bring out as much valuable information as possible."

She struck her hands together. "Lud! What a fool I was! You mean there would have been real value in such information as I might have brought?"

I saw there was nothing to be got in that direction, and inside myself I damned her. For what, I wasn't sure; but I had a persistent feeling that she deserved damning. She deserved it for meddling with my brother Nathaniel, if for nothing else; for she was a lady who had seen a thing or two in her day; and I couldn't bear to think what might happen to Nathaniel if she set her mind to him.

"Surely," she said, "surely you don't mean that those soldiers across the river, in St. John's, haven't yet learned whether Burgoyne's troops have landed in Canada!"

"Well," I said, "that's something I needn't bother my head about. What worries me is why a mystery should be made out of Ellen Phipps! Anybody'd think it was a crime to ask where she's gone and when she's coming back—and worse than a crime to know about her brother."

She laughed lightly. "There's no mystery to it. You see, Ellen went to tell her brother she expects to go soon to Albany—to tell him and to bid him farewell. That's why we questioned you about her brother, you see. We were afraid he might have sent word he was going elsewhere, so that Ellen might have her journey for nothing." Her blue eyes were wide and frank.

"So that was all!" I hoped I sounded both innocent and relieved. "There was no secret about it, then."

"No, no! Nothing could be more absurd!"

"Then when did she go, and when is she coming back?"

Marie de Sabrevois raised her hands and eyes in mock despair. "She went yesterday morning. She'll return when her errand is done—tomorrow, it may be; or the day after."

"Well," I said, "it seems strange to me that you no sooner arrive here than you let her go running off alone to a wilderness like St. Francis—you, who have been so eager to see her for months and months. Strange, too, that you let her go just after Sullivan's troops had come. Didn't you know the roads would be crowded with horsemen and supply carts—crowded and difficult!"

"What's strange about it?" she demanded. "You're jumping at conclusions! Ellen went to the convent at Three Rivers: not to St. Francis. The nuns will arrange to have Joseph brought across the river to see her. But I'm not surprised it seems strange to you! When she felt she had to go, I longed to go with her, but I was worn out by my voyage—exhausted! Even this little walk has quite overcome me! You see, I'm not strong, and fear me I must return to Madame St. Auge's already!"

She sighed pathetically; but to me she looked as though she had known nothing of exhaustion for many a long year. She was as shapely and elastic as a sleek young cat; and sleek young cats have extraordinary powers of endurance.

"I wonder you didn't send word for Ellen's brother to come here?" I said.

She had a ready answer. "No: it would be unsafe for him to travel through American troops—through our troops. They mightn't understand that he isn't really an Indian, and might not believe him friendly to our cause." Then she added softly, "I'm glad you take this interest in Ellen. I'm sure you'll help us on our way to Albany if you should have the chance."

She couldn't help knowing, as well as I, that I was a nobody in the army, and little able to help Ellen Phipps or anyone else. I wondered what lay behind those clear blue eyes; but there was no way, so far as I could see, of finding out.

"Your uncle," I said, "should be able to make everything easy for you. I thought he'd be here before now."

"My uncle?" she asked, and seemed surprised. "You haven't heard from him? You didn't know? Poor man, he has a broken leg, and cannot travel."

"Be damned to a broken leg!" I told myself. "You've got everything figured out, as slick as a whistle!" To her I only nodded gravely and said I was sorry to hear of Mr. Leonard's misfortune. Then I asked: "When shall you go to Albany, ma'am?"

"As soon as we can. As soon as I've recovered my strength after the long sea journey." She coughed delicately, to let me see how weak she was.

And then, as we had reached the door of the château again, I could only bid her a polite farewell and cross the river to the shipyard, speculating helplessly—why she should take no interest in military matters, when in London she had been so knowing about them: why she should have permitted Ellen Phipps to go to Three Rivers at such a time as this: above all whether Mademoiselle de Sabrevois would have been as guarded in her speech and as overcome by exhaustion if I had been Nathaniel.

XVI

Sᴜʟʟɪᴠᴀɴ's forces had moved north to redeem what Sullivan called the shameful blunders hitherto made by American troops in Canada. After they left, St. John's became a sort of open-air madhouse. Half-clothed and leaderless soldiers, remnants of the regiments that had fled from before Quebec a month ago, appeared from nowhere and wandered from farm to farm, begging for food. Frantic supply-officers squabbled day and night over a pitiful mixture of supplies, each officer declaring that he and he alone must have the food, since the men of his regiment were most in need of it. The place was a porridge of rain, mosquitoes, mud, and rumors of smallpox, enough to make any man wonder whether anything worse could happen.

What it was that befell me, however, was the last thing I would have expected.

I had gone to Hersom, on the waterfront, to pick up the day's news along with the meager rations I was allowed to draw for Tom and myself. News had suddenly become more important to us than ever, not only because we felt we had to learn something that might offset the horrible tales we heard of the smallpox—tales almost as sickening as the disease itself—but because all the new regiments we had seen arrive had been sent down the St. Lawrence by General Sullivan to capture Three Rivers, so to prevent British troops from passing that important post.

We were hoping to have word that General Arnold would be sent to lead them in place of those who had started to do so—a General Thompson, who had appeared from God knows where, and of whom nobody seemed to know anything except that he was an Irishman; and Colonel St. Clair, who had been in the British army many years ago. We were suspicious of Thompson and St. Clair. Our troops, we knew, were not inclined to have the greatest of faith in Irishmen or English-men—especially in Irishmen or Englishmen of whom they had never heard. That was why we hoped that Arnold would be put in command of the new regiments. Not only would men follow him anywhere, and against any odds; but he alone, of all the high officers left with this stricken army of ours, was familiar with the country and the people.

He knew how to lead, and where to lead; and we suspected he was the only one that *did* know.

As I stood in front of Hersom's warehouse, I was flabbergasted to see Nathaniel come striding along the river road as if he well knew where he was going, and was in a hurry to get there. He had on a white jacket with a fringe at the edge, and brown leather breeches with brown stockings pulled over them and made fast below the knee with bands of red wool. There was even a long queue, half hair and half rope, hanging down his back.

When I ran out and took him by the elbow, he clapped his arm around me, as affectionate as ever; but on the instant he seemed to lose all of his hurry and purposefulness, and sauntered toward the warehouse with me as idly as though he had nothing on earth to do.

"I was wondering whether I'd see you," he said; and as soon as he said it, I knew he had hoped he wouldn't.

"What are you doing here?" I asked. "You were sent down the St. Lawrence, weren't you?"

He laughed. "Always the same old Peter! Forever bound to treat me as if I was still twelve and you fifteen!"

"Look here," I said. "The last thing I heard, you were sent to get information. Did you get it?"

"Of course I got it! There's only eight hundred British troops at Three Rivers—men from Halifax regiments."

While this news didn't explain Nathaniel's presence, it was welcome; for it meant the fine new regiments sent forward by Sullivan would drive eight hundred men down river as easily as driving a flock of yellow-legs.

"Have you told Arnold?" I asked.

"Not yet. Where is he?"

"Not yet! You haven't told him yet? What in God's name are you thinking about?"

"Don't be a fool, Peter! I can't tell him till I see him, can I? He's here in St. John's, isn't he?"

"He's in Montreal, and you know it!"

Nathaniel looked pained. "Don't get so excited! I was told he'd be here; and even if he isn't, it's no farther to Montreal this way than by the St. Lawrence—that is, not much."

He might easily, I knew, be stating the case correctly; for the St. Lawrence swings to the southward just above the mouth of the Richelieu River, and runs almost parallel with the Richelieu. Thus it is little shorter to travel direct from Three Rivers to Montreal than to travel by way of the Richelieu and St. John's. I had heard, too, that Arnold was galloping all over the country trying to assemble enough supplies to feed his wretched remnant of a garrison in Montreal; so the rumor might indeed have got abroad that he was in this God-forsaken town.

"Now look here," I said. "You knew Arnold's headquarters were in Montreal, and that's where you should have taken your information!"

Nathaniel made a contemptuous sound. "You can't build this mole hill into a mountain, Peter! The information I've got isn't worth much. Verrieul stayed down the river to hear more news; and we decided I'd better take back what we'd learned, just to show we were working."

"Nathaniel," I said, "I don't want to see you make a fool of yourself. You're supposed to obey orders, always. What would Arnold say if he found you hadn't come direct to him?"

Nathaniel shrugged his shoulders.

I looked at him straight. "Where were you going just now when I stopped you?"

"Where?" He laughed. "Why, I was hunting for Arnold."

"Headquarters in this town," I told him, "are in the square stone house you passed two hundred yards back. That's where they are when there *are* any. What made you think you'd find Arnold down this way, provided you found him at all?"

Nathaniel made no answer.

"How did it happen you were laying your course with such assurance? If you'd asked any of our men, you'd have learned that De Woedtke's supposed to be in command here, and you'd have learned his headquarters aren't down this far. You haven't come here to see Arnold at all, Nathaniel!"

Nathaniel stared at me. His eyes were hard. "I don't know what call you've got to interfere with me!"

There was no question in my mind. He had learned Marie de Sabrevois was in Iberville, across from St. John's, and he had come here to see her.

I put my hand on his shoulder. "I don't propose to see my own brother shot for disobeying orders. Turn yourself around and set out for Montreal."

Nathaniel looked bored. "Shot for disobeying orders! If everybody in this army that disobeyed orders was shot, there wouldn't *be* any army! Anyway, I'm not disobeying orders. If we'd discovered anything new, maybe you might stretch a point and say I wasn't exactly obeying orders; but the way things are, where's the harm if I stay in St. John's a few hours to get some rest?"

"Where's the harm—after what Arnold said to us about obeying orders? You heard him speak of Butterfield and Bedel, didn't you? You heard Steven Nason give his word to Arnold that he could depend on us?"

"Oh, for God's sake," Nathaniel cried, "I'm sick of hearing about Arnold! How Arnold marched to Quebec; how he did wonders at the Cedars; how he'll raise hell with the British—Arnold, Arnold, Arnold—you'd think that damned horse-jockey was the only officer we had!"

"What was that? What was it you called Arnold?"

Nathaniel's face and voice were sullen. "'Horse-jockey' was what I said. That's all he was before the war—a cheap horse-trader and horse-jockey. Everybody knows it. That's why he went to war—to make money out of it!"

"What in God's name are you talking about?" I demanded. "Arnold's a sea captain and shipowner—a man of property and position. His father before him was a sea captain and shipowner. His great-grandfather was Governor of Rhode Island—a gentleman of the highest character and distinction. Arnold himself is the same sort of person, Steven Nason says."

"I don't care what he says! Steven Nason's an uneducated man, just the way Arnold is. Arnold could tell him anything, probably, and Nason'd believe him."

"Don't say anything you'd regret," I told him. "Steven Nason may not have what Harvard calls an education, but he can talk the Abenaki language, and drive a straight furrow, and keep a company of soldiers under control, and get along with his neighbors. He doesn't believe everything he hears, like some educated dunces I've met; and he knows the difference between what's good and what's worthless, though that's something colleges don't seem to be able to teach. And to top it all off, he's had a year of war. It's hard to believe, but there's those who'd prefer Steven Nason's education to that of some who've spent four years in college and almost learned to read the Bible in Greek." I eyed him severely, to let him know he could apply my words to himself if he so desired. Then I asked him, "Who told you Arnold was a horse-jockey?"

Nathaniel was contemptuous. "A horse-jockey and a gymnast! That's all he was—just a common gymnast. He used to travel around giving exhibitions. Anybody can tell you how he used to give exhibitions jumping over loaded ammunition wagons. That's all this great general was —nothing but a circus performer!"

"My God!" I cried. "You're mad! Wherever did you hear such tales for children! Somebody's been stuffing you with fish-feathers! Who was it?"

"It's common knowledge. Everybody knows it. You hear it everywhere."

"I don't hear it everywhere," I said. "Is it some of the information you've been collecting for your commanding officer?" I took him by the arm, and would have said more; but the sound of a hoarse voice, bellowing from the river road, stayed me. It roared unmelodiously a familiar song about three beautiful ducks and a ball that rolled, rolled, rolled interminably.

A moment later a fat white horse strained into sight from behind the warehouses, dragging a cart piled high with bundles. The cart thumped and bumped on the logs with which the road was paved. On top of the bundles sat two men, one of whom, a Canadian, slumbered deeply, resting precariously against the shoulder of Cap Huff, who swayed as though balancing himself against the thrusts of a heavy sea. He whacked the rump of the white horse with the ends of the reins in time to his singing, and all the while he darted sharp glances at everyone in sight. Seeing us, he bawled a hearty greeting.

When he had drawn up beside us, he eased the body of his companion down among the bundles, descended from the cart, peered solicitously into the brown face of the recumbent figure: then gave it an earnest slap with an open hand. The Canadian sat up with a start, looked around him and reached wildly for the reins.

"Liquor!" Cap said to us, jerking his head toward the Canadian. "You can't depend on 'em! They keep drinking it. They got just that much sense." He coughed virtuously, but the virtue was expended in the sound alone of the cough; for its spurting smell made one think a vast quantity of rum had been exploded into a gas too thick to disperse quickly.

He looked from one to the other of us, and finally his gaze focussed on Nathaniel. "Oh yes! I remember! Well, you must 'a' seen 'em! You must 'a' seen the King's troops Sullivan was talking about."

"King's troops?" Nathaniel asked. "What King's troops? I didn't see any King's troops!"

Cap Huff rubbed his eyes with sausage-like forefingers. "Then Sullivan's a liar! I kind of figured he was a liar! He wrote Arnold last night there was King's troops between him and Three Rivers, ready to attack, and for Arnold to send down all his spare men and be damned quick about it. Arnold figured he was a liar, too, on account of not having heard from you. He said if there'd been troops, you'd have reported 'em."

The blood seemed to leave my heart, and I held my breath; but from the look of blank surprise on Nathaniel's face I knew my fears were groundless.

"I just came here from Three Rivers," Nathaniel said. "There weren't any troops on the road; not any."

Cap stared at him, shot a quick glance at me; then went to staring at him again. "Well, that's interesting! You don't suppose it would interest Arnold, do you? Or do you have to tell everything to your brother first?"

"Aren't you a little free with your tongue?" I asked. "This boy was told he'd find Arnold here. He was just starting for Montreal when you came in sight."

Cap grunted, "By God, he'd better! I've had about all I can stand for one day! Here, come along and show me a place to store these bundles. Your brother can take this cart back to Montreal, and carry word to Arnold that'll make him bite somebody."

I led him to the shipyard, where Tom Bickford had rigged a shelter, for although the marked timbers were safely on their way to Crown Point, the yard had come to seem like home to us. On the way Cap cursed so passionately that his voice cracked and became shrill. "You wouldn't believe it!" he told us. "You wouldn't believe any man could be so rotten as that Hazen!"

He jerked his thumb at the cart. "See those bundles? They're full of what this army ought to have, but ain't got: powder, bullets, buckshot, shoes, shirts, blankets, cloth for breeches, nails, stockings, rum. See 'em? On each one there's the name of the feller it was taken from, and what's in it, and how much the feller's to be paid, all neat and regular. Me and Doc and Major Scott, we been rounding 'em up. Scott took three cartloads to Chambly day before yesterday, and Arnold sent an order by him to Hazen, telling Hazen to accept 'em and take care of 'em. Last night I set out after Scott with this load; and when I got to Chambly nice and early, there was all of Scott's bundles dumped beside the river, no guard over 'em nor nothing, and a feller walking away from 'em, sort of innocent-looking. A couple of the packages was broke open, so I ran after the innocent-looking feller and kind of looked in his breeches pockets. He was all stuffed full of stockings!

"Yes sir! He'd been stealing, and I can't stand stealing, especially when it's done from me. If I'd left this with the packages, he might have got this, even!" He worried a tin box from his breeches pocket and pried off the cover. It was full of a sickish-smelling brown paste, seemingly made of rotted leaves.

"What's that?" I asked.

"Opium. Doc Means, the old catamount, said it was the only drug worth a hoot, and if I saw some, to pick it up for him. I happened to come across this, so I picked it up."

He stuffed it back in his pocket and stared at me indignantly. "When I saw that feller stealing stockings, I told him a thing or two about being dishonest. Well, sir: he wouldn't pay no attention: said the packages didn't belong to nobody.

" 'Not belong to nobody!' says I. 'They belong to the Continental Army: that's who they belong to.'

" 'No,' the feller says, 'they don't belong to nobody, because Colonel Hazen wouldn't receive 'em when Scott brought 'em in. He made him dump 'em beside the river, and then he ordered Scott off to Sorel to help dig trenches. That's how I know they don't belong to nobody.'

" 'What's your name?' says I to the feller.

" 'You better ask Colonel Hazen,' the feller says.

"With that I seen a light. Yes sir! I seen it was high time I got away from Chambly before Hazen, the old stink, made me dump my goods beside the river and ordered me off to Sorel too. So I set off for St. John's, and here I am!" He began to toss the packages from the cart to the ground.

"How could Hazen do it?" I asked. "Is he half-witted, or is he a traitor?"

"Brother," Cap said, "he's a pig-nut! Look around at the officers in this army and you'll see the greatest lot of pig-nuts there ever was! Some are good ones; but most of 'em ain't nothing but pig-nuts!"

"Pig-nuts?" I asked.

"Pig-nuts," Cap repeated. "It takes a sledge-hammer to crack a pig-nut, and when you get inside it, there ain't nothing you care to use. Besides being like pig-nuts, most of the officers are like women in not being able to stand getting told they done something kind of wrong. You ever tried criticizing a woman much? Arnold, he knows how to do things; and when he sees a pig-nut doing things wrong, he tells him. Tells him loud, so everybody hears it. The trouble is, you can tell a man with brains he's wrong and he'll try to fix things up; but you take and tell a pig-nut he's wrong, and he'll spend the rest of his life trying to have something heavy fall on you when you ain't looking."

"You mean Arnold's spoken to Hazen?" I asked.

"Spoken to him!" Cap cried. "He damned hell out of him for not being willing to attack the English and Indians when they was on the run after the Cedars; and he damned two hells out of him for pushing Jerry Duggan out of the army. Duggan was the only American officer the Canadians would follow, but he was a barber. Canadians never shave nor fix up their hair. They never see no barbers, so they think they're nice, and they took to Duggan. Hazen, he said he wouldn't be in the same army with a barber. Made so much trouble for Duggan, he did, that Duggan had to resign. Duggan's worth ten Hazens! Hazen's the king pig-nut, and he hates Arnold because Arnold tells him to his face what he is, and because Arnold's the only good general that's been seen around here since Wolfe stopped a bullet."

Absent-mindedly Cap lifted a board from one of the boxes and took out a dusty bottle. It had been opened before; for he drew the cork with his teeth and helped himself freely to the contents. After that he passed the bottle to us.

While I was drinking, Nathaniel said to Cap: "If he feels that way about barbers, maybe he doesn't like gymnasts, either."

The cart was empty, except for the Canadian driver; and with no gentle hand I helped Nathaniel up into it.

Cap eyed him dubiously. "What was that? What is it he maybe doesn't like either?"

"Gymnasts," I said dryly. "He means acrobats. Nathaniel heard that Arnold used to be a gymnast, but of course there's nothing in it."

"Oh, ain't there!" Cap cried. "Well I hope to die if there ain't! This feller Arnold can skate better than any Canadian that ever lived. Even with a hole shot through one leg he's stronger'n quicker'n any other three men in the world! He's the only feller ever I see that could jump all the way over an ammunition wagon without touching a hand to it."

He moved closer to the cart and stared at Nathaniel with bloodshot eyes. "If you don't believe there ain't nothing in it, just take your time going back to Montreal! If you don't get there quicker'n scat, that gymnast'll jump all over you. You'll deserve it, but you won't like gymnasts any more than Hazen does."

He hiccupped portentously: then stingingly slapped the white mare on the rump; and the last I saw of Nathaniel, he was sprawled with the pig-tailed Canadian in the bottom of the cart, and the cart itself was bouncing around the turn in the river road on its way to Montreal.

XVII

If st. john's had been a madhouse during early June, it became far worse in the next few nightmare days.

First came the smallpox regiments, sent back from Sorel to die or get well—Greaton's Massachusetts regiment and Poor's New Hampshire regiment. For the most part they had inoculated themselves, so that some could walk, and some had to be carried; but in the regiments there were less than three hundred men able to be out of the hospital. They had the look of men dug out of graves, as they dragged themselves into town.

Hard on their heels came the reports that Sullivan's new regiments had been hacked to pieces at Three Rivers. We had the news fragmentarily, some from Ellen Phipps, who had been there when it happened; some from deserters, who pretended to be sick, and were trying to make their way on foot through the wilderness between St. John's and Albany; and some from Canadians, who turned their coats with the news and now jeered at us openly.

They had gone down river, those beautiful regiments, eager to fight and confident of driving to Quebec through any force that might oppose them. In the dead of night they had landed a few miles from Three Rivers. General Thompson and Colonel St. Clair, leading the advance, had picked up a Canadian Frenchman as a guide. He led them into a swamp, through which they struggled for hours, up to their thighs in mud and tangled roots that wrenched their clothes from them.

They escaped from the first swamp only to stumble into a second. When dawn came, they were still far from Three Rivers; and at Three Rivers, rushed there the night before from Quebec, were not only the whole British fleet, but freshly arrived transports carrying an army that was trooping ashore, boatload after boatload, even as the Americans marched up to the assault.

Sullivan's troops attacked, only to be overwhelmed by numbers; and when they broke and ran for their boats, the boats were gone. They took to the swamps, foodless and exhausted. General Thompson and Colonel Irvine were captured by the British; and when the remnants of those once-proud regiments at last straggled into Sorel, they were

as destitute, ragged and dejected as the sorriest specimens in all that
sorry camp.

. . . At the first report of the disaster, I had gone to the Château de
St. Auge to urge Marie de Sabrevois to set out for Albany as soon as
Ellen Phipps should return from Three Rivers. This time I was admitted without question; and when Marie de Sabrevois entered the
bare room in which I waited, Ellen Phipps was with her.

I knew from the thumping beneath my smock that Ellen had been
more in my mind than I had realized, and that I had feared she might
come to some harm on her journey to Three Rivers. I would even have
liked to say something of the sort to her, but since she hardly looked at
me when she came in, and since her aunt was there, I said nothing.

Marie de Sabrevois had no sooner set eyes on me than she asked,
"Where's your brother?" and there was a haughty look about her, as
if she were provoked.

"I don't rightly know," I said. "He takes his orders from General
Arnold. He might be in Montreal, and then again he might not."

"Haven't you seen him recently?"

She and Nathaniel, I realized, must have met when she was journey-
ing from Quebec to St. John's. She must have expected to see him again
on the day when Cap and I had sent him back to Montreal. When I
hesitated in replying, she dropped the subject like a hot coal and
turned to another. She was a smart woman: the smartest I ever knew.

"You had a message for Ellen's brother, didn't you?" she asked. "You
can tell her now, and she'll see he gets it."

"Yes," I said, "we had word that Congress had resolved to raise three
thousand Indians for service in Canada, and I thought Ellen's brother
might like to know about it."

"Oh, indeed!" she said. "Three thousand Indians! Three thou——
Who told you Ellen had a brother?"

"Why, Ellen told me," I said. I looked at Ellen; but she was busy
creasing a fold in her coarse gray dress.

Marie de Sabrevois laughed. It was a pleasant laugh.

"Ellen's brother would think twice, no doubt," she said, "before joining those poor soldiers that ran from Three Rivers. Ellen saw them,
running before the guns of the British ships. Tell him, Ellen."

Ellen continued to crease the folds of her dress. In a low voice she
told what she had seen from the house in which she and her nun-
companion had taken refuge on their return journey—American troops,
mud-stained, dog-tired, like sheep without a leader, bombarded by the
British fleet whenever they came out from the swamps onto the river

road. "They fought with their muskets against the ships' cannons," she said. "We could even hear the soldiers on the ships, laughing when the Americans fired."

"Poor men! Poor men!" Marie de Sabrevois sighed. "How could they expect to stand against England's finest regiments!"

"They'd have stood against them, and whipped 'em, too," I reminded her, "if Arnold had led 'em, or if they hadn't trusted one of these pig-tailed Frenchmen!" I waited eagerly for her reply, but she made none.

"Well," I said at last, "that's what I came to talk about. You spoke of going to Albany with Ellen. I wanted to tell you what had happened, in case you didn't know about it, so you could get started. It wouldn't be pleasant for either of you, would it, if you were caught in a retreat?"

"No, it wouldn't," Marie de Sabrevois admitted, "and it's kind of you to have us in mind. When do you think we should start?"

"Right now," I said. "As soon as you can."

She nodded. "Yes, I can see you're right. If there should be a retreat, the town might be burned or looted. We'll do what you say." Then, while I racked my brains for a way to get a word with Ellen alone, she added musingly: "We're both so sorry, my little girl here and I, that your brother is away; that we can't see him whenever we wish—which would be often, of course. Do you think he'll be coming back to St. John's soon?"

"It's war time!" I reminded her. "Men can't come and go as they like, Mademoiselle de Sabrevois." Then, with a grudging sort of gallantry I looked at her significantly and said, "Otherwise I have no doubt Nathaniel would be in St. John's all the time."

"Ah, you've noticed it too?" she asked amusedly, and to my great puzzlement, she glanced at Ellen. "These young people!" she said, and added, "Well, I cannot see the harm. Ellen likes your brother very much —don't you, Ellen?"

Ellen acquiescently murmured something inaudible to me. Her aunt gave me a merry glance, a look benevolent, as people do when they teasingly encourage an affair of young love. At that, Ellen blushed.

My heart suddenly felt weighted with buck-shot; and I thanked God I had not had the misfortune to become overly attached to this brown-haired girl. She had reminded me of my sister Jane, being so different in every way. That, I told myself, was probably why she had come to occupy so large a part of my thoughts. Certainly my interest was nothing more than brotherly; nothing more!

"Well," I said cheerfully, "I'll keep an eye out for Nathaniel. I guess we can probably contrive for Ellen to see him somehow."

Ellen glanced up at me then with an odd expression; but since neither she nor her aunt had anything to say, I left the Château de St. Auge, wondering why Ellen's look had touched a familiar cord in my memory. I was halfway across the river before I remembered having seen the same look on my sister Jane's face when she felt called on to thrust out her tongue at me.

I didn't wonder that Ellen was attracted by Nathaniel; for I had often noticed that his cultivated voice and the crinkle in his brown hair made him sought after by every lady who saw him. We were supposed to look alike: yet seldom indeed did any woman ever give me a second glance when he was near; or at any other time, either, for that matter.

I was spared over-much thinking by the voice of Cap Huff, which I began to hear long before I reached the shore. "Where the hell you been?" he shouted. "Get up to headquarters quick! Arnold's in town! He wants you!"

. . . To hear Cap talk, Arnold was always in a passion over something or other; but the truth was that he was as kindly and forbearing a gentleman, under most circumstances, as I have ever seen—even under conditions that would drive most of his critics, particularly those who have attacked him most bitterly, into an apoplexy.

When I rapped on the door of the dingy headquarters room in which I had talked to General Sullivan two weeks before, I expected to find Arnold in a rage over the defeat of the new troops and the supplies Hazen had refused to handle at Chambly, but the voice that bade me enter was mild. The general was alone in the room, writing at a rickety pine table. He cocked an eye at me as I came in, and said: "I'll be only five minutes—this letter to Schuyler——" He went on writing, a half smile on his dark face, his broad-shouldered figure crouched over the table as if he intended to spring up in a moment.

I have known hard workers in my day, but never one like Arnold. He could ride fifty miles; talk for hours at a Council of War, cajoling the stubborn and bulldozing the weak-spined; then ride another fifty miles and lead troops into battle; and on top of it all sit down and write a dozen letters with a hand as steady and a brain as clear as though he had just risen from sleep.

I wondered, as I watched him, how any man could call him a horse-jockey, as Nathaniel had heard him called; for he was handsome, and there was a proud look to him—a look of distinction, that made it clear why he should be admired by such persons of breeding as General

Schuyler and General Washington, and hated by boors like Bedel and Hazen.

He pushed back from the table at last, folded his letter and gave it a thump with his fist.

"So you got the vessel off!"

"Thanks to Tom Bickford," I said. "Tom did it. I had to stop."

He wagged his head and looked distressed. "Poor Sullivan! He must have been in a state, pitchforked into this mess! What was it he had you do?"

When I told him, he raised his eyebrows. "Hardly necessary, was it? The Canadians are with us if we're winning and against us if we're losing. And wherever we lose an inch, Montgolfier contrives for every Canadian in the world to hear about it. I'll say this for Montgolfier: he always makes that inch sound like a mile!"

The name Montgolfier struck me hard. That was the name in the letter Nathaniel had brought to Madame St. Auge from Marie de Sabrevois. I had it by heart. "To Monsieur Montgolfier," she had written, "I send my respects, and to you eight thousand kisses."

"Who's Montgolfier?" I asked.

"He's director of the Seminary of St. Sulpice in Montreal," Arnold said, "and if he could arrange it, he'd have every last American strangled in his bed this night! He gets information from all parts of Canada and America: yes, and sends it out, too; but I'll be damned if I know how! If I did——" With his fist he made the motion of wringing a bird's neck.

"At all events," he went on, "it'll be no loss to Sullivan if I set you to doing something else; and that's exactly what I'll do. De Woedtke was told to fortify this town, and the drunken sot hasn't done it. Today I laid out lines to the north. Works must be thrown up. We've got to have some sort of breastworks and trenches here in case of a retreat; but there don't seem to be men to build 'em.

"Well, we've got to find 'em. They tell me deserters from Sullivan's camp are going through here fifty a day. That's your task. Round up deserters and put 'em to work. Here!" He reached for his pen and scribbled on a sheet of paper: then tossed it to me. It read:

Capt. Peter Merrill has authority to employ unattached soldiers on fortifications. This is for the good of the Colonies, and Capt. Merrill is authorized to use all necessary force.   B. Arnold, Brig. Gen.

"There you are," Arnold said. "Orders and commission, too. You're an army captain now, as well as a sea captain. I've got no right to appoint officers. Only Congress can do that; but if I need officers, I don't know how to get 'em unless I appoint 'em. Go ahead, now! Get men; and if they won't work, beat 'em! I don't propose to have my soldiers sacrificed because a lot of damned renegades refuse to take orders. You can work with Cap Huff. He——"

Outside the window Arnold's black horse, tied to one of the posts beside the entrance, whinnied shrilly. Far off we heard the clatter of hoofs. Arnold went to the window. "Ho!" he said. "Here's a friend of yours with something on his mind."

The sound of hoofs grew noisy and came to a scurrying stop. Arnold threw up the window. "Send him in here," he shouted. "Come in here!"

It was Joseph Marie Verrieul, one-time student of the Revrint Dr. Wheelock at Dartmouth, who opened the door. He smiled at Arnold confidingly. "They told me you might be here, or maybe at Sorel or Nicolet," he said. "I'm glad you're here, because I'm near beat out."

"What's your news?"

"It's the British," Verrieul said, almost happily. "It was difficult to find out about them because of the cloud of Indians around them, most of them drunk. Oh, very drunk! It's a good thing for unworthy Joseph Verrieul that he learned at Dartmouth how to hold a quantity of liquor."

"I'll take your word for that," Arnold said. "What about the British?"

"Yes," Verrieul said, "the British. I thought it best to wait until I learned definitely about them. Now I know. They have just arrived at Three Rivers. They're starting upstream at once, a great fleet. Sixty vessels."

"How many men?" Arnold asked. "How much of an army?"

"How much of an army?" Verrieul repeated. His eyes wandered. "There was never anything so fine: nothing they haven't got! A hundred and twenty-five thousand gallons of rum! Plenty for everybody. Cannons and muskets, everything polished, so the sun glitters on them, and the red coats." As an afterthought he mumbled, "Silver facings on the Germans. Blue with silver lace and facings, all shining."

Arnold slapped his table sharply. "How many men?"

"Eight thousand, they say," Verrieul said. His voice wavered. "I think ten thousand, counting Canadians and Indians."

Arnold kicked his chair closer to the table, slid into it and picked up his pen. "Captain Wilkinson!" he shouted. "Captain Wilkinson!"

The door opened and Wilkinson's grave face appeared, the muscles over his jaws working like the gills of a fish.

Arnold jerked his pen at Verrieul. "Take this boy out and get him some food and a place to sleep. He's half starved."

As the door closed behind them he spoke without looking up. "Your orders are changed. I want you to take this letter to General Sullivan. Sit right where you are."

I watched the mosquitoes dancing against the dirty window-pane. A cold breeze seemed to blow across the back of my neck. Eight thousand troops—all shining—nothing they haven't got! Eight thousand! The number of kisses Marie de Sabrevois had sent to Montgolfier, the man who received information from all parts of Canada and Europe! No: she had sent the kisses to Ellen Phipps: not to Montgolfier. Why had she dragged Montgolfier's name into it? There was something wrong; but if Arnold didn't know, neither did I.

Eight thousand troops! The end was not difficult to see, with sickness ranged against health, destitution against plenty, defeat against confidence, paper against gold!

I thought of our house at the bend of the river in Arundel. The mid-June run of pollocks would be on. All along the river road there would be fish-frames, with split pollocks on them, raising havoc with the scent of sweet-grass and new-cut hay. Swallows would be hovering before their clay nests under the eaves of the tool sheds in the shipyards, trusting that nobody would lift a pole and knock their whole world to dust. We and the swallows, I dimly perceived, had much in common.

Eight thousand men! Cannon and muskets! Everything polished! And deserters going through, fifty a day! Where was Nathaniel, I wondered, and how would this news affect him? I could almost hear my mother's voice saying: "Look out for Nathaniel."

Arnold picked up his letter, waving it to dry it. "You'll have to read this," he said. "In case anything happens, you've got to be able to repeat what's in it." He tossed it across the table and at once went to writing another. I ran my eye over the one he had given me. It was an appeal to Sullivan to retreat immediately from Sorel.

The British had at least ten thousand men, Arnold wrote; to risk a battle against such numbers would only result in the loss of everything. "I am content," he told Sullivan, at the end, "to be the last man who quits this country, and fall, so that my country may rise. But let us not fall together."

I read it again: then folded it and put it on the rickety table.

Arnold threw down his pen and dried his second letter. His face, when he spoke, had a queer lumpy look to it. "Sullivan doesn't want to go! He wants to stay right where he is, and fight the British. He thinks they'll do what he wants them to do; but they won't! If he stays where he is, they'll sail past him up the St. Lawrence. He can't seem to realize the St. Lawrence turns south, beyond Sorel, so that for every mile the British sail, once they're past him, they're a mile in his rear as well!

"If they pass him before he starts to retreat, he's lost—he and his men and his guns and his stores! We're all of us lost—ruined! They'd capture every last man of us—every last man! There'd be nothing between them and Albany! All they'd need to do would be to go there, march down the Hudson, join Howe, cut Washington's forces to pieces, and start hanging rebels. They'd have nothing to worry about except which of us to hang!"

He jumped to his feet, took his sword from the table and fastened it to his belt. "Well, they won't do it, not if I have anything to say about it! I'm going back to Montreal. I'll do what I can to protect Sullivan's rear until I'm ordered out or wiped out. I can't do much with three hundred men—not against ten thousand; but I might delay 'em a little!" A light seemed to glow behind the swarthiness of his face. "I'll kick up a dust somehow!"

He pulled on his gauntlets. "Get a horse somewhere! Seize it if you have to! Take that letter to Sullivan; and on your way, stop at Chambly and give this"—he pushed his second letter at me—"to Colonel Hazen. He's to move all his supplies and stores back here at once! Damned quick, too!"

He bolted from the room. By the time I reached the front door, his black horse was pelting down the river road at a gallop; and Captain Wilkinson, his jaw-muscles throbbing, was still hard at work freeing his own brown mare from a hitching post.

My heart and head, I knew, should have been filled with martial and patriotic emotions; but what I felt was a great wistfulness, wholly personal to me. I was ordered to Chambly and thence to Sorel, with an ache inside me that longed for me to carry it back to St. John's—St. John's and Ellen Phipps, who had blushed and assented when Marie de Sabrevois asked her whether she didn't like my brother Nathaniel.

XVIII

CHAMBLY and St. John's are twelve miles apart. St. John's is the end of navigation for vessels going north from Lake Champlain, and Chambly is the end of navigation for vessels coming south from the St. Lawrence; and between the two towns the Richelieu leaps down from the level of Lake Champlain to that of the St. Lawrence in a series of shoals, ledges, rapids and tumbling cataracts.

Those twelve miles are a barrier to an invading army wishful of moving from Canada to Lake Champlain; for no vessel can pass over them; and the army that attempts it must disembark at Chambly, abandon its vessels, march to St. John's, and there build new vessels for the transporting of men, guns and supplies.

Therefore Chambly is a strategic point, and a fort was built there during the old French wars—an ugly square thing on a weed-grown plain between the upper and lower rapids.

When I came down the road on that hot June afternoon, there were tents on the plain, pitched with no appearance of military neatness; and on the river bank were piles of unguarded supplies. There was a rumpled, deserted look about the whole place, such as is seen around an ill-kept tavern early in the morning.

I kicked my plow-horse in the ribs and rode up to the drawbridge of the fort. A ragged sentry sat on the planks, staring into the weedy water in the ditch.

"Message for Colonel Hazen," I told him.

He jerked his head toward the open gateway of the fort, so I gave him my horse's reins and entered the dark interior. In the guard-room I found a man mending rips in his trousers; but when I asked for Colonel Hazen, he shook his head absently and remained engrossed in his needlework. "Busy," he murmured. "In quarters—talking to somebody."

"I've got to see him quick," I said. "I've got a message from General Arnold. It's important."

He looked up at me. "From General Arnold? You'll be welcome here! Welcome as a pole-cat! Hazen's got Bedel with him—Bedel and Colonel Easton and Major Brown."

"I'm not here to be welcomed," I said. "I'm here to give him this message."

He eyed me queerly, made a neat knot in the twine with which he was sewing, sawed it off with a jackknife, wrapped his needle and twine remnant in an old rag, and led me down a passageway smelling of ammonia.

"Is Colonel Bedel the one that was at the Cedars?" I asked.

"The one that *wasn't* there, you mean," he whispered. "Yes, that's him."

"I thought he was being court-martialed for cowardice."

The man made no answer, but stopped at a door behind which I heard mumblings. He jerked a thumb at the door and went away, stepping softly. When I knocked, the sound ceased: then a sulky voice said, "Come in."

The room was a cell, dimly lighted by one small slit of a window and two candles. Two men occupied chairs at the table, and two more sat on a bunk built against the wall. They were just sitting, all four of them, as if they had nothing else to do. When one of the two at the table snapped, "What's your business?" I knew he must be Colonel Hazen. He was red-faced, thick-necked, quick and impatient in his movements, and he wore a handsome uniform—as good as those worn by the officers of the Pennsylvania troops cut to pieces at Three Rivers.

"A despatch from General Arnold," I said, and gave it to him.

One of the two on the bunk, tall and long-nosed, snorted and said, "Speak of the devil!"

The officer at the table with Hazen looked dusty and farmerish. His face was round, and so was his body; and his eyes squinted as if he could say something smart whenever he chose; and he chose at this moment. "Ain't that a leetle weak, Major?" he asked. "Generally you git violent inside of three words!" At this all four guffawed, as idlers guffaw when one of them achieves a gem of rudeness.

The tall officer with the long nose, therefore, was a major, and must be Major Brown; and I remembered, then, that someone had spoken of Bedel as being the best hay-pitcher in New Hampshire. Thus Bedel had to be the round, dusty-looking, farmerish one; for the fourth officer, the one who sat on the bunk beside Major Brown, was thin, with a bitter twist to his mouth, which was set in a perpetual sneer. He must, I was sure, be Colonel Easton, for I could tell by looking at him that he would be no better at pitching hay than at doing a generous deed.

Colonel Hazen placed Arnold's letter on the table, smoothed it: then turned it over and examined the superscription. "'Captain Peter Merrill.' That's you, is it?"

"Yes sir."

"Whose commission do you hold, sir? Congress or Provincial?"

"General Arnold gave me my commission. It was necessary in the performance of scout duty."

The four officers looked at each other: then concentrated on me.

"So you're a scout, are you?" Major Brown asked. "You have special qualifications, no doubt, if the *general* commissioned you." He stressed the word "general" in such a way that I knew he would willingly cut Arnold's throat if he could do it undetected. I made no answer; and in an instant he was on his feet, as if he had me in a court of law. "We'd be interested to know, Captain, about your special qualifications."

"Well, sir," I said mildly, not wishing to have trouble with any of these four officers, "well, sir, I don't rightly see what that has to do with you, or with my present duties."

"You don't?" Major Brown cried. "It has *this* to do with it! It's contrary to law for General Arnold——"

"I'll answer your question," I said. "I've got another despatch to carry, and it won't stand delay. I was a sea captain." I had an itch to ask them for their own qualifications, but dared not—which is what the army does to most.

They glowered at me.

"Sir," I said to Colonel Hazen, "I'd like a receipt for that despatch."

When he ungraciously gave it to me, I went out of the fort on the run and without saluting. All four were emphatically what Cap Huff called pig-nut officers—all rind and a little meat, and that worthless. I knew next to nothing about them; but I was sure of two things. They hated Arnold because he hadn't found them competent, and had let them see he knew their incapacities; and to my mind Arnold alone was worth all four of them stirred together, with another ten thousand like them added to the mixture.

. . . Because of the thousands of smallpox sufferers that had poured back on us from Sorel, and the tales of starvation, defeat and desertion that had reached us daily from Sullivan's camp, I expected to find something terrible when I reached it. It might have been worse; for although the men in sight were thin and dejected-looking, they were clean shaved, and their hair and breeches were tied, showing they were subject to discipline.

Nonetheless the camp at Sorel was miserable. It occupied the sandy marsh where the Richelieu runs into Lake St. Peter. The broad St. Lawrence lay before it, the far shore lost in a heat haze; and against the haze quivered distant marshy islets. The air was moist and stagnant, and had the smell of a dirty water-butt on a hot day—foul and sickish.

Through and over everything seemed to run a faint yet shrill moaning. This was the sound of the countless mosquitoes with which the country swarmed.

Yet the place was orderly. Two hundred brown bateaux lay in regular ranks along the river; three schooners and a pair of cumbersome flat-bottomed gundelos were tied up among them, like five curlews looming above a flock of sandpipers. The camp itself was neat, and enclosed with earthworks and trenches. Behind the earthworks, close to the water's edge, were five cannon, three of them great guns and two just big enough to kill geese.

All around me, as I rode through the wretched shelters under which this pauper army lived, were the Pennsylvania troops I had seen entering St. John's two weeks before. Already the uniforms that had shone so brightly against the brown Richelieu were faded and tattered, and the men themselves had the look of being tattered in spirit.

There were sentries at the door of headquarters; and when one of them bawled that here was a despatch-bearer come from General Arnold, I was taken at once before General Sullivan. There was little amiability to be seen in his broad lynx-like face as he glanced from the superscription on the letter to my rough clothes, and even less when he had opened the letter and run his eye over it.

To me he said: "It was you, wasn't it, Captain, who was taking the vessel to pieces because Arnold thought it might be needful in a retreat?"

I said "Yes," whereupon he remarked grimly that there seemed to be a conspiracy on somebody's part to persuade him to retreat without firing a gun. With that he sighed and spoke to me kindly enough. "I suppose it's your duty to return to Arnold with an answer to his message. Well, I can't let you have it now: you'll have to wait. Meanwhile, find yourself quarters with Wayne's officers. I'll have use for every healthy man obtainable, and soon, too!"

It seemed plain to me that what Sullivan meant was that he intended, in spite of Arnold's warning, to fight the British. If he had any other intentions, I was sure he would have moved at once.

But in spite of Arnold's warning, Sullivan would not stir. There in that steaming, sticky fry-pan of a camp he waited, silent and lynx-like, studying the pallid surface of Lake St. Peter. He seemed to be set upon waiting, with his inactive army, perforce, waiting with him.

. . . On the day after I brought him Arnold's message the whole army seemed to stare breathlessly into the heat haze that smudged the northern sky, and wilt as it stared. A sun of molten brass glared down on torrid marshes that spewed mosquitoes into the quivering air; and on every side there was muttering and grumbling; for word had spread as to the numbers of the British and the size of the guns they were bringing against us—guns big enough to let them lie well out of range of our little pea-shooters and batter us to a jelly.

At mid-morning we heard that a column of British had been sighted on the far shore of the St. Lawrence; a long column, attended by supply carts and artillery, marching up the river. If this was true, it meant the British were moving on a long curve that would bring them in our rear. It meant we would be cut off.

Officers went to Sullivan, where he stood on the earthworks, peering like a basilisk into the north. St. Clair, worried-looking and grayish, talked with him, and Wayne, a tall, chesty officer with a bold, jeering look. They waved their arms and pointed; and we knew they were urging Sullivan to retreat while there was yet time. But Sullivan just went back to his tent, his lips tight and perspiration dripping from him, and wouldn't stir. He would not stir.

Early in the afternoon sentries on the earthworks shouted and pointed across the pale blue waters of the lake. The distant haze had lifted—cooled, perhaps, by a fresher breeze—and beyond the sandy islands that crowd the upper end of Lake St. Peter there rose the white sails of such a fleet as I had never seen.

The whole horizon was solid with topgallantsails and royals, score upon score of them. There were more than fifty vessels in the fleet. Their sails were big and square: not the sails of small merchant vessels, but of ships—war vessels: frigates, beyond question, and sloops-of-war. This vast spread of canvas hung there, shining in the scorching afternoon sun, like the silvery rim of a thundercloud: a great armada.

The breeze was light but steady. In three hours, if it held, every last one of those tall vessels would have passed between the islands and would be close enough to open on us with big guns. I wondered whether Sullivan had gone mad with the heat. In no other way, it seemed to me, could his unwillingness to move be explained.

He climbed the parapet again, surrounded by officers who gesticulated furiously and argued hotly with Sullivan and each other; but Sullivan stood immovable among them, his gaze fixed on the countless sails in the north.

I felt half suffocated by this Gehenna in which Sullivan's stupidity had embroiled me, and feveredly wondered what the British would do to us when they captured us: where they would take us.

I wondered about Nathaniel: whether he had seen Ellen Phipps yet: whether he would escape the British, or whether they would capture him too. I wondered about Ellen—whether she would get away to Albany: whether I would ever see her again.

Within me I cursed this lynx-faced general, who was putting all of us in a corner like a lot of helpless rats—putting us where we could neither fight nor run—and doing it in spite of Arnold's warning: in spite, now that the odds against us were actually in sight, of the warnings of all his officers.

The group around Sullivan burst apart, almost as though a bomb had scattered them. Some of the officers shouted. A drummer ran toward them: then stopped, hitched his drum into position and beat a rattling, rasping roll that seemed the embodiment of irritation. It told everyone within hearing that Sullivan had yielded at last and ordered a retreat.

The whole camp boiled with men, and for the first time I saw the specters that had lain hid in the huts and tents. Some crawled out on hands and knees; others were drawn out by men who looked near as sick as those they drew. They had the smallpox, and there were hundreds of them. For every well man, there was one with smallpox, lying on the hot sand in front of tent or hut from which he had been dragged.

They looked dead. Their ragged fragments of uniforms were loose on them, almost as though there were nothing inside but bones; their limbs, sprawled at odd angles, seemed lifeless. Flies and mosquitoes crawled on their unprotected faces, but they lay without moving—a dreadful festering host—an army barely alive.

. . . The things that were done by men called well on that sweltering fourteenth day of June were more than I can believe when I cast my mind back over them. Even if they had been in perfect health, their accomplishments would have been miracles. But the well were sick from scanty food, discouragement, exposure—so sick that if they had been aboard a ship of mine, I would have hesitated to let any one of them go aloft to hand a sail for fear he would have lost his hold from weakness.

Yet those men leveled the earthworks they had been weeks in building, and filled the trenches. They trundled cannon from embrasures and stowed them aboard the schooners; carried the sick to bateaux and placed them tenderly in the bows and sterns; took out powder, shot and supplies from rickety warehouses and loaded them in schooners and gundelos; packed up every last thing in tents, huts and headquarters—every entrenching tool, every shovel, every blanket, every kettle.

They struck and folded tents: crawled over that baking, mosquito-ridden, stinking marsh like fumbling human ants, weak, drenched with sweat, but tirelessly salvaging every usable thing.

The sun was a blazing ball in a leaden heat haze when the schooners and gundelos, loaded with guns, stores and men, set off upstream. The British fleet, crowded by now into the channel between the islands, was close. We could see the fighting-tops of the ships in the van, and riflemen in them, waiting to pick us off.

When there was nothing left in the camp but huts and warehouses and an expanse of foul and trampled sand, we set fire to everything burnable. The smoke rolled down over the throngs that wrestled with the bateaux at the river's edge; and in the hot red light of the setting sun they looked like lost souls struggling on the fringes of hell.

We went into the bateaux like cattle, helter skelter, urged on by Sullivan, who marched up and down on the bank, as cheerful as though the British were in England, instead of a whisker's width behind us. The sick lay at our feet, moaning and complaining; for not only were they seared and tortured by the internal fires of smallpox, but the bateaux were like furnaces from lying in the glare of the sun.

There was a sickening odor to those poor men, the overpowering stench of smallpox, and they were terrible to look at, because of the sores and swellings that made their faces unrecognizable. They croaked hoarsely for coolness and water, and for a hundred things we had no way of giving them; and to the accompaniment of this piteous faint chorus we pulled out into the swift current of the Richelieu.

XIX

Even though years have passed, I sometimes wake, even now, drenched with perspiration, from dark dreams that I am on the Richelieu once more, toiling until my muscles crack to reach the double goal that hangs like an unattainable mirage before me—for not only was I possessed, like all the others, to reach a place where we would no longer be at the mercy of the British, but I knew I could have no peace until I had again made inquiries at the Château de St. Auge.

The heat, the weakness of the men, the weight of the clumsy bateaux, made us slow enough in our struggle up that river; but slow as we were, we crept like giant waterbugs past the even slower schooners; for the wind, dropping with the sun, had left them nearly helpless. Anyone could see with half an eye that their progress soon must cease, and that unless something should be done about them, they must inevitably fall into the hands of the British.

Fortunately there seemed to be no end to the Canadian twilight; and Sullivan, slipping among us in a canoe, made a selection of bateaux—a hundred of them, and among them mine. We transferred our sick into other bateaux; and the well, all but the oarsmen, went ashore to make their way upstream afoot. Then back we pulled to the schooners; and far into that sultry simmering night we worked at shifting boxes and barrels, powder and shot, guns and gun-carriages, sick and well, from their decks and holds into the bateaux.

It is hard enough for healthy men, well fed, to lower heavy weights from a large vessel into a small boat in the bright light of day without accident. For hungry, weak men to do such work in darkness is not possible—or so I thought until the determination to escape the British burned like a flame in these men's minds.

I expected every moment to hear that a cannon had fallen through the bottom of a bateau, or that a barrel had burst itself on the heads of those who stood waiting for it with upstretched arms; but for hours those ragged, sweating specters fumbled safely at their labors, making profane jests about the fat King whose troops were at our heels; and one by one the bateaux, deep in the water, dropped away from the larger vessels and pulled slowly upstream again.

When we were done, there was nothing left in the schooners. We took off their sails, even, and stripped them of their cordage; and at last we set fire to them, so that the final bateaux to cast off were lighted on their way by the flames that poured from the hatches.

It was like dawn, for in the light of the burning vessels we could see apple trees, white with blossoms, on both banks; and robins waked to trill their quavering morning melodies. It wasn't dawn, alas, but only midnight, and before dawn had come we had tied rags around our hands and the rags were bloody.

We rowed all night through a sultriness that pressed upon us like hot wool, and all through the scorching glare of the following day. It is fifty miles from Sorel to Chambly, against a swift current; and for hours on end each stroke we took with our clumsy oars seemed the last that could be endured. Still we took one more, and then one more: always one more stroke, our arms and backs like hot lead; and inch by inch we lumbered on, another inch farther from the British: another inch closer to Chambly—another inch closer to the rapids, beyond which British vessels couldn't pass.

Toward dusk a black wall of clouds rose in the west—a wall from which emerged an angry smothered roar, with only such breaks as a growling animal might make to catch its breath.

The growling was louder when we came to the pool at the foot of Chambly rapids, where massed bateaux wallowed uneasily in the swirling, foam-streaked water, waiting to go up. They were a sad flotilla in the shadow of the coming storm, and the men in them, both sick and well, were strangely silent—perhaps because, like me, their muscles trembled with fatigue and they were too spent for speech.

While we waited, the black wall in the west towered up over us and seemed to burst. The whole sky blazed. Thunder pounded at our ears and heads like padded hammers, while the rain had the solidity of falling lakes. There was an inhuman yet personal intensity to the storm, as if the devil had sent a legion of water-witches to torment us. There was no slackening of the rain; the stabbing of lightning was incessant, and it was to the unremittent crashing of close thunder that we were drummed to our battle with Chambly rapids.

Before that night it had been thought no bateau could be taken through them; for they were a sloping rampart of raging, tumbling, yellowish water, its upper end as far above its lower as is the masthead of a ship above its keel. Where there are ledges and boulders in the stream, the water slips over them like brown glass, seemingly without motion; but having passed the obstruction, it hurls itself upward in angry spouts, as if to leap back over the rock that hindered its descent.

Thus the sloping rampart of the rapids is like a beaten desperate army, tumbling down from heights it cannot scale; and it was up those heights that we must go, with all our bateaux, supplies and ammunition.

There could be no failure; for if we failed, we would have no means of escape, and would be doomed to wander, without arms or food, in the trackless wilderness to the south.

How we did it I scarcely know; but it was done. With fingers bloody from our rowing, we lashed ropes to the bateaux, bow, stern and amidships; and as many as could laid hold of the ropes, regardless of rank or military observances. Ordinarily, that is to say, no love was lost between the Pennsylvanians and the New England troops, and I have known times when Pennsylvanians would see Massachusetts men in hell before they would lift a finger to help them. But at Chambly rapids there was no thought of differences; and once, while I dragged at a rope with raw hands that seemed to clutch hot nettles, the man who grunted and puffed beside me was General Sullivan.

The men on shore hauled; in each bateau, men with poles strained to hold it from the rocky bank; while in the rapids, waist deep in the surging flood and clinging to the gunwales, went other men. Inch by inch they worked forward, half supported by the bateau and half supporting it. The heavy boat tilted upward in the churning, thrusting torrent, rearing like a restive horse; and inch by inch it climbed that rampart of water that leaped at us and showed white fangs in the crackling flashes of lightning; then hid for a moment in impenetrable dark before leaping at us once more.

The pole of a bateau-man would often slip; and its wielder, plunging over the side, would go down through foam and over boulders, to be fished out, choking and gagging, by those below.

Those who waded would lose their footing, swing backward against the legs of their fellows, and whirl away, half submerged, until they floundered among the boats that waited in the pool. The bateau would hesitate and lurch; there would be a strangled chorus of shouts from those who labored with it. Once more it would move upward almost imperceptibly, quivering and fighting in the lightning's glare.

There was agony, even, in watching the painful slow ascent of those unwilling bateaux, held by main strength on that sloping wall of water at an angle as unnatural as it was impossible; for with each one that went up, we said to ourselves a score of times that it could go no farther —that it must topple backward and whirl down among us, sinking others before it sunk itself. Yet every last one of them went up, and over the brink at last into the smooth stretch of water that flows through the plain in front of the square stone fort.

. . . It was a strange sight, that plain, when we had hoisted our bateau up the rapids and dragged its nose ashore, our legs trembling and muscles throbbing.

It had the look, in the blue flashes that seared our eyes, of a battle-field; for human figures covered the treeless space before the black fort that glistened in the rain. They sprawled grotesquely in the mud; and with each blaze of lightning we saw them stabbed by a thousand watery darts. Rivulets ran over and around them; but they lay like sodden corpses, conscious of nothing. Here and there a body moved; struggled to its knees and crawled a little: rose to its feet, even, to stagger blindly and then sink again.

Groups of men came slowly into the plain from down the stream, or clambered like clumsy demons over the river bank. They groped and stumbled: then sank down among the prostrate figures, or dragged themselves away toward St. John's. It was not an army: there were no officers: no sentinels—nothing but human cattle, palsied from exhaustion; sick with overexertion and despair.

The night before I had drunk a cup of paste, made from flour mixed with the water of the Richelieu. Since then there had been nothing to eat. I picked my way toward the fort through the recumbent bodies of those miserable skeletons, wondering whether Hazen had obeyed the orders I had brought from Arnold—the orders to send all supplies and sick to St. John's. If he was so quick at disobeying, it might be there were still supplies remaining in the fort. I could have eaten anything. The walls of my stomach seemed to grind together, and to squeak in the grinding.

I tried to remember when it was I had spoken with Hazen and his officers. A week or more ago, I thought at first: ten days perhaps. No: it was less: six days—five days. Then it came to me that it was only two days before. Two days! I stood and stared at the drawbridge that spanned the ditch before the fort; it was down, and the lightning showed me that the heavy gates stood open, unguarded by any sentry.

Behind me I heard the chupping of a horse's hoofs in the mud, and almost at once the rider's voice shouting, "Aren't there any officers in this army? Where's the general?"

The voice was cracked with excitement. By the vivid flashes I saw that the rider was Captain Wilkinson.

"I don't know," I said. "I just got here."

"Look," Wilkinson said, "hold my horse, will you? He'll be cut off—Arnold'll be cut off—by Heaven, sir, when did you start—this is damnable—when did you leave Sorel?"

"Two nights ago."

Wilkinson groaned, hoisted a leg over his saddle and slid stiffly to the ground. "Why in God's name didn't Sullivan let us know?" he demanded, military forms forgotten. "Why didn't he tell Arnold? We only got word this afternoon! This afternoon, two days late! By God, sir, this man is trying to ruin us! Why, Arnold'll be captured if I can't get five hundred men to cover his retreat! Where in God's name can I get five hundred men out of this rabble?"

"Let's have the reins," I said. "Tell it to somebody inside."

Wilkinson rushed across the drawbridge and disappeared through the yawning gateway. His steed, a plow-horse, hung its head almost to its knees and slumbered. I felt in the saddlebags for food, but found only a greasy fragment of paper that had been wrapped around salt pork. I chewed it until it grew pulpy and trickled down my throat. It seemed to put strength in my knees, but not much. I could have eaten a whole pig. Yes, I could have eaten Wilkinson's horse.

When Wilkinson came out again, he had recovered some of his calmness. "They're there," he said. "Sullivan, Hazen, Maxwell and St. Clair. They say De Woedtke's supposed to be in command of the rear. D'you know anything about him?"

"No," I said, "I don't, but if you're going looking for him, look for a place where rum can be bought, because that's where he'll be."

For the only time during our acquaintance, Wilkinson favored me with an approving look. "It's quite possible," he said. "Where's your musket and pack?"

"St. John's," I told him.

"In my opinion," he said, "you'll do well to go there and get them. Those gentlemen inside didn't even want to believe me when I told them how close the British were to Montreal. You're liable to be wasted if you stay around *them* much longer."

He scrambled into the saddle and went clopping off in the direction of the rapids.

Presumably I was still at General Sullivan's disposal, and waiting to be given a message from him to be carried to General Arnold; but under the circumstances, it seemed to me that to bother my head further about such a message were to transform a military formality into a symptom of insanity.

It was twelve miles from Chambly to St. John's, I knew. My desire for food vanished. If I walked all night, and if the monstrous thunderstorm that had crackled overhead for four long hours would last a little longer to light me on my way, I might still reach the Château de St. Auge by morning—and it might be before Marie de Sabrevois and her niece had vanished from my sight forever.

XX

Usually I saw nothing but dislike in Madame St. Auge's eyes when she opened the door to me; but on this occasion I saw horror. Until then I had given no thought to my appearance; but now, when I looked at myself, I could see I was as badly off, nearly, as any of the wretched creatures with whom I had fought my way over Chambly rapids.

Thanks to the rain, which had ceased at last, I was almost clean; but there was nothing left of my stockings, and my shoes were a muddy pulp. My breeches, minus their knee buckles, were dangerously ripped, and fastened here and there with string. I had lost my hat; my hair was matted; my face, between my beard, my lack of food, and the weariness that weighed on me like lead, felt like hot glue. All in all, I couldn't blame Madame St. Auge for staring at me as she did; but I couldn't waste time apologizing for clothes or the lack of them.

"Where's Ellen?" I asked.

She raised her eyebrows. "Ellen? You expect to see Ellen? You?"

"Look here," I said, "I've been on the move all night—for days—ever since I can remember. The British are close behind us! Where's Ellen?"

She lowered her eyes, folding her hands over her protruding stomach, and looked smug. "I don't know where she is. I don't know."

"You *must* know! Do you mean they've already started for Albany?"

She looked stupid; it seemed to me she deliberately looked stupid. "For Albany? I don't know."

"You don't know! She's with Marie de Sabrevois, isn't she?"

Madame St. Auge was sickeningly pious. "Our poor Marie!" she sighed. "She's ill with exhaustion. In her bed, she is, alas! Allowed to eat only the simplest foods."

Fatigued as I was, I had an impulse to take her by the shoulders and shake her. She knew it, too, for she backed away apprehensively, murmuring, "You must excuse me, if you please."

"Did my brother come here?" I asked. "Do you know where *he* is?"

Madame St. Auge smiled faintly. "Oh yes: your brother was here. Naturally! How could Ellen have gone away with him if he had not come here for her?"

"Gone away with him! In God's name, where?"

"I cannot tell you."

A thought struck me. Was Nathaniel to see her safe to Albany, since Mademoiselle de Sabrevois herself couldn't go? Then, as Madame St. Auge did nothing but stare at me, I answered my own question. "No, he couldn't do that! He's on duty with the army! And he couldn't take a girl like Ellen with the army! Do you know what this army is? It's starving! It's trying to save itself! There's no discipline or order in it! It's rotten with smallpox!"

"I'm very sorry," Madame St. Auge said. She started to close the door in my face; but I prevented her by putting my foot upon the threshold.

"So am I sorry," I told her harshly. "I intend to see Marie de Sabrevois."

"I have told you she is in bed."

"I don't care where she is! I'll see her!"

But the woman stood in my way, and I was unwilling to lay a hand on her.

"You should be the last to make a disturbance at this door!" she said. "It's your brother's affair; not yours. If he sees no harm in taking her with him, you should be content. If your brother takes away and hopes to protect a young girl to whom he is betrothed with the consent of her guardian, it is for you to show respect: not excitement and interference!"

"Betrothed? You're telling me that Mademoiselle de Sabrevois wishes this young girl and my brother to be betrothed!"

"Why not? And why not? Why should they not be betrothed, and why should he not take her away to protect her?"

"I can't talk to you," I said. "You'll have to let me see Mademoiselle de Sabrevois."

"No, you can't."

I heard the thumping of a drum from across the river, and the sound of shouting. I was getting nowhere, and I felt I had to speak my mind. "Look here," I said. "I doubt if you've told me the truth. What's more, I doubt that Mademoiselle de Sabrevois is sick, and I'm going in to see her!"

Madame St. Auge spoke suddenly in French, raising her voice. A man came out of the room in which Nathaniel and I had first seen Ellen. He was a drab man in unnoticeable snuff-colored garments— the sort of person at whom one seldom looks twice. He might have been anything—a farmer: a small merchant: a servant; but I remembered seeing him before. He had been one of those waiting in Arnold's headquarters on the afternoon when I had gone in with Steven Nason and Cap Huff to report to Arnold.

He answered Madame St. Auge in French, holding up his hands as if horrified; and to me he added, in English: "I forbid! That poor lady is so helpless that she would sicken at excitement—oh, very dangerous! I am a doctor. You must go away now. It is bad for her, even, to hear your voice."

The sound of the drum came more plainly to my ears. There must be two drums, I realized, or even three. "You're a doctor?" I asked. "You live here in Iberville? I didn't know there *was* a doctor in this place."

He shrugged his shoulders. "Many people know nothing of doctors until they have need of one."

"If you live here," I said, "what were you doing in Montreal two weeks ago?"

He looked at me with an air of compassion. "Young man, you are sleepless and hungry. It has made a fire in your head. You imagine things, I think. Two weeks ago I am in Montreal, of course; yes! To ask that care be exercised, lest our people take the smallpox from your soldiers. Is there something wrong in that?" He spoke more gravely. "You must go somewhere for food, and sleep well."

He and Madame St. Auge stood staring at me steadily. I whispered the words—"food, and sleep well." Both of them nodded.

The distant drum-beats throbbed in my brain. I might find some sort of help with those drums, whereas I could look for nothing in the Château de St. Auge—nothing.

I turned from them and stumbled down the steps, repeating the words to myself, over and over—"food, and sleep well; food, and sleep well." There was something ludicrous about them. What in God's name did such people know about it, I thought: they who had food, and gave it to no one: they who spoke about sleeping well when they had never had a brother who was going to marry a girl like Ellen, and had taken her out of a safe refuge into a broken and retreating army—to protect her!

I got back to the river somehow, and rowed myself across. Along the road, in twos and threes, shambled an unceasing procession of ragged, emaciated soldiers. They paid no attention to me when I stumbled among them, to walk with them. I felt empty; limp. Something seemed to have hit me in the head. I had no mind of my own. Whatever these silent, dirty, tattered soldiers might at that moment have done, I would also have done unquestionably. If they had run, I, too, would have run. If they had fallen, I might have fallen as well.

I was surprised when a huge hand grasped my shoulder and turned me into the shipyard. I saw Cap Huff's moist red face close to mine, and behind him a group of men in tow-cloth smocks like my own—except that mine was in shreds. So great was my relief at finding myself among friends again that I began weakly to laugh.

At the sound of this silly laughter of mine, they came close around me, while Tom Bickford took me by the arm. I tried to understand how anyone connected with this army could still look as fresh and clean as Tom.

"You better come and lay down, Cap'n Peter," he said, and tugged at my elbow. "You get some food and sleep!"

"Have you seen Nathaniel?" I asked.

"You better come right away and lay down, Cap'n Peter!"

A powerful odor of asafoetida reached me. Doc Means came and felt my pulse, and Joseph Marie Verrieul took my other arm. They only irritated me. "What's the matter with you?" I asked. "Can't you hear? Where's my brother Nathaniel?"

"He's been sent with Major Scott and Zelph way down to Crown Point, at the other end of Lake Champlain, Cap'n Peter," Tom said, "to help guard supplies General Arnold seized in Montreal for the army. They been shipped down there to keep 'em from the British. Nathaniel's on that duty."

"When did he go?" I asked. "How long's he been gone? Who went with him?"

"Why, he's all right," Doc Means said. "You better worry about yourself, not him, Cap'n Peter. We got a nice eel stew on the fire, over in the work-shed. Tom's been saving it for you. I'll drop in a little mite of Sympathetic Powder to kind of straighten you out."

The ground seemed to heave under me: I thought I was back on shipboard. "I'll straighten all of you with a belaying pin unless I get an answer," I told them. "You say Scott and Zelph were sent south to Crown Point with him? Just those three men?"

"Doc's right," Tom Bickford said solicitously. "You better worry about yourself: not Nathaniel. Him and Major Scott and Zelph aren't in any danger at all, and the trip's even so safe that some young girl's folks took advantage of it to send her along with 'em to be took care of that way. Name of Phipps or something. You quit worrying about Nathaniel, Cap'n Peter."

I was in no condition to think calmly. All I could do was have confused thoughts. Something seemed impossible and incredible. For no reason I had understood, Marie de Sabrevois had seemed to consider it important that she and Ellen should go to Albany; and now here was Ellen in Crown Point with Nathaniel, only halfway to Albany, while Marie herself remained in St. John's.

I had been suspicious of Marie de Sabrevois. I had thought her a spy in the interests of the British. Perhaps she was: I couldn't tell. I had thought her a cold-hearted, calculating woman, although I had no inkling of the object of her calculations.

I had thought she wanted Nathaniel to be in love with her—possibly so that she might use him in the obtaining of information. But how could that be, when she had practically stepped aside to let Ellen be with Nathaniel? Perhaps, after all, Marie de Sabrevois was a noble and self-sacrificing woman. Perhaps she had seen that her ward was in love with Nathaniel; had placed Ellen's and Nathaniel's happiness above her own. Perhaps, as Madame St. Auge had said, she was indeed sick: sick from the shock of making a great sacrifice.

It was all too much for me, especially in my exhausted state.

Cap Huff put his ham of a hand on my shoulder. "Worry about me a while. Nathaniel's had the big luck to get sent to Crown Point, all safe and nice, with as handsome a looking young lady as you'd care to see to play cards with him when he's tired, or sing to him when he ain't feeling well, just so's he gets her safe to Crown Point, which is the same as walking up Dock Square with her on his arm, pretty near. While me, I'm left here among all this trouble and destruction and dissipation of a busted army, and can't get away, and neither can you, nor any of these pore worthless fellers that's standing around us, waiting to see you get hysterical with joy over Doc's eel stew."

He turned from me abruptly to resume his scrutiny of the ragged soldiers who shambled past in twos and threes. I sat on the ground. They brought me a bowl of eel stew. I drank it slowly, leaning back against some piled timber, and began to be conscious of returning sanity. Strangely enough, I was not so dead for sleep as I had been, and became curious about Cap.

"What's he doing?" I asked. "Counting the soldiers as they go by?"

"He's been watching this road ever since we got word Sullivan had started to retreat," Tom explained. "He or one of the rest of us has stood right here, day and night, watching for Steven Nason and you. Cap was afraid one of you might have got took sick. He said he didn't propose to have either of you rolled into one of the dead pits by mistake."

"Whose men are these?"

"Arnold's. They say he rushed 'em across the river and away, like ghosts, right under the noses of the British."

I thought, as I looked at them, that Tom was not far wrong when he spoke of them as ghosts. Some half carried, half dragged, sick men between them. Others hobbled as they walked, seemingly sunk in meditation. They were ragged and draggled, and there was a dreadful suggestion of decay about them, as if they had been corpses that had hung on gallows in wind and weather; and then, cut down, haggardly marched in this retreat.

I saw a cart piled high with supplies; another cart loaded with sick, their faces bloated and discolored with the smallpox: then more supply carts, and more armed stragglers. In their rear was a detachment trying to march in columns of fours, but not succeeding. Gaunt officers marched alongside and exhorted them; while two drummers, thumping wearily on drums the shape of wine-kegs, beat the time. The men slouched along, half asleep, yet wakeful enough, sometimes, to glance back, hollow-eyed, over their shoulders.

As the column passed us, I saw that they were the last of all, so I knew they were Arnold's rear guard. Far down the road behind them I saw a single rider, pelting lickety-split on a black horse. He drew rein just before he reached the last rank, near where I sat, finishing the eel stew.

It was Arnold, in a blue uniform and high boots. His silver gorget glittered, and there was something hard and bright about him, as if he had been newly polished from top to toe.

"All right, boys," he called in a voice that might have been considered harsh, but had more of an exciting quality to it than mere harshness—a quality that drove away the last of my numbness and confusion. "All right, boys—keep at it, boys! Not a Britisher within ten miles, and the last bridge burnt! Another hour and we'll get a full meal into you!"

One of the men in the ranks coughed. "What you got for us today, General? Half an ounce o' salt pork and one bean?"

There was a sound of sniffing in the ragged lines; and I knew the men must be in fair spirits in spite of their appearance; for in some parts of New England, notably in New Hampshire, a sniff is the equivalent of a hearty laugh in other sections.

Arnold touched his black horse with a spur. As it broke into a canter, Cap Huff thrust out a vast hand and shouted, "Hey, General!"

Arnold gave us a cold glance; then turned his horse in mid-stride and set him down close to us as neatly as a seaman lays a ship's gig against a dock. "You needn't wait for further orders," he told Cap. "Take the first boat you can get to Isle aux Noix and send it back here for another load."

"General," Cap said, "where's Steven Nason?"

"He's been up with the St. Francis Indians, keeping them neutral. He and Natanis. They'll get through somehow."

"General," Cap said defiantly, "I'd like to wait right here till Stevie comes."

Arnold nodded, and there was a gleam in his eye that told me he took pleasure in Cap's blundering ways. "I've got no objection. You can stay here till I go. That'll not be till Sullivan's troops have come in and passed south. But I'll tell you this: don't stay after I've gone unless you want a free trip to England in chains."

"General," Cap said, gesturing in our direction, "these boys are handy with oars, all of 'em. What you say we pick you out a good boat and row you to Eel Ox Nox when you're ready?"

That was how Cap called Isle aux Noix, then and forever after; and because of the society he later formed—the Eel Ox Nox Club—the rest of us always referred to it in the same way.

Arnold nodded again. "Good! Good idea! Get a boat and keep it here. Stay here yourselves, all of you, so I'll know where to find you when I need you." He swung his lather-streaked black horse and went clattering along the river road toward the brick barracks before which his men were already dumping their supplies and arms.

. . . The next two days were hideous. The sun beat down on us as if it had come close to enjoy our troubles. There was no breeze to dispel the hot steam in which we moved; but toward sundown a bank of clouds rolled down from Lake Champlain and into the valley of the Richelieu. Then, through the night, the lightning stabbed and crackled around us, the rain beat through tents, roofs and windows until we were parboiled, and the violence of the thunder was like some hell-minded giant trying to smash the world to pieces.

Throughout those two days the retreat still stewed about us. Sullivan's troops came hobbling in, ready to drop in their tracks and sleep wherever they halted, whether in broiling sun or drenching cloudburst.

Somehow Cap Huff contrived to keep a fire burning perpetually in a lower corner of the shipyard; and by its changeable light in the rain, we could see, all night long, if we were wakeful, those half-clad, groping, draggled skeletons lurching past in twos and threes, a dismal and pitiful thing to watch.

When the thunder was still for a while, and we woke, we could hear the mutter of their voices, the clink of their camp kettles as they stumbled, the shrill squealing of the Canadian carts that helped to carry baggage and supplies, the clack of oars in bateaux, the thudding of the cannon wheels.

The sick went past in boatloads that moved dimly on the black water; and no lost souls, rowed by Charon on a darker river, could have complained more dolefully.

Last of all to come were what was left of Wayne's men. Tom Bickford, standing beside me to watch for Steven Nason while Cap Huff snatched an hour's sleep, hissed when he saw the rags of blue and white that once had been their uniforms. Indeed, it was beyond belief, what had happened to those men since we had first seen them; and even now, in the coldest nights of winter, I sometimes lie and sweat with rage at the thought of how they were thrown away by Sullivan, a brave man, no doubt, but a blunderer whose sum of military knowledge was less than that contained in the smallest joint of Arnold's smallest finger.

Where the British were, no man seemed sure, though there was not one of us but knew they were close. The cannon had come down from the barracks again and been placed in the road, just beyond us, behind a barrier of baskets filled with sand. They were four-pounders, those guns, nice for leaning against a door to hold it open, but not the best means for stopping a British army.

The river front had turned into a veritable hugger-mugger of aimlessness and turbulence. Bateaux came downstream constantly, back from Isle aux Noix; and loaded bateaux pushed out from the bank, colliding with everything in sight in their eagerness to be off.

It seemed to me, at times, that men had lost the power of speaking any word except "Get in!" though they were always able to bellow mere sounds. Majors, lieutenants, common soldiers, sergeants, captains, in inextricable confusion, ran here and there: getting into bateaux and getting out again to shout, "Get in!" at someone, or to push at someone else: picking up boxes and barrels and ammunition, only to drop them and pick up others; and through it all shouting at each other, "Get in! Get in! Get started! Get in! Never mind that, get in! Why the hell don't you get in! Get in yourself! Go ahead: get in!"

Night and day the boats pushed out, filled with men that shouted: men that groaned and babbled in delirium: men that laughed and cursed. By day the sun scorched us: by night the rain nearly drowned us. Gradually the milling crowds on the river bank grew smaller: the mass of bateaux dwindled: the piles of baggage and stores dropped away to nothing.

Cap Huff, perched on the upturned bateau he had commandeered for Arnold, fretted perpetually about Steven Nason. "Somep'n's happened to Stevie," he kept saying. "He'd be here by now if somep'n hadn't happened to him! By God, if those illegitimate lobster-backed Royal 69th Footsore Dragoons of His Majesty's Personal Backhouse have done anything to Stevie, by God, I'll pull 'em off into the bushes one by one and stake 'em out on a ant-hill! If ever this army needed I and Stevie, it's now, when there ain't but one general in sight that don't fall face down in a cowflap every time he starts to go anywhere or do anything! If anything's happened to Stevie, by God, the war's as good as over—and somep'n *has* happened to him! I *know* somep'n has!"

His complaining made me think he might be right.

The last of Sullivan's men had hobbled down the road and tumbled into bateaux, three full days since Sullivan had consented to retreat. The barracks below us had been set afire, as well as Colonel Hazen's mansion across the river. I wished, in my despair, that we could somehow burn the Château de St. Auge, and Marie de Sabrevois with it.

When the smoke poured up from the barracks, we looked for Arnold among the officers who hustled into bateaux and were pulled off upstream—that is, to the southward, toward Lake Champlain. It was not until they were all afloat that he came pelting out of the barracks yard on his black horse. Behind him rode Wilkinson, extremely military on a bay mare afflicted with wind.

Arnold clattered through the mud and puddles from last night's rain and waved to us. "Put the boat in the river! We're getting out of here!"

Wilkinson stopped to hand me Arnold's field-desk: but Arnold went straight for the barricade across the road and seemed to sail over it: then reined in his horse and spoke to the major who commanded the battery of four-pounders. "Put those guns in boats and get started! Don't get caught! You've got five minutes—no more!"

He bolted down the road, leaving Wilkinson still skirting the barricade on his windy mare. The artillery company swarmed around the pieces, hustling them back to where we wrestled with our bateau. In two seconds we were all of us struggling to be in the same small spot at the same time.

A bateau-man, perched on the stern of the nearest bateau, leaned back on his setting pole to keep the bow against the shore. He danced on the stern thwart with excitement. "By God!" he shouted. "It's thum—it's thum! A million of 'em!"

Cap Huff let go his hold on our bateau to shoulder himself free of the jostlers. "Keep those damned guns off my feet!" he roared. Stooping, he heaved at the spokes of a cannon-wheel. The whole piece rose in the air and toppled into the boat beside us. The boat lurched beneath the sudden shock; and the bateau-man on the stern thwart shot overboard.

He scrambled out, wild-eyed, and pointed downstream, sputtering, but we didn't need his pointing.

Far down the river road there moved a column in scarlet coats and

white breeches. There was a shimmery glitter in the air above them—
the reflection of the setting sun on their bayonets. There did indeed
seem to be a million of them; they filled the road as far as we could
see, an endless stream of scarlet.

Between us and that slowly flowing column there was nothing except
Arnold and Wilkinson—two small horsemen, motionless in the middle of
the long road that curved like a snake beside the river. Around us the
sweating artillerymen argued and cursed, balancing their guns and
trimming their bateaux. One boat pushed off; then another.

We stowed our belongings, wishing Arnold would stop watching that
scarlet flood. The men in the next bateau bawled at us to push them
off; and Cap, setting his foot against the bow, shot it out into mid-stream.
We were alone, then, on the muddy river bank, a nervous and uneasy
crew. We could see people edging out from the farm houses, silently
eyeing us in the sunset glow; but they stayed half hidden, either from
fear or hatred.

All of us were fretful over small matters. Cap Huff was in a stew, not
only because of Nason, but also because Doc Means persisted in saying
how it should be as easy to inoculate people against the bites of mosquitoes and black flies as against the smallpox; and I was in a rage because Cap Huff went from one to the other of us, asking in a husky
whisper, "What do you think's become of Stevie? What do you think we
ought to do about Stevie?"

He must have known that none of us knew anything at all about
Nason, and that there was nothing to be done about him. Yet he harped
on the subject interminably; and to me, attempting to pursue certain
thoughts that had come into my head concerning Ellen Phipps, it
seemed as though he would never stop.

When Verrieul, standing on a thwart, said softly: "Now they come,"
we got ourselves into our places. Arnold's black horse came sailing over
the abandoned barricade, with a clatter of hoofs, Wilkinson scrambling
close behind.

Arnold swung himself out of the saddle and stood looking down at us,
his bridle over his arm. Far off we heard a bugle call and excited shouts.
A few of the Canadians came out into the road to wave at the advancing
troops; then dodged back again into the shelter of houses.

"You're all here, are you?" Arnold asked. He looked at the blazing
barracks: at the smoldering ruins of Hazen's house; cocked an eye at
the sky: then turned back toward the approaching British.

"They've thrown out their light infantry," he said to Wilkinson. "If
there's anything else to be done, I don't know what it is—only this."

He unbuckled his saddle girth and hauled the saddle off his black horse. As he passed the saddle to Cap Huff, he lifted a holster flap and took out a handsome silver-mounted pistol. He stripped the bridle and bit from the horse's head, tossed them to Cap, stroked the horse's nose, put the muzzle of the pistol close above its eye, and pulled the trigger. The poor beast went down with a thump, kicked once and never stirred again.

Wilkinson cleared his throat and did nothing.

"Come, Captain," Arnold said impatiently. "There's no time to lose!"

Wilkinson stared at him. The muscles over his jaws throbbed uncertainly.

Arnold laughed. "If you don't feel up to it, Captain Wilkinson, we'll have it done for you. It's got to be done! Whatever the British get of ours, whether it's horses or land, they've got to fight for! Put a bullet in her brain and come ahead!"

Wilkinson stripped his mare, then, and shot her. When it came to getting into the bateau, he made a great show of formality, standing to one side so that Arnold could precede him. He was the fussiest young man I ever saw, and so eager to help officers above him in rank that he was always underfoot.

"Oh for God's sake, Captain!" Arnold cried. "Stop nursing me and get in!"

Wilkinson climbed in, and I thought I saw Cap Huff rock the boat intentionally. At all events, Wilkinson fell among our feet, and while he was picking himself up, I certainly saw Cap Huff slip something out of a pocket in Wilkinson's saddlebags—something that disappeared in the recesses of Cap's own garments.

Then Arnold gave a heave at the stern of the bateau and vaulted into it as it slid out into the stream. "Pull!" he ordered. "Those light infantrymen aren't as slow as they might be!"

We needed no urging; for the body of redcoats that had moved out ahead of the main column had already passed the warehouses. Even in the twilight we could see the buckles on their belts, and hear the voices of their officers. They were beautiful to watch—as beautiful as the troops Nathaniel and I had seen parading in St. James's Park before the King, but more dangerous.

The water hissed at the bow and along the sides as we dug in our oars. I could feel the whole boat lift when Cap Huff pulled and grunted.

"Roll on, roll on; my ball, roll on," Verrieul sang softly behind me.

"What the hell you think this is?" Cap growled. "A funeral? Sing faster!"

He broke into a hoarse bellow about the three beautiful ducks—
"*Rouli, roulong, ma boule roulong—on roulong ma boule!*" He went on

with the song, singing it so rapidly that parts of it sounded like the gobbling of a turkey; and to that tune the clumsy brown boat went rapidly on its way to Isle aux Noix.

The scarlet-coated infantrymen came to a sudden halt abreast of the smoking ruins of the old barracks. "That's right!" Arnold said, watching them. "Stop there! You might strike an ambush if you went on!" He turned from his scrutiny of the British troops and spoke to Wilkinson, who was fumbling unbelievingly in the pockets of his saddlebags. "Where's my field-desk?" he asked. "I'll write a few letters while the light holds."

XXI

Valley forge, from what we heard of it in later days, was no health resort for the troops who wintered there, thanks to a Congress unable to supply them with food or money, and to the unwillingness of certain godly Quakers to sell to anyone but the British, who paid in gold. We heard a lot about it, too, especially from folk who had not been there; but less has been said about Isle aux Noix—possibly because its name is difficult to pronounce, but more likely because those who knew it best were glad enough to forget it.

As to which was the worse, Isle aux Noix or Valley Forge, I won't try to say. It takes a wiser judge than any man I know to determine whether frozen feet are worse or better than smallpox, or whether it is more enjoyable to be starved by Quakers in the bitter cold or eaten alive by insects in the broiling heat. All I know is that since my sojourn on Isle aux Noix, I am no longer impressed by such preachers as threaten me with hell fire.

It was nearly midnight when we drew up to sentry-fires that seemed to float in mid-stream and were told by a sentry that Sullivan had taken the barn near the center of the island for his headquarters. When we moved down abreast of the barn and backed in to let Arnold jump ashore, we were conscious of a strange sound, a sort of complaining noise. It was like the wailing of a westerly gale in the top-hamper of distant ships; but there were no ships in this place, and no wind either.

Arnold tapped me on the shoulder when the boat grounded. "I'll want you," he said. "See Wilkinson tomorrow, so I can find you in a hurry when you're needed."

We overturned our bateau to make a shelter, and lay with our heads beneath it. The ground was soggy, and soon the nightly thunderstorm arrived to drench us. Yet it was not this that kept us wakeful, but a nightmare quality in the very air: a quality that filled us with a restless apprehension.

The complaining sound we had heard was the moaning and raving of the sick, who seemed to lie everywhere around us. What with that, and the dreadful smell of the place—a blend of every terrible smell I

had ever smelled, with several new and awful smells added—and the
faint, unending whining of the unseen mosquitoes that covered us, and
the sticky, steamy misery in which we lay, I was more than a little sick
myself.

As for Cap Huff, he floundered and flopped among us like a great fish
out of water, and finally rolled himself over two men to lie next to Doc
Means, explaining that he hoped the asafoetida would drown out some
of the other smells, and so give him a chance to sleep.

"If it wasn't for Stevie Nason," he said, "I wouldn't stay five minutes
with an army that smelt like this! An army ought to have a smell that
you could get used to; but this army keeps getting new ones, and the
newest one's always the worst! I can't get to like it, and I'm about ready
to go home. I'd go home right now if Stevie was here. That is, I would if
he'd let me. No, by God, I'd go anyway!"

"Where is it you live?" Verrieul asked politely.

"Who, me?" Cap said in a tone of surprise; and, lifting himself on one
elbow, he seemed to be fumbling in his garments. We heard the sound
of breaking glass, and a prolonged gurgle. Then he handed me a neck-
less bottle, warning me not to cut my lip. "Pass it around," he added. "It's
brandy—just the kind of brandy a feller like Wilkinson *would* have. We
got to get rid of it before he comes snooping around in the morning.
We'll all have a drink to Stevie."

While I drank, Verrieul asked again the whereabouts of Cap's home.

"My home?" Cap said. "My home? Well I've usually lived most any
place, or thereabouts; but if I hadn't ever lived nowhere, I'd rather live
wherever that is than here! I'd get up right now and go there, too, if it
wasn't for expecting Stevie!"

I think that was the case with most of the men on Isle aux Noix that
night. They would have gone home or anywhere else if they could—if
there had been boats to carry them, and any manner in which they
could have stolen the boats; and if they had not been held where they
were by circumstances beyond their control.

That, I think, is the case in all wars: at some time or other, everyone
would run away if he dared. I know that I would have helped myself
to a boat and got away somehow, if Arnold had not said he wanted to see
me; for more and more I felt an urging within me to find Nathaniel
and Ellen Phipps.

. . . All through the night we longed for daylight; but when daylight
came, we would have been glad to go back to the darkness again, because of what we saw around us.

Isle aux Noix is a flat pancake of an island, a mile long and a quarter mile wide. Near the middle of it were a house and a barn and a few out-houses grouped around a heap of manure that seemed ancient enough to have been piled there in the days of Champlain himself. Plowed fields surrounded the house; but the rest of the island was lowland and brush.

In Cap Huff's opinion it was a floating island, anchored to the bottom of the river by the roots of the bushes; and he stuck to this idea because no matter how hard the rain fell, the surface of the island always re-mained six inches out of water. If it had been a solid island, Cap insisted, it would have been six feet under water after we had been there a short time; for it seemed to be a custom of Canada to have thunderstorms every night—storms so violent that the island shook beneath us when the thunderclaps were overhead. We would do better, Cap said, to live at the bottom of a well where, comparatively, we'd be nice and dry.

On this marsh were eight thousand men—eight thousand American soldiers, or men who had once been soldiers. Two thousand of them had smallpox; and two thousand sick men, crowded together in a small space, is a staggering number.

The six thousand who were not sick when they arrived were weary beyond all telling; for no weariness compares with the exhaustion that follows failure; few things are more weakening than the condition of mind that men get into during a retreat.

The truth is that men who were called "sick" on Isle aux Noix were all but dead, whereas those who were said to be "well" were only well in that they were able to drag themselves around without assistance.

There were not enough tents for the sick, even, and nothing with which to cover them except overturned bateaux, or a thatch of grass and branches, laid across poles. Since there was no way of fastening the thatch firmly in place, it fell down whenever the wind came up, and this usually happened late at night, in the midst of a heavy thunder-storm. Thus the sick men were wet both day and night; for since they were too sick to protect themselves against mosquitoes and black flies if left naked, their blankets could not be dried during the day.

To tell about Isle aux Noix is not easy. To speak of one miserable circumstance brings to mind a host of others, equally miserable; and to describe the place honestly, one would have to tell a thousand horrors, little and big, and use a lifetime in the telling.

There was no food except a small amount of flour and salt pork. The pork was sour and bad, hard to eat unless a man held his nose; and even this carrion could not be properly cooked because firewood was scarce on the island. There was only brush, not nearly enough to make fires for eight thousand men three times a day, even if it had been burnable, which it was not, being green.

Consequently we made the flour into paste with the brown water from the river, and spread the paste on stones, which we put in the sun. When the paste was dry, we peeled it off and ate it.

Across the river, staring us in the face, was pine growth enough to provide fuel for all the armies in the world; but it might as well have been in Arundel, or in England, for all the good it did us. We couldn't get at it; for although the British, having no boats with which to follow us, had stopped their advance at St. John's, they had sent out a force of Indians, commanded by a Frenchman, to keep watch over the island—a fact that was forcibly impressed on all of us when a party of officers crossed over to the mainland to look for firewood and provisions, and had hatchets driven into their brains and their scalps ripped off within three minutes of landing.

During our first night on this devil's island we expected that with the dawn, the moaning of the sick would become less terrible; but instead of that, it increased. The reason it increased was because many had died during the night, and those still alive wished the dead removed, which is not hard to understand. They feared, too, that vermin would leave the dead for the living, who were already infested beyond all belief; and the sick-tents were so packed with sufferers that the survivors hoped to be more comfortable if so much as one body could be removed from among them.

Another reason they moaned was because with the daylight they were able to see the inroads the disease had made on others during the hours of darkness, and they feared for themselves—particularly for their eyes, which are destroyed in bad cases.

Also they wanted water, and dressings for their sores, and medicine, and human companionship, and some sort of surcease from the anguish of homesickness that intensified their burning and itching.

As soon as it was possible to see we went to work helping these sufferers; and I truly believe there was no tent or shelter into which we looked that did not contain a corpse or one who would be a corpse within the hour. In the case of a dead man, we drew him out on his torn and horrid blanket, knotting the lower corners across his feet, so there would be no slipping. Then two of us laid hold of the upper corners and dragged him to the dead pits, which were at the lower end of the island: the end nearer St. John's.

A pale and sinister-seeming mist rose from the surface of the river and the soaked earth of the island. It shrouded everything until the sun came up to burn it off; and since there was no breeze, it hung heavily, in layers. Those who walked through that billowing, drifting shroud seemed at times legless and headless bodies, and at others mere floating heads, disappearing and reappearing in a gray Purgatory.

Therefore, as Doc Means and I went down the island, dragging our dead man behind us, we might have been moving into a land of specters —a colorless place, a place of groaning and moaning, in which other dim figures moved, dragging burdens like our own.

The dead pits were trenches, shallow and a scant six feet in width. Because of the great number of sick, and the frequency with which they died, the pits were always open, until they were full.

The one to which we came was only partly filled with close packed ranks of swollen carcasses that lay there grinning, as if at some appalling joke. We stood above them, half strangled by the stench, and swung the blanket between us: then tossed the poor body in among the others. A billion flies leaped upward, as if in protest at this new arrival, and such was their buzzing and hissing that the row of dead men seemed to whisper and titter at their uninvited guest.

It came to me that this dead friend of ours was on the verge of speech. His eyes were open, staring above us as if horrified at what his soul must meet.

Who he was, I do not know. Certainly there was no one who seemed to care. The same thing must have been true of all the others in those pits. There were no names written anywhere—just a long row of bodies, already worse than hideous: men who had done as well as any men could do under the circumstances, and received nothing for it—neither pay nor food nor clothing nor thanks: not even decent sepulture.

There were shovels standing in the loose dirt beside the pits. When I picked one up, thinking to cover those bloated and revolting forms, a man stopped me: one of a pair who had brought another body. He wore the fragments of a blue and white uniform. His face bristled with a straggling red beard, and he crouched, as if something gnawed at his stomach. "No dirt," he said. He panted and grunted. "Don't cover till night. Makes rows irreg'lar." He held his middle and moved an elbow toward the blanket which he and his companion had dropped.

"Put him in straight," he begged. "We can't do nothing but roll 'em in, all crooked." He sat down suddenly at my feet. His companion staggered away through the mist. Doc Means and I swung the body into the pit: then turned our attention to the sitting man.

"What's the matter with him, Doc?" I asked. It seemed terrible for a man to die here on the edge of the dead pits, though I cannot tell why it seemed so, when in reality it was the handiest place in which to die.

"Lemme be!" the man said. "I had smallpox and got over it. There ain't nothing wrong with me now, only the flux. Everybody's got it that ain't got smallpox."

"Isn't there something he could take for it?" I asked Doc.

"H'ist me up," the man said, as if fearful we might try to give him medicine. "I can walk if I'm h'isted up." We hoisted him to his feet, and he lurched off into the mist, past other pairs of men dragging corpses.

We went back to the bateau; and as we went, Doc Means shook his head. "Armies," he muttered, half to himself, "armies was created special to encourage disease. You don't rest good in an army, and you're kind of scairt most of the time; and when you ain't scairt, you're either mad or homesick. What's more, you're always too hot or too cold or too wet, and there's always some pitt-whistle of an officer making you do something disgusting, and your food's rotten, if so be you get any food at all; and all those things together fix it so you can't help getting took sick. Then when you're sick, those same things fix it so medicines don't do you no good, even when there *are* medicines, which there usually ain't. The way to cure these fellers of what ails 'em is to stop the war and send 'em home. There ain't hardly one of 'em but what would be healthy inside of a week."

We were two hours dragging dead men to the pits and doing what we could for the sick close to us—though there was nothing we could do but admit air to their shelters: air that wouldn't choke them with its foulness. They were from Poor's New Hampshire regiment, and near every man in the regiment was down with smallpox—so many that when they moved on, there weren't enough of their own men to row them, and their bateaux had to be manned out of the Pennsylvania regiments.

How any man who was sick with smallpox came alive off this island is more than I can understand. There were no medicines, and so few doctors that the camp could have been little worse off if there had been none at all. I saw only two, and in my opinion they left something to be desired. One seemed to me to be doing nothing but weeping. Another, having heard Verrieul speak enthusiastically of the abilities of Doc Means, came to enlist Doc's assistance in caring for the sick; then wrangled with him angrily over theories of medicine.

The first question he asked Doc was where he had studied; and when Doc said he had got all his information by word of mouth, and out of almanacs and from reading Culpeper's Herbal and a medical book by Thomas Tryon, the doctor said "Pfaugh!" in an offensive voice, adding that Tryon was a crank and a quack.

"Well," Doc said, "maybe he is, but he's good enough for Ben Franklin, and what's good enough for Ben Franklin is good enough for me. Howsomever, I ain't making no effort to be a doctor in this army. It's a fact I brought along my Venesection Mannekin and my Almanac and my Digby's Sympathetic Powder, but only because——"

The doctor burst into angry laughter. "Digby's Sympathetic Powder! It's useless! It's worse than useless! There hasn't been a reputable physician use it for pretty near a hundred years."

"Is that so?" Doc said. "Well, you'd be surprised, the results I've got with it! It never did nobody no harm, and that's more'n regular doctors can say for most of their drugs and powders."

The other looked at him haughtily, but changed the subject. "What system do you use for reviving drowned persons?"

"It depends," Doc said. "It depends how old they are, and whether they're male or female."

"In what way does it?" the doctor asked.

"If they're male and young," Doc said, "I hang 'em to the side of a house, by the feet, and bend 'em up from the waist a few times. That dreens 'em out. If they're old, I lay 'em over the edge of a bed, if I got one."

"Good God!" the doctor cried. "The suspension method! Why, it's no better than murder, especially if the body's been under water more than an hour."

"According to my experience," Doc said, "anything or anybody that's been under water more than an hour, excepting of a fish, I'd let alone on account such few results could be expected."

The doctor stared incredulously from Doc to the rest of us, and then back to Doc again. "Do you mean to stand there and tell me," he whispered, "that the judgment of the greatest physicians in Europe—the judgment of Réaumur, Stoll, Murray, Cullen—is inferior to your own? Do you mean to tell me you've never heard of the marvelous cures effected by blowing smoke up into the insides of persons who have been under water for five hours—yes, for an entire day and more?"

"Down our way," Doc said mildly, "people drowned over an hour don't get well. It may be their own fault, but my opinion is, it's ordained; and all them judgments of Mary Cullen and all them Europe doctors you talk about wouldn't give satisfaction to them or their relations either, except if they happened to be kin to the undertaker."

The official medical man, already crimson with indignation, looked dangerous. "May I ask," he said, "whether you ever heard of the Humane Society of London? Of course you haven't! You're not aware that the Humane Society of London has denounced the suspension method! The Humane Society of London recommends the injection of smoke, tickling with feathers, scorching the cuticle and putting the fingers and toes out of joint. I give you the information, but no more trust you to execute such recommendations than I would trust a tadpole to prescribe for General Washington! If I hear of your attempting to practice medicine or surgery in this camp——"

God knows how long this doctor, forgetful of the groans of the sick, would have continued to bully Doc; but fortunately a bugle blew near the middle of the island, and the outraged practitioner felt compelled to depart in the direction of the bugle.

It was blowing for parade; and, knowing there would be less of a crowd at headquarters during parade than at any other time, I bolted a noisome piece of salt pork and set out to report to Wilkinson.

. . . The mist had burned away, and I had a clear look at four companies that were forming. There was next to nothing left of their uniforms; but from the rags of faded blue and soiled white that hung on them, I knew they were the wreckage of Anthony Wayne's regiment. I was surprised to see how many men were standing at attention; and even more surprised that they should have the strength to do so, for they were bearded and emaciated, and their eyes had the look of blue smudges in clay-colored faces. The officers looked little better than the men: but they rapped out their commands sharply enough, and the men formed lines that were almost straight.

I could hear the order that was being read—something about the colonel being determined to punish in the severest manner every man who came to parade with a long beard, slovenly dressed or dirty. I wondered how long a beard had to be in order to be considered long, and also what sort of severe punishment Wayne proposed to inflict on men in the present situation. He could take away their salt pork, I knew, but I didn't see what else he could do that would be considered severe—not unless he buried them alive in the dead pits.

In the midst of the reading, a man in the front row pitched forward to lie with his face in the mud. A sergeant crawled between the ranks, got him by the arms and dragged him back out of sight.

Then the whole front rank wavered; two men in the rear rank stumbled forward and fell with a clatter. Man after man went down in the other three companies, to be dragged out of the way of those still able to stand. But when I moved on, all four companies still stood rigidly at attention, listening to the orders from that wind-bag of a Wayne, and the ground behind them was littered with what looked like dead men. Before the night was over, I had no doubt, some of them *would* be dead, and well out of this hell-hole of an Isle aux Noix.

. . . Wilkinson leaned in solemn meditation against a corner of the barn.

His jaws were clenched, as I could see from the faint movement of his cheeks. If he was not thinking great and important thoughts, he at least had the air of being thus engaged.

"General Arnold said I was to see you," I began; but Wilkinson frowned, pointing toward the warped boards beside his head. His lips formed the words "Council of War!"; so I held my tongue and listened.

I recognized the querulous voice of General Sullivan. He was pleading almost petulantly, as a child pleads with its mother to be allowed to eat something forbidden.

"There's nobody," he complained, "who doesn't want us to hold the country. Why look here, gentlemen! What's to become of the poor Canadians who've helped us—who've fed us and carted our belongings and loaned money to us, in the hopes we'd take the country from the English? What's to become of them? If we desert them, the British'll hang 'em! My God, gentlemen; you can't hold Canada unless you *hold* some part of it, and this island's the last bit we can keep a grip on. Congress wants it held! General Washington wants it held! The American people want it held! What's to happen if we let go?"

Arnold's voice followed closely on Sullivan's. There was a hoarseness to it that made my heart thump faster.

"With all due respect, General," Arnold said, "you're looking at it wrong end to. We've got eight thousand men on this island; and if there ever was an army that size with as many enemies to fight as we've got, I never heard of it! We can lose every man in half a dozen different ways; and as I see it, our first duty is to save 'em if possible."

There was a growl of assent, but Arnold's voice drowned it. "It's not what Congress wants, or what they'll think if we don't do exactly what they want. What they want doesn't matter! They want one thing today, and another thing tomorrow. They don't know what's going on up here. Most of 'em wouldn't know if they were here, looking at it. They haven't got the sort of brains that lets 'em see what they're looking at. We're the ones that know; and what we know is this: in two weeks, if you try to hold this island, there won't be enough well men to row your sick! The place is full of dead already, and God only knows what sort of plague you'll get from 'em if you add to 'em for another two weeks. All your men, sick and well, are eating rotten food and drinking rotten water; and in my opinion they'll *all* rot if you keep 'em here!"

The rumble of agreement grew louder.

Arnold's voice was contemptuous. "But the main point is this: the British are twelve miles from us—only twelve miles! In three days they'll have their full force in St. John's—half a day's march; and they'll be ready to move. It's beyond me why they haven't moved already! If I had command of that British force, I'd take you and every one of your men prisoners today—this afternoon! Either that, or I'd wipe you out! That's how strong your position is, General!"

He paused, and in my imagination I could see him staring with pale eyes at General Sullivan. The barn was so silent that I heard the rustling of a wasp, investigating, with palpitating rump, a knot-hole close to Wilkinson's shoulder.

"There's a road from St. John's to this island," Arnold went on. "How in the name of God do you propose to stay here with that road undefended? There's no way of doing it, General! They can take us, just like reaching into a henhouse and taking a sick hen at midnight! All they need to do is send a few light guns—a few four-pounders—past us. I don't have to tell you what would happen, General! They'd cut off our line of communications! There'd never be another ounce of provisions reach us—never another ounce! Then you'd have two choices: starve or surrender!"

Sullivan cleared his throat. "We could strengthen the old French entrenchments. We've still got men able to do duty."

"Yes," Arnold said, "but you won't have 'em long! Last night twenty-seven officers locked themselves in a hut with a barrel of rum, and drank themselves blind so they wouldn't have to listen to the groaning of the dying men they couldn't help! Get these men out of here, General, while you're still able to move 'em—while they're still able to move themselves! Don't for God's sake turn the whole island into one big dead pit! Get 'em to Crown Point, where they'll be of some value to the United Colonies. They're worth nothing as British prisoners! Dead, they're worth even less! Get 'em away and give us a chance to fight! We haven't got it here! No matter what you say, we haven't got it here!"

When Sullivan spoke, I wondered what in God's name was in his head in place of brains, and I longed to have him on board ship, where I could pound some sense into that iron skull with a belaying pin. "With men able to do duty," Sullivan said, "I can't in honor abandon this position. Considering the desire of General Washington and the Congress, I cannot retreat farther—not on my own responsibility."

There was another silence. I looked at Wilkinson; but he only stared at me owlishly, his jaw muscles throbbing. I think he saw something reasonable and noble in Sullivan's willingness to sacrifice the lives of eight thousand men in order to save the pitiful vanity that he miscalled "honor."

When Arnold spoke again, his voice was deferential: almost too deferential. "I think I see what you mean, General. You can't retreat unless

General Schuyler or General Washington orders you to retreat: that's what you mean, I take it."

"If General Schuyler should order it," Sullivan admitted, "I would, of course, obey."

"In that case," Arnold said, "I have only two suggestions. One is that you start your sick for Crown Point at once. At once! You can do that without orders. The other is that you send me to Albany to tell General Schuyler what's going on. You've got to have those orders with no loss of time, or orders won't do you any good—not any good at all!"

"You think he'll order a retreat?" Sullivan asked.

Arnold only laughed.

"Then I suppose you'd want to go tomorrow, General?" Sullivan said.

"Tomorrow!" Arnold cried. "I'm a seaman, General, and I'll take seamen with me. We'll go today and sail all night."

"Good!" Sullivan said. "I'll start the sick for Crown Point—ah—I'll start them tomorrow."

XXII

W<small>E FOUND</small> a twenty-seven-foot bateau and calked her with old rags dipped in pork fat. We made a rudder for her, and a tiller, and ballasted her with cannon balls. We made sail from tarpaulins—a patched leg-of-mutton that looked as if it might have done duty as a staysail for Henry Hudson himself, and a jib fit for nothing on any deep-water vessel except to swab the galley stove. We bought a door from the Frenchman who lived on the island, and decked her forepart with it, in case she tried to put her nose under water.

In this craft we pushed off into the gathering dusk and headed toward Champlain, the general and Wilkinson, with the rest of us as crew —Tom Bickford, Doc Means, Verrieul, Cap Huff and myself. I knew she was rickety from her wobbly feel when we overturned her for calking; so I put in an oar for each of us, to give us something to hold to if she sank. How rickety she was I didn't know until we reached the lake, and there caught a light breeze from the northwest. Slight as it was, it made our lobster-pot of a vessel squeak with pain, and flap like a flounder.

Arnold was in good humor; he wanted to talk, and not about the awful situation of the army on Isle aux Noix, or the mischances that had brought it about. That was Arnold's way—to cast his thoughts into the future, and dwell as little as possible on the past. What's done is done, he argued. It's water under the bridge. Lay your plans; and if the plans go wrong, it's the fortunes of war—not something to be wept over.

He was a great planner, able to see farther and straighter into the future than any man I ever knew. He was a great soldier and good company, too. When he put his hand on the tiller to feel our crazy craft I saw he was a good seaman as well.

"Feels as if Noah might have used her as a tender," he said. "What's her best point of sailing, do you think?"

I took the tiller and worked her a little. "I wouldn't want to commit myself," I said, "for fear I'd have to prove it."

He nodded. "That's the way she feels to me, but you can't always tell about a bateau. Did you ever sail one before?"

When I said I hadn't, he grinned. "They'll surprise you. They'll stand pretty near anything. They're almost as good full of water as when they're tight and dry—just wetter to sit in, that's all."

This was a relief, as Tom Bickford had started bailing with his camp kettle.

"So don't be afraid to push her," Arnold went on. "It's a hundred miles to Crown Point and another hundred to Albany. I'm counting on reaching Crown Point in two days at the outside."

I said nothing, knowing we would either make Crown Point in two days or never make it at all.

Arnold was restless. His brain, it seemed to me, was never still, not even when he was asleep.

"About that vessel you sent to Crown Point," he said suddenly. "How long would it take to put her together and finish her?"

"Finish her fit to cruise?"

"To cruise and fight."

"If I could have twenty men from our shipyard," I said, "I could have her ready for sea in two weeks, provided I rigged her as a sloop."

"Yes," he agreed. "That would be about right: two weeks! That's fast! We'd have to build 'em quick—quick!"

I had no idea what he was talking about.

"Yes sir," Arnold said meditatively, "yes sir! It's got to be done! Somehow we've got to do it! It would take three hundred ship carpenters: three hundred of the best."

I thought he was joking. "Three hundred! You could build a fleet with three hundred!"

"That's right," Arnold said. "If we can get three hundred good carpenters, and lumber and nails and sails and rope and guns, and enough sailors to man 'em after they're built, we'd have a fleet. Well, that's what we've got to have!" He eyed me sardonically.

"A fleet of how many?" I asked, remembering the cloud of sail we'd seen bearing down on us at Sorel.

"Well," Arnold said, "we'd have to build enough to delay 'em. We've got a few small vessels already: enough to hinder 'em a little. There's the *Royal Savage* schooner, that Montgomery seized at St. John's when he came up to join me last winter; there's the *Enterprise* sloop I took at St. John's last summer; there's the *Liberty* schooner, that used to belong to Skene, and that Captain Oswald captured in Skenesboro a year ago.

"They're small and out of repair; but small as they are, they're enough to control the lake until the British build something bigger. The hell of it is that the British could offset those three with flat-boats—gundelos—provided they're big enough to mount heavy guns."

"How many would you want to build?" I persisted.

"As many as I could," Arnold said. "As many as we'd need to keep 'em from reaching the Hudson and joining Howe! We wouldn't necessarily have to build big vessels. We might be able to stop 'em with gundelos, even. Haul your wind a little: see if you can't get more speed out of this tub!"

We jockeyed her a little, but she was doing the best she could.

"Yes sir!" Arnold went on. "If we could delay 'em: if we could get control of the lake for three months—for four months, so they'd have to build a fleet and make a fight for it, they'd be no further ahead a year from now than they are today, because they'll never dare to operate against us in the winter. Why, by God, sir, if we could delay 'em, it would be as good as a victory!"

For the first time I fully understood his plan; and more than that, I understood that here might be a chance for me to get my fingers on Nathaniel at last, and keep him close to me, where he would be in no trouble.

"I don't see why you can't," I told him. "I know a shipyard inside-out, and so does my brother Nathaniel. He and I could build a gundelo in two weeks, just the two of us, I do believe, only in my opinion a gundelo isn't worth the powder to blow it to hell."

"Ah, yes," Arnold said, "but it's cheap and easy to build; and an eighteen-pounder in the bow of a gundelo can kill just as many men as an eighteen-pounder in a fort."

"Yes, but it's flat-bottomed," I reminded him, "and it slides like a pie-plate. It's neither speedy, handy, nor seaworthy. If I let off an eighteen-pounder from the bow of a gundelo, I'd need a kedge-anchor to keep her from kicking ashore and fouling herself in a pine tree. I'd rather have one Spanish row-galley, like those you see in the Tagus, than twenty gundelos. They're lateen rigged, with a main and foremast: just two sails to handle, and two yards, and no bowsprit. A handful of farmers could make sail on 'em, provided they had just one mariner to give 'em orders."

Arnold eyed me speculatively. "I never saw one. It doesn't sound like the smartest rig in the world."

"It's good enough for Spaniards," I reminded him, "and for Italians and Algerines too. They like to hug the shore pretty tight, but they can beat to windward as well as anyone. You know where you'd be if you tried to beat to windward in a gundelo: about ten miles south of hell's kitchen."

"That's so," Arnold said, "but gundelos are better than nothing, and any damned fool can build a gundelo."

"Yes," I said, "and Nathaniel and I can show almost any damned fool how to build a Spanish galley, just so he knows how to handle an adze and doesn't pound his fingers every time he drives a spike."

When Arnold made up his mind, he made it up quick. "Good," he said. "Good! Now let's see: I sent your brother to Crown Point, didn't I? He's in charge of your ship timbers. All right: good enough! When we get to Crown Point, I want you and your brother to draw plans for a few Spanish galleys. Maybe we can contrive a way to show Mr. Burgoyne there's some slight difference between Lake Champlain and a Thames Regatta."

. . . We labored past Cumberland head and the steep sides of Valcour Island; then cruised across those fretful waters toward Crown Point, where this narrow inland sea is pushed together by the mountains of Vermont and New York.

The crumbling fort at Crown Point and the patched stone barracks within it stood forlornly on land that appeared to have been spread out, like butter, as a support for the rolling hills behind it. The lake became a canal that twisted among mountains to connect the waterways of Canada with those that join the Hudson. A few miles ahead we could see the heights of Ticonderoga, beneath which, we knew, the canal opened once more into narrow lakes—on the right Lake George, and on the left the long lagoon of South Bay.

We had made the run from Isle aux Noix to Crown Point in a day and a half—half a day better than Arnold had stipulated. Considering that our bateau was only a little more seaworthy than a washtub, and that Tom Bickford and Verrieul had never stopped bailing in all that time, we had done well.

I thought Arnold had no appreciation of the manner in which this argosy of ours had been nursed along. As we approached Crown Point, he stood up in the stern, staring at the sorry fortifications. The closer we came, the more restless he grew, sitting down only to pop to his feet again and make faint sounds of exasperated amusement.

"Nothing!" he finally exclaimed. "Not one damned thing! Now what do you think of that!"

He tapped my hand. "Look at it! There's a lesson for you in how far a pee-wit can see! Take a good look at it!"

It wasn't much to look at; but it was better than Isle aux Noix.

"Properly fortified," Arnold said, "that point controls the lake. Put a decent fort there, properly manned, and no invading army could ever get past. And *now* look at it! Half a year's work to be done on it, and no time or men to do it!"

"I don't understand about the pee-wit," I said.

Arnold laughed. "I haven't seen this place for sixteen months! Sixteen months ago I commanded it! A hundred men, I had. I took ninety of 'em and invaded Canada." He slapped his knee. "Yes sir! Invaded Canada, captured St. John's, destroyed the shipping, and cut the British off from the lake."

He eyed me with that hard, pale stare of his. "It beats all how people can't see beyond their noses! I had hell's own time making folks realize these lakes were worth holding—that the safety of all the colonies depended on it. I had to write letters day and night to make 'em believe it: letters to Congress: letters to Connecticut: letters to Massachusetts: letters to Albany: letters to everyone—For God's sake, send men! Send men so we can fortify Crown Point and Ticonderoga and hold 'em! That's what I told 'em. Then I did what I could to fortify the place—me with my hundred men! Dig, dig, dig, dig! That's all we did, dig, until New York and Connecticut listened to my letters and sent up a thousand men under those three she-rabbits, Hinman, Easton and Brown. By God, sir: there were enough healthy men to make this place impregnable in four months, if commanded by anyone but Hinman, Easton and Brown! They wanted my place, and they got it! And then they sat here, they and their thousand men, and wondered whether it wasn't too warm to go fishing. They did nothing! Not one damned thing! No fortifications: no entrenchments: no sentries! Any quiet, nice little boy could have taken the place by hammering on a child's drum and squeaking, 'Surrender or I'll fire!'"

I thought of Easton and Brown, sitting with Hazen and Bedel and glowering at me like sulky children. "I've heard it said," I told him, "that Easton and Brown aren't favorably disposed toward you."

"Favorably disposed!" he cried. "I should hope not! Easton's a tricky, intriguing coward. I told him so to his face, here at Crown Point, over a year ago and kicked the seat of his breeches by way of proving it. Brown's a bad officer—no foresight: no vision: no more than Easton had. What they didn't do at Crown Point would be enough to prove it. But there's more than that. Montgomery told me Brown was a bad officer, and now Brown wants to be promoted: wants to be a lieutenant colonel. Well, he can't be: not if I have any say! I'd sooner see a cow made lieutenant colonel!"

He snorted and made a whisking motion with his hand, as if to sweep Brown and Easton from his life forever. A few moments later I laid the bateau alongside the shaky wharf beneath the ruins of the fort, and Arnold jumped ashore to get something to eat before pushing on for Lake George and Albany. He beat his breast, as if on the verge of exploding from long hours of inaction, and immediately turned two one-handed cartwheels, first on his left hand and then on his right—a difficult thing to do, if you have never tried it.

. . . The timbers of the vessel we had shipped from St. John's were stacked in two large piles close by; and between them was pitched a tent. In front of the tent stood Nathaniel, alone, still wearing his white Canadian jacket. We shouted and waved to him. He seemed to hesitate, and finally sauntered down to us.

I didn't fully understand why, but a great weight lifted from my chest when I saw Ellen was not with him. He must, I thought, have sent her to Albany—to the friends of whom Marie de Sabrevois had talked so much.

Because of the general being with us, I had less than my usual greeting for him; and it seemed to me he eyed me with something of defiance. He was a fine figure of a soldier, tanned and handsome, wholly unlike those of us who had been battered by Chambly and Isle aux Noix.

Arnold, I could see, liked Nathaniel's looks, but only nodded to him. To me he said: "I'll be here one hour: no longer. Pick up another bateau—one that doesn't leak, and see to it that the men are ready when I am."

With that he set off toward the barracks, Wilkinson cat-footing along at his elbow. His back was no sooner turned than Cap Huff poked Nathaniel in the ribs and bawled: "Where's your young lady? I got a present for her!"

Arnold wheeled. "Young lady? Has one of you been married?"

XXIII

WE STOOD in a sort of frozen silence.

Arnold came back, looking from one to the other of us. "I always like to know when one of my men gets married during a campaign. Which one of you was it?"

Cap Huff cleared his throat. "I said 'young lady.' I didn't say 'wife'! I wasn't accusing nobody of being married! I wouldn't do no such thing as that, General!"

Arnold ran his eye over us: then stabbed a finger at Nathaniel. "What's all this evasion? Seemingly you're about to be married to some young lady. Well, it's no crime to be married. Some of the best men I know have had wives."

"Yes sir," Nathaniel said. "I mean No sir! This young lady and I, we've decided not to be married. There's certain difficulties—that is to say——"

"Oh, indeed!" Arnold said. "Let's see about this! Where is this lady you aren't going to marry?"

Nathaniel nodded toward the tent. "Yonder, sir."

Arnold turned on his heel, contemptuously repeating, under his breath, "Certain difficulties! Certain difficulties!"

He marched into the tent, looked around: then popped through the back flap and disappeared. Nathaniel went in after him, and the rest of us skirted the tent to the open space behind it.

There was a fire in the middle of the space; and over it, spitted on a ramrod, hung half a dozen medium-sized hornpouts with a savoury-looking white froth edging their crinkled tails. Hunkered down before them was Zelph, black and worried-looking.

In the shade of one of the piles of lumber, so stacked as to leave a wide shelf about two feet from the ground, sat Ellen Phipps, knitting a gray stocking. When she looked up and saw Arnold standing in the rear opening of the tent, she leaned forward to examine the hornpout. "Move them back, Zelph," she said. "Don't let them get cold."

I think perhaps I hadn't fully known until that moment what had ailed me for so long—why I had felt such a strange restlessness: a restlessness so powerful that I seemed to have had it within me forever. But in that moment I knew, and knew beyond any doubt. I knew there was no one so beautiful as Ellen; knew I would never again have a happy moment unless I could be near her. There was something of suffocation about the feeling for her that suddenly swelled and throbbed within me.

"So you're the lady!" Arnold said. He whipped off his hat and made her a quick bow. "I had to see for myself when I heard one of my men had been fortunate; but I couldn't dream how fortunate, ma'am! We seldom find gems of loveliness in these forests."

Hitherto, I had seen Arnold hard at work, in the company of men. I had found him pleasant and considerate; but it had never occurred to me he could be as courtly as any of the be-ruffled Englishmen Nathaniel and I had seen at Ranelagh. I now saw that he could; and I well understood, later, how he won the heart and hand of such a belle as Peggy Shippen, daughter of the Chief Justice of Pennsylvania.

Ellen's eyes opened wide at Arnold's speech. "Why, that's beautiful! I could listen all day to such talk!" She glanced at the hornpout, at Nathaniel, standing close behind the general: then at those of us who had crowded up on either side of the tent. When her eyes met mine, I felt a singular weakness in my knees.

Arnold went to sit beside her on the shelf of ship timbers. "Well," he said, "I venture to say you'll have your share of such talk. I think it would come natural to any man—if you looked at him, ma'am."

His speech was airy; but his eyes, studying her, were intent. I saw that her quiet self-possession amused and pleased him.

Ellen pulled a needle from the gray stocking, adjusted the stitches carefully on the remaining needles, and glanced thoughtfully at me.

"There's one point I'd like to have explained," Arnold went on. "Something was said about difficulties—difficulties in the way of your marriage, according to my understanding. Difficulties in the way of your marriage to young Merrill, here. Now there shouldn't be any difficulties of a serious nature, it appears to me; and if there *are* any, perhaps I coud help to iron 'em out."

Ellen said nothing: merely continued to knit placidly. Nathaniel's face wore a set, mulish look with which I was only too familiar: a look that meant he would listen reluctantly to whatever might be said about the subject in hand, and pay attention to no word of it.

When his offer went unacknowledged, Arnold raised his eyebrows and tapped a plank with his boot. He rose to his feet suddenly and fixed Nathaniel with a pale and angry eye. "Well!" he rasped. "What *is* the difficulty! I'll have an answer and I'll have it quick!"

"Mercy!" Ellen said. "You've frightened me!" Since her voice was un-

perturbed, and her eyes still fixed on her knitting, I gathered her fright
was not serious.

"The only difficulty," Nathaniel said, "is that we decided we wouldn't
be married just yet."

"Not just yet?" Arnold cried. "Not just yet? What are you talking
about! If this lady left her family and friends to go away with you, there
can't be any talk of 'not just yet.' I won't have it! Not in any detachment
under my command!"

He made puffing sounds and glared at Nathaniel: then turned to
Ellen again. "Were you a party to this decision, ma'am: this decision
not to get married 'just yet'?"

Ellen sighed, nodded, and slid an anxious glance toward the hornpout, over which Zelph still crouched morosely.

Arnold rounded on Nathaniel. "Then the whole business is your
fault! If you intended to be married in the beginning, and the lady now
feels she doesn't want to be married just yet, then you've fallen short as
a suitor. It must be your Maine coldness! That's what it is: it's that
terrible chill you Maine men have in your blood! Damnation, sir, do you
mean to tell me that if a lady's well disposed toward a gentleman to
begin with, she can resist him if he won't take No for an answer? You're
different, you young people, from what *we* were—no sentiment any
more—everything taken for granted! One of you says 'Let's get married,'
and the other says 'All right, but not just now.' Pah! Where's the romance
in that! Press her, sir: press her! That's all that's necessary! Press her
enough and there'll be none of this 'not just now' talk!"

He slapped the ship timbers. "Tell her about it! Don't expect her to
guess how you feel! Hurry to her in the morning and tell her, and keep it
up all day! Don't let her forget it! If you have to go away for five minutes, write her a letter. Write her two letters!"

Ellen, removing a needle from her knitting to start a new row of
stitches, glanced at the half-circle of faces that stared at Arnold: from
Wilkinson, with his air of portentous gravity and his steadily moving
jaw muscles, around to Cap Huff, who stood beside me, breathing heavily, his mouth open and a look of concentration on his crimson counte-
nance, as if he strove valiantly to hold each syllable in his memory.
When her eyes met mine, they clung for a moment. Her eyebrows, I
thought, lifted almost imperceptibly. Then she went at her knitting
again, her needles twinkling and clicking.

Arnold moved an impatient shoulder. "As I see it, your difficulty's no
difficulty at all. I have no objection to a reasonable number of ladies"—
he coughed delicately—"accompanying my troops, but I have to insist
they be married. Unattached, they promote dissatisfaction—yes, and

dissension. There's enough of that among our troops without any outside help. Therefore I'll have to ask you to stop balking at trifles, and get married."

"But General!" I protested. "I'd hate to see my brother or this lady forced into something against their wills." I fished in my mind for a likely reason why they shouldn't be married, but could only add weakly, "It may be they feel they're too young."

"Too young!" Arnold exclaimed. "I never heard of anyone feeling too young to be married—no, nor too old, either!" He glared at all of us: then bowed to Ellen, clapped his hat on his head and slapped it to set it in place. "Your servant, ma'am. When I return from Albany in a few days' time, I'll be glad to hear pleasant news of a conjugal nature."

To Nathaniel, with more tartness, he added, "See that I do hear such news, sir!" On that he turned, limped back through the tent, and bolted off for the barracks as if enraged at the time he had wasted. Behind him stalked Wilkinson, full of disapproval of everyone in the world but himself.

Cap Huff hooked his thumbs in his belt and with his fingers rapped a tattoo on his stomach. "By God, he's right!" he told Nathaniel. "In case you don't know what he means, I'd be glad to show you." He looked at Ellen. "Maybe I better show you anyway."

"You big damned fool!" I said. "You've raised enough hell for one day! Take these men out and hunt up a seaworthy boat for the general, and have it ready within the hour, or he'll yank off your skin and use it for a wallet!"

"Oh, he will, will he?" Cap growled; but for all his bravado, he unhooked his thumbs from his belt and went lumbering off with Tom Bickford and the others.

As soon as they were out of hearing, I turned to Nathaniel. "If we've heard the truth of what you both feel, why in God's name did you bring this girl down here alone? And why haven't you sent her on to Albany?"

Ellen stamped her foot. "Zelph!" she cried. "Why have you cooked those pouts? For practice, maybe! Get plates this instant!"

Zelph leaped to his feet, and Ellen came to stand between Nathaniel and me, placid again. "For my part," she said, "I'd better explain to you, Captain Merrill, that I'm not the spiritless little girl you saw at the Château de St. Auge. Since I left there, I've had only men to deal with, and that's taught me a little independence of spirit. If you understand that, we can go ahead and help you to understand a few more things, but I'll have to ask you to be discreet about speaking of them."

"I understand you've changed since I first met you, and appear to be another person entirely," I said, "or what's more likely, I saw but a very little of you in St. John's, and misunderstood that little. I'll not speak of anything you tell me."

At that she smiled with a sudden brightness. "Good! Then we'll tell you everything, and you'll find it very simple. My dear aunt, Mademoiselle de Sabrevois, wished to send me to Albany. She and I had intended to go there together; but ten days ago she became ill, and so couldn't go herself, but was very anxious for me not to delay. On that account she chose your poor brother Nathaniel for the office of my escort."

She laughed. "He was not very gallant; never did I see a gentleman less anxious to perform such an office."

"What!" I said. "What!"

She laughed again. "The conditions were not to his taste, you see. He is very ardent, poor Nathaniel; but he burns for the aunt: not for the niece. That was his misfortune—and mine! There seem to be rules for some of these armies that permit ladies to be present only if they are married or about to be, as that officer with you made almost embarrassingly plain a little while ago. My aunt said that poor Nathaniel and I must pretend we were only waiting for a priest, and that nothing in the world except not being able to find one after we left St. John's, where we were too hurried, was the cause of our lack of matrimony."

She pointed at Nathaniel and laughed outright. "Look at him! Just as he stands now! With that miserable look of trying to be dutiful! That is as near as he has come at any time to the appearance of an adorer."

I let out a great breath: my shoulders seemed to straighten of their own will; and I looked affectionately at Nathaniel, who smiled sickishly.

"Now I truly begin to understand," I said.

She eyed me gravely. "I think that must be unusual. This is the rest of it. Poor Nathaniel, Major Scott and his little troop brought me here to Crown Point with the supplies; but here Nathaniel himself must stay, for he couldn't disobey his orders.

"But I, too, have orders that must be obeyed. My aunt has ordered me to go to Albany. Therefore I wished to proceed to Albany with Major Scott, his men and the supplies. But Major Scott made a misfortune for your poor brother Nathaniel and a comedy for me. He turned out to be a very strange man—so strange that he made love to me; and it happened that most of his men had found something to drink."

She looked at me almost inquiringly, I thought. When I was silent, she continued, "Major Scott said many things to me that were too polite, and having something to drink himself besides, showed no regard for the state of affairs supposed to exist between Nathaniel and me. Therefore Nathaniel and I both decided it would be better for me to remain upon his wretched hands a trifle longer, and wait for a more trustworthy escort to Albany. It happens that since Major Scott and his men went through to Albany, we haven't seen anybody else going that way who appeared to be of a kind to entrust with my precious person. There, that's all, and I'm hungry."

Zelph placed a sheet of corn bread on the shelf of timbers from which Ellen had lately risen, set out birch-bark plates and maple forks, and served us with hornpout whose sweet and juicy flesh would have made the tenderest trout taste coarse. It was the first good meal I had eaten since that day, far back down the corridors of time, when the lot of us, innocent as a herd of sheep going to the slaughter, had first arrived in St. John's to have our little fling at the glory and splendor of war. And when I glanced at Ellen, sitting small and straight beside me and staring out of round brown eyes at the wreck of my tow-cloth jacket: when I sniffed the sweet, warm scent that came slipping down from the pine forests on the heights at our backs: when I looked across the glassy narrows before us to the swelling blue hills of the New Hampshire Grants, I was conscious of a feeling of contentment such as I had never known.

It was Ellen, singularly enough, who disturbed my composure, though not unpleasantly. In a grave manner she asked me an unexpected question. "When I said that we were told to pretend to be betrothed, your poor brother Nathaniel and I, it seemed to me I saw a change in you. A small change, like that." She measured off, with her thumb, a portion of a pink finger. "You might have been displeased, I thought, if we had been actually betrothed." It was a statement, and yet a question.

"In a way," I said lamely. "In a way, because this is no time for Nathaniel to think of marriage."

"You thought I was not a fit person, perhaps? You think I wouldn't make a good wife for your brother!"

"No, no! It wasn't that! Not that at all! No, no, no!"

Ellen took her ball of wool from under her arm to free a strand. "I have heard so. I've heard the *Bostonnais* think, always, that each one of us who has learned her lessons in a convent is decorated with horns, like a little Mefistofele. Such a thought would be without foundation. Look!" She placed her hand on my upper arm and turned me toward her, bending her head forward so that her cap of glistening brown curls was close—so close I might have touched them with my lips. A faint fragrance rose from them. I could have said nothing coherent—unless, perhaps, my life had depended on it.

"You see!" she said. "There are no horns. We're little different from those who go to school in Boston, we who are educated in convents! I think of only two differences. It is perhaps difficult for us to speak in

English without first saying the words to ourselves in French, and then translating into English. Also I think we learn to speak more freely: to ask questions about things we do not understand, rather than be silent about them."

Nathaniel laughed. "There's no doubt about that: no doubt you learn to ask questions!" He addressed me almost with bitterness. "Just when a person wants a little quiet, she starts asking questions!" He poured out a flood of them, making his voice ladylike, in what he doubtless conceived to be an imitation of Ellen: "How old is your sister Jane? What does your mother look like? How old was she when she was married? How old is Captain Peter? How does it happen he's named Peter? What day is his birthday? How long has he been a sea captain? What did he do before that? Does he stay at home part of the time or does he go sailing always? Where does he sail to? What's Spain like? Are the girls in Spain beautiful? Do you speak Spanish? Does Captain Peter speak Spanish? Has he been in love, ever?"

Ellen's reply was tranquil. "It is impossible to learn without asking. My brother Joseph says that Indians are ignorant because they are too proud to ask questions. Besides, I asked you no questions except when you were all gloom and darkness, through thinking of my dear aunt." To me she added: "Many of those questions I asked for no reason at all except to make your brother forget himself in replying to them. We were taught to do this by the good sisters at the convent."

Nathaniel looked sheepish; but I smiled benevolently, greatly pleased with him—not only because he was safely beyond the reach of Marie de Sabrevois, but because he was wholly uninterested in Ellen.

"It seems to me," I said, turning to Nathaniel, "that all of us must give some serious consideration to your orders from General Arnold. He's going to Albany today: at once. It might be just possible that he'd consent to carry Ellen with him, if she feels she must go there. He was right about unmarried women traveling with the army; and Arnold doesn't talk for the fun of hearing himself talk, as you should well know."

Ellen dropped her hands in her lap and stared round-eyed at me. "Arnold!" she cried. "General Arnold! That was never General Arnold!"

"Who did you think it was?" I asked her. "Didn't you see he limped? Of course it was Arnold: the man who made the greatest march that ever was—who'd have taken Quebec if he hadn't stopped a bullet when he was needed most."

Nathaniel laughed: contemptuously, I thought.

"But he seemed a pleasant man!" Ellen exclaimed. "He was handsome, too, and a gentleman."

"What's wonderful about that?" I asked. "What did you expect to find? A chimney-sweep?"

Ellen's nod was half a yes and half a no. "But I have heard about him. An awful man! A ruffian, who gives orders to kill women and children!"

"Bless your heart," I said, "he does nothing of the sort! He's the kindest of men—except to cowards and liars."

"Oh, Peter!" Nathaniel said. "What's the good of trying to stand up for Arnold, after what's happened!"

I looked at him closely. "After what's happened? You mean after what he did to save our troops at Sorel?"

Nathaniel smiled pityingly. "He's no fit man to hold high rank in the American army. Everybody knows he's to be arrested for what he's done! That's why I paid no attention to what he said to me about Ellen. He won't be allowed to hold a command: not after Congress hears of his conduct."

I sat down on the shelf of ship's timbers and whistled a stave of Cap Huff's ball rolling song to keep my temper within bounds.

"Nathaniel," I said, "this is the second time you've belittled Arnold. What's the reason for it?"

"The reason? The reason? Why it's common knowledge."

"No! That won't do! It's not common knowledge, and you'll have to be clearer. What do you mean by saying 'When Congress hears of his conduct'?"

"I mean just that, Peter. When Congress learns about the supplies he stole in Montreal, there'll be trouble. No officer who stole what he did should be allowed to command any part of an army. Everybody says so."

"So Congress is going to learn about the supplies, is it? Who's it going to learn from?"

Nathaniel shrugged his shoulders. "How should I know? Somebody's bound to tell."

"Tell what? What is there to tell, when those supplies, as we all know, were seized by the orders of the Commissioners of Congress? They're supplies for the army! That's why they were sent to Chambly and St. John's first. Now they've been sent to Schuyler in Albany, because the army's retreating—God knows where to—and it's Schuyler who has charge of all supplies. He pays for 'em and distributes 'em."

"Indeed!" Nathaniel said with exaggerated politeness. "I suppose the sable-skin coat Arnold stole for himself is being sent to Schuyler in Albany! And the diamond-studded sword-hilt—that'll get to Schuyler! I suppose Schuyler'll pay for *that!*"

"Look here," I said. "You had charge of part of those seized supplies!

Did you see anything among them that wasn't for the army? Any diamond-studded camp kettles or any sable-skin breeches?"

"No," Nathaniel admitted, "but everybody knows——"

"Who told you? Who was it said Arnold's no fit man to be an American officer? Who's going to send word to Congress about him? Who said he's going to be arrested? Who said he stole a sable coat and a solid gold sword or whatever it was? *They* say he stole? *Who* says it?"

"Why, everybody!"

"Tell me one!"

"I don't remember any particular one, but everybody says it."

"Don't say that, Nathaniel! Anybody remembers who makes charges of that sort. This is a serious business! Arnold's the one good fighting general there is in our whole Northern Army! Do you know where we'd be, right this minute, except for Arnold? We'd be locked up in Montreal, all of us, with British regulars to give us a smell of their bayonets every time we showed our noses at a window! God knows it's not much of an army right now, thanks to Wooster and Sullivan and Congress and the smallpox; but bad as it is, it's still an army. If it wasn't for Arnold, it wouldn't exist at all! There wouldn't *be* any Northern Army! I want to know who it is that accuses Arnold of being a thief!"

Nathaniel was furious; but thanks to his shipboard training he gave me a fair answer. "If you don't mind, Peter, I'd rather not name any names."

"Listen to me!" I said. "What you're saying is a lie! Understand? It's a lie! I've been two days on a bateau with Arnold, and he's no robber. He took no sable coats and no diamond shoe buckles, or whatever it was you said. He's the only man in sight I'd trust to lead me! The only man! I know a leader when I see one; and that's what Arnold is! Now for God's sake be careful! Don't spread these lies about Arnold, or they *will* reach Congress. Then, the first thing you know, we'll be under the command of one of those pig-nut generals that Cap Huff talks about—maybe one of the foreigners that Congress loves so much, like De Woedtke, or the Frenchman we came to America with! He'll get us into a corner we'll never get out of—another corner like Isle aux Noix, where we'll be rolled into dead pits by the thousands; and there'll be nobody on God's green earth to know what becomes of us. We'll be gone like the flame of a blown-out candle—and with as little to show for our lives!"

Nathaniel sullenly studied his shoes. Ellen's glance was calm and level. I was swept by the feeling of hopelessness that burdens every man who speaks of war to those who have insufficient knowledge of what war is.

XXIV

When they turned from me, seemingly indifferent to my words, I climbed to the top of the pile of timbers to put my thoughts in order. I watched Nathaniel strop a razor against his palm: then set off, all unconcerned, no doubt to make himself more handsome. I watched Ellen, too, seat herself in the shade of the tent and busy herself with her knitting. Except for a trim whaleboat that drifted into sight around the rocky point above us, the lake was empty—flat as blue milk in a pan.

While I studied the whaleboat, a burly figure sat up in it, dug violently at the water with a paddle, and vanished again below the gunwale. It was Cap Huff; so I knew he had borrowed the boat to avoid tiresome formalities. I saw Tom Bickford and Verrieul run up the shore to help him; and the three of them worked it to the bank beneath me, out of my sight. The whole place, then, lay dusty and wilted in the noonday heat, and well-nigh deserted—as far removed from the sights and sounds of war as though the British army, as well as the groans, stenches and open dead pits of Isle aux Noix had never existed.

Yet my mind was beset by questions that were closer to the war than I liked: questions the answers to which seemed important. Not only did they seem important to my own welfare, which was a small matter; but I had the distressing suspicion that the answers I sought might be of vital consequence to the very cause in which I was enlisted as a soldier.

The foremost of the questions was this: Was Nathaniel's prejudice against Arnold evidence of a consistent spreading of calumnies intended to undermine our best officer, and to set his own troops against him? If so, who were the agents engaged in distributing the slanders? Of what did Marie de Sabrevois and Nathaniel talk when they were together, and not engaged in coquetries?

I thought farther back: as far back as our first meeting with Marie in Ranelagh Gardens. It was a meeting, of course, that might have happened to anyone. Yet it had happened to us, and because Marie had chosen to have it happen. Why? I wondered. What was the reason? It seemed likely there *was* a reason; for I knew by now that Marie had a quick and clever brain.

What was her purpose? Who was the quiet Leonard? When I spoke

of him to Madame St. Auge, she had said "Ah, Lanaudiere?" and then
denied she had meant Leonard. Who was Lanaudiere? If he was Leonard, had Marie created the meeting with us, and sent the man with us
to America because in our company he would land safely and unsuspected? Unsuspected of what?

I could not answer. But the questions kept pressing upon me.

Why had Marie de Sabrevois wished to take Ellen to Albany; and
what errand had they there? Nay, what errand had Ellen there, now
that Marie de Sabrevois wished to remain behind? And there was always that letter Nathaniel had carried—that letter about Montgolfier
and the eight thousand kisses; and so I came back to the first and most
important of all the questions: Who was serving a British employer by
spreading the calumnies against Arnold?

My thoughts pursued themselves in circles, getting nowhere and accomplishing nothing.

Zelph, I saw, had burned the birch-bark plates and smothered the
fire with sods, and now was ambling along the shore of the narrows
with a fishing line protruding from the pocket of his moose-skin
breeches. On the shore below I could hear a rattling and thumping,
and the hoarse voice of Cap Huff issuing orders and countermanding
most of them as soon as issued; so I knew Tom Bickford and the others
were transferring Arnold's baggage to the borrowed whaleboat. Nathaniel, newly shaven, had returned to stand by Ellen in the shade of the
tent; and the coolness and freshness of his appearance made me the
more conscious of my own bewilderment.

It was probably that very coolness of Nathaniel's that sent Ellen's
eyes toward my scarecrow figure and my beggar's garments, stained
and tattered by our labors on the Richelieu.

"If you must think so fiercely," she called to me, "you would do well
to let me stitch at your jacket while you think." As an afterthought she
added: "Then something, at least, will be accomplished."

I came slowly down from the pile of timbers, wondering whether I
was really as tiresome as I must appear to these gay young people.
"You can do more than that for me," I told Ellen. "You can answer
some of the questions that have worried me: questions about yourself."

"Worried?" she asked. "You have worried about me? There are questions about me that have worried you?"

I was certain, when I saw the candor and innocence of the eyes she
raised to mine, that with a little care I could ask her what I pleased,
and never arouse her suspicions.

"Yes," I said, "I was worrying about your journey to Albany." I
coughed, to let her see I was wholly at ease. "I was worrying, and

wondering, too. I was really wondering why your aunt was so anxious to have you go to Albany, even when she was well. Were you perhaps to be put in charge of Mr. Leonard there?"

"Mr. Leonard?" Ellen asked. "Mr. Leonard? I do not know any Mr. Leonard!"

I chanced a shot in the dark. "Perhaps you know him as Lanaudiere. It may be that you are only to deliver a letter to Mr. Lanaudiere."

She looked genuinely blank. "Lanaudiere? No; I have never heard of anybody of that name; and as for letters, my aunt said I would be expected by her friends in Albany, and there was no need for me to have a letter to them. The only two letters I carried had nothing at all to do with any Lanaudiere, and were not even written by my aunt, because she sent them with me to oblige a friend of hers who wrote them. No, they were not to anyone with a French name."

"Now wait," I said to myself. "Now wait! Here it is! Here's something at last!" If I could see those letters, I might have something to open Nathaniel's eyes to what I feared was the truth. As carelessly as I could I asked Ellen whether she still had them.

She shook her head placidly. "They have gone. Major Scott, he said both of the gentlemen were in Albany." She laughed. "And so, though I wouldn't go with him myself, I thought he could carry the letters for me, and he took them."

Nathaniel had been looking at me sulkily and shrewdly. "You won't make anything out of this, Peter," he said. "Those letters were written by a friend of Marie's—a Mr. Baudoin, whom I know; and he had known those two gentlemen in Canada, and had favors from them, and merely wished to send them a message of greeting and thanks after they had left."

To myself I said that this was a likely story, all my eye and my elbow. To Nathaniel I said nothing of the sort, though it sickened me to realize he was so infatuated with Marie de Sabrevois that he failed, even now, to see the weak point in what she had told him—to realize that her very insistence on the innocence of the letters ought to be sure proof of their guilt.

"Very well," I said. "It's not my business, and I didn't mean to seem prying if a Canadian gentleman asks Mademoiselle de Sabrevois to forward two letters to American gentlemen, friends of his, who've been traveling in Canada during the war. I'm sure that's very natural! Why shouldn't she?"

I spoke as easily and quietly as I could, and in as matter-of-fact a tone, as though I were dismissing the matter; but Nathaniel's color deepened.

"What do you mean?" he asked me challengingly. "What do you mean by talking about Marie's forwarding letters to American gentlemen who've been traveling in Canada during the war? I don't like your tone, Peter, and you'd better understand respectfully that the two gentlemen at whom you seem to sneer are among the most important, finest and best-considered officers in our army. I'd have you know, if you please, that one of 'em was Colonel Easton and the other Major Brown—Major John Brown."

"No!" I said. "Not Easton and Brown!"

Nathaniel was triumphant. "Certainly: Colonel Easton and Major Brown."

I stared at my shoes, so that Nathaniel mightn't see my eyes. Easton and Brown—who, with Hinman, were to blame for the lack of fortifications in the very spot where we sat! Two of the three inefficients responsible for ousting Arnold from Crown Point at the moment when he had started to make it an impregnable barrier against English troops and English vessels! Easton, kicked by Arnold for being a trickster and a coward: Brown, blocked from promotion by Arnold for being an officer without foresight: both of them intimates of Hazen, the man who couldn't obey orders, and of Bedel, the poltroon of the Cedars!

Once more, in my mind's eye, I saw the four of them, birds of a feather, flocking together in that small, dark room in Chambly Fort, glowering at me because I had brought a message from Arnold, the fighter who had damned them all for cowards or blunderers.

"Important," Nathaniel had called them in all seriousness; "finest and best-considered officers in our army!"

I decided there was something incomprehensible about an army—dangerous currents, like the wild rips off Ushant: forever letting fools and incompetents come safe to port, while shattering the best and bravest men on the rocks of jealousy and suspicion.

"Easton and Brown!" I said to myself. "Easton, Brown, Bedel and Hazen! God help Nathaniel!"

. . . Beyond the tent I heard a rasping voice. It was Arnold, on his way from the barracks to the shore with Wilkinson and a strange captain. He stopped and faced the latter. "Waste no time!" he cried, wagging a finger in the captain's face. "Start your camp today! Chop foundation logs! Cut poles and pegs: lay out the logs—here and there and there"—he pointed to the spots.

"Send out your men to shoot anything they can get—deer, bear, raccoons, porcupines, woodchucks, rabbits, crows! I tell you there'll be three thousand on the verge of death with smallpox! You'll have a town of dying men here: a whole damned town! You never saw such a sight in your life; and when you've seen it, you'll hope to God you'll never see it again!"

Wheeling, he limped to the whaleboat. Three soldiers, heavily laden with bundles, plodded after him. As they set down their burdens at the water's edge, I heard a triumphant bellow from Cap Huff. "Beer! Mutton! Cheese! By God, General, this is the kind of a war I *like!*"

By the time I reached the landing to see them off, the whaleboat was already on its way toward Ticonderoga, Tom Bickford at the tiller. Arnold had his field-desk open on his knees, poking among his papers. He seemed to see me out of the back of his head.

"I've been thinking about those row-galleys," he called. "They ought to be pierced for eight guns to a side, and carry eighty men. Give 'em stern and bow ports."

I waved my hand to show I understood. The whaleboat grew small upon the hazy lake, and I had another question to ask myself.

There, moving irrevocably beyond my reach, was the means by which I could have sent Ellen safely on her way to Albany. Why hadn't I asked Arnold to take her with him? Again I wasn't sure of the answer.

. . . "Row-galleys to carry eighty men!" Nathaniel exclaimed when I returned to the tent. "I heard what he called out to you. What is it he aims to do?"

It came to my mind, suddenly, how I could make sure of pressing Nathaniel's nose against the grindstone and keeping it there. "If we can build the proper ships, and build 'em quick enough," I said, "it wouldn't surprise me at all if Arnold went back and took St. John's."

"St. John's?" Nathaniel asked. He swallowed. "St. John's! How quick would we have to build 'em?"

"How quick *could* we build 'em? How quick could we build lateen-rigged row-galleys like those we saw in the Tagus on our voyage to Lisbon?"

Nathaniel turned and looked into the north, along the pale blue lake. "With any kind of carpenters," he said, "I'll bet it wouldn't take a month to build enough row-galleys to knock St. John's into a hoorah's nest!"

I went through the tent to where Ellen Phipps still sat, busy with her knitting. This, I felt, was the proper time to find out what I wanted to know: whether her trip to Three Rivers, just after Sullivan reached St. John's, had been due to her own wishes, or whether she had been sent by Marie de Sabrevois. If the latter was the case, then she—innocently, I was sure—had been the bearer of intelligence concerning the arrival of the new American regiments. At Three Rivers, I knew, she had stayed at a convent; so if she had unwittingly carried a message from her aunt, the mother superior would have passed the word along, just as Montgolfier disseminated information from the Seminary of St. Sulpice in Montreal.

While I stood looking down at Ellen's chestnut curls, wondering how to begin, she said tranquilly: "I've been thinking, and I'd like to tell you what I think, because I don't wish to think mistakenly. See if I'm right: From the time I first met you, you have now and then had a few thoughts about me, haven't you? Were they kind ones?"

"Kind?" I said stupidly. "Yes, but that's not the right word"; and then, forgetting all about putting questions to her concerning Three Rivers, I blurted out, to my own surprise, "Ellen, why did you blush when your aunt asked you, at the château, if you liked Nathaniel?"

She blushed again. "Did I? It may be. I think perhaps my aunt was teasing, because she knew I liked Nathaniel, but liked you better. Or no—I'm not sure she was teasing: perhaps she wanted you to think I liked Nathaniel, so that you'd stay away from me. I think she understands that you have a dislike for her, just as well as she understands that I haven't one for you."

"You think she wanted to keep me away from you—and from her, too, perhaps?"

"I think it might be," Ellen said gravely. "I think perhaps she's right. And this has something to do with what I've just told you I've been thinking. You've said you had kind thoughts of me. That means you like me, doesn't it?"

"Like—like you?" I was caught aback by her question. Out of the ocean of affection that struggled for utterance within me I was able to bring only one other word, "Yes!"

She nodded. "Yes, I was almost sure your thoughts of me were kind. Now I wish to tell you something else. The first time you came to the Château de St. Auge and sat beside me on the floor to speak about your sister, I noticed you thought about other things beside yourself. You thought about your brother, and about me. The questions you asked— they touched me. I thought for a time you wished to make talk; but no! For my sake, you wished to hear about my brother—about my mother. You were eager, even, to know about them. I found this very unusual— and pleasant to think about afterward. It set me to thinking about you; and I've thought about you often ever since. You see, I'm trying to make you understand something."

"Yes," I said, my heart quickening. "Yes, I want to understand."

She frowned, and her earnestness increased.

"Well, then; I must tell you one thing more before I come to the point. I am very slow-minded. At first when a thing is said or something happens, I seldom seem to understand it; but after a little while, if I *do* think hard, then it seems to me that I *do* understand it. Something like that has been happening now. I have been thinking over many things you have said, and I'm afraid I'm beginning to understand them."

"Afraid? Afraid you'll understand what?"

She drew a deep breath. "I'm afraid I understand your feeling toward a person who is everything to me, and to whom I owe a great loyalty. I love her very dearly." She laid aside her knitting and clasped her hands tightly.

"I could never wish anybody to like me or have kind thoughts of me who had—had ugly thoughts of her. No, and I could not like anybody myself who had an ill feeling for her, or suspicions; who—asked ugly questions about her."

"Ugly questions?" I said heavily, for I knew what she meant. "You heard me asking ugly questions?"

She nodded sadly in affirmation. I saw a glimmering beneath her downcast thick lashes. She turned away her head; and when she spoke I could just hear her voice. "If suspicion smirches her, it stains me too. That is how I would wish it. Do you think I would be less loyal to her than to wish it?"

I could only protest clumsily. "Suspicion? Ellen, I'd as soon have suspicion of my mother as of you. I admit I've had—some strange thoughts—I hope they're wrong ones—maybe they are; but they're never strange when they're of you."

"Ah," she murmured, "they're only strange when they're about one I love!" She kept her face averted and sighed shiveringly.

When I caught at her hand, she turned reproachful eyes upon me.

"No," she said, "I am able to use my mind, though perhaps you think women can't. At the convent we were taught to think: you mightn't believe it. We were taught the logic of Plato, the logic of Bacon; and I've learned to use my powers of reason a little. You have no kind feeling for Mademoiselle de Sabrevois; you must have none for me! You think she is wicked; so must you think me wicked! That is how I feel when I love people; I share whatever comes to them."

"Ellen——"

"No, no!" she said hurriedly. "You and I can't be friends! You mustn't like me—I don't want you to!"

Upon that she went quickly into the tent, and let the flap of canvas fall behind her.

I could only stand there, feeling like a beggar-child who has forgotten his cold and his rags while he looks through a window at a brilliant Christmas tree, and then is shut out from that fairyland brightness by the closing of a curtain across the pane.

XXV

In the next few days the narrow strip of water in front of our camp at Crown Point was the clogged throat of a double-ended funnel, one end in Canada and the other end open to Albany and the whole New England coast. Everything under God's heaven seemed to be pouring into both ends, overwhelming us with a deluge of smallpox patients, commissioners, committees, curiosity seekers, orders, counter-orders, starved and half-naked troops, scanty supplies, wild rumors, heat, thunderstorms and frenzy.

Tom Bickford and the crew that had taken Arnold to Albany returned; and Tom, in great haste, stopped long enough before departing northward to toss me a written message from Arnold. Tom was carrying orders back to Sullivan from Schuyler to abandon Isle aux Noix and come south to Crown Point. He had no time, even, to eat. His craft was a wooden canoe with two masts and two lug sails, queer-looking because Tom kept Cap Huff perched on the windward gunwale to hold her upright; and long after he was gone we could hear Cap bawling to Tom to ease her off and give his breeches a chance to dry.

To Captain Peter Merrill at Crown Point [the message read]. *Get the ship timbers to the southern tip of the lake at once. You will find a sawmill at Skenesboro, and can start getting out more timbers with no loss of time. We have sent to New England for ship carpenters, who are hard to come by on acct. of so many privateers building. I have sent an express to Steven Nason's wife to help us get a few men from your part of Maine. Lay down keels for ten row-galleys. If we can get enough men we will build a 38-gun ship, a frigate, and kick up a dust with her. As everything depends on speed, you will not let any grass grow under your feet.*

B. Arnold, Brig. Gen.

. . . I thought we'd never get a vessel to transport our timbers; for whatever would float was in use on business that would allow of no interference. Every empty craft was hurrying north to salvage Sullivan's army before it was gobbled up by the British. They straggled past, day and night: bateaux, canoes, longboats, even whaleboats that had been dragged over to Lake George from the Hudson.

All south-bound boats were loaded with the sick; and with the arrival of the first of them, I had Nathaniel and Zelph strike the tent and move it out of sight and sound of the landing place, so that Ellen might not fall sick herself.

These men had been five days on the journey from Isle aux Noix, five days of broiling sun in a cloudless sky. The bateaux were sieves, hurriedly built to begin with, and therefore badly built. Water stood ankle deep in them, making them hard to row. Because of the scarcity of healthy men, there were only two oarsmen for each bateau—and they had little time for bailing, and less to tend their miserable freight: time for nothing except to push at their heavy oars.

So these bateaux crawled in toward Crown Point, as sick-appearing as the men they carried. They moved as slowly as the hour hand on a chronometer, and there seemed to be no end to them. They crept along the shore, all day long, all through the night, and all the next day as well.

Looking at the shapeless figures that were lifted from those boats, I marveled that life remained in any of them. For five days they had wallowed in bilge-water with nothing to protect them from the sun. Their only food was raw pork and musty flour—the worst of all possible foods for men in their state.

They had no clothes except the rags in which they lay; and these, unwashed and unchanged, were caked to the suppurating pustules that covered them, from head to foot, like dreadful swollen coats of mail, so that their slightest moves wrenched at their sores and ripped their flesh.

The Point was filled with the animal howlings of these festering men: their inflamed skins torn as if by red-hot tweezers: blind from the swelling of their faces: their tongues and lips like scorched leather, dark brown and hard, so that coherent speech, even, was denied them.

I spent my days and nights at the landing place, thinking that when the last of the sick had arrived, I might help myself to boats; and I thought those three thousand moaning, half-dead soldiers would never cease coming over that rocky bank, like an army of the damned, flayed and blasted by the devil himself.

It's easy to speak of three thousand sick men, but not so easy to understand the meaning of the words; for three thousand smallpox cases seem like all the sick in the world.

Even when all three thousand were stowed at last in rude shelters at Crown Point, with no medicines to ease them and no nurses to tend them, I was still unable to get boats; for those that brought the sick had instantly pushed off again and headed back north, the weary oarsmen dragging at their sweeps as if their arms had turned to wood and grown to the handles. There was no rest for them while men were still left in the steaming swamps of Isle aux Noix, with nothing to prevent Burgoyne's regiments from hacking them to pieces.

Not until the main army itself had begun to come ashore was I able to get a boat, and that a slow one: a small gundelo, slower even than a bateau. The important thing, however, was that she floated; and once I had my hands on her, I lost no time getting her down to our camp.

I found Ellen on her knees at the lake rim, washing clothes by rubbing them with ashes and slapping them against a rock.

When she looked up and saw me, she slapped the rock even harder. She hadn't forgiven me, I realized, so I turned from her to Nathaniel, who was writing a letter in the shade of the near-by tent. So absorbed was he in his task that my voice startled him into covering his letter with his hand. I overlooked this movement of his, and spoke casually.

"I've got a boat at last, Nathaniel! We'll give her a light load; and you and Ellen and Zelph can be on your way to Skenesboro in an hour. You and Zelph can row and Ellen can steer."

Ellen stopped her washing. "I think you forget," she said coldly. "I'm waiting for a chance to go to Albany. Your brother has been trying to arrange that for me."

I shook my head. "He hasn't succeeded, Ellen. Country that's the very heart of a war campaign doesn't offer many chances for a young girl to travel safely. My brother and I are responsible for your——"

"You?" she interrupted. "No—only your brother. You have no responsibility for my safety, and I ask you not to concern yourself with it."

"I do, though," I said. "What's more, Nathaniel knows, just as I do, that it's folly for you to talk of going to Albany until either he or I can take you, or we can put you in charge of someone we know as well as we know ourselves. Until that happens, you'll have to stay with us, and we're going to Skenesboro, so you'll have to go there too."

"Skenesboro?" she repeated, and her expression became haughty. "I shall not go to any such place!"

"Why not? What do you know about Skenesboro?"

"Nothing. I never heard of it, but I'm glad you're going there, because I'm going to stay here. Do you understand I'm going to stay here?"

I tried gentleness. "I thought you were going to Albany."

"Yes, certainly, in a little while; but first I'm going to stay here as long as I think proper."

Nathaniel folded his letter and spoke impatiently. "You may as well

let her alone; I've found you can't argue with her. The truth is that since
you came here, she's harder to get along with than ever. She wants to be
rid of both of us and free of our care of her."

"Is that true?" I asked Ellen. "Is Nathaniel right?"

She bent to her washing again, humming a tune, as if alone at the
water's edge. I looked helplessly at Nathaniel.

"Didn't I tell you?" he asked. "She thinks her brother Joseph can
work wonders and she's depending on him to help her. That's what's
in her mind. He's one of the few St. Francis Indians that's favored the
American cause since the beginning; and she's sure he'll turn up here
before long with some part of the army. So she intends to stay here, on
the ground that a sister's got a right to wait for her brother and to join
him, and you'll waste your breath trying to get her to go to Skenesboro
—or anywhere else we go, for that matter."

I turned to Ellen. "Is it true you're staying here just to get rid of us?"
But she continued to hum and to wash clothes without paying any attention to me.

"All right, then," I said. "We'll use force."

At that her humming stopped and she looked at me open-eyed and
open-mouthed.

"How?" she asked. "How would you use force?"

"With a rope," I said. "Two ropes, it might be: one for the ankles
and the other for the elbows."

She stared at me incredulously; then color rushed to her cheeks, her
eyes flashed, and she whispered huskily the one word "Shame!"

"Yes," I said. "It would be a shame indeed for a woman who's joined
an army to be so insubordinate that she'd need to be tied elbow and
ankle and put into a boat because she wouldn't take orders."

"Orders!" she cried, and jumped up to face me. "From whom?"

"From me," I told her. "You haven't noticed it, but I'm an officer on
special duty, and I'm empowered to press unattached persons into the
service in order to perform a special military duty assigned to me. I'm
sorry, but now that you've come into the field of operations, you'll have
to do your share. I don't mean I'm so military I have no humanity left
in me. I'll leave word here for your brother, if he comes this way, that
you're at Skenesboro, because that's where you're going to be—and as
soon as we can get our boat there with you and the ship timbers in it."

Her eyes, fixed on mine, had become contemptuous. "I'll not go! You
and your ropes!"

"I'll give you an hour," I said, "to finish your washing. Maybe you
can dry it on the boat."

"Never!"

She meant it, and I think her fury would have lasted, and she would have made a great deal more trouble about leaving if an inspiration hadn't just then come to me. I looked satirical, or at least I tried to, and I think she was too indignant to perceive that it was bad acting.

"I believe I understand," I said. "Nathaniel's told you that I'm not going in this boat myself, but design to send you in it with him, while I stay here to get more boats for the rest of the timbers. Well, you may do as you please; but if you stay because you prefer to be near me, I'll warn you that in spite of my wishing to be as much with you as possible, I'll be busy most of the time and won't have the opportunity."

Her eyes, already wide and round, grew wider and rounder. "Oh," and she made a long-drawn-out syllable of that exclamation. "Oh! I'll go!"

Without another word she began to roll her wet clothes into a ball; and an hour later, when I went with Nathaniel to the boat, there she stood at the water's edge, an angry little figure with a ball of damp clothes in one hand, and a packet of dry ones in the other.

*   *   *

. . . I said good-bye to her in a gentle voice and received not even a nod in return. She kept her back to me as she got into the boat, and I never saw another human back so eloquent. I would not have believed that merely a back could express all that dislike, all that scorn, and the clear conviction that behind it there stood an insignificant creature so puffed with egregious vanity that the rebuke now being administered to him would probably not improve him.

I watched the boat move off toward Ticonderoga and South Bay, and I foolishly hoped that maybe—just once—before it passed from my sight, Ellen would turn and look back. But she didn't; and so, after a time, I sighed and set off toward the landing.

I went a little out of my way; in fact, I went to the very spot where Ellen, busy with her knitting, had sat when I had come back with Arnold from Isle aux Noix. The place was pleasant then, I had thought, with its tall elms, and the distant pines marching up the swelling hills behind us; but now it seemed cheerless and somber; colorless and dusty. There was nothing pleasant about it. It was a terrible hole.

. . . I had help in sending the rest of the timbers to Skenesboro.

That evening while I stood at the landing, keeping an eye on the bateaux that still pulled slowly in, laden with the last of the soldiers from Isle aux Noix, I heard, far out in the silvery haze, a hoarse voice bawling words in the French tongue. Harmonizing with it was a sweeter, thinner voice that I recognized as Verrieul's.

"*Trois beaux canards s'en vont baignant*," Verrieul sang softly, whereupon Cap let go with the bellowing chorus,

> "*Rouli, roulong, ma boule roulong,*
> *On roulong ma boule roulong,*
> *On roulong ma boule!*"

I suspected that Cap's journeyings with Verrieul, who was a gay and likable youth, had caused him to affect a French manner; and my suspicions became a certainty when I heard him bellow: "You tend to the eels, Doc! I'll take the keg, and we'll have supper *toot sweet!*"

. . . I went to the water's edge and watched two canoes slide out of the twilight mist.

They were half-canoes: passenger canoes, that is to say, probably from St. Francis—a size larger than a light canoe, but a size smaller than a North canoe, so that they can be easily handled by two men, and yet be used without hesitation on deep water. In the first one were Tom Bickford, Verrieul and Doc Means.

The second, I thought, held strangers and a pile of baggage, but I soon saw that what I had mistaken for baggage was Cap Huff, holding a keg in his lap. On recognizing Cap, I looked more closely at the others and realized that the painted Indian who also sat in the bottom of the canoe was not an Indian at all, but Steven Nason, and I suspected that the red man who paddled stern was Natanis.

I couldn't recognize the young man who was paddling bow. He was dignified and handsome; but his appearance was marred, to my way of thinking, by what he wore. He had on a large beaver hat, sadly in need of brushing, and a green coat, full skirted and elegantly cut, but narrow in the shoulders, so that it hiked up around his ears with each upswing of his arms. Under the coat was a flowered waistcoat of pink brocade with glass buttons. In spite of all this finery he wore next to nothing beneath the coat and waistcoat—no shirt: no breeches: no stockings: only a handsome pair of moccasins ornamented with scarlet porcupine quills. Thus he seemed more undressed than a newly born baby.

When I held the canoes to keep them from scraping, Cap monopolized the conversation. "What's the news?" he roared. "What's going on here?"

Knowing he was more interested in food than anything else, I told him it looked as though the pigeons might arrive soon: scattered birds had been seen flying across the lake, and someone thought he had seen a flock above the sky-line of Ticonderoga, though he might have seen smoke and imagined it to be pigeons.

"Hell," Cap said, "we ain't blind! Joe Phipps"—Cap jerked his head toward the young man in the green coat—"he saw a flock three miles long this afternoon going north over the Winooski. That ain't what I'm talking about. Where's Arnold, and when's your brother going to get married?"

So the half-clad young man was Ellen's brother Joseph! He had jumped ashore and squatted on the shingle, holding the canoe in place, his brilliant green coat and brocaded waistcoat clutched up around his middle to keep them dry. Now that Cap had spoken his name, I could see in him a likeness to Ellen, though his garb made the resemblance seem grotesque. His eyes were a velvety brown, with a golden spark in them, and though his mouth was set in a line which he doubtless considered grim and stoical, there was a pleasant softness about the corners of his lips.

He returned my stare calmly enough, and when I nodded to him, he smiled and said something I knew must be in an Indian tongue.

"Nice clothing he's got on, ain't it!" Cap said patronizingly. "Up in St. Francis, that's the big *à la mode* for attending routs and drums consisting of eel-spearings!"

"Don't laugh!" Steven Nason said quickly. He looked coldly at Cap. "If you've got any remarks to make about friendly Indians, no matter whether they're white or red, go off into the woods and talk to yourself. Don't make 'em where anybody else can hear! We're trying to keep this boy's friends neutral, so we won't have to fight them as well as the Mohawks—so they won't use their carving knives on top of you to help you not to have such a thick head!"

"He don't speak educated English!" Cap protested. "He ain't at home in the language, the way I am."

"He doesn't have to speak English—not to understand what *you're* talking about!" Nason said. "This boy can read a moose-track and tell you the size of its horns, and what it had for dinner last Tuesday. 'Tisn't likely he'd have any trouble reading a face like yours, is it?"

"Like mine?" Cap said wonderingly. With a puzzled air he passed his hand over his face, looked at his fingers and became slightly offended. He said nothing more, however, but with a dignified air balanced his keg on the gunwale of the canoe and stepped into the water. Unfortunately he stepped into a hole, and disappeared; then emerged to the surface, spouting like a whale and threshing the water with unbelievable energy.

Joseph Phipps slapped his knee and howled with laughter. Cap scrambled into the shallows, rose to his feet, glared contemptuously at all of us; then salvaged his keg and, with it in his arms, climbed the bank and stood before us, dripping indignation.

Nason had preceded him. "They told me you'd been ordered to Skenesboro to start building a fleet," he said to me.

"I couldn't get a boat till today," I said. "That's what I'm doing here: waiting for more boats, so I can send off the rest of the timbers. They're hard to get. Nobody wants to let go of a boat for fear of needing it to escape from the British." I fished in my pocket and handed him Arnold's letter. "Here; this'll interest you."

He set down his pack to read it. When he gave it back to me, he turned to Cap, who had dropped his keg on the ship's timbers and was picking at the bung with a knife. "Phoebe's coming to Skenesboro!" Nason told him. "We'll go there ourselves first thing in the morning, and these timbers ought to go by boat at the same time. Boats are scarce, and I want you to pick up a few—borrow 'em, maybe—so be careful with that rum."

Cap Huff eyed us indulgently. "Careful? What would I be careful for? It ain't the careful people that do the best borrowing. The harder a thing is to borrow, the carelesser you want to be about it." He whacked the keg with a club to loosen the bung.

"Arnold doesn't say your wife's coming to Skenesboro," I reminded Nason. "He only says he wrote to her to drum up some men."

He nodded. "I know. I know her, too. She'll pick up the carpenters and then go with 'em to make sure they get here."

Joseph started a fire: the others made camp: Doc Means took a dozen eels from the canoe, scoured each one with a handful of ashes, chopped them into five-inch sections, skewered them on ramrods and hung them before the fire—and then we had a piece of luck. There was a scrabbling and clappering in the elms behind us, as though a whirlwind had struck them.

Cap Huff pounded on his keg. "Pigeons!" he bawled. "Pie! Pigeon pie! Pigeon soup! Get your guns!"

The western sky was alive with pigeons, millions of them: an endless cloud, hovering and whirling as wet snow-flakes swirl in a gust of wind. They fluttered into the elms by the thousands, as if sucked into insatiable maws. From the trees came crashings, as branches, overloaded by the weight of pigeons, broke and fell. At such times billowing clouds of birds puffed from the foliage, only to vanish again among the leaves. There seemed to be no limit to the numbers the trees would hold.

Thus our wretched fare of sour beef and moldly flour was ended at last; for when pigeons of this sort arrive at a given spot, the flight always lasts three weeks, and with proper equipment a sufficient number can be killed to feed an army twice the size of ours. In this very spot, one year later, a British army of eight thousand men lived three full days on nothing but pigeons.

"Pigeons! Pigeon soup!" Cap went on bawling; but Nason had other ideas.

"Stop your noise!" he told Cap. "There's more than pigeons in those trees! Before we get through, we might get a boat or two out of 'em if we're still as smart traders as we used to be before we went to war." To those of us who had run for our muskets he said, "Let those guns alone. What we need now is ladders: not guns. A pair of ladders! Give your guns to Cap'n Peter, and everybody else help with the ladders." He took the men away, all but Cap, who worked hard at his rum keg and philosophized: "Stevie always claimed bad luck couldn't last forever, and maybe he's right! First I found this keg of rum, and now these pigeons come along! It kind of looks as if something favorable might happen."

"Where in God's name did you ever find a keg of rum?" I asked.

"Eel Ox Nox," Cap said.

The bung came out noisily, spattering him. He cupped his hands around the bung-hole and inhaled ecstatically. "That's English rum," he announced. "There ain't as much bite to it as to good Medford rum, but there ain't no question about it being rum. Verrieul and me, we deserted to the British up at Eel Ox Nox, and I picked up this rum. They have it lying around everywhere, the British do. Verrieul, he heard at Three Rivers that they brought a hundred and twenty-five thousand gallons over from England with 'em, in case some general got faint on the march to Albany."

"You deserted!" I said. "You're here, so you couldn't have deserted!"

"Certainly we deserted!" Cap said. "There wasn't a drop of rum at Eel Ox Nox; not a drop! So when Verrieul spoke about the hundred and twenty-five thousand gallons, I said I'd row over and see about it, and Verrieul said he'd come too; so he did, and there was the rum, just as he said."

I thought he was making game of me. "So you made a social call on the British! No doubt you found them happy to see you, and in good spirits."

Cap nodded. "Fine! That's a fine army! They got fine clothes and fine muskets and fine rum. Fine-looking men, too. Terrible thick in the head, they are; but fine! We hollered at 'em, and they come out, and we says we wanted to be on King George's side in all these troubles, whatever they was, and they said we was nice men, and that's the only time when they showed any sense at all; because everything else they said was stupid.

"Right away they gave us a drink of rum and asked us what was happening on Eel Ox Nox; and we told 'em we was the President and Secretary of the Eel Ox Nox Club, composed of the smartest officers in the whole damned army, and if we could show a keg of rum to the other members, they'd all desert, maybe.

"Maybe the whole army'd follow our example and desert, Verrieul told 'em. He said the Americans thought all the rum in the world had been drunk up, and when they learned different, it would be easy for influential people such as those in the Eel Ox Nox Club to persuade their acquaintances to like King George again, and want to be on his side too. That feller Verrieul, he's quite a feller! Fine face he's got! Innocent! No matter what he tells you, you believe it."

"The Eel Ox Nox Club!" I exclaimed. "You're not serious!"

"Why ain't I?" Cap demanded. "I hope to die if I ain't! Me and Verrieul decided we'd have a club for people like those up at Eel Ox Nox, who'd stood as much as they could from politicians. What we wanted, Verrieul said, was a political club without any politicians in it."

When I expressed disbelief, Cap became eager. "Let me tell you about this club. If a feller's in politics, and wants to stay there, he's got to spend all his time making promises he don't ever intend to keep, and doing damned fool things just so's to get some damned fool's vote, ain't he?"

I admitted that this seemed to be the case.

"For sure it does!" Cap said. "Well, me and Verrieul, we don't neither of us want to be politicians, but we want a club that'll kind of encourage us to act like politicians in special cases—p'tickly towards those that need to be acted that way towards.

"Verrieul says it's kind of a public duty to act like a politician once in a while—towards the English, say, and towards Indians and York troops, and towards other politicians. One of the good features of a club like that, Verrieul says, is that we can raise money the way politicians raise it, and then spend it on ourselves the way politicians do. Then it ain't stealing."

"That's one way of looking at it," I admitted.

"Oh," Cap said, "that Verrieul, he certainly is an educated feller. When I hear what he thinks up, it kind of makes me sorry I didn't go to Dartmouth College myself. He made up a motter for the Eel Ox Nox Club. It goes 'Nulla die sine something or other.'"

"What's it mean?"

"Mean? Well, as near as I can remember, it means 'Don't never tell an Englishman the truth because he'd get it wrong anyway.'"

He seemed to consider the matter closed, for he tilted the keg with a view to drinking from the bung, but desisted, choking, when a cupful ran down his neck.

"Well?" I said.

"Well what?" Cap asked.

"What happened at Eel Ox Nox?"

"Oh," Cap said, "the British, they talked over letting us take a couple kegs back to show the Eel Ox Nox Club and get 'em fond of King George again; but that night when Verrieul and I come away, there was only this one around loose, and Verrieul said if we asked 'em for the other, they might notice we was leaving. So they still got about a hundred and twenty-four thousand, nine hundred and seventy-five gallons left, if I ain't weak on arithmetic—and if they're still saving it for that general in case he contracts the vapors.

"When we got back to Eol Ox Nox, Verrieul and me talked it over, and he said what's the use electing anybody to the club just now, or being a tempter in any other way; and I says yes; and besides, I says, what's the use us tempting anybody that could get his own as easy as we got ours, I says.

"That's the way it come about we didn't make no distribution excepting just a little now and then between I and Verrieul when it got to be necessary. Practically, we ain't more than smacked the taste of it, because it's more than half full right yet."

He turned from me to address Doc Means. "What you say, Doc? You got medical brains; but you wouldn't hold with rum being harmful on the innards, would you?"

Doc examined the keg with watery blue eyes. "Plain rum?" he asked. "Just plain rum?"

Cap looked worried. "There ain't no other kind, is there?"

"What I mean," Doc said, "is I wouldn't recommend rum, not unless it was took as a remedy. Maybe you noticed, when we walked up from the landing, that there was some Melancholy Thistles growing alongside the path. How'd you like to make an infusion of those thistles, and mix the rum with it and have it for supper: not hot, but just about blood heat?"

"Thistles!" Cap expostulated. "Melancholy Thistles! Who ever heard of Melancholy Thistles! Any time anybody speaks about drinking rum, you always have to talk about mixing it with something! What's the matter with drinking just plain rum? What'd be the good of mixing it with Melancholy Thistles, even if there was any such thing?"

"I'll tell you what would be the good," Doc said. "Those that know about herbs say there ain't any herb much more important than Melancholy Thistles. I ain't tried 'em, but it appears to me this would be a good time to experiment with 'em. They say there ain't anything in the world so good for curing melancholy. That's why they're called Melancholy Thistles."

"Are they in the book?" Cap asked.

"Certainly they're in the book!" Doc fumbled in his canvas smock, brought out his Culpeper's Herbal and removed it from its protecting stocking leg. "Here!" he said. "Here it is!" He read in a quavering voice: "'Melancholy Thistle . . . grows in moist meadows . . . flowers in July . . . under Capricorn, and therefore under both Saturn and Mars. Saturn rids Melancholy by sympathy, Mars by antipathy!'"

"Wait a minute," Cap said, and rubbed his head. "What's all that about Slatterns?"

"Saturn!" Doc said sternly. "Saturn!"

"Oh," Cap said, disappointed. "I thought it was going to be something interesting right there. Go on."

Doc resumed his reading. "'The decoction of the thistle being drank in wine, expels superfluous melancholy out of the body, and makes a man as merry as a cricket. Superfluous melancholy causeth care, fear, sadness, despair, envy and many evils more besides; and seven years' care and fear makes a man never the wiser nor a farthing richer.'"

"I ain't got any Saturns or Mars's or superfulous melancholic or none of those articles you was reading about," Cap protested.

Doc seemed surprised. "You ain't? How do you know you ain't? Maybe you just ain't had enough trials to bring out your melancholy."

Cap's reply was thoughtful. "No, maybe I ain't. Maybe if we had a little real hard luck, I might catch superfulous melancholic." He seemed to toy with the thought. "I dunno: maybe I got just a touch of melancholic right now, seeing as how you insist on it so hard. Do you suppose if I put a piece of this thistle in the keg, it would work right on a man, no matter whether he had superfulous melancholic under Mars or not? Do you suppose 'twould make him merry as a cricket if he had just a light case of melancholic?"

"It stands to reason it would!" Doc said. "If the book's right, the less melancholy a man had in him, the merrier he'd get."

Cap gave the keg a resounding slap. "Get a mess of thistles and put 'em on to boil! We'll soon find out whether the book's right or not!"

Doc chopped tall thistles and set them to steep in his camp kettle. Nason and the others returned, each one dragging a slender pine from which all the branches, with the exception of a single row of butts protruding two feet from each trunk, had been trimmed. Thus the pines had the look of enormous combs.

We lashed these together in pairs, the butts of the branches mingled, so that we had two long ladders with irregular-spaced rungs. These we took to the pigeon-filled elms and stood against the trunks.

By now it was almost dark, and the trees were impenetrable silhouettes overhead; but when we loaded two muskets with small shot and fired into those black shadows, they seemed to explode above us. A million pigeons, disturbed by the noise and the shot, flapped blunderingly about, struggling for new resting places. Out of each tree tumbled twenty or thirty birds, dead or wounded—not nearly enough, considering that those who needed them were numbered in thousands.

But when the birds went back into the trees, they lit on the ladder rungs in such quantities that the timbers sagged. Reloading our muskets, we pointed them to rake the ladders. Then when we fired, a torrent of pigeons cascaded down to thump and flop beneath the trees. By the time the cripples had been knocked on the head and thrown in a heap, the ladders were again covered with those stupid, fat, long-tailed birds, all of them near bursting from the berries they had eaten.

To slaughter them in such numbers seemed sinful at first; then it got to be like knocking apples from a tree. There was no way of telling, when we stopped for lack of small shot, how many birds there were in the four piles at the foot of the elms; but they were mounded shoulder high, and any one of the piles would have filled a good-sized farm cart. A steadily increasing crowd of officers and men had come over from the camp, to see what we were up to. They stood around us in a half circle, their eyes glittering in the light of the fire we had kindled to make sure of finding all the birds; and from their looks, none of them had eaten a square meal in months.

One of the officers, a tall, thin, simple-looking lieutenant, came to Nason. "Name of Whitcomb," he said, "attached to Burrell's Connecticut regiment. Was you planning to eat all those yourself? If not, I got a few men could use some." He coughed and added, "I guess we all could."

"I guess so," Nason said. "That's what we've been shooting 'em for." He stared calculatingly at Whitcomb—at his broad shoulders, his light brown hair, his leather breeches, his long blue vest with capacious flask pockets. It was as if, almost, he had asked a silent question of Whitcomb and received an equally silent answer that more than satisfied him, for he added, "Tell somebody to build twenty of these ladders tomorrow. Then everybody can live on pigeon stew. In case you don't know it, the best way to eat 'em is to cook 'em with beans."

"Beans?" Whitcomb asked. He was as harmless and benevolent-looking as could be, and as innocent-appearing as though he scarcely knew what was being said to him; but if ever there was a dare-devil, it was Whitcomb. We didn't know it at the time, however; and from the way he said "Beans?" we thought he must have come from a family that had religious scruples about eating them.

"Plain white beans," Nason told him. "You put a quart of beans in a kettle with some water and the breasts of a dozen pigeons and a little salt pork and an onion, and put another kettle over it, and bury the whole business under a fire all night. Then you got something."

Lieutenant Whitcomb swallowed. "So I've heard tell. It must be nice if you got the beans."

"Well," Nason said, "maybe we could find you some beans, even. What you better do now is have your men get a few old sails: then they can drag these pigeons to camp in three or four trips."

The lieutenant stared. "All of 'em? We can have all of 'em?" The half circle of human scarecrows scattered into the darkness, running.

"Yes," Nason said, "you can have all of 'em if you'll do a little something for us in return—if you'll find us some barges, so we can load those timbers and get 'em to Skenesboro tomorrow for General Arnold."

When Whitcomb was silent, Nason added, "All these men here, they're scouts for Arnold. It's all regular and above board, only if we wait to get boats through ordinary channels, we may lose a week."

Whitcomb turned to look at the piles of lumber, which showed clearly in the light of the fire beside which sat Cap Huff and Doc Means, taking alternate sips from a tin dipper. "Barges?" Whitcomb asked. "You want to get those timbers to Skenesboro on barges?"

Longboats, I reminded Nason, would do as well.

Whitcomb nodded. "I'll get 'em for you. When things get a little quieter, I know where I can pick up all the boats you need." Hopefully he added, "I aim to be a scout myself. I aim to scout around and get me one of those German soldiers—the kind that's all weighted down with cutlery so's he can only march two miles an hour." He looked so helpless that we felt sorry for him.

We took him to our fire, where Cap Huff and Doc Means, in a singular silence, removed the ramrods from over the coals and set our supper before us. The eels were juicy, having been cooked slowly, as should always be the case.

Nason picked up Cap's tin cup, filled it from the mixture in the kettle and gave it to Whitcomb. Then he filled his own cup, and so did the rest of us.

Cap watched us closely as we drank. "What do you think of *that?*" he demanded.

" 'Tisn't bad," Nason said. "What's in it?"

"Thittles," Cap told him. He hiccupped and tried again. "Thithlsh." He dismissed the matter with an airy wave of his huge hand. "Now look here, Stevie, wha's use going to Skenesboro? Doc'n I been talking, 'n' here's what we think. Le's g'w'up to Eel Ox Nox tonight, juss us, 'n' have a meeting of the Eel Ox Nox Club. Doc, he's been elected, and everybody here can be members." He hiccupped, focussing his eyes on Whitcomb. "O' course, we dunno about this frien' of yours, this gellaman here."

Verrieul interrupted Cap's maunderings. "Make him a non-resident member."

"Tha's juss what we'll do!" Cap cried. "Make him a non-resonant member!" To Nason he added enthusiastically: "After we hold our meeting, Stevie, we wouldn't need to build a lot of row-galleys or nothin'. Save lot of work, Stevie, and be great help to Arnold." He leaned back proudly and surveyed us with a triumphant leer.

"I don't follow you," Nason said. "Arnold's orders were——"

"Listen, Stevie!" Cap leaned forward to drop a confidential hand on Nason's shoulder. "I'll 'splain everything to Arnold. Arnold don't listen to many men, but one of the things people look up to me for is how I talk to him. 'Listen, Arnold,' I say, because I'm an outspoken man; and he always says, 'What you want?' he says. I never see him yet, I couldn't go right up to him and have him ask me what I wanted. He ast me that once on the trip to Albany, juss on account of the way I was looking at him; and he says if I didn't want nothing, to quit looking at him that way. Thass how I stand with Arnold—juss like that!"

He interlaced the fingers of his two hands: then looked at them interestedly and inquired, "How you unfasten your hands after you get 'em fixed that way? Anyhow, it shows you the friendship between I an' Arnold."

Upon that his hands seemed to separate of themselves; for he looked surprised. "There!" he said. "They've quit! If it's a sign me 'n' Arnold can't agree about this matter, don't worry! Juss disregard his orders, an' le's get back to Eel Ox Nox, where it's all nice, and close enough to the Bri'sh to borrow from 'em. I wouldn't ask for more obliging neighbors than them Bri'sh when you want something."

A fresh thought seemed to strike him. "Stevie," he said thickly, "all we'll do is g'w'up to Eel Ox Nox, and then us club members'll cross over to the Bri'sh and steal us some of their gerranals——"

"How's that?" Nason asked. "Steal their what?"

"Some of their gerranals," Cap said, frowning. "We could tell the Bri'sh we juss wanted to borrow 'em. We could steal Gerranal Burgloyd and dress nice afterward, because he's got fourteen suits of clothes they're carrying through the woods for him, along with what goes with 'em. Some of their other gerranals only got six or seven suits of clothes, and only use two or three soldiers apiece to carry 'em. But le's don't hurt feelings by juss borrerin' Gerranal Burgloyd—Burgoyle—alone. Le's borrer *all* their gerranals."

Doc Means looked troubled and cupped a hand about an ear. "I never heard the term. What are these articles you're talking about? Did you say journals?"

"Whyn't you listen to what I say?" Cap shouted angrily. "I said 'gerranals'! A gerranal's a man among the Bri'sh with fourteen carts full of suits of clothes and hats, and four wagonloads of champagne and napkins, and two bottles of ink to write home to King George about what disgusts him. If we steal enough gerranals, Arnold wouldn't worry about boats, would he? Because the Bri'sh wouldn't have nobody left to carry nothing for, and they'd go home."

He turned politely to Whitcomb. "You 'quainted with Gerranal Arnold? Greatest man ever was!"

Whitcomb stared gloomily into his empty cup. "Not personally. We all heard how he stole the communion cups out of the church up in Montreal."

Cap shook his head as if an insect buzzed about his ear: then, focussing a hard eye on Whitcomb, made as if to struggle to his feet. Nason pushed him back again and looked carefully at Whitcomb.

"Lemme up!" Cap said thickly. "I'll show him who stole any commulion cups! I'll commulion cup *him!*"

Nason snapped his fingers in Cap's face. "You'll fight the British and no one else: no one else! Understand?" He turned to Doc Means. "What was put in that rum? There was something in it!"

"Thils," Doc Means said, indistinctly. " 'S cure for splerfrus menkolly. 'S like all these urrer doctors' cures—don't cure nurrin'! Lotta splerfrus liars, 's what doctors are!"

Nason reached for the kettle and spilled its contents on the ground. "That's the place for it, whatever it is!"

To Whitcomb he said quietly: "Now here! That's not the first time we've heard the story about Arnold stealing things from Montreal. Where's it come from: that's what we want to know!"

"You think it isn't true?"

"We *know* it isn't! What we don't know is how any such stories came to sift all through the army! Who started them, and why? My God, it couldn't have been any of his men in Montreal! They knew better, every damned one of 'em!"

"I guess there's no call for profanity," Whitcomb said coldly. "I'm only telling you what I heard."

"Listen!" Nason said. "If we ever lose Arnold out of this army, you'll find plenty of cause for profanity! You say you aim to be a scout; but when I ask you where you got your stories about Arnold, all you can do is tell me there's no cause for profanity. A hell of a scout, *you'd* make. If somebody sent you to scout for Indians, you'd probably come back with a hoorah's nest."

Cap Huff hiccupped. "Took the words right out of my mouth, Stevie! Feller like that, he'll prob'ly resign from the army if somebody tells him all the Bri'sh are bastards!"

"That's enough for you," Nason told Cap. To Whitcomb he said, "I'll take the information I asked for, and I'll take it now."

There was a trace of surprise in Whitcomb's voice. "I guess maybe there's something in what you say. Let's see, now. Most of those stories about Arnold came from folks that got a good deal of sympathy for Colonel Easton and Major Brown. Appears to me I never heard anybody talk so violent about anyone as the colonel and the major did about Arnold when they went through here."

"Where were they going?" Nason asked.

"Near as I could make out," Whitcomb said, "they were going to Congress to complain about Arnold and try to get higher rank."

"Higher rank for Easton!" Cap Huff cried. "What rank's he entitled to? Regimental wet-nurse?"

Whitcomb shrugged his shoulders. "I don't know anything about that. There's a lot of New Hampshire officers been listening to Easton and Brown, on account of the things Arnold's been saying about Bedel and Hazen. They stick together pretty well, the New Hampshire officers do. There's a good many of 'em think we'd get along better if the war could be put in the hands of New Hampshire men, without too much interference from strangers. They're the ones that tell you how Arnold didn't do anything in Montreal except steal. If Arnold ever gets into a court-martial, he'd better make sure there ain't any New Hampshire men on the court."

Nason stared at Whitcomb and Whitcomb contemplated the fire, in which eel bones still burned blue. I pretended to be half asleep; but I was a turmoil inside, wondering and wondering about the letters Ellen had carried from St. John's for Easton and Brown. I dared not speak, for fear I might somehow set Nason on Nathaniel's trail—somehow involve Nathaniel, and Ellen with him, in disaster.

"I don't like it," Nason said. "I don't like any of it! There's something queer in all this. It's like a bad dream—one of those that make you say, 'This happened before.' Ever since Arnold made his first attack on Canada, nearly a year ago, lies about him have poured out of Canada. They poured out of Quebec; and now here they are, pouring out of Montreal!"

"They're scared of him," Cap Huff said. Apparently the effect of the thistled rum was wearing off. "It ain't worth lying about anyone unless you're scared of him."

Whitcomb was thoughtful when he rose, and in his voice was a trace of discomfort. "I better go along with these boys and pick up the boats you need." He slapped the remaining timbers calculatingly.

"That's good," Nason said. "We'll be obliged to you." Then, as if to ease Whitcomb's embarrassment, he added: "If you still want to be a scout, you'd better get leave and come to Skenesboro, where we can say a good word to Arnold for you."

XXVI

Skenesboro, Doc Means said, looked to be afflicted with something halfway between the yellow-jaundice and rigor mortis; and the place caused so much anguish before we were finished with it that Doc's description came to seem high praise.

The southern end of Lake Champlain is a narrow appendix, more like a river than a lake. For twenty miles it holds the center of a pleasant valley; but at Skenesboro a ragged limestone mountain rises abruptly in its path, and the lake, as if overawed, crawls into a rocky ravine and ceases to exist.

The Philip Skene for whom Skenesboro was named was an English army officer who had married a rich wife and been granted thirty thousand acres of land at the tip of the lake, by the King; but because of his loyalty to the English, he and his family had been arrested early in the war and imprisoned in Hartford.

On the lower slope of the mountain, sheltered from north winds, stood Skene's house and barn, built out of yellowish stone that did indeed have a jaundiced appearance. They looked down on the narrow lake-end and on a cove into which the waters of Wood Creek tumbled in a cascade of yellow foam. Wood Creek was more important than its name implied, for there was a sawmill, an iron-foundry and a gristmill at the falls, and the creek itself was the one natural roadway between Skenesboro and the south. Once past its cascade, travelers could row from Skenesboro to Fort Ann; and Fort Ann was halfway to the Hudson. If we received supplies for building ships, they could only reach us by way of Wood Creek. Consequently Wood Creek, to our minds, was the very heart and forefront of Skenesboro.

When, however, we rowed our timber-laden whaleboats into the rocky ravine beneath the limestone mountain, we were appalled. The gristmill and iron-foundry were empty and haggard-looking. Scattered among the trees were cabins in which lived Negroes imported by Skene from the Sugar Islands. Except for Nathaniel and Zelph, who waved us to a landing near the falls, Skenesboro seemed lifeless and hopeless— the last place in the world in which to conjure into existence a fleet for the halting of the British. Yet a fleet must be built, for in no other way could the British be stopped.

I'm often asked why the British should have waited for us to build a fleet: why they didn't row after us in small boats, if they were so determined to pursue us; or why they took the trouble to row at all: why, in short, they didn't march immediately along the shore of the lake and scatter our sick and frightened army like a flock of pigeons. Or why, for that matter, they didn't bring down upon us the splendid fleet we had seen through the haze of Lake St. Peter while we lay on the sandbanks of Sorel.

It's no wonder these things aren't clear to all. Even such military experts as Lord Germain and his advisers saw no reason why their regiments couldn't march from Quebec to New York in a week's time. Consequently it is not astonishing that our situation puzzles those who were neither soldiers nor seamen, with a knowledge of ships and guns and weight of metal.

It's for the sake of those fortunate souls who know nothing of war that I tell here the things which seemed to us so clear and simple, but might never have been seen at all if Arnold had not been there to understand them.

In the first place, most of the British vessels we had seen at Sorel drew too much water to enter the Richelieu. Those small enough to sail up the river were obliged to stop when they reached Chambly rapids; for ships cannot climb rocky hills. They could not even be dragged around the rapids on wheels or sledges; for the British tried it and failed. Therefore if the British wished vessels on Lake Champlain they were obliged to build them, or to carry them over the road in sections, as we had carried the ship timbers from St. John's—a task as arduous, almost, as building them.

But the Americans already had three vessels on the lake: the schooner *Liberty*, taken from Skene by Arnold's men in May a year ago: the sloop *Enterprise*, captured by Arnold in his dash to St. John's the same month; and the stout schooner *Royal Savage* with her twelve brass cannon, captured by Montgomery at St. John's when he took it from the British in the preceding November, on his way to join Arnold at Quebec. They were in bad condition; but they were vessels, and could quickly be made seaworthy by capable ship carpenters. Their guns, moreover, were in place; so if handled by seamen, and the guns manned by proper marksmen, nothing could compete with them except vessels equally well armed. If the British had tried to send an unprotected army down the lake in canoes and bateaux, we could have sailed alongside them in these three vessels of ours and blown them to pieces at our ease and pleasure.

And use the lake the British army must—not only use it, but gain complete control of it before they could send their army south to join Howe and cut the colonies in two.

There were no roads along the lake; and even if there had been roads, the British would never have dared to march men and supplies along them—for one reason because they would have had to protect their line of march from attack, or had the line cut and be left to starve in the wilderness. Such protection would have required the use of all their troops for guard duty, and left none for fighting. For another reason, they would have been obliged to build a hundred and fifty miles of road, from St. John's to Ticonderoga, across swamps and rivers, and through trackless forests. The roads would have had to be stout enough to provide passage for artillery, for the carts carrying wines, uniforms and household equipment for their officers, as well as rum, potatoes and mutton for their soldiers, and to stand up under the burden of their Hessians, each of whom weighed, Cap Huff swore, close to half a ton on the hoof.

If, therefore, the British had attempted any such task, they would have been three years at it, and been eaten by mosquitoes a dozen times.

Consequently there was no way out of it: the British had to use the lake for the transportation of their men and supplies, but they couldn't use it until they controlled it. The only way they could do this was by setting to work at St. John's, building more ships than we could build, and doing it in a hurry, making it possible for their regiments to strike at us late in the summer, hack us to pieces and march down the Hudson to join Howe.

There was no way of knowing how large a fleet the British would build at St. John's; but it would certainly be one that would give us plenty of trouble. They had everything with which to work—timber easily transported from the St. Lawrence; a fleet full of sailors on whom to draw; as many ship carpenters as they wanted from Quebec and Montreal and Three Rivers, as well as from their fleet. They had naval stores ready to hand on the King's ships that had driven us from Sorel, and as many great guns as they wanted, and above all as many naval officers as they needed to command their vessels when built.

. . . We gave no thought to such things when we pulled our whaleboats into the cove of Wood Creek on that hot June afternoon, but were only filled with dry-mouthed wonder as to how to commence our work.

There we were, nine of us, in the whaleboats: Verrieul, Natanis, help-less-looking Doc Means, Cap Huff, Whitcomb, Nason, Tom Bickford and that oddly garbed white Indian Joseph Phipps. On the shore stood Nathaniel and Zelph; and so far as we could see, whatever fleet was built would have to be built by the eleven of us.

Except for the timbers of the one vessel we had brought with us, we had nothing with which to work: nothing, that is to say, except a sawmill without logs, an iron-foundry without iron or workmen, a grist-mill without corn, and space for shipyards without carpenters, unless Nathaniel and Tom Bickford and myself should be counted as carpen-ters, and perhaps Zelph, who had worked a little around ships.

We had no canvas, no nails, no cordage. Barring the hatchets in our belts, we had no tools—no felling axes: no grindstones to keep them sharp: no adzes or hammers. We had no oars, no sailors, no money. And in spite of all that, we pointed out to each other likely locations for stocks—stocks for the vessels that must somehow be constructed out of God knew what.

When my whaleboat slid into the shallows, Nathaniel and Zelph hauled her bow to land. "Zelph's got two axes," Nathaniel said. "He thinks maybe he can find more. A man came over from Albany this morning to say there'd be thirty carpenters here tomorrow. He's up at the barn, finding places for 'em to sleep."

Cap Huff waded ashore, his keg of rum cradled in his arms. "Thirty carpenters?" he asked. "Thirty carpenters from where?"

"From Albany," Nathaniel said.

Cap Huff shook his head ominously. "Yorkers! I better see about get-ting us some place to live: some place where those Yorkers can't steal everything we got!"

He hurried away with his keg of rum, and with him went Natanis and Joe Phipps to hunt food for our suppers; while the rest of us went to work.

By sunset that evening, the timbers we had brought were stacked on either side of a rough staging hacked from the slopes of Wood Creek with Zelph's two axes and our tomahawks, and lashed in place with wattape. We had cut blocks and placed them at the proper height and inclination. On these we had set the keel of the St. John's vessel, erected her stem and sternpost and made six ladders to let us start work on the following morning with no loss of time.

Nathaniel told me enough about Ellen to let me know she was com-fortable in a three-room house on Skene's property, with a farmer and his wife. He might have told me more if I'd pressed him; but this I wouldn't do, for I'd made up my mind that her likes and dislikes were too violent and stubborn for me, and that the less I saw of her, the better off I'd be.

Since I didn't press him, he was full of a strange tale about the Negroes left by Skene on his place: how they seemed to be entirely without brains, knowing nothing and understanding nothing when he had sought their help in finding axes and other tools. Zelph, said Nathaniel, had sat down with a few of them, and played with his dice, and shown them how to play. They had played for hours. Zelph had lost nearly all his money. Then, suddenly and surprisingly, he had won it back, together with two axes which Skene's Negroes had unearthed from beneath their cabin floors.

"I wouldn't be surprised," Nathaniel concluded, "if those black men know more than they pretend to know. I wouldn't wonder but what, if you and Steven Nason went and talked to 'em, we might find they had more than axes hidden away."

It takes a Negro, I knew, to understand a Negro. "Zelph," I said, "if those black men of Skene's have tools, we need 'em. You quit work right now and go to see 'em. I'll give you till tomorrow night to get all their tools. If you don't get 'em, we'll tear down their cabins and dig up the floors."

Zelph fished his dice from his pocket, worked them tenderly in one black paw: then dropped them deftly onto a flattened pink palm. "Nick!" he said. The dice showed a five and two—seven. Zelph laughed in a way that presaged ill for the belongings of Skene's Negroes.

Cap Huff, smelling strongly of rum, peered over Zelph's shoulder. "You can't do that again," he said.

Zelph closed his paw over the dice. "How much you bet I can't?"

"I bet you a million dollars you can't."

"How much real money?" Zelph persisted.

"How much?" Cap asked. "Why, ten dollars Continental."

Zelph shook his head. "Ten dollars Continental ain't worth throwing for." He again dropped the dice into his outspread palm. They showed a six and a one—another seven.

Cap watched Zelph depart, his elbows thrust well out, after the manner of Negroes when they feel important. "By God," he said, "it ain't natural, the way those things act! I'll bet he does something to 'em, and I got to find out what!"

. . . Cap had chosen one of Skene's horse-sheds for our living quarters. He had brought hay from the barn and spread it on the floor, and in one corner he had buried his keg of rum.

The horse-sheds faced the south and were open to that side, the arched openings set off with uprights. Thus they were airy and cool on hot nights; and we could look out at our cook-fire from our bunks, which we built of logs along the sides and back, and filled with balsam tips.

Thanks to the multitudinous thoughts that filled my brain that first night I couldn't be comfortable in my bunk, but turned and fretted, wondering about tallow, spikes, cordage, files, bitts, adzes, seamen, belaying pins, pulleys and a million other things we needed. To think of any one thing we lacked was to think of a dozen other things, all equally unobtainable, and all vital to the building of a vessel.

"What you breathing so hard for?" Cap Huff asked. "One of the reasons I was so anxious to come here was because I thought it would be quiet enough to let me catch up on my sleeping."

"If we had axes and could start getting out timbers," I told him, "we could build gundelos. They're flat-bottomed, so we won't need bolts or half spikes for a week or so; but we'll have to have tools and stores before we can do anything about row-galleys. Two hundred miles those stores must come, from Boston and Salem, maybe, or even New Haven and Providence, over roads not fit to be called roads. Maybe there isn't any way we can get any of the things we need."

"Listen," Cap said, "how long you got to be in the army to find out it ain't no good to worry about getting something? Either you get what you need, or you don't get it. Most generally you don't!"

Nason was more encouraging. "We don't have to do everything ourselves," he said. "Arnold must have written a million letters by now, asking for what we need. He never overlooks anything. He thought of Phoebe, even, and she won't disappoint him. She'll find some way to pry ship carpenters away from privateer builders, and it won't be long before she's here. There's shipyards at Newburgh and Albany; and Schuyler'll make 'em let us have supplies. He's as smart as Arnold, almost. There'll be officers here, just as Cap Huff says, and they'll have to do the worrying. All we'll have to do is work on a vessel."

Somewhat easier in my mind, I stared up into the blackness above me, wondering and wondering how the miracle of a fleet could ever be accomplished here in the heart of a forest, where the scent of tar and seaweed had never penetrated.

. . . A mist still hung over the lake when we went to work the next morning, long before sun-up. Before it had burned off, we had staked out the ways for six gundelos, each to be sixty feet long on a fifty-five-foot keel.

While we staked out the last of them, we heard the shouting of a noisy company on the Wood Creek road. They straggled out of the forest and down to the shore of the lake, all in dusty brown, with wrinkled gray stockings and hickory shirts black beneath the arms and on the back with sweat. Felling axes were made fast to their waists. They carried bundles of tools wrapped in blankets. There were thirty of them; and their leader, a genial, stooped man with no teeth to be seen in his upper jaw save one yellow one, asked who was giving orders. I said quickly that I was. He took my word for it, which he would never have done if he had been a soldier. A soldier would have wanted to know all about it, and by what right I gave orders, and when and where I received my commission; and until satisfied, he would have done nothing whatever, not even though the British had been on the verge of overwhelming us.

By midday we could hear the distant whanking of axes, and by mid-afternoon logs were coming into the sawmill, thanks to the help of four horses Cap Huff had somehow persuaded near-by settlers to lend us. What was more, the sawmill was running, and those of us at the water's edge worked to the rumbling clank of the treadway and the whining rasp of the saw biting into oak.

In a week the quiet serenity that had once brooded over this small backwater had wholly vanished. Bateaux crawled in, both by lake and by creek, bringing a little of this and a little of that. Messengers, gray with fatigue and caked with mud, rode in from the Atlantic coast on lathered horses. To whom they reported, we had no idea. The place seemed to have no head; nor did there seem to be need of giving orders. Every man, in those first days, did one of the thousand things there were to do, and the row of keels on the stocks somehow sprouted ribs and grew a skin of planking.

Seeing that the gundelos were progressing, I took Nathaniel and Tom Bickford from their work and we set up stocks for two row-galleys; for I hoped we soon might have both timber and stores with which to build them.

Commissaries arrived from Ticonderoga, and suddenly there was food to be had from them—real food, such as none of us had seen since we left home—beef, mutton, butter, cheese, greens by the boatload, and best of all, punch and porter to slake the fires that burned within us after our hours of lumber handling, hammering, chopping and pounding in the sultry July heat.

Ship carpenters appeared as though hatched out by birds. While we worked on our gundelo, short-handed, a new worker would appear beside us, sweating and cursing as if he had been there always; and before we could ask him who he was, he would be gone and two others would have come to take his place.

There were fifty carpenters from Connecticut and another fifty from Rhode Island. They had worked on privateers, and were contemptuous of these little vessels on which we toiled: contemptuous of us, too, because we worked for nothing, whereas they had been given fabulous wages to lure them from the building of privateers. Five dollars, hard money, for each day's work, some of them bragged, with a cow apiece to boot, and free food.

It made no difference to me how much the carpenters received, so long as we got carpenters; but Cap Huff felt differently about it. At night, lying in his bunk, he complained bitterly. "Damn it, it ain't reasonable for those people to get five dollars a day, hard money, and us not get nothing but a chance to stop a cannon ball. We ought to take and do something, such-like as raising hell about it."

Nason rebuked him. "Be grateful," he told Cap, "for the blessings you've got. You can't do anything about the wages these carpenters get, so it's no use fretting about it."

Cap kept on grumbling, however; and he spent all his nights with Zelph, playing with Zelph's dice.

In a short time Skene's barn was filled with workmen, who built themselves bunks alongside the walls, and peevishly demanded better quarters. From morning to night the place was a turmoil of hammering and shouting; and in the cool of the evening, when the leaves hung dark and motionless, men brawled and howled and went stumbling down to the lake to splash and thrash in the milk-warm water.

Into the midst of all this there came, finally, a terrible curse—a portly officer with a pot belly, pursed-up lips and a face the color of a crab-apple, a sort of velvety reddish-purple. He came in a whaleboat, rowed by four men; and to see us the better he stood in the bow of the boat, dressed in a blue uniform coat too tight for him, gold swabs on his shoulders like robins' nests built out of tarnished gold thread. His appearance would have been more impressive if he had hidden the pipe that hung from the corner of his mouth—a big-bellied affair the shape of a Canadian stove, and even more smoky. I was unhappy to learn, that night, that this was to be our commander, not only in ship building but in fighting; that he was a Dutchman from Albany who signed his letters "Jacobus Wynkoop, Commander of Lake Champlain."

My unhappiness was greater on the following morning, when he came down to see us, his pipe sending up smoke that smelled of burnt feathers. He was accompanied by a young secretary who looked and acted uncomfortable, and clumsily bumped into and stumbled over almost everything in sight.

What Wynkoop saw seemed to cause him neither enthusiasm nor

disturbance until he reached the stocks for our new galleys. When he saw them, he blinked and sniffed, and shot a question at me that might have been in a foreign tongue for all I understood of it. I was saved from embarrassment by the secretary, who asked the question again in English, saying, "What's this here now?"

I said it was a row-galley, whereupon Wynkoop shook his head decisively and said, "Ve ken't built 'em: ve ken't built row-gellies! Sdob id, und built gundelos!"

"Sir," I said, "General Arnold specifically asked for row-galleys. He asked me to design row-galleys, so he'd have vessels fit for maneuvering."

Wynkoop snorted. "Vat you going to fessen 'em togedder mit? Sdring? Vair's der nels? Vair's der boldts? Vair's der sbyges? Vair's der sells und ricking?"

"Well," I said, "we're bound to get spikes and bolts sooner or later and I figure to get sails on 'em somehow. General Arnold wants row-galleys. He told me——"

Wynkoop snatched his pipe from his mouth and glared at me. "Cheneral Arnolt! I dun't gif a demn for Cheneral Arnolt! He en't der feller dot hess to vite dis vleet! Id's me!" He thumped his chest. "Me! Vite it, chess, und maneuffer it! Id's as issy to maneuffer a gundelo ass a row-gelly. Und ve ken built dree gundelos vile you're drying to built vun of dese demn row-gellies, und nod gedding it built, neider! Zum teufel mit! I vun't heff it! Nudding but gundelos I vun't heff!"

So there was an end of our row-galleys. I wondered where Arnold was, and what he would say when he found I hadn't obeyed his orders to build galleys; but there was nothing to be done about it, for his orders had been superseded by Wynkoop's.

That's one of the unfortunate but inescapable things about an army. Half the orders are given by men incompetent to give orders; but for the sake of maintaining the discipline without which an army is worthless, the orders must be obeyed on pain of public disgrace or even of death.

We went back to work on the vessel whose frame we had brought from St. John's. Here, at least, was something so near finished that not even a Wynkoop would want to stop her. Since she was small, we had given her as much deck space as possible, arranging to rig her as a sloop; and now we pierced her for eight guns. Between the gun-ports we made oar-ports, five ports to a side. Thus in spite of Wynkoop's desire for gundelos, we had one row-galley after all—a sloop row-galley; but a row-galley none the less. Her hull was so near finished that if we could have got oakum, we could have plugged up her seams somehow and tossed her into the lake so to lay down another vessel on her stocks. But having no oakum, we had to leave her as she was and work on her powder-magazine and fo'c'sle, which was like working in a hot corner of hell.

Not content with stopping our attempt to lay down row-galleys, Wynkoop took carpenters from shipbuilding and tree-felling in order to build a fort and barracks for additional ship carpenters and the troops who were expected to arrive to man the fleet. The fort was a stockade that rambled over hill and dale—a stockade so long that a dozen regiments would have been required to man it properly; and the barracks were dark and airless; perfectly designed to bring sickness and discomfort to any so unfortunate as to live in them. Thus, although those of us who were left to work on the vessels did more and more each day, our progress became slower and slower, and our despair over Wynkoop greater and greater.

❀   ❀   ❀

. . . It was not the stifling heat in the fo'c'sle of the unfinished row-galley that made me eager to escape from it and work on a gundelo, where I could be in the open; but the fact that I could no longer keep an eye on the activities of Ellen Phipps.

Each day, since our arrival in Skenesboro, she had descended the hill-slope near Skene's big house, gone around behind the shipyards and come down to the lake, sometimes with her brother Joseph and sometimes alone. Each day she carried a small bundle with her, a bundle that held clothes; and I could see her, at times, kneeling on the shore and scrubbing white garments against a rock, while Joseph sat idly by, fishing. Her every moment held a vital interest for me. My mind was in a perpetual ferment as to what she was doing, and why. I was restless if I couldn't see her, and equally restless if I could. My curiosity extended even to Joseph Phipps and the peculiar garments he wore when with Ellen.

He did her the honor to wear his green coat; but beneath it he wore no shirt, nor did he so much as own a pair of pants. Thus he had the look of being naked—or would have had that look if his skin had not been as brown as a musket-butt from exposure to the sun.

I am, I hope, tolerant of the peculiarities of others, but Joseph's pants-less state disturbed me. Something, I felt, should be done about getting pants on him. This feeling became stronger than ever after I had worked for two days on the fo'c'sle of the row-galley, and so been without sight of Ellen in all that time. I am free to say, now, that I recognize what lay behind this sudden dissatisfaction at Joseph Phipps's

garments, or lack of them. It was only, of course, the desire to say
something, no matter what, to somebody who had recently been with
Ellen: the vague longing to hear from her, somehow: to speak her name
freely, even, as an easement for the emptiness within me. But like all
people in my condition I could not, at that time, admit this, even to
myself; and it is possible that I might have said nothing to Joseph about
his pantsless state except for an unguarded speech of Cap Huff.

Cap had a habit of returning early from his work in the shipyard in
order to dig up his keg of rum to see whether anybody, as he put it,
had been at it. On such occasions he took Doc Means with him to do
the digging, while he himself kept a look-out to make sure nobody
spied on their activities.

On returning from the shipyard, I found their labors had been successful; for the two of them, squatted before the fire, were taking alternate sips from a tin cup. They were overseeing the roasting of a small
pig; and while the pig sizzled above the coals, Cap, in his roaring voice,
was singing the praises of Steven Nason's wife, who was being anxiously
awaited—not only by Nason, but by all of us, since she was expected to
bring more ship carpenters to help us in our labors.

"Yes sir," Cap bawled, "she was smart, and it ain't no good my telling
you about it, because you can't get no idea how smart she was from
what I say—not that I ain't a powerful speaker! She was smart, and she
had to be smart to beat the hellcat that Nason was preossified in."

Doc Means blinked. "Pre-whatted in?"

"The one that had him engroppsed," Cap explained. "For years he
was engroppsed in this hellcat—she come from Arundel, too, though
you'd never a-guessed it when we found her in Quebec, smelling of
perfume enough to knock you over, and wearing a dress that showed
her off like a brick powder-magazine!" Cap passed the tin cup to Doc
and made a series of gestures with his vast palms, as though he caressed the exterior of a giant hour-glass.

He wagged his head, as at a dangerously pleasant recollection. "Yes
sir; she was an Arundel woman, too, same as Phoebe. We got all kinds
in Arundel, like everywhere else. Women ain't no different, wherever
you are. They think the same things, and you handle 'em the same
way."

"I s'pose so," Doc Means sighed. "How was it you handled this hellcat?"

Cap cleared his throat. "By God, she done a good deal of handling
herself! Before we got through with her, she had some of us handled
nigh into hell—her and that Frenchy she was living with up in Quebec!
It's God's wonder she didn't talk Nason into being a British major. You

ought to heard what she called Nason when he wouldn't be one! Called
him a pheasant and told him to go back to his cesspool and eat fish-
bones."

Doc Means passed the tin cup to Cap. "She sounds kind of talkative
to me," he opined.

"No," Cap said, "she didn't say much, but what she *did* say made
you damned uncomfortable." Cap growled and spat. "Pretty as a picture of Philadelphia as Seen from Cooper's Ferry, too—big blue eyes, and
yeller hair, and freckles like inside a lily, sort of, and a smell like delicious flowers. Made you want to bite her, kind of." He spoke with
gusto, exclaimed "Hoy!" enigmatically; then drained the tin cup and
licked his lips unctuously. "She thought she could do damned near anything with Nason; but she couldn't! Phoebe wouldn't let her!" He stared
hard at Doc Means. "A hellcat: that's what she was, and an Arundel
woman, by God! Just plain Mary Mallinson; but she Frenched it all up
and stuck a 'de' in it: Marie de Something—Marie de Summlething—Sub-
blething—don't it beat hell how those Frenchies think up names you
can't even remember, let alone pronounce?"

A picture shot into my brain with knifelike sharpness. I saw Nathaniel, in the box at Ranelagh, holding up a rosy, paper-thin slice of ham
and pretending to read my father's letter through it. I heard his voice,
even: "Dated from Arundel in the Province of Maine," he had said.
Those were his first words; and they had been heard by Marie de Sabrevois, blue-eyed, golden-haired, perfumed, with "freckles like inside a
lily," standing beyond our box in her dress of pink brocade, beside the
silent, sleepy-looking Mr. Leonard. Mr. Leonard had volunteered, later,
that they had heard what Nathaniel had said, and so had Marie de
Sabrevois; but she had denied any knowledge of such a place as Arundel.

"The name wasn't Marie de Sabrevois, was it?" I asked.

Cap's jaw dropped; he stared at me from round eyes. "That's just
what it was! Where'd you ever know that poison ivy?"

I contrived, somehow, to keep my face expressionless. "It's a common name in Canada," I said. "There's a place of the same name not far
from Isle aux Noix."

Cap nodded. "It's just as well you don't know her. There wasn't *anything* that hellcat wouldn't do! She learnt it from the feller she lived
with. He was her brother, she said. Brother hell! No sir! You're well off
not to know her! She don't like Americans, and she don't like Arundel
people, and she don't like Arnold."

"Why not?"

Cap scratched his head thoughtfully. "Why not? Well, she don't like

Americans because she used to be one herself and then stopped being one. That's one damned good reason. For another thing, we killed the feller she lived with. Leastways, it was Steven killed him, kind of by accident; but I say 'we' because if he hadn't, I'd 'a' done it on purpose!"

"That doesn't account for her not liking Arnold."

"No," Cap agreed. "Well, she don't like Arnold because Arnold's a friend of Stevie's for one thing, and because Arnold went up to Montreal, years ago, and dragged her out of a convent to see if she was the same one that used to live in Arundel, and by God, she was!"

Cap's voice rumbled on, telling Doc about Phoebe Nason; but I, possessed at last of definite knowledge of the things I hitherto had merely suspected, went to my bunk and sat upon it, wondering what to do.

In my foolish pride, I had refused to ask, even, where Ellen lived. I must see her, and I must see her without Nathaniel's knowledge; for what I had to say to her could not be said in his hearing. It was only Joseph Phipps that I could trust to take me to her and make sure that I saw her; and at once I realized how I could turn Joseph's lack of pants to good account.

It was not long before Verrieul returned with Nathaniel; and when Verrieul hurried in to get his tin plate and spoon and horn cup from beneath the blanket in his bunk, I caught him and told him he must interpret for me to Joseph on a matter as delicate as it was important.

That was how the three of us came to find ourselves, after supper, at the base of the limestone mountain, looking down on the score of campfires that glowed along the edge of the lake, where the workmen had gone to catch and cook eels and hornpout, which bite better at night.

"Now," I said to Verrieul, who translated my words to Joseph in French, and gave me back the answers, "now this that I say to you is said for your own good, and not to give offense. I hope you will understand."

Joseph said that he understood.

"When a man walks with a lady in my country," I said, "it is considered proper for him to cover up his legs. Therefore I shall be glad to make a gift to you of pants, so that there may be no appearance of impropriety when you walk with your sister."

"He thanks you," Verrieul interpreted, "and he will be pleased to accept the pants. He prefers red ones. He says to be sure to have the pants made with a seat in them, as he wishes to cut out the seat himself."

"Cut out the seat!" I exclaimed. "If you cut the seat from a pair of pants, they're no pants at all!"

"But they cover the legs," Joseph explained. "That is the only reason my people wear pants: to cover the legs in the winter, or when traveling through rough country, full of thorns. In warm weather, or in open country, pants are unnecessary, uncomfortable, and foolish."

"Foolish!" I exclaimed. "Look around you at all these men. They're from Albany and Rhode Island: from all parts of the civilized world! All of them wear pants! Do you think they'd all wear pants if there were anything foolish about it? What do you think your sister would say if I went calling on her without pants?"

Verrieul was slow in interpreting Joseph Phipps's answer to this question, and they spoke back and forth until I became impatient at the delay. "Well, what's the matter? Can't he answer a simple question?"

"Yes," Verrieul said, "but your question put him in mind of something else. He says your question doesn't require an answer because he is making no effort to persuade you to go without your pants. For him it is foolish to wear pants; but it is for you to do as you please, without worrying about what he will think, or what his sister will think. He also says that yesterday, in passing the shipyard, his sister was unable to see you at work in your usual place, and spoke of it to him. Today she looked even more carefully to discover where you were working, and expressed surprise that you should be absent. She asked whether you had gone away, or had fever. Because of her persistence in speaking of the matter, he says, it is more than likely that she wishes to talk to you about something."

"Well for God's sake," I said, abandoning my concern over Joseph's pantsless state, "what made him delay telling me? If I hadn't had occasion to speak to him, I might have been weeks learning about it! This is a hell of a way to treat an important message! There's no time to be lost! I'll go at once to where she lives! At once!"

Even before Verrieul had interpreted my reply, Joseph Phipps was off through the scrub that fringed the foot of the limestone mountain, and Verrieul and I followed as best we could through the thick hot darkness of that July night.

The house we sought was in a field—that I could tell from the sweet smell of drying hay—and through the kitchen window we saw Ellen, seated at a table on which burned three tallow dips. Near her sat a worn, stooped woman, her grayish hair slicked back on her head like thin silk. The two of them were sewing; and Ellen, I could see, was talking; while, on the far side of the hearth, a man sat asleep in a barrel chair. The man, Verrieul said, was the woman's husband.

When Joseph Phipps tapped on the window, the husband sprang from his chair and flattened himself like a squirrel against the chimney-piece, reaching for the musket that hung against it. At a word from Ellen he ceased his effort and stood peacefully enough on the hearth-stone, yawning and scratching the back of his neck.

Ellen came to the window to peer out. Her brother said something in French. Her hand went suddenly to her throat; then fluttered up to touch her brown curls, a touch behind and at the side, such as women find necessary, no matter how their hair is dressed. She came out, then, and stood in the doorway, a slender gray shape.

"Ah," she said, "it's you!"

I put out my hand, thinking she might give me her own. When she didn't, I touched her arm, but she just stood there, motionless. I heard Verrieul's and Joseph's voices, speaking softly in Abenaki, as they went back through the darkness toward the lake. My hand that had touched her sleeve felt rough and clumsy. I waited for her to speak; and the two of us were so long silent that I was in a panic for fear she might go back into the house.

"Joseph thought——" I began, but the loudness of my voice, in the dark stillness, choked me and I was silent again.

Ellen moved a little, and I imagined a heavy warmth came out from her and struck against me. "Evidently it was not important, what he thought."

"I came as soon as I could," I said. "I didn't know—I was surprised—he thought you wanted to see me."

She moved impatiently. "That's true, in a way. I was very much put out because you didn't come here to inquire concerning my wishes."

"Of course," I said, "I'd have come if I'd suspected—I mean, I was afraid you wouldn't be pleased if I—that is, I was afraid I wouldn't be welcome."

"Not welcome? Why do you raise the question of being welcome? I did not wish you to come here so that I could welcome you, but so that I might learn how long it would be before you proposed to send me to Albany."

I wondered how to speak to Ellen of the things Cap Huff had told me, and I couldn't figure how to do it.

When she spoke again, her voice was graver. "How long do you expect to be here in this place?"

"I don't know. Until the fleet is built."

"And how long will that be?"

"God knows! If we can get enough men from Maine, we'll build it in a month!"

"Men from Maine?" she asked politely. "I have seen nothing about men from Maine to make me think they're more capable than men from other parts of America."

I saw fit to ignore the implication in her words. "They know how to build ships, and that's more than can be said for a lot of the men they're sending us. If we get many more Yorkers and Dutchmen, we'll be here forever!"

"I see," she said coldly. "So you'd be willing to leave me here forever, too, if you can't get your wonderful men from Maine. I think you've forgotten I'm to be sent to Albany when I can be sent safely. Since that's now possible, why don't you send me?"

"Ellen," I said, reluctant to answer because of my unwillingness to hurt her, "this doorway's no place to stand and talk."

"I'm quite comfortable," she assured me. "When am I to be sent to Albany? Does the doorway prevent you from answering a simple question?"

"No," I said, "I can answer your simple question if you'll answer one equally simple. What is it your aunt wants you to do in Albany, Ellen?"

"Ah! So you're at my aunt again!"

"Yes, I am! Until I know what you're supposed to do in Albany, I'm—well, I'm afraid to have you go there."

"You're afraid?" Ellen asked softly. "You're afraid of something that might happen to me?"

"Not exactly. Not in the way you mean. But I'm afraid for you—afraid that innocently you might—afraid that through something you might innocently do——"

"What are you trying to say! Do you think I'll understand you better if you hem and haw?"

"Very well," I said, "I'm afraid you might innocently do something to hurt the American cause."

"I see," Ellen whispered. "You know that I love my aunt, and you choose to think she's a spy."

"Wait, Ellen! You've spoken of Marie de Sabrevois, again and again, as your aunt; but in reality, she's nothing at all to you. You know nothing about her. You don't know where she was born, or who her father and mother were. That's true, isn't it?"

Ellen's reply was quick. "Such a question is even more foolish than it is insulting. My aunt is the sister of the gentleman who purchased my mother and me from the Indians. He was a great gentleman, Henri Guerlac de Sabrevois. I can't remember my mother, or Monsieur Guerlac; but my aunt Marie came to me, often and often, in the convent, to tell me how kind he was, and how generous and brave, and how he wished me always to be a lady, like my mother."

She stopped. I was uncomfortable, not knowing whether or not she was weeping; but when she went on, her voice was almost expressionless.

"I'll ask you to remember that I know nothing about you, and yet I've trusted you, though you haven't been punctilious in repaying my trust. Therefore I see no reason why you should feel free to complain that I know nothing about my aunt, who has had me fed and clothed and educated all my life! I ask myself why it is you should try to turn me against my aunt, who has been always sweet and always kind; why you should say I know nothing about her. If you'll think a moment, you'll see that I know her brother was an officer in a great French regiment, the regiment of Béarn. I know she loved and honored him. I know she was kind to me: kinder than anyone. What more is there for me to know? Do you, perhaps, know more than that about your mother?"

I touched her arm again: felt for her hand and took it in mine. It was clenched and, in spite of the warmth of the evening, cold. "Ellen, you don't understand. I've heard things——"

She freed her hand carefully. "Heard! You've heard things! I understand the things you've heard have not been reliable. I understand that if you wished to learn about my aunt, you'd listen to me. I know better what she is than anyone alive! But you won't listen to me! You try to poison my mind against her! You try to poison your brother's mind against her! And I think I understand even more! I think I know why you want to cast suspicion on her! I think I know why!"

"You think you know why?" I was stunned and laughed harshly. "I see. You mean I'm jealous of her as a man might be jealous of his mother-in-law."

It was a shot that told; there was silence for a moment. Then she said huskily, "Well, you promised to send me to Albany. Will you send me?"

"No," I said, "I can't. It's—well, it's not safe. Ellen, I want you to listen——"

There was the sound of a light thump, and the click of a latch.

I felt for her in the darkness, but found only the weather-beaten wood of the door she had closed in my face.

"Ellen," I called. "Come back, Ellen!"

I held my breath and listened. Beyond the closed door I thought I heard faint footsteps, mounting a stair. I ran to the kitchen window. It was dark.

"Ellen!" I called again. "Ellen!" I stood there and stood there, straining my senses for a sound or a sign, but found neither. My lips were dry, and my back drenched with perspiration from the discomfort of my thoughts.

How much, I asked myself, could I tell Ellen, even if she relented? Marie de Sabrevois was using her: of that I was certain. What else she was trying to do, there was no way of knowing. . . . A hellcat, Cap Huff had called her. There was nothing, he had said, she wouldn't do.

The house was dark and silent. I turned and took my bearings from the stars: then stumbled back around the shoulder of the limestone mountain.

XXVII

The sun, striking down on the deck and sides of the sloop row-galley on the following afternoon, made her into an oven hot enough to bake beans; and I, helping to fit lockers in her powder-magazine, was more than half blinded by sweat. When I climbed on deck to clear the caked sawdust from my throat, the first person I saw, standing disconsolately among the litter of chips and shavings that surrounded the gundelo on the adjoining stocks, was the stooped, slick-haired woman I had last seen sitting across the table from Ellen Phipps.

Distress was so marked, both in her attitude and the expression of her face, that I went straight to her. "What's wrong?" I asked. "Is anything wrong with Ellen?"

She eyed me doubtfully. "By your looks you're related to Nathaniel Merrill."

"I'm his brother. What's wrong?"

"If you know where he is, you better find him. Ellen's gone."

"Gone? When did she go?"

She shook her head. "Some time between sun-up and dinner. That heathen brother of hers, he was around, half naked; and pretty soon they went off together, same as always, and they never come back."

I would have spoken, but she forestalled me. "When she wasn't back for dinner, I looked in her room. She tooken a dress with her, and the moccasins she made, and some night things. She ain't coming back: that's certain!"

Assuming a confidence I was far from feeling, I assured her Ellen was in good hands and would come to no harm. When the woman trudged away, stoop-backed from her labors and apparently not even aware of the hammering and shouting and half-built vessels that surrounded her, I went in search of Nathaniel on the run. He was, I knew, squaring timbers for the last gundelo to be laid down, because I had heard him complaining to Verrieul that he was doing it with a felling axe, and that it was hell's own job, which was not far from the truth.

From the defiant look on his face, when I found him, I could see he knew what had happened.

"Come down to the edge of the lake," I said. "I want to talk to you."

He came quietly enough. We waded out to a boulder where we could sit and sharpen his axe with a flat rock. Thus we were free from interruption, and there was no make-believe to our work, since even still we were without grindstones, and our axes, as a result, duller than hoes most of the time.

"Nathaniel," I said, "Ellen's gone, and Joseph Phipps went with her."

Nathaniel scooped up water and trickled it on his axe-blade, but said nothing.

"Since Joseph was subject to your orders," I said, "I suppose you knew he was going, and with whom."

"Yes."

"Nathaniel," I said, trying to choose my words with care, "why didn't you speak to me before you gave Joseph permission to go? You must have known that if I'd wanted Ellen to go to Albany, I'd have sent her myself."

Nathaniel laughed. "What was the use of speaking to you? She was bound to go to Albany. Nothing you could have said would have changed her. Why wouldn't she be bound to go to Albany, knowing that the sooner she went there, the sooner she could get back to see— to see her aunt."

"Oh, so that's it! After she goes to Albany, she's going back to St. John's."

Nathaniel was silent.

"I begin to understand your willingness to have her go," I said. "I don't doubt you were *eager* to have her go, even, seeing that she could carry a letter to Marie de Sabrevois for you."

Nathaniel's glance was hard and level. "Well, what's the harm in that?"

"Harm? What's the harm in it? Can't you see the harm in it, without my telling you? Doesn't it seem to you possible that you've done a dangerous thing? That innocent child knows all we've been doing here in Skenesboro! And what'll she do? She'll tell Marie de Sabrevois!"

"Well, why shouldn't she?" Nathaniel asked. His voice sounded half strangled. "Why shouldn't she?"

"Why shouldn't she? I'll tell you why she shouldn't! Do you know who Marie de Sabrevois is? Do you know what she's done? Who she was with when we——"

Nathaniel jumped up to stand over me, his axe in his hand. His eyes were hot.

"Sit down on that boulder!" I told him. "What are you trying to do? Let all Skenesboro find out what a fool you've been?"

Nathaniel seated himself slowly, his tanned face a sickly yellow. "Listen," he said softly. "She's the—she's all I—she's the purest, noblest—if you dare—don't you dare to try to tell me anything else, or by God, I'll kill you!"

"You're insane!" I said. "That woman has driven you out of your head!"

"That's not true! I see things more clearly than I ever did! I see things in their proper proportion! It's you that's out of your head! You, with your pig-headed ideas: you're doing your damnedest to ruin everybody you pretend to love!"

"What in God's name are you talking about?"

He swung his arm toward the seven partly finished hulls ranged along the shore like the picked carcasses of giant turkeys. "I'm talking about these little walnut-shells of boats we're trying to build, so to fight the greatest nation in the world—trying to build without men or nails or tools or cordage or sails; that we're going to try to sail without sailors!"

He laughed contemptuously. "Fighting England! Us fighting England! How long do you suppose we can fight England with men half armed, half clothed, half fed! With men rotting away with smallpox! With money worth next to nothing, and nine-tenths of our people unwilling to fight—unwilling even to give a keg of nails or a coil of rope to help *us* fight! How long? How long can we fight England?

"Out of my head, am I? They'll hack us and hang us! They'll wring our necks as if we were a flock of pullets, and *then* what'll happen? *Then* what'll happen to Mother—to Father—to Jane and Susanah: to *my* father—*my* sisters—*my* mother! They'll be hanged for rebels! Our land'll be confiscated. They'll be driven out—driven to Halifax, as our people drove out the Loyalists. Insane, am I? Why you fool, we haven't a chance!"

"Lower your voice," I said. "I don't choose to have every Patriot between here and Crown Point know I've got a traitor for a brother!"

Nathaniel shivered. "Now wait, Peter! This is my country! It's as much mine as it is yours. I was born in it and brought up in it! It's mine! I love it just as much as you love it! Do you think, for God's sake, that somebody made a special deed of gift of it to you? That you're the only one entitled to have affection for it?"

"Certainly not," I said, "but——"

"Listen," Nathaniel said, "it's my country! I wouldn't live anywhere else in the whole damned world if you gave me all of it! What right have you to call me a traitor! Do you think you're the only person in existence with eyes and judgment—the only person competent to think?

"Do you think it's because I love the British that I say we can't whip 'em? All the people with brains have been sent out of the country, and we're being governed by rats. From the way this army has been treated, what we need is a rat-charmer to coax the rats out of Congress and drown 'em!"

"Now look here!" I said. "Wait a minute! You can't talk like that!"

Nathaniel's voice trembled.

"Why can't I? I'll say what I please about people who leave me in Canada with nothing but dried peas to eat and no rum to warm me—no powder to put in my gun in case the British catch up with me—no clothes or shoes or medicines! Is there *anything* too bad to say about those that sit at home, with full bellies and in comfortable houses, putting incompetent muttonheads over me as officers, like this Dutch donkey Wynkoop—that expect me to stand up here sick and naked and fight the British with my bare fists? What should I call 'em? My friends? My government? I say they're rats; and I say the British'll tear us to pieces as easy as they'd tear a rotten sheet!"

"You'll lower your voice," I said, "or I'll give you a thrashing!"

Nathaniel eyed me defiantly. "Can't you see?" he pleaded. "Can't you see that all we've got to do is wait—wait till we're no longer shoeless, powderless, shipless, naked paupers—wait till we're stronger, so we can laugh at England and turn our backs on her without forcing thousands to die of smallpox, and making other thousands starve to death, and standing still other thousands up to die in front of British muskets? That's all we need to do: wait until these valleys are filled with settlers, and thick with villages and roads—wait till there's enough mines and mills and stores to buy an army that *is* an army in place of this helpless rabble! When that's done, *ten* Englands couldn't stop us from doing as we pleased!"

I stepped off the boulder into the milk-warm water: doused myself in it to soften the shell that seemed to have stiffened on me at my brother's words. I could hardly think, let alone speak. I climbed back on the boulder, somewhat clearer-headed, to study Nathaniel. What I had heard was bad—bad! Yet there was so much truth in it that I couldn't let myself think about it.

"Nathaniel," I said, "it sounds to me as if you considered going over to the British. In that case I've got this to say: I won't have it! Before I'd——"

"Save your breath!" Nathaniel said. "I gave *you* my word I'd go with you, and so I will; but I didn't give my word to stop having my own thoughts! I didn't give my word to think the way Wynkoop thinks, or De Woedtke thinks, or the way *you* think, for that matter. I'll think as I wish, and you can't stop me! I'll think as my conscience dictates, just as you do, and you'll do well to remember you're not the only person with a conscience! Don't *you* try to tell me how I must think! Wiser men than you have thought as I do! Let me alone, and I'll keep my thoughts to myself, because of what I promised. But keep your hands and tongue off me; and what's more, keep your slanders off Marie! Otherwise I'll do what you're doing: I'll follow the dictates of my conscience! I'll do what I think ought to be done, instead of what a lot of rats tell me I ought to do!"

I sat and stared at him. I could do nothing but stare, for his words had stripped me of all coherent speech. For a moment Nathaniel returned my stare: then he climbed off the boulder and went splashing toward shore.

As I followed him to the shipyard, the intensity of my thoughts was such that I slipped and stumbled as I walked.

What to do about Marie de Sabrevois was the question that engrossed me. I longed to speak with someone about her; yet I knew Cap Huff might somehow have been mistaken about her name. It was even possible that there might be two Marie de Sabrevoises. After all, there was a settlement of that name, not far from St. John's. And of course, I told myself, it was possible that Ellen was right about her aunt's goodness: that Nathaniel was right about her purity and nobility. It was certain I could not talk about her to Nathaniel or to Ellen. It was equally certain that for their sakes I dared not speak about her to anyone else. Nor, I said to myself, could I prove what I knew about Marie de Sabrevois; but know it I did; and dodge and squirm as I might, there was no escaping it.

XXVIII

Gɪᴠᴇ a man enough work to do and he forgets his sorrows. He ceases, even, to complain about his food, for if he works long enough and hard enough, any food becomes savory, just as any bed feels soft and welcome.

We had worked hard enough before Ellen went away; but she was no sooner gone than the seeming hopelessness of the task that lay before us set us to working harder than ever, with Wynkoop ordering us to do something, and almost immediately deciding to have us do something else; so that even had we possessed the tools and materials with which to build ships properly, much of our efforts would have been wasted.

As it was, the vessels on the stocks seemed no further advanced, each day, than they had been the day before. Nothing existed for us save the building of ships: nothing else, it almost seemed, had ever existed, or ever would. To me, the marshes and the cool breezes of Arundel became misty memories: Ellen, even, seemed as remote as those long-gone days when I walked my own quarterdeck, bound for the Spanish ports.

Those who came up from Ticonderoga brought us diversified information—how Pennsylvanians were fighting daily with New Englanders; how General Gates, after replacing Sullivan as Commander of the Northern Army, had ordered the entire army out of Crown Point and back to Ticonderoga, giving Arnold the job of moving it back; how Congress, early in July, had signed a Declaration of Independence, making us free and independent of Great Britain. What we wanted to know, however, was when in the name of God we'd get blacksmiths, oar-makers and the million other things that we needed; but they didn't know the answers. It was as Cap Huff said: a Declaration of Independence was a nice thing to hang on the wall, maybe; but if somebody didn't send us a few tons of spikes and oakum before long, the British would blow hell out of us, the Declaration and everything else; so what was the use of mentioning a Declaration of Independence before we got a few spikes?

We had our first encouragement on a cool evening in mid-July, when we heard shouts from the Wood Creek road and the sound of a fife playing *Yankee Doodle*, extremely brisk and cheery. We ran down the hill, and so did most of the carpenters who were sitting around the new barracks and Skene's barn; for a fife was something we hadn't heard for many a day. There, coming into the ravine, was a company of fifty, swinging along in double file as fast and regular as soldiers, only instead of muskets they carried axes. At their head was Dominicus Davis, the best calker in our Arundel shipyard. Beside him, tooting the fife, was one of James Gould's children, though I could never tell them apart, he having had twelve by his first wife and eight by his second.

It was not Dominicus, nor the fife, however, that moved me, but a small flat-backed figure, marching beside the column and nearly at its rear; nor did I recognize that figure until I heard Cap Huff bawling for Steven Nason, and saw Cap galloping down the road like a moose to fall in step beside it.

It was Steven Nason's wife, Phoebe. She wore tow-cloth leggins tucked into moccasins and held up with a red sash over tow-cloth breeches; and her blue-checked shirt was open at the neck. A blue handkerchief was knotted around her head; and at her throat was a string of brown beads. When she came nearer I saw that dust had caked black on her lips, so I knew she had traveled hard through the hottest part of the day. Nevertheless there was a cheerfulness to her smile that put me in mind of an eager spaniel: never too weary to be alert and gay.

"I promised these men they'd have the best there is," I heard her tell Cap. "Find Steven and look after it, and I'll see you after we've reported and got 'em settled."

She left Cap and trotted ahead to the front of the line. I saw her pointing to Skene's big house. The sound of the fife was smothered in the hurroaring and whistling that greeted these welcome newcomers as they swung up the slope.

. . . Just to look at Phoebe, later, as she sat beside our fire, eating Zelph's pone and catfish stew, was enough to hearten us; but she had news that was more heartening still.

She had come by way of Rumford; then had cut across to the Hudson and up it, so her charges might have good roads on which to make forced marches.

"There were two regiments in Saratoga," she said. "Connecticut regiments, with a brigadier general in command." She eyed Cap Huff meaningly. "They're bound for here, so to stand guard over you and see you tend to work, instead of spending your days in riotous living."

"Connecticut regiments!" Cap growled. "Pirates! They'll be trying to work off their clay coffee beans and wooden nutmegs on us!"

"Who's the general?" Nason asked.

"Waterbury," Phoebe said.

"My God," Cap bawled, "there's *another* general I never heard of! Why in God's name don't they send us a general that knows something— somebody like Arnold or Schuyler?"

"I don't know how true it is," Phoebe said, "but Waterbury's men claim they're coming to join Arnold. According to them, it's Arnold and Waterbury who'll be in charge of building the fleet."

"In charge hell!" Cap muttered. "They can't chew hay and spit spikes and oakum, can they?" More hopefully he added: "If that's true about Arnold, maybe he'll let us undress those two regiments, if they got clothes, and calk the vessels with their pants."

"You seem to think," Phoebe said, "that oakum and nails grow on trees down our way, and can be picked and sent up to you on five minutes' notice. If I didn't know you'd spent most of your life in Kittery, I'd think, from all these foreign ideas of yours, that you must be some kind of foreigner—most likely an Englishman. Oakum and nails aren't too easy to find during the best of times; and now that everybody's got the privateering fever, you're as apt to stumble on a hundredweight of oakum as on a litter of sables. Don't think you're the only people in the world that have troubles! You don't know what trouble is till you start interfering with somebody who's making money out of the war!"

"Well, for God's sake!" Cap roared. "They expect us to fight for 'em, don't they?"

Phoebe ate the last of her corn pone and rose to her feet to re-tie her red knitted sash.

"I wouldn't put it just that way," she said. "They don't know any more about war and fighting than a five-year-old girl knows about having a baby. They know they've got a lovely chance to make money privateering, and that's all they want to know. What they expect is that somebody'll keep the war from stopping till they've made all the money there is."

She added dryly, "Their idea of a nice war is one that'll last about fifty years."

The semi-circle of men, sprawled on the ground before our bunkhouse, stared at her. Their eyes were glassy in the red glow of the cookfire. Nobody, seeing their tattered breeches, their stockingless legs, the shreds of cloth that hung around their upper bodies, masquerading as shirts, could have dreamed that they were men who had known comfortable homes and a decent way of life: that Nason owned an inn, and a good one; that Verrieul had won the approbation of the president of Dartmouth College; that Tom Bickford had set his heart on being a clergyman; that Whitcomb had been a justice of the peace; and that my brother would even still be welcome in the mansions of his Salem class-mates.

We looked to be, every last one of us, what Carleton called us in an open proclamation within that very month—"rebels, traitors in arms against their King, rioters, disturbers of the public peace, plunderers, robbers, assassins, murderers."

And not only had all this happened to us in three short months of war, but it was only by the grace of God we were not rotting with a thousand other smallpox victims in the dead pits of Isle aux Noix.

"Fifty years?" Nason asked softly. "They want the war to last fifty years? It's not quite that bad, I guess."

Phoebe smiled at him, a lop-sided smile, and twisted her fingers in her brown beads. "No, you naturally wouldn't guess so. I only mention it so you won't be impatient with those of us that aim to help you. There's a lot of talk, at home, about patriotism. If you believe all you hear, every-one's a Patriot; but when you try to get somebody to give you fifty dol-lars to prove his patriotism, that's another story! Fifty ship carpenters marched up here with me to work on these ships, and only seven came of their own free will, to help the army! Only seven! You couldn't get the rest of 'em away from the privateersmen unless you filled their hats with money and gave 'em as much live-stock as Noah carried in the Ark. Dominicus Davis and my cousin Theodore Marvin, they came for what-ever pay we want to give 'em, and they'll ship on the fleet when it's ready to sail; but Enoch Cluff, from Wells, he wouldn't come till he'd got fifty dollars hard money and nine cows, the cows to be let out to the persons that paid 'em, and doubled in four years' time. Do you know how many cows Enoch Cluff'll have by the time this war's over?"

Cap Huff heaved himself about, and produced from some portion of his rags the stub of a pencil. "I know how many you think he'll have, Phoebe," he said, "but you're mistook! Just let me have the names of the seven that come of their own free will."

Phoebe ignored him. "Why, we had to offer 'em more than money and cows. Money and cows wasn't enough! When we offered 'em money and cows to come up here and help stop the British from splitting the colo-nies in two, they shook their heads and said No, they guessed they'd stay where they were, on account of their labor's being so valuable to the country! Valuable!"

She hitched at her red sash and shook her fist at Steven Nason. "Do you know what I'd do in time of war? I wouldn't let anybody—not any-body—make more money than a soldier makes! I'd oblige every man to go in the army unless he could swear he was so poorly he hadn't eaten but one meal a day for a month, and that a small one!"

Doc Means stared up at her pathetically. "I wouldn't advise letting anyone off on that account. Half a meal a day is all you get in *this* army, and it ain't harmed us yet."

Nason looked at his wife as though lost in perpetual admiration of her, which I think he was. "How'd you contrive to get 'em to come, Phoebe?"

She tossed her head. "We scared the privateer builders! We went to 'em and showed 'em what would happen unless they made sure we got ship carpenters. After we scared 'em, they told off carpenters to go to the fleet. Sometimes they even gave us the money to pay the wages the carpenters demanded."

"How'd you scare 'em?"

"We told 'em the truth. Told 'em that if they didn't help us build a fleet on the lake, their privateers wouldn't ever make any money for them on account of not having any home ports to come back to. We proved to 'em that the British would hold all the ports in America, so there wouldn't be anything for the privateers to do but sail around in circles in the middle of the Atlantic."

Cap Huff looked at me. "I told you she was smart!"

Phoebe eyed him darkly. "That shows you what shipbuilders have come to on the coast. I wouldn't choose to see people in this section making fools of themselves in the same way. I hope I won't hear of anyone whining, or being afraid of shadows, or such-like nonsense. So far as I can see, you haven't anything to be afraid of. The fifty ship carpenters I brought up here today are as good ship carpenters as you'll find anywhere, and I want 'em treated right, because the better they're treated, the more work they'll do."

She stared hard at Cap, who set up an unmusical humming, like an enormous bee. "What's more," she went on, "you've got a Connecticut general coming up here, and two regiments of men that can handle felling-axes, unless they were brought up to be nursemaids or hairdressers, which they probably weren't."

"Felling-axes!" Cap bawled suddenly. "Where do you think——"

He breathed heavily and was silent when Phoebe brandished a brown forefinger in his face. "Twelve hundred felling-axes left Albany yesterday, thanks to Schuyler, and two tons of oakum! Let me tell you, too, I'd rather be you, sweating over nothing worse than how to build ships without spikes and oakum, than be Schuyler, and be responsible for getting the oakum and the nails! Yes, and that's not all! Connecticut may be full of pirates and wooden nutmegs and clay coffee beans, as you imply, but you can thank your stars for her governor! He's sending eight hundred more felling-axes by way of Bennington; and Waterbury's men claim he's sending the best privateer captain in the state to sail one of your vessels. If New York was half as patriotic as that little mouse of a state, and had a governor a third as able as Trumbull, New York could whip three Englands, all by herself!"

A soldier in a brown uniform with crossed belts came out of the darkness to stand on the far side of the fire. We recognized him for one of those who had accompanied Wynkoop from Ticonderoga. "Steven Nason," he said. "Steven Nason hereabouts?"

Nason got up quickly. Phoebe moved close to him and stared at the soldier from behind her husband's broad back like a child peering around a tree.

"Message from General Arnold," the soldier said. He held out a letter. Nason took it, going down on one knee beside the fire to worry it open and read it. Phoebe leaned against him and looked over his shoulder.

When Nason rose slowly, Phoebe hooked a finger in his belt. "I could stay here till you got back, Steven. I could stay here and sail with the fleet. I can sail as well as anybody."

He shook his head. "Start back early tomorrow morning. They need you at home."

His eyes traveled from one to the other of us.

Whitcomb jumped to his feet. "I ain't much of a carpenter, and seeing as how there's so many Connecticutters coming up here, and seeing as how I'm a Connecticutter myself, it appears to me the thing to do is to get rid of a few Connecticutters, starting with me."

Nason looked unimpressed.

"It was me that got you the boats for the ship timbers," Whitcomb reminded him, "and I was told that if I came down here, I'd get to go out on scout duty. That's what your letter's about, ain't it?"

Nason nodded. "All right: I'll take you. Pack up. We're starting north tonight." He himself followed Whitcomb into the bunkhouse, and Phoebe went too, her finger still hooked in her husband's belt.

The rest of us, silent around the fire, could hear Phoebe telling small, homely things: how Nason's mother had a felon on the third finger of her left hand from jabbing herself with the scissors, but was otherwise well; how the dog Ginger had eleven puppies, and two had been saved, both black with white waistcoats: how six barrels of herring had been salted for fear the winter would be a hard one; how she had brought him a woolen shirt from his mother and woolen stockings from his sister Jane, and a package of needles, yarn and darning cotton from herself.

"It doesn't seem quite right, Steven," we heard her say, "for you to rush off like this before I have a chance to do your mending, even."

Nason laughed. "You'll have enough of that, Phoebe, before you're through."

"Well," she said, "there's generally something to be thankful for. Thank goodness I got here when I did! Thank goodness I didn't get here two hours later."

What the others thought, I had no way of knowing, for not even Cap Huff had a word to say; but what I thought was that we, too, had more to be thankful for than I had hitherto realized.

XXIX

Phoebe's information proved to be as accurate as it had been welcome, and in two days' time Skenesboro was not only alive with Connecticutters; but from a distance the little row-galley and two of the gundelos had the appearance of pale bee-hives a-swarm with bees. Men clung and crawled on them from bulwarks to keelson, plunking the new oakum into them with calking irons Steven Nason had made in Skene's old iron-foundry.

General Waterbury, attended by Wynkoop, came down among us, a gray-headed man with gray sidewhiskers, walking with his left shoulder thrust a little forward, as if pushing into a gale of wind. He was as old as my father, nearly; and from the way he eyed Wynkoop, he was no more favorably impressed by this fresh-water admiral than the rest of us had been. I could hear Wynkoop talking and talking, in that strange, half-foreign language of his, telling about gundelos, and about some mighty brave fighting he had done in the last war against the French.

It seemed to me that Waterbury's face, as he listened, grew grayer and grayer; but he said nothing: just went pushing ahead, crab-like, his eyes darting quick glances at the partly finished vessels.

There was a sour look about Waterbury's mouth that should have been a warning to Wynkoop; but being the sort of man he was, Wynkoop talked on and on, making no effort to understand the things he saw.

Now I don't know whether Waterbury sent for Arnold, sensing that there would be grievous trouble and delay unless Wynkoop was removed entirely from the neighborhood, or whether Steven Nason, on reporting to Arnold, had told him how Wynkoop had insisted that only gundelos be built and so spurred him to quick action. The fact remains that Waterbury was scarcely settled in Skene's big house when a human bombshell burst in the middle of our shipbuilding.

. . . It was five weeks to the minute from the time when we had left St. John's, half a jump ahead of the British light infantry, that a bateau with a patched lug sail came running into the narrow end of the lake on the wings of a hot northwest wind. She headed straight for the finished row-galley, veered sharply inshore and hit the shingle with a clatter.

The lug sail came down on the run, and at the same moment the stocky, blue-clad figure of Arnold leaped from the bateau, ran limping to the galley, and, without bothering with a ladder, went up one of the posts of the staging hand over hand.

He shot himself in over the bulwarks as easily as a boy vaults a fence, ran to the main hatch and peered down it: then turned to the quarter-deck where I, working on the taffrail, stood open-mouthed, wondering whether to tell him about the row-galleys now, or wait until later.

He laughed silently, his teeth tight together. "Good! A tidy little craft! When'll you put her in?"

"Any time," I said. "Tomorrow."

"That's right! Get her in! Where's the plans for that Spanish galley?"

"In my bunk up yonder."

"Get 'em!" he said. "Get 'em!"

He limped aft, down the steep slope of the deck, to stand beside me: hung over the larboard taffrail to squint forward: crossed to the starboard taffrail and did likewise: then faced me and nodded approvingly. "Good!" he said again. "Come up to headquarters, right away! We'll get at it!"

He sprang up on the taffrail, jumped into space, caught at the staging, and went down a post, hand under hand.

Regardless of the questioning of the carpenters who swarmed around me on his departure, I scrambled to the ground and ran for the bunk-house. The very act of running brought home to me the difference between Arnold and every other officer with whom I had dealt. When other officers gave orders, men obeyed them. When Arnold gave orders, men ran to obey them.

. . . The windows of the front corner room of Skene's big house were open as I came up the slope, and Arnold's high, rasping voice brought me up the steps in a hurry. In the corner room I found General Waterbury, slumped in a chair behind a roughly made table, his lips pursed in a sour smile, while Arnold leaned over the table and thumped it with his fist to emphasize his words. At the end of the table sat Wynkoop, stolid and motionless, except for his beady black eyes, which followed Arnold's movements as if hopeful of catching him in a blunder.

"Why," Arnold said, as I came in, "if they'd put a tenth—yes, by God, a *hundredth*—of the effort into building this fleet that they do into building their measly, pocky privateers, we could blow Burgoyne halfway to Portugal!"

He turned and saw me. "Here he is!" Over his shoulder to Waterbury, he added, "This is Captain Peter Merrill of Arundel. He sailed his
own brig to Spain, and I figure on having him handle one of ours for
us." To me he said: "Where's those drawings?"

I handed him what I had—drawings made on cartridge paper. He unrolled them and spread them on the table in front of Waterbury, weight-
ing the corners with rocks; then shot a quick glance at me.

"As I understand it," he said, "you haven't laid down any row-galleys
yet."

"No sir," I said. "We started to do so, but there wasn't sufficient material to let us get forward with them."

There was nothing to be gained by telling tales on Wynkoop. Arnold
was a smart man, and a smart man knows what's going on without being
told much.

Arnold nodded. He went to stand beside Waterbury and study the
plans.

"Yes," he said. "That's more like it! This vessel's keel ought to be laid
tomorrow—tomorrow!" To Waterbury he said, "This is a Spanish galley,
General. The Spaniards use 'em, and the Algerines too. Just fitted for
our purpose, they are: short masts: lateen sails: a minimum of canvas
and cordage to bother the landsmen that'll have to sail 'em. We can't do
any better so long as we're forced to build small."

Wynkoop reached for the plans and drew them over where he could
examine them.

"I've given her extra heavy scantling and a square stern, General," I
said, "so she looks like a watering-trough; but she'll carry two great guns
in the cabin and as heavy a piece as you want to put in the bow. I've
given her twelve ports amidships. You can traverse your midship guns,
and use 'em where you see fit. What's more, she'll handle easy, for all
her clumsy looks."

"How much of a crew did you figure on?" Arnold asked.

"About ninety. I've allowed for mounting eighteen swivels, so she'll
need eighty to ninety."

"Ve ken buildt four gundelos in der time it dakes for vun uf dese gel-
lies," Wynkoop objected. "Alretty ve got tree big wessels!"

Arnold balanced on his toes, pushing his lower lip out and in, as if
feeling a roughness on his upper lip. "Big?" he asked politely. Then he
laughed. "We've got two schooners and a sloop, all mounting sparrow
guns! Sparrow guns! That's how big they are! Four-pounders and two-
pounders: that's their armament! What do you expect to sink with two-
pounders, Colonel? You couldn't sink a washtub with two-pounders, not
unless you boarded it and scuttled it to boot!

"As for our gundelos, what good would they be against a vessel like this?" He thumped his fist on the plans. "They'd have no more chance than a privateer brig would have against a frigate! You know, Colonel, that a frigate can fight and sink half a dozen war brigs! It's weight of metal that tells, every time, allowing that the ship with the guns is able to shoot—and the British have German artillerymen, damn 'em!"

"Der more gundelos ve heff," Wynkoop said heavily, "der more ve'll sgare der British. After ve sgare 'em, ve'll heff to vight 'em on lend, enyvay. Loogit all der wessels der English het at Quebec, und der whole ding het to be zettled on land by Volfe, wessels or no wessels!"

Arnold glanced wryly at Waterbury, who scratched the corner of his mouth. To Wynkoop Arnold said: "I'm glad you spoke of that, Colonel. I've had occasion to give considerable thought to the manner in which Wolfe took Quebec."

He tapped the table. "Wolfe wasn't the man that took Quebec, though he'll always get the credit for it. The man that took Quebec was Admiral Saunders—Charles Saunders, moving his fleet up river with every flood-tide, and down river with every ebb, perpetually threatening to disembark his men here, there and everywhere, day and night. He wore Montcalm out. Montcalm was in a panic for fear of what Saunders might do. If it hadn't been for Saunders, Wolfe wouldn't have had one chance in a thousand of even *reaching* the Plains of Abraham! Not one chance in a million!"

Wynkoop puffed and made sounds of expostulation.

"If you want the real truth about Quebec," Arnold said, "here it is: Wolfe should have been court-martialed for putting his troops where he did, and Montcalm should have been court-martialed for abandoning an impregnable fortress to fight in an open field!" He laughed harshly. "Wolfe and Montcalm! Montcalm and Wolfe! Two blunderers! It was Saunders and his sailors! Saunders and his ships! Saunders and his naval discipline! D'you think either Montcalm or Wolfe could have got their regiments to do the work that Saunders' sailors did—up all night: making sail; shortening sail; anchoring; heaving up the anchor; hauling around the yards? Not by a damned sight! They'd have deserted! Saunders and his sailors took Quebec, and the wrong man got the credit, as usual!"

Nothing that Arnold said, I knew, was making the smallest dent in Wynkoop's stubborn Dutch mind, though it was the simple truth.

Arnold eyed him narrowly and spoke cautiously. "In all likelihood, Colonel Wynkoop, this year's campaign will be settled on Lake Champlain, and I take it that all of us want it settled conclusively in our favor. There's only one way in which that can be done, and that's for us to build a fleet superior to anything the British can build. That wouldn't be difficult if we had the men and material, because there's one thing the British can't build, and that's a frigate. They haven't the depth of water to build a frigate at St. John's. If we could get the men and the supplies, I'd build a 38-gun frigate, and the British couldn't pass. Since it's out of the question to get either the supplies or the workmen, we've got to do the next best thing: we've got to outbuild them, and it's my information that they've already brought two schooners from the St. Lawrence to St. John's in sections—schooners bigger than any of ours. That means we've got to build vessels that can maneuver with their schooners. That means row-galleys, Colonel, and it means we can't delay any longer! They've got to be laid down tomorrow!"

Wynkoop settled himself in his chair as if he intended to stay there all day. "Cheneral Sguyler gafe me der commend uf Lake Shumplain," he said stolidly. "In dot gepecity I belief der broper wessels iss gundelos. Dey're more mople, und petter aple to selegt der bettle ground."

Waterbury looked puzzled. "They're more *what?*"

"Mople. Dey ent so heffy."

"Mobile!" Arnold exclaimed. "Gundelos *mobile?* In dirty weather they'd be as mobile as lobster-pots!"

He glared at Wynkoop, his lips pressed tight together, his swarthy face lumpy. Suddenly he smiled. "As senior officer at this post," he said carelessly, "I order an immediate Council of War to consider the form of ship construction best adapted to our needs—the council to include all officers above the rank of lieutenant colonel. The council will be in order. General Waterbury, what are your views on the type of vessel that would be of greatest service to us?"

"Chust a minute!" Wynkoop objected; but his objection was unheeded by Waterbury, whose reply to Arnold's question was magisterial.

"I'm in favor of completing the gundelos now under construction, and in devoting all our efforts to the construction of row-galleys similar to this plan." He slapped my drawing with his open palm.

Wynkoop, breathing heavily, made explosive sounds.

Arnold nodded thoughtfully at Waterbury and said, "Those are my opinions exactly, General, and since that disposes of the business before this Council of War, the council stands adjourned. Captain Merrill, lay down the keel of that Spanish galley tomorrow and remain in charge of her until she joins the fleet."

XXX

SKENESBORO was an ante-room of hell in the weeks that followed; and our labors turned into a confused and fever-ridden struggle such as sets dreamers to groaning in their sleep.

Wherever Arnold could find a sea captain, he laid violent hands on him and hustled him to Waterbury, who put him in charge of the building of the vessel he was to command. He called on the regiments at Ticonderoga for seamen and marines; and as might be expected, the ones sent were those who could best be spared—the sickly and contentious: the thieves and rascals: the worst clad and least trustworthy: men who looked unable to shoot, march or hand a sail—men so pocky and so vermin-ridden that to pull their own weight at an oar seemed beyond their powers.

Poor as they were, they were marvels of physical perfection by comparison with those collected in New York to serve aboard the fleet—or purchased, rather; for the latter were raked out of alleys and gutters by the offer of a bounty; and if ever there were human beings who deserved the title of "sweepings of hell," which one of our officers gave them, it was they.

Like all such sorry offscourings, they held themselves superior to all other men in wit, wisdom and ability; and when the barracks and the huts were filled with them, there were perpetual howlings and riotings, and fights of terrible ferocity, which nobody seemed able to quell. I longed, often, to see Cap Huff's hulking figure charge into a brawling, cursing mass of those ragged, uncontrollable creatures, but he had gone away to Ticonderoga to testify in a court-martial which General Arnold had demanded so that Colonel Hazen might be punished for refusing to accept the supplies seized in Montreal, as a result of which the supplies had been plundered.

The only genuine seamen to be sent to us, so far as I could see, came marching in through a thunderstorm one afternoon, headed by a quick-moving man with enormous arms: a man seemingly unable to look at anyone or anything without feeling the back of his neck and casting a quick glance at the sky. Nathaniel and I, working in the bow of our galley, found his appearance familiar. When he caught sight of us, he pawed at the back of his neck, and raised a long arm in greeting. I remembered, then, that the same gesture had been made to us from the battered rowboat we had picked up off Old York a mere three months ago.

It was David Hawley, the Connecticut privateersman who had escaped from the Halifax prison, and rowed five hundred miles in a week.

We were glad to see him; glad, too, to have the Connecticut sailors he had brought. Since all the other vessels had captains, Waterbury complimented him by putting him to work with Captain Warner, who was also from Connecticut, on the *Trumbull* galley, whose stocks were next to ours. Ours, being the largest, had been named the *Congress* by Arnold; the other three were named for the three mainstays of the Northern Army—General Washington, Governor Trumbull of Connecticut, and General Gates.

The galleys were growing rapidly, though not as rapidly as they would have grown if we had been free of the attacks of intermittent fever that laid workmen flat on their backs by scores, their teeth chattering and their faces as white and pinched as though the blood had been drained from their bodies.

There were times when, between our sick, the endless feuds among Pennsylvanians, Yorkers and New Englanders, and the heat and the mosquitoes, we were sure that none of the vessels would ever be finished.

Yet the little *Lee* galley, built from the timbers we had brought from St. John's, was pushed into the water and went off to Ticonderoga, unballasted, unmasted, ungunned—a raw hulk, rowed by a mob of Yorkers who fouled their oars, cursed, and tumbled about the deck under the apparently unseeing eye of red-headed Captain Davis. Davis gave us a wink as his craft moved slowly northward—a wink that indicated he was less put-upon than he seemed.

Thatcher, captain of the *Washington* galley, stood with Hawley and me, watching the *Lee* pull out. Thatcher laughed ironically. "They got considerable to learn," he said, "and I shouldn't wonder if Davis learned 'em."

Hawley caressed the back of his neck. "You got to be charitable at a time like this. You got to let 'em get aboard ship. When you get 'em there, you can explain to 'em about not making unnecessary noises, and how Satan finds some mischief still for idle hands to do. If you try to explain to 'em *before* you get 'em there, as I understand it, they might write home to a Congressman about it, and you'd get put in jail for conduct unbecoming to something or other."

The gundelos *Connecticut* and *Spitfire*, too, were thrown in by main strength, they being too flat-bottomed to slide on the ungreased ways; and off they went to Ticonderoga for guns, sails, powder, shot and the rest of their equipment.

And so, in spite of everything, Arnold had the beginnings of a fleet two months from the day when we had started south from Isle aux Noix.

Two months to a day had passed when Cap Huff returned from Ticonderoga—a strangely mild and soft-spoken Cap Huff—with a message from Arnold. He drifted into our bunkhouse about an hour after sundown, as quietly as a shadow, and hoarsely whispered, "I got a message for Hawley. Anybody here know Hawley?"

Nathaniel offered to get him, whereupon Cap said, "All right: tell him he's got to go to Crown Point to take command of the *Royal Savage*. Where's my rum?"

Doc Means said somebody had discovered Cap's rum and taken it, but that there had been only a small amount in the barrel anyway—maybe two quarts.

"How do you know there was only two quarts?" Cap asked, but the question was perfunctory: he had other things on his mind.

"Sit down," I said; "sit down and give us the news. You must be tired after your long trip."

"No," Cap said, "I got to have some rum. I been subject to so much discipline up in that damned Ticonderoga that I'm pretty near dried up. Come on, Doc: let's go over to see the ship carpenters. They got rum, ain't they?"

He added absent-mindedly that there was no news.

"No news!" I protested. "What's the reason Arnold sent for Hawley? What happened to the captain of the *Royal Savage*? What happened to Hazen? Didn't you go up there to testify on the Hazen court-martial? Where's Steven Nason? Where's Whitcomb? What's the news of the British fleet? How many vessels have they got? What are they doing? How are our vessels getting along?"

"I need some rum," Cap persisted. "I got a couple of new dice tricks I want to try on those ship carpenters." He seemed uneasy. "You ain't heard anything about Whitcomb?"

We said we hadn't.

"Whitcomb killed a general," Cap said. He looked behind him, then sat down close to the fire and asked softly whether anybody had a touch of rum—just the merest touch.

Doc Means brought him a flask, and Cap drained it at a gulp. He hiccupped grandly, staring absently into the fire.

"Whitcomb killed a general?" I asked. "What kind of general did he kill?"

"Listen," Cap said, "did any of you ever hear me tell this feller Whitcomb he ought to kill some generals?"

I said I didn't remember it.

"Well," Cap said gloomily, "he claims he got the idea from me, and being as how there's hell to pay and no pitch hot, I ain't had a minute's peace for a week, for fear of what else I might have said to him when I was feeling my rum a little."

Exasperatedly he added, "I don't see nothing so terrible about killing a general, if you go behind the British lines to do it, and do it in daytime, all clear and open. The British, they claim it ain't sporting, but I don't see why it ain't. They'd 'a' killed Whitcomb fast enough, if they'd caught him!"

Then he told us. Whitcomb and Steven Nason, sent by Arnold to bring back a prisoner, had traveled all the way to St. John's, circled the British camps and hidden themselves on the road between St. John's and Montreal. Whitcomb stayed in one spot for a day and a half, and at the end of that time a general came riding down the road on horseback. Since Whitcomb was afoot, he had no chance to overtake him: yet he ardently longed to take back a general to Arnold. Consequently, as Cap said, he plugged him through the shoulder so not to stave him up too much. He did not, however, plug him hard enough, and the general got away. As for Whitcomb, Cap said, the British learned his whereabouts and set guards across all the roads, in spite of which he came safely through them and back to Ticonderoga, as did Steven Nason.

"The British were awful mad," Cap said, "but eight days later they were madder, because they had to bury the general. Here was this feller Whitcomb making the war so dangerous that not even a British general could be safe! Yes sir: they'd come three or four thousand miles to fight this war, and hired Hessians and Indians and everything, so to make it a good one, and they certainly didn't propose to have the whole business ruined by this feller Whitcomb! They got so nervous over Whitcomb, they offered a hundred pounds to anybody who'd get him, dead or alive."

"How'd you learn all this?" I asked.

"That misbegotten Hazen used to live in St. John's," Cap said. "One of his acquaintances wrote him a letter and told him about it, and the first thing we knew, all of Hazen's friends were hollering about what a terrible thing Whitcomb had done."

"His friends? Do you mean Easton and Brown?"

"Yes, damn 'em!" Cap growled. "Easton and Brown and Wilkinson. You remember that little antimire Wilkinson, that little pissmire as was Arnold's aide in Montreal?"

We said we did.

"Well," Cap said, "in the first place, he drinks. Yes sir! If you let that damned little tit-pot smell the cork of a rum bottle, he'd get drunk and blab everything he knew and a lot he didn't know; so Arnold wouldn't have him around any longer. He's Gates's aide now. He don't like Arnold, naturally—hates him worse than poison, the way you hate anybody that says you drink."

Cap shook his head. "It certainly beats hell the way these fellers blame everything in the world on Arnold, and how they find out so many things to blame him for! They couldn't been madder about Whitcomb shooting the general if the general had been their own dear little sweetheart. It was all Whitcomb's fault, they said, but it was all Arnold's fault, too, for sending Whitcomb to Canada. Wilkinson and Hazen and Easton and Brown, they were talking about how Whitcomb wasn't a gentleman, and ought to be turned out of the army. They're afraid if he's kept, the British army'll look down on us for low, general-shooting riffraff. I think they heard some Englishman say so. By God, there's people in this country that just ain't right in their heads! They'll believe anything an Englishman or a Frenchman tells 'em: anything! The foolisher an Englishman talks, the apter they are to believe him. Wilkinson's one of 'em. If some Englishman told Wilkinson that pork wasn't being baked with beans no more, Wilkinson would go around hollering that nobody who et pork with beans oughtn't to be associated with, not by nobody!"

Cap spoke plaintively. "Now you take this general that Whitcomb shot! He wouldn't have died, ever, if one of those damned doctors hadn't got hold of him; so what's the use trying to blame Whitcomb for it! And for God's sake, what did they expect Whitcomb to do: wave his handkerchief at this general? If Englishmen want to be so all-fired sporting, why don't they hang the doctor that couldn't cure the general of a plain ordinary gunshot wound in the shoulder!"

"How did Arnold feel about all this?" I asked.

"Arnold? Why, Arnold felt just the way I did! He knew the doctor done it. He never accused Whitcomb of killing no general! Arnold's a sensible feller! He's got more sense than all the officers in both these armies, all put together. Arnold said it was too damned bad Whitcomb didn't bring the general back. Whitcomb felt bad, too. He said he and Stevie'd go up to St. John's again and catch a couple of live ones. Yes sir: it certainly was a disappointment to Whitcomb. He said when he winged that general and saw him go riding off, hell bent, he felt as bad as he did the time he missed his first moose. Anyway, Whitcomb's safe, because he's gone back to St. John's, where there ain't nothing to worry about but the British; but I ain't going to feel safe till I get afloat—not while Easton and Brown and Hazen and Wilkinson go snooping around Ticonderoga, thinking up lies to tell about Arnold or anybody that works for Arnold!"

He stood up, swayed perilously close to the fire, and sat down again suddenly. "I ought to be getting over to see those ship carpenters," he said. "I got some dice of my own now." He leaned over and dropped a hand on Doc Means's shoulder, adding, "Got a pair for you, too, old Catamount! Me 'n' you, we'll go over and see those carpenters. I took eighty-six dollars, hard money, off of one Pennsylvania regiment up at Ti, and anybody that can take anything off a Pennsylvanian, he could skin a ship carpenter right down to the belly-button."

"You can't go yet," I said. "You haven't told us what's happening!"

"There ain't a thing happening!" Cap protested. "Not one damned thing! You don't have no time to do anything, because the second you start doing it, somebody catches you and puts you to work rigging a ship or carrying powder and shot and guns aboard! Arnold's got ten vessels ready to sail, but they ain't sailed yet."

He ticked them off on his fingers: "*Royal Savage* schooner, *Enterprise* sloop, *Liberty* schooner, *Revenge* schooner, *Boston* gundelo, *New Haven* gundelo, *Providence* gundelo, *Connecticut* gundelo, *Philadelphia* gundelo and *Spitfire* gundelo. Fifty-eight guns, most of 'em small, and four hundred and fifty men, without nothing to sit on except themselves on account of not having enough pants to set down on nothing with."

Hawley came out of the darkness, piloted by Nathaniel; and at the sight of Nathaniel it occurred to me that here was a heaven-sent opportunity to put him in a safe place by sending him with Hawley, who could use him to good advantage. In Hawley's company he would have no occasion to see Easton and Brown; and he'd be free of this fever-ridden pest-hole in which we worked.

"What's all this about the *Royal Savage?*" Hawley asked.

Cap got to his feet. "Orders from Arnold. I left the letter up at headquarters. Wynkoop, he ain't Commander of Lake Champlain no more. In fact, he ain't nothing no more, and you're wanted to take his place."

"What happened to him?" I asked. "Did you suggest that Whitcomb drown him?"

Cap was indignant. "I never suggested nothing to Whitcomb! I don't hardly know the feller! What happened about Wynkoop was that when Arnold was all ready to have Hazen court-martialed, the court was packed with New Hampshire men—friends of Hazen and Bedel. They objected to everything Arnold started to do. Wouldn't admit his witnesses—wouldn't listen to Arnold—wouldn't do a damned thing! When Arnold complained, they got all excited, and said they'd never been so insulted by nobody, not in all their whole lives, and if Arnold didn't apologize, they'd take their dolls and go home!"

Cap tugged at the collar of his shirt. "By God, if ever there was a court that ought to have been shot, it was that one, starting with the president of it—Colonel Poor of New Hampshire!"

"What's that got to do with Wynkoop?" Hawley asked.

"It's got this to do with it!" Cap said. "Gates dissolved the court, it being made up of old women; and if he'd done what he ought to done, he'd 'a' set 'em to sewing shirts and breeches for the fleet! Then, on account of Arnold having done all the work on the fleet, and being the only officer fit to sail it and fight it, Gates put Arnold in command of everything. He made Arnold admiral of the fleet, but he neglected to explain it to Wynkoop so's Wynkoop could understand it. The only way to make Wynkoop understand an order he don't want to understand is to open up his skull with a splitting wedge, and pound in the order with a sledge-hammer. So Wynkoop, he just didn't pay no attention to Arnold. Seems as though he figured the Wynkoop family owned Lake Champlain, and nobody else had no business giving orders on it. So when Arnold sent two schooners down the lake on a scout, Wynkoop lays the *Royal Savage* broadside to 'em and fires on 'em for sailing without his orders. Fires on his own ships!"

"Oh, here! Here!" Hawley said. "You don't expect us to believe *that!*"

"Listen," Cap said, "maybe you'll believe it when I tell you Arnold climbed aboard the *Royal Savage* and cussed Wynkoop for ten minutes without taking breath; then put him under arrest and sent him back to Gates, to be tied up where he couldn't interfere with the war! This Wynkoop is a pig-nut—a Dutch pig-nut, twice as bad as an ordinary pig-nut. Brown and Easton and Hazen and Bedel: they're all pig-nuts: all rind and nothing inside; but the nothing that's inside Wynkoop is solider than what's inside Easton and Brown."

"Easton and Brown!" Nathaniel exclaimed incredulously.

"Poop-heads!" Cap said quickly. "Poop-heads, pure and simple! Best specimens of poop-heads you'll find anywhere, outside of Dutch ones. Dutch poop-heads are biggest and best, of course."

"Why," Nathaniel protested, "I heard——"

I interrupted him, knowing he had heard lying praise of Easton and Brown, and heard it from Marie de Sabrevois. "Nathaniel," I said sharply, "pack your belongings. The *Royal Savage* is flagship of the fleet, and if Captain Hawley'll take you, you'll be more helpful with him than here."

"Take him!" Hawley exclaimed. "You bet I'll take him!"

Nathaniel looked stubborn and I saw I must use strategy.

To Cap Huff I said quickly, "You told us the fleet was sailing for St. John's in a few days?"

"Well," Cap said, "you know how Arnold is when he makes up his mind to do something. If he decides to go to St. John's, he sails in five minutes!" To Hawley he added: "If I was you, and wanted to be sure not to have to chase him a hundred miles in a rowboat, I'd start for Crown Point right now!"

At the mention of St. John's Nathaniel, without another word, had turned and gone to the bunkhouse for his blanket and musket. That night I could rest without keeping myself awake with disturbing thoughts. I'd had fears that Ellen Phipps was a means of communication between Marie de Sabrevois and my brother. What messages might thus pass, I dared not think; but if Ellen came back from Albany now, charged with a secret errand to Nathaniel, he'd be away, thank God!— and on that thought I slept.

XXXI

The heat and thunderstorms of August gave way to September's clear days and cold nights. The young maples were frost-nipped; the air heavy with the scent of dying leaves. Skenesboro was a desert of stumps and scrub, stripped of trees for Wynkoop's preposterous stockade and barracks, as well as for ships, stocks, cabins, firewood, oars. The slashings lay everywhere, like wreckage; war had put a blight upon the land, as upon the people.

Barracks and cabins were filled with shipwrights, soldiers and sailors, flat on their backs with intermittent fever: shivering fit to shake themselves to pieces, their fingers dead white, their nails blue, their eyes black-ringed in pallid faces—and the next minute burning up with heat, howling for water, unable to talk sensibly; and we, knowing the day was not far off when the British would attack, were begging for doctors to cure these men so they could help us with the galleys.

Of all the vessels we had built, only five were left in Skenesboro: the four big row-galleys, crouched in a group, as if at bay at the bottom of this devastated valley, and beside them a single gundelo, like the unweaned calf of one of the larger hulks.

How we got them in the water, God only knows. Zelph persuaded Negroes to come in from the hills and help. Farmers, in for a day to sell corn and potatoes, lingered to pass up planks to the few of us who still could work. Waterbury himself, lame from falling off a ladder, toiled with a hammer when free of commissaries and letter-writing.

On the 10th of September the *Trumbull* galley slid in. She was sturdy, and though high in the water because of her lack of guns and ballast, she was steady as a rock while her crew ran aimlessly about her deck and clapped onto ropes to work her back to shore. She was no yacht; nor was there anything about her that was beautiful; but with her guns aboard, she would at least be dangerous.

There's one thing of which I've been certain since those days: no task is sufficiently difficult to baffle really determined men.

Carpenters fell from the stagings, toward the end of our labors, struck down by fever. It was a common sight to see two men carrying a plank, and for one to drop in mid-stride, as if sickness had leaped upon him.

Those of us who were left were ragged skeletons, our clothes rotten from perpetual sweating: our bodies covered with the sores and bruises caused by over-speedy labor with poor materials and worse tools.

Workmen were so few that we were sure we couldn't finish the last three galleys; and yet we finished two of them, if it was possible to call such hulks "finished."

Truth to tell, anything that floated was considered "finished," and the *Congress* and *Washington* floated beside the landing stages on the 18th of September, three months exactly from that sticky day when we nailed the barn door over the bow of our bateau at Isle aux Noix.

The *Gates* was a shell, still, with another week's work to be done on her deck, bulwarks and bulkheads before she could take to the water; but the *Washington* and the *Congress* were ready to move; and from the urgency of the messages that Waterbury had from Gates, we knew they had to move fast.

Aboard the *Congress* Cap Huff had twenty marines—or so he called them—amidships. Tom Bickford, my first officer, was gentle with the ragged, noisy seamen who fumbled with the oars, slapping them clumsily in the water—gentle, even, when he wagged his forefinger at them and begged them to be more seamanlike and so spare him the pain of thrashing them.

It was dusk when we cast off. We were no better than a wreck, listed to starboard, ungunned, unpainted, unloaded; our masts mere stumps; the decks a litter of odds and ends.

Tom ran up and down, calling to the oarsmen, who pushed and grunted at the sweeps. I moved the tiller over, and her head swung slowly into the north.

Skene's yellow house, a blur against the hillslope, moved backward to blot out the dark bulk of Wynkoop's monstrosity of a fort. Smoke from the cabins lay in the valley of Wood Creek, a pale shroud for the havoc we had wrought. No admiring throng was gathered to see us slip away: only two commissaries, some farmers, and a little knot of Negroes.

In my head were no heroic thoughts; merely forebodings and dark fears: forebodings as to Nathaniel: as to Ellen Phipps: as to what lay before us on these narrow waters, hidden in the chill mist that seemed to me to smell of death. And ironically I remembered Cap Huff's words to Zelph, back in the peaceful days of long ago: "That's the nice thing about a war: there ain't no regular work to do—only wear a uniform, walk around a lot, and camp out."

. . . We rowed twenty miles that night, Verrieul and Doc Means conning us from the bow. A gill of rum was issued to the rowers every two hours; and while the mists of early morning still wreathed the dark hills above us, we pulled into the narrow cleft beneath the heights of Ticonderoga to see a sight that looked like war indeed.

All the waterways to north and south are pinched together at Ticonderoga, as if some clumsy god had squeezed the end of Lake George and the narrowest portion of Lake Champlain between enormous fingers. The earth is gathered up in abrupt folds; the waterways twist between them; and overlooking the narrow channel are the gray walls of the old French fort.

When we had come down from Crown Point, three months before, carrying the ship timbers to Skenesboro, the fort had been a ruin, overgrown and crumbling, and all the other hills were thick with trees. The place had been a wilderness, without a house or sign of life.

Now, as our galley came slowly into that moat between the hills, the fort's gray walls had been rebuilt, and from its ports and parapets black guns protruded. Redoubts and magazines squatted on the rocks, and sentries walked a score of posts. On our left, the shores of Mount Defiance were stripped of trees; and the once-wooded heights of Mount Independence, at our right, had become a city of tents and cabins from which the smoke of campfires rose to undulate in layers against the hills.

Under the guns of the fort were docks; whaleboats and bateaux by the hundred were stacked along the shore. Among them lay the *Trumbull* galley, fully rigged and ballasted, and partly painted. On the docks were cannon: brass carriage guns in rows; spars and masts; piles of cannon balls. Men ran and shouted as we drew near.

A barge put out to meet us. When it came under our counter, I saw the officer in the stern sheets was Captain Wilkinson, whom I had last seen with Arnold.

"What ship is this?" he asked, his jaw muscles fluttering. I told him we were the *Congress* galley; that the *Washington* was close behind us.

"Run her in beside the pile of spars," he ordered. "Send your crew ashore under guard. They'll camp by themselves on the flats to the north until you're rigged and ready to sail."

"I'd like to keep 'em aboard ship," I said, "so to get 'em accustomed to the craft."

Wilkinson shook his head. "Your men are New Englanders. The riggers are Pennsylvanians. They can't work while there's New Englanders around."

"That's too damned bad about the Pennsylvanians!" I said. "What's their objection to New Englanders?"

"They don't like the way you enlist old men and blacks and Indians."

"Well, for God's sake!" I cried. "Do you have to be elected to this war by the Pennsylvanians? When did they decide nobody could fight the British unless registered as gentry?" I was furious to think that Pennsylvanians or anybody else should question Doc Means's age or Zelph's color, since either of them was as valuable as any Pennsylvanian I had ever seen, bar none.

Wilkinson raised his eyebrows. "I'm not responsible for the way they feel, Captain. But I *am* responsible for keeping order among the troops. If Pennsylvanians are obliged to work with New Englanders, there's always a fight, and somebody gets killed; so take your men ashore under guard: then report to the general."

"To General Arnold?" I asked.

Wilkinson's voice was chilly. "General Arnold has no authority at this post, as you doubtless recall, now that I mention it. General Gates is commander-in-chief of the Northern Army."

Dignified and disdainful, he turned his boat and left us; but his pomposity made no impression on Cap Huff, who emitted an unseemly noise between compressed lips, and hoarsely whispered, "Poop-head!"

By the time the galley had been made fast to the dock and the crew marched off to barracks by Tom, Verrieul and Cap Huff, shears had been set up for handling the guns, and a swarm of shipwrights, armorers, riggers and blacksmiths were hard at work.

A company of York troops, lined up in a row, rolled 18-pound shot from man to man, moving them to a spot abreast of our main hatch, looking and acting like children playing a queer game of marbles. Eight other ragged soldiers lashed a long 18-pounder to four poles, preparatory to bringing it aboard.

I made myself as military as I could—a difficult task, since my tow-cloth smock, long ago worn to shreds, had been replaced by a buckskin shirt whose tails had been cut off to make patches for the shoulders, so that I had to wear it outside my breeches. The latter, bought from a farmer, were too small, and for footgear I had only moccasins, since shoes were impossible to get. I had a ribbon for my hair, however, and Joseph Phipps's gold-laced hat, which he had let me have in return for a pewter snuff-box.

Wilkinson was waiting in the ante-room to the general's quarters inside the fort on the hilltop; the general, he told me in a hushed voice, was almost ready for me.

I disliked Wilkinson for his unwarranted solemnity, but he was a good aide-de-camp, able to look busy when doing nothing, even while taking a nap: able, also, to soothe impatient persons by leading them to think he was about to perform something miraculously important for their sole benefit. He was more profound over inconsequential matters than any man I ever knew—an excellent trait for a soldier, and one that brings higher rank to the person who practices it than mere bravery or ability. It was a great boon to Wilkinson; for in one year's time he was sent to Congress with a message, and such was the ponderosity with which he delivered it that Congress made him a brigadier general at twenty-one, when he deserved a brigadier generalcy about as much as our village idiot.

When Wilkinson ushered me in to see Gates, I found him fumbling nearsightedly among his papers. He was gray and stooped, with a sly side-glance that returned and returned to the person with whom he spoke. He looked crafty, as if hopeful of stealing up on a person's thoughts, instead of asking frankly for them. Yet he was bluff and hearty, and seemingly eager to do everything possible to make things easier for those who had to do the fighting.

He got up to shake hands, quite as if my rank were equal to his own: then threw his arms apart in an old-womanish gesture, staring petulantly at my clothes.

"Captain! Captain Wilkinson!" he called querulously. "Here! I want you, dear boy!"

Wilkinson appeared as neatly as though he had shot up through the floor.

"Now look here, Captain," Gates complained, "look at this!" He flung his hands out before him, seeming to spill from them a burden of disgust. "A captain in our fleet, obliged to fight against soldiers like Carleton and Burgoyne in a teamster's shirt and wearing tobacco-pouches on his feet! Now for God's sake, Wilky, do something about it! Get him a coat somewhere! Get him some breeches and stockings! And try to find some shoes for him. Damn it, Wilky, fix him up with some shoes!"

Wilkinson looked dubious. "Yes, General," he said soothingly. "You know such things are scarce: scarce!"

Gates's reply was testy. "Well, of course they're scarce, dear boy! If they weren't, he'd get 'em himself, wouldn't he? Now look here, Wilky: if you can't find clothes in the fort, go over to Mount Independence and talk to some of those York troops. They've got clothes, some of 'em have, and they'll sell anything! They'd rather have money than breeches, and they're no better with breeches than without 'em, so there's no reason why we shouldn't deprive 'em. We'll equip Captain Merrill out of the public funds: that's what we'll do; but for God's sake, Wilky, don't bring back clothes that are lousy! They tell me all the York troops are lousy, so if you get clothes from 'em, be sure to have 'em examined, especially the seams. Have the seams well looked at, dear boy!"

In spite of Gates's kindness, I could never think of him, after that, except as something of a fussbudget—too much of a fussbudget to be a good commander-in-chief.

When Wilkinson had departed, grave and splay-footed, Gates sat down at his desk again and pawed among his papers. "Well, we thought you'd never get here in time to fight!" He eyed me slyly over the tops of his spectacles.

"The fever took all our carpenters, sir. We were lucky to finish the *Congress* and the *Washington*."

"When'll the *Gates* be ready?"

"In a week, I hope, sir."

"By cracky! I hope so! We need her! General Arnold's been making life miserable for us, shouting for those galleys! We get a letter from him every fifteen minutes. He wants those galleys!" He poked irascibly among his papers.

"When does he expect to fight?"

"Whenever he has to," Gates said, "and I don't want you to lose a minute—not a minute! We're putting everybody to work on your galley and Waterbury's. By cracky, it'll be a shame if the *Gates* isn't fit to fight!"

"Sir," I asked, "what's known about the British fleet? Have they built vessels bigger than ours?"

I waited his answer with a shrinking feeling; for on the size of the British fleet depended, in all probability, my safety and Nathaniel's. More, even, than our safety hung on it: our very lives might be at stake.

Gates pounced on some papers with a grunt of satisfaction. "Now then, here's General Arnold's requisitions. For your galley: two eighteens, two twelves and four sixes. For the *Washington* galley, one eighteen, one twelve, two nines and four fours. Right?"

"No sir," I said. "The *Congress* galley can carry more guns. She ought to have two long nines in addition to those named."

Gates made the note on the requisition. I tried again to ask what strength the British would bring against us, but he interrupted me. "According to my understanding, all these row-galleys have an outlandish rig."

"Lateen," I said. "Two masts, with a lateen sail on each."

Gates shook his head. "Never heard of such a thing! You'll have to keep watch on the riggers and see you get what you want. Don't spend a minute here that you don't have to! Not a minute! It'll be terrible if the British come down from St. John's, and catch Arnold without the ships he's counting most on!"

"Sir," I said, "I'd like to know whether I can depend on the services of one of my best men—Steven Nason. He went north on a scout a month ago and——"

Gates stopped me with an uplifted hand: then rose from his desk and went to the narrow window that looked out on the parade ground. The sentries on the battlements were staring down at some common object of interest; and I could hear a confused gabbling and cheering.

Wilkinson came into the room with an appearance of exaggerated coolness, but his jaw muscles were throbbing.

"Sir," he said, "before crossing to Mount Independence, I ventured to prosecute my search for Captain Merrill's——"

"What's that noise?" Gates interrupted. "For God's sake, Wilky, get to the point!"

"Sir," Wilkinson said, "it's a messenger from General Arnold with two prisoners—two officers."

Gates peered from the window again: then turned an exasperated glare on Wilkinson. "*What* two officers?"

"British," Wilkinson said. "Two British officers. It's that Whitcomb again. Whitcomb took them." There was disparagement and expostulation in his voice.

"Whitcomb!" Gates exclaimed. "Whitcomb!" He hopped slightly, ejaculating, "Ha! Whitcomb! Ha, ha! Whitcomb!" as if in uncontrollable delight.

The gabbling and cheering grew louder. Through the window we saw soldiers sweep through the gate of the fort and spread out, fan-wise, on the parade ground, to stare at three figures in the center. One was Steven Nason. The others were blindfolded and wore gaudy scarlet coats. Their waistcoats were scarlet as well, and their white breeches snugly bound with black gaiters. On their heads were close-fitting caps of black leather with a metal plate sticking up in the front, as if to protect their foreheads from bullets. They might have been snatched straight out of St. James's Park instead of captured in the middle of a wilderness.

I was as interested in them as was the crowd; for they were the first Britishers any of us had seen at close range.

Gates fussed about his desk, straightening his papers. "Go back to your vessel, Captain," he told me. "This is an omen; a good omen! You asked me for Nason, and yonder he is, with conquered British—very pat! very pat! Yes, we'll take it as a sign from heaven!"

He edged himself into his desk chair, looking up slyly. "That Whitcomb!" he said. He chuckled and chuckled, slapping his hands softly against his desk. "Now we'll learn something! Now we'll learn what they're up to!"

XXXII

It was late that night before Steven Nason came to the officers' quarters beside the crew's barracks; but he could have delayed until daybreak and still found Cap Huff awake and waiting.

In spite of his reckless and blustering ways, that great ox of a man had such a regard for Nason that he behaved, in Nason's absence, like a dog deprived of his master: he was forever wandering to the door to sniff the outer air, or growling to himself uneasily, or scratching himself out of pure fretfulness.

He practiced dice-throwing with Doc Means, for both had worked interminably to perfect themselves in the finger-twists Zelph had taught them: twists that, if properly executed, caused the dice to fall as the thrower wished them to fall; but he put no heart in his throwing—not even enough to curse when Doc beat him, which he seemed to do almost by accident, especially at such times as large sums of money were supposedly at stake. Since the day Cap had given Doc the pair of dice, Cap had become indebted to Doc in the sum of eight thousand dollars (Continental).

When Nason at last arrived, Cap was more than ever like an enormous clumsy dog, wagging himself before Nason, patting him with his huge paws, and almost panting with joy. Unknown to any of us, he had (to use his own words) picked up four flasks of rum: and these he produced when Nason joined us.

"Stevie," he said, his big face glistening with apprehension, "I hope to God you're through running around with this feller Whitcomb! He ain't a safe feller for you to be with! I ain't had a minute's peace since you went north the second time, knowing the risks he takes."

Nason laughed. "Risks! I suppose you weren't taking risks when you and Verrieul paid a visit to the British and came away with a keg of rum!"

Cap was scornful. "That's different! We had to have that rum. Nobody has to have British generals. Whitcomb thinks he has to have British generals; but that ain't no regular human need, like rum or shirts, or getting your feet warm. It's just his imagination. Anyway, besides, we wasn't hiding nothing, and we walked right up to 'em in the daytime.

That's different from getting around behind 'em and hiding in the bushes, the way Whitcomb does. That's something I just can't stand, Stevie—somebody hiding in the bushes and watching what I do—and I ain't the only feller that feels that way! Hiding in the bushes is plumb risky, Steven, no matter where it's done!"

"Where's our fleet," I asked Nason, "and how's it look?"

"It's moving south, hunting for a likely place to fight, and it might look worse—lots worse! General Arnold's a seaman if ever I saw one, and he's got another seaman to help him. His name's Wigglesworth. He's a colonel, but he used to sail ships for Nathaniel Tracy in Newburyport. I wouldn't wonder if Arnold and Wigglesworth are better than anybody the British can produce." Meditatively he added, "They've got some smart men, though, the British have. They've got a man named Schanck. He's made himself a flat-bottomed boat that he can turn into a keel-boat in five seconds."

"How, for God's sake?"

"There's a little slot of a well in the center of it," Nason said. "There's a board pinned in the well. If he takes out the pin, the board drops down and makes a keel, and then he can beat to windward. He calls it a centerboard."

While I was storing this discovery in my mind for future reference, Cap Huff snorted. "Hell, that ain't nothing! Anybody could 'a' thought of that—if he'd ever just a-happened to think of it." He was almost right, and I was surprised it had never occurred to anyone before.

"Did you find out anything about the British fleet?" I asked Nason, little dreaming he had acquired information of even greater moment to me than the number of vessels we must fight.

Nason nodded. "They've got seven real vessels. They're big, but we couldn't be sure how big. It was hard to tell from where we were. Then they've got a lot of little gundelos, each one mounting a single heavy gun. Six of the big vessels are in the water, and one's on the stocks still. Whitcomb says the one on the stocks wasn't even started three weeks ago. They must have laid down her keel after they saw our vessels."

"How many guns do the big ones carry?"

"We couldn't be sure. There's so many British troops around that it's kind of risky to try to see all you'd like to see. There's women, too, and children! Their regiments brought three hundred women from England with 'em: camp followers. Nearly every soldier brought a dog, and some of the officers brought two or three. Seemed as if you couldn't get within a mile of the shipyard without falling over a camp follower or stepping on a dog! To tell you the truth, there were times when we felt kind of shaky, trying to keep those lobster-backs from catching us."

"That ain't such a hell of a lot of women!" Cap said. "Only three hundred?" Then he brightened. "What kind of looking women was they, mostly?"

Nason ignored him. "So far as we could make out, the two biggest vessels were schooner-rigged. We couldn't tell about the new one. She looked deep enough to carry a lot of sail. If they started her less than three weeks ago, the way Whitcomb says, it's hard to see how she's going to be of much assistance to 'em this fall."

I breathed more easily, but not for long.

Cap eyed Nason coldly. "I s'pose you was hiding in the bushes when you caught those two fellers."

"Of course we were," Nason said. "We went up past St. John's, and out on the Laprairie road, between St. John's and Montreal."

"Gosh!" Cap cried. "Whitcomb went right back where he shot Gordon!"

Nason nodded. "Yes: he figured that was the safest place. He hid in the same clump of bushes that he shot Gordon from. He said the place was so well known that nobody'd ever expect to see him there, and he was right."

"Gosh all hemlock!" Cap bawled. "I wouldn't have nothing to do with a feller as reckless as that Whitcomb! Who were these fellers he took?"

"One was quartermaster of the 29th Foot—name of Saunders. The other was his servant: a corporal. Not bad men, once they got broke to our ways."

"I s'pose they was born out of wedlock," Cap said, "like so many in the British army."

When Nason eyed him sternly, Cap assumed a jovial air. "Listen, Stevie; there ain't no earthly use getting touchy over these fellers. There ain't nothing I can say about 'em, no matter how hard I try or how dirty I talk, that'll be half as bad as the things they'll say about us when they go home. Prob'ly this Saunders offered you half a dollar to turn him loose."

"Well," Nason admitted, "they offered us twenty dollars apiece to let them go, but we didn't see fit to accept."

"I should hope not!" Cap said virtuously. "They'd 'a' given you counterfeit money!"

"I doubt it," Nason said. "They seemed good men: as good as you'd want to meet. We had to swim across a couple of rivers; they couldn't swim for sour grapes, but they had no complaints. They didn't even complain when we had to go two days without food."

"Why would they?" Cap demanded. "Would I 'a' complained if I'd been in their boots? Not by a damned sight! The recollection of what happened to that General Gordon would have kept me awful polite and helpful."

"I sort of hated to leave 'em," Nason said. "They were pleasant to talk to. Some of the things they claimed to know about America would almost make you die laughing. Whitcomb and I, we had considerable trouble keeping our faces straight."

Cap looked politely interested. "I s'pose they think we got six toes on each foot, and all our womenfolks follow the army, and it's a half hour's walk from Maine over into Virginia, and it takes a whole afternoon to row around Rhode Island."

"Yes, just about," Nason said. Then he added something that made my flesh crawl. "They think nobody in America can build ships except people from Maine. They told us they knew we'd never be able to build a fleet that amounted to anything, because we couldn't get enough Maine men to build it."

At this Cap slapped his huge thighs and bellowed mirthfully; and at the sound of his laughter everyone laughed with him—Tom Bickford, Doc Means, Joseph Marie Verrieul, and Nason too. They drank from the rum bottles, choked, coughed and laughed until the tears ran down their cheeks; but I, remembering the thoughtless extravagance of my speech to Ellen Phipps, dimly sweet on the doorstep of the farm house in Skenesboro in the dark of a hot July night, found nothing at which to laugh.

My lips stiffened with horror at this final proof of all I had long feared and known, but had refused to face squarely, as is the way with most of us. Hopefully I had told myself that I *might* be wrong: that Nathaniel *might* not be in danger: that there *might* be two Marie de Sabrevoises. Now there could be no more such hopes.

I heard again the words of idle bombasto with which, thinking to bring a smile to her lips, I had replied to Ellen's question as to how long it would take us to build the fleet.

"If we can get enough men from Maine," I had told her, "we'll build it in a month."

And when she had scoffed at the abilities of men from Maine, I had added, with more than a little truth, "They know how to build ships, and that's more than can be said for a lot of the men they're sending us."

And now here were these words, these idle, jesting words, incapable of being uttered by any American in sober truth, brought out of St. John's by two Britishers, one of them a high officer, free to have access to the highest.

I knew exactly what had happened. Ellen, having performed her aunt's commission in Albany, had been taken by her brother back to St.

John's—back to Marie de Sabrevois. No doubt, in all innocence, she had carried letters with her from the Loyalists that infested Albany, making life hideous for Schuyler with the same sort of lying rumors that had been spread about Arnold. Reunited with her aunt, whom she loved and trusted, she must have told her all that had happened during her travels—how she had almost been forced to remain in Skenesboro until enough men from Maine could be obtained to build the fleet. Possibly she had said she feared she might be forced to remain there forever, waiting for men from Maine who would never come. And Marie de Sabrevois had told the British! In no other way could my words have reached the officer captured by Whitcomb and Nason!

I was right: I had always been right. Marie de Sabrevois was a spy. She had used Nathaniel and Ellen to further her own ends; and thus information had been given to the enemy through Ellen's act and through Nathaniel's.

I was thankful for the dim light in our small cabin—the faint yellow flame of a single candle, that cast fantastic wavering shadows of my companions on the rough walls; for otherwise they must have seen in my face that I was afraid. And I *was* afraid; afraid of what would happen to Nathaniel and to Ellen if this knowledge, strangely shared by me with a woman from my own town—a woman who had once attempted to make a traitor of Steven Nason—should become public property.

XXXIII

THE *Trumbull* left us in a week, a low craft, long and raking. Her dark red sides and her two big triangular sails, with yards that slanted backward like twin quill pens held by invisible hands, gave her a foreign air, so that she seemed out of place amid the flaming foliage of these rugged northern headlands. She might have been a pirate from Algiers, stealing into the north on some desperate adventure, except for the ragged beat of her twelve long sweeps. So roughly did these scrabble her over the water that she looked more like a giant red bug, confused by her own ungainliness.

Why Waterbury, Captain Thatcher and I didn't become stark, staring lunatics in the week after her departure, I can't say. Everything went wrong. The *Gates* galley had failed to join us, for every last ship carpenter in Skenesboro had fallen a victim to the flux and intermittent fever. Our own efforts to outfit our vessels seemed merely laughable, for most of the things we wanted couldn't be located, while such things as could be found weren't the right ones. Gates himself came down the hill to show us a despatch from Arnold, who had taken post on the western or inner side of Valcour Island. The galleys, he insisted to Gates, must be sent—they *must* be sent!

When we heard Arnold's peremptory words, we knew we must make shift with anything we could get. We seized whatever we could lay hands on: shouted ourselves hoarse for rope and more rope: for rammers and hand-spikes: wads, priming-wires, tubes: worms, ladles, gun tackles: for cartridge paper, sponges, grape shot, round shot: for breeching-hooks, cartridge boxes, musket and pistol cartridges: for powder and more powder: for rum, provisions, extra spars, seizing, spun yarn, water-kegs.

On the 5th of October Wilkinson brought us word that Arnold could wait no longer: willy nilly we must sail as we were; so we worked all that night with blazing pine-knots lashed to the bulwarks, and at dawn we set sail for Valcour.

After the blinding sweat, the unending turmoil, the ceaseless labors of the past three months, the silent reaches of this narrow lake seemed a part of some new land—unreal, even, with the endless ragged wall of snow-clad mountains to the east, and the glaring colors with which the shores were painted—the bands of golden yellow, blazing orange, silvery greens and blues, patched here and there with furry browns that had the look of huge animals sprawled asleep among the rolling hills. Splattered on the browns and golds were gouts and smears of crimson and scarlet, as if a stricken giant had tramped, bleeding, high and low, hunting those who had come with guns and swords and axes to put the curse of war upon him.

I wished with all my heart that it might prove unreal indeed—that we might cruise on and on, out of these constricted waters and into the open sea, away from the raggedness, hunger, disease, cruelty, tumult and death that must come crowding up around us as soon as we ceased to sail.

. . . Valcour lies halfway between Ticonderoga and St. John's, on the New York side of the lake; and by noon on that peaceful October Sunday we raised the high hogback of the island. It looked, from a distance, like a shaggy prehistoric buffalo, standing belly-deep off shore to feed.

For a time I thought there had been a mistake as to the whereabouts of the fleet, even though Waterbury, a mile ahead of us in the *Washington*, held his course due north, straight into the insignificant passage between Valcour and the mainland. I saw no fleet in the passage, nor anywhere near it.

Then I saw Waterbury haul his wind. At the same moment a puff of white bloomed amid the reds, greens and yellows of the island. Another white ball blossomed, and another, and the heavy boom of great guns struck against us. By looking hard I found a mast. Then, as if that one had been a key to a puzzle, a whole grove of them was visible, and the dull gray of furled canvas.

The guns roared on, saluting the *Washington*. She slid in among the masts. As her sails came down, she, too, seemed almost to vanish.

The men, hunkered beneath our low bulwarks for the warmth denied them by their torn and scanty garments, grumbled among themselves. I think Cap Huff spoke an almost universal thought when he dropped from the mainmast look-out steps with a thud that shook the quarterdeck, declaring violently that you might as well cooper a fleet in a hogshead as hide it behind an island where nobody could see it.

Tom Bickford had been exercising the men on the furling and lashing of lateen sails. He hurried back to the quarterdeck, his face all smiles. "Well, sir," Tom said, "that's the smartest anchorage ever I saw! How'd you like to have to root *them* out, Cap'n Peter?"

Nason turned on him. "Look here! If you haven't anything good to say, don't say it."

"That's right!" Cap bawled. "If there's anything I hate, it's sarcasm! If you got anything to say, say it—unless it ain't fitten to say, as Stevie says."

Tom took the tiller from the helmsman. "I better take her in, Cap'n Peter," he said. "We wouldn't want to make any kind of mess: not with everybody there watching." He turned a puzzled gaze on Cap Huff. "Sarcasm? When was I sarcastic? I don't aim to be sarcastic about anybody."

"No, I s'pose not!" Cap Huff said. "I s'pose when you called that the smartest anchorage you ever saw, you just wanted to utter a Christian sentiment."

"What's the matter with the anchorage?" I asked.

Cap eyed me doubtfully: then turned to peer into the channel between Valcour and the main. By now we were in it, almost, running fast before the smart south wind. With each passing moment we saw more clearly how the fleet was ranged.

Midway of Valcour a shoulder juts out toward the New York shore. South of the shoulder is a cup-shaped bay; and it was across the mouth of the bay that the fleet was stretched in half-moon formation.

"The matter with it?" Cap asked. "Why, look at it! How would they get out of that corner, if they had to get out in a hurry? Considering the sailors they've got aboard, they'd be too busy bumping into each other and running ashore to do anything else. Do you think they could ever run out and chase the British?" He laughed hoarsely.

"I wouldn't be at all surprised," I said. "Those vessels have been cruising for a month. It doesn't take long to make a sailor, not if you've got seamen in charge. A man soon learns the ropes, when he knows he's going to get a rap with a belaying pin if he doesn't. If that's your only objection to the anchorage, stop worrying about it."

"That anchorage ain't worth a hoot!" Cap said coldly. "Can't I see what it is? Once you're in there, you wouldn't know what was happening anywhere! You might as well be up on the Chaudière as behind that island!"

"Not quite," I said. "Not quite. I hate to mention this in your hearing, but it takes a seaman to understand ships, just as it takes a tailor to make a coat. You pay eight hundred dollars for a keg of rum because Congress printed money without knowing anything about money. They printed it the way they'd print newspapers, and that's why it's worth no more than newspapers."

Cap breathed heavily. "Newspapers! Money! Eight hundred dollars! What's that got to do with this anchorage?"

"It's got *this* to do with it. That anchorage was selected by a seaman. Look at it carefully. A squadron coming down from the north can't even *see* this fleet, not unless a scout boat should be sent right down the channel and into the jaws of the crescent."

"Ain't that just what I say?" Cap demanded.

"Wait. You don't understand. The British won't move against us unless they have a favorable wind—a wind from the north. Once they've got it, they'll keep all their vessels together, probably, and expect to find us lying out in the open somewhere. They'd never think of looking in here for us, because from the north this channel looks like nothing at all."

Cap was exasperated. "That's what it looks like, and that's what it is! Don't you think I can see?"

"All right," I told him. "If you can see so much, you can see what's going to happen when the British ships go past the island."

Cap's eyes wavered. "When they go past! Once they're past, they're past, and they do as they damned please, don't they?"

"Not at all! The British can't move a man or a gun of their main force until they're safe from our fleet. If their ships should go on to Crown Point without finding us, we could sail to the Richelieu and blow their army to pieces; so they've got to find us and try to put us out of the way. They've *got* to. If they come down from the north, and run past this island, and then discover us after they've got past, they've got to come back again. They've got to beat back against the wind, into this narrow channel; and with the wind against 'em they'll have a hell of a time doing it. The island's so high that when they get into the channel, their wind'll be all whichway, and they'll have trouble maneuvering. God knows how many ships they'll send against us; but no matter how many there are, we'll have a chance against 'em, thanks to whoever picked that anchorage."

Cap put his hand under his hat and scratched his head. Then he said intolerantly, "Who do you think picked it? When you see a good anchorage like that—so good that right the first minute a person looks at it he don't see the virtue in it, and only finds out it's good after he studies it out himself and has second thoughts that show him it couldn't be better, why, what you go to look for in the man that picked it is *brains!* Arnold picked that anchorage! But I wouldn't have told it on him if it hadn't been a good one. Whenever you see brains used around this army, you'll find they belong to just only about three or four men: more likely three. One of 'em's Arnold, and one of 'em's Stevie Nason! Arnold and Stevie Nason is two of 'em, anyhow."

We had hauled our wind and were headed straight for the curved line of vessels. We were so close we could see the tattered coats of the crews that swarmed on ratlines and gun-carriages. Fastened to the bulwarks of every vessel was a fringe of inverted evergreens, a collar of spruce or hemlock, so that the fleet had a holiday flavor.

Our own men lay aloft in the ratlines and manned the rails, waving their disreputable caps, so that there must have been a lively look to us as we came slashing down into the little bay.

All the vessels of the fleet, when they left Skenesboro, had been un-rigged and at loose ends, unballasted and ungunned, just short of total wrecks. Now they were shipshape and handsome, their canvas neatly furled and the new striped flag of the United Colonies whipping out from every masthead. It was a miracle, this crescent of fourteen armed vessels, their black guns staring open-mouthed at us—this makeshift fleet manned by half-clad landsmen, whose white skins showed through the slits in their beggars' rags, but who still could swing their arms at us and howl a hearty welcome.

A ball of smoke popped from the side of the *Royal Savage*. A torrent of cheering echoed from the high slopes of Valcour, to vanish in the roar of the guns that saluted us and the thunder of our own replies, only to burst on us again as the smoke clouds drifted backward to cling in wisps among the pines and birches.

A boat slid out from under the counter of the *Royal Savage*. In the stern sheets sat a stocky, broad-shouldered figure, brightly uniformed, all blue and gold and buff. It was the general. He pointed to the center of the line, making a circling gesture.

I looked at Tom. He nodded. "She'll go as she is," he said. We shot into the middle of the crescent, like a rabbit plunging into a hole. Close on one side was the *Washington*, her yards already lashed and her sails brailed up: on the other side a gundelo with a single 12-pounder in her bows, two 9-pounders amidships, and a newly broached keg of rum in her stern. We were so close that the gabble of the crews was loud in our ears.

Tom turned our vessel on her heel and laid her between the *Washington* and the *Royal Savage*. "What's the anchorage?" I asked the quarterdeck of the *Royal Savage*.

"Six fathom and good bottom!" they shouted.

By the time General Arnold came aboard, our anchor was down, our sails were clewed up against our two raking yards, and we rode as neatly between our neighbors as though our snub noses were made fast to the same boom.

Nason lined up the men for the general; and, considering that some of them were Bounty Boys who, less than a month before, had been called the very sweepings of hell, they made a smart appearance—as smart as any body of men can make when their breeches are in shreds and their coats no better.

The general was all business when he climbed over the side. He came to a stop before Nason's marines, pushed his under lip out and up, and balanced himself with feet far apart. It was always hard to guess what he was thinking; and when he stared at something as he now stared at Nason's scarecrows, his thoughts were usually miles away.

"Good!" he told Nason. "We'll make something out of these men! There's a barrel of rum in my boat. Have it brought aboard."

He turned abruptly and came aft. "So this is it!" he said, looking from Tom to me. "You did better than I thought you would. This isn't a bad vessel!"

"She's a good vessel," I said. "She'll sail rings around the *Royal Savage*."

Arnold laughed. "To tell you the truth, the *Royal Savage* is about as wild as they come. In a breeze she bumps everything in sight, larboard, starboard, dead ahead or dead astern. I made up my mind when you were a mile away. This is the vessel for me." He looked aggressive, as if he expected a protest.

"You've made no mistake," I said. "She can sail, and I think these men have learned to sail her."

"Can they fight her? They'll have to do both."

Nason had come to the quarterdeck with Cap Huff. Cap spoke up eagerly. "General, that's the first thing I taught 'em. 'Either you can fight the British,' I told 'em, 'or you'll fight me!' That was enough for 'em; they'll be wildcats for fighting, General, if ever you show 'em any British to fight."

"I think I can show 'em some," Arnold said. "I wish I could be as sure of showing 'em some decent coats and breeches."

His face was lumpy. "Damn 'em! If they'd only give me what I ask for, there'd never be an Englishman get as far as Crown Point, not unless he floated there dead! Ask for a frigate and they give you a raft! Ask for sailors and they give you tavern waiters! Ask for a thousand pairs of breeches and they send you a dozen waistcoats. Ask for supplies and they call you a thief!"

He seemed boiling mad: then unexpectedly he smiled. "We'll fool 'em! We'll fool 'em yet! Try to keep the men supplied with rum, so they won't freeze. I've asked for clothes, but I can't get 'em."

"General," I asked, "have you heard for certain how many vessels the British have built?"

He stared at me, pushing out that under lip. "Look here: I'll move into this vessel today. What sort of quarters are there?"

"Nothing to brag about," I told him. "There's one big room aft, for officers. I didn't bulkhead it, in case we had to use it for a hospital. We sleep on the floor; but there's a mess table, and you could sleep on that."

"That's all right," Arnold said. "I'll go back, get my things, and move right over."

Zelph came aft, tenderly carrying a round-bellied kettle. "Lobscouse, Cap'n Peter!" he shouted. "Lobscouse, all hot'n thick! Thickest lobscouse I ever see. We eat now, guess we better."

"Lobscouse!" Arnold cried. "What's in it?"

"Gennle," Zelph said, "they's twict as much in this lobscouse as ever I got into the same size lobscouse before. They's some ducks and some pigs' feet an' a big snapper turkle, biggern your hat, Gennle, an' a pecker potatoes, an' a mess ship braid all busted up. Yow!"

"Don't keep that lobscouse out here in this cold wind!" the general said sharply. "Get below with it!" To me he added, "After all, I won't need my clothes and papers. They're better off in the *Royal Savage*, where there's a cabin to stow 'em. Now I'm here, I might as well stay."

I think we looked surprised at this decision; for he laughed. "Come, come! Once the wind changes, the British'll be down on our necks. We don't want to lose a minute getting at that lobscouse!"

In the cabin, warmed by a plate of lobscouse and a tumbler of rum, the general told us some things that opened my eyes. I'd known he was a better leader than any officer in our army; but now it dawned on me that he was something more. He was a great man—a great captain, in whom burned a flame of genius: a flame that fevered and provoked the brains of small, mean men, filling them with envy and malice. This is something I cannot explain: all I can say is that those who admired him and recognized his worth were generous gentlemen—Washington, Schuyler, Joseph Warren, Silas Deane; whereas those who hated him with undying bitterness were human shrimps—Easton, Wilkinson, Wynkoop, Hazen, Bedel and others of whom I shall speak in due course.

When he had been talking to us and we to him for a time after finishing the lobscouse, he put his fists on the table and stared at us.

"Well," he said, "I guess it isn't necessary to feed you any pap. You've been through the mill, and don't have to be babied. I think I can do you the compliment of telling you the truth."

Cap Huff looked concerned. "It ain't nothing serious, is it, General? We ain't going to get our pay or nothing like that, are we?"

"Certainly not!" Arnold said. "All available money had to be paid to the militia and ship carpenters. You don't think there'd be anything left over for such as you, do you? You're supposed to fight: not to go around whining for pay! You ought to know it's the loud talkers and the light workers that get paid for wars: not the fighters."

"I'm glad to hear it," Cap said. "If all these men got paid, and I had to take their money off 'em the way I did off the ship workers, I'd have to get out of the army and look after my estate." He took a package of currency from his brown frock and whacked it against the table. It was about the size of two Bibles.

"Good!" Arnold said. "If that's ship workers' money, accept my congratulations for a patriotic act! Only don't let it interfere with your duties! That's one bad thing about money: if a man has much of it, it's apt to make him too careful when he gets into a fight. I'd hate to see anyone too careful aboard this vessel when trouble starts, though I want no precautions overlooked! We're going to need 'em before we leave this anchorage!"

Tom Bickford had a word to say. "We spoke about it coming in, General—about the anchorage. It's as if you'd had it made! Cap'n Peter was saying they'd have a dreadful time beating in here after you!"

The general slapped his knee. "Why, you're seamen after all! Thank God for that! We've got one or two sailors aboard this fleet, but damned few seamen! Damned few! Yes sir! This is one anchorage in a million! I wore grooves in this lake, running in and out of every cove and around every island, before I found it. It's the only place on this part of the earth where they'll have to hunt for us, and then have their noses bitten off before they—before they——"

"Then they're stronger than we are," I said. "How much——"

"I didn't say so!" he interrupted. "Don't misunderstand me!" He shot a quick glance at me. "As a matter of fact, they *are* stronger: a little stronger: not much, probably." He dismissed their possible superiority with a wave of his hand. "The point is that their strength has almost bankrupted 'em. They thought they were ready to sail a month ago! If they could have done so they could have occupied Crown Point and taken Ticonderoga. The war would have been over—Pht! Like that!"

He shook his fist at us. "But they couldn't sail! They couldn't do it! Thanks to your work in Skenesboro, gentlemen, they had to go to building again. When I sailed up to Windmill Point and let 'em see my wares, they had to lay down three more vessels, starting a month ago; one of 'em a——"

He interrupted himself. "If I could have got the shipwrights, if I could have got the stores and the men, I'd have built a frigate, as I wanted to in the beginning; and then, by God, let 'em try to find a hole in the north gate!"

"You don't mean to say they've built a frigate in a month! A frigate! Why, a frigate could knock all of us to pieces in half an hour!"

"There you go," Arnold said, "getting things hindside foremost! What do we care about a frigate, even if they *have* got one, or a *dozen* frigates, for that matter! What we care about is delay. Delay! Why, look here! Today's the sixth of October! There's snow on the Green Mountains! It's cold! It's nearly winter; and the British aren't started yet! Before you know it, there'll be snow on the New York shore, and then it *will* be winter! They can't carry on a winter campaign! They'd be beaten by snow and cold, and they know it! A little more delay and we've got 'em! They can't get through! We're safe for nearly a year! Delay! Delay! That's all we want. Every day we delay 'em now is worth a month's delay earlier in the season!"

He jumped up and banged his fists on the table. "What's more, there's no price too high to pay for it! No price!"

Tom Bickford's hands were clenched. Cap Huff hitched at his belt, then rubbed his red face with huge hands. Nason, his lips compressed, stared into space. Arnold, I saw, could have whatever help they could give him in purchasing delay.

Arnold saw it, too. He patted Cap's shoulder and smiled at the rest of us. "I've got to row around the fleet. Keep after 'em: that's the only way! Keep after things! Maybe you noticed: there's only one thing wrong with this anchorage."

"It looks all right to me," I said.

"Trees!" Arnold complained. "Those trees behind us! When the trouble comes, those trees might put us in a box! If you climb one of 'em, as I did, you'll find you can look right down on the deck of this vessel. That won't do! We can't have that! Carleton might take it into his head to land a few scouts on Valcour; and before we knew it, they'd be up the trees picking us off! You've seen the evergreen decorations of the others; do likewise. Cut young spruces and fasten 'em, butts up, around your ship, outside the bulwarks, so they make a six-foot palisade. They'll give you shelter from musket fire, and they'll be discouraging to anybody who tries to board you!"

He gave us a confident nod; and before we could do him the courtesy of rising, he had run up the companion ladder, as spry as a cat. He stopped at the top and looked back at us, his dark face framed in the hatchway.

"Waste no time! Get yourself ready! All they're waiting for now is a north wind! That may start to blow tonight."

Not until after he had gone did we realize that although he had talked as freely and easily with us as though he held no higher rank than ours, and was just our hearty comrade, he hadn't told us the one thing we all wished most to know. He hadn't told us how much chance we would have to be alive after the British fleet came down upon us from the north.

XXXIV

THE wind was in the north the very next morning, but it was weak and soft: not glittering and knife-edged from northern snows. Our bulwarks were high with the butts of spruces, their branches trimmed off on the inner side. Over everything there was a soothing scent of greenery reminiscent of home and Christmas.

Arnold had us knock together a plank table on the quarterdeck; and there he sat, writing letters, issuing orders and watching every vessel in the fleet—especially the *Revenge,* which was doing guard duty, running down the channel, and then beating up around the outside of the island, all her men on deck, and gun-crews at their stations with lighted matches.

Whenever the *Revenge* sheered in to report, Arnold had a look of hawk-nosed fierceness that put me in mind of an eagle.

Those pale eyes of his were sharper than an eagle's. He had the *Trumbull* moved, for fear the *Royal Savage* would swing against her. He sent Tom Bickford to report a chafed backstay on the *Lee.* He watched them exercising the guns on the *Washington* and sent word to the first lieutenant that the guns were laid too high. He saw a boatload of potatoes rowing out from the New York shore, and nothing would do but he must examine all of them, to be sure we were getting proper value.

He was as busy as a hen who has hatched out a brood of ducks, but calmer. With all his peering about and giving of orders, the words flowed smoothly and rapidly from his pen.

He called to me, shook the sand from a letter and handed it over. It was to General Schuyler, complaining of the manner in which the fleet was treated.

The Atlantic States [his letter ran] *expect this fleet to protect them from the British, and evidently they think we can do it by shouting "Boh!" and making faces. Where in God's name is the powder we should have? Where are the blankets? My men are sleeping on bare decks and the nights are bitter. Where are the woolen stockings and breeches? My men are bare-legged and bare-footed. I could make warmer clothes for them out of a lace curtain! We're expected to fight, but given nothing*

*to fight with. . . . Is it possible my countrymen can be callous to their
wrongs, or hesitate one moment between slavery or death? . . . I have
received your letter about Major Brown's charges against me, presented
by Colonel Easton. I am at a loss to know where these tales originated.
You know the falsity of them, and so do the Commissioners of Congress,
but I will take it as a favor if you will continue to deny them at every
opportunity.*

Arnold tapped the page. "It's this last I want you to see. Did you hear
any of these slanders in Skenesboro? Did you hear I robbed the citizens
of Montreal of their belongings?"

"Yes sir," I admitted. "Those stories were going around as far back as
July."

"July! They've been calling me a thief since July!"

"That's an overstatement," I said. "Some damned fool starts a rumor,
but nobody believes it—nobody with sense."

The look in Arnold's eyes was worse than distressing. "I suppose," he
said, "you never had occasion to suspect the source of these rumors."

"Well, sir, I heard Brown and Easton mentioned, just as in your letter."

Arnold waved a contemptuous hand. "No, no! I mean where Brown
got his crazy notions. Somebody supplied him with them. He never
thought 'em up himself! He's dull—a thick-witted ass! I know him! He
went to Yale when I was in New Haven. Twenty-seven years old, he
was, when he graduated from college—a noisy oaf, all muscle and no
brain! A great man in college, because he could kick a football over
the college buildings; but he can't think for himself, and never could!
Indignant, he was, at those who threw overboard the tea in Boston Harbor! He called it contrary to law and order, and above all a great waste
of tea. It wasn't till he heard other people talk that he decided it was a
patriotic act. No, Brown never thought up those charges! My God, man!
Listen to them!"

He snatched a paper from beneath a stone on his table. "Wants me
arrested for 'following crimes'—hm, hm,—'subjecting him to serve in an
inferior rank'—inferior rank! The muddle-headed blunderer! Listen—
'for permitting smallpox to spread before Quebec'—who does he think
I am? God, able to stop smallpox from spreading? He wants me tried
for 'plundering the inhabitants of Montreal to the eternal disgrace of
the Continental Army'—I suppose if he'd been in command he'd sat still
and let his men starve—and here's a gem: 'for giving unjustifiable, cruel
and bloody orders, directing the inhabitants of whole villages to be put
to death by fire and sword, without distinction to friend or foe, age or
sex.'"

He looked purely exasperated. "That probably refers to the time I ordered De Haas to run the Indians out of Canasadauga for being a party to the murder of four prisoners at the Cedars: that must be what he means, the jackass!

"And here's the climax: I was guilty of 'great misconduct from the camp at Cambridge until I was superseded by General Montgomery at Pointe aux Trembles, near Quebec!' God knows what *that* means! Maybe somebody told him I was misconducting myself when I got my feet wet crossing the Height of Land, and had the indescribable carelessness to let myself get shot in the leg when we stormed Quebec!

"Those things don't sound like Brown to me! Somebody's been filling Brown with lies, up to the muzzle. They sound more like that Frenchman in Quebec who made us think Natanis was a spy, so we'd shoot him instead of using him for a guide. We damned near did it, too!"

"Who was that?" I asked.

Arnold put his papers back beneath the stone and half rose to peer toward the upper end of Valcour—looking, evidently, for the *Revenge*. "Oh, it's not he! He's dead! Clever, he was, too; but he miscalculated Nason's powers. Guerlac, his name was. Didn't Nason ever tell you about Guerlac?"

I shook my head.

"No," Arnold said, "I suppose not. I suppose he wouldn't. There was a woman in it—one he'd never talk about. Well, it couldn't be Guerlac, because Nason killed him. That's who it sounds like, though. I'd give a good deal to find out what's behind all this!"

He gnawed his thumb, his eyes focussed on something miles away. "These charges sound like the ravings of an idiot: they're so preposterous I can't dignify them by taking public notice of them, any more than Gates or Schuyler can; and the hell of it is, they're dangerous! There's always somebody to believe anything about a man—anything! If these reports ever reach Congress, there'll be plenty to believe 'em! Plenty! And God knows what they'd do! They might put that old gray mare Wynkoop back in command of this fleet. They might let a Frenchman have it—a Frenchman who wouldn't have time to fight because of having to tell everybody what a fighter he was!"

"They'd never do that!" I protested.

He looked at me pityingly. "Congress wouldn't? Why wouldn't they? Look at what they *have* done! Haven't they just made St. Clair a general, for God's sake? And for what? For what? Damned if I know, unless it was because he voted to abandon Crown Point, or because his name sounded French to 'em! The way to get quick promotion in this army is to go to France and take a French name; then Congress would make you a major general."

I laughed, thinking of the Chevalier Mathicu Alexis Roche-Fermoy, who considered himself superior to General Washington.

"It's no laughing matter," Arnold said. "They don't care *who* they promote, so long as he's no damned good!"

I told him I was laughing because of Dr. Price's book, which contended that people who have a parliament that subjects itself to any kind of foreign influence aren't free at all.

"Price on Civil Liberty?" Arnold asked eagerly. "Have you got that book? I've heard of it, and I'd like to look at it. That's the book supposed to be responsible for the signing of the Declaration of Independence!"

When I produced my copy, he read a few words: then clapped it shut. "Of course! Of course! He's absolutely right! This government of ours isn't a government at all!"

He tucked it in his sash and got to his feet to study the sky. "South!" he exclaimed. "No British with a south wind! We'll exercise the galleys —once around the island! The prize'll be a keg of rum! I'll pay for it out of my own pocket! We'll show Waterbury a thing or two!" He rubbed his hands together, balanced on his toes as if bursting with energy. "I'll sail this hooker, and we'll drink the rum ourselves!"

. . . The next day was the 8th, and the wind was in the south again; and there it stayed on the 9th and the 10th—a gusty, moist wind out of a heavy sky, moaning ominously in our top-hamper and sighing mournfully in our spruce-decked bulwarks.

On the night of the 10th the breeze fell. Arnold, stretched on our mess table, was wakeful and read Price's book by the light of two candles. I was wakeful, too, so that I knew that we were in for a change of weather. The wind was raw and smelled of snow, and it swung into the northeast just before dawn. It was a wind that made our legs ache, even though we had a blanket apiece.

The mountains on the New York shore, on the morning of the 11th, loomed white against a pale blue sky. Down the channel between Valcour and the mainland rushed an endless procession of white-caps, all of them soiled-looking, as is the way of white-caps on fresh water.

Arnold wanted his breakfast, and he wanted it in a hurry. "None of your humming-bird breakfasts, either," he warned Zelph. "I've got to have something to stick to my ribs! This feels like a busy day!"

"Lansakesalive, Gennle," Zelph said, "they ain't nothin' aboard this here vessel, only a pail of coffee an' a nice slab o' salt poke an' that ship braid I cooked on shore yesdy. What you say, Gennle; coffee an' poke?"

"Look," Cap Huff said. "I saw you playing around with a twenty-pound salmon last night—a salmon the size of a shark. Where is it?"

"Salmon ain't for breakfast," Zelph said. "Salmon's for supper."

"No it's not!" Arnold said. "It's for breakfast. Make a quick chowder: pork scraps, ship bread and potatoes. We'll eat him now while we've got a chance."

Zelph snorted. "Chance! Chance! That all we got, chance! Lay around and lay around, not doing nothin': that all we do, Gennle!"

"You make that chowder!" Arnold said. "Before you know it you'll have so much to do you won't even have time to *say* 'fish,' let alone cook one!"

The general was right. We were finishing Zelph's chowder when the whole fleet set up a tumultuous shouting, and we hurried on deck to find every ship's crew perched on the guns and in the ratlines, peering into the north. They were watching the *Revenge*, and from the manner in which she was tearing down to us, like a little old lady with her skirts hoisted up to let her run the faster, she had news.

Arnold took one look at her, then turned to Nason. "Run up a white pennant, and while you're doing it, pass the word to the *Washington!* All captains aboard the *Congress* for a Council of War!"

Cap Huff let out a roar that turned every face aboard the *Washington* in our direction.

"Hey there! Wake up! Tell Cap'n Thatcher and General Waterbury they're wanted for a Council of War!" His voice, echoing from the cliffs of Valcour, frightened a fish-hawk from a towering pine and sent it screaming into the north. "Send the word along! Don't be afraid to holler!"

Arnold groaned. "That's no way to speak to officers!" he told Cap severely. "'Holler'! 'Wake up'! 'Hey there'!"

"General," Cap said, "I can't keep military words straight in my head; but I'll get those captains over here if it's the last thing I do!"

The *Revenge*, abreast of us, let off a two-pounder with a thump, came about in the gun's white smoke, and dropped her jib.

The captain shouted through a birch-bark trumpet: "They've come around Cumberland Head! The first one was a ship—a full-rigged ship!"

Arnold, astride our taffrail, raised despairing eyes to heaven. "And you, you damned fool," he growled, "you had to fire a gun! Why didn't you put a match to your magazine, so they'd be sure to see you?"

"A full-rigged ship," the captain of the *Revenge* repeated, "and two schooners, maybe sixteen guns each!"

"Did they see you?" Arnold shouted.

"I guess not! They didn't haul their wind!"

"Is that all you saw?" Arnold called. "Three vessels?"

"That's all I waited to see. One was a full-rigged ship!"

Arnold made a funnel of his hands. "Get away to the southern tip of the island. Anchor behind the island. Understand? Anchor where you can watch 'em. If they keep on going, let 'em go! Understand?"

"I'll let 'em go," the captain said.

"If they come about and start for you," Arnold shouted, "fire a gun and make sail. Fire a gun and get back here with no loss of time. Understand? When you're seen, fire a gun, and beat back up the channel. Take your place in the line of battle. Understand? The moment you see one of the enemy come about, fire a gun and get away!"

The voice of Captain Seaman came faintly to us against the wind—"Fire a gun—beat back——"

Arnold shook his fist at us. "Now, then! Wet the blankets and double-shot the guns! We'll show these British there's somebody in the world besides themselves!"

XXXV

I WATCHED the captains come over the side: David Hawley, feeling the back of his neck; sleepy-looking Thatcher of the *Washington* galley; puckery-lipped Captain Warner of the *Trumbull;* red-headed Captain Davis of the *Lee;* General Waterbury, second to Arnold in command, gray and sober-looking, his left shoulder thrust forward, crab-like: Colonel Wigglesworth, third in command, a stocky, sedate man with quick blue eyes that belied his sedateness and a nose so hooked that he had the look of an amused hawk. I knew him for a sea captain of ability, as a sea captain had to be to sail one of Nathaniel Tracy's ships.

The others I knew by sight only: Captain Dickenson of the *Enterprise* sloop; and the gundelo captains—Grant of the *Connecticut,* wearing a bearskin coat; little Ulmer of the *Spitfire;* Simonds of the *Providence,* pale and shivering with an attack of intermittent fever; Reed of the *New York,* whose clothes, I suspected, were in worse shape than mine, since they were concealed beneath a linen overall; Rice of the *Philadelphia* and Grimes of the *New Jersey,* captains who had commanded galleys in Pennsylvania's river defense, a year before; Sumner, of the *Boston,* a Bostonian with a thoughtful look frequently encountered in Bostonians, even when least thoughtful,—good men, all of them, though some had never been beyond lobster soundings.

With a full-rigged ship maneuvering against us, however, our seafaring knowledge would be of less account than our ability to keep our heads above water.

Our own vessel, like all the others, was a turmoil of preparation. Men ran among the guns; casting them loose; setting tubes, fuses, rammers, water buckets in place; falling over the water buckets and each other.

Cap Huff's scarecrow marines were herded amidships, drawing the charges from their muskets and reloading. Cap himself lay full length on the deck, his head down the main hatch, watching the screening of the powder-magazine with wet blankets; bawling directions in a voice that set the whole belly of the galley to booming.

I followed my fellow-captains down the companion ladder. The cabin was dim, and the thudding of bare feet on the deck above gave me the feel of standing within a drum that rumbled a hurried call to arms.

"Come, come, gentlemen!" Arnold said. "Find seats if you can!" He sat at the end of the mess table, gripping it as though to pick it up and bang it on the floor out of pure exuberance. There was no doubting his cheerfulness.

We found seats between the gun-carriages, or on them, or astride the guns themselves, as poverty-stricken in appearance as sardine fishermen.

"Now then," Arnold said, "you heard the *Revenge:* a full-rigged ship and two 16-gun schooners passed Cumberland Head. By now they're abreast of us on the far side of the island. The rest of the fleet's with 'em—no question of that! It's what I expected, gentlemen: what I figured on! They haven't observed proper precautions! They've over-rated themselves! They haven't kept proper watch, and so they're going by. Let's decide: what's best to be done?"

There was some clearing of throats.

"Quick!" Arnold said. "They're going by!"

Colonel Wigglesworth spoke up, which was proper, he being a young man, if not the youngest; and the youngest is entitled to speak first in a Council of War. "What's your opinion, General?"

"You'll have my opinion fast enough! What's yours?"

Wigglesworth coughed. "Pretty hard to beat this anchorage. We could fight 'em right here."

"If we do," General Waterbury protested, "we'll never get away if we're outgunned! They've got a full-rigged ship, so I guess there's no doubt they're superior. A running fight, I say! On the lake we'll have a chance to haul out if we're sinking. Why, we're cornered, here."

"You want to fight 'em on a retreat?" Arnold asked.

Waterbury coughed. "Isn't it better to save some ships than not save any?"

The captains clamored among themselves. Their words were lost in the clattering and thudding on the deck above.

Arnold stood up and thumped the table. The captains were silent. "All right!" Arnold said. "That's what some of you think; and here's what I think! The object of this fleet isn't to save itself! We've got just one job—to keep the British from getting through to Ticonderoga and the Hudson on this campaign—to save the lake from them for this year. What happens to us doesn't matter, as long as we keep them where they are! If luck's against us, which I trust under God it won't be, then we can talk of retreat, but not till then! That's my opinion!

"Let's suppose, gentlemen, we abandon this anchorage and fight the British on a retreat. What have we got to do it with? You know as well as I do! We have vessels of varying speeds, sizes and batteries, manned by landsmen no more capable of laying guns than of laying eggs! If the British are superior in ships and guns and men, as General Waterbury thinks, any attempt to engage them openly on the lake can result only in disaster. They'll catch us separately and pound us to pieces! We'll never have a chance of winning or escaping either! We wouldn't delay 'em half an hour!

"On the other hand, gentlemen, suppose we remain at this anchorage. The British go past us. The wind's in the north. We've got the weather gauge! We can jump out at 'em, those that are fastest, chop up the slow ones and get back here to the anchorage!"

He banged a fist on the table. "Then let 'em come, by God! Let 'em beat up into this strait! Let 'em stick their heads into this crescent! They'll never board us! They can't do it! They've got to stay out in front of us: swap shot for shot with us! If our men could only shoot—by God, if they'd sent us the tenth part of what we needed—if those damned mercenary rats on the seaboard hadn't put all their sailors and all their dirty damned money into privateers, so there was nothing left for the defense of their country—we could fight off twice our strength in ships and guns! Yes, and we can do it now! Now! Now!"

His voice rose until the air of the cabin seemed to shiver. He clenched his fist and shook it in our faces. "At this anchorage we can meet 'em with concerted fire! I don't care how strong they are! I don't give a damn how many officers, seamen and gunners they got from the St. Lawrence fleet! No strength, no skill can help 'em work up to us in an orderly manner! They'll have to come up piecemeal—every which way! We can fight 'em all day; and with any luck we can beat 'em off! If we can't, we'll find a way of delaying 'em again—delaying 'em and delaying 'em, till we've saved the lake!"

He dropped his head. His eyes were round and fierce. "I say fight 'em here and fight 'em now! What have you got to say to *that*?"

Being New Englanders and sea captains, they had little to say. Most of them coughed dryly, waiting for others to do the talking. Colonel Wigglesworth slowly turned his sharp blue eyes and his hooked nose from captain to captain, like a watchful hawk. Then, to Arnold, he said: "It appears we're all willing, General."

Waterbury rose from his bench and jerked his cap hard down over his ears. "That's settled! We'll fight 'em here!"

Arnold went to the companionway and stood there, one foot on the ladder. "There's just one more thing! This is the time for the British to discover us, because of the wind. We might unstep our masts and hide here till tomorrow; but tomorrow the wind might turn south.

Then *they'd* have the weather gauge. We've got it now, and I propose to keep it! When the ship and the schooners are a mile or two to the south'ard, they'll see the *Revenge* and bear up toward her. Then, gentlemen, a few of us'll have to sail out and see what we can do. Unless we do so, it may occur to the British to tack back to the northward and come down on us from the northern end of the channel. We don't want that: so we'll let 'em see us pop out and pop back again. Then, unless I'm greatly mistaken, they'll never think there's any way of getting at us except to follow us in. There's four that can go out fast and come back handily: the *Congress,* the *Trumbull,* the *Washington* and the *Royal Savage.* If there's no objection, we'll do it."

Colonel Wigglesworth laughed grimly. "Objections! Good grief, General! There ain't time to think of any!"

He was nearer right than he knew. The words had scarcely left his lips when there was a distant thump; a penetrating thud that fluttered the air in our crowded cabin. The British had sighted the *Revenge* and come about in chase of her.

We scrambled for the companion ladder. Arnold's voice above us spurred us on. "Hoist away! Foresail and mainsail! Haul aft the sheets! Clap on there and haul! Clap on and haul!"

XXXVI

WE WENT down in an echelon, our own vessel in the lead, hugging the Valcour shore; the *Washington* a little behind us, nearer the center of the channel; then the *Trumbull* and the *Royal Savage*, each farther to the rear and nearer the New York side.

Because of the branches above their bulwarks, they had a shaggy wild look.

Arnold watched them contentedly. "Good!" he said. "They look as if they could stand a power of pounding!" He stood on tiptoe to peer at the point of the island. So far as I could tell, he was wholly unmoved at the prospect of going into battle.

With me it was different, I am free to say. No gun had ever been fired at me with serious intent, and the prospect of having God knows how many fired at me before the day was over left me with a liquefied feel in my stomach.

I was uneasy, too, because Nathaniel was in the *Royal Savage* instead of aboard our own vessel. I wanted him where I could watch him; perhaps steady him if anything went wrong. To tell the truth, I felt that if I had him to watch, I might be steadier myself.

As we opened out the sweep of lake to the south, the men at the bow guns set up a sudden shout. In the same moment we sighted, far away, to the southeastward, a full-rigged ship—a sloop-of-war—working back toward us on the larboard tack.

When we cleared the sheltering shoulder of Valcour we saw two schooners, big ones, pointing toward us as if racing. They yawed as we came out and let off bow guns. I didn't even look to see where the shot went, for just then we passed entirely beyond the southern tip of the island, and the whole broad expanse of lake lay before us, swarming with craft of every size and shape, as a marsh pool swarms with waterfowl when the moon is full in October.

In a long line to the eastward, their shining sails half blending with the snowy whiteness of the distant mountain wall, a throng of gunboats were converging on us. They were gundelos, each with a single cannon in its bow; but they were long guns and loomed up in that clear air, as big, almost, as the boats themselves.

Towering up above these smaller fry, like a goose among teal, was a floating fortress, low in the water, high-sailed, bristling with heavy guns. There was another large vessel: a sort of overgrown gundelo. We counted seven guns on her: great guns—more than twice as many as any of our gundelos carried.

Behind this swarm of vessels moved a phalanx of bateaux and canoes, drifting slowly southward, waiting: biding their time. The canoes, even at that distance, looked monstrous. They had high bulging bows and sterns, and the paddlers were thick in them, like teeth in a jawbone. Verrieul, from his perch in the ratlines, shouted that they were *Canots du maître*—Master canoes. That meant Indians—hundreds of Indians.

"Well, well!" Arnold said. "So *that's* what they were up to!" He glanced over his shoulder at the other galleys: then stepped up on the bulwarks to have a clearer look at the armada of gunboats bearing down on us.

We seemed to be the hub of a girdle of vessels; a belt that was inexorably contracting, intent on our destruction.

The gun-crews, at their stations, were understandably restless; for the north wind howling in our top-hamper must have cut like knives; and that rim of gunboats, their sails fang-like against the eastern shore, wasn't soothing.

They shuffled and shivered, these shoeless, red-nosed gun-crews. Their eyes and heads turned constantly from us to the onrushing Britishers.

Arnold made tapping motions with his forefinger and counted— "twelve, thirteen, sixteen, twenty, twenty-three, twenty-four——

"Twenty-four gunboats, I make it," he said. "Maybe fifty bateaux with troops. Light infantry, probably. See what you get." He took the tiller from me.

Nason came aft. "Sir, the bow gun's double-shotted."

Arnold nodded. "Try it once. Then take two gun-crews aft to the cabin guns. We'll haul our wind and get the eighteen-pounders into play as we go back to the anchorage." He thrust out his lower lip. "They've got a few more than I figured on—a few more. Too many to run risks with."

Through our fringe of spruces I tried to count. One of the distant schooners yawed again, puffing out a cloud of white smoke. The shot struck off our starboard bow, a quarter mile away. It seemed to me too close. I lost count, but contrived somehow to arrive at what I considered a fair estimate. "Twenty-two, I make it," I told Arnold.

The bow gun let off with a crash that almost brought us to a stop.

"All right," Arnold said. "Let's turn."

Tom Bickford ran forward, shouting orders. We hauled our wind and crossed the bows of the *Washington* galley. She went off a little: then rounded into our wake. The *Trumbull* and the *Royal Savage* did the same, as pretty as a picture. In five minutes' time the four of us were running back into the channel in the face of the sharp northeast wind, close hauled on the starboard tack.

"Now then," Arnold said, "we'll have a try at those schooners."

We went into the cabin and set the cabin tiller in place. The schooners showed up bright through the cabin ports, like a sailor's half-model in a frame. Arnold rubbed his hands together cheerfully, and the gun-crews, ranged around the two long eighteens, stared at him open-mouthed, as though they watched a figure in a play.

He looked a little like that, too, with his hat cocked on one side, his handsome blue coat, half open over a long waistcoat of yellow fur, and breeches of buff deerskin. Arnold was always neat; and being a rich man, with means to indulge his whims, he was always uniformed as a soldier should be—but as few were, in our poor army. He was one of those persons who seem neat, no matter what they wear, and he took pride in his appearance.

"If you're going to lead troops," he told me once, "you ought to try to look like a leader." I could see, now, what he meant. In the fascinated stare of the two gun-crews there was something more than admiration for their confident, smiling commander. Like myself, they were sure he'd bring us safe through the coming battle.

Arnold tinkered with the quoin beneath the breech of the larboard eighteen-pounder: threw his weight on the gun to raise the muzzle: wrenched at the carriage and said, "Off a little: off a little!"

I altered our course the merest whisker.

Arnold nodded to the gun captain, who slapped his linstock against the breech. The cabin flooring jerked: the galley lurched: the gun roared and sent white smoke rolling and tumbling astern. Arnold ran to the other stern gun and struggled with the quoin.

We heard a gun slam from the *Washington*: two thudded together from the *Trumbull* and the *Royal Savage*.

Arnold peered through the port. "Missed!" he said. He stooped, squinted, threw up his hand. The linstock slapped, and our heads rang with the crash.

He turned the guns over to Steven Nason and motioned me on deck.

A seaman in the main top hung over the edge to bawl, "Splinters under the schooner's larboard cat-head!"

A voice far forward—the voice of Cap Huff, I would have sworn—

shouted "Rum!" Another voice took it up, and another, until the whole forepart of the vessel was clamoring for rum.

The galley stood up well to the cold north wind, slashing through the chop with cheery chucklings. Far behind us the British schooner let off another gun. We saw the shot kick up a spout between the *Royal Savage* and the *Trumbull*. War, I thought, wasn't so bad, after all. The *Royal Savage* seemed slow, but she was better built than our rough galleys; and I was glad Nathaniel could see a battle under such favorable circumstances. It couldn't help, I felt, but give him a greater sense of loyalty to those for whom he fought.

We were in the channel by now, close over to the New York shore. When we came about on the starboard tack, we could see the American fleet clearly, about a mile away.

The wind seemed to jump from north to northeast: to eddy around us. Our mainsail slapped against the mast, and the galley swayed. Arnold came beside me and felt the tiller. The men continued to shout for rum.

"I don't like the feel of that wind," I told Arnold. "It bounces off the cliffs. I think we ought to get the canvas off her when we're in midchannel, and row the rest of the way."

"Do so!" Arnold said. He stepped to the break in the deck and spoke in a rasping, high-pitched voice. "We're taking in sail. Then we're rowing to our anchorage. All you've got to do, to get that rum, is brail up those sails in a hurry and clap onto your sweeps!"

Under bare poles the galley moved steadily over the last half mile. The pursuing schooners had worked out into the lake on the larboard tack, and were hidden from us. So, too, was the sloop-of-war. Except for the black smears around the mouths of the spongers and rammers, who had rubbed their noses with powder-stained hands, and the salty powder-smoke that clung in our throats, we might have been returning from a pleasure cruise.

The *Washington* and the *Trumbull*, following our example, furled their sails and crawled along behind us. The *Royal Savage*, having no oars, took in her square topsails, and continued to make short tacks under her fore-and-aft sails. I was sure Hawley felt the same insecurity about the wind that I had felt.

That crescent-shaped line of vessels, absurdly enough, seemed like home to me, and I couldn't get back to it fast enough. I thought of it as a sort of shelter from the unknown.

As we crawled slowly into place in the curving line of gundelos and schooners, the turmoil on our decks was deafening. To present our broadside to the vessels in pursuit of us, we must, before anchoring, get a spring on our cable by making fast a line to the anchor, running it through a stern port so to haul ourselves around at right angles to the wind after the anchor should be let go; also it was necessary to drop our boats over the side, out of the way of the enemy's fire, and to move our heaviest guns to the gun-ports that pointed down channel. Since our seamen were still green hands, all this movement required more running, shouting and giving of orders than can be imagined.

Yet Arnold seemed to find the uproar pleasing. He stood at the break of the deck, speaking mildly to those who came near him, telling them to take it easy: to take it easy.

There was a confused shouting from the gundelos on the eastern side of the crescent. One of the tall black schooners that had pursued us had hove in sight at the far end of the channel. She let off three guns in quick succession at the *Royal Savage,* who had a sluggish look, as though a current held her near the Valcour shore.

Arnold, watching her through our fringe of hemlock, shook his head. "Look at her! Where in God's name did Hawley learn to judge distances?"

"She ought to make it on the next tack," I said.

"I hope so," he said sourly. "All my papers are aboard her: all my accounts. My clothes, too." As an afterthought he added, "She'd *better* make it unless she wants an eighteen-pound ball in her tail!"

He beckoned to Cap Huff, who, now that the guns had been traversed, stood at the break in the deck, restlessly waiting permission to draw the promised rum. "One gill to each," Arnold told him, "and mind you don't help yourself too freely."

The *Royal Savage* came up into the wind. I tried to find Nathaniel on the quarterdeck, but couldn't. The vessel made me nervous, hanging there. Her sails shivered. I heard myself shouting, "Put your helm over! Over! Drop your anchor!"

"She missed stays," Arnold said. "She's gone."

I pulled hard with my stomach muscles, trying to help her around somehow.

Her sails filled. She fell off and moved slowly to the eastward, close to the island. Then she stopped. Far away as we were, I could see her masts bend. She stood there, motionless: then canted over on her starboard side.

"She struck!" I said foolishly. "She's ashore!"

"That's right," Arnold agreed. In a thoughtful voice he added, "This is a hell of a time to lose one of your best vessels."

I muttered that it was the wind, and racked my brain for something I could do to help Nathaniel.

"Wind be damned!" Arnold said coldly. "It was rotten bad seaman-ship!"

Into our line of vision came one of the small British gunboats, her gun high on her bow like a duck's head. She bored up into the channel with the help of a lug sail and four long oars. Another slid from behind the shoulder of the island, beyond the stranded *Royal Savage:* then three in a clump: then another and another.

A boat put out from the stranded vessel, an anchor balanced across its bows; so Hawley was sending an anchor astern, in the hope of warping her off. Nathaniel, I was sure, would be in command of the boat.

The black schooner let off a gun. The shot landed close to the boat's bows, sending a spout of water as high as the *Royal Savage's* main truck. The boat capsized and the anchor disappeared. We could see men swimming back to the *Royal Savage*.

Our marines, hunkered down in the shelter of the bulwarks, between the guns, scrambled cautiously to their feet to look. Cap Huff and Steven Nason worked on one of the long eighteens, slewing it so that it bore on the black schooner, and casting anxious glances at Arnold.

Arnold shook his head. "No hurry! You'll have as many chances as you want before the day's over: better ones than that!" Beyond the black schooner the southern end of the channel was choked with gunboats, each with its single big gun. There must have been twenty-five of them. Of the ship there was no sign, nor of the other schooner, nor of the strange floating fort we had seen.

Arnold limped up and down the quarterdeck, swinging his arms. "By George," he said, his voice high-pitched and triumphant, "I believe the sloop-of-war fell so far to leeward she can't get in!"

The whole fleet lay in a frozen silence, as if struck with horror at the black schooner driving so implacably toward the *Royal Savage*. I knew the fleet was silent only because the captains waited for Arnold to commence firing. By now it was impossible to fire, since the schooner was in line with the *Royal Savage;* and even had she been in range, we couldn't fire without endangering our own men.

But the *Royal Savage*, canted though she was, could fire, and did. Spurts of smoke jetted from her tilted side. The thud of the guns came slowly to us. Her guns were small, mostly four-pounders, and they sounded feeble, hopeless.

There was something unreal and dreamlike about the scene. The tall black schooner came slowly into the wind, as if forced to do so by the guns of the *Royal Savage*. She fell off on the starboard tack—on a course that would take her across the front of our crescent and put her in a position to rake the helpless *Royal Savage*.

Arnold watched her come about: then limped from the quarterdeck and ran to the bow gun: a twelve-pounder. He stooped and sighted along it: pulled at it a little: then came back to the next gun and did the same. He laid all the guns of the broadside; and to Nason, who stood by the sternmost gun, I heard him say, "When she crosses that line, let her have it. Then keep on till you're told to stop."

He had no more than spoken when the black schooner fired her broadside at the *Royal Savage*. Smoke, trailing out behind her, gave her the look of a ghost-ship. Hawley hadn't taken in his sails, probably thinking they might help him get clear of the land. We saw holes open in them. Her rigging flew apart, here and there, and a staysail came down on the run; but one of her stern guns popped defiantly.

It was sickening to see her chopped up. The very broadside whose smoke I still saw might, I knew, be the end of Nathaniel.

Three of our guns let off together with a bellowing roar; then all the guns of the crescent went into action. Confined, as we were, in a narrow strait, between cliffs and tall pines, the thunder of the guns was like a helmet of sound crushed down upon us.

A thick fog of white smoke rolled out from the crescent to hang between the tumbling waves of the channel, whirling and eddying, driven onward less by wind, it seemed, than by the stupendous roaring of the guns—a roaring that shook the planks beneath our feet.

What the intention of the schooner might have been, I couldn't tell. She may have thought to rake us all: then go about until her consort and the sloop-of-war could come to her assistance. Certainly she was passing across our front with all sail set and no thought of stopping, when the treacherous wind turned against her.

She swerved surprisingly into the north—then into the northeast. As if a blind crew had snatched her from the hands of those who sailed her, she came straight for the center of our crescent. Arnold jumped from the quarterdeck to join the men who pushed and milled about the sternmost eighteen-pounder. I would have gone too, except that Tom Bickford and Verrieul had gone with Steven Nason to help lay the guns, leaving the quarterdeck empty of all officers but myself. I did what I could to help the eight seamen working frantically at the four little swivels on our larboard taffrail. Amid the roaring of the cannon, the popping of those swivels sounded like puppies yapping at thunderclaps.

The schooner's crew seemed impotent to bring her back on her course. On both sides of her, and dead ahead, the water boiled and spouted, hurled upward by the hail of shot. Our cannon smoke drifted down upon her, caught in her upper sails and blew along her deck. A gash opened in her mainsail, as if slashed by a vast knife; her canvas flapped in the veering wind.

She could have held no straighter course for the middle of our line if she had been drawn by a cable. Voices, shrill and piping amid the uproar, rose in exultation from our main deck. The swivel gunners tore at the ends of their cartridges with their teeth. The sweat ran down their faces, smearing the powder grains around their mouths into black daubs. I found myself tight-muscled and sweating with desire to see that black schooner blown to pieces before my eyes.

A covey of gunboats had come across the channel and opened all together on the *Royal Savage*. Their more distant bellowing joined with ours to make a diabolic din. I saw the *Royal Savage's* fore-topsail lean; then crumple, swing down and hang motionless against her ratlines.

Black dots fell to the water from the *Royal Savage's* bowsprit. Her crew, or what was left of it, was abandoning her. My anxiety over Nathaniel was leavened by my overwhelming desire to see the end of the black schooner which still, miraculously, towered unharmed amid the shot-lashed waters.

Arnold ran up the companionway. His buckskin breeches were sponge-smeared, his right eye circled by a powder smudge. "What's she doing? Anchoring?" he asked. "We can't see for the smoke."

That was what she was doing, and when her anchor went over the side, it had a spring on it. A moment later her stern began to come in sight as the men clapped onto the spring and walked it in through the after port.

"Now we'll get it," Arnold said. He scratched his swarthy jaw and eyed the nearing gunboats. All of them, by now, had turned from the silent *Royal Savage* and were moving up, strange misshapen waterfowl, their long guns stretched forward like eager heads, bent on reaching their distressed mother, the black schooner.

"What about the crew of the *Royal Savage?*" I asked. "Their boat capsized. They had to go ashore."

"Yes, send our boat," he said. "Send Bickford. No, I need Bickford to lay guns. We've only got three men who can lay a gun properly. You'd better send Verrieul. Tell him to take boats from the other galleys. Tell him to bring Hawley back here, and some of his men. Divide the others among the galleys."

He watched the black schooner swing slowly broadside to us, his swarthy cheeks vibrating from the unceasing explosions of our cannon. "We'll need extra men before we're through!" he added ominously.

He turned to the companionway. "Keep your eye on the dead and wounded. Get the dead overboard as fast as you can. The men don't like 'em around. Oh, and take off their clothes before you put 'em over the side. We'll need 'em." He ran back to the guns.

Verrieul prowled up and down behind Cap Huff's marines while Cap, bawling his loudest, directed the activity of four sharpshooters, perched on the lookout steps of our stumpy masts. Ropes, encircling them and the masts, made it possible for them to use both hands for loading and firing. When I told Verrieul he was to lead the rescue party to the *Royal Savage*, he took affectionate leave of Cap. He must have thought he might never see Cap alive again.

Verrieul picked out four seamen, and they ran aft to the boat, bent over as if by the stupendous roaring of the guns. Above me I heard a penetrating thump. I looked up. One of the sharpshooters sagged in the rope that held him, jerked convulsively: then fell straight down, striking the deck with a crunching sound, and sprawled motionless, his limbs at odd angles, like a broken scarecrow. One of his arms was gone at the shoulder, and from the raw socket gushed blood that trembled with the trembling of the deck. It was Zelph.

I stepped over the widening pool of blood, took him by the remaining arm and lifted him up. He opened his eyes, gasped for breath, and screamed. There was something unreal about the shrillness of the scream. It seemed impossible that it could have come from a person known to me. The Zelph with whom I had grown up was incapable of making such a sound.

He stopped, drew a shuddering, rasping breath, and screamed again. Cap ran to me and got him by the feet. I took the front of his tattered moose-skin jacket, and we dragged him aft.

We carried him into the dark cabin and put him on the table. He gasped and screamed, gasped and screamed, while Doc Means, a dim figure in that low-ceiled room, peeled back Zelph's jacket to eye the ragged hole from which blood welled in dark jets.

"For God's sake," I said, "tie him up!"

Doc, wiping his fingers on a piece of sacking, turned mournful eyes upon me. "He's gone. His chest's caved in. There's ribs in his lungs, and nothing to be done. Seeing you're a friend of his, maybe you'd like me to help him get it over with."

"Get it over with? Get it over with?"

"Every time he breathes," Doc said, "he'll scream. He'll scream till all the blood's out of him. He'll scream a long time, maybe. You better let me help him."

"Help him? Let you help him?"

"Yes," Doc said. "With opium. Or a knife. A knife's quicker."

We stared at him.

"It's the best way to treat him," Doc said mildly. "The best and kindest. You go on deck, both of you."

Zelph screamed once more. The sound was horrible.

Keeping tight hold of me, Cap turned me toward the stairs and pushed me on deck, into the thundering tumult that surged, like invisible waves, over the rim of spruce butts that ringed us. One of Cap's marines, clutching his jawbone with a bloody hand, stumbled against us, moaning.

"Here!" Cap said. "What's the matter?"

The marine removed his hand from his face to let us see a three-inch splinter protruding from his cheek.

Cap's comment was contemptuous. "What you going to the hospital for *that* for?"

"To have it took out," the marine said angrily.

"There's only one way to take it out," Cap said callously, "and that's this!" He seized the splinter and pulled.

The marine squealed.

"Here," Cap said. "Here's your splinter. Keep it to show the folks at home." He slapped the marine on the shoulder and pushed him toward the bow. "Go on! Get to work, now! Remember you ain't allowed but one wound when you fight on fresh water!"

He turned to look at me. "You all right?" We stared at each other. Behind us the cabin was like a tomb.

XXXVII

THE black schooner was the *Carleton,* one of those transported in pieces from the St. Lawrence and put together again in St. John's. The ship-rigged sloop-of-war was the *Inflexible,* and the other schooner was the *Maria,* both brought to St. John's in sections in the same way, and rebuilt there. At moments when there were rifts in the clouds of smoke that jetted from a hundred cannon, we could see, at the far end of the channel, the *Inflexible* and the *Maria* riding at anchor like toy vessels, unable to beat up to us. There were seamen of distinction aboard those vessels; but for all their reputation and experience, not one of them equalled Arnold.

In everything he did, Arnold outthought them and outplanned them, and it wasn't his fault that he didn't, even with his inferior force, destroy them and get safe away. It was the fault of those Patriots on the seacoast, so busy building privateers that they had failed to give him the carpenters, seamen and supplies for which he had never ceased to ask.

Arnold had said the British would not keep proper watch: would run past us; and so they did. He said they couldn't beat up to us in that narrow strait, and they didn't. He said that if they knew enough to sail around the island and come down on us from the north, they'd be more likely to go aground on the shoals northwest of us; but instead of sailing around the island, they lay anchored at the southern end of the channel, as if their brains had jellied. He said they'd underrate us; and this, too, they did.

On the *Maria* were Commander Pringle and Sir Guy Carleton. On the *Inflexible* was the Lieutenant Schanck of whom Steven Nason had told us: the one who invented the centerboard. In the *Carleton* schooner was Lieutenant Dacres, destined to command some of England's greatest ships, and Edward Pellew, who became Lord Exmouth, and destroyed Algiers and commanded all of England's squadrons. Yet all these splendid seamen from the grand British navy, and all the German artillerymen in the gunboats and all their twenty-four-pounders, which were bigger than any gun we had, were not sufficient to silence Arnold, or to overwhelm this ragged rabble at whose head he fought—those sweepings of hell who had been worthless on land but had, in less than one short month, been pounded into usefulness by shipboard discipline.

How it was that Dacres and Pellew and every other man aboard the *Carleton* schooner escaped being torn to fragments by the incessant battering of our guns is more than I know. For an hour she lay there, broadside to us and within easy gunshot, a target for every gun in our crescent. We splintered her booms, shot away her running rigging, smashed her longboat, broke her gun-carriages, threw solid shot and grape shot against her until her black sides were scarred from stem to stern with yellow pock-marks.

Up and down behind our guns went Arnold, a demon of energy. His face was smeared with powder smudges; from his hat hung a strip of gold lace, ripped loose by a passing grape shot; his shoulder was crusted with a smear of brown, the blood of a gunner shot through the throat as Arnold crouched beneath him to sight a gun.

His biting voice, shrill and harsh, drove the gun-crews as though he lashed them with a whip. "Double-shot!" he told them. "Double-shot! Give her another! We've got her now! Hurry it up! One more, boys! Double-shot! Don't waste time! She can't get away! Hurry, boys, hurry! Double-shot! Double-shot!"

Whenever one of the three sternmost guns was loaded, the gunner shouted, the crew fell back beside the gun and Arnold ran to the carriage, sighting and wrenching; giving the word to fire. As the linstock slammed down and the gun jerked backward, Arnold was off again: up and down, making jabbing motions with his fist: urging the gun-crews on: urging them on.

There was something about his violent determination that was catching. It was like a sort of flame, searing all those exposed to it. No longer were my nerves and muscles rigid with the expectation of death: I burned with an eagerness to see our shots go home against the black schooner. So hot was this desire that it parched my lips and tongue: singed my cheeks until they seemed half charred.

I forgot, even, to watch the shore of the island for the boats that had gone to get Nathaniel and the rest of the crew of the *Royal Savage;* for the black schooner was in trouble. Half her guns had ceased to fire, and she was listing—not much, but listing nonetheless. Even the eighteen-pounders on our afterdeck seemed to sense, from the shouts and caperings of their crews, that there was an advantage to be pressed. Their stupendous belchings became sharper and more hurried, or so I thought.

We could see what had happened. The *Carleton's* spring had been shot away, and because of it, she was swinging head to wind once more: swinging bow on, into a position where she could bring no gun to bear on us, and where we, for the same reason, could rake her with every shot.

The black schooner hung there, head on. "Sink her!" the men shouted. "Sink her!" They cursed the schooner, as if she had been a disobedient dog.

One of her jibs went up. It would not fill, but flapped and shivered in the northeast wind. An officer scrambled out on the bowsprit, seized the stay and kicked at the jib to make it draw. He threw himself against it, whipping at it with his body. The schooner hung there. Her head would not pay off.

Arnold shook his fist at the gun-crews, spurring them on: then turned and came up the gangway to where I stood at the lee swivels. "Get me a bucket of water," he said to one of the swivel gunners. To me he said in a strained, hoarse voice, "Let's have some rum: rum all 'round. My God, I'm dry!"

I sent Tom Bickford for the rum, and thought to myself that Arnold was a caution. Exertions, losses, disappointments, danger, death—nothing seemed to disturb him. He looked at his shot-pierced hat, tore off the hanging piece of gold lace, winked at me, and dropped the hat to the deck while he pulled up his sleeves to rinse his blackened hands and face in the bucket of water the swivel gunner brought him.

Flapping his hands to dry them, he stood on tiptoe to peer over the spruce butts at the black schooner. There was an oily glare to the water between the two fleets. Smoke layers undulated above it, and a pale sun threw a silvery glitter in our eyes. From the position of the sun in the south, the day was only half gone. It seemed incredible that this could be so, since the battle had only just begun. It occurred to me, then, that the *Revenge* had warned us of the approach of the British fleet this very morning; and that warning now seemed something that had reached us long ago, in the dim past.

The thought of Nathaniel came back to me with a sudden shock. It seemed ages since I had seen those small black figures moving ashore from the stranded *Royal Savage*. I climbed on the rail to look shoreward, wondering what in God's name could be keeping the boats that had gone for the castaways. I saw the splash of oars, then, close to the rocky banks, and made out the boats, moving toward us at last.

I turned to tell Arnold.

Against the glare of that southern sun the black schooner took on an added blackness. She hung head to wind, still, unable to make sail. Around her the water foamed from the skittering of grape shot, or spouted up in liquid plumes at the impact of solid shot. On her bowsprit the small black figure had ceased to struggle with the jib, and was making its way to the tip of the jib-boom.

"There's a brave man," Arnold said. "He ought to go far if he lives five minutes more."

The figure that stood so carelessly at the end of the jib-boom, with no apparent thought for the shot that howled around him, was, we later learned, Pellew. Two gunboats moved slowly towards the schooner's larboard bow; and Pellew, clinging to the preventer stay, leaned far outboard to heave a rope to one of them. The boat crew snatched at it and missed. Pellew drew it in, coiling it neatly, and threw it out once more. The boats turned and rowed off, dragging the *Carleton's* head around at last.

Angry howlings rose from our main deck as the schooner crept from the line of battle, listed over like a man who leans heavily to ease his hurts.

Arnold shook his head. "No use; no use! We can't sink her: not with these pop-guns. She's got some dead aboard, though; and she's out of the fight. That's something. That's something! Now we can tend to those gunboats."

Tom Bickford brought the bucket of rum and water and set it at the break in the deck. The men crowded up to it, unhooking tin cups from their belts or drawing them from hidden corners of their garments. They were a motley company, in their tattered travesties of clothes. Splinters had gashed them, and the blood was caked brown on the untended scratches. Some wore dirty, blood-stained rags around their heads: around arms and legs. Their faces were smeared with black: streaked with sweat and with the tears that powder-smoke had brought.

Tom handed up a cupful. Arnold took it and gulped it down. One of the men, watching him, smacked his lips and exhaled ecstatically.

Arnold gave them a tight-lipped grin. "You fought well!" he said. "You've done well! You've outfought a British fleet! There's nobody that can say more! See you keep it up!" He drank his second drink.

One of the ragged seamen shouted, "You done well your own self, Ginrall!"

Cap Huff herded a handful of his marines to the rear of the tattered group. "What was it he said?" he bawled. "Hey, General, tell these fellers of mine! They got to be encouraged!"

Arnold laughed. "They don't need it! All they need is something to shoot at!"

The ragged group cackled and drank their rum. Their eyes glittered and were restless. They scrambled back to the guns, whose explosions, now that the *Carleton* had escaped, seemed labored; more disgruntled.

I turned to look shoreward again. The boats which carried the *Royal Savage's* crew had separated, one heading for the *Washington* galley: the other holding a course that would bring her under our counter. The boatmen were rowing raggedly. Their heads were turned, not toward us, but astern; toward the rocky, pine-clad shores from which they had come. Something, I knew, had threatened them.

I called to Tom Bickford to man the shoreward guns. Arnold came to stand beside me, scanning the dense growth of spruces that rose like massed spears above the brown rocks.

From halfway up a tall spruce a jet of smoke puffed out, turned a pale blue and vanished. Our shoreward bow gun let off with a bellowing cough. As if the gun had released a spring on shore, a dusky, reddish figure popped out from behind a tree. Near him appeared another: then two more. They seemed enormous; too large, almost, for men, and the color of animals: of sleek young bucks. They capered and made gestures, and suddenly were gone, like demons dissolving into thin air. We heard faint, wailing howls—howls vaguely like those of a lynx, squalling in the night from hunger or frustrated love.

Arnold spat over the side and eyed me slyly. "I was afraid those hellions wouldn't show themselves."

"Afraid?" I asked. "Afraid?"

"Listen!" he said. We listened, and again we heard those distant quavering howls: howls whose shrillness seemed to set insects crawling behind my ears.

He jerked his head toward the sound. "Nobody'll ever leave this fight of his own free will, not while those gentlemen are co-hooping and co-hopping around on shore!"

He was still in a good humor when Captain Hawley, followed by Nathaniel and a dozen members of the crew of the *Royal Savage*, clambered over the side and came aft to report. They were draggled and dirty, but unwounded. Not wishing to make an exhibition of myself or embarrass Nathaniel, I said nothing to him: merely eyed him severely when he winked at me, looking mightily pleased with himself.

Arnold sent the men forward to report to Cap Huff: then turned a hard eye on Hawley. "Well, you weren't much help to us."

Hawley shook his head. Being behind him, I could see his hands were locked together, and his thumbs digging at his palms. He felt badly: no doubt of that.

"Why didn't you come about sooner?" Arnold demanded.

Hawley only nodded. I could see his throat muscles work.

Arnold's swarthy face was puffy, as if he was near exploding.

Nathaniel spoke up. "We'd have gone ashore, even if we'd been anchored. I never saw anything to beat her crankiness."

Arnold turned to him almost deferentially. "I suppose you didn't, by any chance, save my papers?"

Nathaniel looked horrified. "Your papers! Were your papers aboard?"

"Every document that bore on this campaign," Arnold said gently. "All my accounts: that's all."

Hawley cleared his throat and drew a long breath. "I—General—I didn't know—these British——" He cleared his throat once more, stared at the sky and tried again. "They had me in Halifax, General. I was real anxious to fight 'em. Real anxious to fight."

He stopped. I felt sorry for him. Arnold shook his head and turned away.

"We figured on taking her again," Nathaniel broke in. "We figured on swimming out to her. We would have, too, only when we started back, we found those red skunks had cut us off—hundreds of 'em! The biggest men I ever saw!"

Hawley fumbled at the back of his neck. His eyes were fixed on his feet, and his voice was indistinct. "I'll board her now if I can get enough boats. I'll get your papers for you."

Arnold jerked his thumb over his shoulder in the direction of the *Royal Savage*. From her canted side slow jets of smoke puffed toward us: hung, billowing: then rolled up over her bulwarks and drifted south in ragged streamers.

"See that?" Arnold demanded. "They boarded her, and now they're killing our men with our own guns!" He seemed to fly into a fury. "By God, if I have to abandon a vessel, I see to it that nobody else gets her!" He shook his fist at Hawley and Nathaniel. "Why didn't you set her afire! Why didn't you blow her up? What in God's name was the use of making the British a present of a schooner and guns and powder and shot!"

He ran to the companionway. Steven Nason straightened up from the aftermost gun, his face a black mask except for his eyelids, which were still white. "Lay your guns on the *Royal Savage*," Arnold shouted. "I want every gun in this fleet laid on that vessel! Send word along the line! They can't have her! Blow hell out of her!"

All along the deck the men turned the guns. We payed out two fathoms of spring, to let them bear more easily.

In his eagerness to have the *Royal Savage* destroyed, Arnold seemed to have forgotten Hawley and Nathaniel.

On the side of the British line closest to Valcour, one of the British gunboats was in trouble. The men aboard her were scurrying like tor-

tured ants. A puff of smoke rose from her stern, and two men fell overboard.

She surged slowly and distressingly. A dark mass of smoke rose up
from her, and riding on the smoke was a powder chest. The smoke
glowed and burned at the base, and spread enormously, as if pressed
flat by the chest on its crest. It enveloped the boat. The chest popped
sideways into the air, turned end over end, and fell into the lake. With
the crash of the explosion came a tumult of shouting from our own and
the British boats.

The smoke rolled away from the gunboat, and we saw that not only
had her magazine exploded, but she was ablaze in her amidship section. The other British boats moved toward her, and she toward them.
One of her men, in the water, made clutching motions with his hands
and vanished.

When I turned my eye shoreward for a moment, to watch for Indians,
I saw that Hawley stood alone, feeling his neck and staring up at the
sky, as if the cannon that pounded on all sides of us were to be found
somewhere in the heavens. I went to him, suspecting that he was, in a
way, in greater distress than the British gunboat.

At the touch of my hand on his arm he drew away, walked past me
and spoke to Nathaniel. "I got to take back the *Royal Savage*," he said
flatly. "If I can get the men, I'll take her! Will you go to take her?"

Nathaniel looked from Hawley to me. "You'd better go," I told him.
"You'll be safer in a small boat than you'd be right here."

Hawley went to Arnold, who had his head through the hemlock
screen on our taffrail, counting the shot-holes in our hull. When he
pulled his head back, he seemed to have forgotten he had ever spoken
sharply to Hawley. "Mark the holes," he said, tapping Hawley on the
chest. "Get 'em marked right away, and in an hour you can take your
men over the side and put on some patches."

"Sir," Hawley said, "lend me three bateaux and I'll take the *Savage*.
I'll get my men off the other vessels and take her back."

Arnold eyed the western hills dubiously. A wall of dirty gray cloud
had pushed up above them, and the sun had gone down into that dark-
ling shroud. The color of the lake had changed to that of the slates on
which we wrote in school; and in the gathering gloom the puffs of smoke
that jetted from our own guns and those of the British were shot with a
pinkish orange glare. The spruces on the island no longer stood out
clear and distinct, but were a black barrier behind us: a threatening,
saw-toothed barrier.

"No," Arnold said. "By the time you've rounded up your attackers, it'll be night, and I'll need you right here. We've all got work to do—unless we want our bones to rest permanently at Valcour."

Hawley clasped his hands behind him. I marveled at the length of his arms. His stubby fingers, twisting together, seemed to reach nearly to his knees. "I wouldn't choose to have the charge of—the charge of cowardice stand against me."

"Nobody's accusing you of cowardice!" Arnold said quickly. "If it'll make you feel any better, take two boats and half a dozen active men and try to get through her cabin windows just at dark."

XXXVIII

Wₕₑₙ darkness came at last, we had fought for five everlasting hours. The *Royal Savage* was in flames, set by the British when they saw Hawley's and Nathaniel's boats approaching. The British gunboats, battered and leaking, had pulled slowly away to the shelter of the ship and the schooners, which lay at the entrance of the channel, watching our shot-torn crescent like three cats sniffing a basket of sardines.

The ship, her view of us at last unobstructed by her own gunboats, fired five broadsides before night shut down. The solid shot screamed above us; a few, almost spent, thudded against a hull with the sound of a gigantic horse kicking a cavernous barn. Such, however, was her distance that we made no answer, but lay there licking the wounds we could see and hunting for the others whose existence we suspected.

Notwithstanding our plight, there was something cheerful about the darkness and its myriad of small sounds, after the uproar of the day. Nine wounded men were stretched aft of the main hatch, with a staysail over them. Three had lost legs—one close to the thigh; and one was shot through the stomach, but he was out of his head and obsessed with the belief that he was building stone walls on his farm. Doc Means swore that since none of them had taken anything more nourishing than rum and water since the night before, and probably would receive nothing but water and rum for some time, they would all recover. Seven dead men had been thrown into the water and were already as good as forgotten, and the blood and litter had been swabbed from the decks. A score of seamen were over the side in bateaux, nailing lead over shot-holes by the light of the column of fire that whirled upward from the *Royal Savage*.

We had twelve shot-holes, some big enough to put your head through; and to get at two of them it was necessary to tilt the galley by traversing the guns. Cap Huff, red and noisy from rum, superintended the cleaning of the fore part of the vessel while Nason worked a crew on the pumps. Cap kept his men in a good humor by telling them how he planned to go ashore as soon as he had time and catch an Indian and roast him for supper. Cap's talk of Indians made our hunger easier to bear, especially since we could see the glimmer of fires far off among the trees of Valcour, and hear a steady yowling drifting down on the northeast wind. The sound was like the squalling of distant seagulls.

Arnold had called a Council of War, and he waited for it in the cabin, scratching away at a letter by the light of a smoky lantern. The cabin had been swabbed down after Doc's labors, but it reeked of blood and saltpetre—an odor that would cling to it for many a day.

Arnold's curly black hair was draggled, and his pale eyes sunken, but he was tilted forward on the edge of his bench, driving his quill across the paper as though freshly risen from a nap. There were times when he seemed to me to be made of steel, wire and teak, rather than flesh and blood.

Even when a blinding flash of light left the outlines of the stern windows seared blue against my eyeballs, Arnold's pen scratched on without a break. "There she goes!" he said. The flash was followed by the roar of the *Royal Savage's* exploding magazine. It echoed from the cliffs of Valcour and from the New York shore, rolling from shore to island and back again in swelling waves of sound; and through all its booming and reverberating Arnold kept right on with his writing.

The captains who had that morning assembled in our small cabin had been an odd-looking lot; but they were even odder now, as they came straggling down the companion. Waterbury had hurt his back, so that he was humped over like an old, old man, supporting himself on the handle of a gun-swab. Burning powder had fallen on his coat, covering it with neat round spots, not unlike the dapplings of a young fawn. Wigglesworth, hook-nosed and sedate, had washed the powder from his face, but done it over-hastily, so that his nostrils were black, still, as well as his ears and his neck, and the inner corners of his eyes, which gave him the staring look of a startled owl. Poor Hawley, his hands swathed in dirty bandages, due to his efforts to board the burning *Royal Savage*, sat silent against the bulkhead, stroking one bandage with the other.

Captain Dickenson of the *Enterprise* sloop came down holding the skirt of his coat before him, to show us where an Indian's bullet had struck a button at the small of his back and run halfway around him, leaving his coat tail hanging by a thread. Since the *Enterprise* had been on the right of our line, she had been close to shore, and those aboard her had seen more than they wished of the Indians.

"By Jody," Dickenson said, wagging his coat tail at us, "they looked eight feet tall, and they had black faces! If I hadn't known they were Indians, I'd have said they'd been spewed up from the bottomless pit!"

Red-headed Captain Davis of the *Lee* galley had a bandage around his head: a bandage so caked with blood that his hair seemed pale beside it. Simonds, who had been white and shivering with ague when we last saw him, was burning with fever now, and perpetually clearing his throat and muttering to himself, so that I think he was a little out of his senses.

Captain Rice might have been drunk, so thick was his speech: his eyes were glassy; and only the repeated nudgings of his friend Grimes kept him awake. Evidently he had been badly shocked. Grimes was smeared with blood from neck to knee, doubtless from helping a wounded man. Little Ulmer of the *Spitfire* wore a bandage on his thigh. Sumner of the *Boston* had been deafened by the close passage of a cannon ball, which had broken his ear-drums. Thatcher of the *Washington*, Warner of the *Trumbull*, Reed of the *New York* and Grant of the *Connecticut* were not to be seen.

Arnold spoke impatiently. "We'll wait no longer. I wanted to make public acknowledgment to all of you together, but under the circumstances the missing ones will understand how it is. Gentlemen, you fought well! I'm proud of what you've done this day. I hope your country'll have the sense to be grateful!"

An epidemic of throat-clearing broke out among the captains. They shuffled their feet and studied the rough boards on which they sat.

"Now, then," Arnold said, "we've lost the *Philadelphia*. Captain Rice tells me she sank half an hour ago. And we've been so unfortunate as to lose the *Royal Savage*"—he glanced quickly at Hawley's rigid face—"in spite of Captain Hawley's effort to retake her. A brave effort, Captain Hawley: a brave effort against heavy odds."

Hawley made a strangled noise in his throat and cast a pitiful glance at Wigglesworth, who sat beside him. Wigglesworth nodded soberly and said, "Good work."

"From the appearance of things," Arnold said, "they were a little more lavish in their attentions to General Waterbury and this vessel than to some of the others; but none of us were overlooked, I suspect." He hesitated. "Captain Reed of the *New York* sends me word that all his officers were killed, and Captain Warner and Captain Grant have a few splinters in them, but the rest of us didn't do so badly. Not so badly. What's your situation, General?"

Waterbury tried to straighten up. The effort made him groan. "Bad! Captain Thatcher's seriously wounded and the sailing master, too. My first lieutenant and three others are killed. I've got a twelve-pounder through my mainmast and God knows how many through the hull. My sails are shot to pieces, so far as I can see."

Arnold disposed of Waterbury's troubles. "I'll give you Captain Hawley. He'll get sail on her if she's got a rag to set."

Hawley laughed abruptly. "I guess we can get some on her somehow."

Arnold nodded. "Yes, that's right! Get some on her, even if you have to use the men's breeches for sails, because we're going to move."

Feet clattered on the companionway, and Tom Bickford's face appeared. "Fog!" he said. "It's drifted so thick we can't see the Indian fires on the island." He vanished.

"There you are!" Arnold cried. "Just what we need! I take it there's none of you anxious to stay where we are!" He opened his mouth in a wide and silent laugh.

General Waterbury spoke sourly. "If we *can* go, we'd better. I don't believe there's a vessel in the fleet with fifty rounds left. I don't believe I could fight two hours more—if it was the kind of fighting we did today."

Arnold's eyes, in that dark cabin, seemed to absorb most of the light from our tin lantern. "Look at that, now! Everything's turning out just as it should! We've got a northerly breeze still, a fog to hide in, and there's no moon till tomorrow. What's more, none of us want to stay, and the British think they've got us bottled up!"

He laughed again, that silent, open-mouthed laugh: then abruptly became grim.

"So we'll get away! We've *got* to get away! We've delayed 'em one day: we've got to delay 'em some more! Their army can't move while we're at large on the lake, and the way to stay at large is to get away—give 'em the slip! And we'll do it! We'll do it, because they'll never expect us to do it!"

He banged his fist on the table. "By God, gentlemen, I'd like to see the faces of those British captains when they wake up tomorrow and find their noses stuck in an empty fox-hole!"

The captains chuckled. In a few short sentences Arnold had banished all their doubts and filled them with confidence and eagerness to be gone.

He took a paper from the table. "Listen to this, now, and for God's sake make no mistakes. I want every captain to take the helm of his own vessel, and I want each one of you to put his best officer in the bow with a lantern screened in a canvas sack. We've got to go through that British fleet without a sound: understand? Without a single damned sound! If any of you runs ashore, the whole British fleet will be down on us like hornets, and have half of us aground in ten minutes. If anyone shouts: if anyone talks: if anyone shows a light, it's all the same! We're gone! Our goose is cooked! Understand?"

Nobody said anything.

"All right, then," Arnold said. "I want each of you to put six stout men on your starboard bow with six spare oars. That's to fend you off if you start to run ashore. Tell 'em to keep their mouths shut in case they have to do any fending, unless they want their gizzards blown out. Put your wounded under cover, where their groans can't be heard, if they're inclined to groan. Put 'em in the cabins, if you've got cabins. Put your look-out on your larboard bow with his screened lantern, to give you your steering directions. If he moves his lantern up and down, go straight ahead: if he circles it to larboard, steer to larboard: if to starboard, go to starboard. That's easy enough, isn't it?"

The captains agreed that it was.

"You'll want one more lantern in your stern," Arnold told them. "Screen it well, so it can only be seen from dead astern. Then all that's necessary is for those with square sails to set 'em, along with your steering sails, run before the wind, and follow the lantern. Those with lateen rig need only the foresail. Understand?"

"Oars out or in?" Hawley asked.

"Be careful of your oars," Arnold warned. "You'll have to have 'em out, so to hold off in case you run up too close on the vessel in front of you; but don't use 'em till you must. And whatever you do, plug shirts and breeches around the oars, so they won't rattle if you need to use 'em."

General Waterbury coughed dryly. "If they discover us——"

"General," Arnold said, "I know the British pretty well. They don't think much of us. They're tired tonight—tired and battered; and when Englishmen are tired and battered, they like to have a cup of tea or a quart of rum and go to sleep. Since they don't think much of us, that's just what they're going to do, General. They're going to sleep. I think we'll go through them without the least trouble: without any trouble at all." He stared around at us: then he, too, coughed. "If they *should* discover us, I know you'll make it as expensive a discovery as possible."

He moved close to the lantern to read from the paper in his hand. "Here's your sailing order. It's the same order in which you now lie, barring the *Trumbull*, the *Washington* and this vessel. Colonel Wigglesworth in the *Trumbull* will pass across your front at seven o'clock. When he reaches the west shore, he'll turn due south, and the rest of you will follow. You're to keep as close to shore as possible. There's six fathoms of water ten yards off shore. I sounded it myself. With this northeast breeze there'll be waves on the rocks, and you can gauge your distance from them." He read the order in which the gundelos and the schooners were to follow: then read it again, more slowly. "All clear?" he asked.

The captains muttered that everything was clear.

"The *Washington* and the *Congress* will bring up your rear," Arnold said. "You can depend on General Waterbury and me to do all we can for you in case—in case——" He changed the subject abruptly. "If there's any uncertainty, or any doubt about anything, this is the time to speak."

The cabin was silent, save for a faint creaking from the rudder case and the thump of the pumps.

Waterbury, favoring his lame back, moved stoopingly toward the companion. Arnold jumped to assist him, as spry as though weariness and he were strangers.

He laughed and winked at us, as he helped along his crippled second in command. "A pleasant trip, gentlemen! I trust we'll meet soon at Crown Point."

XXXIX

THE lantern under the *Washington's* stern was a trembling yellow glow through the fog that drifted with us, pressing against our eyes and faces like clammy fingers, beading our eyelashes with drops through which the gleam of the lantern doubled and trebled and melted back to a single point again. The fog bit through our scanty clothes and blew its damp breath against us until, with that and the suspense, we shivered and shook. On our right we could feel the loom of the shore, and hear the waves climbing among the rocks, clicking and clacking with the sound of bayonets rattling against barrels of muskets: clucking like ramrods dropped against charges of buck-shot. We were close enough to feel the impalpable pressure of protruding headlands. Their pressure swelled and diminished as the shore-line approached or fell away.

Nathaniel, lying close beside me in the bow, held the lantern, shrouded in a cone of canvas. I wanted to throw it overboard because of the stench of whale oil and hot tin that rose from it in a reek that must, I felt sure, advertise our passing to all the British on the lake.

Except for the smell, we were a ghostly crew on a phantom vessel. Above us was the faint slapping of the cordage against the mast, and a little flutter, now and again, from the rips left in our single big foresail by the passage of enemy shot—a flutter as elusive as the sound of a swallow's wings. We seemed to stand motionless in a thick wet world—a black, muffled world that surged past us, laughing coldly at our painful straining after the single smudge of yellow light that hovered out of reach.

I seemed, indeed, to be a ghost myself: a wraith lacking substance, incapable of further exertion: nothing but a brain without human habitation, and that brain a dull one, thinking small and hopeless thoughts—that all our labors were futile and unreal: that Ellen Phipps was lost to me now, forever: that Nathaniel's affairs would distress me no longer, since we were taking leave of the British and this northern country: of how the river flowed past the shipyard in Arundel in the summer dusk, dimpled with the quick movements of rising minnows. Our efforts were like the marks of minnows in the water, I thought: gone as soon as made, and of as little value.

Even the stealthy sounds around me might have been made by disembodied spirits, murmuring in apprehensive sibilants of the bourne to which a silent ferryman was bearing them.

I could hear Verrieul's muted murmur, a breath; no more: Cap Huff's hoarser note, like the scrape of leather on a lichened rock, warning him to be still. Whisperings ran along the deck and suddenly ceased, just as successive waves of flutterings and of calm sweep a birch thicket on an August night.

There were hurried footsteps in the leaves on shore: an abrupt stillness: then a scurry that brought my heart into my throat and put an end to my thoughts of wraiths.

"Deer!" Verrieul whispered.

Cap cursed softly; and as if in answer a shriek rose from the darkness at our right, quavered in a crescendo of agony, and fell away into the hiccuppy snoring with which a horned owl rounds out his scream of protest against existence.

We were all familiar with these sounds of the forest; but into each one of them I read the whoops of Indians, the tread of British infantry, the rattle of ambushed guns waiting to blow us to fragments.

I hissed for a messenger. Nason pressed in between Nathaniel and me.

"Tell Arnold I figure we're close to the British line," I whispered. "I'm going to dowse this light."

Nason crawled away. Nathaniel unhooked the door of the lantern. The light gleamed on his thin brown face; then vanished. Drops of water spattered from our top-hamper. The fog hung slack: then puffed into our faces in a way I misliked, since it foretold a changing wind. The galley dipped twice and the foremast creaked.

Off to our left I heard a hollow thump, followed by a splash. Somebody had dropped a bucket over a vessel's side. The trembling yellow glow ahead of us vanished. The *Washington,* too, had heard the splash. We were alone, then, floating in space: suspended in the unknown.

The breeze was faint—so faint that our lateen sail slapped the mast. We had way on us, but little more—perhaps a mile or two an hour.

We lay and shivered in the fog. Cap set up an interminable whispered discussion with Verrieul about French Canadian cookery. It was his belief that there was no taste to French Canadian dishes save of garlic, and that if the taste of garlic should be removed, everything would have the flavor of straw, not only soups, but meats and vegetables as well. They whispered and whispered about food until I, not having had any for a matter of thirty hours, would have swapped my breeches for one of the soups that Cap derided.

Among the gun-crews—at their stations but stretched on the deck for greater silence—men slept and snored, great ripping, gargling snores, until their mates kicked them, or shut off their breaths, at which they choked, groaned, muttered, and instantly fell asleep again.

Around ten o'clock—I felt I'd lain on my belly for a year—Tom Bickford crawled up to say Arnold wanted me. Tom took my place in the bow and I went aft, over the bodies of the men who lay like logs along the narrow deck.

Arnold had a compass in a bucket with a lighted candle, and over the whole a funnel of canvas lashed to a stick. In the canvas he had cut a flap, so he could see into the bucket and get his bearings. He was crouched down, peering at the compass, when I came to him. His face, in the dim light that shone from the peep-hole, had a look of pleased anticipation, though our situation was far from pleasurable, to my way of thinking. The truth was that Arnold took pleasure in anything dangerous, and seemed forever hopeful that something more dangerous would soon appear.

"What do you think?" he asked.

I told him I thought the wind was changing; that if we couldn't get our pumps working, we'd soon be down by the head and making no progress whatever, except toward the bottom of the lake.

"Yes," he said, "this is all a lot of nonsense. There isn't a Britisher in sight, and there hasn't been. We're safely through them."

He gave me the tiller and walked forward. "Get those sweeps in the water," I heard him say in a high, repressed voice. "We're safe away, but there's to be no shouting or talking. There'll be rum all round."

The oars caught hold. The galley lurched a little from the water in her. In half an hour the pumps were thumping again. Behind us, where the British slept, there was silence, heavy and profound.

We kindled our lanterns once more, and in a short time made out the lights of the *Washington,* dead ahead. We rowed along beside her. The banging of her pumps sounded like coopers pounding heads on barrels. On her far side wallowed three gundelos in bad condition. Hawley left the wheel to speak to us. When the *Washington* passed the British, he said, she was a whisker's width from sinking. He was not sure, even now, he said, that she could stay afloat till dawn.

We, too, shared his doubts when the wind shifted into the south and blew hard against us, kicking up a dirty chop against which we made small progress.

We clung together, five mangled wrecks, pumping and rowing, rowing and pumping through the endless hours.

When the pale morning broke, the *Washington* looked to us like the corpse of a vessel. Seen through the fog, she was the gray of a corpse. Her two triangular sails were in rags. Shreds of cloth, remnants of her muffling of the night before, hung draggled from her oar-ports. Holes yawned in her sides, where planks had been splintered by British shot. The hemlock fringe above her bulwarks was smashed, as if a moose had gamboled in it. She labored wearily against the head wind and the abrupt fresh-water waves, rolling from side to side, gravid with the water that filled her.

Inshore, when the light grew stronger, we dimly saw, as through a veil, the rounded hump of Schuyler's Island. We were both glad and sorry to see it—glad because it offered a convenient anchorage: sorry because it showed us that in our ten hours of ceaseless labor we had brought our sinking craft a mere eight miles.

When Cap Huff learned how far we had come, he roared strickenly, swearing we had rowed twice around the lake, to say nothing of pumping out enough water from our one galley to float all of Britain's mighty navy.

. . . There was still a fog when we came to anchor at the northern end of Schuyler's Island, sheltered from that damnable south wind; and we prayed to God the fog would hold until the wind changed—until we could patch our mangled craft—until, in short, we could somehow earn for ourselves another chance for life.

Until the fog lifted, we knew, we were safe; for the British, waiting hopefully to pounce on us at Valcour, now that the wind favored them, would never dream that we were gone.

There were five of us in that little bay—the *Congress* and the *Washington*, and three battered gundelos, the *Providence*, the *Jersey* and the *New York*; and there was so much to be done to make each vessel seaworthy that a shipyard, fully equipped, would have needed a week for the task.

Arnold, stripped to breeches and fur vest, was all over the five vessels like a squirrel, almost before they had time to swing head to wind. He rowed around the *Washington*, thumping her shot-torn planking with his fist. He scrambled through one of her stern-ports: then, as if by magic, appeared at the mast-head of the *Providence;* and somehow, in another moment, he was hanging, head-down, from the taffrail of the *Jersey*. In ten minutes' time he was back on the quarterdeck of the *Congress* with a full knowledge of what needed to be done, and how to do it.

In those days, even, there were some who hated Arnold for no reason that anybody could see, just as many hated General Washington, and

just as there have always been and always will be people who take
pride in hating the best and kindest of men with a hatred that stops
short of nothing. But even those few who hated him—Nathaniel among
them—could never deny that his was the genius of a true commander-
in-chief. We had a chance to see many leaders before the war was over,
but we never saw one like Arnold. When a crisis arose—when something
had to be done on the instant: something bound to have a serious effect
on subsequent events—most of the others, by comparison with Arnold,
were no good. In one way or another, paralysis struck them. Either they
couldn't make up their minds; or they were assailed by doubts; or in
seeing a part of the picture, they were blind to other parts. But Arnold
saw everything. He made up his mind in an instant; and he did everything without doubting or flinching.

Not daring to trust the work to anyone else, I had taken Nathaniel
to fish the mainmast pierced by British shot; and before we had finished
cutting our plank, Arnold had called all the others around him on the
quarterdeck—Nason, Tom Bickford, Verrieul, Cap Huff and Doc
Means. He rapped out his orders as if he had been through this same
situation a dozen times before: two men to the mast-head with the
telescope to watch for British: two men ashore from each vessel to boil
all our remaining potatoes so that we might have something to put in
our stomachs: a measure of rum and water all round—mix it two and
one. . . . All the time he talked, he worked at his field-desk, opening
it up and propping it against the carriage of a stern gun, sharpening his
quills with a silver pen-knife, prying up the cover of his ink-well, setting
out a pad of paper: driving his words at us with stabbing movements of
his pen. . . . The *New York* and the *Providence* were beyond repair:
lay 'em alongside the galleys: take from 'em the canvas necessary to
repair our sails, the planks needed to plug our shot-holes: sway up the
guns from the gundelos and mount 'em at our spare ports; transfer powder and shot; send off the gundelo captains in boats to take a message
to Crown Point, asking for bateaux and men to tow us the next day,
in case the wind held southerly; scuttle the gundelos so the British
wouldn't get 'em; carry a letter to General Gates——

Men crawled fumblingly on the sails to patch them, looking like
clumsy slow caterpillars. Ragged scarecrows thumped and banged at
the pumps. Seamen silently spliced and knotted rigging, contemplative
specters in the fog.

Toilers in the gundelos swore exasperated oaths; boards came loose
from broken bulwarks with the screech of reluctant nails; hammers
slammed a hurried tattoo against the hulls; and Arnold sat at his desk,
writing, watching everything, jumping to his feet at intervals to send

that shrill, hoarse voice of his like a whiplash among the workers; and always returning to his eternal writing.

There were wisps of blue sky overhead by eight o'clock, and the wind was stronger from the south, whirling the thinning fog in streamers around the rocky point of Schuyler's Island. Then, in a moment, the fog was gone, and to the east of us the white walls of the Green Mountains were like a distant cloud against the pallid blue that accompanies a south wind.

Arnold craned his neck to see the men at the mast-head. They were plainly anxious. One took the telescope from the other, wiped it well against the rags of his jacket, and stared and stared into the north. Arnold went back to his letter.

"Sail!" cried one of those at the mast-head. My heart sank. It was not yet nine o'clock, and the British had only eight miles to come.

Arnold laughed. "By God! I'd give a hundred dollars, hard money, to see Carleton's face right now. If I could hear him as well, I'd make it a thousand!"

He chuckled. "Two blunders in one day—passing us to leeward in the morning, and not keeping a proper watch at night! That's something to be proud of!"

He called up to the look-out, "What are they doing?"

"Ship and two schooners beating to the eastward on the starboard tack," the look-out replied.

Arnold fixed me with a speculative eye. "It seemed to me that there was something more than blundering to the failure of that other schooner to get in and attack us. I don't know who commanded her, but if I'd been his superior officer, I'd have had him court-martialed for his day's work!"

He went back to his letter, read it, added a few words with a neat flourish, and folded it carefully. From his manner, no one would have dreamed the British fleet was threatening him again.

He called the captains of the gundelos, gave them his letters and told them to tell Wigglesworth to hurry on to Ticonderoga with all possible speed.

He sent them off in their boats—Simonds of the *Providence*, his face death-like because of his intermittent fever, which would set him to shivering again on the morrow: Grimes, his clothes still smeared with blood stains: Reed, neat in his overall.

He watched them step their little leg-of-mutton sails in their long-boats and go reaching off into the south wind: then hustled from end to end of the *Congress*, urging the men on, and lending a hand where there was need of it.

That was another good thing about Arnold: in spite of his pride in his dress and his personal appearance, he would work like the commonest laborer, but twice as fast and twice as hard as any laborer was able to work, in order to achieve an end on which he had set his mind.

He stopped when the look-out bawled that the British had put back toward Valcour.

"Back?" he shouted. "You mean come about on the other tack, don't you?"

"Not by a damned sight," the look-out said. "They went back. They all went back!"

Arnold scrambled up the mast to see for himself. One quick glance was enough for him, and he dropped to the deck, as light as a cat. "He was right," he said, examining the plank we had fitted to the mast. "Every Britisher's on his way back to the anchorage! Every last one of 'em turned around!"

He showed his teeth in that soundless laugh of his. "I'll bet you a dollar Carleton was so mad he went off and forgot something! I'll bet you anything he had to go back to tend to it!"

That, we later learned, was the fact. Carleton had been in such a rage over our escape that he forgot to leave orders for the troops and Indians that had been landed on Valcour; and, lacking definite knowledge of our whereabouts—for our bare poles were invisible against the pines of Schuyler's Island—he had returned to rectify his blunder.

Arnold was in high good humor. "Now," he said, "we can eat our potatoes in peace; and if God only sends us a north wind in place of this damned draft out of the south, we'll play hide-and-seek with those gentlemen until they're frozen stiff!"

Three potatoes apiece we had, without salt, and two gills of rum and water to wash them down. In spite of being half blighted and half cooked, those potatoes seemed to me the sweetest fare I had ever eaten. They melted to a delicious paste on my tongue, and vanished almost like a mist. Even the skins were sweet, and disappeared as quickly. I could have eaten a hundred, I thought, and then slept for a week.

Sleep, alas, was scarcer than potatoes. By noon our sails were mended, our masts fished, our broken sides patched. We scuttled the *Providence* and the *New York;* then laid the *Congress* against the *Washington,* so to help her in her tribulations. That sorry vessel put me in mind of an ancient farm wagon tied together with rope, its spokes and axles nailed and wired: on the verge, to the unknowing eye, of falling to pieces at a touch; yet able to screak and wabble onward for months if not for years.

By half past one we had done a month's work on her, and we tumbled back aboard the *Congress* with Arnold shouting to us to get up the anchor and put all hands on the sweeps. Like two Algerine pirates we stole around the headland of Schuyler's Island and wallowed southward once more, against a dirty brown sea that slopped over our blunt bows and flooded the decks with water.

Behind us the *Providence* and the *New York* lay fifty fathoms deep, where the British could never get them; but the *Jersey* had foundered on a rock from which she wouldn't budge; and when we tried to set her afire, she was too waterlogged to burn. Five vessels we had so far lost; so that somewhere ahead of us, struggling against that cruel wind and the thirty-four-mile stretch of angry water that lay between us and Crown Point, were the nine remaining vessels of our little fleet; and not one man aboard the nine was more certain of seeing the light of another day than were we.

. . . No galley convicts, chained to their oars and lashed by French slave-drivers until the skin curled from the bones, could have tugged and sweated as our men tugged and sweated through the afternoon of that 12th of October, and the long night that followed. Hail squalls stung us, striking like bullets through our ragged clothes. The monotonous thumping of the pumps beat at our ears until we drowsed as we worked.

Sometimes we rowed; sometimes we tacked and rowed together, striving to gain against the wind that puffed us backward, and seemed, in its puffing, to howl scornfully at our dry-throated efforts. Whether we rowed or whether we tacked, we might have been moored, almost; for we moved as slowly as a vessel dragging its anchor.

All through that endless night the men toiled on and on. Packed in between the guns, they swayed at the oars in a slow and staggering dance. They might have been animals, milling in a panting, clattering drove upon our hail-swept deck—a half-seen herd that had a skunklike reek, what with its weariness and hunger, its foulness and its sweat: a herd from which strange noises came: howls, coughs, groans, high-pitched laughs: prolonged and senseless mutterings.

The voices of the officers, from lack of sleep, were mere croakings. Cap Huff wheezed like a giant porpoise as he shoved at an oar here and an oar there. Steven Nason, Tom Bickford, Verrieul and Nathaniel went up and down between the rowers, waking those who slept on their feet, shaking them, promising rum to them, saying anything to keep them going.

Arnold limped and slipped from end to end of the quarterdeck, coughing, whispering to himself, watching the sails, watching the row-

ers, peering behind him and peering ahead; taking the tiller from me
and giving it back; sniffing the wind; making sounds of exasperation in
his throat, or of amusement, or of expostulation, as if prying into every
nook and corner of his brain with indefatigable persistence, hunting for
a way to bring us out of the hole we were in.

We didn't know it then; but on what we were doing, with the help
of Arnold's grim determination, depended the life of the Revolution,
and the very existence of what we know as freedom. If Arnold had
failed us, or if we had failed him, I think that no American who reads
these lines would be in the position of life in which he finds himself
today.

. . . With the coming of the dim dawn of Sunday, the 13th of October,
the wind went down; and as it died in fitful, lessening gusts, hope rose
in all of us—even in the dullest landsman who tugged at the oars; for
even he knew that if the wind would turn into the north, we might yet
be safe.

We moved alone in the fog, so far as we could tell; but the men took
heart, laughing the silly laughter of fatigue, cursing the British and their
fleet, as if contemptuous of such trifles. I knew how they felt: they
had come through a battle that could have been no worse: nothing had
hurt them, and so they couldn't be hurt. That, I am now willing to admit, is how I myself felt when the wind died down; but I felt different
when it came up again.

All these Champlain fogs vanish as soon as the early morning chill
is gone; and as this one lifted, we strained our eyes and twisted our
heads like owls. We found the battered *Washington*, half a mile behind; and what was worse, ahead of us we saw four gundelos, four
tattered hulks, fallen back from Wigglesworth's squadron. Unable, with
their flat bottoms, to keep up with Wigglesworth's more seaworthy vessels, they had slipped so far behind that they were now our charges.
For one ungenerous moment they seemed to me like poor relations
who appear at the most inopportune of moments, confidently demanding support, and determined to let themselves be saved, no matter what
the cost to someone else.

The thinning fog revealed the western shore, bleak and gray. The
leaves were stripped from the birches and the maples: the mountains
beyond were somber with pines that broke the whiteness of the snow.
Arnold uttered a grunting laugh when he saw it, and my heart was as
heavy as my stomach, already leaden from hunger.

We were abreast of Willsborough. In sixteen hours of rowing we had
come six miles and were still twenty-eight miles from Crown Point.

INSTEAD of turning, the wind came up from the south again. It rolled back the remnants of the fog-bank and thinned it to nothing. To the north the lake was flat and blue, and on it we saw the British, white against the dark pines of Grand Isle like snowy icebergs. Their very snowiness was heartbreaking: for it showed us their sails were full and drawing: they were running free, while we labored against a head wind. Where they were, the wind was north, bringing them straight down on us.

Before the fog lifted, I thought we had almost escaped. Now I saw we were worse off than ever; and I damned dramas and romances in which misfortunes quickly pass: in which troubles vanish like a morning mist, to leave life smiling and golden, free of care and pain.

Things aren't like that in life and war. In life we struggle, shattered, from disaster, only to plunge headlong into fresh disasters. In war, soldiers fight until they can fight no more, and then go on fighting: men exhaust themselves with superhuman labors and then go on working regardless of weariness.

It seemed to me that if any men deserved to escape, we did—that if any men had ever earned peace, victory and a happy end, we had earned it; but war and life, alas, take no account of what men earn.

We were silent, staring at those distant snowy sails, and by our silence revealed our knowledge that here was the end of all our labors. I dared not even wonder what that end might be.

Arnold broke the silence. "They've got a breeze, so sooner or later we'll get it, too. Don't forget that! Cast loose the guns in the cabin."

He went down among the rowers, who had stopped rowing to watch the British. "Now then," he called, limping up and down between their haggard ranks, "now then, we'll drink the last of our rum and get at it again! It means hard work, but not for long! Only till the wind comes up with us!"

There was something indomitable about him, always. He wouldn't be beaten: he *couldn't* be beaten. He couldn't even *think* of being beaten; and those who saw or heard him in a trying hour caught from him a sort of reckless hardness.

Those at the oars were still powder-caked from the cartridges they had ripped open with their teeth at Valcour, and from the greasy black powder-wetness of guns and swivels. Their cheeks bristled with beard: their necks and arms, emaciated from work and lack of food, protruded awkwardly from stinking rags. Their hands were all gurry sores and blisters, their feet and legs battered from stumblings and collisions in the battle.

I have heard it said that God took a hand in our defeat of England: that Providence fought for us because our cause was just. That may be so; but God and Providence seemed far away on that sunny Sunday morning; for they did nothing about our adverse wind: took no steps to deprive the British of their fine north breeze. I am, I hope, one who fears God and respects religion; but having a regard for truth, I have never, since that day, blamed my misfortunes on either God or Providence.

Inch by inch we struggled against that devilish damned wind, while the British bore down on us with a speed that filled us with cold forebodings.

When, at last, the south wind died and we finally caught the same breeze that had done so handsomely for the British, a scant mile separated us from the foremost of the onrushing vessels.

Even then we made poor progress; for the four gundelos ahead of us, shot-riddled and water-logged, were slow, and the *Congress* hung behind them, herding them like four reluctant sheep.

Arnold, watching their laborings, shook his head. "These rear-guard actions aren't pleasant," he admitted, "but there's no escaping this one. If we can find a corner to dodge into with these gundelos, we may be able to save their guns and crews, and certainly we'll make it possible for Wigglesworth to get through to Ticonderoga with the *Trumbull*, the *Enterprise* and the *Revenge*. He must have another gundelo with him; and the *Gates* ought to be equipped by now; and the *Liberty's* there; so if Wigglesworth gets safe away, we'll still have enough of a fleet to keep the British from being over-reckless."

His eyes were pale and expressionless as he studied the approaching British. There were three of them in the lead—the *Inflexible* sloop-of-war, with her three towering masts and her press of canvas, and the two big schooners, the *Carleton* and the *Maria*. Far behind them was the swarm of gunboats, gathered around the floating fortress like ducklings paddling contentedly beside a swan.

It was eleven when Arnold gave the word, and the stern guns, in the cabin beneath us, let off with a jerk. The *Washington*, behind us and steering wildly, let off her guns as well; but to neither of us did the

British reply. The two schooners hauled their wind so that they were between us and the western shore.

"Well, well!" Arnold said. "Look at that! They've made up their minds they won't let us land on the New York side!" His face wore an expression of exaggerated concern.

"Think of it!" he said. "Crown Point and Ticonderoga are on the New York shore, so they figure the only way we can reach those places is to go ashore on that side! Strange! Strange they persist in thinking there's only one way to skin a cat!"

When at last the British vessels opened on the wallowing *Washington*, Arnold turned away. I think he felt, as I did, a sort of sickness, as at the sight of a comrade hurried to his death by quick water in which no man can swim.

Not far from us was the sharp outline of Split Rock, cloven from the mainland as by a giant axe. Beyond it we saw the blue folds of bays and headlands that might, if we could reach them, provide a sanctuary.

"Run out those sweeps again," Arnold shouted to Tom Bickford. He turned back to watch the *Washington*.

From the side of the *Inflexible* jutted a cloud of white smoke, through which darted the pale flashes of her guns. The *Washington* yawed; her foresail split and flapped. The stuttering roar of the broadside came down wind to us, a warning of what we ourselves must soon expect.

"It's no use!" Arnold said. "Waterbury's got to do the best he can. If we turn back to help him, we'll never get the gundelos away. And he's gone, anyhow! There's nothing that can save him!"

As we passed Split Rock, the *Inflexible* drew closer to the *Washington* and gave her a broadside at close range—a broadside that heeled her over. Arnold shrugged his shoulders, a gesture of resignation. He knew what must happen next, and so did I. So did all of us. I was sorry for Hawley, but glad Nathaniel was aboard the *Congress* with me.

The *Inflexible* came about and passed into the wake of the laboring *Washington*. The two big schooners were on her flank, between her and the New York shore. If the *Washington* stayed as she was, the *Inflexible's* larboard battery would pour its fire along her shattered decks. If she could contrive to turn her broadside to the *Inflexible*, she would be raked by the two schooners. Whatever she did, she was helpless.

The *Inflexible* was close under the *Washington's* stern. The pounding of her guns, hurling destruction into that battered hulk, sounded like the hollow slamming of iron doors.

The *Washington* yawed again; her fore-yard broke at the mast, so that the sail hung in useless folds; her guns were silent.

We, watching this sad performance, were silent too. The four vessels behind us were fixed immovably in a welter of smoke. A mastodonic thudding came from them. Every eye was fastened on the striped flag that floated at the peak of the *Washington's* tattered mainsail; and when it moved downward, a vague sound, a blend of resignation and relief, arose from our decks. The *Washington* had struck, and our turn had come.

. . . The next two hours were horrible hours of smoke, groans and thunderous frenzy: of panting, tugging and cursing: of guns that leaped, guns that roared until our eardrums seemed to be wooden plugs wedged into our heads and calked in place with masses of greasy wool, of shot that screamed over and between us, splintered bulwarks and gun-carriages, crushed men into broken wrecks that we stuffed through the nearest gun-port.

Our progress was like that of a wounded dog, bleeding and dizzy, struck and roared at by three bears, yet still able to keep beyond the full sweep of their claws: able, even, to snap desperately at his tormentors.

The three British vessels, now agonizingly near, poured in their broadsides at point-blank range; and we, working both our larboard and our starboard batteries, and our swivels as well, did what we could to hold them off.

Every last man worked on the guns; for a third of our crew was gone: either dead in the waters of the lake, or shot-riddled in the cabin, Doc Means at grisly work upon them. Such was our plight that Arnold wouldn't leave the tiller, but clung to it like a chained animal.

Steven Nason had charge of a gun on one side of me, Nathaniel on the other. They were dreadful to see, because of the glassy, drunken look that filled their bloodshot eyes. The vessels on which we laid our guns seemed wavering mirages, thanks to our three foodless, sleepless days.

What I couldn't understand was how any of us could escape the hail of grape and ball that hurtled around us; and what surprised me most was that I had no longing to escape it, but only a weary eagerness to have the end come soon.

I think the British vessels planned to close with us and board us. They seemed to swell abruptly, though at the moment I thought this strange enlargement was one of the tricks my eyes had played me for an hour past. The blasts from their guns hit harder; there was a crackling in the air like the snapping of whiplashes; men went down, along the deck, as though invisible hands had caught them by the ankles and tripped them. Some went down hard: others staggered drunkenly, then sprawled grotesquely underfoot.

Beside me Nathaniel clutched nothingness and stood swaying, his hands groping and groping. When I caught his arm, he went down like a felled tree, dragging me with him.

I fumbled at his chest, but there seemed to be no blood on him. The sponger from my gun-crew pulled at my shoulder. I got up and laid the gun on the *Inflexible*. She seemed to have a thousand sails, each with a thousand shot-holes in it. The gunner fired the gun.

I licked caked powder from my lips and wondered desperately what to do about Nathaniel.

Tom Bickford took my arm. When I shook him off, he caught at me again. "Arnold wants us."

"Nathaniel's hurt," I said.

Tom looked at Nathaniel, quickly looked away and again said, "Arnold wants us, Cap'n Peter."

I stumbled aft, half pushed by Tom.

Arnold, one knee hooked over the tiller, was re-priming his pistols and watching the ever nearing British vessels.

"We're abreast of Buttonmould Bay," he told us. "That gives us a chance to pull to windward. They expect us to run for the New York shore; so we'll pull to windward where they can't follow, except in their boats." He laughed. "We'll fool 'em again!" The shrillness of his voice gave me strength.

To Tom he said, "Hoist the pennant to pull to windward: then brail up your sails and run out the sweeps. Hurry!"

To me he said, "What's the matter with your brother?"

When I shook my head he said, "Take the helm. I'll work the stern guns while you run her ashore. Drive the men! Drive 'em! We'll have to work fast."

Then he said, "I'll give you a minute or two before we come about, so you can tend to your brother!"

That was like Arnold. He thought of everything, and he was as kind a man as ever lived.

I hurried to Nathaniel. He hadn't moved. I swabbed his face with water from a gun bucket. So far as I could see, there wasn't a scratch on him. When I tried to listen to his heart, I could hear nothing for the slamming of the British guns and the sandy rasp of my own breath.

I tried to pick him up, but couldn't because my legs and knees were weak. I took him by an ankle and dragged him up the gangway and onto the quarterdeck, where I could keep him from being thrown overboard.

"Here!" Arnold said. "Try to beach her so she lies level." He gave me the tiller and hurried to the cabin without a glance at Nathaniel. The four gundelos ahead of us turned into the wind, and we turned too, hammering at the three Britishers as they went sliding past. The suddenness of the maneuver caught the British napping. They were a quarter mile beyond us before they came about; and then they were almost helpless, since they could only make short tacks far in our rear, hurling distant broadsides after us as we rowed desperately into the bay, straight into the wind.

That was our advantage over them: we had oars, and they didn't. They depended on sails; and if they had attempted to follow us into shallow waters with which they were unfamiliar, they would themselves have been in trouble.

My dulled brain told me that we were still ten miles from Crown Point; that in spite of rowing and fighting for eighteen miles, we were still ten miles from safety. I vaguely wondered whether any place in the world was any longer safe.

The jerk of the guns, pounding from our stern with slow irregularity, helped kick us into the shelter of the headland. The four gundelos, sails brailed up and oars all awry, moved before us, disheveled and wild-looking, like ragged mad women. Our deck, except for the gabbling of a man with a bullet through his hand, was nearly silent. The pumps had stopped at last, since every man was needed on the oars.

The oarsmen, now that the end of all our labors was at hand, panted and pushed hard at the sweeps. With each British shot that passed us, howling an angry malediction at our final effort, they crouched over their oars to make themselves smaller.

Behind the northern point of the bay I saw a shelving beach: one on which we might almost run our bow on land and still be sheltered from British fire. I called a seaman to take the tiller, and went to the cabin. The place was a sulphurous corner of hell. Wounded men groaned in the corners; and at the far end, gun-crews moved like demons against the smoke that filtered through the ports.

"One more!" Arnold said, when I told him we were close to shore. He dragged upward at the gun's breech. The gunner tapped the quoin; the crew jumped clear, and the gun bellowed and bounced back among us like a black dragon.

"All right!" Arnold shouted. "Get the wounded forward! Cut off the sails to use for stretchers!"

He climbed the ladder into the bright afternoon sunlight. A British ball passed near us with a diabolical squeal. I felt the rasping wind of it. Arnold's hat fell off, so he must have felt it more than I.

Steven Nason stood on a bow bulwark, hacking strips from the lateen sail that hung in brails above him. The long yard of the foresail, struck by the same shot that so narrowly missed us, whipped around like the tail of a windmill. It struck Nason and hurled him backward, in spite of his size, as if from a catapult. His body turned slowly in mid-air, cleared the bulwarks, fell against two sweeps, which broke short off, and dropped straight down, out of sight.

I ran forward, but Tom Bickford was before me, hanging over the side where Nason had vanished. He jumped back on deck, ran around two guns, scrambled onto the bulwarks and dove overboard. When I hung over to look, I saw, between the slowly moving oars that drove us onward, Nason's dark bulk, under water, distorted and wavering against a background of gray sand, and above him Tom Bickford, sprawling and kicking, reaching and reaching for him.

I unshipped an oar and made fast a rope-end to it. Cap Huff came charging aft, caroming into oarsmen and upsetting water buckets. His sweaty great face was distorted, so that he had the look of a blackened moon-faced baby on the verge of bursting into tears. He took me by the front of the shirt and shook me. "Why don't they stop the ship? Is he dead? He ain't dead, is he?"

"Get back to your marines where you belong," I said. "Tom Bickford's got him."

He clung to me, breathing heavily: then, almost fearfully, looked over the side. What he saw seemed to frighten him, for he whimpered and clumsily threw a leg across the bulwark. When I looked too, I saw Tom not only had Nason by the arm, but had hooked his fingers into one of the ragged shot-holes that honeycombed our side.

I pulled Cap back. "Can't you see Tom's got him? Go forward and get your men ashore."

Cap hiccupped. "By God, if Stevie's dead, I'll take it out of England's hide!"

He lumbered forward. We were close under the headland by now, so close that suddenly and strangely there was the odor of pine woods in our nostrils. The four gundelos were drawn against a marshy bank, their crews pouring from them like ants, and, like ants, carrying heavy burdens we knew to be wounded men. I felt our own bow scrape bottom. Our stern settled a little, and slowly the deck canted to starboard.

Arnold had a canvas speaking trumpet, and through it he shouted to the gundelos, ordering that they be set afire. We might have lain at a deserted dock, for all the excitement in his voice when he issued his orders—for marines to be lined up on the bank to hold off the British in case they tried to attack in boats before the vessels burned: for ten men to remain on board with him to set the ship afire: for the wounded to be lowered from the bow in canvas slings. . . .

To me he said, "You'd better look after your brother yourself. I don't believe he's dead."

That picture of him, haggard, hollow-eyed and unshaven, hungry and sleepless, but always steady and calculating, taking us ashore at Buttonmould Bay after days and nights of planning, fighting and responsibility such as might drive the best of men insane, is one that has never left me.

At that time I knew only one thing: that he was a seaman and a general fit to rank with the world's best. I know more now, after years of meditation in the quiet of a vessel's cabin.

I know battles are not great because of the numbers engaged in them, or because of the heaps of slain. Some of the greatest have been between small bodies of men, but are great because of deciding matters of moment to the world. I know the battle we fought at Valcour Island was momentous indeed, and that no force, great or small, ever lived to better purpose or died more gloriously than the force that manned Arnold's fleet on Lake Champlain. It had saved the lake for that year; and it had done more: it had won the delay that brought us the chance to fight at Saratoga—a chance that otherwise must have been forever lost. All of that was due to Arnold. Every last bit of credit goes to Arnold; for no other man could have effected the building of even the small fleet we *did* build; nor could any two—or ten—others have planned the fight that Arnold planned, or held our untrained forces to a resistance as dogged and heroic as any in all naval history.

. . . When the wounded were safe ashore, Doc Means and Verrieul came to help me with Nathaniel. Doc's ragged tow-cloth smock was belted around him, its back bulging with the bundles of his profession. He peered nearsightedly at Nathaniel; then nodded encouragingly.

"No," Doc said, "he ain't dead, but he's been pretty close to it. I shouldn't wonder if a cannon ball come past his head and pushed the air against him so hard it was kind of like being kicked by two-three mules all together. That's how it looks to me. If we don't jolt him, and if we can get him laid down in a quiet place, where there ain't somebody tripping over us every minute, or falling dead on us, I'd prob'ly have him up and walking in half an hour, lively as a chipmunk."

The two enemy schooners and the ship maneuvered at the entrance to the bay. Streamers of white smoke drifted down wind from their black hulls as they threw shot at us—shot that passed overhead, wailing, to smash among the pines.

I kept an eye on the British vessels, fearing they might attempt what I, under the circumstances, would have tried to do: come into the bay on a long slant, so to be closer—so to capture these beached hulks of ours, and their guns, with boarding parties. To this day I cannot say why they held off, firing uselessly, when they might have scudded to Crown Point in pursuit of the *Trumbull* galley and the four smaller craft still afloat. But hold off they did; and it was to the angry roaring of their distant guns that Doc and I swung Nathaniel down into Verrieul's outstretched arms.

As I clung to the bows, waiting for Doc to clamber down, I saw Arnold and his seamen, standing by the cabin, peering within. They started back, and a puff of smoke surged upward from the cabin. I let go and dropped into two feet of water.

The beach swarmed with men, all black and tattered. Of the eighty who had been aboard the *Congress* at the beginning of the fight at Valcour, there were less than fifty now. The other crews had suffered less than ours, but not much less. More than half our ragged crew had been killed or wounded, and it seemed incredible to me that any of us were still alive.

Nason lay white-faced on the beach, a draggled wreck, one arm grotesquely bent. Tom Bickford, almost as pale, knelt above him. Cap Huff blundered out from the milling figures on the upper beach, clutching a strip of canvas to his breast. It hung between his legs, so that he constantly tripped and stumbled on it.

He dropped to his knees beside Nason. "Put him on this," he told Tom thickly. "We'll hang it on a pole, like a hammock, and lug him."

Doc Means went quickly to Cap. "What's the matter with you?"

Cap stared up at him. "Stevie got hurt. He got hurt bad." He hiccupped and added wildly: "They killed him! They killed Stevie!"

Doc slapped Cap's cheek—a stinging slap. "Pay attention to me! Nason ain't dead—not yet he ain't! What happened to *you?*"

"Nothing! There ain't nothing happened to me! Why don't you fix up Stevie?"

Doc slapped him again. "Stop your hollering! Take off that coat!"

Cap fumbled at his ragged jacket, groaning as he dragged it from his naked shoulders. Beneath his arm was a purple welt that oozed dark blood.

"Look at that!" Doc said. "You're pretty near as bad off as Nason! You got a grape shot in you."

"I ain't had any grape," Cap said dully. "I could use some."

Doc peered nearsightedly at Cap's ribs, whipped out a knife and flicked the point against the thick muscles beneath the shoulder. From Cap's lips came an anguished grunt.

Doc held out his hand. In its palm lay a flattened leaden ball. "There it is! Now mind what I tell you! Don't try to carry nobody! Tend to your own affairs and keep away from Nason. Understand? If you try to carry him, you'll bust yourself open!"

"Why don't you tend to him?" Cap bawled with sudden surprising fierceness.

"I'll tend to him when you get away from here, and not before!"

Cap rose to his feet. His naked torso was smeared with blood. He rubbed the red stains fumblingly, examined his crimsoned fingers in blank amazement, and stumbled off toward the ridge above the beach. Along its top lay his squad of scarecrow marines. They were as business-like, waiting there to protect us against British landing parties, as though they wore clean uniforms instead of lousy rags.

Doc watched him go; then shook his head and spoke to me. "Take your brother over the ridge behind the headland. Pick a spot where we won't be interfered with. We'll be out of range of the guns there. After I've done what I can for Nason, I'll follow you."

As Verrieul and I carried Nathaniel over the ridge, I turned to see where the British were. The *Inflexible* was coming into the wind, pre-paratory to tacking, far out beyond the headland. She fell off slowly on the other tack, working her guns with grim persistence. The shot splashed astern of the beached vessels. All of them were burning, the smoke and flames rolling and crackling from cabins and hatches. At their mast-heads flew our red and white flags, each with its rattlesnake and the words "Don't Tread On Me."

There was satisfaction in the knowledge that in three days of fight-ing, the British hadn't been able to make us haul them down. And there was something in the sight of them that seemed to half strangle me. I think the scores who lay behind such shelters as the beach af-forded, waiting for the fire to take those flags, must have felt as I did; for when Arnold, standing alone in the bow of the *Congress* to watch the progress of the flames, turned and stepped up on the bulwarks, the men burst into a shrill and quavering cheer that sounded as choked as my own throat felt.

On the far side of the ridge, there was nothing to remind us of the battle save the slow and distant thudding of the British guns, firing uselessly at our burning ships. Verrieul motioned with his head toward a stand of young pines, sprouting from a fallen tree. It offered a shelter from the wind; so we took Nathaniel to its lee and lowered him to a patch of pine needles. He was limp and heavy; but his hands were warm, and a slow pulse beat in his wrists.

It seemed an hour before Doc Means came lurching to us. Without a word he stooped and pawed at my brother's chest, neck and shoulders.

Nathaniel's face was the dull silver color of a fish on the beach. Doc worked away at the base of his skull for a time, but it did no good.

"We got to get him breathing," Doc said. His tone frightened me.

He showed us what to do. Verrieul raised and lowered Nathaniel's arms, while I pressed against his ribs, forcing air out so that fresh air might be drawn into his lungs. I feared, from the way Doc drove us, that life was almost gone; and I wondered, in a detached way, what I would say to my mother. The thought of her grief—of the sorrows that would crowd her long days and her longer evenings when she sat sewing at the low table by the fire—goaded me to working at Nathaniel's chest until my shoulders ached and the sweat poured from me.

His death-like inertness filled me with a tireless endurance. In my determination to save him, if he could be saved, I lost all sense of time. Hours may have passed before Doc caught our wrists and pulled us to our feet.

"I saw his eyelid move," Doc said.

We hung over him, breathless.

He opened his eyes, staring straight up into the pines above him. He stared and stared—just an empty stare: then a bewildered gaze. He turned his head and saw me.

"I'm all right," he said thickly. "Go on back to your gun."

Another sort of look came into his eyes, and he feebly put out his hand to touch my knee. "What's this?" he whispered. "Are we—did they——"

I could see he thought he was dead, and that we were in another world.

"You got hurt a little," I said. "We had to run ashore. We're only ten miles from Crown Point."

It came to me suddenly that I had heard no shouting from the beach: no sounds of gunfire: that I had heard not even the distant banging of British guns.

The silence of the pine thicket was more than the quiet of an October twilight: it was an unnatural silence, so heavy that there must have been a cause for it. It was the sort of breathless hush that enfolds a countryside before the bursting of a storm.

XLI

I TURNED and ran back over the ridge where I could have a clear view of the beach. It was empty—a trampled strand, with here and there a rag, and at the edge of the water a broken musket. In the shallows the five vessels still burned, but they were dismasted hulks, their bulwarks charred so that the guns stood high in air.

As I watched, a gun-carriage on the *Congress* collapsed in a flurry of sparks. The gun slid sideways, hung for a moment, then pitched into the water with a sharp hiss. A burst of steam floated off shore.

The crews that had covered the beach and the ridge had gone: Cap Huff and his marines had gone: Nason and Tom Bickford and the rest—they were all gone. I remembered the rapidity with which Arnold always acted. He must have rounded up the crews and rushed them off for Crown Point—and thought, of course, that we were among them.

By carrying Nathaniel pig-a-back we might catch up with the column, unless our legs gave out from hunger.

I went back across the ridge, moving as rapidly as a dead-tired man could. Beneath the pines, where I had left Nathaniel and Doc and Verrieul, there was nobody. I thought I had come to the wrong place, but I saw I hadn't. The pine needles bore traces of our labors over Nathaniel.

I looked at the spot stupidly, stared about me like a fool, then called loudly, shouting Doc's name, and Verrieul's. There was no answer. I took a few steps forward among the pines and shouted again. Then I held my breath and listened.

A squirrel whisked into sight on a tree trunk overhead. He flattened himself, his tail all a-twitch with nervousness, and peered down—not at me, but at something on the opposite side of the tree.

I looked at him dully and scratched my head, thinking: "Yes, he's looking at something—— No, at somebody; there's somebody on the other side of that tree!"

Then for a moment or two I had a strong conviction that I was asleep —asleep at last, somewhere, I wondered where—and that this was a dream.

I've often heard people say, "I thought I must be dreaming," but for those few moments after the vanishing of Nathaniel and Doc and Verrieul, and the squirrel's peeping down the wrong side of that tree, I believed in sober truth that I was having a dream—an ugly dream, too —and that I'd wake from it presently and find out where I really was. I'd been passing through thunderous nightmares in which I knew I was awake; here was another, but in so curious and ominous a silence that I couldn't credit its actuality. Then I said to myself suddenly, "Look out!" I felt my heart thudding, was awake and had a hint of the grotesque reality.

I moved softly backward, loosening my hatchet in my belt.

Behind me I felt a silent movement—the loom of a body near at hand. I whirled. An Indian was so close on me that I could smell his oily, sweetish smell. His face was painted black, and he seemed enormous. He held a musket almost against my stomach. When I gave ground before him, another Indian grasped my arms from the rear. Two others came from among the trees and looked quietly at me.

Never had I seen bigger men—though they looked more like devils than men. Their faces were black; their hair rose from their shaved heads in a sort of crest. The crest was stiffened with clay and painted bright red. It was like a horse's mane that had been clipped close, or like the crest on a dragoon's helmet, so that it gave them a look of fierceness that was horrible. They wore buckskin leggins and red belt cloths; and the tops of their bodies were not only bare, but shining with grease. Under the left arm of each one was tied a bag made from the whole skin of a bird or animal. There was a peculiar sweet smell to them: a smell that might have been a blend of wood smoke, sweet grass, fur and rancid oil.

The sight of those black-faced figures appearing so suddenly out of nowhere held me paralyzed and speechless. I made no protest and no resistance when two of them took me by the arms and hustled me through the pines to the shore on the northern side of the headland. I seemed to be numbed and in a daze as they dragged me along.

I think the truth was that I must have been, in reality, half asleep; and in the haze of this stunned drowsiness, I dimly heard the four Indians cackling in high good humor.

On its side behind a stand of birches was a long North canoe with something that looked like a bird daubed on each end in red paint. Two more Indians were hunkered down beside the canoe. One was tending a newly made fire on which a pot rested; the other was kneeling over Doc Means and fumbling with the bundles inside his smock. Doc was bound hand and foot, as were Nathaniel and Verrieul.

When the two by the canoe saw that another captive was being brought in, they yowped and howled like animals; but since the one continued to tend his fire and the other to fumble in Doc's smock, their howling seemed perfunctory.

I was tied and thrown down beside the others; and at that our captors ignored us. One went to sniff at the pot over the fire. Scooping out some of its contents with his fingers, he licked them noisily.

"For God's sake," I whispered to Doc, "where did they come from? Did they hurt Nathaniel?"

Doc's face was pressed into a patch of moss, so that his speech was indistinct. "They stopped his circulation again. He ain't moved since they jumped on us. He's got to be bled. He's got to be bled right away. Where's all that Injun lingo that Verrieul claimed to know?"

Verrieul sighed. "You gain nothing with these people by hurried speech. To be frank with you, the suddenness of the thing was upsetting to me. I need a few moments to compose my thoughts."

"Upsetting!" Doc said. "They scairt the living tripe out of *me!*" He groaned and added, "Something's got to be done—damned quick, too —if we don't want 'em to spoil all my medical supplies!"

"I know," Verrieul said. "I'm watching them. There are more things to be considered. They are from the west. I recognize some of their speech, but not all of it. They're not Hurons or Iroquois. They speak an Algonkian tongue, like Abenaki, but they aren't Abenakis. The longer I can go without speaking, the more I'll learn. Also their chief man has gone ahead on a scout, to watch Arnold's retreat, and it's best to say nothing until he returns. He'll be the wisest of them. Two of these that took us are very young: not more than fifteen years old. To speak with them would be a waste of time. They're not yet possessed of good sense."

I looked more carefully at the six red men. In the beginning I had been unable to distinguish between them. All seemed equally tall: all of an age: all equally horrible.

Now I saw differences. Because of the black paint and their crested heads, they had a look of uniformity; but two, beneath their paint, were full-skinned, their cheeks smooth and unwrinkled from jawbone to the lower lids of their eyes. They were, I realized, young boys. The others were men of twenty-five or thirty.

While I stared, I was conscious that I myself was stared at. A seventh Indian had come quietly up behind us. His face, too, was black, with three red marks, like scowl marks, drawn across his forehead and centering on the bridge of his nose, which added intentionally to what seemed his naturally murderous expression. His hair was crested, like the others, rising in a stiff red mane above his shaved skull. When I studied him, I saw wrinkles on his upper lip, and depressions under his eyes. He had a little more stomach than the others; and the backs of his hands were wrinkled and bony.

He made an unintelligible grunting sound; then moved around us to stand with the others. He, too, nosed at the odor of the pot, tested the contents with his finger: then picked up a piece of bark, and dusted it on his naked thigh. With it he scooped a sample from the pot, blew upon it to cool it, and gulped it down.

The Indian who had rummaged in the back of Doc's smock stepped close to the new arrival and exhibited the package containing Doc's extra asafoetida bags. The two of them stood there, sniffing at it as though it were some rare perfume they had smelled before, but couldn't quite remember when or where.

I was almost as surprised as they when Verrieul spoke. His voice was deep and rich, unlike his usual manner of speech, which was simple and engaging. It was not only the voice of an actor, but the voice of an old actor, who cannot even say "Good morning" without investing the words with a quaver of emotion.

The two who had been sniffing at Doc's asafoetida bags immediately dropped them on the ground and stared intently at Verrieul. When he spoke again, moving his bound hands and feet suggestively, they all made coughing sounds that seemed to rise from their stomachs. The oldest Indian—the new arrival—hurriedly went to Doc and untied him.

Doc scrambled to his feet. "By Grapes!" he said—and it was the first time I had ever seen him angry—"I been around a good deal, here and there, but that's the first time I ever see a sick man treated *that* way!" He stood swaying before the oldest of the Indians, and his faded blue eyes were hard as glass. "Ain't you got no sense?" he asked bitterly. "Don't you know *nothing*, you jabbed smut-faced weasels? If I raked hell and strained the ocean, I couldn't find a meaner set o' minks than you! Where's my supplies?"

There was no mistaking the tenor of Doc's remarks. All seven of the Indians stepped uneasily away from the bundles.

Doc gathered them together; then turned to Nathaniel. For all his apparent feebleness, Doc could move as fast as anyone, if not faster; for when he seemed to be stumbling and falling, he was in reality engaged in getting somewhere in the manner he found most expeditious. He stumbled and wavered above Nathaniel; and almost before I knew what had happened, he had jerked the rope from his wrists and ankles.

"Here," Doc said to the oldest Indian, "make yourself useful, why don't you!" He pointed to Nathaniel and made imperious motions. The Indian obediently took Nathaniel under the arms and held him up. From one of his bundles Doc unwrapped a trigger lancet and a small chart. The chart was his Venesection Mannekin; and when he opened it, the other Indians crowded close to stare open-mouthed at the veined figure it portrayed, surrounded by signs of the zodiac, and the various legends explaining the benefits of drawing blood from different sections of the body.

"That's right!" Doc said to the Indians. "Push right up and lean your-selves all over me, so we can make as much of a mess of things as we can!" He turned irately to the oldest Indian. "Tell 'em to keep away from us! How'd you like to have me shove a lancet into *you* with six smut-faced weasels standing around and joggling me while I did it."

The Indian spoke harshly to his six companions and they obediently withdrew a few feet to stand gawping at Doc.

Doc ignored them and studied his Venesection Mannekin. "Accord-ing to this," he said thoughtfully, "you're supposed to take the blood from behind the ear, being as how it's his head as seems to be troubling him; but I ain't never done it, and I don't propose to start now. If a ship's leaking, it don't matter what part you pump water out of!"

He raised Nathaniel's arm, tightened the skin, set the lancet against it and pulled the trigger. The blood oozed out in a slow dark stream which soon ran more swiftly. Doc solicitously watched Nathaniel's face.

As for the Indians, all of those horrible, black-faced creatures clapped their hands tightly over their mouths and stood so, like children strug-gling to repress unseemly mirth—except that their gesture was one of amazement: not of merriment.

Nathaniel groaned, raising a hand uncertainly to his head.

"There," Doc said comfortingly, "you'll be all right now, just as soon as we get a little food into you! What is it these red pole-cats think they're eating, anyway?"

He staggered back from the circle of onlookers, stumbled to the fire, and, as if to save himself from falling, put out his hand and lifted the pot from the forked stick on which it hung. "Why," he said, "I believe it's succotash!" He helped himself freely with a piece of bark; then nodded profoundly. "Yes: it's succotash: not bad, either!"

He dipped out a little and fed it to Nathaniel. The very sight of a person eating made my stomach squeak like an ungreased boot.

"Here," Doc said testily to the oldest Indian, "put him on the ground, where he can lean against the canoe!" He motioned impatiently, and the Indian did as he said.

Doc, hunkered beside Nathaniel, fed him slowly; and the seven red men, wilder and more malignant in appearance than any human beings I had ever before seen or imagined, stood there without a word and watched this high-handed disposition of their food.

Verrieul coughed apologetically. "When you're finished," he reminded Doc, "you might pay a little attention to us. It was I who told them what a great medicine man you are."

Doc hung the kettle back over the fire and came to us. "By Job," he said plaintively, "these red rattlesnakes certainly make me forget myself. I guess maybe it's because they kind of startle me and get me all upset!"

He rounded furiously on the leader of our captors. "Look here, you old Sponge-belly! What you want to keep these boys tied up this way for? Ain't you got no trace of decency?" He pulled and twitched at our fastenings, and in a moment we were loose.

We sat up and stared at Doc and the Indians, and the Indians stared back at us. I wondered how long it would be before they drew hatchets from their girdles and split open our skulls.

Verrieul scrambled to his feet and said something to them in passionate and moving tones, at which the Indians looked puzzled. Then the one Doc had called Sponge-belly took his hatchet from his belt and hefted it thoughtfully. Instead of using it on us, however, he went to a birch tree and peeled off a sheet of bark. He folded up the edges, so that it made a crude bowl, and into it he poured nearly half the contents of the kettle. When he made signs that it was ours we pulled our spoons from our breeches pockets and spooned succotash into ourselves and into Nathaniel. To me, after my three foodless days of endless labor, it seemed the sweetest food in the world.

While we ate, the seven Indians stood around us, waiting for us to finish. When our portion of the succotash was gone—no more of a satisfaction to the aching void within us than a shrimp would be to a starving seagull—Sponge-belly took the bark bowl from us, filled it with the remainder of the succotash, and the seven red men huddled around it, picking up the soup-like mixture of corn, beans and bear fat with their fingers, throwing back their heads to gobble it down, dribbling the juice on their chins and chests, and freely splattering it on each other.

Cautioned by Verrieul, we, too, sat silent while they ate. When they were done, they removed as much of the remnants of the succotash from their necks and bodies as they could without rubbing off the black paint.

The six younger Indians sprawled negligently on the ground, but Sponge-belly hitched up his belt cloth and made coughing noises in his throat, as if to loosen his talking muscles. He walked back and forth before us, stiff-legged, like an enormous red rooster preparing to crow.

He spoke at last in deep tones, similar to those Verrieul had used; and during his speech Verrieul threw us phrases here and there, to give us an idea of what was being said.

"They belong to the greatest Indian nation in the world," Verrieul whispered hurriedly. "That's what they all say—they're Saukie-ok: Sacs: part of the nation of Sacs and Foxes—very important people—great fighters—this gentleman is a great fighter—he's bragging—he once drove an arrow all the way through a buffalo—he once traveled eight days without food and entered the town of his enemies and went into the house of the man who had killed his brother and stuck a knife into him—he has the handsomest horse ever seen—he has four beautiful wives—he has taken twenty-seven scalps—he's the one that thought of coming to this place and capturing us—everybody fears him because he's cunning and full of stratagems—he thinks we're fortunate to be taken prisoner by such a great man—he will now take us back to the camp of those who fight under the flag of the Great Father in England —and out of consideration for the ancient medicine man—he means Doc —he will permit all of us to travel unbound. We must be quiet; not try to escape."

At pauses in Sponge-belly's speech, his six comrades made labored grunting noises. They sounded like forerunners of seasickness, but they were intended to show admiration and approval.

At the close of the speech, Doc eyed us mildly, but his voice trembled a little. "He's a wind-bag and a sponge-belly! If he drove an arrer all the way through a buffalo, it must 'a' been a buffalo that didn't have no bones. I guess I know that much anatomy! He's a sponge-belly, you tell him!"

"I'll tell him what will be most apt to save us from harm," Verrieul said. "I shall tell him again that you're a great medicine man: that we're all great men."

He struck a pose, as dignified as a man can contrive who is dead from sleep, whose breeches are in rags and who hasn't shaved for four days. When he spoke, he gestured grandly, mouthing his words; raising his hands toward the heavens. I was asleep before he finished.

I half woke from time to time and was aware that the gold and crimson of the sunset turned to rose and then to pale blue above the hills on the New York shore, dimly visible to us through the laced branches of the birches. A cold mist came up from the lake and, in our fitful periods of half wakefulness, set us all to shivering.

XLII

THEY put us in their canoe at last and set off to the northward. We fell asleep the moment we were in the canoe and stayed so until our captors prodded us awake with their paddles. It was late at night when we staggered ashore and into a tumult more suggestive of madmen at large, celebrating their freedom from restraint, than of any portion of a British army.

We were on the southern point of Grand Isle, and through the trees shone the lights of many campfires. Around the fires were hundreds of Indians, turning, gesturing, bending, capering, prancing. They were dancing to the tune of incessant yowlings, the thudding of wooden drums and the monotonous dry rattling of pebbles in turtle-shell rattles.

Their caterwauling was contagious; for no sooner had our captors lifted the canoe from the water than they humped their backs and began a jerky stamping, emitting piercing yells—"Ow! Ow! Ow! Ow!"—as if suffering excruciating stomach pains.

At sight of us, those who sang and danced became more violent, whooping and cavorting in a frenzy of triumph.

On rising land beyond the campfires were four tents, recognizable as officers' tents because sentries marched before them. The sentries were brown-faced Canadians in greenish buckskin hunting shirts; and as sentries they were not a success, for Sponge-belly and his six Indians, with us in their midst, pushed contemptuously past them, and scratched and picked at the flap of the nearest tent, thrusting their fingers through the openings.

Knowing something of the rancorous nature of British officers, I wasn't surprised when the tent flap was violently thrown open from within to reveal a tall, buckskin-clad man in a boiling rage, bellowing imprecations in obscene French.

The man himself was a surprise indeed. I recognized him instantly, even in the dim candlelight against which he was silhouetted, and with something of bewilderment and wrathful indignation; for he was the silent, self-effacing gentleman with whom we had traveled to America on the *Beau Soleil*—Mr. Leonard.

When, in my astonishment, I spoke his name, this extraordinary personage slowly fastened up the flap and went back to stand behind the rough table which, with two camp stools and the bearskin spread over a pile of spruce tips in the corner, comprised the almost luxurious furnishings of the tent.

When our captors pushed us in, there were twelve of us in that small canvas structure; and immediately, what with the Indians, Doc's asafoetida, and our own weary and unwashed state, it smelled like a den of foxes. Whether it was that odor which caused Nathaniel to lean more and more heavily against my shoulder, or the sharp memories of Marie de Sabrevois that the sight of Mr. Leonard brought to his mind, I couldn't tell. The fact was, however, that Nathaniel was slipping away from us again.

Mr. Leonard's eyes, I thought, avoided mine. Thinking he might not have recognized us in our dilapidated condition, I said to him: "Mr. Leonard, you may not remember me——" but he smiled and stopped me.

"It would be impossible to forget your kindness and hospitality," he said. "This is truly an unexpected pleasure. And by the way: I fear you misunderstood my name when we were introduced. It is not Leonard, but Lanaudiere." He raised an eyebrow. "The fault may have been mine. I seem to recall now, that I was even glad, in England, to be called Leonard, because of the difficulty with which an Englishman pronounces a French name."

"My brother has been hurt," I said. "Will you let him sit down?"

His expression was compassionate as he helped Nathaniel into one of the chairs. "In just a moment," he assured him, "we will give you the attention you should have. First we must dispose of these gentlemen who brought you in. They are singularly impressible: almost like sensitive plants in their susceptibility to oversights. At one rude touch they often wither."

"Sensitive plants?" Doc Means asked. "Ain't you thinking of skunk cabbages?"

Lanaudiere glanced coldly at Doc: then reached behind the bearskin in the corner and drew out a bottle of rum. At sight of it, Sponge-belly made a speech in which he obviously referred admiringly to his own bravery and our importance. He got the bottle, and with it a few sharp words of advice and warning from Lanaudiere. In his manner there was no hint of the sleepy, reticent Mr. Leonard we had known in London and on our voyage from France. He had become a commander both feared and respected; and if his remarks were not satisfactory, Spongebelly gave no indication of it.

Tucking the rum bottle into his belt, Sponge-belly turned in an almost

friendly way to Doc Means, bringing up from the depths of his stomach a farewell eructation; then lifted the tent flap and herded his black-
faced companions into the night.

Lanaudiere went to the opening and watched them go. For a moment he stood there, looking down at the scattered campfires on the
point, listening to the yowling and drumming. Then he fastened the
flap and studied Nathaniel, who seemed to be scarcely breathing.

"You said he was hurt. You mean he's been wounded?"

"There's no wound on him," I said. "He acts stunned. We think a
cannon ball grazed him. We were doing what we could when those
red hellions——"

Lanaudiere stooped suddenly and swung Nathaniel up against his
chest. "I think your brother only needs food and care. If you will excuse
me a moment, I'll see he receives both."

With Nathaniel in his arms, he went to the opening in the rear of
the tent, then turned to face us. In a kind voice he said, "I do not need
to tell you, of course, that it would be unwise to leave this tent. My
charges are sometimes over-hasty—just a lot of thoughtless children."
He smiled and went out.

"Just a lot of red wildcats!" Doc Means muttered. "Just a lot of
thoughtless rattlesnakes!"

Verrieul's face was haggard. "If this Lanaudiere is a friend of yours,"
he said, "I hope you'll remind him that now is the time to show it.
From the way he speaks to Indians, he's one of their highest officers.
They're under his orders—as much as any Indian can be under anyone's orders."

"But we're free of Indians, now," I reminded him.

"I don't know," Verrieul said uneasily. "They're difficult to deal with,
sometimes. Those that captured us have taken a liking to Doc. They
want to carry him home with them—and us, too."

"By Grapes," Doc protested, "they better leave me be! I can't stand
much from those pole-cats! How was it you said they called themselves?
Sox and Pox?"

"Sacs and Foxes," Verrieul said.

Doc grunted. "I guess there's no doubt they're Sacs: Wind-Sacs!" He
raised his voice to a mincing mealiness. "Just a lot of Foxes with the
hydrophoby! Just a pack of thoughtless, boyish Wind-Sacs!"

Verrieul appealed to me. "I tell you frankly, I do not like the way
Doc speaks to these Indians! It is true that my experience with Hurons
and Abenakis has so far been pleasant, but I know nothing about Sacs
and Foxes, and I prefer to be elsewhere if Doc intends to continue to
speak unpleasantly to them. That's not how Indians like to be ad-

dressed. What is more, the Sacs and Foxes live so far to the westward that if we are obliged to go with them, we'll be old men before we get back—if, indeed, we ever get back!"

I wondered whether fatigue and hunger had unhinged my mind. Not only did Verrieul's words sound fantastic: not only did the incessant yowling of Indians seem maniacal; but I thought I heard, somewhere near at hand, a woman's voice: a voice familiar to me. This, I knew, was impossible.

Lanaudiere came back with a slab of venison between two half loaves of bread, and under his arm a bottle of rum. His manner was paternal. "This is the best we have, and I know there is no need to apologize for it—not to gentlemen who have led such precarious lives for so many days!"

The venison was thick and dark red; as soft as cheese; and when we had eaten every last scrap of it and the bread, washing it down with rum and water, I felt almost rested. My muscles still shook with weariness, but my agony of uncertainty over Nathaniel was at last ended— or so I fancied.

He was safe, I said to myself. Nathaniel was safe. There had been no woman's voice. My wits had been rambling. And then, as though my tongue formed the words independent of my wishes, I found myself saying to Lanaudiere: "I thought I heard a lady's voice while you were gone. It couldn't be your niece I heard, surely?"

Lanaudiere smiled. "My dear friend! All your questions will, of course, be answered in due time; but first I hope you will consent to satisfy my *own* curiosity. We are in the dark, you see."

I knew, then, that I *had* heard a woman's voice, and that it had been the voice of Marie de Sabrevois. Otherwise he would have given me a fair answer. Marie de Sabrevois was with Lanaudiere, among these advance scouts of the British, up to some deviltry or other. It was to her that Lanaudiere had just carried Nathaniel, and my thought was: "God help my brother now!"

"We heard the ships' guns," Lanaudiere said, "but we have no definite news yet. I take it your fleet was destroyed?"

I tried to think fast. Lanaudiere had imposed on us: had somehow used us when he landed in America, though I was not certain how he had done it. His niece—if she *was* his niece—was a spy. A hellcat, Cap Huff had called her. If they could use me again, they would do so, and I had no intention of being used again.

"Destroyed?" I asked. "Why, no! One of our galleys was a little crippled, and we had to run her ashore."

"*One* of your galleys!" Lanaudiere cried. "You mean to say we sank only *one* of your galleys?"

"I don't believe there was more than one," I said. "To tell you the truth, after I saw a number of our vessels safely on their way to Crown Point, I paid no more attention to them. There was a good deal to attend to on our own galley."

Lanaudiere stared up at the roof of the tent and smiled faintly.

"Of course," I said hastily, "we didn't much care what happened, since we'd accomplished our object."

"Indeed!" Lanaudiere said. "And what was that, if it's not asking too much?"

"I thought everybody knew," I said. "We only wanted to delay you so your army couldn't cross the lake this year. That being done, we have no further use for the fleet."

Doc Means yawned. "There's been some discussion about auctioning off what's left of it, on account of not needing it after the 12th. Let's see: yesterday was the 12th, wasn't it?"

Lanaudiere stared from one to the other of us with the same faint smile.

"Look here, sir," I said. "I was captain of the *Congress* galley. I've had about five hours' sleep in three days, and I need more. I'm a prisoner of war. What are your intentions concerning us?"

"My intentions?" Lanaudiere asked. "My intentions are to send you back to Isle aux Noix under guard until such time as you're exchanged. Why do you ask?"

"For one thing," I said, "I know your Indians want to get their fingers on us; and for another thing, our little experience with you last spring has—well——"

I stopped, knowing we were in too delicate a position to be strictly truthful. Lanaudiere helped me out. "You mean you have no confidence in me?"

I nodded.

"My dear sir!" Lanaudiere said. "You must remember several things. I helped you reach America safely with your specie, which you might otherwise have had difficulty in doing. What was more, we were then not actually at war——"

"Do you mean this is the first time you have fought against us?" I asked. "Weren't you in Quebec last winter, with your niece?"

It was more in the manner of the reticent, self-effacing Mr. Leonard we had first known that he passed over my question. "Surely you've heard the old adage to the effect that there are times when all is fair."

My brain seemed all fog and sawdust. Lanaudiere's words, the yowling of the Indians, had blank spots in them as waves of sleep washed over me. I could hardly speak for yawning, let alone think.

"My brother——" I said. "You'll send a letter—they'll exchange for us—we helped General Arnold—very worried about my brother——"

Lanaudiere took his bearskin from the corner. There was a bed of spruce tips beneath it. "You are troubled by lack of sleep," he said soothingly. "In the morning these worries will seem like nothing! You shall have my own tent, the three of you, for tonight."

It was possible, I sleepily realized, that I had misjudged him. He had deceived us and spied on us; but now he was doing his best to be both kind and good.

I tried, in a heavy way, to thank him; but he wouldn't listen. "There are other tents where I can sleep. Here, it's merely a matter of posting extra guards." He absent-mindedly repeated the words "extra guards," and went out, his bearskin over his shoulder.

With one accord Verrieul, Doc Means and I staggered to the bed of spruce tips. Since I cannot remember how it felt, I think my senses must have left me before my body reached it.

. . . It was probably not one thing but many that woke me at dawn the next morning—habit, perhaps; or uneasiness about Nathaniel, or hunger, or the stillness of the place, even. In my dreams I had been conscious of the incessant squalling of the Indians; but now I heard nothing but the metallic scream of a jay.

I went to the tent flap and looked out. Two swarthy sentries in buckskin eyed me morosely. The lake, through the trees, was a milky blue in the early morning light; and on it, close to the point, lay a flotilla of canoes, drifting—waiting, evidently, for a leader. They were full of Indians, and so far as I could see, there were no Indians left on the point, though two fires still smoked on the shore.

From the rear of the tent the view was even less encouraging—three other tents with no signs of life, and two more sentries, French Canadians—sullen-looking, pigtailed men. Of Lanaudiere there was no trace.

I woke Verrieul and Doc, and at Verrieul's polite request, the sentries led us to the lake-shore and glowered at us while we shaved and scrubbed the grime of battle from ourselves as well as we could, considering that we had no soap. We had, in fact, next to nothing, barring the bundles to which Doc had clung through thick and thin. We had no blankets, no hats, no money. Frayed twigs, dipped in salt or ashes or gunpowder, whichever was handiest, served to clean our teeth. Except for the ragged clothes we stood in, and the razors, long knives, spoons and horn cups we carried in our pockets, we were as destitute as mendicants.

I was framing the words I intended to say to Lanaudiere, when Doc moaned. He had discovered Sponge-belly on the bank above us; and since Sponge-belly was joined immediately by his six companions of the day before, I suspected that they had kept watch on us through the night.

They came as close to us as they could; and although their faces were still smeared with black paint, there was no mistaking their expressions. They were benevolent, no doubt of that; and Sponge-belly's smirk, as he gazed at Doc, was almost silly in its affability.

They had added shirts to their garb of the day before; and although the shirts had once been of different colors—some striped and some checked—they were so daubed front and back with grease, food remnants and traces of paint of every hue that they looked about alike.

When Doc, still groaning, went for his clothes, all seven red men pushed along beside him, grinning, nodding their crested heads, and bringing up guttural retching noises, clearly intended to indicate friendliness and admiration.

Doc's aversion to these attentions was such that he stuffed his bundles into his smock, gathered up all his clothes, and set off naked for the tent, walking with that wavering, staggering shamble of his. His seven red friends hurried along beside him, regarding him with delight. With them went one of the sentries.

As we hurried into our own poor garments, Verrieul shook his head. "I'm disturbed because they stay here, instead of setting off to the southward with the canoe fleet. When an Indian wants something, he is the most persistent of mortals, and I think it would be well if you saw your friend, Lanaudiere, and asked him to hide Doc from them, before they quarrel over him."

I, too, wanted to get to Lanaudiere promptly: not only to ensure Doc's safety, but to learn what had happened to Nathaniel; so I urged Verrieul to ask a sentry where we could find Lanaudiere.

He spoke to one of the French Canadians, who ignored him. He tried again and again, but those sullen, swarthy-faced guards of ours never opened their mouths. Their eyes were blank, like those of a dead cod.

"You can see," Verrieul said uneasily, "they've been ordered not to speak to us."

My own uneasiness returned a hundredfold. How many times Mr. Leonard, during our short acquaintance, must have deceived us and lied to us! Hand in glove, he had been, with Marie de Sabrevois.

"We'll go to the tent," I told Verrieul, pretending a confidence I was far from feeling. "I've got to find out about Marie and Ellen Phipps. There must be some way of getting word to Lanaudiere."

At the tent, Doc was safely under cover. He had tied the flap, and his Indian friends were crowded around the entrance, peeping through the openings.

The voice of Marie de Sabrevois, the night before, had reminded me poignantly of Ellen; and today, for some strange reason, I found the thought of her almost an obsession. The sound of the wind in the leaves, the whispering of the waves of the lake, were surprisingly reminiscent of her voice. The gray of the beech trees was exactly like the gray of the convent dress in which I had first beheld her. I had a singular feeling that she might be near me: twice I looked over my shoulder, I knew not why.

I imagined that I saw a fold of her gray dress protruding from behind one of those gray beech trees. It wasn't, of course: it was only a shadow on the trunk: a ridge on the bark. I knew it couldn't possibly be a dress: yet I couldn't take my eyes from the tree that had played such a trick upon me.

As I watched it, the gray shadow swayed a little. I ran forward, half choked by the pounding of my heart.

To my inexpressible joy it *was* Ellen! She was waiting behind the tree, her head bent above knitting needles that flashed in and out of gray wool.

We just looked at each other. There was an intent, strained look in her eyes, such as I have seen in the eyes of dumb persons.

One of the sentries, pulling at my arm, gabbled French. Ellen quickly moved between the sentry and me. "Go slowly to the tent," she told Verrieul. "Then one of these men will have to go with you. The two who remain can't stop me from talking, and won't be able to decide what to do."

She widened her eyes at me, a way of hers that never failed to make my heart skip a beat. "It is disobedient, this that I do, but it was necessary that I should speak with you."

She was silent again, and again we just looked at each other. Truth to tell, I could not stare enough; for although her brown curls, her brown eyes, her pointed chin had remained in my brain as though etched within it, the image was a pale thing beside the warm and glowing reality.

One of our guards jabbered furiously. Verrieul had gone; and with him, as Ellen had predicted, had gone the third sentry.

Ellen turned on the jabberer. She stamped her foot: stamped it twice, ordering him to be silent. He quailed visibly before her indignation.

She turned her back on the sentries and spoke rapidly to me. "Last night, when Monsieur Lanaudiere brought your brother to my aunt's tent, I knew you were here. I wished then to see you, knowing your feelings for your brother; but Monsieur Lanaudiere forbade."

"He's your aunt's uncle?"

"No. He's one of the commanders of the Indians—he and Monsieur Langlade and Monsieur Campbell. He was General Carleton's aide in Quebec last winter; but when his father-in-law, Monsieur de St. Luc, was captured by General Montgomery and put in prison, Monsieur Lanaudiere was so angry that he took his father-in-law's place as a leader of Indians."

"I met him in England," I said. "I must tell you this. He was with your aunt. She called him her uncle."

"Yes," she said. "Yes. Now I must tell you something, too. You were right about my aunt. She is what you said she was."

When I would have spoken, she stopped me. "Wait! I must tell you how kind she is. In spite of everything, she is kind. I wish you to realize her great kindness, so that you will understand why it is that I have loved her so much."

"She used you," I said. "You loved and trusted her, and she took advantage of you. She used you to send messages to Albany. She used you to stab innocent people in the back."

"I know," she said. "I wish you to believe that I do not like to be underhanded. What is more, I do not wish to remain longer among people who fight against you and your country. I must tell you how I arrived at that thought. I imagined myself a mother, whose son was marching out with Indians and Germans so to make poor people obey rulers and laws they did not wish to obey. I saw at once that it would be impossible for me to feel pride in what he was doing. Because of that, I shall get away from here whenever I can. I shall go into the colonies—into your colonies."

"Get away? Are you——"

"What you must understand," she interrupted, "is that what I did— the taking of letters to Albany, and speaking to my aunt of what I had seen—was done because she was so sweet, always: how could I think she would do what she has done?"

"It's not necessary for you to explain——"

"Yes, it's necessary. I can't be at peace until I hear you admit that I was obliged to trust in her goodness because of her kindness." Almost wildly, I thought, she persisted. "And she *is* good! She *is* good!"

"Ellen," I said, "what did you mean when you said you'd get away from here whenever you could? You meant your aunt won't allow you to leave, didn't you?"

"Listen," she said earnestly, "I must tell you this: I had a horror last night, when I learned from Monsieur Lanaudiere that you were here— I had a horror you'd be sent away with the Indians: that they'd be permitted to take you."

"What made you think that, Ellen?"

She shook her head. "I fear for you, always. I imagine the worst. If I hear of a battle, I think always that you'll be killed: not that you may come out of it unhurt, or only a little wounded." She put her hand on my arm. "Was it a very terrible bad battle that you've been in on the lake?"

"Where would you go in the colonies?" I asked. "You haven't any relatives, have you?"

"No, I have no relatives. The first time you spoke with me, you told me about your sister Jane." She shot a quick glance at me and then added hurriedly, "I could make myself useful, and I'm said to have an even disposition. Would your mother find a place for me in your house, do you think?"

I looked around at the sentries. They stood stolidly at my very shoulder. I wanted to kill them—to do anything that would let me be alone with Ellen.

I fumbled for words. "Why," I said, "my mother—my sisters—they'd be—I mean, they couldn't—we'd love you—everyone——"

She nodded tranquilly; so I knew she understood; but the knowledge made no easier the choking fullness of my heart.

"Now," she said, "I've saved my best news for the last. When I had a horror for you, I went to Marie at once. As soon as I had told her what was in my mind, she made me a promise. She promised immediately, without a moment's hesitation, that you would have the best of treatment—you and your brother also. It will be necessary, perhaps, to allow the Indians to take away some prisoners, she said; but not you. They shall not take you or your brother. That shows you how kind she is; how good. She knows you dislike her; and if she wished, she could do you great harm. She has great influence, my aunt has. General Burgoyne sees her often and asks her advice. He thinks highly of her— highly."

"No doubt he does," I said. "She seems to have ways of making gentlemen feel indebted to her—Mr. Lanaudiere for one, and my brother for another."

"Now you're bitter," she said. "I ask that you won't feel bitter—that you'll forget her political views and think only of her nobility and kindness. You see, she's too generous to revenge herself on you because you have suspected where her sympathies lie; and you have her to thank for your safety."

"Ellen," I said, "I hope you'll waste no time getting away from people who see no wrong in turning Indians loose on helpless settlements. As for me, I'll take no favors from her."

Ellen rolled up her knitting and thrust it in a pocket of her gray dress. "But you would from me?" she whispered.

"Yes," I said. "I can take anything from you—anything!"

She turned and ran lightly up the path to the tents.

XLIII

From the manner in which the seven Sacs and Foxes pulled at the tent flap and peeped through the slits, I feared they might drag the canvas and poles down on us. "For God's sake," I told Verrieul, "speak to them! Tell them Doc's making magic. Say anything that'll keep 'em quiet! It's enough to drive a body crazy, the way they peep and pry."

Not a word had we been able to get from our surly French Canadian guards; and when I had tried to push past them and go to the other tents to look for Lanaudiere, or Nathaniel, they threatened me with their bayonets. It was easy to see they would have taken pleasure in shooting all of us, and there was nothing to do but sit in Lanaudiere's tent, waiting.

What Verrieul said to the Indians, I didn't know, being too engrossed in my own thoughts to ask; but when I drew aside the tent flap in half an hour, hoping to see Lanaudiere, the red men sat in a half-circle, staring fixedly at the entrance, as though they expected something wonderful to burst from it.

When Lanaudiere came to us an hour later, he was diplomatically evasive. "You've had a taste of war," he said, "so you'll understand that a man's time is not his own in the heat of a campaign. It's been unavoidable, all this delay; but we'll have no more of it." He sighed, as a man sighs over work well done. "I'll warrant you'll be glad to leave this camp, too."

"You mean you're going to send us to be exchanged?"

He nodded benevolently. "Of course, there'll be a few formalities, but we'll see you're well looked after while they're being arranged." His thin brown face, surmounted and softened by his neatly clubbed white hair, had the benignity of a clergyman's.

"Well looked after?" I asked. "Who'll look after us? Where shall we be looked after?"

"These things are difficult to arrange satisfactorily," he said. "I thought of sending you to Isle aux Noix, but that's damp and unhealthy, and the place will be in a tumult, day and night, with troops and bateaux passing. You'd be ill, I fear! Then St. John's occurred to me; but really, you know, St. John's is no better. When all is said and done, Montreal's the place." He repeated "Montreal" contemplatively.

"Montreal! You're sending us to Montreal? How do you expect to exchange for us if we're in Montreal? The river'll be frozen in less than a month! Don't for God's sake send us as far as Montreal!"

"My dear Captain Merrill," Lanaudiere protested. "You speak as though Montreal were at the ends of the earth! It's a charming city, I assure you! In your place I'd consider myself fortunate to be sent to Montreal. It was only last winter that my poor father-in-law was taken prisoner: you've heard of him, no doubt? Monsieur de St. Luc?"

He raised his eyebrows politely when I shook my head, speechless.

"No? Ah, well! You'll be more familiar with his name eventually, I have no doubt. He's the greatest of our Indian commanders. Yes. Well, do you know, he was sent to Esopus! There truly is an abomination of miserableness in the heart of nothing! Why should you complain at the prospect of Montreal!"

"But my brother! He's in no condition to travel to Montreal—to be carried around Chambly rapids and over those miles of corduroy roads!"

"Poor fellow!" Lanaudiere said. "He'll have the best of care. Make your mind entirely at ease about him."

"For God's sake," I said, unwilling to believe my ears, "you're never going to separate us!"

"Military necessity," Lanaudiere reminded me, "obliges us to do things we'd prefer not to do. You can depend upon it, your brother will be as well nursed as in his own home."

I took a deep breath and held it, knowing I would only harm all of us by speaking frankly to this gentle-appearing soldier.

"If we have to go to Montreal," I said, "I'd like a few minutes with Nathaniel. When would we have to go?"

"By a stroke of good fortune," Lanaudiere said, "we're able to send you in great comfort, and quickly, too. It just happens that seven of my men feel they must start home to do their autumn hunting; and they've consented to carry you as far as Montreal. You'll find it an interesting experience, traveling in a North canoe."

"North canoe! Autumn hunting! Seven of your men! Do you mean you're sending us to Montreal with the seven Indians who captured us?"

Lanaudiere's face was indulgent. "I envy you the trip! They're like friendly children—gay and generous."

"You'll send an English officer with us, I suppose," I said.

Lanaudiere sighed. "I'm afraid we can't spare any of our officers at the moment. Besides, it would be entirely unnecessary! Entirely!"

"Look here!" I protested. "You can't turn us loose with those—with those——"

Our tall, white-haired host was patient with me. "My dear Captain, you mustn't take this attitude! We've done what we could to make things easy for you, and in return you seem to imply there has been something shameful about our efforts."

"You know mighty well," I said, "that there's nothing those red devils won't do if they take a notion."

"Devils?" Lanaudiere asked courteously. "Devils? They're a part of our army, just as other Indians are a part of *your* army. Your Congress authorized the employment of some thousand Indians, not three months ago. Surely your Congress would never solicit the help of 'devils.' No, no, Captain Merrill! You'd never speak so harshly if you knew them."

I knew that further protest was a waste of breath.

"I'm asking no favors," I said, nevertheless, "but I think we're entitled to be treated as other prisoners of war are treated. What's become of the men that were captured when the *Washington* galley struck her colors? She must have had a hundred aboard, at least. They haven't been brought back here, so they must have been taken to Crown Point. I demand that you let us join them."

Lanaudiere's voice was regretful. "I'm sorry. I know nothing about the prisoners made by the fleet. I'm obliged to follow the course that seems wisest to me—the course that seems safest for you."

A suspicion that had been forming in my mind became more definite. I began to believe that Marie de Sabrevois, in spite of what Ellen had told me, had resolved to rid herself, once and for all, of a person who might some day interfere dangerously with her plans.

"I hope you're not forgetting," I reminded Lanaudiere, "that we made you free of our house in Arundel only six months ago. Because of that, if for no other reason, I think I'm entitled to make a reasonable request and have it granted."

"You are, indeed! You may be quite, quite certain that I shall immediately grant any request you make, if it's within my power."

"It's not much that I'm asking. I'd like to write two letters, and give them to Nathaniel to forward for me, in case we're held in Montreal all winter."

His distress seemed sincere. "I cannot tell you how sorry I am. Your brother's condition was such that we felt he should have medical attention, so we sent him to the encampment on the mainland."

"So I can't see him?"

"To my great regret——"

"Yes," I said. "Can I see Ellen Phipps?"

Lanaudiere shook his head. "Nothing would please me more, my dear Captain, than to say 'Yes' to everything you ask me; but Ellen, you see, is here no longer. She's kind, and a good nurse; so when she offered to go with your brother to the mainland——"

"I see," I said. "You sent her away because you knew she'd spoken to me, didn't you?"

"My dear Captain Merrill! She was kind enough to go because she's a good nurse."

"Yes," I said. "It's completely clear."

Lanaudiere smiled faintly, rose from his table, lifted the rear tent-flap and went out. As he went, I saw him motion to someone near at hand.

On the instant the opening was filled with the black faces of Sponge-belly and his six Indians. Their vermilion crests seemed bristling with savage eagerness.

They crowded through the opening, and the tent was filled with the sweetish, oily, furry odor of their bodies. One caught me by the wrist. I felt my other arm seized.

When they hurried me from the tent, Lanaudiere had already disappeared.

Two of the Indians held Verrieul by the arms, as I was held; but on Doc, lurching along between Sponge-belly and another red man, there was no restraint. Because of the bundles in the back of his smock, he looked like a pale and ancient bear humped over in fretful contemplation. Above his head his two guards exchanged triumphant glances, and from time to time Sponge-belly's hand reached out, almost timidly, to touch the misshapen lumps Doc carried.

When they had us at the water's edge, the seven Indians stripped off their shirts, swung their North canoe into the lake and neatly stowed their fur robes, muskets, mats of woven rushes and other belongings amidships.

"Well," I said to Doc and Verrieul, "God knows how this happened to us, but I feel somehow it's my fault for having known Lanaudiere in the past."

"To be frank with you," Verrieul said, "I felt it was my fault for bragging concerning our abilities."

Doc eyed us pathetically. "No, it ain't nobody's fault, only England's. If she hadn't hired these red weasels to fight us, we'd be all right." He hitched his bundle-filled smock into an easier position, and looked appraisingly at Sponge-belly. "I dunno but what I could get along with these people all right, if only they didn't smell. They got a way of smelling I can't seem to like."

"For our sakes," Verrieul warned him, "I hope you'll try to like it. They're gentle with you now, because you, too, have a powerful smell, and they think you're as powerful as your smell. Have you never seen a dog proud of himself because he has rolled in a long-dead fish, and respectful of another dog that has rolled in a fish even longer dead? That is how they look upon you; but they're quick to change their minds if you displease them, and you're sure to displease them if you talk so much."

"I don't believe it," Doc said. "Don't they do a lot of talking themselves?"

"Well," I said, "we'll be in Montreal in three days, and I don't believe they'll lose interest in Doc in such a short time."

Sponge-belly urged us toward the canoe. At Verrieul's suggestion we wiped our feet carefully before we stepped in to seat ourselves on the bottom between the padlers on their little seats.

Sponge-belly pushed us off with his steering-paddle. The six paddlers grunted—"Heh! Heh! Heh! Heh!" Their paddles rose and fell in time to their grunting, and so swiftly did the canoe slide northward that I told myself we might reach Montreal in less than three days.

. . . We never saw Montreal, except as a jumble of houses on the far side of the St. Lawrence.

I hadn't thought, when I talked with Lanaudiere, that the day would soon come when Montreal would seem a desirable town, close to my friends and everything I held dear; yet that was how it seemed when our canoe, skirting the southern bank of the river, drove all too swiftly past the high island on which the town is built.

It was bad enough to travel all the way down the Richelieu, past Isle aux Noix, St. John's and Chambly, past British encampments, British provision-boats, canoes and bateaux carrying British officers and men; disheartening to turn to the west against the tremendous roiled St. Lawrence. But when the arms of our paddlers never faltered as we drew abreast of Mount Royal, we were in despair.

"It's no use," Verrieul said, when I told him to remind Sponge-belly that Lanaudiere had promised we'd be taken to Montreal. "It would do us more harm than good. They hate to be talked to while they're paddling. They say a person who talks in a canoe is an old woman. That's the worst thing they can say of anyone. It's worse than accusing a man of getting lost in the woods. I'll speak when they go ashore for the night, but it won't help us."

Verrieul was right.

When he told them what Lanaudiere had said, and asked them to deliver us to the British in Montreal, according to Lanaudiere's promise, Sponge-belly seemed faintly amused. His reply was terse; and when Verrieul heard it, he turned to us with such a pleased, contented look that for a moment I thought his plea had been successful.

"Pretend you're hearing good news," Verrieul said. "And maybe it is. We're none of us wounded or sick, and we have Doc to look out for us. If we're careful, we'll be well treated, probably. By great good fortune, I can make myself understood to them, and they can speak to us, so they'll never have to kill us for disobeying orders. Now you must make noises such as you've heard them make, showing you're satisfied."

We made yowping sounds—"Howl Howl Howl" The making of them gave Doc the hiccups.

"Then Lanaudiere lied to us?" I asked.

"Yes, he lied," Verrieul said. "He never so much as mentioned Montreal to any of these seven. He just gave us to them. We're theirs. What's more, I don't believe he expected us ever to get away—as long as we live."

We contrived, somehow, to keep our faces cheerful; but that night I lay long awake—not because of the penetrating cold that bit into knees and shoulders, but because of my fears that Lanaudiere's expectations might be realized: that we might be fated to wander in the wilderness, like beasts, for the remainder of our days.

XLIV

THE next day we went on, and the day after that we went on, and the day after that, and the day after that. We went on endlessly: always on: always on and on, and still on. It seemed to me our western journey was perpetual; that we were doomed to hurry eternally up rivers and across lakes; past meadows, swamps, islands, mountains, forests, cliffs, cataracts, landslides, blowdowns, forts, settlements.

We pressed onward from dawn to dark, in rain that drenched us, hail that hammered our bowed heads, snow-flurries that left our faces hot and smarting: in blinding sun, and in wind that cracked our lips.

The seven red men toiled incessantly, like animals driven by an unresting instinct; dragging their long canoe from the water to crawl with it over weary miles of trails: embarking on inland oceans whose further shores were below the horizon.

My mind was staggered at the vastness of the country we traversed, and at the numbers of people who had pushed so far west into what I had always thought an empty wilderness. It was no more a wilderness than our Province of Maine. Daily, almost, we sighted the cabins of settlers, or trading stations; and the route we followed, Verrieul said, was yearly traversed by hundreds of traders, to say nothing of Indians, who moved constantly along these waterways during warm weather, going to trade or visit friendly nations, or merely traveling for pleasure.

When we passed canoes or skirted trading posts, we lay flat in the canoe, at Sponge-belly's orders, so that we became almost hopeless in our realization that our captors were determined to keep our whereabouts a secret. I'm bound to say these Indians were kind to us from the first, but my feelings won't be hurt if I never again see an Indian, or smell one.

We met travelers aplenty; voyageurs, carrying supplies; hunters and trappers, hard-faced men who never took their eyes from our Indians; but we were warned not to speak to them under pain of death.

Verrieul urged Doc to make wise-sounding speeches to the Indians now and then, so that our lot might be improved. At first Doc said helplessly that wise speeches were beyond his powers, since he knew none, though he could say a great deal about how we had nothing to cover us at night, whereas our seven captors had a bearskin apiece, and how it would be a wonder, now that the nights were getting colder, if all of us didn't die of pneumonia before we got wherever we were going.

"You'll find it easy," Verrieul insisted, "if you remember that Indians are less impressed by the things we consider valuable, than by what seems commonplace to us. Money, to their way of thinking, is nothing by comparison with a long memory. Fine clothes, or a high position in society, are of no importance in the sight of an Indian; whereas one who has unusual knowledge, or has traveled to far countries, is a person of distinction, worthy of respect and consideration."

All that day Doc meditated, contemplating the ducks and geese that rose continuously before us and circled over us, with the sound of enormous whisperings. These wild-fowl were as numerous as the blueberries on our cut-over lands in Maine. There were times when their passage above our heads cast heavy shadows, as if clouds moved between us and the sun: other times when the splatter of their rising, on our approach, was like the rushing of quick water in an angry river. Their monotonous movement seemed to stimulate him, and his lips moved spasmodically.

He rid himself of his first speech after we had finished our dinner by the campfire that night.

He got out his Vonsection Mannekin, as we had told him to do, and studied it with an air of profundity. He consulted his Culpeper's Herbal and drew designs on the ground with a twig, muttering what must have sounded to the Indians like incantations. This, Verrieul said, was the way to impress Indians, though you had to be sensible about it, as well as mysterious, or in time they would become suspicious. But the most important thing, Verrieul said, was for Doc to sound wise, yet be sufficiently enigmatic to make the Indians scratch their heads a little.

Verrieul sat quiet until Doc's mutterings grew outrageous. Then he announced to Sponge-belly that Doc wished to make an oration. Sponge-belly nodded, and the Indians, sucking at their pipes, fastened eager eyes on Doc. It was not what Doc said, however, that benefited us most, but what he did.

He made a valiant effort to look proud and ponderous; but since he was gentle and kindly when unenraged, his words, at first, were almost apologetic.

"Well, gentlemen," he said, blinking at Sponge-belly, "what I got to say can be said quick. All the rivers run into the sea, yet the sea is not full."

When Verrieul had translated, Sponge-belly and the others set up a yowping, like seals in a cage, howking for fish. It seemed to cheer Doc, and make him freer.

"We come from a distant country, me and my children," he went on, pointing at Verrieul and me. "Our country is far to the eastward, close to the home of the Great Spirit. We're glad to travel to the westward, me and my children, even though it's kind of upset our plans. We're glad to travel to the home of Sponge-belly and these other weasels of his. It's about the only place in the world where we ain't been. Only by traveling all over hell an' gone can we find out whether the pictures in this book of healing are fitted to be used in Sponge-belly's country as well as in our own country, close to the home of the Great Spirit."

He opened his Culpeper's Herbal and peered into it absent-mindedly while Verrieul translated.

The Indians barked when Verrieul had finished. "How! How! How!" they ejaculated, humping themselves far over, to give the sounds greater volume.

"There's just one little point I'd like to bring up," Doc continued. "You can build a better barrel out of staves than out of bung-holes. Here you got us all the way out here, hoping to make use of this magic that me and my children carry. Yet you ain't doing nothing to keep us from freezing to death. There it is, gentlemen! There it is, my friends and brothers! If we freeze, you're building your barrel out of bung-holes! You'll have this and this and this"—he pointed to his Venesection Mannekin, Herbal and lancet—"but they won't do you no good! Lemme remind you of this, too: He that soweth sparingly shall reap also sparingly, and he that soweth bountifully shall reap also bountifully."

The Indians howped agreeably.

"Yes," Doc concluded, "nobody can't make you give more'n your heart tells you; but kindly bear in mind that the Great Spirit loveth a cheerful giver. What I'm getting at is this: unless you want to lose us and the great magic herein contained"—he slapped his medical supplies—"you got to give me and my children something to sleep under at night!"

Sponge-belly made a terse reply to Verrieul's translation of these words of Doc's. "He says," Verrieul told us, "that we could have had part of their blankets whenever we asked for them. He says he had no way of knowing that our magic wouldn't cure cold as well as other things. He says, too, he would like to look into the magic book of healing."

When Doc relinquished his battered Culpeper's Herbal, Sponge-belly and his companions examined it in the flickering firelight.

In Culpeper's Herbal are colored drawings of hundreds of plants, leaves and flowers. The text tells how to use flowers, roots and leaves in the curing of every known ailment, from falling hair to cold feet. In it, too, is an appendix explaining the proper astronomical time to gather all these growing things—not only the best day of the month but the most fitting hour of the day: also how to mix potato pudding, take away little red pimples from the face, make icing for tarts, and so on.

The Indians were entranced by the pictures, and pointed first at one and then at another, exclaiming in amazement. They were particularly taken with the likeness of the mullein, which, because of its steeple-shaped spike of yellow flowers, was handsomer than adjoining pictures of mugwort, mustard, motherwort, maidenhair and wild marjoram. They made belching sounds, pushing at each other so to examine the page more closely.

"They want to know what that's good for," Verrieul translated.

Doc took back the book and eyed the picture with professorial calm. "That's mullein. That herb's as valuable as it is common. It's good for pretty near everything there is."

He read gravely from the Herbal, pausing from time to time to let Verrieul translate. "The common white mullein is under the dominion of Saturn. A small quantity of the root, given in wine, is good for fluxes of the belly. The decoction thereof drank, is profitable for cramps and convulsions, and for an old cough. If gargled, it easeth the pains of toothache. An oil made by infusing the flowers is excellent for the piles. The decoction of the root in red wine wherein red-hot steel has been often quenched, doth stay the bloody flux: doth also open obstructions of the bladder when one cannot make water. Three ounces of the distilled water of the flowers drank morning and evening for some days together, bringeth relief from the gout. The decoction of the root, and so likewise of the leaves, is of great effect to dissolve tumors or inflammation of the throat. The seed and leaves boiled in wine, and applied, speedily draw forth thorns or splinters gotten into the flesh. The juice of the leaves and flowers, laid upon rough warts, doth easily take them away, but doeth no good to smooth warts. The powder of the dried leaves is an especial remedy for those troubled with bellyache."

Doc closed the book with a slap. "Quite a herb, ain't it?"

Verrieul, flinging his arms about, translated to the open-mouthed red men.

"Does it do all those things?" I asked him.

"I guess mebbe it would," he said, "if you thought it would. There ain't nothing that does you much good unless you think it does."

Delighted as the Indians were over Doc's oration on the mullein, they were more deeply impressed by magic powers he then displayed. They asked again to see the book, and when they had it in their hands, they hunted patiently for the picture of the mullein, only to have it elude them.

"What they looking for?" Doc asked Verrieul. "What is it those red minks want to find?"

When Verrieul told him, Doc reached over Sponge-belly's shoulder and turned the pages to the letter M. There, on page 220, was the mullein.

The Indians, astounded, howped and yowped; and Sponge-belly went to counting the sheets between the front of the book and the mullein's picture.

"What's he doing, counting those pages?" Doc wanted to know.

Verrieul, too, was at a loss; but on asking, he discovered that Sponge-belly wished to be able, in the future, to locate the mullein with no loss of time, and could only do so by counting, one by one, the sheets that preceded it.

Sponge-belly's lips moved with the earnestness of his counting. It seemed impossible that any human could be as ignorant of printed numbers and the insides of a book as Sponge-belly was.

"Well," Doc said, "if that don't beat all! You tell that red rooster he don't need to count. All he's got to do is ask me how many pages it is from one place to another, and I'll ask the book, and the book'll tell me. It talks to me, that book does. Saves a terrible lot of time, too."

When Verrieul interpreted, Sponge-belly coughed up a guttural exclamation of disbelief.

Doc, nevertheless, held to it that if he was allowed to see only the corner of any page, it would whisper to him its location.

When Sponge-belly gave Doc a glimpse of the corner of the page containing the picture of a knapweed, Doc instantly said that it was separated from the front of the book by ninety sheets of paper.

To find out whether Doc told the truth, Sponge-belly counted the sheets. It was a skeptical lot of red men that counted with him. I must admit, too, that my own heart thumped and perspiration stood heavy on me, after they had counted beyond eighty, for fear Doc had failed to reckon the unnumbered pages at the beginning of the book, or had in some way been mistaken.

By the grace of God he had not miscalculated, and when Sponge-belly had turned ninety sheets, there was the likeness of the knapweed, flanked by a goldenrod and a lungwort.

Our captors had never doubted, I think, that they had a rare prize in Doc; but this astounding piece of magic convinced them that they possessed the leading magician of all time. They made guttural noises at each other and at Doc; and for half the night they sat around the fire, telling one another all about it, and trying unsuccessfully to catch Doc in a mistake. They gave us two of their beaver blankets, which had a high smell, compounded of grease, sweat and singed hair; but despite the smell we slept in comfort for the first time in weeks.

XLV

THERE are so many Indian nations, scattered through that beautiful western country, that I never learned the names of half of them. The Sacs, certainly, are the biggest in stature and the best natured, and the Sioux and Winnebagoes the most peculiar, speaking an ugly, uncouth language. The Sioux and Winnebagoes are so different from the other Indian nations that they are said, by traders and travelers, to be the descendants of Tartars who somehow came from China in ages past. The Pawnees, too, are odd, being the only Indians who can endure to live as slaves. Therefore every Indian nation has Pawnee slaves, and some of the traders too.

Of all the others, however, I learned only of the Ottawas, the Chippeways, the Menominees, the Ioways, the Illinois, and the white Indians to the south—the Mandans. All of these people had been kept in an unending turmoil by the French and the English since early days, and had been encouraged to go out and remove the scalps from their neighbors —a diversion in which they indulged without much urging. Such nations as spoke different languages hated each other with a deep and bitter hatred, and made war with unfailing regularity. Those who spoke the same languages occasionally stole horses from each other, or trespassed on their hunting grounds, which also resulted in wars of considerable virulence. In the matter of fighting, in short, they were strikingly similar to the French and the English, who are perpetually fighting someone, though in a more expensive and wasteful manner, and in a style designed to bring misery and ruin to a greater number of innocent people, and over a wider extent of territory.

One singular thing about all these different Indian nations was that every white man who lived among them was convinced, and took oath, that the particular Indians with whom he associated were gentle, kindly, truthful, honorable, brave, virtuous, dependable and noble, but that all others were sneaking, murderous, treacherous, dirty, lying, stealing, debauched wretches. If I had based my opinion of the Sacs and Foxes on the testimony of such of their enemies as the Sioux and the Winnebagoes, I would have considered crucifixion or burning alive too gentle a reward for their misdeeds. Since my opinion is based on my own observation, I am bound to say that all the Sacs and Foxes I saw were more charitable and better companions, after we got to know them, than any of the many Frenchmen and Englishmen I have known, and wiser, both in speech and thought, as regards their private affairs.

As near as we could gather from what they told us, the Sac or Saukie nation was the greatest in all Canada, long, long ago, and fought fierce wars with the Hurons and the Iroquois, in which the Hurons and Iroquois were roughly treated. It is my understanding that every Indian nation considers itself to have been, at one time, the greatest in the world. From what I have seen of European nations, they hold to the same idea even more tenaciously than Indians.

It was mid-November when Sponge-belly, after piloting us the length of a narrow, bright green lake, brought us down a swift and winding stream that constantly grew wider; then into a broad river, crystal clear.

There is, I know, a widespread idea that Indians are silent and solemn people, never speaking except in monosyllables. It is true that the Sauk ies are silent when talk is fruitless, as, for example, when they return from a long journey and are surrounded by a hundred relatives and friends. They have learned that conversation, at such a time, is a waste of breath. In their public utterances, too, they are slow to speak, believing that since their words will be repeated, they must be chosen carefully and thoughtfully. But when playing at dice, or traveling, or sitting with their families, or racing their canoes, they are garrulous and cheerful, quick to show surprise, amusement or contentment, and no less backward at displaying disapproval or chagrin.

When we came out on the broad, clear river, all seven of the red men howled, thumping their paddles on the gunwales of the canoe, and their eyes had a foggy look, as though the sight of the river moved them. When they were through yelling, they ran the canoe to the riverbank, disembarked with their packs, and set about decorating themselves, as businesslike as a troupe of actors preparing for a performance.

They laid out mirrors and paints, and went at themselves with hairpullers, which were corkscrews made from a split piece of metal.

They pulled out each other's hair, not only next to the crests on their heads, but from their chests and chins as well, though the latter was thin and straggly, and not much to brag of. They singed their manes until they were smooth and neatly rounded; then filled the crests with red mud. Like seven strange crested birds they sat in a row in the sun to dry their hair, daubing themselves with paint and admiring the results in their handmirrors. They acted, Doc said, like a bridegroom painting a privy.

When we took to the water again, they were a gaudy company. In place of the black faces they had affected when they captured us, their chins and lower ears were vermilion, and white stripes ran upward from their black noses and over the tops of their heads, parallel to their bright red crests. Thus they had the look of enormous red-headed woodpeckers. The similarity, Verrieul learned, was only partly intentional. The white paint was used solely because they belonged to the White Party. Every male in the entire Sac nation, he discovered, was made either a White or a Black at birth. Thus the nation was evenly divided into ready-made factions, who were forever striving against each other, in hunting and war and games; even in dancing or the singing of war songs. In this way the spirit of patriotic competition was not only instilled in every boy as soon as he was able to walk, but kept alive in every man until his dying day.

After our endless journey, this country to which we had come seemed even more beautiful than New England. The stream itself was clear as glass, so that when we passed deep pools, we saw the black and white edging to the fins of the trout far below: the white and red spots on them: the backward movement of their eyes as they rolled them calculatingly at the shadow of the canoe.

The valley through which this river flowed was broad enough for ten rivers, and was laid out to natural terraces, rising and rising until they terminated, in the far distance, in a long chain of hills, pearly blue in the warm November haze.

The terraces, and the hills too, were wooded with maples, elms and birches in small clumps and groves, separated by rich meadows, so that both sides of the river had the look of a cultivated estate.

The chief town of the Saukies was built at a fork in the river. The houses stood on the second and third terraces above the river; and on the terraces above and below the houses were plantations of corn, beans, melons and pumpkins.

The houses were the size and shape of a New England barn built by a carpenter who had forgot the proper proportions for a barn.

They were too long, too low and too narrow; but they were built of hewn plank, covered with overlapping bark; and in front of the door of each house was a sort of porch where the occupants could sit in good weather, smoking their pipes and looking down on their fields and the river. All along the fronts of these houses were spears and poles, thrust upright in the ground, so that the place had a queer, bristly look.

When we came in sight of the settlement the whole town erupted Indians—pigeon-toed squaws, befeathered braves, stark-naked copper-skinned boys and girls, all joining in a discordant chorus of welcome underlain by the yapping of innumerable wolf-like dogs that gamboled among them.

When at last our canoe swerved in to the bank, the youngest and largest of our Indians, known to us as Tiny, stepped over the side to draw us ashore. He stepped on a rock, and his foot turned under him, so that he floundered and fell. At his fall a singular sound rose from those who watched us; and when he limped as he rose, the moan became almost a wail.

When I got out, and Sponge-belly had me by the arm, urging me up the slope, I was conscious of hands touching me: hands tapping and poking and feeling me. From shoulder to ankle I was kneaded and prodded. On both sides of us ran women, boys and children, stumbling and tumbling down: staring wide-eyed at us, regardless of where they placed their feet; and perpetually fondling us, as if to make sure we were flesh and blood.

Sponge-belly took us to the council house, a long, narrow barn near the center of the town; and behind us crowded the entire throng— men, women, children and dogs. The interior of the building was smoky from a fire smouldering in its center. Sponge-belly settled himself beside this fire, and motioned to me to sit near him. Tiny sat near me, breathing hard and holding his ankle, which was swollen. Doc, Verrieul and the others huddled there as well, while the crowd came pouring in to gather around us and stand staring.

Sponge-belly took his pipe from his belt, loaded it with tobacco, lighted it at the fire, blew the smoke straight into the air above him: then at the earth. He handed it to me, and from me it passed around the silent circle.

The silence was broken by the arrival of an elderly Indian, tall and a little stooped, decorated with enough beadwork and quill-work and hair-fringe to supply a dozen men. The fringes of his leggins were edged with black hair and so was his buckskin shirt. Around his neck was a string of bear claws and above each elbow were silver bracelets. His leggins were fastened below the knee with bead garters colored red, blue and black. His moccasins were embroidered with colored porcupine quills, and their tops turned over in loose cuffs edged with brass bells that tinkled with every step. His hair was long and wavy, as was that of another man who followed him. The latter, however, wore a buckskin vest edged with beadwork, and the open seat of his leggins was concealed by an enormous medicine bag made of black hawk skins.

The first one, Verrieul whispered to us, was the Peace Chief of the

Sac nation, Pahokuk, and the second was the chief shaman or magician, Wahoway, father of Tiny.

They sat down with us to stare silently at nothing. Sponge-belly loaded his pipe afresh and started it around again. We sat there and sat there. Nobody asked questions: nobody seemed curious about anything except our appearance. We must have sat there an hour before Sponge-belly unexpectedly coughed, and plunged into an oration. He spoke deliberately, giving Verrieul an opportunity to translate his words.

The Great Spirit, he said, had smiled on their journey to the eastward. There had been a great fight. Later the White Father in England would send a special belt to the Sac nation, with medals for the chiefs.

The white men, he said, had fought with lightning and thunder, and the howlings of the storm. They fought in wooden canoes, each one larger than twenty of the largest canoes in all the country of the Saukie-ok. In the wooden canoes were guns that held more powder than a thousand pistols, vomited smoke in clouds, and hurled bullets the size of pumpkins—bullets that traveled a mile and shattered men to nothing.

The battle had raged, Sponge-belly told his incredulous countrymen, for three days. It was a battle of giants. Because of the white man's medicine, their war canoes moved with the aid of giant mats, not only in the direction of the wind, but even against the wind.

Of all the braves who had fought in the battle, Sponge-belly concluded, none had equaled the exploits of the Saukie-ok; for they, alone and unaided, had captured three of the Long Knives, one a great medicine man: another a great sorcerer, familiar with the magic which caused a war-canoe to move against the wind; the third an orator who spoke with many tongues—with the tongues of the English, the French, the Iroquois, and the Hurons, as well as in the language of the Saukie-ok.

In short, Sponge-belly referred to us proudly, after the fashion of a man who seeks to enhance his own importance by bragging to acquaintances of the accomplishments of his friends—friends whom he will never willingly relinquish. The Sacs in the council house stared at us with friendly glances that recalled the faint indulgent smile of Lanaudiere, and I feared that now I knew the full meaning of that smile. Behind those sleepy eyes of his had lurked the amused certainty that henceforth I would be held where I could never again have a finger in the war—held where I could nevermore meddle, by accident or design, with Marie de Sabrevois or any of the plans that she and he together might evolve.

XLVI

I HAVE no doubt Doc's magic would have made him popular with simple and credulous people under any conditions; but none of us could have anticipated the wave of popularity that inundated him.

At the end of Sponge-belly's speech, he signaled us to rise; and when we did so, Tiny, too, got up. Then his leg bent beneath him, and he pitched to the earth floor. He clutched his ankle with both hands. It must have been painful, for his painted face was contorted.

Doc reached him by crawling between the legs of the throng of sympathetic onlookers. He got to his feet to stand astride Tiny and shake an angry fist at the copper-colored faces pressed almost against his own.

"Ain't you got no sense?" he cried. "Git back away from this boy before he suffocates in addition to what he's got! How'll I make an examination with a hundred of you red minks sticking your knees in my back every time I stoop over!"

Verrieul spoke to him quickly. "Be careful, Doc! Tiny's the son of the medicine man! The medicine man might take a dislike to you."

"That won't be nothing new!" Doc said placidly. "That's the way doctors are. Anyway, seeing as how Tiny's a friend of ours, we'll fix him up first and do our worrying afterwards."

He handed me his lancet and rolled up his sleeves. "Now then," he said to Tiny, "let's have a look at that leg."

He crouched over the boy, prodding and fumbling at the puffed ankle, while Tiny sank back on his elbows to stare up sheepishly at the ring of silent spectators.

"Why," Doc said mildly, "that ain't nothing!" He gave Tiny's toes a sudden downward twist, at which Tiny winced and grunted.

"There," Doc said. "That's practically all there is to it. Now there ain't nothing to do but reduce the swelling." He kneaded the ankle, twisted the foot from side to side and pulled at the heel.

Tiny relaxed and stared stolidly into the smoky dimness above him.

Around us the silence was broken by whisperings. Pahokuk crowded up to peer over Wahoway's shoulder.

Doc gave the foot a final twist. "There," he said, "let's see you move that limb." Tiny waggled his foot delightedly.

Doc scratched his head. "Gimme my lancet," he told me. "There ain't no particular need for it, but seeing as how these red vermins expect me to do something wonderful, it don't seem right to disappoint 'em. Give 'em a look at the Mannekin."

He took his Venesection Mannekin from me, opened it and gave it to Verrieul to hold. At the sight of this representation of a naked, veined figure, a frozen silence fell on all the Indians in that dim, smoky lodge.

Doc studied the Mannekin. "Mm!" he said profoundly. "I better stick it into him where they can all see it. Now here's a nice vein." He traced, with the tip of his lancet, a faint white line that passed down the left leg of his Mannekin. Almost absent-mindedly he pulled the trigger, and the blade licked out and in, like a serpent's tongue. All those who watched, even Pahokuk and Wahoway, clapped their hands over their lips, as if to restrain themselves from bursting into howls of astonishment.

Five minutes later Tiny, relieved of a cupful of blood, was walking without assistance, while Doc, Verrieul and I moved triumphantly toward Sponge-belly's house, escorted by a vociferous crowd of Indians.

During the remainder of the day we sat beneath the open shed at the front entrance, while close in front of us sat or stood or walked hundreds of Indians of all ages—children with dirty noses, stark naked: foppish young men in white buckskins, their ears slit, with handfuls of eagle feathers thrust through the slits: bleary-eyed old gentlemen whose leggins, garters, headbands and tobacco bags were a blaze of color: fat squaws who brought mats to sit upon so that they might stare at us with more concentration: giggling girls in sleeveless coats ornamented with silver discs and breastplates.

Sponge-belly's wives brought us food—succotash cooked with buffalo fat; we sat and smoked; and with the assistance of Verrieul we talked politely with Sponge-belly and a score of others.

From them we learned the reason for the profound interest in Tiny, and for the demonstration of grief when he had hurt his ankle. In spite of his youth, he was, it appeared, the greatest of the Sac ball-players: and in three days' time there was a ball game to be played against the Foxes—a game that probably would last all day, and on which tremendous wagers would be made. Tiny, we gathered, was able, because of his height and strength, to throw a ball the better part of a mile; and if the Sac nation had been deprived of his services, it would have been a national calamity.

Because of Doc's success at curing Tiny, a throng of Indians constantly surrounded us through the rest of that long afternoon, listening respectfully to every sound that fell from our lips.

Pahokuk came, sat and smoked with us. Wahoway left us. When he came back, he handed Doc a coat of buckskin, beaded on the breast and shoulders: then seated himself and sucked at Pahokuk's pipe.

"Here, what's this?" Doc asked, eyeing the coat longingly. "I ain't got no money to buy nothing!"

"It's your fee," Verrieul said. "You cured his son: therefore he gives you a coat. That's *his* fee when he's called to make medicine over the sick; for difficult and important cases, one coat or a beaverskin blanket. For women and unimportant people, half a coat. For children, quarter of a coat."

Doc stared unbelievingly at Verrieul: then back at the coat again.

It was a handsome one, soft and almost white. In the middle of the back was painted the thunder-bird—the small bird no larger than the joint of my forefinger, but so powerful that the cracking of her eggs in the nest is the crashing of the thunder.

Doc blinked. "Why," he said, "durned if I ain't tempted to practice medicine around here, if these red minks got that much sense!"

Verrieul looked pityingly at Doc. "To practice medicine you must first be a shaman, and to be a shaman you must be taken into the Midewiwin—the Grand Medical Society that has chapters among all the Indian nations."

Doc shook his head doubtfully. "I dunno about that!" he said. "I dunno about that!"

"You may say so indeed!" Verrieul said. "To join the Midewiwin is a great honor, and one seldom conferred."

Doc flirted his hand airily, as if contemptuous of the exclusiveness of the Midewiwin. "The trouble with belonging to this Middywinny, or whatever it's called, is that you'd probably have to agree to be a regular doctor, and being a regular doctor is one of the most ticklish businesses there is, for everybody concerned, and even for outsiders like patients, on account of the ethics connected with it. Leastways, regular doctors call it ethics. If one doctor sees another being careless, or purging a patient to death, or bleeding him to a shadder, or otherwise murdering him without good and sufficient reason, he can't tell nobody about it, not if he's a regular doctor. He's got to keep his mouth shut, because that's what doctors think ethics is. I guess if I was a regular doctor and took to curing Injuns, all simple and easy and without no fuss, it would be pretty bad ethics. No, I don't believe I'd want to be a regular doctor."

"But Indian doctors are different from regular doctors," Verrieul explained. "They're put to death if they lose too many patients."

"Then they ain't regular doctors at all!" Doc cried. "How do you get into this Middywinny or whatever it is? It sounds good!"

"You must be elected. There are seven shamans in this town, because seven clans live here. Each clan has a shaman. Tiny's father is head shaman, and has the greatest influence. Because of what you did for his son, he may help you; but all seven must vote to admit you to the Midewiwin. I think it's impossible."

"No it ain't," Doc said. "If these folks like to bet on ball games, they'll bet on dice, and once they start to betting on my dice, they'll have to elect me to their society, because I'll own pretty near everything they got, including the society."

Then he became thoughtful. "I wonder if they'd turn us loose if I made 'em a present of the Talking Book and the Venesection Mannekin and the lancet? I got a notion to ask 'em."

"Why *should* they?" Verrieul asked. "They can take those things from you whenever they want to. They're in possession of them and us too." He paused, then finished in a low voice, "And they'll keep us forever."

"Forever?" Doc repeated. "Not me! I belong in a war that's going on, some particular hell of a long ways from here, and I got to get back into it. Looks difficult, but I got to!"

"They'll keep us forever," Verrieul said again.

And I, unhappily, could see no hope that he was wrong.

XLVII

Doc's good deed in curing Tiny's ankle made it possible for Tiny to play in the ball game between the Sacs and Foxes, and because of that we were adopted into the Sac nation with unparalleled rapidity—a circumstance whose influence upon us was far-reaching, as without it we might never have turned back to white men again.

The game was played three days after our arrival, before thousands of spectators—played with three hundred men on a side, not one of them hampered by any garments except a strip of cloth in front and a horsehair tail lashed on behind to curve gracefully above his rear. Each player carried a snowshoe-like bat that was frequently used as a weapon, during the arguments that took place between the players. The goal posts were a third of a mile apart and the side which won was the first side to make 100 goals. The game lasted from nine in the morning until sundown without intermissions; and Tiny, by making the one hundredth goal for his side, brought riches to the Sacs, the wildest gamblers among all Indian tribes. They won fifty ponies, a score of Pawnee slaves, innumerable bowls, pans, pots, coats, pipes, leggins, muskets, tobacco pouches, belts, spears, bows, arrow cases and God knows what-all that the Foxes had wagered on their powerful team. Hence Doc Means's prestige increased; and Verrieul and I, as satellites of his, shared a reflected credit.

After the game there was a feast of rejoicing, held in the long dance house, a house a hundred and fifty feet long, with fires burning down the center, so that we could scarcely see for the smoke.

The *pièce de résistance* was the greatest delicacy that can be served at an Indian banquet—dog meat boiled with dried blueberries in bear fat.

After the feast three beaver robes were spread on the floor of the council house, whose atmosphere by this time was rich, and Doc, Verrieul and I were seated upon the robes. Then Pahokuk addressed us, Verrieul translating.

"My sons," Pahokuk said, "you have come a great distance. In your travels, we are told, you carried yourselves with patience and dignity, as the warriors of this nation are taught to bear themselves. Before that, we have been told, you fought well. Because of this we have decided you are worthy to become members of the Sac nation—though the things we heard about your former nation at first led us to doubt the wisdom of such a step.

"We understand your Great Spirit gave you a book, the Bible, telling you how to live peacefully together, but that your people are too stupid to obey this book. Even without a book, we are able to do as our shamans tell us, and so to live in peace. In your country, we hear, men persecute other men for holding beliefs contrary to those which are popular. We hear your countrymen claim to be fighting for freedom and liberty, and yet hold innumerable slaves. We are told your most honorable men deprive Indians of their lands by fraud and misrepresentation: then sell it to their own people for large sums. Others, we hear, hold beaver skins in greater veneration than bravery or honor, and employ men to poison and kill Indians in order to add to their store of beaver skins. In your country, we hear, wrong-doers are choked to death like dogs: men shut up in prison when they cannot pay a debt: little children whipped for ignorant mistakes. Your Great Spirit, we are told, is cruel, and showed his love for his own son by allowing him to be tortured and killed. We are told that when a man does wrong, your Great Spirit punishes that man's sons and grandsons and great-grandsons. None of these things are proper or just, according to our views."

"Me too," Doc muttered.

Pahokuk went on: "We hear that in your country a man is admitted to the highest councils if he has succeeded in stealing or hiding more pieces of money than his neighbors. We hear men put such a value on food and clothing that the poor often freeze and starve, even when thousands have plenty. We have heard nothing is so sacred in your country as the pursuit of wealth; that in its pursuit, a few men are permitted to dirty the waters of a river so that no other man can take fish from it, or to make a smoke over the land so that all others find it hideous. We cannot credit it, but we have heard young men from your country will not fight unless paid for doing so, even when their homes are threatened: that only one-tenth of your young men will go to war, though your nation be on the brink of ruin."

I didn't dare meet Pahokuk's eye. I was too ashamed.

"When you are taken into this nation," Pahokuk continued, "you will find that our councils are designed to promote the welfare of all, without regard for the wishes of those who have more shirts and ponies than the rest of us. We are told by Shabonock that the country from which you come is governed by a number of men called a Congress;

that this Congress is supposed to be wise and honest, and has the power of naming your leaders in war, but does not name those who are brave: only those who possess influential friends or a few extra beaver skins. He tells us, even, that your Congress would sacrifice young men by thousands—sacrifice even your entire nation—rather than act contrary to the wishes of those with wealth and influence.

"We have heard this Congress orders its armies to do things without providing the wherewithal to do them; sends soldiers into battle without shoes on their feet, powder for their muskets, or food to eat; places leaders from other countries over your own leaders, just as if we took a Winnebago, of whom none of us had ever heard, to lead us in battle; that it publicly declares Indians to be bad men, but privately hires Iroquois to help fight against the Great Father in England. We have been told that this is the way in which your Congress customarily acts, and that it is almost always wrong in its deliberations. If these things are true, then it will be a privilege and a relief for you to become members of the Sac nation; for the Sac people are sensible and honorable. They do not tolerate such imbecilities."

Doc Means grunted. "Putting all his arrers right into the bull's-eye, ain't he?"

"Hush," Verrieul said. "Look indifferent, and watch, now: the ceremony of taking us into the tribe is going to begin."

Pahokuk made a signal. Two braves seized each of us by the arms, hustling us from the long house and into a sweat-lodge that stood outside. They removed our clothes, poured water on hot rocks until we nearly melted: then, howling and whooping, dragged us down the slope, and threw us into the cold, black river. On emerging, we were hurried to the long house, and at the door blankets were thrown around us. When we were brought back into the smoky interior, and placed on our backs on beaver robes, three shamans pulled the blankets from our chests and Pahokuk stood over us with a pointed stick, charred at the tip. With it he drew on our chests something supposed to be an eagle; and the shamans tattooed it upon us with murderous-looking instruments. When they were finished, we were decorated with red and blue birds that looked more like buzzards than eagles.

After we had been thus frescoed, we were salved, and Pahokuk placed strings of blue wampum around our necks. He lit a pipe, held the stem to Doc's lips; then to mine, and finally to Verrieul's.

"My sons," he said, "you are now flesh of our flesh and bone of our bone. By the ceremony performed this night, every drop of white blood has been washed from your veins. You are taken into the Sac nation and adopted into a great family. One of you, being a shaman, is re-

ceived in the room and place of a great man, and by this ceremony
receives his name—Wasawmesaw, the Roaring Thunder. To the others
I give the names"—he touched me with the stem of his pipe—"Wa-
hongashee, No Fool, and"—he touched Verrieul—"Miaketa, Little Soldier.

"My sons, you have now nothing to fear: we are now under the same
obligations to love, support and defend you that we are to love and
defend one another. Therefore you are to consider yourselves as a part
of the Sac people."

Neither Doc nor I believed what Pahokuk said—neither as to the
white blood being washed out of us, nor as to being supported and
defended. Yet from that day they made no distinction between us and
themselves. If they had plenty of food and clothing, we had plenty.
If there was a scarcity, we all shared one fate.

. . . It is easy enough to be an Indian in the summer, if one can be a
warrior and travel to the eastward, unburdened by women, children,
old men and innumerable dogs; sleeping comfortably beneath an overturned canoe; taking fish and shooting game whenever the need arises.

But we three captives became Indians in the winter; and in the
winter it is hard work being an Indian—harder than building ships,
or sailing them, or trading, or any other calling I know.

The house, in which one end of its single long room had been given
to us for our own, was seldom free of smoke, either by night or by day.
When we tried to sleep, the place seemed alive with dogs, all determined to lie heavily against a human. Thus we were continually waking
to cuff a dog that refused to be discouraged, only to have him pillow
himself against us when we were once more quiet. Moreover Doc's
admirers and patients freely came in at all hours to sit silently against
the wall of the house and stare at him.

Doc's prestige, among the Indians who remained in the town, was
enormous. He cured their simple ailments by putting them to bed and
refusing to let them eat—a sure remedy, he privately assured us, for
every human ill—and with his dowsing rod he discovered a lead mine
half a mile from the village. The only lead mines in that western country belonged to the Sacs and Foxes; and the nearest, until Doc used his
dowsing rod, was fifteen miles away. When, therefore, Doc unearthed
another close at hand, the Sacs were grateful. The shamans permitted
him to take the first degree of the Midewiwin, which made him an
assistant shaman and gave him the right to wear a headdress made
out of buffalo horns, eagles' feathers, strips of red flannel and braided
rattlesnake skins.

Indians, we found, own all their property in common, even to making equal division of the food they kill and raise. Thus some are worse than lazy, knowing they will be fed by the harder workers. Some, too, are unfortunate, forever hooking fish that get away, knocking over deer that somehow escape, and felling bear trees from which the bear has decamped. Others are helpless or incapable. Thus the competents, among Indians, are forever doomed to see the fruits of their labor gobbled up by gluttons and incompetents. Unfortunately for ourselves, Verrieul, Doc and I were competents. We worked for that Indian tribe like slaves, helping to get food for the entire town, and enough to make pemmican for future use—pemmican that necessitated the drying of elk and deer meat over frames, pounding it to bits on rocks, and packing it in deerskin containers with bear fat that necessitated, too, cutting wood for the fires, making deerskin kettles, frying bear fat into grease. Between times we turned our hands to light chores such as collecting birch and elm bark for utensils, keeping moccasins and snowshoes in repair, making cartridges, tending and feeding horses, and cutting down trees to get at bears and raccoons.

January was on us and gone in a never-ending round of labor. In February we made utensils and weapons in preparation for sugar making and the spring migration of buffaloes. In March we made sugar, carrying sap buckets from trees to kettles until it seemed to each one of us that we had walked a million miles.

By the time the sugar was finished, the rivers were open; April had come, and with it the buffaloes, as well as wild ducks and geese in such quantities that the noise of their passing was as the noise of many waters. In April, too, the dancing began—the Buffalo dance, the Corn-planting dance, the Religion dance. There were ducks and geese to be shot and their breasts dried; eight hundred acres of ground to be prepared for the annual crop of beans, melons, pumpkins and corn; canoes to be built and mended; buffaloes to be hunted down, killed and made into pemmican, their hides cured and the rest of them saved; for these Indians, whom some call lazy and good-for-nothing, utilized every scrap of the many buffaloes we killed, even to the hoofs, intestines, horns and bones.

Most of the Indians hunted far afield; but we three white men were kept always near the village; and in spite of our supposed equality as brethren of the tribe, the three of us were not allowed to go out together in the same hunting party. And so it happened that when a party with whom I had been spearing buffaloes returned to the village one June afternoon, I had a singular surprise.

Outside our long house sat an old Indian who looked strange to me.

His head was shaved, except for a patch of hair in the center of his skull; a patch about four inches across. There was a bone ornament fastened to the patch of hair, and up from the ornament rose a flaming crest made of deer's tails. He was a gay old thing to look at, for the crest was bright scarlet, while his face and his shaved skull were painted with bright colors, mostly yellow and blue stripes.

This old gentleman made a howking noise; then addressed me in the familiar quavering voice of Doc Means. "There's some paint behind the door. Get yourself covered up with it, and try to make yourself as handsome as what I am. We got visitors. If I ain't mistaken, one of the visitors is a Britisher; and another is your old friend Joseph Phipps."

. . . The Britisher, Doc told me while I painted my face, was Charles Gautier de Verville, nephew of Charles Louis de Langlade, and he was only British in that he wore a British coat and commanded Indians in the British army. In reality he was the grandson of a Frenchman who married an Ottawa squaw. He himself, when not leading Indians to the wars, was a trader, and a successful one; but seemingly there was more money to be made out of leading Indians than out of trading with them, which is one of the surest roads to riches.

He made a specialty of helping Langlade to bring western Indians all the way to the east. In his younger days he and Langlade had brought them to fight for the French against the English. Now the two of them brought Indians to fight for the English against the Americans; for when in need of Indians, the English paid well for them. He, like Langlade, must have been both brave and able, for Indians never follow an incompetent or a poltroon. He was, however, like all other Indian leaders, unable to control the tribesmen when they were drunk or in a passion—or to speak more properly, he knew enough not to try. He and Langlade, men said, had been in command of the Indians who massacred Braddock's troops on the Monongahela: he, too, had helped to command the western red men who had slaughtered the women, the children and the unarmed soldiers at Fort William Henry.

"This Gautier," Doc said, "he's been around to look at me. I don't like him and he thinks the same of me."

"Why?"

Doc eyed me innocently. "Well, I told him us three was really English sympathizers—Tories; but we'd got pressed into the American service: kind of dragged along with Arnold against our will, because if we hadn't, our American neighbors was fixing to take us out and hang us, so we had to. I told him first chance we had after we got ashore after fighting on the lake, we sneaked off by ourselves, meaning to join the

British troops in that neighborhood, or get to Canada; so when Sponge-belly and them six others come out of the woods, we went with 'em peaceful and glad. What's more, I said, he could ask Sponge-belly or any of the others if we ever made any resistance—we come right along with 'em and joined the tribe."

"What did he say?"

"Didn't say much. Kind of glared at me out of the corner of his eye like a bad colt: said he'd inquire of Sponge-belly and the others, and if they corberated what I'd been telling him, he might up and take and believe it,—maybe."

"What else?"

"Well, I said I was a Tory, but also a practicin' doctor, so I'd like to get with the British troops so's to see how they treat a feller that gets hit with a cannon ball."

"And what did he say to that?"

"He said a French word. I don't understand no French, but I got the drift of it. It meant he didn't reckon on making it easy for me to go."

"Then that's the end of us," I said.

"No," Doc said. "I don't believe it. I don't care nothing about this Gautier, nor no other Frenchman. I don't like 'em. They got a mean streak in 'em when it comes to fighting. They're suspicious of every-body, and they act dirty to everybody, whether they need to or not. It wouldn't do this Gautier any harm to let us go back, but he's made up his mind he's going to fix us so we can't. Well, I ain't going to let him do it. I can fix him first. Fact is, I got him fixed already."

"Fixed? How have you got him fixed?"

Doc's reply was placid. "You remember that old idea of mine—that idea about how these red vermins maybe might turn us loose if I made 'em a present of the Talking Book and the lancet and all the rest of my medical supplies?"

I said I did.

"Well," Doc said, "I called a meeting of the Grand Medical Society right away; and me and Verrieul, we talked to the shamans. We talked to 'em as pretty as they ever got talked to. I asked 'em how they liked my magic, and they said they liked it. I said, Well, they'd done well by me, and I wanted to do well by them, and the best way to do it, as I saw it, was to divide my magic among 'em. The trouble was, I says, that I didn't have but just enough magic to go around, and if I divided it, there wouldn't be nothing left for me. Therefore, I says, what I'd ought to do was to go east with the boys that are going to do their spring fighting and try to pick up some new magic, and meanwhile leave the Talking Book and all the rest of it with them, so to make sure I'd come back."

"They didn't believe *that*, did they?" I asked.

Doc coughed. "Well, it sounds different when Verrieul tells it to 'em in Indian. I can't tell it the way Verrieul does. You ought to hear Verrieul tell it!"

"But don't they know they could have all your magic, just by taking it away from you?"

"How could they?" Doc asked. "They can't roll dice the way I can. Everything they own, pretty near, I won from 'em and then gave it back; and they ain't never won nothing from me. They can't use my dowsing rod, can they? That's what I told 'em: they can't learn how to use any of my magic till I show 'em how, and I ain't going to show 'em how till we start east with Sponge-belly—all three of us."

. . . When the drums summoned us to the council house that night, we looked as much like Indians as any of the Sacs. Verrieul's face was bright green; his eyes two discs of white. My chin and lips were blue against a background of vermilion. We even smelled like Indians, for our buckskins were black with grease and smoke, and our pouches stuffed with summer killikinnick—tobacco mixed with powdered wintergreen leaves—which has a sweetish smell.

Among the hundreds of Indians gathered in that long house—some flat on their backs, with their knees crossed, some hunkered down, some sprawled on their bellies, or disposed in any way that suited their convenience—my eager eye at once discovered Joseph Phipps and Gautier de Verville. I was impatient to see Joseph and speak with him, but I was even more anxious about Gautier; for it was he who would assist Langlade in leading such Sacs as elected to make war on the side of the English: he might, even, hold in his hands the power of life and death over Verrieul, Doc and myself—for if he prevented us from returning to the eastward, our existence among the Indians would be a living death forever.

Gautier, like most half-breeds, had a muddy complexion and a hard black eye; and he used that eye on Doc and Verrieul and me from the moment we entered. He wore a scarlet British coat and a brass gorget the size of half a pie, and a gold-laced hat. He was short and bandy-legged, but the Indians clearly held him in high esteem. This, Verrieul learned, was because he was almost as great a fighter as Langlade, and had fought like a lion for the French against the English on the day Montcalm was defeated at Quebec.

As for Joseph Phipps, he looked more impressive than on that distant night when he had guided me around the limestone mountain in Skenesboro to see his sister. He wore a buckskin coat, with the head of a moose painted on its back and front; and on his blackened face white moose-horns had been drawn so that they seemed to sprout from his nostrils. His wampum necklaces and headband were blue, his leggins and moccasins stiff with porcupine quills. Whether or not Joseph recognized me, I couldn't be sure. From time to time his gaze passed lightly over me, only to return admiringly to Gautier. I feared his feelings toward us were bound to be colored by those of Gautier; and Gautier's certainly were hostile. My heart was low and the outlook far from promising.

When Gautier rose to speak, he followed Indian custom by placing before him, as a gift to the Sac people, a broad band of glass beads, as large as a bell-pull. Verrieul told us what he said.

"Brothers," Gautier began, "I come to you with a message from your brother Langlade. The white chief in Quebec has sent a messenger to Langlade to ask the help of his red children in the west. This messenger"—he pointed to Joseph Phipps—"is here. He has brought the belt which I give you. Already we have visited the Ottawas, Sioux, Pottawattamies, Menominees, Chippeways, Winnebagoes. Now we come to ask the help of the bravest of the western nations, the Sacs and Foxes.

"Brothers, the white chief in Quebec asks that many braves be sent to fight for the English against the Americans. It would be a terrible thing for the Sac people, brothers, if the English should not win the war against the Americans, for the Americans are bad. They lie to Indians, break their promises to Indians, steal from Indians whenever they have a chance.

"Brothers, the Chippeways, Ottawas, Pottawattamies, Sioux and Winnebagoes have agreed to go to the assistance of the English. They are already assembling at Green Bay. The Sacs and Foxes I have saved for the last not only because they are most important, but because I wish the honor of leading them. It is Langlade's desire that we set out tomorrow for Green Bay. It is his desire that as many warriors as possible from the great Sac people fight in this war; for if the war is lost, the Americans will steal Sac lands, kill Sac women and children, drive buffalo and elk from Sac hunting grounds and empty every lake and river of its fish. They will make slaves of the Sac people and leave them with nothing—without land, food, canoes, guns, or places to lay their heads."

Gautier's eyes stabbed at Doc and Verrieul and me, but we returned his gaze stolidly.

Pahokuk took up the belt Gautier had offered, and gave him a kind reply.

"My friend and brother," he said, "the Sac people are not united concerning the need of helping white men settle their difficulties. They have too many difficulties, anyway.

"Many of us, brother, believe it will be all the same for the Sac nation, no matter who wins this war, since we see no difference between the English and the Americans. Those who come to trade with us are all alike. Not one of them has ever done us a kindness unless he hoped to get something of much greater value in return. Probably, brother, they will never change. Therefore there seems to be no reason why we should fight for either side in preference to the other. Nor does it seem necessary, brother, for us to travel far to the eastward, looking for trouble, when the Sioux and Pawnees are close at hand, trespassing on our hunting grounds. There is always plenty of trouble near at hand, brother, without going beyond the far horizon to seek it.

"Therefore, brother, we have decided to do no more than we did last year. Shabonock is a great war chief. It pleased him, last year, to travel to the eastward with some of our young men who wished to learn more about the white man's way of making war, and although their numbers were small, their deeds were great. This year Shabonock has again decided to go, and we are happy because of it, since it will show the white father in England that we are his children still. With Shabonock will go one of our shamans, a shaman whose medicine is strong and powerful, so that those who go will have the assistance of a great manitou, and will do wonderful things."

In spite of the chorus of approval that greeted Pahokuk's speech, Gautier made an immediate protest, though he was careful about it, for fear of irritating the Sacs, who, like all Indians, are quick to take offense when their decisions are questioned.

"My brothers," Gautier said. "There are three among you who were not, at this time last year, members of your nation. Today, although they are members of your nation, two are not yet familiar with your speech. In a manner of speaking, the three are strangers. I have learned that they wish to go to the eastward with your fighting men. Oftentimes, brothers, it is a mistake to transplant a tree too soon. Therefore I say to my brothers that it would be better if these three were kept among you until they are more familiar with your language and customs."

Doc spoke up quickly in an aggrieved voice, and Verrieul translated. "Ain't every drop of white blood been washed out of my veins? Ain't I flesh of their flesh and bone of their bone, the way we was promised?

Ain't I got a right to do what I want to do, the way all the rest of the
Sacs do? They ain't going back on their word, are they?"

Gautier ignored him. "Brothers, you are sensible men; and I hope
that I, too, am a sensible man. I have questioned the oldest of the
three strangers, and learned from him how the three came among you,
and why they wish to return to the eastward. Brothers, I am not impressed by their story. It is the sort of story that might be told by men
who wished to escape, and could escape in no other way."

Doc raised his eyebrows. "Hoy!" he exclaimed lightly. "Us shamans
don't think much of that kind of talk!"

Gautier leveled a hard black eye at him. "One little moment! You
will oblige me by remaining silent for one little moment." He turned
to Sponge belly. "I have been told that when the three strangers were
taken prisoner, they were not with the Americans: that they had hidden
from their own war party: that they made no resistance on being captured."

Sponge belly's voice, I thought, was eager. "It is the truth. The white
men had gone away, taking their wounded with them. Only these three,
who are now our brothers, and a sick man they had with them, were
left behind."

Gautier stared from Sponge-belly to us. He shook his head. "Brothers,
there is something about this story that is not right. I believe these
three should be kept here in the west until bound by ties that can never
be broken—until they have wives to keep their fires burning; children
to make their lodges gay with shouts and laughter."

Wahoway got to his feet. "Brothers, you have not been told the whole
truth. Our brother from Green Bay is our friend, but the secrets of the
Grand Medical Society are hidden from him. Thanks to the medicines of
our brothers from the east, we discovered a lead mine close to our village, we won the ball game from our brothers the Foxes, and we have
had good hunting since they have been with us. They have dealt honestly with us; used their medicine freely for our benefit. They are our
brothers in fact as well as in name. Now they wish to go to the eastward, not only to fight, but to get new medicines, even stronger than
those they now have.

"Our brother from Green Bay says they wish to escape from us. This
cannot be so, since they have offered to leave with us their medicines
as guarantees against their return. If they go, we shall have their medicines. Is there any man so foolish as to think that such powerful medicines as these would ever be willingly abandoned? No! It is clear that
our brothers intend to return! They are our people. All our people are

free to do as they wish. Therefore these three are free to do what they wish."

Gautier was a clever man—too clever to suit my taste—and he persisted in his opposition. "Brothers," he said, "we are friends of long standing. As your old friend, I ask that this question be submitted to the judgment of all the braves together, but that those on whom you sit in judgment be sent from this council house. Their medicines, you say, are powerful. If that is so, they might, by remaining here, confuse your minds with their magic."

"Hi-yi!" Doc exclaimed when Verrieul translated this to us. "This feller's going to try to make me out a wizard instead of a medicine man! If he does that, he'll have us tomahawked, all three of us. Well, you tell him this before we go out: you tell him we ain't none of us wizards, because if we was, we'd have used our magic on him to shut him up, instead of being willing to trust our red brothers to do the right thing by us!" He nodded amiably at Gautier, then herded Verrieul and me from the crowded council house.

Outside, he drew a sleeve across his forehead. "By Grapes! If I ever get out of this, I ain't never again going to tell nobody I'm a doctor! It's the most ungratefullest profession there is, and if I had it to do over again, I'd ruther be anything than a doctor. Yes sir: I'd even ruther be in that there Congress in Philadelphia!"

XLVIII

WHILE we waited apprehensively outside the council house, I felt a touch on my sleeve. A quiet voice, close beside me, whispered, "Say nothing. We go where nobody hear." It was Joseph Phipps, who had somehow contrived to follow us.

When we stood in the center of the gruesome dance enclosure, Joseph laughed silently. "This place long ways from anywhere! I was think I become to be old man before I catch up with you!"

"She sent you?"

He nodded.

"Have you a letter for me?"

"No," Joseph said. "No chance. My aunt—like hawk!" He made a clutching gesture.

"Yes," I said. "Yes. I understand. But you saw Ellen, didn't you? She's well, isn't she?"

"She all right."

"And my brother Nathaniel? You saw him too?"

"One-two times."

"He's well?"

"Didn't ask about health," Joseph said.

"They exchanged him? They sent him to Ticonderoga?"

"No," he said, and then, disjointedly, in his mangled English, he made me understand that he had taken Ellen to Albany when the two of them had left Skenesboro. In Albany she had remained for two days with people she had never before seen—people to whom she had been directed by Marie de Sabrevois, and with whom she expected to remain until her aunt should join her. At first these strangers had been hospitable; then had changed. They had told Ellen that Albany was not a safe place, and had insisted that she return to St. John's. They had given her letters to take to her aunt.

Ellen had accepted the letters without protest; and since the two of them had been at a loss as to what else to do, they had made the journey to St. John's. On the way they had discussed the letters. Ellen had told him, Joseph said, how I had accused her aunt of being a spy, and how I had feared Ellen might be used to the hurt of the American cause. She had begun to suspect that I had been correct; and that the letters she was carrying were not innocent ones. If this was the case, Ellen had said, it was not right that she should have been asked to carry them. They held a long discussion as to what should be done. Ellen was for destroying the letters: Joseph for opening them. Joseph prevailed; but when they were opened, there was nothing in them. The pages were blank.

"Blank?" I cried.

"Trick," Joseph said. "Old trick! Everybody know! Write in onion juice."

They had heated the letters over a fire and the writing had appeared. One letter contained a map of Albany with certain buildings marked: the other a list of names. In Joseph's opinion it was a list of Tories in Albany who could be depended on to take up arms against the rebels in case Burgoyne broke through. There had been two hundred and eight names in the letter.

Ellen was furious, Joseph said, but he himself had thought more of the results of being caught with such letters. He had destroyed them with no loss of time.

I was sick at the thought of the danger to which Marie de Sabrevois had subjected Ellen. "Where were you when you opened the letters?" I asked.

"Bouquet River," Joseph said.

Bouquet River was almost opposite Split Rock, not far north of Crown Point.

"For God's sake," I said. "You knew I was still in Skenesboro at that time! Why didn't you turn around and come back to me?"

Joseph smiled ruefully. "She ashamed. She think you too much good man."

"Too much good man!" So that was what Ellen thought of me! It was not entirely satisfactory, but it was better than nothing.

"Joseph," I said, "I hope you were careful not to let your aunt know what you'd discovered."

"You think I pick up rattlesnake by middle?" he asked. "My aunt bad woman. My aunt do anything. Woman like that in St. Francis, we cut off nose."

I had already learned enough about Indian customs from Verrieul to know that nose-cutting was reserved for Indian ladies whose morals were not what they should be.

"Lanaudiere's no relation to her, is he?"

Joseph shook his head. "Friend. Lanaudiere, friend; Burgoyne, friend. Friend have money—give much money—she like money—much money. She like money very much. Rich soon, I think."

"What happened when you got back to your aunt? How'd Ellen explain not having the letters for her?"

"Ellen angry," he said, "so she tell big lie. She tell my aunt big American devil Whitcomb follow us in woods, so we hide letters under big rock. Mark place so sometime she go get 'em. I say I show her rock sometime. She say letters not important now, right quick." Joseph chuckled.

"My aunt bad woman," he repeated. "She try send Ellen back to Albany again, with letters. Ellen say no. Ellen big fool. I say take letters, go see Captain Merrill. Ellen say No: she not do that way." He sighed. "Ellen know nothing: she great fool. When she refuse, my aunt know Ellen find out something—maybe find out something from you. That's why she take Ellen with army—so she not run away somewhere: not tell anybody something dangerous. My aunt no fool: she know Ellen angry: she know Ellen honest: always want do what right. My aunt know girl like that, she tell somebody something!"

There had been, Joseph said, no open break between his aunt and Ellen, until the Sacs had brought us back to Grand Isle after the battle. Then Lanaudiere had come to his aunt's tent with Nathaniel in his arms, and had told her the Indians had also captured me.

"When he say that," Joseph said, "my aunt look at Lanaudiere and Lanaudiere look at her. They say nothing; but Ellen know what they think. They think, 'Here is chance to get rid of man we don't like. Here is chance to put that man where he never bother us no more.'"

Thereupon Ellen had pleaded for us: had begged her aunt to have us treated as prisoners of war should be treated. She even threatened, if we were not so treated, to send word to the Americans so that they could retaliate on such British prisoners as were in American hands.

Marie de Sabrevois, Joseph said, had become powerful because of her relations with Burgoyne. Night after night, he said, she dined with him. Their intimacy was known to every high officer in the English army. She could do as she pleased, and it pleased her to run no risks from an American, or from a girl like Ellen Phipps. To keep Ellen quiet, she had promised her to protect me from the Indians, but within the hour the Indians had taken us away.

So Ellen knew at last that Marie de Sabrevois was as ruthless as she was beautiful, without virtue, without respect for her word of honor, without regard for human life.

There was apprehension in my next question. "You say Marie de Sabrevois would run no risks from me or Ellen, Joseph. Do you mean anything could happen to Ellen if she considered Ellen dangerous?"

For the third time Joseph said, "My aunt bad woman. She do anything."

I tried to understand exactly what he meant, but couldn't. The truth was that I was afraid to think clearly: afraid to think what might happen to Ellen if Marie de Sabrevois ever made up her mind the girl could continue to be dangerous to her.

"Does Nathaniel know what's become of us?" I asked.

Joseph nodded. "Yes. I think he sorry. Not very long, maybe. I think, maybe, he like aunt very much."

"Where's Ellen now?"

"Locked up," he said. "My aunt say Ellen sick here." He tapped his forehead.

I fumbled helplessly for words. "Sick! Sick! Damn that hellcat to a million hells!"

"Yes," Joseph said. "Hellcat. Ellen locked up same convent St. John's. That Montgolfier, he keep her quiet there! I see her, though. Brother, they can't keep out; so she ask me if I can find you. I say Yes. I say I give somebody black squirrel robe. Then somebody send me to Langlade with message. Then if you with Indian, I see you. She say I must do that, so I come. I'm here—stay with you now to help. You get away? We can't tell!"

From the council house on the far side of the dance-enclosure there came a cheerful murmur like the murmur of a west wind in the rigging on a summer morning. We heard Doc's quavering laugh; heard him set out across the dance-enclosure, shuffling clumsily. "Cap'n Peter!" he shouted. "Cap'n Peter!"

Joseph Phipps left me, slipping away into the night.

"Here!" I called. "Here!"

Doc drew near, smelling disgustingly of asafoetida, to stand swaying before us. With him came Verrieul and Sponge-belly. In spite of himself, Doc gave utterance to a squealing yell of triumph. "Hi-yi! I'm going back to that war I belong in! I guess it's still running! Or else Gautier wouldn't be fixin' up for all us red warriors to take part in it. Hi-yi! Come on, now!"

"Where?" I asked him. "Come on where?"

"To the distribution party," he said, "I got to give them shamans of the Medical Society all my scientific equipment to hold for me and wreak damage with till I get back to the east where I ain't coming back from—only they think I certainly am.

"Come on! I got to distribute my own personal asafoetidy among 'em, and teach them poor souls how to use Old Sir Kenelm Digby's Sympathetic Powder in connection with wounds——"

"Wait a minute," I interrupted him. "What's in that powder? We don't want to poison 'em."

"Hi!" Doc cried. "It wouldn't poison nobody! I made it! It ain't nothing but maple sugar and cooking soda; but it's better'n anything Digby ever made. It'll do you good, too, if you believe in it. Come on! I got to show 'em how to use the Talking Book, and how to handle the dowsing rod, and use the lancet with the Venesection Mannekin—Lord have mercy on 'em! They ain't going to learn these points very good, I don't suspicion; but that's their look-out; not mine."

"What'll happen to us if they can't make those medicines work?" I asked. "I'm afraid they'll——"

"Hi-yi!" Doc shouted. "Nothing to be afraid of! That's all looked out for! They been told all those articles works only by virtue of being infested with my manitou. They know my manitou is naturally goin' to be tollable sulkish on account of getting left behind with them and separated from me. They told Sponge-belly he's got to keep us fed awful good on the war-party, and treat us the nicest in the world all the time we're away, on account that manitou of mine being so affectionate toward me. My manitou, he'll know what's happenin' to us; and if it ain't good, he won't do nothing at all he's asked to till I get back. That's goin' to be never, but not mentioned. Come on! Hi-yi!"

XLIX

W<small>E, THE</small> war-party, moved up to Green Bay amid a flotilla of canoes; for twenty-two Sacs and sixteen Foxes had decided to follow Gautier to the eastward to help the British, and triple that number of relatives and friends accompanied those thirty-eight to Green Bay, not only to speed the warriors on their way, but to exchange the winter's accumulation of furs and sugar and bark at Langlade's trading post, he being what was known as an honest trader, content with a mere five hundred percent profit.

In the canoe commanded by Sponge-belly were Tiny, Joseph, Verrieul, Doc and myself. This time we were not passengers, but workers. Doc held the post of bow-man, not only because he was a shaman and lucky, but because he was a good bow-man. Sponge-belly wielded the steering-oar. The rest of us were middlemen, driving our short paddles at high speed. Forty strokes a minute we averaged, rising to sixty and even higher when the current was against us.

"Hi-yi!" Doc shouted from time to time. "Hi-yi! Old Shaman Means, going east fast! Hi-yi! Old Shaman Means goin' back to the war! Put your backs in it for Old Shaman Means! Hi-yi! Good Old Shaman Means!" He was full of vanity.

We seemed, somehow, to have become Indians. Our bodies were blackened with soot and grease, which stuck to us even when we leaped in the rivers and lakes, which we regularly did twice daily and frequently oftener, following the example of our red companions. Our faces were painted, we were stripped to belt cloths and moccasins. Yet it was not our paint and our nakedness that made us feel like Indians, but rather our state of health. Never at any time in my life had I felt myself so wholly a healthy man, with a body so light and yet so able to endure fatigue.

. . . Gautier, we knew, would watch us unceasingly. If we were ever to escape, we realized, we must never betray our sympathies. Like spies, we must forever sing the praises of the things we most feared and hated; and in this occupation Doc and Verrieul became proficient, bursting into tirades against Americans whenever they suspected they were overheard.

At our camp on Fox River, one night, we heard a faint rustle behind our overturned canoe, beneath which we sat. Doc rolled a suspicious eye at the sound, and immediately began to talk loudly for effect.

"I do believe," he said, "that there ain't nothing as hypocritical as an American. The Philistines were pretty bad, but they couldn't hold a candle to Americans."

"A low set," Verrieul agreed heartily.

"Why," Doc said, "there ain't a gentleman among 'em! Practically every one of 'em works!"

"Impossible!" Verrieul murmured.

"Well, it's the truth," Doc said. "They got the idea that one man's as good as another, and that a feller like you or me has as much right to walk right plum down the middle of the road as the Duke of Buggerum."

Verrieul seemed shocked. "I had no idea it was as bad as that!"

"It's worse'n that," Doc insisted. "America's a nation of shopkeepers! What you think of a country that not only ain't got sense enough to have a King, but ain't got enough sense to have any important offices at all, like the Queen's Bedchamber Women, or Wet Nurse to the Prince of Wales, or Porter of the Back Stairs for the Princess Amelia, or Heater of the Water for the Horses, or an Honorable Band of Suberannalated Gentlemen Pensioners at five hundred dollars a year apiece, like you can read about in my Almanack! Why, Americans don't pay their generals as much as His Royal Majesty, God bless him, pays the Cistern Cleaner to His Majesty's Household!"

"They don't understand such refinements," Verrieul said. "They're mere money grubbers."

"And brag!" Doc complained. "You never heard so much brag! To hear 'em talk, you'd think they had a chanst of licking England!"

"*Canaille!*" Verrieul said.

Doc was mystified. "Can you what?" Then, when Verrieul had explained, Doc said "Oh!" a little feebly, and added, "Yes, you're right! They're the worst Can-I's there is! With them Americans it's all the time Can-I this and Can-I that; and the truth is, they can't. They can't lick nobody without they hide behind a tree and do it long-distance! They ain't sporting!"

"Purely barbarous in action and speech," Verrieul assured him. "It's agony to be near such uncultivated fellows, talking through their noses about trade, trade, trade!"

"Hypocrites!" Doc exclaimed.

"You said 'hypocrites' once before," Verrieul said. "Don't repeat yourself."

"Why not?" Doc asked helplessly. "If I don't repeat myself, I got to use profanity."

He yawned and stumbled to his feet to look behind the canoe. When he returned he had a satisfied air, and I hoped that Gautier, too, had been satisfied.

. . . The settlement of Green Bay, on the shores of the beautiful Fox River, is a handsome piece of country only marred by the perpetual thunderstorms that hover above it, day and night, during warm weather.

On one side of the river were cabins, built of whitewashed logs, and in front of them narrow fields of brilliant green. Growing in the water were acres of wild rice; and the flocks of geese and brant and ducks that circled above the rice surpassed belief. The bottom of the river was covered with sturgeon the size of sharks, while trout and whitefish flirted over and among them. The place was a Paradise of game.

Opposite the settlement were camped the Indians who had agreed to go east with Langlade. Like the Sacs and Foxes, they had brought friends and relatives in such numbers as to make a populous Indian town, each nation distinguishable from the others by the manner in which their lodges were built. The Sioux stretched tanned skins over stakes; the Ottawas erected wigwams out of sheets of bark laid on poles; we Sacs and Foxes used closely woven mats of rushes in the same manner. Chippeways, Menominees and Winnebagoes for the most part slept beneath their overturned canoes.

All these people visited among themselves, smoking each other's pipes, sampling each other's food, swapping bracelets and brooches. All enmities, even the bitter hatred of the Sacs for the Sioux, were forgotten in making common cause against the Americans.

It was early in June that the last of the Ottawas came in from the northward. That night the nations danced their war dances, all of them different, but all equally terrible.

The songs to which they danced were dissonant and ominous; and their movements and appearance, too, were menacing. Some were naked, except for such covering as was to be had from the skin of a woodpecker or golden robin, or some equally trifling bird. From head to foot they were painted to suggest the raw flesh of open, festering wounds.

The dances had a peculiar rhythm that grew heavier and faster, just as the songs and the drums became louder and swifter. It was a rhythm so firm and heavy that it set the earth to throbbing beneath the feet of the onlookers; and as the drumming and the threatening songs increased in speed, there was somehow a corresponding quickening in the heartbeats of us who listened.

The faces of the dancers, hideously painted to begin with, were more and more contorted as the dances became more swift; and so, too, did the warriors gesture more and more ferociously with their tomahawks.

The songs rose to a crescendo and ended in a scream so violent that the scalp crawled. Only by an exercise of self-control could a spectator keep from howling with excitement that was half anger and half eagerness to fight anything and anybody. It was a performance from which the senses shrank, dismayed; yet in it was a horrible contagion.

All night these tireless red men danced and whooped and ate; and in the morning, after we had eaten our fill of sturgeon boiled with wild rice, the canoes were launched and we all moved off in a body into the narrow bay to the music of unending distant thunder.

Langlade, a bald, huge-shouldered, squat man in a canoe with Gautier, led us; and it was a wild company that followed—a hundred and fifty warriors, gleaming with paint and feathers, all singing in a mournful minor key. Our flotilla was surrounded by the canoes of relatives and friends, who wailed a discordant accompaniment; while along the shore ran the rest of those who had come from distant nations, howling dolorous farewells.

From the foremost canoes came slow musket-fire; and amid that slow thudding and a final lugubrious yowling we took up our long journey to the eastward.

L

To ME that journey was like the turning of a wheel—a wheel beneath which we had once been caught and crushed, and which now, as it slowly began to turn back, still weighed hard upon us.

We had been in torment when carried into captivity, beneath the gray skies of autumn. We should have been elated now, with gleaming June clouds above us, and waterways calmly blue between fields and forests: yet we were not, because of the fate that awaited us three at the end of our long journey, unless we escaped before Langlade and Gautier reported us to Lanaudiere, as they inevitably would.

Always our canoe traveled in the rear; for no sooner had Gautier told Langlade about us than Langlade put Sponge-belly in charge of the rear guard, making it impossible for us to race on ahead and escape. It was the place of honor, Langlade told Sponge-belly; but from Sponge-belly's glumness, as we moved eastward at the tail-end of the flotilla, we knew he considered our position a reflection on himself.

Doc took comfort from Sponge-belly's lowering face. "Leave him be!" he said to me, when I suggested fanning his indignation. "Leave him lay! He's stuffed with sulks, like a barrel stuffed with gunpowder. Pretty soon he'll bust!" Softly, and to himself, he added, "Hi-yi! Old Shaman Means'll touch him off! Bong!"

One by one the landmarks fell behind us—the Grand Traverse, the Beaver Islands, Michillimackinac, Grand Manitoulin Island, French River, Lake Nipissing, the Mattawa River, and at last the Ottawa River —the one Frenchmen call La Grande Rivière.

It was when we emerged from this beautiful river into the broad St. Lawrence that we had an unexpected glimpse of the war. At the embarking place on the westernmost point of Montreal Island there was an army of British troops and Indian warriors. A whole flotilla of bateaux and canoes were ranged along the shore; and on the bank above was a staggering assemblage of redcoats, voyageurs, teamsters, axe-men, and great store of baggage wagons, hogsheads, ammunition boxes and supplies.

The scouts and advance guards of this force were already on the move, to the westward, up the St. Lawrence, which was mystifying to us, whose goal was in the opposite direction.

It was hard to remember, when British scouts shouted at us and waved their paddles, that we were not Americans, in perpetual danger of being shot out of hand—that we were, to their sight, friendly Indians bound for the war.

Among those scouts, in addition to French Canadians and Indians, were big men in strange green uniforms—different in appearance from the English regulars, who are apt to be scrawny, as if fed on carrots in their youth.

On the point of the island the main body of troops was embarking beneath the eye of a British officer. He was a general, with a face as red as the coats of the infantrymen who were getting themselves into the canoes. It may be that the heat of the day had upset him, for he was tongue-lashing his red-coated soldiers in terms that would sound offensive when applied to a dog, let alone to a human.

There were vast numbers of Indians in addition to the regulars; but by comparison with our own red men from the west, they were a scurvy-looking crew. To one who had never before seen Indians they may have seemed good enough, since they were painted as gaudily as our own companions; but they were small, and truly dirty. There was something disreputable about them, as though they had been drunk for a week, and were of no account at any time.

Joseph Phipps knew some of these Indians; and Sponge-belly laid our canoe alongside one of the scout canoes to find out why this army was traveling west whereas we traveled east. What Joseph learned was that the force before us—seven hundred British and eight hundred Indians, led by General St. Leger—was bound for Lake Ontario and Oneida Lake: then for the Mohawk Valley, by which route it proposed to smash into the colonies by the back door and join Burgoyne's army at Albany. From Albany the two armies would march triumphantly down the Hudson to New York, destroying any armed rabble that dared oppose them.

The Indians, Joseph said, were riffraff from St. Francis and Caughnawaga, outcasts from the deep woods north of the St. Lawrence, and Iroquois driven from the Mohawk Valley into Canada by Americans. With them was Sir John Johnson and his regiment of Royal Greens —Tories ousted from their Mohawk Valley homes earlier in the war. These were the green-uniformed troops we had seen. All these men, Indians, British and Tories alike, considered the war as good as over.

They had seen Burgoyne start for Lake Champlain two weeks ago; and his army, they predicted, would pierce the Americans as a knife cuts liver. They gave us a fraternal salute of whoops and paddle-thumps; and as we turned from them to resume our journey, they shouted that they'd see us soon in Albany.

"They'd see us soon in Albany!" That meant Burgoyne would join Howe, and the two of them together, back to back, would scatter our half-clad, half-paid, half-armed, half-fed regiments: roll them up: crush them: drive them like hunted foxes into swamps and thickets.

It meant Tories would come out of hiding by the thousand and the hundred thousand, to retaliate on the rebels who had bullied them, stolen their property and made them into harried, helpless fugitives for two long years.

My own thoughts were apprehensive; but Doc Means, strangely, was in the best of spirits. He flourished his bow-man's paddle, and cocked his horned shaman's bonnet rakishly on the side of his head; and when we were out of hearing of the last of the British troops he sang a quavering song—a reminder of his remarkable memory, which had fastened on a casual word let fall by Verrieul more than a year ago, and now turned it to our advantage. It was just the sort of song that Indians were always singing to boast of their exploits, and it also told Verrieul and the rest of us how we could escape from Langlade and Gautier, and get back to our own people again. "Listen, listen, listen," Doc sang—

> Listen to the magic of Old Shaman Means!
> Old Shaman Means talked to his manitou—
> Had a little talk with his personal manitou—
> Little White Fawn, his personal manitou!
> Listen to the manitou of Old Shaman Means!
> We'll go to Caughnawaga, Caughnawaga, Caughnawaga
> With the personal manitou
> Of Old Shaman Means!
> Remember Caughnawaga where Verrieul had friends!
> We can go to Caughnawaga
> And get started toward the war!
> Spread the news of Caughnawaga
> Where we got to go ashore,
> Or Shaman Means's manitou
> Won't let you go to war!

. . . When I saw Verrieul transmitting Shaman Means's message to Sponge-belly, I had a sudden superstitious faith in Doc's magic that made me wonder whether I myself had become part Indian.

Caughnawaga was already in sight on the right bank of the river;

the great flotilla of canoes to which we belonged, sweeping to the left, was preparing to land on the left bank to carry over the rapids; but Sponge-belly, looking sullen, was sending our own canoe to the right and Caughnawaga.

T̲ʜᴇ Indian town of Caughnawaga lies on the southern shore of the St. Lawrence, nine miles above Montreal, at the point where the river bursts into the thundering turbulence of Lachine rapids.

The word "Caughnawaga," in the Algonkian tongue, means "town where Christians live"; and since Indians, unlike white men, insist on applying sensible and truthful names to towns and rivers, Caughnawaga is inhabited by Christian Indians who hold religion in higher esteem than tribal bonds. Thus, in Caughnawaga, one finds Iroquois, Hurons, Abenakis and Ottawas living happily together in the Indian manner; and one also finds white men and women who have become Indians and risen to positions of importance among their fellow Indians.

As Indian towns go, Caughnawaga wasn't bad. It had a chapel with a bell-tower, several warehouses, some dilapidated fortifications, left over from the old French wars, and a varied assortment of houses and wigwams made from rough boards, bark, skins or rushes, depending on the fancy of the builders, scattered haphazard around the point where Turtle River falls into the St. Lawrence.

The inhabitants struck me as peculiar. Certainly they were different from the red men to whom we had been accustomed. They were smaller, and their color was muddier, showing that their blood was mixed.

Indians are said to be filthy, but the houses of the Sacs had been cleaner than the cabins of most white men, whereas the very simplicity of their belongings had given their homes an air of neatness in spite of the meagerness of their furnishings.

The Caughnawagas, however, were surrounded by cheap and useless possessions acquired from the white man, so that their houses were cluttered with trash. In place of furs, they used tawdry calicoes and stamped cloths. The garments of the men were incongruous, and worn without rhyme or reason—buckled shoes with the toes slashed to give the feet greater freedom; breeches without stockings; shirts hanging outside the breeches; shapeless beaver hats, too small for the wearers, tilted forward on long and greasy hair; cinnamon-colored coats disgustingly wrinkled and spotted.

I know now that this happens to all Indians, with a few exceptions, when they have the benefit of the white man's civilization, religion and education. It was as Verrieul said: the closer they are to civilization, the worse they become. Good Indians, he insisted, grew constantly fewer in number, and those who are avaricious, treacherous, debauched, diseased and brandy-ridden multiply like rabbits. The same state of affairs, I find, is likely to occur among whites who are encouraged, as Indians have always been, to expect gifts and to be free with brandy.

The Caughnawagas who greeted us when our canoe landed remembered Verrieul and were overjoyed to see him. They led us at once to the house of Mr. Tarbull, the oldest chief among the Caughnawagas.

That was how he was called—Mr. Tarbull. He was an old man, decently dressed in buckskin. His hair was white and he himself nearly so. He had been captured by Indians, he told us, seventy-five years before, in the town of Groton. He asked, from time to time, whether any of us had ever been in Groton, and although we always said No, he hopefully continued to ask the same question.

With Mr. Tarbull lived his son, Captain Phillips, and his grandson, John Phillips, and a number of female relatives, all of whom had Indian blood. Captain Phillips had a shifty eye; and I gathered that he would accept military titles or gifts from English, French and Americans, indiscriminately, and fight for or against any or all of them on the following day, provided he happened to feel like fighting.

The grandson, John Phillips, had an open admiration for Verrieul. He too had been to Dartmouth College, though from his dress and behavior nobody would have suspected he had ever been ten feet from Caughnawaga—and that, too, I discovered, was another Indian peculiarity. No matter how much they might be educated to follow the customs of the white man, they never permanently acquired those customs. In Dartmouth, Verrieul said, Indians behaved like white men much of the time, but when they went back to their own people, they instantly became Indians again, not only in the way they acted, but in the way they thought.

A dozen young men came to speak to Verrieul; and though all of them had been his fellow-students at Dartmouth, they would have been unhesitatingly called savages by the sorriest fisherman in Arundel.

As the news got about that Verrieul had arrived, more and more Indians came in to see him, among them several bearing the good old New England name of Stacy, and a number of Williamses, all of them descendants of white captives.

How Verrieul accomplished what he did, I don't know. One of his

Dartmouth friends spoke with him a while, went away, and shortly thereafter returned with a peculiarly stupid-looking Indian who, I later suspected, had been told what to say. He was as large as a western Indian, with skin the color of new copper. His hair, hacked off at the nape of his neck, was made fast around his forehead with a band cut from an old beaver hat. He wore a belt cloth, leggins, moccasins and a tobacco bag the size of a woodchuck. His manner toward Verrieul was almost insulting, which seemed to me strange. Then I learned that he was Lewis Vincent, the Huron with whom Verrieul had become drunk at Payne's Tavern in Hanover. Thus I realized that his insulting manner had been assumed to help us.

"What is the reason," Lewis Vincent asked Verrieul, "that our brothers were placed in the rear by that great officer Langlade? The rear is where old women are placed, and children."

He spoke in the Abenaki language, as Verrieul explained, hastily translating, and Sponge-belly and our brothers of the Sacs understood Abenaki well enough. Thus the conversation proceeded; and with the aid of Verrieul and what knowledge of Indian languages I had picked up, I understood pretty well myself.

Verrieul's reply was dignified. "We are neither old women nor children. We are led by a great chief, the great chief Shabonock."

"Then Langlade is afraid," Lewis Vincent said. "He is afraid the great chief Shabonock, unless placed in the rear, will be recognized by the white men as a greater warrior than himself. He is afraid that if Shabonock is seen first by the British, it will be Shabonock who will receive the rum and medals that Langlade wishes for himself. I suspected he was afraid when he said to one of our braves that he was going to Quebec."

"Quebec!" Verrieul exclaimed. "Langlade's going all the way to Quebec?" He turned inquiringly to Sponge-belly, who looked murderous.

"I know one thing," Lewis Vincent added. "If Langlade called me an old woman by placing me in the rear instead of in the van, I'd teach him a lesson!"

"Would you?" Verrieul asked. "And what would you do?"

"I'd cut across to the Richelieu River from here," Lewis Vincent said. "I'd let him go on to Quebec without me. To go to Quebec is a waste of time. He must come back again to Lake Champlain in order to fight, mustn't he? I'd let him waste his time; and while he wasted it, I'd join those who needed my help! I'd go straight across to the Richelieu, and arrive at the front of Burgoyne's army weeks ahead of Langlade! Then I'd ask the white chief Burgoyne which was the old woman: Langlade or me."

"How!" Sponge-belly said. "How! How!"

"Hi-yi!" Doc Means cried. "Let Old Woman Langlade go to Quebec! Let's us get back to the war!"

Verrieul spoke indulgently to Lewis Vincent. "No doubt you'd do great things; but if you were traveling in a North canoe, as we are, you could never carry it across to the Richelieu from here. That's certain! It would be too big; and the carries are long."

"Am I a fool?" Lewis Vincent asked. "Do I know nothing? I'd give my North canoe to my friends in Caughnawaga, and in return they'd give me one of the canoes they keep laid up, away yonder on the Richelieu. Then all I would have to do would be to walk across country to the Richelieu, find the Caughnawaga canoe, get into it and paddle away."

Verrieul turned to Mr. Tarbull. "Is it true, what my brother Lewis Vincent says? Do the Caughnawagas have canoes laid up on the Richelieu?"

Mr. Tarbull nodded. "Yes: on the Rivière La Colle. It enters the Richelieu near Isle aux Têtes, halfway between Isle aux Noix and the northern end of Lake Champlain." Looking benevolently at Spongebelly, he added: "Our brothers from the west are welcome to one of the canoes at Rivière La Colle. Our brothers have been wronged, and it is our duty to help right that wrong."

Both Lewis Vincent and John Phillips were determined to guide us to the laid-up canoe on Rivière La Colle, and they had words about it.

Verrieul spoke confidentially with Sponge-belly. "Each one wishes to go across country to the Richelieu and then in the canoe with us to join Burgoyne, so to see Langlade's face when he finds you have been among the British for days, receiving the rum and presents which he expects to receive. They wish you to say which one shall be permitted to go."

"Langlade's face will be worth seeing," Shabonock said darkly. "They shall both go!"

How right Cap had been, after his rum-stealing expedition to Isle aux Noix, in saying that Verrieul had such an innocent face that anyone would believe anything he said!

And how right I had been to say, the day Verrieul joined us, that none of us could dream how useful he was to be!

He'd only saved our lives: that was all!

LII

At dawn on July 2nd we drove our freshly pitched Caughnawaga canoe down the narrow La Colle and out onto the brown Richelieu. Our faces were newly painted, and for the most part we were in high spirits—Sponge-belly because, by a stratagem, he had cut in ahead of Langlade; Lewis Vincent and John Phillips because of being with Verrieul and hoping to join the American army, which they had secretly let Verrieul know they proposed to do.

Doc, Verrieul, Joseph Phipps and I weren't so high-spirited, because we knew that in order to reach our own people once more, we must pass through the entire British army.

As the sun mounted higher, the wind blew hot from the north, so we took two setting poles from the bottom of the canoe, rigged blankets to them and skimmed out into the open lake, overhauling gundelos, bateaux and canoes—British couriers; Canadians directed by Britishers in scarlet and white: provision-boat crews in tow-cloth overalls: sutlers, commissary workers, and even women now and then. They eyed our painted faces with a sort of fascination, and cheered us on our way with friendly shouts.

Their gaiety, I knew, came from confidence. It was the gaiety of conquerors: of an advancing, victorious army.

All through the morning we passed supply-boats, couriers, canoes, bateaux, moving up and down the lake—a sight that filled me with reluctant admiration for the English, who were able to come three thousand miles and do more, even, than our army had been able to do.

Our rapid passage over the lake seemed more than ever like a wheel, turning familiar scenes into my brain—Isle La Motte, where I had camped with Nason and Cap Huff: the high landmark of Cumberland Head, by which I had steered: the long wall of the Adirondacks beyond the western shore: the jagged tumbled masses of the Green Mountains, not green at all, nor yet white as we had last seen them, but a pearly blue: the high mass of Valcour Island, behind which we had fought—behind which, now, Zelph's white bones must lie scattered on the bottom of the channel; Grand Isle, on which I had had my last glimpse of

Ellen, and where the gently smiling Lanaudiere had, as he no doubt imagined, disposed of us forever.

Mid-afternoon, thanks to the hot north wind, found us abreast of Bouquet River: the narrow cleft of Split Rock was just ahead: yet the British army was nowhere to be seen. I wondered whether it had somehow found a way to circle around Ticonderoga and march on toward Albany.

Beyond Split Rock loomed the bays and headlands for which Arnold had steered the shattered *Congress* galley, her decks all bloody, and her tattered flag still flying.

Beneath the lofty headland, where Sponge-belly's men had sprung on us to snatch us from safety and from civilization, I saw the canvas of tents; and before those tents moved figures less haggard than the scarecrow sailors who had fought at Valcour.

I felt Sponge-belly's steering-paddle press hard to larboard.

Doc reached between his feet for his shaman's headdress, and pulled it on. "Hi-yi!" he muttered. "Hi-yi! There's women in this war! It's time we got back if this is what's going on!"

. . . A soldier can be sure of only one thing in a war: nothing ever looks the way it should, or happens as expected.

I was ready for red-coated sentries, for prowling Indians, for scowling officers, but not for anything as strange as those offscourings who were following the British army. They were all at Buttonmould Bay, on the ridge where Cap Huff had drawn up his marines to fight off the British fleet. Some portion of the army must have occupied this camping ground before the camp followers moved up to it; for it was stripped of brush and trees. The tents, in orderly array, were ranged in an amphitheatre, so situated as to look down on the very spot where we had dropped from the bow of the *Congress* galley. Even now a dozen blackened ribs protruded from the shallows, a sad memorial to a gallant fight.

The inhabitants of the tents were mostly women whose faces had the hardness that comes with long experience. They were scattered along the beach, some with skirts kilted up, wading in the water and hunting beneath rocks; others washing garments; a few bobbing for catfish. Some had the swarthy, defiant look of gipsies. Others, the noisiest, were Irish. Most of them, whatever their nationality, had voices rough as wood-files.

Several were drunk, and I suspected that a few who were stretched on the gravel, asleep in the rays of the westering sun, were sleeping off the effects of rum. It was easy to see where they got it; for the nucleus, so to speak, of the amphitheatre of tents was a group of sutlers' marquees, rigged as shops, boards laid on packing cases forming counters across their open fronts.

How many women there were in this encampment, it was hard to tell, but from the number of bateaux stacked in the shelter of the headland, there were three hundred. The only men we saw were sutlers and a few French Canadians in buckskin, drinking at one of the marquees. While we lay off, drifting toward the beach, watching this motley assemblage of females, the Canadians launched their canoe, climbed in and came out past us, heading toward Crown Point, jocosely waving brandy bottles.

I was concerned only over one thing. Had Marie de Sabrevois placed Ellen among these women? The only way we could find out was to buy rum and use it freely.

"What we ought to have," I told Verrieul, "is rum to drink the health of the one who has brought us so far in such a short time." I indicated Sponge-belly. Rum-drinking, in Indian circles, requires a special coat of paint, so all of us went ashore, took our paint and mirrors from our blankets and hunkered on the shingle, Indian fashion. The women gathered to watch us, and, on being asked, brought us kettles from which we scraped the soot that formed the basis of all our decoration. A few made scoffing remarks about our unbearable vanity—"Bejasus," I heard one say, "ain't they beauties! They'd sour vinegar, even!"—but for the most part they eyed us with a sort of fascinated repulsion, as they might have stared at snakes.

While Sponge-belly and the rest of our companions squatted by the canoe, still busy with their colors, Joseph Phipps and Doc and I went to the nearest marquee and stood before it. Our appearance made an impression upon the sutler.

"Well, by God," he said, staring at my clay-filled crest and Doc's buffalo-horn bonnet, "where'd *you* come from! Why ain't you up in front? Ain't you heard there's a war?"

Joseph Phipps answered. "Me St. Francis. These Sacs. We go fight."

"Sacs, hey!" the sutler said. "Well, you Sacs'll find you've come a hell of a ways, all for nothing, if you don't get on up to Ticonderoga. This war's liable to be over tomorrow: maybe even tonight!"

"Me want rum," Joseph said.

"I don't doubt it," the sutler said. "We ain't allowed to sell rum unless we get money for it. Got any money?"

"Hi-yi!" Doc Means said. "Me big shaman! Me big medicine man!" He took a bracelet from his arm and threw it on the counter. "Heap big medicine, that bracelet! You give rum!"

The sutler picked up the bracelet, tapped it with a knife-blade, dug at the back with the knife-point: then threw it down contemptuously. "One bottle," he said.

Doc's howl was anguished. "That bracelet heap big medicine! Squaw wear that bracelet, every man love her! Hi-yi! That bracelet worth big keg rum! Big keg! Big, big keg!"

The sutler guffawed. "Keg! That bracelet ain't worth a thimbleful of this rum I got here."

Doc grunted. "You got damn bad rum, like all rum! Damn big ugly man! Damn bad rum! Somebody buy one keg rum, he only get poisoned. Squaw buy my bracelet, everybody love her all rest of her life! I sell bracelet to squaw!"

"Say!" the sutler complained. "You're a pretty wise Injun, you are, like hell."

Doc turned to eye the interested women who had crowded up to stare at Doc and his bracelet.

"Look here," the sutler said hastily, "I'll give you three bottles. How's that?"

Doc just stood there, looking off into space.

"For God's sake!" the sutler cried in exasperation. "How much rum you expect to drink, anyway?"

Doc glanced toward Sponge-belly and the others, hunkered down beside our canoe, still busy at their painting. He counted on his fingers. "Nine nice Injuns," Doc said. "Nine nasty bottles."

The sutler looked mulish. I untied my medicine bag. It was made of two mink skins, soft-tanned and almost black, so that it had value. I tossed it on the counter. "Six," I told him, pointing to the bag and Doc's bracelet. "You give six."

Before he could answer, there was a heavy muffled thump, a distant thud, such as could only come from the far-off explosion of a big gun. Hard on its heels came a burst of thudding that struck against our eardrums like padded hammers.

The sutler laughed triumphantly. "Hear that? They're blowing hell out of 'em down there—seven thousand of the finest troops this rat-hole of a country ever saw! I'll give five bottles for your damned Sac gewgaws; not another drop!"

The women gathered in groups, staring into the blue haze to the southward. The thudding tumbled against us with a soft turbulence. Other women ran down from the tents to join the throng on the curved beach.

"Take it or leave it," the sutler said, setting five bottles on the counter. "Come on: take 'em and go on up to Ticonderoga where you belong."

Doc picked up the bottles and contrived to stuff all of them in his medicine bag, which, being a shaman's bag, was large.

"You know my sister?" Joseph Phipps asked suddenly. "You know Ellen Phipps?"

"Your sister!" the sutler exclaimed. "What the hell you talking about! Damned if you ain't the damnedest Injun ever I see! We don't keep squaws in this camp."

The thudding of the distant guns ceased as suddenly as it had started.

"Now what's the reason for *that?*" the sutler cried. He made shooing motions. "Go on! Git out o' here! I got to pack up this truck and get ready to move up with the army. They'll knock hell out of these Americans in about half an hour, and then they'll need food and licker."

"My sister," Joseph Phipps repeated. "She got brown hair. She kin to Burgoyne's friend. You know that lady?"

The sutler stared at him, open-mouthed. "Burgoyne's friend! Burgoyne's friend! Now what in the name of God do you know about Burgoyne's friend? Who do you think you're talking about, anyway?"

"Marie de Sabrevois," Joseph said.

The sutler laughed. "Well, if Sacs and Foxes know about things like that, I guess we got to be careful what we say! I ain't so well informed as you seem to be. All I know is, the lady you speak of, she comes back here to see another lady that's crazy. Understand?" He made a circular motion with his finger against his forehead.

"Where's her tent?" Joseph asked.

"How the hell would I know where her tent is?" the sutler demanded. "You ask too damned many questions! If you want to talk to any of the women in the camp, wait till after the attack. We'll join the army after Ticonderoga's been took. Then you can get an officer to go along with you, all regular."

He leaned over his counter to shout at someone beyond us. "Sir! Sir!"

I turned and saw my brother.

. . . Nathaniel had been running toward the boats on the southern end of the beach. At the sutler's words he stopped and looked at us impatiently. "What is it? I'm in a hurry."

The sutler jerked a thumb toward Joseph Phipps. "This Injun here claims to be related to a friend of yours. It don't sound right to me."

Nathaniel looked thinner than I had remembered him, even after our summer of endless labor and our three foodless days on the *Congress* galley. He looked neat, though, in a loose green coat, belted at the waist with a black sword-sash, and plain black breeches and boots—

the garb a young gentleman of property might wear if he were following an army out of curiosity.

He came a step toward us, staring incredulously. "To a friend of mine?
Related to a friend of mine?"

I had a queer wonder that he didn't recognize me. In spite of my
paint-daubed face, my naked, blackened upper body, and my peculiar
head ornament, I still felt like Peter Merrill; and that feeling alone
should, I thought, reveal me to Nathaniel.

Rather uncertainly Nathaniel said, "Joseph Phipps?"

Joseph grunted. "Yes. Joseph Phipps. That's me." He tilted his head
toward the sutler. "This trader, he pretty thick, head like punkin—nothing inside, only big hole."

Nathaniel clapped a hand on Joseph's shoulder. "Where've you been?
We sent over to St. Francis to find out, and couldn't learn anything!
We thought maybe you'd been killed."

Joseph grunted. "Where's Ellen?"

"Ellen?" Nathaniel asked. "She—she—you knew she'd been sick, Joseph?"

"What kind of sick?"

"Why," Nathaniel said, "she's not quite responsible. She says things
—dangerous things. If she wasn't watched, she'd come out with talk
to cause trouble for anyone she ever heard of—for you, or me, or General
Burgoyne, even. For her own aunt, for that matter. It's terrible!"

"I go see her," Joseph said.

Nathaniel hesitated. "I don't know," he said uncertainly. Then, per-
suasively, he added, "You heard the guns, didn't you? Your aunt wants
to get back to Ticonderoga tonight, in case the fort's taken. Burgoyne
depends on her a good deal."

Doc, tall in his horned headdress, stared impassively at his feet, as if
he had heard nothing and seen nothing.

"I go see her now," Joseph said.

From the south there was another burst of far-off gunfire—a dull, irregular throbbing. The sutler swore softly, pulled the boards from the
packing cases, and hurriedly started stowing them with goods.

"Wait till tomorrow," Nathaniel urged Joseph. "Ellen'll be up near the
army then. Your aunt doesn't like to have anyone see Ellen while she's
in this state. You don't need to worry about her. You can't do her any
good by going to see her, anyway. There's a woman with her all the
time, to see she doesn't need anything."

"I go see her now," Joseph repeated. "You show me tent."

He took Nathaniel by the arm and turned him toward the high
ground, in the direction from which he had come when we first saw

him. Nathaniel, I perceived, was both reluctant and troubled. He became more so when he glanced over his shoulder and saw Doc and me following.

"Look here," he said, stopping short. "Send those men back where they belong! It's bad enough for Ellen to see *you*, all painted up this way, without having to look at those devils! Your aunt won't like it, I tell you!"

Joseph laughed. There was something grim and terrifying about him. "They good men," he assured Nathaniel. "You stop thinking about my aunt. I take care my aunt!"

Again he urged Nathaniel forward, but in a moment he ceased to urge him and went on ahead, for from one of the highest of the tents came the sound of a sweet, soft voice—a voice I recognized as that of Marie de Sabrevois.

As we came closer to the tent, I heard Ellen speak. There seemed to rush suddenly into my brain, to obliterate all thought, a host of sounds: sounds associated in my mind with scenes I loved—the roaring and rushing of breakers on a ledge: the drone of bees among apple blossoms: the humming of a fair breeze in the rigging of a vessel.

"Marie," Nathaniel called. "Marie!"

I heard Marie de Sabrevois say gaily, "In just one minute!"

Then Nathaniel said, "Here's Joseph Phipps."

There was a quick movement inside the tent. The flap was drawn back, and Marie de Sabrevois stood there, as innocent and pretty as a china doll with yellow hair.

"Joseph!" she cried. "You've come back at last!" She stood before the tent flap, as if to bar his path. Joseph, however, walked straight at her; and she, confronted by this menacing, paint-smeared figure, gave way before him and let him pass. Joseph walked into the tent, and Nathaniel after him; and before Nathaniel could drop the tent flap, I pushed Doc in as well and went in myself.

LIII

THE tent was small and hot, and smelled of women and dry grass. On a rolled bearskin in one corner sat Ellen Phipps, and at sight of her I was afraid the thumping of my heart might drown all other sounds in that cramped shelter. I fixed my eyes stolidly on an Indian squaw who squatted on her heels at the back of the tent. A rope was coiled around her waist, and I somehow knew she used the rope for tying Ellen.

Ellen wore an Indian woman's jerkin, too large for her, and beltless, so that she seemed to be huddled in a shapeless buckskin bag. Her feet were bare.

I saw her make the word "Joseph" with her lips; then felt her eyes on me. I gave her a fleeting glance. Her eyes were wide and her lips a little parted. She looked away with such startled suddenness that I knew she recognized me, in spite of my panoply of soot and grease and the painted white rings around my eyes: in spite of my shaved head and my crest of hair, stiffened with clay.

Marie de Sabrevois had come into the tent after us, and made an affectation of being glad to see Joseph. "You mysterious boy! Away from us these months, and nobody knowing where! Now it seems that all the time you've been with friends!" She smiled and added, "Don't you think, Joseph, you might ask these two comrades of yours to go outside? They make the tent a little crowded."

She drew a handkerchief from the breast of her caped and belted smock—an absurd imitation, both in cut and material, of the rough tow-cloth hunting shirts worn by woodsmen. I caught again the familiar penetrating odor of violets. She pressed the handkerchief to her pretty nose, and the look she threw us wasn't kind.

Joseph eyed her. "Why Ellen dressed like this way?"

Marie de Sabrevois turned an amused glance on Nathaniel, as if calling him to witness how absurd an Indian could be.

To Joseph she said, "I'm afraid, my dear boy, you've been coarsened by your travels. Perhaps, if you speak in French, it will help you to achieve politeness."

"I speak English," Joseph said. "Why you keep my sister in tent like this way? Why you call her sick? She no more sick than me."

Marie made a helpless gesture, "Oh, Joseph, don't you understand you can't, in a moment's time, deliver a judgment on your sister's health? You've been away for months. We've been with her all those months, and we know the poor child isn't well."

She came forward to place a caressing hand on Ellen's shoulder, and there seemed to be genuine tenderness in her voice. "The poor child isn't right in her head. She thinks we want to harm her! We, of *all* people! That's why she's dressed as you see her: so she can't run away! That's why we have her watched! She might go running alone into the wilderness!" Marie smiled sadly at Ellen's downcast head. "Think what it would mean, Joseph: wolves, mosquitoes, bad soldiers! She'd never be heard of again!"

"That true, what she say?" Joseph asked Ellen.

Nathaniel spoke up eagerly. "It doesn't do a bit of good to ask *her*, Joseph! Of course she says it's not true! She doesn't know!"

Ellen said nothing.

Joseph spoke to her again. "What they say true? You sick?"

"No," Ellen said. "No."

Marie de Sabrevois made a little fluttering, appealing gesture. "You see?"

Joseph Phipps grunted. "Ellen, how you like go live with Indian women in Indian camp?"

Ellen rose quickly. So large was the buckskin jerkin in which she was clothed that it almost slipped from her shoulders.

"Indian women would be kind," she said. "Can you take me there?"

Marie de Sabrevois made a sound of exasperation. "You can't do it!" she told Joseph. "Every person of importance in the British army knows Ellen is sick! General Burgoyne himself knows, and wishes her to be treated by the best army doctors. Ellen remains where I can watch over her and be certain she's cared for properly."

Joseph's painted face was malignant; and she added hastily, "Another thing you've forgotten: white Indians are under suspicion in this army. Even if I permitted it, you wouldn't be allowed to take Ellen away from here! You may think your paint makes you an Indian, but those who know enough to look at the palms of your hands must see the truth."

Involuntarily I clenched my fists. I would have stopped the movement, once I had begun it, but it was too late. In the same moment I saw Doc Means haughtily fold his arms, so that his own palms were hidden.

Marie de Sabrevois's eyes flashed from Doc's face to mine. Without a word she moved quickly and lightly to the closed tent flap. I saw that she, too, had recognized me at last. More than that, I saw that if she went from the tent before we did, our chances of escape were gone.

I caught the tent flap and held it down. "Don't make a sound!" I said. "I don't want a sound from anyone. There are people in Albany whose lives depend on your keeping quiet!"

Marie de Sabrevois moved back from between Doc and me. When I turned from her to tie the tent flap shut, she laughed a little. "I do believe," she said to Nathaniel, "it's your brother Peter!"

Nathaniel came to me, frowning almost grotesquely.

"That's right," I told him. "She's right."

"For God's sake!" Nathaniel exclaimed. "For God's sake!"

Then, comprehending the expression of his face, I knew he took me for a spy, inside the British lines. "Nathaniel," I said, "we've been prisoners of western Indians all winter. We're on our way to our own people if we can get to them. I don't know why you're here. I won't ask any questions about that; but I want you to come back with me."

"You've been prisoners of western Indians," he said in a bewildered voice. "But I was told—I heard——"

"I know what you heard," I said. "It was a mistake." I glanced at Marie de Sabrevois. She had the look of a cat watching a bird in the grass.

"I want to make this all clear," I said hurriedly, well aware that I must either lie or use force; aware, too, that the use of force would help me none with Nathaniel. I'd remembered something Joseph Phipps had told me on the night when he first talked to me in the village of the Sacs, and I thought that now I might use it for our present preservation.

"Just by chance," I said, "I came across a letter, hidden near Bouquet River. It had the name of two hundred Albany Tories in it—Tories that might join the British army if it ever got as far as Albany. I want it understood that this letter has been sent forward. If we reach Ticonderoga safely, it'll go no farther. If we don't reach Ticonderoga, I wouldn't give a dollar for the lives of all two hundred."

I was pleased at this lie. It had so much the sound of truth that it cheered me and gave me as much confidence as though it had indeed been true. And there was enough truth in it, I knew, to keep Marie de Sabrevois quiet.

"I don't know what you're talking about," Nathaniel said.

"I know that, Nathaniel. I speak of it only so that we may have a chance of getting to Ticonderoga. You'll take that chance with us, won't you? Don't answer quickly."

I went to Ellen and took her by the shoulders. "You're all right?" I asked, and the feel of her set me to shaking inside, a strange and disturbing sensation. She looked at me and nodded slowly.

I dropped my hands from her and said, "Then everything's all right. Can you stand it, like this, a while longer?"

She nodded again.

I untied my killikinnick pouch from my belt and dropped it in her lap. It was two feet long and a foot wide, beaded in blue, red and yellow. "Since they're so careless about giving you decent clothes," I said, "maybe you can make yourself a belt and headband out of this. Maybe moccasins, even. You'll find a stone awl in it."

She put the thing about her, smiled and said, "Don't worry about me. Don't worry about me. Take care of yourself."

I turned to my brother.

"Now, Nathaniel," I said, but I looked beyond him at Marie de Sabrevois. "I want five minutes alone with you, just outside this tent."

Marie said "No!" quickly, and Nathaniel seemed to waver. But I gave her a second glance; she thought of the letters that for all she knew might be, as I had told her, at Ticonderoga; and I had my way.

Nathaniel followed me outside; a few women looked at us curiously, but they were more interested in the recurrent sound of firing from the south, and Nathaniel and I spoke in lowered voices.

"You can't get through to Ticonderoga," he said earnestly. "You're right in the middle of the British army. Don't you know that?"

I looked at him. "Nathaniel, I said I wouldn't ask any questions."

"You can if you wish," he said. "I haven't joined the British." He hesitated. "Thanks to that lady"—he glanced back at the tent—"thanks to that lady's great kindness, neither am I prisoner on parole. Everybody's been very kind to me, thanks to her. I'm—I'm treated as a noncombatant. Officially I'm a guest of General Burgoyne's."

"Good God!" I whispered. Then I laughed harshly. "A guest of General Burgoyne's!"

"Wait," Nathaniel said. "Don't jump at conclusions. They're the kindest people in the world, the British are. After the battle of Valcour, Carleton and Burgoyne treated all the prisoners like guests: gave 'em food and clothes and rum. Carleton talked to 'em like a father! When they were sent back to Ticonderoga, the Americans were afraid to let 'em land, for fear they'd convince the whole garrison that they should never have fought England. Gates sent 'em home, every last man of 'em."

"Well, well!" I said.

"Of course," he went on, "I wasn't sent back with them, on account of being hurt. They gave me medical treatment—the best."

"Where'd you spend the winter?"

"Quebec."

"In the hospital?"

He crimsoned and shook his head. I knew he had been without money when we fought the battle of Valcour Island. Now he had good clothes; and to have spent a winter in Quebec he must have had money: he must have had a place to sleep . . . I tried to keep my thoughts away from Marie de Sabrevois. I must take this easy, I told myself. Morally Nathaniel was in a mess, and that's something any man may get into at some time in his life.

"I suppose," I said, "you've seen Burgoyne and talked with him."

"Oh yes! You see, he'd offered to let Marie travel to Albany with the army, so she persuaded him to let me go along as well."

"I see," I said, "I see. Of course, I don't know what's been going on all winter, but there's one bad side to being Burgoyne's guest, Nathaniel. Anybody who finds out about it is liable to misunderstand your position——"

"Who's going to misunderstand it?" he interrupted. "I haven't been able to write home—nobody knows but what I'm dead, any more than they know about you—and after Burgoyne's marched down the Hudson, there won't be anybody left whose wrong opinion makes any difference."

He took me eagerly by the arm; then snatched his hand away to stare at the greasy black smears on his fingers.

"Yes," I said, "but suppose he doesn't!"

"Doesn't what?"

"Doesn't march down the Hudson!"

"That's what I'm trying to tell you," Nathaniel said. "It's all over! For God's sake, don't go running your head into a noose, just at the eleventh hour! Remember we've got others besides ourselves to think about!"

"Surely," I protested, "surely it's not all over! Nothing's over till the last gun's fired!"

"I tell you it's all over!" Nathaniel insisted. "There never was any such crew of lunatics as this Congress that's been trying to run things for the Colonies. Do you know how many men they've got at Ticonderoga? Thirty-five hundred! Not a quarter enough! Do you know who they've got in command there? St. Clair, a turncoat British officer: one of the stupidest numbskulls that ever lived!"

"Why, that's not possible!" I said. "St. Clair was nothing but a colonel last June, at Sorel, and not much to brag about, either."

Nathaniel laughed. "That's what I'm trying to tell you! This Congress of ours is crazy!"

"There must be some mistake," I said. "Somebody must have misinformed you. Nobody'd be so foolish as to leave a garrison of only thirty-five hundred men in Ticonderoga, with Burgoyne getting ready to attack!"

Nathaniel shrugged his shoulders. "It's what Congress *has* done. They didn't think Burgoyne *would* attack. They heard he was going to sail around to New York from Quebec, and they believed it!"

So Nathaniel had learned of secret information received by Congress. Who, I wondered, had sent that information, which had proved to be false? I thought I knew. I pretended to ponder his words; but what I really did was rack my brain for a plan that would turn him from his infatuation. The tents around us were a soft pink from the setting sun. The distant booming of cannon had again ceased.

"What would happen," I asked, "if we stayed on this side—if we didn't go back to the American side?"

"Happen?" Nathaniel asked. "Nothing! When Burgoyne joins Howe and Clinton, as he'll soon do, the war'll be over, and you and I'll be free to go home and see that nothing happens to Mother or Father or the girls. There'll have to be trustworthy, loyal people put in charge of things everywhere, and it'd be a godsend to a place like Arundel if we could have the say in building it up. Why, I've been thinking it over, and I know how it could be made into a real seaport: one of the best." His words sounded reasonable and sensible: yet they filled me with a sort of despair.

"Nathaniel," I said, "listen to me. I've heard you say yourself that in fifty years' time no power on earth could keep us from having our freedom, no matter how England might feel about it."

"Yes!" he said eagerly. "There'd be nobody powerful enough to stop us, once we were stronger; but the devil of it is, we can't *ever* be stronger while we're governed by such a Congress!"

"But," I said, "if we stop now, we're stopping before we have to. Those men up at Isle aux Noix didn't stop till they had to. We wouldn't either of us feel right, ever, I don't believe, if we stopped before we'd tried everything!"

"I tell you there's nothing more to try, Peter!" Nathaniel cried. "The war's lost! The American troops won't fight; and even if they *would*, they've got no generals fit to show 'em what to do! Burgoyne's officers are soldiers, and they say there isn't a real soldier on the whole American side—not one of 'em capable of planning or fighting a battle."

"How about Arnold?" I asked.

Nathaniel whisked away an imaginary obstacle. "Arnold doesn't have to be considered. Congress heard so many things about him that they promoted five officers over his head!"

Then, observing the expression on my face, he added, "They're lunatics, I tell you! That's the way they govern! If they have their way, they'll make America into a madhouse!"

"Nathaniel," I said, and I contrived to keep my voice gentle, "come with us! In lots of ways, there isn't anything more important in life than being able to say 'I have fought a good fight, I have finished my course, I have kept the faith.' It's better to die with your own people than to live in torment forever for leaving them when they need you most."

Nathaniel caught my wrist. "I'm *not* leaving them. Damn it, Peter, but you're stubborn! I'm working *for* them! Look here—you don't know what's happening! You show it when you talk about our own people! There's twenty-five thousand Loyalists under arms, Peter, fighting to keep America from being wasted and thrown away by lunatic Congressmen! Twenty-five thousand—as many as there are in the whole Continental Army! Aren't *they* our people too? Aren't *they* fighting the good fight? Aren't *they* keeping the faith? Certainly they are! Major Peters, the commander of Burgoyne's Canadians—he's a Yale graduate; a fine fellow. There's the Jessups and the DeLanceys and the Van Courtlands and——"

Doc Means put his head out of the tent. The buffalo horns on his shaman's headdress waggled, giving him an uncanny look. "This ain't getting us nowhere," he said, in a voice strangely mild for one of his hideous aspect.

"For God's sake, Peter," Nathaniel persisted, "can't you see I know what I'm talking about? I don't want you hanged!"

As Doc had said, we were getting nowhere: there was nothing to do but go. "I know you don't, Nathaniel," I said. "You're thinking of my welfare, just as I'm thinking of yours. Now there's something I want you to remember. We're desperate, Doc and I. We're going through to the American lines tonight. Of course you know that one careless word or one small scream out of any one of you, before we're started, might put an end to all our chances." I looked at him expectantly.

Nathaniel nodded.

"Very well," I said, and I drew him back with me inside the tent. Then, although I spoke to Nathaniel, my words were intended for Marie de Sabrevois. "Since that's understood, you'll understand this, too: in spite of the two hundred Albany Tories who'll be hanged if we don't get through, I'm going to take a few ordinary precautions, even though they may seem unnecessary and even unpleasant. Remember I don't want a sound from you, Nathaniel, or from that Indian woman there— or from any other!"

Before he could reply, I turned to Joseph Phipps and Doc. "Cut strips from the back of the tent. Bind 'em and gag 'em—all of 'em. Ellen, you too, or you'll be blamed for it when they find you." Then I said to Doc, "I'll watch at the flap of the tent; and if one of 'em makes a sound, hit her with the flat of your hatchet and run for it."

LIV

Sponge-belly and Verrieul were already looking for us; and, five minutes after Doc and Joseph and I came out of the tent, we left Buttonmould Bay to the tune of three hundred friendly female voices. The voices were raucous and shrill; and in words as coarse as they were pithy they urged us to knock the bloody heads off the bloody Americans. To Doc and me the very friendliness of the voices made their eldritch yells sound sweeter than music.

When we were clear of the bay, Doc smashed the neck from a rum bottle. It held a little drink for each of us; and Doc, draining the last drop, threw the bottle far behind with a quavering whoop. "Hi-yi! Ten miles to Crown Point! Five more to Ticonderoga! We'll have another bottle halfway to Crown Point! We'll have another when we pass it, and another when we're halfway between Crown Point and Ti——" He hiccupped. "And then we'll have our last one after we've got ashore. Just tell 'em that, Verrieul, and see if it don't get a little speed out of this here waste-basket they call a canoe!"

There was still light in the western sky when we passed Crown Point —light enough to let us mark with our thumbs the measure of rum we were supposed to drink from the third bottle. The liquor had no more effect on me than so much tea. I thought at first it was the fault of the rum; but when Doc, in a strident voice, began to sing a mournful melody, I knew the rum was all right.

When we rounded the broad elbow at Crown Point, we had no more need of daylight for measuring our rum. Ahead of us, winding along the shore and extending up the slopes of the hills on the western side of the narrow strait, were the lights of countless campfires and the shimmer of innumerable tents. They looked, against the dark hills, like holes punched in a somber screen behind which glowed a golden radiance. Here, at last, were the British in all their strength; and at the sight of that city gleaming in the wilderness, I felt a sort of triumphant relief which led me to join in the howling of my Indian companions, as if I, too, were delighted at the spectacle. My relief, however, was due to the knowledge that Ticonderoga was still safe.

Apart from that, too, there was something heartening about the sight of this enormous, brilliant camp. We could hear a band playing gay music, as though upon some gala excursion. A band, tootling tunes in a trackless forest, within sight of enemy guns! The English, I told myself, were a strange and incomprehensible people!

We had our fourth bottle of rum. "Take it easy," I called to Doc.

His reply was indignant. "I ain't hardly touched the stuff!" He coughed weakly and hiccupped again, a hiccup that sent a tremor along the canoe, as if we had scraped a rock.

We pressed on past the glittering lights. They must, we knew, belong to the main army, whereas what we wanted was the light troops—the advanced corps, with whom the scouts and Indians always traveled, thrown out as a protecting cloud to screen the movements of the heavier troops behind.

The camp we sought seemed to burst out at us from the dark shore, as fireflies appear from nowhere on a hot spring night. At one moment there was nothing ahead of us, only darkness: then lights flickered and moved. They were on and then over the water: then on all sides of us. We could feel the loom of Ticonderoga, dead ahead. The lights over the water were the lights of vessels: of a fleet stretching all the way across the strait. I could see, dimly outlined against the star-sprinkled sky, the masts and yards of a ship; of another ship; of a brig.

Sponge-belly muttered and turned the canoe toward shore. I took a deep breath and tightened my stomach muscles, to quiet my misgivings.

"Don't let 'em talk to white men," I whispered to Verrieul.

He laughed. "They'll talk to whoever they want to talk to, but you'll find the white men won't want to talk to us!"

A sentry challenged from the dark bank: challenged hurriedly again. I braced myself for the shot. Doc whooped hideously from the bow. Tiny, Sponge-belly and Verrieul howled discordantly, rattling their paddles on the gunwale. We heard nothing more from the sentry.

Then we slid in among a nest of bateaux, from which sweating Britishers were dragging supplies by the light of blazing pine-knots, held by perspiring soldiers. The workers stared at us, stumbling with their burdens.

Tiny stepped clumsily over the side, reeled, and recovered himself. He stood there grinning, clutching the canoe so it might not scrape upon the shingle. Doc staggered ashore, waving his last bottle of rum. Lewis Vincent and Verrieul, ruffled and malevolent in appearance, stamped unsteadily in the shallows, brandishing drawn knives and squalling.

"They're drunk," I heard a soldier say. "They ain't never nothing else!"

An officer, accompanied by a scarlet-coated torch-bearer, ran up to us—a fine-looking boy, as neat and tidy, in spite of the heat of the night, as though bound for a play. By the light of the torches I could see the sight of us disgusted him.

"Speak English?" he asked. "Wrong place! You in wrong place!" He made motions, circling toward the silent hills beyond.

We ignored him.

Sponge-belly splashed out, stepping high and haughtily. Then he moved grotesquely in a circle, uttering spasmodic cries. The rest of us spurred him on with whoops, while the officer watched him helplessly.

Doc clumsily placed the neck of his rum bottle against a rock and, with a wavering tomahawk, sheared it off. Sponge-belly stopped his dance to drink; and the officer was struck with a sudden thought. He left us, running; and before our bottle was empty, he was back with another—a full one. He held it up before us. "Brandy!" he said. "You come! I give brandy!" He backed away, luring us with the bottle.

We took our packs and muskets from our canoe, overturned it, and stumbled after the officer. He led us inland, over a newly cleared road, and across steep ledges. We were a noisy and hilarious crew. Some of us, certainly, were drunk; and all of us had the air of being far gone in liquor. From the distrustful looks the officer cast back upon us, it was plain to be seen that Indians had not yet endeared themselves to their British employers.

I think we climbed a mile through the hot forest before we came to sentinels. Beyond the sentinels we saw the lights of more campfires. Between us and the fires capered the figures of dancing Indians. We had climbed high above the lake; and if my judgment was sound, we had come around to the back of the American fort at Ticonderoga, and were on a level with it.

The young officer spoke to a sentry, then handed the bottle to Sponge-belly, who stood looking at it with an air of profound bewilderment. The officer gestured toward the dancing Indians, favored us with a final contemptuous stare, and left us.

. . . Wonderful indeed are the ways of an eagle in the air, of a serpent upon a rock, of a ship in the midst of the sea, of a man with a maid; but these are as nothing beside the way of an Indian in the grip of rum. His dignity, judgment, honesty may vanish: his religious beliefs, respect for old age, love of ceremony may fall entirely from him: in a moment he becomes quarrelsome, insane, murderous. No sober Indian attempts to cross a drunken Indian; and no Indian nation holds any Indian accountable for what he does when drunk.

We three white men reckoned on this when we bought rum at Buttonmould Bay. We reckoned that, if we could make our Indian companions drunk, and seem drunk ourselves, the three of us could somehow, in the darkness, take French leave of the British and make our way within the American lines. We hadn't counted on finding a hundred drunken Iroquois dancing a Bacchanalian war dance at the very front of the advanced corps of the British army. Yet that was what we did find; and when Sponge-belly reeled among those rum-soaked dancers and burst into an oration, telling how brave and important he was, I thought we had lost our opportunity to steal off quietly.

At the end of his oration, Sponge-belly waved his brandy bottle, drew his hatchet from his belt, and screamed to be shown the Long Knives— to be led against the Americans. His screaming set the others to screaming. They stamped, leaped and howled. Like madmen they gathered around Sponge-belly and, still leaping and howling, hustled him off among the trees.

Since Doc was with him, there was nothing to do but follow; so follow we did, howling and leaping too, but cursing Sponge-belly and those fuddled red fools.

. . . Verrieul stayed close to me. Joseph Phipps was somewhere ahead, watching over Doc. Where Lewis Vincent and John Phillips were, I had no idea. The whole dense, hot forest was a bedlam of howling maniacs.

We ran on and on. We ran until there was no longer a canopy of treetops above us. We saw stars overhead. The smooth pine needles underfoot gave way to meadows. We were in open country, and I suspected we were on dangerous ground.

I knew it when the silent darkness before us was split by a musketshot. The howlings came to a sudden end. The report of the musket echoed as if imprisoned in a vast tin kettle. The shot, I realized, must have been fired by an American outpost.

I caught Verrieul by the belt and pulled him to the ground. Far ahead there were more stabbing flashes; a stuttering rattle of reports.

All around us there were quick movements: the rush of feet through young undergrowth: cracking twigs: grunts, and a heavy thud or two. We saw the dark forms of staggering, tipsy Indians as they turned and fled back past us into the shelter of the forest whence we had come.

Verrieul and I lay still and listened. We heard someone approaching, noisily and laboriously. He tripped and fell: then resumed his journey

on all fours, muttering and moaning. I recognized the voice of Sponge-
belly. He crawled off, snuffling and grunting. Far away, to the rear, I
could hear a British officer imploring those red zanies to be quiet.

Again we lay and listened. Human life, in the space around us,
seemed suspended. Above us I felt the furry beat of an owl's wings, and
damned myself for having lacked the foresight to arrange with Doc and
Joseph Phipps for a rallying-call in case we were separated.

Verrieul rolled closer, so that his lips were against my ear. "They must
be out there somewhere between us and the American sentries," he
whispered, "but who knows whether they're alone? We must be sure."

He made a faint, flat chirp, such as a sleepy bird makes in the night;
then murmured, "I'll go to the right; and if I find them, I'll whistle so,
if they're alone." He chirped again, the same dull chirp. "If you find
them, do likewise. This would be a bad time to get a hatchet in the
brain, just as we're near our friends."

He crawled off to the right.

I listened once more. The stillness pressed against my ears. I got to
my knees and felt my way forward, holding my breath, turning my
head this way and that to guard against surprise.

An air-current brought me a faint odor of sweat, grease and rum. I
hesitated, trying to decide whether it also contained the sweetish scent
of Indian. The thick silence was shattered by a hiccup that seemed to
explode almost beneath my outstretched, groping hand.

"Doc!" I whispered.

A hand touched my face, fumbled for my ear, signaled for me to
come forward. I crawled up alongside Doc, and found Joseph Phipps
on my other side.

"Who's with you?" I asked.

"Just me and Joseph," Doc breathed. "Where's the others? Where's
Verrieul?"

"Off to the right, looking for you. I'll call him." I whistled, the reedy
pipe of a drowsy bird in the still watches.

Verrieul answered at once. He was not far off. I located his position
by taking a sight at a star.

"Come on," I told Doc. "We'll join up so we'll be together when we
talk to the Americans."

"Talk to who?" Doc asked with a queer kind of gasp.

"The Americans. What's the matter?"

"My God!" Doc exclaimed, whispering huskily. "Is it as easy as that,
after all? Prisoners forever—thousands of miles, water and land—turned
into Injuns—shaman—British lines, whole British army to stop us—and

now, just because Sponge-belly got drunk, all we have to do is crawl a few yards—and begin talking to Americans! It ain't reasonable!"

"It's true, though," I said, marveling as he did. "That's the way it happens. We haven't talked to those Americans yet, though. Come on."

Doc held me. "What's that?"

Hard on his words a thin jet of flame spurted along the ground, not twenty paces from us. To our straining ears, the bang of the musket that made it seemed as loud as a cannon.

From the direction where I had located Verrieul there came a faint, recurring sound—a sound like the slow brushing of a wing-tip against a leaf—the sound a shoe might make if the foot within it should tremble at the touch of death.

My throat went dry; my heart seemed choked within me. "Friends!" I cried. "Americans! Four Americans! Don't shoot again! Don't shoot again!"

Then, in a hoarse and strangled whisper, I called Verrieul's name. There was no answer. I called again, more loudly, and Doc called too, in a voice I hardly recognized as Doc's.

There were abrupt movements ahead of us; the sound of a ramrod rattling in a gun-barrel; then a muted, rasping shout of "Who's there! Who's that out there!"

"Americans!" I called huskily. "Aren't you an American outpost? One of Whitcomb's scouts, maybe?"

"You wait," the voice said dubiously, then made a hissing sound and addressed someone in the direction of the fort. "Hey! You! Where's Major Whitcomb? Is he there?"

"No, he ain't," a husky and unctuous voice replied. The voice, by one of those incredible miracles of war, was not only unmistakable, but familiar. At the sound of it something seemed to turn over in my stomach; for it was the voice of Cap Huff.

"It's me," he said, replying to the outpost. "Who you got out there in front of you, claiming to be Americans? Don't believe 'em if you got much interest in keeping your hair!"

I rose to my knees. "Cap Huff!" I called. "Don't shoot again! We're friends! I'm Peter Merrill. One of us got hit!"

I scrambled toward Verrieul; and as I went, I heard a heavier scrambling near at hand, and stertorous breathing that must, I knew, be Cap. He was coming toward me.

"It's me, Cap," I said. "I look like an Indian, but I'm Peter Merrill."

"I don't believe you! Did you say Verrieul?"

"Yes, Verrieul. Doc Means is here with me. He looks like an Indian, too, but he's Doc Means."

Cap spoke uncertainly. "Peter Merrill! Doc Means and Verrieul! I guess it sounds like you. I guess you're Peter Merrill." He seemed troubled. "Which one got hit?"

"I'm afraid Verrieul," I said. "I'm afraid."

Cap's lumbering ceased, and I knew he'd found something.

"Verrieul!" he said heavily.

When I reached Cap he was crouched over Verrieul's body. "He's gone," he growled.

In spite of being sure what had happened, I wouldn't let myself believe it. "He can't be! He *can't* be! Not with one shot, and at night."

"We're using buck-shot," Cap said.

Doc Means crawled past me. I heard him push Cap violently away; heard him fumbling here and there. Then he was still.

"Yes! He never knew what hit him."

"Here," Cap said, "put him on my back. We can't leave him here."

The three of us followed Cap and his burden. He took us to a hole in the ground, no larger than the cellar of a cabin. There were two men in it; and one of them, as soon as he spoke, I knew to be Whitcomb.

"Who was it?" he asked.

Cap let Verrieul's body slide to the ground. "Verrieul," he said, and for a moment we were all silent.

It was Whitcomb who spoke first. "Who are these other men?"

Cap told him our names; Whitcomb remembered us, and said thoughtfully, "Missing since Valcour Island."

Then he added briskly, "Never mind. You've come through the British lines?"

"Yes."

"How many men have the British got?"

"They've got seventy-five hundred," I said. "Thirty-five hundred British and not quite that many Germans—the rest Canadians and Indians, mostly Indians."

Doc Means spoke placidly. "Which one of you killed Verrieul?"

Whitcomb cleared his throat. "I'll tell you how it is. We got to go see General St. Clair right away, so we'll bury Verrieul here and now. We'll leave him here and just forget about him."

"I don't know about that!" Doc said. "I'd want to give that a little thought."

"I'll tell you how it is," Whitcomb said again. "We got two militia regiments inside the fort—Massachusetts regiments. We're trying to get 'em to stay and fight. Maybe we can keep 'em and maybe we can't. They say their time's up in two days, and they got to go home. If we take Verrieul's body in, we got to tell 'em what happened—tell 'em we shot one of our men by mistake. Those Massachusetts regiments, they wouldn't like to hear anything like that! They get scared easy. If they heard about Verrieul getting shot, they'd be afraid of getting shot themselves. They know they deserve to be. They wouldn't stay here five minutes after they heard about Verrieul. That's how it is. We can't afford to lose a man: not a man!"

"How many have you got altogether?" I asked.

"Two thousand, not counting militia," Whitcomb said. "Counting militia, three thousand."

"Three thousand!" I repeated. "You've got *three* thousand?"

This confirmation of what Nathaniel had told me—of insane blundering on someone's part—made me sick.

"Three thousand if you want to count militia," Whitcomb said, "but if you know what's good for you, you won't count 'em."

Doc sighed. "Well, where'll we bury him?"

. . . We were outside the old French lines, the earthworks that protect Ticonderoga on the landward side. Whitcomb shouted a warning to those in the works, then led us across a low embankment and into the trenches. There were men on the fire steps. We saw them only as blurs against the stars.

We went down the slope behind the trenches and out to the stone fort, perched on its high point above the black void of the lake. Soldiers with lanterns stood guard outside: within the fort, lighted windows fronted on the drillground. We halted before the very room in which Gates had capered before us like a sly old woman, nine months before, when he learned from Wilkinson how Whitcomb had captured two Britishers. It was like old days when the door across the hall flew open; for there stood Wilkinson himself, his jawbones a-throb, as if he privily chewed some small and savory morsel.

"Where's the general?" Whitcomb asked.

"Perhaps," Wilkinson said in that soothing voice of his, "perhaps I can attend to this for you. The general hasn't had much rest since he sent his little boy to Albany last Sunday."

"You mean he's gone to bed?" Cap Huff asked.

Wilkinson looked hostile. "That, sir, was the implication I intended to convey."

"Well, get him up," Cap said. "Look here, what we got!" He gestured largely toward us. Wilkinson stalked to the general's door with his peculiar careful gait. He tapped on the door with an air of secrecy, listened a moment, and went in. We heard him knocking at another inner door.

"What's this place Wilkinson lives in?" Cap asked hoarsely. "I ain't never seen it." He dodged into the room from which Wilkinson had emerged and was back in a moment, looking innocent.

"His little boy?" I whispered to Cap. "What was his little boy doing here?"

"Well," Cap said, "the general claimed to have brought him up here so to give him a nice education, but he sent him away as soon as things began to get instructive."

I pondered his reply. "If he sent him away," I said, "he must expect the fort to be captured."

I construed Cap's silence as a hint to keep my thoughts to myself.

St. Clair came out to see us at once, half dressed. He was a moon-faced man with a strong English accent, and a look of having all his life worn a collar a little too chokingly tight for him.

I wish to say here that I think an injustice has been done Arthur St. Clair in calling him a coward. He was no coward, nor was he a bad general, either, as generals go. Yet there was no more drive and inspiration to him than to a barrel of pork. I had seen ship captains like him, and usually they were troubled with mutinies because of the frequency with which boatswains, third mates and even ships' cooks considered themselves—occasionally with reason—more competent to do the sailing.

St. Clair's trouble, as I saw it, was one that afflicts many white men: he had never learned to interpret what lay before him. If he read, in a book, a passage of a little subtlety, he was almost sure to misread it: if called on to judge the movements of an enemy, he was apt to judge wrongly: if need be, he could even persuade himself that the likeliest place for the education of a small son was a dangerous post in the wilderness, where all his time and all his thoughts should be spent on defending that post.

He heard what we had to say without comment. He chewed his lip and pondered. I suspected he was feeling sorry for himself: not racking his brains as to how the British might best be confounded; and I thought sadly of the difference between this man and Arnold.

He spoke cheerfully to Whitcomb. "This corroborates what we learned this afternoon, eh? We'll have to let it be known that Abercrombie couldn't carry these defenses against the French, not even with ten thousand men."

I hoped he had benefited by the blunders of Abercrombie, who had been responsible for the death of two thousand men on the very ground where Doc, Joseph Phipps and I had lain when Verrieul was dying.

Still, St. Clair was a kindly gentleman, and he was respectful to Congress, so that he doubtless deserved all the honors he received, though I thank God I never had to fight in any battle he directed. He showed his kindness now.

"Major Whitcomb," he said, "there's things to be talked over, so I'll request the pleasure of your company for a time." To us he said, "Get yourselves clean of that paint and those clothes, before one of our militiamen puts a load of buck-shot through you. Report to Major Whitcomb at noon tomorrow. Somebody'll have shirts and breeches for you. Until then your time's your own—unless the British ignore all the rules of warfare and attack with a superior force tonight."

Wᴴᴇɴ we left St. Clair, Cap borrowed a lantern and led us down to the shore. On the way he gave each of us a square of soap—the first soap we had seen since we used up the pieces we had taken with us from Arundel more than a year before.

Doc Means sniffed at it. "Hoy! It's scented! Three cakes of scented soap! Ain't this something new for you to have that much soap?"

"Who, me?" Cap growled. "I don't never use it. It roughs my skin. That what you've got, that's Wilkinson's. It was in his room, and I figured you wouldn't have any, so I picked it up. Three whole pieces of scented soap, that sissy had!"

When we stood in the black, milk-warm water, we soaped ourselves from head to foot while Cap, a disembodied hoarse voice on the bank, urged us to lather our heads well so he could shave off our Indian crests. "That razor was a piece of luck," he said. "There it was, laying right alongside those three cakes of soap, and it struck me you'd be needing a razor before the night was over, on account of having come away so sudden, without packs or nothing." Then he was silent, and somehow his silence had something furtive about it.

I had thought of Cap, always, as the most outspoken of men, unfailingly ready, when with friends, to be passionately critical of shortcomings in others. Yet now, in spite of being in a dark and comfortable spot, he seemed wholly changed. When we questioned him about the army and the fort and the American cause, he gave us replies so sickeningly cheerful that I wondered what had come over him.

He told us first of men we knew. Nason, we learned, was alive, fully recovered, and now on a scouting party to the eastward. He spoke of others; then generalized.

The army, he said loudly, was fine: the food was fine: St. Clair was a lovely man and a great general: the fort was fine and strong. Everything was lovely.

I was irritable because of the tremendous distance we had come since dawn, our lack of food, and the shock of losing Verrieul, and I couldn't stand his use of the word "lovely."

"Lovely?" I asked. "How about those two Massachusetts regiments that won't fight? Are *they* lovely? Where's Arnold? Where's Tom Bick-ford?"

"They're lovely," Cap said abstractedly. "Lovely: just lovely."

He stumbled to the water's edge to stand close beside us. "Keep your mouth shut!" he whispered fiercely. "Keep it shut till we get over on the other side."

I had no idea what he was talking about. I was silent, more from weariness than from Cap's warning, which to me seemed senseless.

We must have been odd sights when we finished our scrubbing—three bald-headed white men, all smooth, slick and shiny, clad in Indian leggins, moccasins and belt cloths. With the paint gone from me, I felt naked and uncomfortable; and certainly Joseph Phipps and Doc, deprived of their garish decorations and their strange head-gear, seemed to have shrunk in size and lost something of dignity.

"Now," Cap said, "you look civilized again. We'll get across the bridge and hunt up something to eat." He led us along the shore to the spot beneath the fortifications where, in October, the *Congress* galley had been fitted. From what had been the shipyard, a floating bridge jutted out across the dark water toward Mount Independence. Sentry fires burned at either end, and on the heights across the water there were spots of light.

As we crossed the bridge, I commented admiringly on the amount of labor that must have gone into the building of it. Its segments of planking were anchored to piles, which had been driven in clusters, so that their tops seemed like gigantic stepping-stones extending from shore to shore. Thus they formed not only a causeway, but a dam against British vessels.

"Yes," Cap said, "it's a lovely bridge. Lovely. It took a lot of work. There's a chain, too, so ships can't get by—a lovely chain, big enough to be an anchor-chain for the Old North Church." He pointed toward the water. Fastened to a boom of logs was an endless chain of enormous links—a lovely chain, as Cap had said.

Cap looked over his shoulder. "Yes," he repeated, "there's been enough work done here to hold up the whole damned British army for nine years." In a raucous growl he added, "Only it ain't been done in the right place."

He led us up the steep slope of Mount Independence and herded us into a small log house—one of a cluster of several similar houses on the shoulder that looked across to Ticonderoga. There were two bunks in the cabin, made of bare boards, and two stools which were nothing but oak chunks like chopping-blocks.

Cap pushed the door shut behind us, removed his shirt and hung it

over the one small window, reached up into the chimney and drew a
ragged candle stub from an invisible hiding place, and contrived to light
it after a deal of cursing and fumbling with his tinder-box.

"There!" he said. He snatched up the candle and examined it carefully. "By God," he cried, "if that mouse ain't been in here again, chewing at that candle! It seems as if you couldn't lay a thing down for a
minute without having it interfered with! If there's anything makes me
sick, it's an army!"

"When do we eat?" Doc Means asked.

Cap slapped his back. "When you been in the army as long as I have,
old Catamount, you won't ask about getting something to eat. You'll go
get it without saying nothing to nobody."

His laugh was boisterous. He was wholly different from the Cap Huff
who had met us on the Ticonderoga side of the lake. He took his hatchet
from his belt, kicked over one of the oak blocks, and inserted the blade
of the hatchet in a crack. The base pried away, revealing the chopping-
block to be a hollow shell. In the hollow was a five-gallon keg.

"Madeira," Cap said. "Don't be afraid of it. It used to belong to Roast-
Fermoy, and he thinks it does yet." He took two cups from the mantel
and gave them to us. I thought at first they were made from gourds.
Then I saw they had been carved from the tops of skulls. Doc examined
them; then went to the fireplace and unhooked the tin kettle from its
crane.

"Who did you say that Madeira belonged to?" I asked.

"Roast-Fermoy," Cap said. "He's the Frog in command of this Mount
Independence here. I ain't acquainted with many generals, but I bet
this Roast-Fermoy can get drunk quicker and stay drunk longer than
any other general there ever was."

He removed the base from the other chopping-block, applied his nose
to the cavity and sniffed suspiciously. "No," he said, "it's all right. I ain't
been able to get over here all day, on account of these damned Englishmen raising so much hell, and I ain't had a minute's peace, worrying
for fear she'd go bad on me."

He drew out two loaves of bread and a cold leg of lamb. Doc, who
had filled the kettle with Madeira, seized the lamb with trembling
hands; then whisked his knife from his belt. Beneath his skilled attack
the meat seemed almost to fly apart in orderly slices.

"Frog?" I asked. "You mean a Frenchman? Not Roche-Fermoy?"

"That's the one," Cap said. "Roast-Fermoy. He don't get up till noon,
and then he eats and gets ready to drink. When he starts drinking, he's
the forgetfullest and politest officer I ever see, and the persistentest. If
he gets started around four in the afternoon, he keeps it up till four the

next morning. The best time to report to him is around ten or eleven at night, when there's food lying around loose—legs of lamb and brandy and Madeira and everything, and all you need to do is have some of it with you like you weren't hardly noticing what you did, when you go out. I picked up this leg of lamb yesterday, thinking Stevie might be back. This cabin here, it belongs to I and Stevie." He fixed me with a bulging eye. "Where's your brother?"

"I don't know," I said, and felt no qualms, since my answer was the simple truth. I was not sure whether or not Nathaniel had yet left Buttonmould Bay with Ellen and Marie de Sabrevois.

"Funny you ain't asked nothing about him," Cap said. He stuffed his mouth with lamb and kept a protuberant eye on me while he chewed.

Doc raised the kettle to his lips, drank deep: then turned an inscrutable gaze on Cap. "What's funny, not asking you? According to the answers you made to some of our questions over yonder, it ain't no use asking you nothing." He deepened his voice to a quavering counterfeit of Cap's bellow. "Lovely! Everything's lovely! Nice and sweet and darling! Fine!"

Cap dropped a huge hand on Doc's bare shoulder. "Listen, old Catamount! When you know as much about this army as I do, you'll be carefuller than what I was. This is prob'ly the gol-rangdest army for politics that ever was, and all the politics is over at headquarters. Those fellers don't do nothing but tattle on each other, and hunt around for others to tattle on. All the armies I ever heard of, they always tried to have a few generals that knew how to fight scattered around somewheres, so's they could be got at in case of need; but this army—Hell! If this army hears about a general that knows how to fight, he gets coopered up in a hogshead and dropped down a well, so's he can't win a battle and interfere with the political fellers!"

He picked up one of the skull-cups, filled it from the kettle, and emptied it with sonorous sucking sounds. Then he examined the skull thoughtfully. "Thousands of these out back of the fort, where Abercrombie tried to show how good a general he was. I shouldn't wonder if there'd be a lot more lying around before St. Clair gets through with us." He rubbed the top of his own head in a suggestive manner.

"Then St. Clair ain't lovely, the way you said over yonder?" Doc asked.

"Listen," Cap said, rapping the table with his cup to emphasize his words, "St. Clair's a puff-head: that's what St. Clair is! He's a puff-head, and Wilkinson's a poop-head, and all those other officers around here, they're tit-heads. Lemme tell you something——"

"Whitcomb isn't a puff-head, is he?" I asked.

Cap laughed harshly. "Listen: Whitcomb was all right so long as there was somebody to take him by the front of the shirt and say, 'Look, Whitcomb: you run eight hundred miles and get me two Englishmen, one a big one with the gout and the other a little one with buck teeth, and then you run right back here with 'em and be sitting on my front door-step at just five minutes after supper-time.'

"That's the way Arnold used to talk to Whitcomb; and Whitcomb, he'd do it. Now that Arnold ain't around, there ain't nobody knows what to tell Whitcomb—nobody but me—and I don't dast to say nothing, on account of two reasons, one being that nobody'd believe I knew what I was talking about, and the other being that if he took my advice, I might get sent away somewheres and wouldn't never see Stevie again.

"Anyway, Whitcomb's been made a major, on account of him being so smart and brainy about doing what Arnold told him, and he's as big a tit-head as we got, outside of Wilkinson and a few others! Chief of Scouts, Whitcomb is! What he's scouted on the English, since Arnold left, could 'a' been scouted by a five-year-old baby that had been dropped on his head when young! Yes sir! You could write it on a gun-wad with a mop! There ain't been one single damned thing found out about the British till today, when three hundred of 'em came up and asked to be shot at; and thanks to that poop-head Wilkinson, one of 'em was wounded. Somebody filled him up with brandy to make him talk, and when he talked, Whitcomb didn't know whether to believe him or not—not till—not till you come in and told the same story."

He burst into a flux of swearing so violent that the words ran together in a jumble. It was impossible to tell whom he was cursing or why.

Doc looked absent-mindedly into the empty kettle. "So it was him shot Verricul."

Cap poured the kettle full of Madeira; then tapped Doc on the chest. "Listen, old Catamount! Don't start rumors around this camp! There's too damned many rumors already! Don't say nothing you don't *know!* If it wasn't for rumors, maybe we'd have a real fighter to command us instead of this tit-head St. Clair and this pot-poop Roast-Fermoy! Maybe we'd even be lucky enough to have Arnold! Oh, by God, if only we had Arnold in place of these piss-potted, wizzle-headed, tittle-whizzled——" He gasped hopelessly, at a loss for words: then, again dipping his cup in the kettle of Madeira, muttered "tit-wits" in a choked whisper.

"Well," Doc said, "it looks as if things wasn't quite so lovely as I was afraid they was."

I was heartsick; everything Nathaniel had told me, every damning thing he had said of the American campaign, everything I thought a British lie, seemed to be true. I shook my head, to rid my eyes and brain of dull fatigue. The strange experiences of this hot, unending day had made me so drowsy that for a moment I felt Cap's words had been the distortions of a dream.

"Look here," I told Cap, "we can't make head or tail out of anything you say. For God's sake, start at the beginning, so we can know what you're talking about."

"The reason you can't make head or tail out of it," Cap said, "is because it ain't got none."

"It ain't got no what?" Doc Means asked.

"Head," Cap Huff said. "It's all tail. Listen! You remember I was up here with Arnold last summer, when they was trying to prove he stole two shoe-laces and a hacksaw blade while we was all in Montreal?"

"Yes," I said, "I remember. You left Skenesboro just when I was most in need of workmen."

"Yes," Cap agreed, "that was the time. Well, me and Arnold stood over there at the fort, along with some other colonels, and that old she-mule Gates——"

"What were you doing with such people?" I asked.

"For God's sake!" Cap cried in a rage. "Lemme tell this my own way, will you? I was carrying Arnold's spyglass and compass and field-desk and a little something to eat and a couple of books, and an extra stick for him to lean on in case the one he had should get busted over a tit-wit's head."

He glared at us; wolfed down an enormous piece of lamb; then continued: "Young Trumbull, the son of the feller the *Trumbull* galley was named after, he'd got us out there to show how he could shoot off a six-pounder and land the shot on top of Mount Defiance, that damned big mountain sticking up over there, catty-cornered from us and the fort." He jerked a huge thumb over his shoulder. "Trumbull claimed Mount Defiance was the place for a fort—not Ticonderoga. Gates, she said it wasn't. It was wholly inassassible, Gates said."

"Wholly what?"

"Something you can't get up," Cap said impatiently. "Inassassible. Well, sir, Arnold he spoke right out and says, says he, 'General, with all due respect and so on, Colonel Trumbull's right. The first thing the British would do, if they busted through you, would be to put a few guns on top of that place over there; and right about that time, gentlemen, you'd start running, being as how that hilltop commands not only the fort, but both roads to the south.'"

I thought Cap was jesting. "Why should Arnold tell them something anybody could plainly see?"

"Plainly see!" Cap bawled. "Plainly see hell! Those poop-heads can't

see *nuthin'* plainly! They hollered and bellered and laughed at what
Arnold and Trumbull said, fit to bust a gut. Trumbull, being nothing but
a colonel, sort of looked sick; but Arnold, he just stuck out his chest and
kind of showed his teeth. That old she-mule Gates, she snuffed around
and snuffed around and let out a bray, and she says to him, 'My dear
boy,' says she, affectionate, 'I tell you the place is inassassible! If it's
inassassible, however do you think they'd be able to take guns up it? It
ain't utter inassassible; but in order to get to it, they've got to sail their
vessels past the fort, which they'd never do, not while we had a few
guns and men!'

"Arnold, he certainly was polite to that old she-tittle-wizzle; but if I'd
been Arnold, I'd 'a' called her a name she wouldn't 'a' forgot in a hurry.
Anyway, Arnold didn't say much. He said, 'Of course, General, they
could find a way *around* the fort, if they hunted hard enough.' And then
he said, kind of careless-like, 'I wasn't figuring on doing much walking
today, on account of my leg hurting me some, but seeing as how there's a
question as to whether that hill's scalable, I'll walk up it right now with
Colonel Trumbull. If any of you gentlemen care to come with us, we'll
show you a lovely view from the top—a lovely view of Lake George and
Lake Champlain, and the whole insides of Ticonderoga as well, all of
'em close enough to spit into.'"

Cap, his huge face red and shining from the heat of the night and
the Madeira he had drunk, sighed audibly. "It was me as had to carry
the axe and chop paths for 'em, but it was them as got the credit, of
course."

"You mean Arnold actually climbed that mountain with his bad leg!"

"Certainly we climbed it," Cap said. "I and Arnold and Wayne and
young Trumbull. We clumb up, and it was just the way Trumbull had
said. You could sling a twenty-four-pound shot into Ticonderoga like
blowing beans, and you certainly could make things hot for anyone that
tried to get away to the south'ard.

"Arnold, he laughed when he got to the top. 'Why,' says he, 'wherever
did anybody get the idea this peak couldn't be scaled? I've seen *towns*
built in worse places than this! A German or a Spaniard, he can't see a
hill like this without wanting to build a barn on it, unless it's got a castle
on it already, which it most generally has!'"

"A barn?" I asked. "Why a barn?"

"That kind of bothered me, too," Cap said. "Arnold didn't say 'barn.'
He said hoss-piss. 'Build a hoss-piss,' he said. That's just another way
of saying 'barn,' ain't it?"

"Possibly," I said. "What happened then?"

"Nuthin'! We clumb down, and I and Arnold went back to Skenes-boro and built the fleet."

"Didn't Gates put guns on Sugar Loaf?"

"Nary a gun! There she stands today, just the way she was when I and Arnold clumb it; plumb bald!"

He went to the door and threw it open. The gray light of dawn had brought a sad pallor to the outside world. The peak we were on, and the heights of Ticonderoga, across from us, were unfamiliar bulks, islands in white rivers of fog. Looming above everything was the ragged top of Mount Defiance, bristling with trees whose tips were saw-like against the dimness of the vanishing night. It was uncleared, unfortified, an invitation to disaster.

"But why doesn't St. Clair—what's St. Clair been doing?"

"Well, I tell you," Cap said. "He's been educating his little son, and building his bridge and his chain, so the British vessels can't sail past here; but I could blow his damned chain to pieces in five minutes, and his bridge too, if I had me a four-pounder in the bow of a bateau. The rest of the time he's been making up his mind where he'd like to have the British attack him, and he's decided he'd like to have 'em attack right in front. So that's where he thinks they *will* attack.

"Well, I ain't no general, thank God, but I've done some deer-hunting in my day, and I've shot me a few geese, me and Stevie Nason. War ain't much different from hunting, the way I look at it, and when me and Stevie hunt deer or geese, we circle out around 'em, and come down on 'em where they ain't looking for us to come. If that ain't what the British do, in spite of what St. Clair thinks, I'm a female Hessian camp follower, eight months along!"

We had finished the leg of lamb. Doc Means drew his hatchet from his belt, split the bone, and expertly extracted the marrow with his thumb. "You sound plumb discouraged," he said. "I'll make me up a package of Old Shaman Means's Injun Remedy after I've had some rest. If you take a little, stirred into a cup of rum, or even into some of this here"—he drank from the kettle and eyed Cap with red and watery eyes—"you'll feel better."

"Listen," Cap said heavily. "I ain't discouraged and I don't need none of your Injun remedies. All I need is somebody that ain't a Wilkinson or a Roast-Fermoy to do my fighting with. When those three hundred Englishmen and Indians crawled up to the old French lines this afternoon"—he glanced out at the growing brightness—"No: it was yesterday afternoon! When they crawled up, about to where you Injuns and we met up later, they didn't know we was there waiting for 'em, and they *wouldn't* have known, until they was right smack up against our muzzles, if that misbegotten Wilkinson hadn't got itchy and told a sergeant to take a crack at the closest ones. He done so, and right away every American hopped up and let off his musket into the air. Fired cannons, pistols, rifles and every damned thing—right straight up into the air! Colonels and majors and captains—regulars, militia, scouts and the whole damned kit and caboodle—they all banged away, right up into the sky! Never killed a damned Englishman!

"Maybe you think Arnold would have let 'em do that! Maybe you think Arnold wouldn't have kicked Wilkinson's backsides out through his ears! Maybe you think Arnold would have left Mount Defiance standing there without any guns on it! Maybe you think Arnold wouldn't take this Roast-Fermoy and shove him into one of his own rum barrels! Maybe you think Arnold wouldn't find some way to tie these Englishmen up in knots and pull off their breeches! Maybe you think Arnold wouldn't know all about 'em! Why, hell, he'd have knew, weeks ago, how many there was of 'em, and where they come from, and what their names was, and what they think about, if they *do* think!"

"Well, for God's sake," I said, "where *is* Arnold? Why don't they send him up here?"

"Where *is* he?" Cap roared. "Where *is* he? Why, he's down around Philadelphia or some place, trying to find out who in hell accused him of stealing a peck of peas and half a pound of nails up in Montreal—and trying to keep from being arrested or thrown out of the army for doing it!"

"Thrown out by whom?"

"Who do you *think* would throw him out?" Cap bawled. "Congress! That damned, tit-witted Congress—that lousy, God-forsaken, poopheaded Congress that fired Schuyler, then had to call on him for help and put him back in again, and now wants to fire him once more—that nit-brained Congress that sent Roast-Fermoy up here, and that took five officers and pushed 'em over Arnold's head: made 'em major generals—not because they knew how to fight, but because they knew how to be nice to politicians and knew how to kiss a Congressman on the ear! Tit-brains, every damned one of 'em, by comparison with Arnold— St. Clair, Stirling, Mifflin, Stephen and Lincoln! And Arnold, by God, who knows how to fight better'n all of 'em put together—Congress wouldn't do a damned thing for *him!* No, no! Congress left *him* a brigadier general; just what he was before he pulled the army away from Eel Ox Nox, and showed these tit-wits how to fortify Ticonderoga, and built the fleet, and fought the battle of Valcour, by God!"

This mountain of a man shook with fury; and I, too, was in an icy rage, even though I could only half grasp the mass of information he had hurled at us.

"Why, Congress can't do a thing like that!" I protested.

"Oh, they can't, hey? What do you think Congress cares about us? They can do worse than that! They'd no sooner raised St. Clair and those other tit-heads over Arnold, than two thousand Britishers came ashore at Compo, twenty miles from New Haven, and set out to pull Connecticut to pieces. Arnold, he was in New Haven, saying Hello to his sister and children, that he hadn't seen since God knows when. If I'd been treated the way Arnold was, I'd 'a' been too tired to fight; but he hopped on a horse and went hellerin' and bellerin' around, scraping up a few hundred militia. Then he jumped on them lobster-backs at Ridgefield, all spraddled out. Even militia'll fight for Arnold! Yes, and what's more, he fought alongside of Wooster. Wooster was killed, and two of Arnold's horses were shot, and Arnold was damned near killed too, but he beat the British off! They had four times as many troops as he had, and he beat 'em off! Chased 'em back to their ships and kicked 'em the hell out of there!"

Cap picked up the keg of Madeira, emptied the last of its contents into the kettle, and hurled the keg so violently to the floor that the staves were crushed inward from the hoops. He thrust his face almost against mine.

"And then, by God," he cried furiously, "*then* Congress gave him a horse and made him a major general; but the dirty, piss-wicking, tit-pecking pea-brains left St. Clair and Stirling and Mifflin and Stephen and Lincoln ahead of him! Yep: those five still outrank him; and that's why Arnold ain't here, where he ought to be! That's why we're caught in a hole, with St. Clair to get us out of it, and Roast-Fermoy, and Wilkinson, and not a real fighter in the crowd, except a few fellers that ain't generals—fellers you never heard of—Colonel Francis and Colonel Scammel and Colonel Cilley and Major Dearborn. That don't do *us* no good, because tit-wit generals don't pay no attention to nobody but themselves. The trouble with Francis and Scammel and Dearborn is, they got brains and know how to use 'em, but ain't no good at all at politics. They're such damn fools they do their fighting on battlefields, like Arnold, instead of around a Congressman's privy, where you *have* to do it if you want to be promoted in *this* army!"

"No!" I protested.

"I say Yes!" Cap shouted. With a curved forefinger he swept the sweat from his forehead and flung it passionately against the wall. "I say Yes! I swear to my God that there ain't but two persons of any importance in this whole damned country that appreciates Arnold. One of 'em's

Schuyler, and Schuyler's got troubles of his own. He's got brains, so Congress can't rest till they spit on him and insult him and drive him out of the army for good!"

"You say one of 'em's Schuyler? Who's the other?"

"Feller by the name of Washington," Cap said heavily. "General George Washington."

"But if Washington appreciates him," I asked, bewildered, "why doesn't he send him——"

"Oh for God's sake!" Cap bawled. "Ain't you got no understanding of politics? Washington ain't allowed to do nothing without he kisses Congress's ear first. He has to write 'em a letter every fifteen minutes, rain or shine, and he can't make any plans of his own without asking Congress please can he make 'em; and he can't get Congress to let him have enough men or money or clothes or food or powder or guns; and he don't have nothing to say about promoting officers! Washington raised hell when Congress promoted five generals over Arnold's head, but a hell of a lot of good it did him! What the hell you think Congress cares about what Washington wants? Why, you poor damned ijit, he ain't nothing but commander-in-chief of the army, and he ain't got no rights at all except to kiss a Congressman's ear every time he sees one with its pants down!"

I sat on the edge of the bunk, staring at this violent hulk of a man. The American Northern Army, Nathaniel had said, possessed no capable leaders, and Arnold need no longer be considered. Fuddled as I was with fatigue and Madeira, I knew his information must have come from Marie de Sabrevois. What was more, I knew Marie de Sabrevois was a good spy, for she had the truth of it.

Beyond the open door, the mist was thinner in the gash between the dark hills—thinner, and a soft rose color. Above the bluish-pink walls of Ticonderoga I made out the red, white and blue of the flag that hung slack in the calm of this July dawn. A fleecy ball of smoke flew from the corner gun, and the slam of the gun was loud.

Drums rattled. Cap scratched his back against the door-jamb, and the cabin shook. Doc Means, seated on the floor, muttered and fell over on his side, sound asleep. Joseph Phipps was crouched against the bunk, motionless. He opened his eyes at the sound of the gun, looked from me to Cap: then slept again. Another gun slammed and another, all from the fort's north platform.

"Well," Cap said, yawning, "here they come."

❖   ❖   ❖

. . . I went to stand beside him. Through the shredded mist, to the

northward, streams of bateaux moved in toward the point on which we
must have landed last night, since a long line of British ships and schooners were anchored abreast of the point. Every bateau was loaded with
men. It must be, I knew, Burgoyne's main army coming up to the advanced post, ready at last to attack.

"Cap," I said, "you're a friend of mine, aren't you?"

Cap eyed me doubtfully. "We better get a little sleep. You ain't had
much in the last few days, judging from the looks of your face, and you
want to be able to keep your eyes open in case the British get to crowding us."

"I can't sleep," I said. "I want some advice."

"About your brother?"

"Yes."

Cap hooked his thumbs in his belt and slapped his hands against his
broad expanse of stomach. "The way I figure it is this: If your brother
was dead, you wouldn't be so careful about mentioning him. If he'd gone
back to Arundel, Stevie'd have heard about it. He didn't get tooken to
the westward by those Indians of yours, so there ain't many other places
left for him to be. Either he's a prisoner, or he's joined the British; and if
he was a prisoner, you'd be willing to say so. That don't leave much
leeway."

He watched me, hard-eyed. At each report of the guns from the stone
fortress on the opposite hilltop, my muscles fluttered. "No," I said, "he
hasn't joined the British; but thanks to a friend of yours, I'm afraid he—
I'm afraid he——"

"A friend of mine!" Cap exclaimed. "What the hell you talking about!
I ain't got no friends, only Stevie!"

Doc Means grunted and sighed. "You got *me*," he said thickly. "You
got me and Peter Merrill. We're your friends, just the way Verrieul was.
Even if it was you that killed Verrieul, we're still your friends." He
groaned again and snored lightly.

Cap muttered something in which I distinguished only the word
"Catamount." He turned his attention to me once more. "Prob'ly," he said
cautiously, "you don't mean Doc."

"No," I said, "I mean Marie de Sabrevois."

Cap crouched, his hands on his knees. "Marie de Sabrevois! That hellcat! She ain't nowhere around *here*, is she?" In Cap's voice there was a
hoarse mistrust that revealed a deep respect for the talents of Marie de
Sabrevois.

"She's with Burgoyne's army. She's close to Burgoyne. She helped
take care of Nathaniel after the battle of Valcour. She's dangerous. I'm

afraid, Cap, of what she might do to my brother if I can't find some way to get him away from her."

"Listen," Cap said. "That hellcat had Stevie Nason standing on his head for ten years! If she'd told Stevie pine trees was pink in winter, he'd 'a' believed it! Yes, by God; he'd 'a' said, 'Certainly they're pink!' and he'd 'a' wanted to fight anyone that tried to argue they were blue, or even green. You can't tell me much about how dangerous that hellcat is! What's she done to your brother?"

"She's got him believing the Colonies haven't a chance to win this war," I said. "He thinks the British are bound to win."

Cap looked at me strangely and scratched the corner of his open mouth with a massive thumb, then turned to watch the bateaux crawling down on us from the north, like an endless school of dark waterbugs, to spill red-coated Britishers within striking distance of this gateway to the south. I had a sudden sickening realization that Cap, too, thought the British would win.

"Look here," I said. "You haven't any such idea in your head, have you? They *can't* win! Nobody that knows the size of this country would think for a minute that a few thousand Englishmen and Germans can take it and hold it, not if we don't want 'em to! They can't take it and hold it any more than they could take and hold the Atlantic Ocean! I've been out to the westward—I've seen more of it than most. You could drop the whole of England into the middle of it, and she'd be like an acorn dropped on Mount Agamenticus! You don't think that——"

Cap interrupted me. "Shut up! Can't you see I'm trying to think? You don't have to argue with me about who's going to win this war, because I got to keep right on fighting in it, no matter who wins. Stevie says I got to, and I will. I ain't going to do nothing to get Stevie mad, because he's a terrible feller when he gets mad, which ain't often. Stevie says the British'll overreach themselves, sooner or later, like all Englishmen, and then we'll give 'em a crack in the eye; but I don't know nothing about it. All I know is, I got to go on fighting. Now wait a minute: what's this Marie de Sabrevois doing with the British army?"

In my relief at having somebody to whom I could talk about Nathaniel the words burst from me in a flood. "She's a British spy. She's got her claws on Nathaniel, and she's trying to turn him to the British. So far she hasn't done it. He thinks he's in love with her, Cap, and she's tolling him along. He can't get away, no more than a drake can get away from a live decoy. She's planning to use him somehow. I can't sleep for trying to figure what to do about it. I can't figure it out. He's my young brother. If anything happens, he'll be called a spy and a deserter. I just can't find the answer! He's a fine boy, Cap. He's no traitor. He thinks he's doing what's right. He's——"

"Listen," Cap growled, "I know all about it! I went through it with Stevie! There's only one course to foller: we got to get Stevie. Stevie'll know what to do! We're scouts, and we can go where most people can't. Maybe we can get around behind the British lines some dark night and catch this brother of yours and tell him a thing or two. You let Stevie tell him a few facts and he'll come away with us, all quiet and peaceable." He contemplated his knuckles; then dropped a heavy hand upon my shoulder. "Get yourself some sleep."

I took a last look from the doorway. The sun was just coming up. The guns on the north platform had ceased firing. The advance companies of the British had fallen back out of range. A swarm of Continental troops dragged a cannon near the head of the bridge of boats, at the foot of Ticonderoga. In spite of their raggedness, visible, even, from where we were, they worked fast and alertly. The sight of the British forces hadn't cowed them.

All around us were big guns, and plenty of them. Below us, near the entrance to the narrow waterway leading to Skenesboro, were five vessels. Two of them had stubby masts and lateen sails. They were the *Gates* galley and the *Trumbull* galley, which I had designed and helped to build. The others were the *Liberty* schooner, the *Revenge* schooner and the *Enterprise* sloop—the remnants of the Valcour fleet. Crowded around them were bateaux by the hundred. After all, the place seemed well equipped, and the men ready to fight.

Cap was already stretched upon the floor, and I let myself slack down beside him. I had only a moment of drowsiness before heavy sleep came, but during that moment I seemed to have a long experience—to be in the canoe for days and weeks with Sponge-belly and my friends. And through that power we have in dreams to be in more than one place at the same time, I seemed also to be in the council house, a painted Indian myself among hundreds of my painted brothers—yet all the time I seemed to be telling Ellen Phipps that I had got through to our lines and Ticonderoga, while she, sitting willingly bound and gagged upon the ground before me, looked at me with patient eyes and seemed a little glad to hear me talk.

L V I

AT TICONDEROGA, in those next few days, everything was wrong. No
sooner had we crossed back to the fort from Cap's cabin on the steamy
noon of July 3rd, 1777, than Whitcomb took Cap and Joseph Phipps
from me and sent them off on private business. The rest of the day Doc
and I spent in search of clothes, which were scarce as gold gorgets. Half
the Continental troops were garbed in ragged homespun; and the militia
were scarecrows, unkempt and shambling, their officers strangers to discipline, drill and neatness. Yet even the militiamen felt free to laugh at
our leggins, belt cloths and shaven heads.

By nightfall Doc had swapped his shaman's bonnet for a shirt and
something that had once been a coat. I had begged a shirt and a pair
of breeches from two Massachusetts militiamen, and had found and
washed a handkerchief for my naked poll; but at that, Doc and I might
rightly have been considered the worst-dressed men in General St.
Clair's army.

It was on the 4th that the storm began to break. I had gone to Wilkinson to ask for an assignment—something at which Doc and I could busy
ourselves. He still held a grudge against me because of my former close-
ness to Arnold, and regarded me owlishly with jaw muscles all a-throb.
"The general hasn't made up his mind, yet, how to use you, Captain.
You'll have to be patient. The general has a great deal on his mind,
Captain. We've entered you on the rolls." He gave me a condescending
nod. "You'll have your pay as from July 1st."

"I can get along without pay, Major," I said, "but I can't get along
without work—not at a time like this. There's five armed vessels off
Mount Independence, Major. Some of them look pretty familiar to me.
Put me in command of one of 'em. You haven't forgot I sailed the *Congress* galley, have you?"

He shook his head. "That was a most unfortunate affair," he murmured. "Not only throwing away his ships, as he did, but setting his
vessel afire and leaving his wounded to be burned to death."

He moved his jaw muscles in a deliberate manner, a profound ass if I
ever saw one.

"He?" I asked. "Do you mean Arnold? Where did you hear any such story as that, Major?"

"Oh, it was told to Congress on trustworthy authority."

"Trustworthy authority be damned," I said. "Congress was also told on good authority that General Burgoyne had no intention of attacking Ticonderoga this summer. Congress told General St. Clair he needn't look for Burgoyne in this direction; but he's here, isn't he?"

"Yes," he said, "but that makes no difference. We'll beat them off." He was exactly what Cap had called him: a tit-wit.

"Major," I said, "I did the navigating on the *Congress* galley, as you well know. What you heard about General Arnold leaving his wounded to be burned to death is as untrue as that Burgoyne wouldn't attack Ticonderoga. It's a reflection on me and on every man who fought aboard that vessel. Whoever sent that word to Congress is an enemy to you and me and the American people. You'll deny it, won't you, whenever you have the opportunity?"

"Oh, certainly, Captain," he said instantly. "Certainly! Certainly, certainly, certainly!"

I saw I carried no weight whatever with him; he'd repeat the story about Arnold the next time he had a chance. The vainer a man is, the tighter he clings to preconceived first notions; he's afraid of someone accusing him of changing his mind, which would show he hadn't been the all-wise possessor of all knowledge from the moment of his birth.

"Major," I persisted, "I'd be truly obliged to you if you'd try to get me a command on one of those galleys, where my knowledge would be of some value. The British have a fleet, and a strong one. I think I could make myself useful against 'em. I've done a good deal of navigating, Major."

"I'll bring it to the general's attention," Wilkinson said. "Those ships, you understand, have officers aboard. You're asking to have one of them displaced just to make room for you."

I tried not to show how much I'd enjoy knocking his ears off. "Our side needs all the men it can get, don't you think so, Major?" I asked. "I'm a man, Major, and I'd like to be made use of."

Wilkinson's eyes described a slow circle of the room, and came to rest on me with a sort of mulish stubbornness. "I understand your point of view, Captain. We're leaving nothing undone—nothing. Ah—I'll speak to the general; but you have no idea of the mass of detail he's obliged to attend to."

A sentry popped his head in at the door. "There's smoke on top of Sugar Loaf!"

Wilkinson got slowly to his feet, surprised and incredulous. "Sugar Loaf? Do you mean Mount Defiance?"

"Same thing, ain't it?" He was not what I would have called a well-disciplined sentry.

"You can't mean Mount Defiance," Wilkinson said. He went to the door. "You *can't* mean Mount Defiance! There's no way of getting up Mount Defiance. Our maps mark it inaccessible."

"They's somebody got up it now!" the sentry said. "They's a hell of a big fire on top of it, no matter what the map says."

Wilkinson pushed past the sentry and went out to the parade-ground of the fort.

He returned at once, his customary calmness gone, his eyes round and staring.

"Wha'd I tell you!" the sentry exclaimed.

Wilkinson pounded noisily on General St. Clair's door and went in. In a moment I heard the general protesting bitterly. "Good God, Wilkinson! They *couldn't!* How could they ever get to the top of Mount Defiance!"

Arnold's swarthy, laughing face came to my mind. In my imagination I heard his high-pitched voice, saying what Cap had described him as saying—"the first thing the British would do, gentlemen, would be to put a few guns on that height over there; and right about that time, gentlemen, you'd start running, being as how that hilltop commands not only the fort, but both roads to the south!"

I wondered why Arnold seemed to see things his fellows couldn't see—why his brain leaped straight to the heart of problems that confronted him, while others fumbled and failed to understand; closed their eyes; dodged the truth as if it were some terrible disease.

The door of St. Clair's quarters flew open and St. Clair hurried out, followed closely by Wilkinson. They went to the south gun platform, and I after them; for I was more than ever determined, in the light of this latest news, to find berths for Doc and myself aboard one of the galleys.

From the battlements the fort and the waters it commanded, on that hot July 4th, was a heartening spectacle. Beneath us lay the narrow, glassy lake; facing us was the dark slope of Mount Independence, scarred with trenches and surmounted by a fort of palisades. Stretched across the channel, a mile to the northward, was the close-packed line of British vessels, idle and useless-looking. Near at hand the heavy guns on the platforms looked numerous enough and powerful enough to blow all of England to fragments. If ever a place seemed to defy attackers, it was this stone fort.

Except for the line of vessels to the north, there was no sign of an enemy. Every gun was silent: the ragged sentries walked their posts as heedlessly as though every Briton were in far-off Albion. There was nothing to threaten the serenity of the scene—nothing but that wisp of smoke above Mount Defiance. Yet that wisp of smoke was more ominous than any storm-cloud. It meant that the British had marched completely around us, ascended an inaccessible peak, and stood between us and the Hudson.

St. Clair, reconnoitering the mountain-top through a telescope, fumed and fussed. "Wipe off that glass!" he told Wilkinson. "Damn that blasted thing! Here, wipe it off!" He wiped it off himself and again studied the top of Mount Defiance. He handed the glass to Wilkinson.

"What do you see?" St. Clair demanded.

"Two Indians," Wilkinson said. "There's somebody that looks like an engineer officer—yes, and an artilleryman. Blue: he's got a blue uniform. Yes, he's artillery!"

"It's a ruse," St. Clair said. "It's a ruse! They'll never get guns up there! Never! How in God's name could they ever get guns up there? Wilkinson, there's no way of getting guns up there, is there?"

Wilkinson made no reply, only continued to peer at Mount Defiance.

St. Clair stared about him, baffled and helpless. His eye fell on me. "Here!" he said testily. "What are you doing here! I don't want you following us around!"

"Sir," I said, "I'm waiting for Major Wilkinson to tell me what to do. I'm a scout captain, sir, and I haven't a command. He said he'd ask you to put me in command of one of the row-galleys."

St. Clair looked puzzled. "Row-galleys? What do you want to command a row-galley for?"

"Because that's my trade. I'm a sea captain. If you have to retreat, you'll find a sea captain might come in pretty handy on one of those vessels, small as they are."

"Retreat!" St. Clair shouted. Then he lowered his voice. "Retreat? Why should we retreat? Rather than give up these works, every man of us'll die in them!"

Wilkinson returned the telescope to St. Clair and at the same time murmured something to him.

"Of course!" St. Clair exclaimed, as though relieved of a troublesome decision. To me he explained, "You'll have to see General Roche-Fermoy. The vessels are at Mount Independence, and that's *his* bailiwick. See him, my dear Captain! See him and tell him what you want."

As I hurried down the hill toward the bridge of boats, my thoughts were sour ones. More than ever I understood what Arnold must have felt when he found himself subject to the orders of St. Clair and others of similar caliber.

. . . The welcome I received from General Roche-Fermoy was delightful. When I recalled myself to him, he shook me by the hand as if we had been the greatest of friends during our crossing on the *Beau Soleil* from France—as if, even, I had been clad in a splendid uniform of blue and buff, as was he, instead of wearing a nondescript coat with my buckskin leggins, and having a blue handkerchief bound around my head to keep its nakedness from being a public spectacle.

I think Fermoy's greatest trouble was that he was hospitable: he felt obliged to drink a glass of wine with anyone who entered his quarters— felt obliged to prove how charming and democratic a French soldier could be. Such hospitality, at times, has an unfortunate effect on the host.

How he had coaxed a brigadier general's commission out of Congress, God only knows; but he had it, nonetheless, together with the command of Mount Independence, the peak which protected Ticonderoga on the south. With his position went a log cabin so roomy as to have a bedroom and a kitchen as well as an apartment which seemed to be, so far as I could tell, his drinking room—or at least his principal drinking room. He had also acquired a young aide-de-camp, two servants and several sentries, to say nothing of an air of penetrating wisdom such as I had seen in no other general—least of all in Arnold, and little enough in Gates and St. Clair, in spite of their long service in the English army.

We had a glass of wine together, and he was kind enough to ask for Nathaniel, whose name he had naturally forgotten. Some gentlemen, he said, were coming to supper, so he would postpone taking action on my request until the next morning, when he could do full justice to it.

Unfortunately he was unwell on the following morning—which was the 5th of July, the hottest day I ever endured. He was so unwell that it took the best part of a bottle of rum to get him up—or so Doc claimed to have discovered from one of the sentries; and I suspect General Roche-Fermoy would have been unable to get up at all if he had not been called to a Council of War by General St. Clair.

He could not, of course, attend to me while the Council of War was on his mind, nor could he do it when the Council of War was over, because, apparently, of the serious nature of the business transacted at it. What the business was, we were none of us supposed to know; but it was not hard to guess. Not only had the British succeeded in scaling Mount Defiance, but they had also succeeded in taking two great guns to the top.

At one moment there had been nothing on that towering height—nothing but a moving speck or two. A moment later two British guns looked over at us—two guns capable of throwing into confusion any movements of troops or vessels that might be undertaken within their range—two guns that would doubtless, in a day's time, be augmented by a dozen more. The British had done what Arnold had predicted they would do; and nothing—not one single thing—had been done by St. Clair to hinder them.

Arnold, Cap had said, had given due warning of what might ensue. "About that time," Cap had heard him say, "you'll start running, seeing as how that hilltop commands not only the fort, but both routes to the south."

Ever mindful of that warning, I tried again and again to see Roche-Fermoy. The whole place was in a hot and irritated turmoil, with men hurrying here and there, as ants run, suddenly frenzied, when a heavy foot descends too near their nest.

I was in a worse stew; for I could no more catch Roche-Fermoy and pin him down than I could a humming-bird. Doc and I haunted his quarters all that long afternoon, but to no avail. He was obliged to rest, his aide told us, after the Council of War. Then he was reported busy with his maps and papers. Then he was having his supper, at which he could not be disturbed, because he was making important plans—or so his aide said.

Toward sundown there was cannonading from the lake-shore. We saw two British gunboats leave the shelter of the line of British vessels, and advance as if to reconnoiter our boom and bridge of boats. They were driven back by a burst of gunfire; but this activity, and the turbulent banging of the guns, increased my rage at being held helpless by this irresponsible French adventurer.

At last, in desperation, I threw myself on the mercy of the aide, who had doubtless been given the position because he spoke French, and I hoped he knew more about French than about war.

"Look here," I said, "I know you're sick of the sight of me, but I've been promised a command on one of our vessels, and I haven't got it. Can't you write out an order and take it to the general to be signed?"

His eyes wavered. "Just at the moment it's impossible. The general's too occupied to be disturbed."

Doc, standing meekly behind me, cleared his throat apologetically. "If he ain't well, maybe I could help him out some."

The aide shook his head. "He's all right, but he's had a tiring day and can't be disturbed."

"If he's drunk," Doc persisted, "I know how to fix him."

The aide made an effort to look haughty, but only succeeded in looking worried. Unquestionably Doc was right. Roche-Fermoy was drunk—too drunk to be of any use.

"For God's sake, can't you help us out?" I asked the aide. "General St. Clair told me to come to General Roche-Fermoy, and here we are, hung up in the air like kite-tails, no good to anyone. Tell us what your orders are, so we'll know what's going on—so we'll know what to do. It's nearly night, and something's going to happen! What is it?"

The aide looked helpless. "I haven't *had* any orders! General Roche-Fermoy hasn't issued any." What he said was impossible, yet apparently the simple truth.

With the gathering darkness, gunfire from the fort and the water-batteries was increasing, and a hot wind had sprung up—a searing blast straight from an oven, so that the black abyss between Defiance, Independence and Ticonderoga was like the mouth of Gehenna. That howling, parching wind, whirling the cannonading against us, set my nerves on edge.

"Orders or no orders," I told the aide, "you'd better wake the general and start him moving. What's more, you'd better pack up his baggage, because it looks to me as if it might be needed elsewhere, and soon!"

To wait longer in the hope of getting anything for ourselves from Roche-Fermoy was useless. With Doc stumbling behind me, I hurried down the slanting path toward the floating bridge. The closer we came to the water, the more violent was the thunder of the cannon. By the flashes we could see a short distance on both sides of the bridge, but the bridge itself was dark—so dark that not until we were close up to it did we see, shuffling and stumbling out of the smoky, gun-powdery gloom, an endless line of heavy laden soldiers. Except for the quick flashes of the guns, there were no lights. The bridge was packed with men, clattering toward us over the loose boards—dim, grumbling specters, bowed down with burdens.

They were a headless, confused mass, hurrying along under cover of the darkness, the noise and the smoke.

Doc spoke weakly. "Where's all them soldiers going? What's it mean?"

I told him, choking with bitterness. "St. Clair's evacuating Ticonderoga. Ethan Allen and Arnold took it two years ago, but they might have spared the trouble. Ticonderoga's gone! St. Clair and Congress wouldn't listen to Arnold, and so they lost it for America!"

. . . Remembering the tattered rabble that had fled out of Canada with Sullivan, a year before, I knew there was no use in trying to cross the

bridge against this human torrent in order to find anybody on the other
side.

"Come on," I told Doc. "Let's go to the wharf and see what's to be
done."

We hurried along beside the stumbling soldiers. The American vessels were moored to a rough dock near the floating bridge. The dock had
been built since I brought the *Congress* galley up past this very spot, almost a year ago, on my way to join Arnold. As for the five vessels whose
masts and bulwarks showed above the dock-edge, the look and the
tarry smell of them took me back to that dark night when we had
stolen away from Valcour Island beneath the noses of the British,
patched and battered sieves, but unbeaten still, thanks to the indomitable persistence of Arnold.

In the center were the long, slanting lateen yards of the *Gates* galley
and the *Trumbull* galley. The sight of them moved me; for they were
in no respect different from the vessel on which we had fought so hard;
on which Zelph had died, and Nathaniel and Steven Nason had come
so near to death. On either side were the *Revenge* schooner, the *Enterprise* sloop and the *Liberty* schooner, saved to the Colonies because of
the rear-guard action we had fought on that far-off 13th of October.

Dim whale-oil lights hung, screened, on the vessels' masts, as well as
in the lee of their bulwarks, so that the crews could contrive to stow the
burdens that were being lowered through the hatches. By the gleam of a
lantern I saw, perched on a hogshead on the dock, a portly officer in a
good uniform. The lantern was held by a small man—an Irishman, I
judged—with carroty tufts of hair in front of each ear. With his free
hand he clutched the officer's knee to steady him on his hogshead. As
we came up, a group of gangling, coatless soldiers dropped their burdens on the dock and moved off.

"Here, here!" the portly officer said in suppressed tones. "Pick up
those things and put 'em aboard!"

"Go to hell," one of the disappearing soldiers said from the gloom.

The officer groaned. "Speak to 'em, Mullen!"

The red-whiskered man moved his lantern convulsively and dropped
his hold on the officer's knee to shake his fist at the darkness. "Damn
you, you scuff-bellied, pick-winded swill noses! Come back here! What's
your regiment, you toad-heels!" He cursed horribly.

One of the vanished soldiers shouted, in a high, mincing voice, "Listen to our bull beller!" Another contemptuously expelled air between
compressed lips.

"I believe those fellers come from Boston," Doc said mildly.

The officer turned to peer at us. "What's the reason you haven't got

loads?" he asked sharply. "Every man that crossed that bridge was supposed to carry his share."

"We come from this side," I said. "I was told to get orders from General Roche-Fermoy, so to get aboard one of these vessels."

"We're too crowded," the officer said. "General Roche-Fermoy
shouldn't have sent me anyone else, not without consulting me. Where's
your orders?"

"Sir," I said, "he didn't give us any. He couldn't be reached, and when
we found it out, it was too late to cross over to the other side to see
General St. Clair."

"I don't understand it," the officer said. "Who told you to report to me?
Who told you to report to Colonel Long of the First New Hampshire?"

I knew, then, who the officer was. He was Pierse Long, a shipping
merchant from Portsmouth. Every sea captain along the Maine coast
knew of Pierse Long as a man of unblemished Christian character.

"Nobody told me to report to you," I said. "When we couldn't get
orders from Roche-Fermoy, we came looking for the galleys. We
thought——"

"You thought you'd ride?" Colonel Long asked politely. "Well, we
aren't giving rides to healthy men, except such as we need. We have to
take the women and the sick to Skenesboro. Those that can walk are
supposed to walk there, by way of Hubbardton. That's what you can do:
walk!" As an afterthought he added: "What's your regiment?"

"I haven't got one. I'm a scout officer and a sea captain. I know these
waters. I sailed the *Congress* galley last year."

"A sea captain? A sea captain from where?"

"From Arundel."

"From Arundel, eh? What's your name?"

"Merrill. Peter Merrill."

"Peter Merrill!" he said thoughtfully. "Well, well! And you sailed the
Congress galley! We heard——" He broke off. "We heard some mighty
strange things about that battle—mighty strange."

"Then you heard a lot of damned lies!" I said. "Colonel, this man with
me and I want a chance to fight on one of these vessels. That's all we
want."

"Well," Colonel Long said slowly, "I guess it'll be all right, but there's
no berths open on any of 'em. I'll take both of you with me aboard the
Gates. Make yourselves useful where you can. Help to get things
stowed. Tell Captain Kidder I say it's all right. As soon as we have the
women and the sick and the baggage aboard, and can see to move, we'll
push off for Skenesboro. There'll be nine hundred of us. The rest of the
garrison goes by land."

He broke off to stare accusingly at two militiamen who had stopped to drink from a bottle. "Mullen," he said, "Mullen! They've been looting! Tell 'em so!" To us he added apologetically, "Mullen's my servant. I don't hold with profanity, but there's times when it's a relief to the spirit, and this is one of the times, so I let Mullen do it for me."

Mullen bawled at the militiamen in a shrill, insulting voice, "You've been looting, you damned black-bellied fish-faces! I'd like to have you under me for five minutes, by God! I'd pull out your dirty green gizzards and stuff 'em in your ears, you yeller, dirt-eating eels!"

Doc Means stared admiringly at Mullen. "My, my!" he said faintly.

The militiamen failed to pay either Mullen or Colonel Long the courtesy of a glance. As they moved away, one belched and the other broke wind. It could scarcely have been accidental.

The colonel paid no further attention to us. Doc and I went aboard the *Gates*. I hurried aft, hoping to find an officer I knew—Thatcher, perhaps, or Colonel Wigglesworth; but instead I found the quarterdeck in possession of a lantern-jawed fisherman from the Chesapeake who had served as mate under Thatcher on the *Trumbull* galley, a year before. I remembered him as a conscientious mate, though overfond of describing how he purified his blood by eating dandelion greens, and of reciting villainous patriotic poetry written by himself.

When I recalled myself to him and told him what Colonel Long had said, his sour, tight-lipped grin stretched his mouth like a scar across his face. "Glad to see you, Captain, but Colonel Long ain't got no authority over me! I been acting captain of this vessel nigh onto three months, and I wouldn't feel like taking orders from nobody, not unless he had some higher authority."

I began to have an inkling of how a man must feel when somebody whose ability he mistrusts has been pushed ahead of him in the peculiar collection of jealousies and false pride called an army. "Make yourself easy, Captain," I told him. "All Doc Means and I want to do is help these troops get away to Skenesboro safely. If there's anything you'd like done, say the word."

He eyed me suspiciously still. He was wondering, I knew, whether my presence aboard was a threat to his position. "Well," he said grudgingly, "keep an eye on them that's stowing baggage in the hold. Don't let 'em just dump it in, the way they been doing. Make 'em do it ship-shape."

Doc and I went forward. Sick men were coming over the side, some on stretchers: some walking, using their muskets as crutches. "Look after those sick men as much as you can," I told Doc. Then I went to the main hatch and did what Kidder had ordered me to do.

The guns pounded and pounded. Knots of soldiers stumbled out of the darkness to mill around on the dock while officers directed them in subdued, fretful voices; then came aboard, muttering, to lower their burdens to the crew that sweated in the hold. Freed of their burdens, they went ashore again, discussing the whereabouts of Hubbardton. That was where they had been told to go—Hubbardton, then Castleton, then Skenesboro. I wondered how many of them would get there.

At two o'clock in the morning I wondered still more. High above us on the crest of Mount Independence, I saw what, for a moment, I took for the edge of the moon, red through the heat haze. Then I remembered that the moon had been new that day and must, necessarily, be long since set. With the thought, the red sliver of light leaped upward; waned again: then broadened and licked up in a tongue of flame.

All around us, in the darkness, men were clamorous. We heard bateaux bumping into us—men stumbling in them—oars thumping and splashing. Colonel Long's voice called, "Steady, there! By God, sir! I'll have you fired on!" He came climbing over the bulwarks, his blue coat ripped up the back. He seemed tongue-tied.

The flame on Mount Independence rose higher, spread out, pushed up a cloud of smoke above it, cast a hot and angry glow on the under side. As the flame rose, so, too, rose the excited voices of soldiers on shore and in unseen boats around us. Their voices held the hurried shrillness of panic.

The colonel mounted the bulwarks, clutched a stay and once more bellowed orders at the throng beneath him. We could hear them colliding; dropping their burdens. "Bring that baggage aboard!" the colonel called. "Here! Bring that baggage onto this vessel!" He must have repeated his order a hundred times; but no man paid the slightest attention to him. The flame on Mount Independence grew bigger and sent up a shower of sparks. By its light we saw the soldiers, crowded together in a struggling, ungovernable throng.

"For God's sake!" the colonel said. "For God's sake!" He stared helplessly around. "What's that fire! What damned fool did that!"

"If I ain't mistaken," Doc Means said, "that General Roast-Fermoy got drunk once too often. He's been taking a nap all day, so maybe he just woke up and tried to smoke a pipe in bed."

"That's what it is!" the colonel cried. "That's just what it is! It's Roche-Fermoy's house! What in God's name is he trying to do? Send word to the British?"

He shouted more loudly at the shadowy figures. When they ignored him, he climbed heavily back on the dock again and I went with him.

He was an honest and brave officer, but he was helpless in that panic-stricken horde.

We cursed and struck at them, but they only cursed and struck back, fading out from beneath our hands to go stumbling off on the road to Hubbardton. Sick men clutched at our ankles; women screamed and got underfoot. It was like a bad dream, when every effort fails of accomplishment, legs seem made of lead and muscles of jelly, and all the world is heavy with futility.

"When it's light," the colonel said, again and again, "it'll be all right. They're confused by the darkness. As soon as it's dawn, we'll have no trouble."

But at dawn, things grew worse. Bateaux, loaded during the night on the Ticonderoga side, moved slowly past, half hidden in the mist; and scores of bateaux that had lain near by, waiting for daybreak, pushed off without orders and followed the others in a straggling flotilla. The occupants of the bateaux were deaf to the angry orders of officers, and pulled silently southward.

At the sight of the vanishing bateaux, a blind frenzy gripped the soldiers who still moved toward us, laden with stores. As if demented, they cast down their burdens and hurried off, pale and sweating, tripping and falling.

Whether the schooners received orders to move out, I can't say; but move out they did. The colonel scrambled back aboard the *Gates*. "Get the rest of those sick men aboard," he ordered. As Doc Means came to help me, we saw a cart approaching, piled high with bundles and drawn by a single scrawny ox. At the edge of the dock, the waggoner jumped from the front end of the cart and, without a backward glance, was swallowed in the ragged crew that filled the road. At the same moment an officer popped in sight from behind the cart, threatening death and destruction to those who refused to unload it. He caught man after man by the arm, and we heard him saying "It's the general's baggage! Damn you, sir, lend a hand with General St. Clair's baggage! Get this baggage aboard a boat! It's the general's!"

When they profanely wrenched themselves free, he offered them money to unload the cart—offered them rum: all the rum they could drink. They only cursed. They told him foul things to do with the baggage—with the cart—even with the ox. They spoke hideously of his money and his rum, and called the general unspeakable names. They cursed everything and everybody, and kept straight on, an uncontrolled and uncontrollable rabble, toward Hubbardton. The officer gave it up and went away, running.

There was a rosy flush in the eastern sky. From far off, on the far side of Mount Independence, we heard musketry fire—volley firing.

The *Trumbull* galley cast off and moved out into the lake, raggedly propelled by her long sweeps. Kidder ran down from the quarterdeck of the *Gates* and angrily summoned us.

A sorrel mare clattered down the muddy road and onto the dock. The rider was St. Clair himself. His face, white and puffy, streamed perspiration, and his nose and eyes were red. He spurred his horse close up to the *Gates* and looked us over coolly enough. To me he seemed pathetic—a puny, baffled figure against the towering background of Mount Independence. Colonel Long climbed on the bulwarks to receive him.

"Pull out any time," St. Clair said. "If you can do so, save my papers. They're in that ox cart. Pay no attention to the rest of the baggage, but take my papers with you if it's possible." He removed his hat, drew a handkerchief from it, and mopped his face: then stared at the handkerchief as though he expected to find it soiled. I was sorry for him, and I know he felt sorry for himself.

He wheeled his horse and set off toward Hubbardton, cheerfully urging on the straggling, frightened soldiers. Five minutes later we had his papers aboard the *Gates* and were moving slowly southward. Behind us the dock was littered with abandoned stores; and the scrawny ox, dragging the half-unloaded cart, moved dejectedly along the road St. Clair had taken.

LVII

THE unreasoning fear called panic is an appalling thing. In its grip a man behaves insanely. Then, when he thinks himself free of its clutches, he is filled with a revulsion of feeling that makes him slack and careless; and this carelessness and slackness is often more dangerous than the panic itself.

No sooner were we clear of the dock than everyone aboard the galley seemed sunk in a sort of heedless languor. The soldiers, lately witless with confusion, were yawningly tranquil now: the women camp followers who had found their way aboard were quick with airy laughter: even the hopelessly sick men were transformed to hopeful convalescents.

As for Kidder's seamen, they moved abstractedly about the deck as if they might, at any moment, be called away on other weightier affairs; and Kidder seemed reluctant to disturb them in their abstraction—seemed almost grateful that they deigned to travel on his craft. He used only two men to a sweep; and they, as if husbanding their strength for more remunerative labor, put no body into their movements: merely leaned against the oars.

So slight was the galley's headway that she barely answered her helm. At such a rate, I knew, we'd be lucky to reach Skenesboro in ten hours.

I walked the length of the deck. There were men everywhere, packed between the guns, wrangling over nothing, pouring out misinformation on weighty matters, after the eternal manner of soldiers and sailors. If I could have had command of the *Gates*, I'd have put five men on every sweep, and driven them hard. That was Arnold's way of doing things. "Once you make up your mind what to do," I had heard him say a score of times, "do it quick! If you don't, somebody may cut you off! The wind might drop, and leave you high and dry."

The dreadful slowness of our progress set my teeth on edge. I walked back to the quarterdeck, meaning to suggest that Kidder let me put his idle men to work on the sweeps. The colonel was writing—a report of his movements no doubt—and was oblivious of my presence. Kidder saw me; but he pretended not to. He didn't want me interfering with his vessel. I went back to the main hatch and sat down beside Doc.

Once again, on the far side of Mount Independence, I heard musketry fire. To me it sounded like the fire of trained troops—British troops. I liked it so little that I felt I must speak to the colonel, Kidder or no Kidder.

I went aft again and stood there, waiting, until the colonel looked around. "Colonel," I said, "if there were two or three more men put on every sweep, we could make Skenesboro around mid-morning."

"We're doing all right," he said cheerfully.

"Colonel," I persisted, "the British move fast when they start. They built and equipped the *Inflexible*—their full-rigged ship—in twenty-eight days."

The colonel's reply was benevolent. "My boy, we're almost as anxious to get away from the British as you are. Not quite as anxious, but almost!"

"Well, sir," I said, "I'm only anxious to make as good a showing as possible."

The colonel's manner was amusedly superior. "Young man, I don't believe you've been keeping your eyes open! The British fleet can't pass Ticonderoga till they cut through the chain and boom, and force a way between the piling. They'll be a long time doing that."

I knew I was a fool to say another word; but something drove me on —the thought of Nathaniel, maybe, or of Ellen, or of Arnold, or of Marie de Sabrevois: possibly my own pride. "Sir," I said, "those piles weren't much. I could have laid a vessel like this alongside 'em and blown them and the chain and the boom apart within ten minutes."

Captain Kidder muttered something beneath his breath. He and the colonel smiled knowingly at each other.

There was nothing I could do or say to help matters. They were my superior officers, and any soldier who wrangles with a superior officer, no matter what the provocation, loses not only his time but his chance to be of use. I went back to Doc and sat close beside him, a little comforted by his sympathetic silence.

We were three hours reaching the spot where, six miles from Ticonderoga, the lake narrows between high and wooded shores. This snail's progress filled me with apprehension. Another fourteen miles lay between us and Skenesboro; and if we did no better than this, we not only might not get there in ten hours: we might not get there at all.

The other vessels had done no better than we. The *Revenge* idled along abreast of us, her sweeps slapping the water raggedly. One of the crew was fishing from the bow; and so lax were the officers that when the fisher hooked a salmon, all the oarsmen ceased rowing and watched the fish trying to shake out the hook. Soon there were a dozen

fishing from the *Revenge*, and as many from the *Trumbull*. The *Liberty*
and the *Enterprise* were half a mile ahead; and the bateaux, like lethargic waterbugs, crawled on the glassy lake far in advance.

"Doc," I said, "I don't like it."

"No," Doc said, "I don't like it much myself. I been trying to figure
what I'd say to Sponge-belly, in case the British catch up with us." He
eyed me sideways. The possibility of such a meeting was resting heavily
upon him.

"Well," I said, "I'll try it again, but I don't believe it'll do any good."

"It won't do a mite of good," Doc agreed. "These fellers think the English are always slow, just the way the English think we're all a lot of
iggerommuses, and I ain't so sure but what they're right."

I went back to the quarterdeck once more, and I went reluctantly;
for nothing is so hurtful to a soldier's pride as to appear as a persistent
suppliant.

The colonel was in high spirits at the sight of a fat salmon flapping on
the deck. Even Captain Kidder's sourness was less pronounced, now
that the trials of the night were over. They gave me a friendly greeting,
doubtless because I hadn't bothered them for some hours. Captain Kidder had just made a suggestion that met with the colonel's approval.
"A fine idea!" the colonel exclaimed. "We'll have fish for breakfast for
all hands as soon as they've caught twenty more. Send five men ashore
to cook 'em—have 'em row well ahead. We'll take our time catching
up, and by the time we get there, they ought to be done. Salmon for
breakfast! We could do worse, Kidder: a lot worse!" He smiled at me,
a kind, good gentleman. "Not a Britisher in sight!" he said. "No occasion
for all that nervousness of yours, you see. They'll be two days cutting
through that chain and those piles!"

"Yes sir," I said. "I don't doubt you know the chain's capabilities.
There's something I'd like to speak about, though. I know this section
of the lake pretty well, as I told you. Last year, when we took the
vessels through to General Arnold, I figured out a few things."

The colonel nodded affably. "Go ahead, Captain. It'll be a pleasure
to hear what you've thought up for us."

He was being jocose, and my heart sank. "Well, sir," I said, "from here
to Skenesboro, the lake narrows to almost nothing. There's places where
a square-rigger can't go through without scraping."

"Yes," the colonel admitted, "it's narrow, but we'll have no trouble:
not with Captain Kidder at the helm."

"No sir," I said. "That isn't what I mean. What I mean is this: if you'll
let me sink one of our five vessels in the proper spot, the British can't

get by. They'll be weeks clearing the channel, and you can take your time getting away."

"Sink a vessel!" Captain Kidder cried. "Which one?"

"This one," I said. "Any one of 'em. It doesn't matter which, does it, so long as we hold back the British?"

Kidder's face turned gray, and his voice, when he spoke to Colonel Long, trembled with rage. "He's crazy!" Kidder said. "We got only five vessels, and he wants to throw one of 'em away without so much as firing a shot! I'm captain of this galley, Colonel Long, and I won't allow no such talk on this quarterdeck!"

When I would have appealed to Long, he shook his head. "You're going out of your way to hunt trouble," he said kindly. "Captain Kidder's right. We've got too few vessels to waste one."

It seemed incredible that men could be so blind; but even in my despair I remembered how Arnold, on the day I first met him, had said: "Such officers cannot understand the precautions necessary to successful defense." It was barely possible that if these officers were unable to comprehend the defense that seemed to me so sure and simple, they might still be made to realize the advantages of another equally obvious plan.

"Colonel," I said, "there's one place in particular, between here and Skenesboro, where a cliff sticks into the channel. A vessel of any size has to be warped around. It's almost a right-angled turn. Two eighteen-pounders on top of that cliff could tear a vessel's deck to pieces. You could chop up the yards and rigging of a whole fleet—throw it into a tangle it would never get out of. Let me try it, Colonel. Colonel, the British'll be trying to come through there after a while."

The colonel showed signs of impatience. "You're overlooking a thing or two. In the first place, we need all our guns for the protection of the fort at Skenesboro. That's a big fort, with a stockade that stretches over all outdoors. In the second place, two guns wouldn't hold the British back for long. All they'd have to do would be to land a few men, get around behind you and capture the guns and you too. No, no, my boy, it wouldn't do! It wouldn't do!"

"Colonel," I said, forcing myself to make one more effort, "I could hold 'em back two hours. Before the day's over, you might find those two hours mighty valuable. Just that much delay might give you all night to work on the fort. And by the time they get landing parties ashore to cut us off, we could lever the guns into the lake and slip off into the underbrush ourselves."

The colonel sighed. "There you go again! How on earth do you think they're ever going to catch up with us!"

"What about those fish?" Captain Kidder interrupted. "There's nigh onto forty of 'em been hauled in—big ones!"

The colonel turned from me in evident relief. "Yes, tell your cooks to take 'em ashore and get 'em on the fire," he told Kidder. "Everybody'll feel a lot better with a good mess of salmon inside him!"

I wondered bitterly how many cases of stubborn blindness, like that of these two men, were helping to bring defeat upon the American cause.

. . . By mid-morning our straggling flotilla had made another six miles. By noon it had made another six and we were at the sharp turn in the lake, close to Skenesboro. The narrow channel, overhung with rocks and trees, bent at right angles. Heaven, it seemed to me, had put that elbow there as an instrument for the confounding of invading Britons; but we left it behind us, carelessly, as a spendthrift wastes the patrimony that others worked to save.

It was between one and two o'clock when we drew up under the shoulder of the limestone mountain, and saw again the sprawling, straggling stockade of Wynkoop's comic fort. In that pocket among the hills the heat was suffocating, just as it had been in the days when we worked ourselves to skeletons to build our gundelos and galleys, including this very one on which I now returned, an ignored subordinate.

Since I had last seen it, the place had changed, though not greatly for the better. The scars and slashings from our timber-cutting were still in evidence; and Skene's yellow house looked down on them, pallid in the noonday glare. Now there were sister buildings to the airless barracks Wynkoop had built—warehouses, in which were stored supplies for this scattered Northern Army. The rude docks by the shipyards, from which we had rowed away to delay the British at Valcour, were stouter now, and larger—large enough to let all five of our vessels crowd against them.

The colonel hurried off to join his troops. He had seen more than enough of me, I was well aware. I would have helped Kidder get his cargo out from under hatches, but he seemed to have nothing for me to do—nor for his own men, for that matter, since he made no move to break bulk. Food, I saw, was uppermost in his mind.

"Well," I told Doc, "there's nothing to do but go ashore and get ourselves a place to sleep. We'll wait for the rest of the army; and when it gets here, we're bound to find Cap and Joseph Phipps and Tom Bickford, and probably Steven Nason; and maybe somebody'll give us work again."

Doc stared at me out of watery, helpless eyes. "I hope so," he said faintly. "I feel kind of mean and dirty, trying to help people that don't want to be helped." Suddenly he became irascible and shook his fist at me. "You and your wars! I'd be a real doctor, if so be I could cut the throat of every man that wanted to fight a war, and if I could feed a dose of poison to every officer higher than a captain!"

I agreed with Doc. An army was a terrible thing, destructive of a man's confidence as well as his independence. Officers, too, with men's lives in their hands, were no different from lawyers, from carpenters, from business men, from Congressmen, from sea captains, from doctors, from historians. Out of any thousand sea captains or carpenters, or Congressmen or historians or doctors, only a dozen would be worth their salt; and if one out of the thousand had genuine ability, it was a miracle.

Doc caught my arm. "Look yonder! What's that?"

A farmer on a mud-caked plow-horse came up the shore on the dead run. When he was opposite the docks, he shouted; and on the heels of his shout a despairing moan rose from the vessels' crews. The farmer turned his horse and galloped up the hill to the stockade gate. Within the stockade the newly landed troops came running from all sides, and we ran, too.

An angry outcry burst from those who milled around the red-faced horseman. We distinguished the word "British!"

Colonel Long, white-faced, stared up at the newcomer and made sounds of protest.

"God damn it," the farmer roared. "I *see* 'em! I tell you they're three miles from here! They put damned near a thousand men ashore—fellers in red coats. Don't you think I can tell a red coat when I see one?"

The colonel mouthed words which refused, seemingly, to get themselves said. The farmer shook both fists at him, then swung an arm toward the high hill that divided the lake from Wood Creek. Wood Creek, and the narrow road beside it, was the only route by which we could reach Fort Ann and the Hudson.

"They started over that mountain," he insisted, his voice shrill and cracked, "they started over that mountain to cut you off! I tell you they's a thousand of 'em! A thousand! The rest of 'em's pulling the ships around the corner. They're twice as big as yours, and there's twice as many of 'em! They'll have you boxed up here inside of an hour if you don't get out! You got to get out! You got to get out quick!"

This Colonel Long, for all his slowness when there was no enemy close at hand, was a brave man and a willing leader, as he showed now.

He caught two officers by the arm. "I want every damned thing burnt," he shouted. "Burn it! Burn the whole damned place! Burn the stores! Blow up the ships! Burn down those warehouses and that yellow house up there! If you can burn the docks, burn 'em. And start the women up Wood Creek in the bateaux!"

He went on shouting his orders to the men who surged about him. "Set every damned thing afire! Burn up the whole damned place! Send the women down to the bateaux. Tell 'em to hurry up! Send the sick down to the bateaux! Tell 'em they ain't sick any longer!"

. . . We tried to burn Skene's yellow house. We burned the horse stalls behind it where Nathaniel and Cap and Steven Nason and the rest of us lived. We burned Wynkoop's good-for-nothing barracks, and kindled raging fires in the slashings. The whole side of the limestone mountain was aflame. The docks were blazing, as well as two of the vessels moored to them. The rocky ravine was an inferno, in which sooty-faced men ran shouting through the smoke, torches in hand, looking for something more to burn. Out of that inferno, over the falls of Wood Creek, clambered sick and wounded, women and children, barefoot sailors and ragged soldiers.

Through the hot and smoky twilight a straggling throng rowed furiously up Wood Creek to the slamming of British guns, hammering at the *Trumbull* and the *Revenge*, which alone remained unburned. Even as we looked, their flags came down, and that was the end of the fleet that had fought so valiantly at Valcour.

Our stores were in flames: our baggage gone: our cannon abandoned: our ammunition lost. The remnants of the Northern Army were scattered God knew where, without a meeting place. We had neither food, nor guns, nor ships, nor tents—we were destitute of everything; and pressing close behind us were the finest regiments of the British army, led by officers without a peer.

LVIII

It is twenty-three miles, the first half water, the second half land, from Skenesboro to the Hudson, but those twenty-three miles are hard ones. The end of the water part of the journey is Fort Ann, a tumbledown affair on the high land above Wood Creek, at the spot where it becomes impassable for batcaux. Twelve miles farther on, overlooking the Hudson, is Fort Edward, almost as tumbledown as Fort Ann. The road from Fort Ann to Fort Edward, if it can be called a road, winds through pine forests rooted in soil that, in the spring and early summer, oozes water like a saturated sponge. Slow-moving brooks meander everywhere, and the road is cut by a succession of log bridges, upon which an unwary traveler, if he stumble, is like to pitch headforemost into black muck smelling of corruption.

All through the night of July 6th we rowed our clumsy bateaux up the narrowing waters of Wood Creek, lighted on our way by the red glow spread fan-like over the sky behind us; and when we reached Fort Ann, we found Colonel Long ahead of us. I had cursed him for his shortsightedness on the retreat from Ticonderoga, but I blessed him now. It sickens me to think what might have happened, except for Colonel Long, to those hundreds of ill and wounded men and to those other hundreds of women on that stifling July night if they had gone blundering through swamps and deep woods, half blind with unreasoning apprehension. But Long stood on the bank of the creek with his little Irish servant, Mullen, holding a lantern to his face so that the frightened fugitives could see him as well as hear him. He talked to the women and the sick, as they scrambled ashore, cheering them up and urging them forward. "Just keep right on," he said, his voice hoarse from repeating it. "Keep straight on to Fort Edward. Take your time. Nothing's going to hurt you. We'll hold the British back. They'll never get by us. Keep right on to Fort Edward. We'll fight 'em off!" He was a brave man and a good officer. In spite of having a regiment whose enlistment was on the verge of expiring—a regiment which did, presently, march off to New Hampshire, regardless of Colonel Long's pleading and our own desperate need of troops—in spite of that he held his men there at Fort Ann and two days later fought back the British in an action that was small, but that was as sharp and deadly as any action of the war.

So we came safely over the morasses and the countless log bridges of the Fort Edward road, dragging the sick, pulling the women from the mud-holes into which they slipped, fighting the gnats and mosquitoes that droned eternally with us through the steamy breathlessness of those dark swamps, hovering in misty clouds about our heads. All through the 7th of July our ragged, mud-stained companions, remnants of the Ticonderoga garrison, straggled dog-tired from the forest and advanced across the fertile shelf of fields above the broad Hudson toward the shelter of Fort Edward.

I say we came there safely; but the safety that our harried company had hoped to find within the fort was nowhere in evidence. We were back to civilization again: that we knew from the fields of wheat and potatoes that stretched up and down both banks of the river. There were settlers' cabins, near the fort and in the distance. But the fort itself was nothing but ancient log barracks set down in a ring of grass-grown ramparts over which I could have leaped a horse; and near by was a hill from which a score of men with small arms might have picked off anyone who sought shelter within those walls. Therefore it was less a fort than a trap. What was worse, there wasn't a cannon inside or outside it; and its garrison was a single regiment of soldiers that looked askance at us, as though we were Tories instead of fellow-fighters in the same cause. I think the reason for their attitude was partly that we had abandoned the strongest post in North America to the onrushing English, and partly that we were mostly New Englanders, who are loathsome in the eyes of York troops.

At all events, we found nothing at Fort Edward to raise us from our melancholy state; and I, standing beside this waterway to the south, down which the British planned to rush, was filled with a sort of desperate stubbornness—an obstinate determination never to admit that my countrymen could be so lacking in courage and wisdom as to make possible what apparently had occurred.

Here was the Hudson. Burgoyne and his troops were only twenty-three miles behind us. "It's all over!" Nathaniel had insisted to me. "After Burgoyne marches down the Hudson——"

I thought farther back—back to St. Leger's British troops and Tories we had seen setting off up the St. Lawrence, to pounce on the colonies by the back door. It was all over, they, too, had told us: they'd see us soon in Albany.

And here we were, defenseless, backed up against the Hudson, with Albany less than forty miles downstream. Here we were, without food, without powder, without an army, and on the verge of being without a country. Yet I couldn't and wouldn't admit, even to myself, that Nathaniel had been right. It wasn't all over! It would never be all over, not until they had driven the last man of us into the trackless wilderness, or put a bullet through his brain. More than ever I realized how deeply rooted, in many New Englanders, is that strange trait that some call mulishness, others call cussedness, and still others know as bigotry; and for once in my life, I was willing to admit that I had my share of it.

Doc Means and I lay in the smoke of a green-wood fire, that night, to keep ourselves from being eaten alive by mosquitoes and black flies; and Doc was restless, getting up a score of times to tinker with the smudge and peer toward the sentry fires that ringed the fort.

"Go to sleep," I told him. "From the way you're fretting, a body'd think you had a brother within the British lines yourself."

Doc seemed only half to hear me. "I'm fretting because I'm getting to be like a regular doctor. I'm getting so I change my medical ideas too often. Only last year I used to think there wasn't nothing so good for people as rest. I used to think you'd get sick if you didn't get enough rest. Well, I know now it ain't rest that keeps people healthy. It's work. If I can't get me some work pretty quick, I'll get sick. If somebody don't give me something to work at tomorrow or next day, I'll feel obliged to leave this army to get along by itself and go home and start making medicine. I got an idea for a fine medicine to cure fright, worry, falling pains and so on. There's a great field for it in this country, and I bet I could get rich selling it. Old Shaman Means's Injun Remedy—Old Shaman Means's Midewiwin Medicine—Old Shaman Means's Catamount Compound . . . cures homesickness, backbiting, Toryism and feelings like your insides were sinking . . . just a little rum and a lot of water and a pinch of Digby's Sympathetic Powder . . . that's all you'd need . . . there ain't nothing the matter with you unless you think there is. . . ."

In listening to his nonsense I forgot, for a moment, my worries about Nathaniel and Ellen Phipps, and in that moment I fell asleep, as I think Doc knew I would.

✿   ✿   ✿

. . . It was many a day before either of us had occasion to worry over not having enough work to do. There were times, indeed, when I came to think that if health, as Doc now claimed to believe, depended on a surfeit of hard work, the pair of us might live to be older than Methuselah.

Doc, still restless, was up at dawn, grubbing around in the grass for a mess of greens; and no sooner had he washed the grit from them and popped them into a borrowed kettle with a dozen slices of borrowed pork than we heard the sound of drums down river. The drummers marched at the head of four hundred men. What was more, the four hundred were in a hurry; for early as it was, they never even broke ranks, but stood in the rutted road outside the fort while a detail from the garrison went from man to man, giving them ammunition and pouring rum into their canteens. They were York militia from Albany County, under a Colonel Van Rensselaer, and to me they looked no different from the Massachusetts militiamen who had refused to stay more than two days with General St. Clair at Ticonderoga. They were dust-caked, half disciplined, soaked with sweat; and from the state of their clothes, they might have rushed straight from their fields and plows to join the army. When they had received their rum, they hurried on, their muskets trailing or slanted over their shoulders every which way. They were Dutchmen, and when they shouted at Doc and me, we could hardly make out what they said. They were asking how far it was to Fort Ann. When we told them, in plain, simple language that any fool could understand, they looked first baffled and then amused, which gave us an even lower opinion of Dutchmen than they seemed to have of us. Yet I must give these men their due; for before the day was over a number of them lay dead in the swamps of Wood Creek; and Colonel Van Rensselaer, who led them, was nearer dead than alive from a British bullet. It was they who went to the relief of Colonel Long and, with what was left of Long's regiment, drove back from Fort Ann as smart a British regiment as ever held Americans in contempt.

Van Rensselaer's troops were scarcely gone when we heard more drums to the southward; and before that steamy hot morning was over, the grassy plain around Fort Edward was a city of tents of every size and color. Ox carts, piled high with supplies, creaked up the road in a slow procession. Within the fort itself a marquee had been erected, and into it and out from it scuttled officers and aides, all in a tremendous hurry. Despatch bearers freed their horses from the near-by picket line to go pelting off in a lather. From time to time a tall, blue-clad officer with a long inquisitive nose stalked from the tent and seemed to smile defiantly at everything in sight. Wherever he moved, two aides moved with him, one at each elbow. They held note-books in readiness to take down whatever word should fall from the great man's lips, the reason being that he was Philip Schuyler, Commander of the Northern Army of the United States. On learning of our retreat from Ticonderoga, he had snatched up every available man on whom he could lay hand, and hurried north from Albany with seven hundred Continentals and fourteen hundred militia to do what he could to stop the victorious advance of the British. It was a pitifully ill-trained, ill-equipped body of men with which to confront the flower of the British army; and yet to the use he made of that forlorn hope of his, and to the brilliancy and bravery of his friend General Arnold, we owe our existence as a nation.

While on the subject of General Schuyler, I may as well say my say about him and have it off my mind. He was a man of property and breeding, an aristocrat by inheritance and training. New Englanders hated him because he was a Dutchman: because he was a patrician: because he fought against the shortsighted New England policy of trusting the national defense to militia who could be depended on for nothing except to eat more than they were worth, to fail their country in every crisis, and to wreck the nation's currency and credit by the millions of dollars in bounties without which they refused to enlist. But regardless of the back-stairs whisperings of Massachusetts malcontents, the truth about Schuyler is this: he was a tireless, self-sacrificing and uncomplaining patriot whose treatment, at the hands of Congress, was such as to make me ashamed to own the members of that body as my countrymen. What they did to Schuyler was mild by comparison with what they did to Arnold; but nonetheless, it was dreadful. Schuyler devoted his time, his health, his reputation and his private fortune to the American cause: his exertions and firmness, at the hour when we were sinking into confusion and despair, buoyed us up and gave us the strength to fight. And Congress rewarded him by depriving him of his command, elevating a petty plotter above him, and driving him from the army.

. . . In spite of all we had heard about Schuyler's aristocratic notions and contempt for simple New Englanders who consider themselves the equals of everybody—even of God and General Washington—we had no difficulty in seeing him. Sick of our inactivity, we had hovered near his tent from the moment we learned whose it was, hoping someone would ask our business. For a time, seemingly, we were taken for farmers or even—which would not have been surprising, considering our peculiar garb—for horse-traders or gipsies. At length, therefore, I spoke to the sentry outside the tent, and spoke softly, so not to disturb anyone. "I'd like to see the general," I said. "I've been a scout under General Arnold, and——"

The sentry slapped the butt of his musket and bawled, "Scout for General Arnold!"

"Hi!" Doc protested. "What you want to do? Get us throwed out of camp?"

One of the aides thrust his head from the tent entrance, glared at me, and said, "Come in here!"

We went in. General Schuyler was writing a letter. He didn't even look at us. In a dreamy voice he said to one of the aides, "How can he be a scout for General Arnold when all Arnold's scouts have been transferred to other commands? Ask him, Varick."

"That was last year, sir," I said. "It was before the Indians took us that we were scouts."

Schuyler looked up at me. His eyes tilted upward at the outer corners, and his lips seemed on the point of puckering, as if to whistle thoughtfully. "Indians?" he asked in a courteous voice. "What Indians took you, and where?"

I told him the barest outline of our captivity. He stared from me to Doc as my tale progressed. "Just a moment!" he said, at one point. "You say you saw St. Leger's force. How many Indians were with him?"

"Eight hundred," I said.

Doc coughed deprecatingly. "And a lousy lot they were! You give me the proper medical supplies, General, and I bet I could scare all eight hundred of 'em so they'd run three times around Lake Superior without stopping."

"No doubt," Schuyler said dryly. "No doubt." To me he added: "This is a remarkable story you tell me. Have you any documents to corroborate it?"

"Documents!" Doc exclaimed. "Them Sacs and Foxes ain't noted for writing documents much, General. We was lucky to get away with our pants and a layer of paint. We ain't even seen anything that looked like a document since Valcour Island."

I unbuttoned my shirt and silently offered, for the general's inspection, the tattooed eagle on my chest. To Doc I said, "Show him yours."

Protesting modestly, Doc pulled up his shirt and then, abruptly brazen, thrust his naked breastbone almost against Schuyler's long nose. "Old Shaman Means and his favorite pet rooster, General," he said. "I don't give everyone a view of him free of charge."

"There, there!" Schuyler exclaimed testily. "That's enough!" He waved Doc away and sat contemplating us for a moment or two. Then he moved suddenly in his camp chair, as if irritated. "You've earned a rest," he said, "but you can't have it. I can't spare a man from here, so if you're expecting to join General Arnold, I can't offer you much encouragement." He looked at me haughtily, as though ready for a protest. I think he thought that because I was a New Englander, I might make difficulties about serving under him, as did so many of our New Englanders—especially the militiamen.

"General," Doc said, "we're almost rested to death."

"There's several things I can put you to doing," Schuyler said. "I'm sending men out to locate St. Clair, and there's messages to be carried up the Mohawk."

The thought of being sent away to a place where I could do nothing to save Nathaniel from the consequences of his folly—where I could take no steps to help him in case, by some miracle, the opportunity arose —was dismaying.

"Sir," I said, "I had a look at the British at Valcour. I believe I've got the feel of 'em, somehow. I used to think they were something extra special as soldiers—something that only silver bullets would stop; but now I know they're no different from anyone. In view of that, General, I believe I'd be more valuable here than carrying messages to a place where I'd never see a Britisher. I'd like another chance at 'em, General, and I think I'm entitled to it."

Schuyler looked at me, and I felt uncomfortable. He must, I thought, see through these noble sentiments of mine—must somehow sense that selfishness lay beneath them, as it does beneath most windy utterances.

His lips took on that puckery look. "Another chance at 'em? What did you have in mind? Popping at 'em from behind trees?"

"No sir," I said. "There's pines on both sides of Wood Creek—as big pines as ever I saw. There isn't one of 'em that wouldn't make a mainmast for a 74-gun ship. Give me some men and some axes, General, and I'll lay those pines across the creek and across the road so thick that——"

Schuyler stopped me with an upraised hand. "Don't bother to explain. I can see you got your training under General Arnold. When I next see him, I'll tell him you learned your lesson well." He reached for a sheet of paper. "What do you need besides axes?"

"There ain't nothing we don't need," Doc said. "Personally, I ain't had any pay since last September, and if I could get me a little on account, and an axe and a musket and a pair of dice, and maybe a blanket and a kettle, I guess prob'ly I wouldn't need much of anything else."

The general glanced up at him briefly, at which Doc looked apologetic. I saw that Schuyler considered Doc too old for an axe-man, and so said quickly that he was not only a good scout, but lucky, and that if I couldn't have him with me, I'd consider it unfortunate.

Schuyler handed me the orders, which authorized us to draw felling-axes, muskets, powder, shot, hats, shoes, shirts—which classified us, also, as scouts acting under instructions from the commanding general.

"Listen to this, now," Schuyler said. "There are two roads to Fort Ann. Go up the northern road. Go to every farm on it. Tell 'em to drive off their cattle, burn their standing crops: destroy, hide or remove all food. You'll find Tories among 'em. The country's full of Tories! Tell 'em that to give aid or comfort to the enemy will be treason to the United States.

"When you've done that, circle around to Fort Ann. Get as close to it as possible: then do whatever you can to make the road and the creek impassable. By the time you get there, I trust you'll find other of our detachments at work. Work with 'em. Work under the commanding officer in charge of the detachments. I want that country wrecked! I want it torn to pieces, so there'll be no nourishment in it except for mosquitoes and squirrels."

Doc Means cackled gaily.

"What are you laughing at, sir?" Schuyler demanded.

"Well, General," Doc said, "it looked for a while as if this was a pretty sick war we'd took so much trouble to get back to, so it's a relief to see it sitting up and taking nourishment."

Schuyler looked complacent, then said to me, "There's one message you're to learn by heart. Give it to all those who need it, with my compliments. Tell 'em this: 'Keep up your spirits, show no signs of fear, act with vigor; and you will not only secure your country but gain immortal honor.'" I repeated it; and as I did so, I thought, ironically, that Nathaniel would consider his own conduct to be guided by this very advice, just as surely as Schuyler would think otherwise.

"General," I said, "there was one thing I forgot to mention. When we passed St. Leger's scouts on the St. Lawrence, they shouted after us that they'd see us soon in Albany."

Schuyler's lips again took on that puckery look. "Did they?" he asked. "I can only say that if you and the other axe-men can contrive to amuse Burgoyne for a sufficient length of time, his troops won't see Albany this campaign—not in the way they expect to see it!"

LIX

WE plodded back toward Fort Ann, this time going by the northern road, instead of the southern, by which we had come to Fort Edward, and the whole countryside seemed to me to weep at the near approach of war. Leaden clouds trailed through the towering tops of the pines, and we trudged through a downpour that softened the paddle-calluses on our hands. The road was a dun morass that clutched our sodden boots. Our clothes and blankets, water-soaked, dragged at our aching shoulders. Along that sparsely traveled track, the scattered farms would have been nothing to brag about, even beneath cloudless skies. In this steamy downpour the small log cabins, in clearings thick with stumps, were as dismal as the wretched folk they sheltered. I marveled, as we progressed from clearing to distant clearing, how it was that any living human being could sit supinely on his little square of dirt in blank indifference to an enemy that threatened death and destruction to him, his neighbors and his nation. Yet that was how too many of these farmers sat; and in addition they resented us, they and their wives and their mud-streaked children, when we pushed into their dark abodes, which smelled of earth, wet straw and sourness. Settler after settler was sullen and unresponsive when we delivered Schuyler's message—that the British were at Skenesboro and maybe at Fort Ann: that all cattle must be driven off; all standing crops burned; all food destroyed, hidden or removed.

As we splashed onward through the rain, I was filled with a sharp resentment that we should starve and sweat and agonize to save such folk as these; and at the same time I knew it was possible to argue that they were as deserving of help as my own brother, whom I was so bent on saving. Confused, I stopped thinking, as one so often must in time of war.

We left our message at every farm that touched the northern route to Fort Ann, slept in a cow-shed on a heap of straw, and early on the morning of July 10th found ourselves once more on that swampy, brook-intersected road that leads through the giant pines and the soft morasses of Wood Creek valley. The road was silent, empty of human life, but the muddy hummocks that rose, here and there, above the brown pools, were trampled, showing that many men had recently passed that way, all going toward Fort Edward. At frequent intervals, too, were signs and traces—a worthless shoe; a powder horn from which the cord had broken; a bayonet sticking in the spongy soil. These were the marks of a night march; for bayonets and powder horns, even broken ones, were too precious to be thus left, nor would they have been overlooked by troops marching by daylight. Since troops don't march by night unless of necessity, we concluded that the Americans must have retreated from Fort Ann.

We drew the loads from our muskets and reloaded, eight buck-shot to a load, not knowing what to expect. Then we went on through that damnable marsh, lurking behind trees to listen. The whole forest, save for the rushing of Wood Creek, swollen from the rains of the day before, was silent.

Doc, peering from behind a tree, hissed at me. "There's the sawmill, but there ain't no fort there: no fort at all!"

The fort had stood at the spot where Wood Creek grows too narrow for navigation in bateaux. We could smell the odor of wet, charred wood. The place had been burned. We were aware, too, of another odor—a foul, unpleasant stench.

"Look there!" Doc said softly. "What's that! It's red!"

I looked where he pointed, and saw a gray animal, like a furtive dog with weak hind legs, drift silently and for a fleeting moment from behind a bush. "Why," I said, "it's a wolf! There's no one hereabouts if that's a wolf!"

Then I saw what Doc had seen before I saw the wolf. Half sunk in the swamp beside the road was the body of an Englishman, a lieutenant, his scarlet coat darkened by the water to the color of blood, his white breeches tinged with pink. The wolf had been at him.

The sight of this boy, four thousand miles from his home and family, face-down in the dark water of a blood-stained swamp, food for a wolf, filled me with a vague wonderment that any man could of his own free will embark in a war except in defense of his home, or in support of principles that to him seemed vital.

"There's another," Doc said, "and another!"

I began to see bodies, then. They wore the leather breeches and rough shirts of American milita. Here and there among them were patches of scarlet—the scarlet coats of British infantrymen. They had not been long dead; but they smelled horribly; for hot weather and swarms of flies had worked upon them quickly.

"We ought to bury 'em," Doc said.

"We haven't time," I told him. "They'll be gone in a few days, anyway, what with the heat and the wolves. We've got ourselves to look out for, to say nothing of those at Fort Edward. Probably the British went back to Skenesboro for provisions and ammunition; but they might advance again, any minute."

The charred timbers of Fort Ann stood in the narrowest part of the valley. "Here's the place to start," I whispered to Doc. "There's a score of trees yonder, on the far side of the creek, that'll reach all the way across the stream, when they're felled. We'll lay down a fence, right here: five trees across the creek and a dozen criss-crossed over the road, with their tops locked together. Then if the British come back, they'll make such a noise getting past the barricade that we'll be able to slip away."

"What if they use Injuns?"

"That's a chance we've got to take," I said.

We picked out a tree that could be dropped across the road beside the creek, peeled off most of our clothes, sharpened our axes and went to work. It wasn't much of a tree, and in three minutes we dumped it where we wanted it. We moved back twenty feet and dropped two more, felling them so they lay across the first tree, at right angles to it. Their tops completely filled the road. We moved up the hillslope and cut into a tall pine, three feet in diameter at the height of my shoulder. When it came smashing down, its top reached to the bank of Wood Creek. The bulk of its branches lay jammed into the first three trees we had cut, forming a tangle through which a rabbit couldn't have passed. Its heavy trunk extended up the slope. No single wall, built by human hands, could have barred us more effectively from those who might approach by land from the direction of Skenesboro.

We listened for sounds from the far side of our abatis, but heard nothing, only the brawling and muttering of the creek and the furry stirring of the breeze in the high pines.

"Come on," Doc said. "Let's chop down something that's got some size to it before we get chilled."

We dropped a medium-sized pine so that it spanned the creek, giving us a foot-bridge on which we crossed. Opposite the barricade we had first made stood a tree that may have been five feet in thickness at its base. It was a beautiful tree, without a blemish. I could almost have got a schooner from it; or a whole house; or wainscoting fit for a king's palace. Doc took one side of it and I the other. At the end of a few minutes I felt it sigh and shiver, as does any big tree when an axe has reached its heart. Doc took our muskets and moved upstream, while I finished the job. The tree came down with a walloping, splintering crash. It seemed endless, lying there, its top on the far side of the creek, wedged among the bristling tops of those we had first felled.

The result seemed unsatisfactory to Doc. "It looks kind of fragile," he complained. "If we set out to block that creek, let's block it right!" He clambered to a cliff that overlooked the stream, thrust a stout sapling beneath a boulder, and heaved mightily. The boulder came down amid a shower of dirt and stones, and plunged in the creek with a sudden clatter. "Hi-yi!" Doc shouted. "There's something they was never taught how to cope with in St. James's Park! Let 'em write home and ask the London Humane Society how to get rid of *that!*"

His outcries suddenly ceased. When I looked around to see what ailed him, he was crouched behind a rock, his musket cocked. I moved behind a tree myself.

Doc spoke querulously to someone on the far side of the creek. "If you're an American, come out in the open. If you ain't, look out behind you. We got you surrounded."

Across the creek a boy rose from behind a boulder. He may have been fourteen years old. He wore homespun breeches twice too large for him, and a torn brown shirt big enough to be an overcoat. His musket was at the ready, as if he expected a partridge to leap up before him.

"You're a liar," he said loudly. "There ain't nobody behind me. I looked there fust off, soon's I heard your axes."

"You a scout?" Doc asked mildly.

"Yes, I be!"

"Don't go pointing that musket at us, then," Doc warned. "If we wasn't friends of yours, we wouldn't be cutting down trees, would we? Who you scouting for?"

"General Fellows. Schuyler sent him up here with eighty of us Berkshire men to chop down trees." He picked up an axe from where he had been crouching and turned from us to signal largely toward someone unseen by us. "Come on, General!" he bawled. "There ain't nobody here, only a couple of fellers chopping for fun!"

Doc made a sound of disgust. "Look at that! Just when we was working up a little sweat, along comes a general to pick out all the good trees for himself!"

When Fellows came up with us, however, he proved to be one of those rare militia officers who go anywhere, do anything, and sit up all night and every night if necessary in order to carry out orders. Like his militiamen, he wore homespun, and there was nothing military about him except his sword, which hung from a hairy leather harness that must have required the skins of two cows for the making. When we placed ourselves under his command, told him what we had done and showed him the tree we had felled across the creek, he said,

"Quite a tree, ain't it!" Unlike most of our officers, he was grateful for suggestions, and seemed to be more interested in stopping the British than in his own importance, which was a pleasant surprise.

When we showed him how easily boulders could be levered into the stream, and how it was possible to distribute the water of the swamps by cutting trenches through the sides of the waterways that had made beds for themselves, he set a detachment to cutting trenches and another detachment to prying boulders from the bank. Wherever there was a bridge, he had his men break it to pieces and carry the pieces to the rear. He stationed us in squads across Wood Creek valley, each squad in command of a head axe-man, who marked the trees to be felled, drove pegs in the ground to show where each tree should be laid, and warned the near-by choppers when a tree sighed and tottered, ready to fall. He put me in charge of one of these squads, and never did I see men fell trees with greater expedition—perhaps because of the manner in which Doc looked apprehensively over his shoulder from time to time, each time asking, in a trembling voice, "Any sign of 'em, Cap'n Peter?"

The whole forest echoed to the irregular, unending chocking of the axes, the recurrent warning howls of "Mark! Mark!" as a tree began to topple, and the rumbling crashes as they hurtled down to wedge their branches tight against those which had already fallen.

Slowly we left the ruins of Fort Ann behind us. From bank to bank the creek was so thickly spanned by fallen trunks that it seemed impossible the British could ever clear them sufficiently to force their way through. The road was laced and jammed with criss-crossed trees. The little brooks, stripped of their bridges, were turned from their courses by the tree trunks that lay across them. The place was a bedevilment of nature, a dismal and unholy chaos.

When night came, we made fires from the uprooted bridges, so that by their light a part of us might go on chopping. But for the danger of crushing men beneath the trunks in the darkness, everyone would have chopped. We slept in shifts, conscious even in our sleep of the bite of axe-blades into wood; of the rending smash of tumbling timber.

All through the 11th of July we chopped and chopped, and pried boulders into Wood Creek, and destroyed bridges.

We worked all through the night as well, and through sickening heat on the morning of the 12th.

Hell, I am sure, can be no worse than that valley of Wood Creek. My hands were raw and blistered: my wrists and knees a mass of sores from the unending rubbing of damp cloth against my salty body: my mind a turmoil from my perpetual brooding over Nathaniel and Ellen.

Sweat stung my eyes, itching and smarting when it trickled over the countless small injuries that such toil invites. The air was alive with mosquitoes and infinitesimal insects whose bites were white-hot stabs.

At noon on the 12th, General Fellows, surveying our labors, grunted with satisfaction. "How many bridges do you figure the British would have to build in the last two miles?" he asked me. He added, "Provided they're able to clear the road."

"Only one," I said.

"One!" he protested. "One! You must have taken out ten bridges yourself!"

"Yes sir, but there's so many trenches been dug that there's no dry land for bridge-heads. The only way the British can ever transport supplies and artillery across that two miles of swamp is to build one bridge —a bridge two miles long!"

He beamed at me, a sour, reluctant Berkshire grin. "That'll please General Schuyler! I'll have to send him word." He stared me up and down. My unshaven chin, my red and hollow eyes, my insect-bitten face and neck, caked with the blood from countless punctures, my scabbed and swollen hands and wrists, seemed to give him satisfaction. "I'll send you," he added. "We need more men out here, and when he sees you, he'll know it's the truth. We ought to have another five hundred, if this road's to be properly blocked. Do you want me to write him a letter? You can tell him what we've done, can't you, and what we need?"

I said I could, adding that I would like to take Doc with me, as my orders from Schuyler included him.

Fellows glanced at him briefly, and seemed unimpressed. Doc wavered as if with weakness. "Take him along," Fellows said readily. In a kind voice he added to Doc, "A man your age ought to stay with regular troops, where he can get medical attention in case he needs it."

"Medical attention?" Doc whispered; then turned his eyes toward heaven with the air of a man who asks the gods to listen.

. . . Fort Edward, when we returned, was in an even greater turmoil than when we had left it three days before. The place was twice as populous, and the fields around the fort were sprinkled with soldiers so tattered and so slovenly that they had the look of mendicants. Among them were families camping beneath overturned carts or in bough huts.

The families were those of farmers from the scattered clearings to the northward. As to the identity of the haggard troops who sat lethargically around us, hunting in their garments for vermin or repairing the ravages of a weary march, we were not long left in doubt.

Just outside the entrance to the fort stood a spellbound group of militiamen; and as we drew near, we heard a bawling voice, familiarly hoarse, addressing them.

"Those Germans," bellowed the voice, "they're about the size of a haystack, only shaped more like lemons. You got to watch 'em for as much as five minutes to see whether they're alive or not. They got boots that'll hold as much as eight gallons apiece and hats like a leather fire bucket. They got coats made out of felt, so when you fire a bullet at 'em it sounds like hitting a feather bed with a axe-helve; and they hang things all over themselves, thicker'n what you see on a tin-ped-dler's cart. When they're moving real fast, they scoot along as much as a mile every day or so. If them Germans was all fifteen years old and started today to walk from here to Albany, they'd have married grandchildren before they got there! Up at Hubbardton I see one of 'em start to brush a caterpillar out of his hair, but before he touched it, it had a cocoon and then come out and flew around—an awful pretty yellow butterfly! What I mean, them Germans is kind of slow! I'd 'a' tooken one of 'em and brought him along, only I didn't have no am-munition wagon with me, and he'd 'a' been an all-fired nuisance to manage unless you mounted him on wheels like a cannon. The next time I see one——"

The bawler's eye caught mine. It was Cap Huff. He broke off and came pushing toward us through the crowd.

"For God's sake, where you been?" he demanded. "I been standing here watching for you, ever since we got in with St. Clair this morning. If you got any business to do, hurry up and get it out of the way and then come over to my lean-to under the southwest corner of the fort. Stevie's there, and hereafter you work for I and Stevie!"

LX

Wᴴᴇᴛʜᴇʀ Cap Huff had told the truth about the British army's German allies, I didn't know; but contrary to my expectations, he had told it about my own situation in the army. When I reported my news to General Schuyler, I thought I had never seen a man more cheerful or more confident. "A two-mile bridge!" he exclaimed. "Why, they can't build that in less than a week, not even after they've cleared away the obstructions! After all, they might be going to give us time to raise an army big enough to stop 'em!" He puckered his lips and wrinkled his eyes in high good humor, adding that he'd send five hundred men with felling-axes, under General Nixon, to join General Fellows: then, as an afterthought, told me I needn't return to Fort Ann. "We've just had word," he said, "that General Arnold's on his way to join us. He'll need scouts as soon as he gets here, and you're to be among 'em. Until he arrives, take your instructions from Captain Nason."

He dismissed me; and I, encouraged by his optimism as well as by the knowledge that at last I had friends to whom to turn, hurried to the south corner of the fort's grass-grown embankments.

I came suddenly on Tom Bickford, crouched over a slab of curly maple, carving from it a new stock for his musket, and saw beyond him other familiar figures.

Tom, hearing my step, darted a quick, hard look at me—a look in which I saw none of the gentleness that had first drawn me to him. Then he leaped up to clap me on the shoulders. When the others joined us, their faces looked hard and forbidding, as had Tom's. It was a hardness that must, I thought, have come from the trials they had borne. They were a staunch lot—Steven Nason, a half-drawn map in his hand; Joseph Phipps, a trim figure in a green hunting frock; Cap Huff, swinging an eighteen-inch trout fresh from the Hudson; Natanis, respectfully studying the eagle tattooed on Doc Means's chest. The sight of these old friends of mine, all together, was a sharp reminder that Nathaniel ought to be among them; and to conceal my feelings I coughed harshly and said to Tom, "Well, I see you broke your musket."

Tom dropped his hand from my shoulder and glanced at his musket, as if surprised to see it there. "Yes, Cap'n Peter. I broke it on a Britisher up at Hubbardton. We ain't hardly had a minute to call our own since then—not till today." In a hesitant voice he added, "We heard about Nathaniel. Cap told us. He can't be right in his head, Cap'n Peter."

"No." I said. I forced myself to meet the gaze of each one of those who stood before me. Their faces, I suddenly saw, had nothing hard about them. They were no different than they ever had been, and the eyes fixed on mine were both shrewd and troubled.

"That's what I told 'em," Doc said. "Your brother's sick. Anybody's sick if he's in love. He falls in love because he's sick, and just being in love makes him sicker."

"Well," Nason said, "let's get straightened out." He glanced suspiciously at the crumbling ramparts above us: then moved out into the grassy meadow between the ramparts and the river. He sat on the warm turf, motioning me to sit beside him. Tom Bickford came too, with his block of curly maple, and Cap with his trout, which he disemboweled neatly with an expert thumb. The others sat in such a way that no one could approach us unseen.

"Well," Nason said again, "we're mighty glad to have you back. We thought you were dead. I guess you're lucky to be alive."

"Yes," I said, "I am. So are you. We were close to the brink, all of us. You and Cap and Tom and—and Nathaniel."

"Yes, I'm coming to that. I know all about it. Cap told me. He told me who your brother got acquainted with. I used to know that woman."

"Yes, I know you did."

"Yes," Nason repeated, "I used to know her."

"She's a bad woman," I said.

"I guess she is. Yes, I guess she is." He spoke, I thought, without much conviction and his questions began to seem irrelevant.

"How long have you been here?"

"We got here the 7th of July. Then we went back to Fort Ann to chop trees."

"What have the men been saying about St. Clair and Schuyler?"

"Why, the usual things. Some talked about how St. Clair must have been pretty scared of the British if he went so far around 'em that nobody, including himself, knew what had become of him; and you hear a good many say we'll never get any food up here till Schuyler hangs a couple of commissaries."

"Listen," Nason whispered. "Haven't you heard about the silver bullets?"

"Silver bullets? What silver bullets?"

Nason moodily contemplated his stockings, caught together in a dozen places with shoemaker's thread. "You ought to keep your ears

open," he said heavily. Then he went off on another tangent. "Probably
you heard a few things about Arnold last year."

"Yes," I admitted. "I did."

"Yes," Nason said. "We all heard 'em—how he was a horse-jockey
and a cheap gymnast: how he stole the communion cups from Montreal——"

"And the baby's rattles," Cap Huff interrupted, "and all the handles
off the front doors!"

"That's not far wrong," Nason said. "You heard those stories, didn't
you?"

Heard them? Indeed I had, and from Nathaniel! I nodded, almost
afraid to speak.

"It's a funny thing," Nason said thoughtfully, "that those stories
weren't told about everyone. You never heard 'em about Gates, any
more than you did about Wooster or Wayne or the other officers in
charge up here. You only heard 'em about the one officer who could
have taken Canada from the English if he'd had a free hand: about the
one officer who had the brains and the ability to keep Burgoyne from
breaking through last year and putting an end to our rebellion. I'll say
this about those stories, too. They kept Arnold in hot water for over a
year, and they've put him where the British don't need to worry about
him any more. Yes sir! Those stories reached Congress, and Congress
wouldn't promote him. There's so many officers ahead of him, now,
that he'll probably never have a chance to plan another campaign
against the British!"

Cap Huff slapped his trout and spoke obscenely of Congress.

Nason lowered his voice. "Now listen to this. Arnold's out of the way,
or so the British think. They don't need to worry about Arnold any
more. But they've got somebody else to worry about. They've got Schuyler to worry about. Yes, and St. Clair."

"Tit-head!" Cap ejaculated.

"Keep your mouth shut!" Nason said. "Let me hear another word
like that out of you and I'll cram that fish down your gullet, bones and
all!"

"I'd better tell you now, while I remember it," I said. "St. Clair and
Wilkinson hate Arnold like poison. Wilkinson tried to tell me Arnold
abandoned his wounded on the *Congress* galley: let 'em burn to death!
If that's what he's saying, St. Clair's saying it too. When Wilkinson said
it to me, I denied it; and if you want to know what I think, I think I was
kept from a command on the vessels during the retreat from Ticonderoga on that account—kept from a command because I wouldn't hear
Arnold lied about."

"Now wait a minute!" Nason said. "What they think about Arnold makes no difference to me."

"It does to me," I said. "Take Wilkinson: if you don't know who his friends are, you can't steer clear of 'em."

"Let me tell you this," Nason said. "St. Clair didn't have enough men to make a fight at Ticonderoga. He'd known it for weeks. If he'd stayed there and tried to fight, he'd have lost his entire army. The only reason we've got a decent force here at Fort Edward today is because St. Clair retreated instead of trying to fight."

"He'd known it for weeks, had he?"

"Yes, for weeks!"

"In that case, why didn't he retreat three days earlier, and save his guns and ammunition and supplies, instead of leaving 'em at Ticonderoga and letting the British get 'em? Why did he wait until the last second, so the British were within an inch of wiping us out?"

"Within an inch!" Cap bawled. "My good God! They wasn't more than a sixteenth of an inch from me at Hubbardton! There was one of them fellers in a red coat that had his bayonet so close to my breeches that it kept pulling out the threads!" He drew from his pocket a silver watch somewhat like a summer squash in size and shape. He held it to his ear and shook it. It gave out a rattling sound. He showed it to me. "That was his. He kind of fell on it, and I guess maybe he broke something in it."

"Look here," Nason protested, "this is no time for arguments. St. Clair brought us here safely——"

"He brought *some* of us here safely," Cap growled. "He didn't bring Colonel Francis here safely. He's dead, and his regiment's wiped out, on account of that poss-pitted General Poor not being willing to go to his support. He didn't bring the Second New Hampshire here safely. Colonel Hale surrendered the whole damned regiment to a couple of Englishmen that had lost their way and was thinking of heading for Boston so to find out where they were. And how about those Massachusetts militia regiments? The way they was running when I last see 'em, they're all dead of heartburn by now."

"We're here and we're safe," Nason insisted, "and St. Clair got us here. This army, from present indications, will be commanded by Schuyler and St. Clair when it fights; and in spite of what you say about St. Clair, he's an able general. As for Schuyler——"

"As for Schuyler," I said, "he's a Godsend. We'd never have built the fleet last year except for Schuyler; and he's the only general I've ever seen, barring Arnold, that gives me any confidence."

"That's about right," Nason said. "Next to Arnold, Schuyler and St.

Clair are the officers best qualified to stop Burgoyne." He leaned forward and tapped my knee. "And no sooner did we get here than troopers began to sidle up and ask us about the silver bullets—about Schuyler and St. Clair and the silver bullets! You say you haven't heard how Schuyler gets his silver bullets?"

"Why," I said, "Schuyler hasn't even had enough lead bullets to go 'round, and he couldn't have got those for us if he hadn't made the Albany people rip the leaded panes out of their windows and melt up the leads."

"No," Nason said. "You haven't heard the news. He's got silver bullets. When the British came up to Ticonderoga, they loaded their guns with silver bullets and shot 'em into the fort. Then those in the fort got up early in the morning and picked up the bullets and took 'em to St. Clair, and St. Clair sent 'em to Schuyler, and Schuyler melted 'em up and turned 'em into hard money."

"Well, for God's sake! Were all of us supposed to pick up silver bullets?"

"The whole damned kit and caboodle of us!" Cap bellowed. In a mincing tone he added, "We played games while we picked 'em up. The ones what picked up the most silver bullets got pink ribbons to wear in their hair; and the feller what picked up the mostest most, they give him a peppermint to put in his tea!"

"It's no laughing matter," Nason said. "It's supposed to be gospel truth!"

"But what in God's name were the silver bullets supposed to be?"

Nason was exasperated at my density. "Bribes! Bribes! The British were bribing Schuyler and St. Clair with silver bullets to get out of the fort!"

"That's too ridiculous to talk about," I protested.

Nason shook his head. "No: they believe it. People believe anything about a man—anything that shows he hasn't behaved himself about money, women or rum."

"Not people with any sense."

"People don't have any sense," Nason insisted. "Listen to any of 'em talk! There isn't one man in a thousand that doesn't talk himself black in the face about subjects he's completely ignorant of; and the most senseless of the lot, nine times out of ten, are folks that claim to be educated."

"By God," Cap shouted, "you never said a truer word! Ain't people the damnedest?"

"Now listen," Nason said. "That's the story that's going around about Schuyler and St. Clair. They took silver from the British: therefore they're not fit to command our troops. They're traitors and thieves. The sooner we get rid of 'em, the better. That's the story. Does that remind you of anything? Did you ever hear anything vaguely like that about anyone else?"

"Certainly," I said. "It's like the stories that went around about Arnold."

"*Like* 'em? Oh no! It's the same damned thing. And it's the twin of another story that came pretty close to doing us a terrible lot of harm. For all we know, it *did* do us a lot of harm. It may have delayed us just long enough to keep us from taking Quebec!"

He turned and looked at Natanis, placing his hand affectionately on the red man's knee. "This friend of ours," Nason said, "is faithful and brave. He's been my friend since he was a young man. In the whole Province of Maine there isn't a man who knows the trails and the streams and the mountain passes as does Natanis: no man who could guide an army to Quebec so quickly and surely. Yet two years ago, when we set out for Quebec under Arnold—who was a colonel then there were letters sent to Washington and to Arnold, and the letters said that this good friend, this best of guides, was a spy and a traitor. They said he'd taken British gold in payment for his services."

He leaned back in the warm grass, plucked a blade and nibbled reflectively at its tender lower end. "There you are—the same old story. Natanis was the one man who had the brains and ability to guide us to Quebec—but it was only by the grace of God that our own men didn't shoot him. If they *had*, we'd have left our bones in the swamps of Lake Megantic."

"That's right," Cap said. "I went thirty days without a drink of rum, as it was! Yes sir: I was wasted away till you had to look at me twice to see me."

"Now then," Nason said, "all these things fit together. We found out, in Quebec, who it was that wrote the letters about Natanis. It was a man who said he was—a man who claimed to be——"

"It was a fox-faced French bastard named Guerlac," Cap said suddenly. "He lived with this Marie de Sabrevois, just the way I told you up at Skenesboro. We killed Guerlac, and we'd ought to killed Marie." He eyed Nason defiantly. "It stands to reason that if a woman's satisfied to live with a bad feller, she's as bad as he is, and usually a hell of a lot worse."

"You talk too much," Nason said. He turned to me. "Guerlac wrote the letters; but of course Marie knew all about them. There's no doubt that she made herself useful to Carleton in '75, and that she has kept on making herself useful ever since. She learned her lesson from the false information Guerlac sent out about Natanis, and if she's traveling with the British army, it's for no good purpose. I'll bet my last dollar it was she who sent out the false information about Arnold; that it's she who's been sending out the stories about Schuyler, St. Clair and the silver bullets." He looked at me sharply.

"Yes," I said, and I tried to keep my voice calm, "yes, I think you're right. I think I can almost prove you're right. I think I can prove it from what I've noticed about her myself, and from a trick she played on a certain friend of mine, and from several things Nathaniel let fall. I'm glad to be able to tell you what I picked up from Nathaniel, because it shows Nathaniel doesn't know what she's up to. If he'd had any hand in what she was doing, he'd never have told me the things he did. You can't condemn Nathaniel if you know Marie de Sabrevois."

There was an uncomfortable silence. It was Nason who broke it. "We're always glad to make allowances for our friends, but your brother——"

"Nathaniel's our friend!" I broke in. "He's not fighting against us, and he thinks he's going to be in a position to help us. He's misguided—he's made a mistake—he's in love. You've got to understand about Nathaniel —you've got to do it! He's done what every man in the world has done, and may do again tomorrow: he's made a mistake; and there isn't a man alive that hasn't, because of his own folly, hovered a score of times on the brink of disaster, and been saved an equal number of times by the merest chance."

"Yes," Nason said, "but your brother's with the British!"

I tried hard to remember exactly what Cap Huff had told me, long ago, about Nason and his one-time infatuation for Marie de Sabrevois. "Wait," I told him. "Wait! Nathaniel's not so much with the British as with the woman he loves. I'm glad it's you I'm talking to. You're a man of experience. You can understand what it must mean to be in love with a woman who's no better than she should be. You can understand, probably, how a woman like that can seem the most beautiful, the kindest and the most innocent woman in all the world. Probably you know that a man in love with such a woman won't allow a word to be said against her, no matter what she is. Probably you know she could have a dozen lovers; and still the deluded fool infatuated with her believes her incapable of looking at any man but himself."

Cap Huff coughed, a tremendous, racking, affected cough. Nason, his tanned face as red as a brick, eyed him morosely.

"That's the way of it with Nathaniel," I said. "He hasn't fought against us yet; and if I'm any judge of men, he never will. Yet it's not because he's afraid to fight, as you men here well know. You saw him try to take back the *Royal Savage* with Captain Hawley, and you saw him stand up to his guns on the *Congress* galley until a round shot came close to knocking him into eternity."

"Nobody could have fought better, Cap'n Peter," Tom Bickford said.

Nason made an impatient movement. "Then how in God's name can he——"

"I'll tell you how!" I interrupted. "He thinks we'll be beaten; and he thinks you told him the truth when you told him that if we *were* beaten, we'd all be hanged for rebels. That's what you told him. That's what everybody said before we went in the army. In lots of ways, Nathaniel's credulous. He believes what he's told, if he trusts the people that tell him. He trusted you, and believed you. Now he trusts Marie de Sabrevois and believes her. He's like most fine people that haven't had much experience of life—that haven't learned there's merit in bad men and a deal of rottenness in the good. She's told him we're already beaten. He thinks Burgoyne will march down this river"—I swung my arm toward the slowly rolling flood before us—"unopposed. He thinks there's nothing to stop the British from governing this country again. And when that time comes, he told me, he'd like to have our own people —our Arundel people—guided by honest men: not by riffraff."

Nason shook his head. "It's too far-fetched. It doesn't sound reasonable."

"It's the truth! It's the simple truth! Listen! You think Nathaniel's harmed our cause, perhaps. He hasn't! He's helped it! If it hadn't been for Nathaniel, we'd never have known Marie de Sabrevois was with the British: never have suspected what she was doing. Now we know. I know she's hoodwinked people right and left. She hoodwinked you: she had a hand in almost having Natanis shot for a spy: she sent advance information to Montgolfier in Canada—telling the size of the army Burgoyne was bringing, so to keep the Canadians true to English rule: she provided Easton and Brown and Hazen with lies for their attacks on Arnold, whom they hated. She sent an innocent girl, Joseph Phipps's sister, to Albany to get the names of the Albany Tories who could be used against us by the British. As sure as I'm alive, it was Marie de Sabrevois who got the false information through, even to Congress, that Burgoyne's army wasn't coming by way of Ticonderoga, but was going around by sea and join Howe in New York—and that's why Congress hadn't provided a garrison large enough to defend the place. And now, added to all this, is the story of the silver bullets. It fits into what we know of Marie de Sabrevois. That's *her* story! She sent it out!"

"I wouldn't be surprised," Nason admitted. "I guess she did."

"Then you can see," I said, "that in reality Nathaniel has done us a service! We'd never have suspected any of these things, except for Nathaniel; so it seems to me that in spite of his mistakes, you owe him something. It seems to me you at least owe it to him to think fairly of him."

My arguments, I knew, were specious: yet there was more than a little truth in them; and I hoped that Nason, being a friend, would recognize their truth and ignore their weaknesses.

He looked me in the eye. "You think your brother hasn't been a party to any of her schemes?"

"I know he hasn't! I *know* it! He's my brother. His face has come to be like a book to me. I can tell, at a glance, when his feelings are hurt: when he's disgusted: when he's interested: when he's amused: when he's lying. I questioned him about Easton and Brown: about the list of Albany Tories: about Marie's activities in behalf of the British. He knows nothing about them. Nothing! If he'd been lying, I'd have known it. He's just a man in love—just a fool—just a lovesick fool."

"Just the way Stevie used to be," Cap Huff growled. He shot an apprehensive glance at Nason when he said it, and I was grateful to him.

"Well," Nason said uncertainly, "well——" Then he shook his head. "If your brother's not helping her in her schemes, why should she keep him where he is?"

"I'll tell you why. She's keeping him as an anchor to windward—an anchor to help her claw off a lee shore, if she needs to."

Nason looked blank. "An anchor to windward?"

"Listen," I said. "Marie de Sabrevois is a smart woman. Like all smart women, she's going to look out for her future if she can. There's only one way in which a woman can insure her future, and that's by getting married. What'll be the future of Marie de Sabrevois if she stays forever with the British? The British know her now. There must be plenty who know of her relations with Guerlac—who know she went to England with Lanaudiere as his niece. Niece, for God's sake! What she is to Burgoyne is common knowledge. My brother's the only one who doesn't know. Even the sutlers know. Do you suppose she could ever find a Britisher who'd marry her? Never! And she's getting along in years. When a woman passes thirty, she can't afford to waste time—not where marrying is concerned. If she gets a chance, it's apt to be her last. In my judgment, she's planning to marry Nathaniel if she needs to, but she won't do it until the campaign's over. I think that's why she's keeping him near her! That's the answer, and I know it's the right one."

Nason stared at me. "What do you want me to do?"

"This," I said. "I want you to say nothing to anyone concerning his whereabouts. In spite of where he now is, he's one of us—one of our own people. For my sake, and his mother's sake, and the sake of the town we come from, I want you to keep quiet about him, so he won't be branded as a traitor!"

Nason's eyes moved slowly from Cap to Doc, and from Doc to the others.

Doc cleared his throat. "We all make mistakes."

Cap stroked his trout thoughtfully. "I ain't never made any yet, but there's times when I've been pretty close to it."

Nason stared out over the broad Hudson, and the little sandy islands that swam on it pinkly in the light of the setting sun. He seemed to think aloud, disconnected thoughts: "I got you into this—I know Marie: she's all you say she is—anybody that's caught in her schemes deserves to be helped, I guess—I was caught once, myself: when we marched to Quebec I was called a spy and a traitor, and put out of the army. I wouldn't have known what to do if my friends hadn't stood by me. I wouldn't want to see anyone else called a traitor because of her, if so be he isn't one." As an afterthought, he added, "And it wouldn't help me with Phoebe much."

He nodded at me soberly. I drew a deep breath. Friends, I realized, were better than anything the world had to offer: without friends a man was helpless—worse off, almost, than in his grave.

"We'll tell Arnold about Marie," Nason went on, "but about Nathaniel Merrill we'll say nothing. Understand? Nothing! If anybody asks you, tell him you saw Nathaniel fighting—and fighting well—at the Battle of Valcour Island. Say you saw him get hurt. That's all you *did* see. For all we know, he's dead. That's all you got to tell 'em—the truth!"

Cap Huff heaved himself to his knees, so that his words had a flavor of piety. "That's all I ever tell anybody—the truth; but I make it a rule not to tell nobody a mite more than he can stand!" He gestured so violently with his trout that its head came off.

"Look at that!" Doc Means said mildly. "You've wore out your fish! Now we got to catch another for Cap'n Peter's supper."

LXI

THE army to which Arnold returned was hungry, ragged, lousy and pocky, but it was nothing to what it became after Burgoyne's Indians broke through.

We sent Natanis down river to watch, so that the rest of us could do the necessary things—bathe and shave, and trim each other's hair; wash and air our blankets; clean our muskets and grease them; set new flints in the locks; sew up the rents in our clothes, and scrub the grime and sweat from our shirts and stockings. So, warned by Natanis, we were waiting outside Schuyler's tent half an hour after Arnold's arrival in camp, eagerly listening to the sharp tones of Arnold's voice and Schuyler's recurrent laughter. There was something about that voice of Arnold's that worked on our spirits like rum and filled us with restless elation.

When at length he emerged, a stocky figure tense and resilient beside the calmer Schuyler, his eye fell on us at once and he warmed our hearts with his smile. He gave Schuyler a little appreciative nod: then came close to us; and impressive he was in his major general's uniform. Those who say Arnold was a small man are misguided in the use of words. He wasn't tall, but he had the muscle, the nerve, the sturdiness, the endurance of a gaint.

"Well!" he said. "Well! Ready for trouble!" He wagged his head as if in complacent recollection of some brave adventure that he had shared separately with each one of us. To Schuyler he said, "I take this kindly, General! I'm not accustomed to such thoughtful treatment!"

"My friend," Schuyler said, "you may be sure of receiving whatever we have to give." He turned and went back into his marquee. Arnold frowned weightily—to cover his feelings, I suppose.

"The cat must have got your tongues!" he said, as if exasperated. "Not a word have I had out of any one of you! I thought you'd deserted me!" He gathered up the front of my hunting shirt in his hand, feeling its texture; then stood back a little and looked me up and down.

"I couldn't understand about you," he said. "I was positive you'd been captured, and thought you'd been sent back with the men from the

Washington galley, probably. When I wrote you at Arundel, and found you'd never come there, I couldn't believe it! What did you do? Spend the winter with the British?"

"No sir. The Indians carried us to the westward."

"Carried who?"

"Doc and Verrieul and me."

"What's happened to your brother?" Arnold asked at once. He was the sharpest, quickest man I ever knew. His mind worked like lightning, and somehow plunged straight to the heart of everything.

"I don't know what became of him, General. He was hurt, as you know; and when the Indians took us, they left him."

His eyes bored into mine. "They left him, did they? Was he badly hurt?"

"Yes sir. He was unconscious. Doc brought him to his senses, almost, but he slipped away again."

"Well," he said. "Well! And the Indians just left him lying there, did they?"

"Yes sir."

"And they didn't scalp him?"

I shook my head. I had made a mistake, I saw. When captives can't travel, Indians scalp them. They often waste food and powder and rum, but they never waste scalps.

"Well!" Arnold said again. His face was expressionless. He looked slowly from me to the others. "Where's Verrieul?"

"Dead. St. Clair's scouts shot him when we came across from the British lines."

Involuntarily I looked at Cap Huff. Arnold followed my gaze, then glanced at the sentries outside Schuyler's tent: at the militiamen and officers who had gathered silently to stare at him. He shrugged his shoulders. "All right! That's too bad: too bad! Fortunes of war! Fortunes of war! Come along to my tent, all of you. I want to put you to work!"

He turned and went swinging toward the opposite side of the fort. His limp was scarcely noticeable. He had a prowling sort of gait, his chin thrust forward and his arms swinging, almost as though he made his way up a bothersome hillslope.

His tent was an old one, of reddish sailcloth, but a Negro servant had made it neat and comfortable. Arnold had no aides with him. I think he had ridden lickety-split from Philadelphia, stopping for nothing, and bringing only his servant to ride his extra horse and cook his food.

"Now," he said, when he had slid into his camp chair, "sit yourselves down along that side-wall, and let's see where we are." He ordered his servant to stand guard outside. Then, as he unlocked his field-desk and opened it on the table before him, he flung questions at us until I was put in mind of a rainspout gushing water in a squall. He wanted to know everything: where the Indians had taken us; how many there were; how we had contrived to get away; what their leaders were like; what their country was like; what sort of goods they took in trade; who the traders were in the Indian country, and whether they had become wealthy through trading with the Indians. We had to tell him everything we had noticed about St. Leger's forces; and when Doc said, as he had to Schuyler, that St. Leger's Indians were a lousy lot, and that with the proper medical supplies he could scare them into running three times around Lake Superior, Arnold wanted to know all about it. He questioned us and questioned us upon the retreat from Ticonderoga —wanted to know the date when the British had first been seen on Mount Defiance; asked when we had got orders to move, and how the retreat had been conducted. He laughed sourly when I told him how slowly the vessels had moved down to Skenesboro; how nothing had been done to fortify the narrow bends in the lake; how I had been obliged to serve under Kidder, who had been a mate last year, when I captained the *Congress* galley.

"Yes," he said, "I know. All our enemies aren't under English colors. The bulk of 'em are closer than that! Much, much closer!"

In spite of Nason's dark looks, Cap burst into a profane account of the Battle of Hubbardton: how Warner had disobeyed orders and stopped six miles short of where he was supposed to stop; how Hale's regiment had run away and then surrendered; how Leonard's and Wells's Massachusetts militia regiments had cursed their officers, laughed at discipline, fled hell-bent from the British, and finally been sent home by St. Clair because the Continental troops were being infected by their licentious, disorderly behavior.

Arnold cut short Cap's violent ravings with a wave of his hand. "That's nothing! Nothing! Men are bound to get out of hand in a retreat, unless they're under proper discipline, and led by men who know their business—know how to give 'em confidence. As for militia, it's God's wonder they ever fight at all, when every last one of 'em's counting the days before he can go home." He grew suddenly irascible. "I'll say this for 'em, too: they've never failed me yet, which is more than I can say for some gentlemen who consider themselves vastly superior to militia—too superior to provide them with clothing, food or bullets!"

He was, I knew, referring to Congress, but Cap breathed heavily beneath Arnold's sharp glance. "General," he said defensively, "I ain't been any place where I could pick up enough food to provide for all these militia around here. I can't even get nothing for myself, General!"

Arnold cocked a quizzical eye at Nason and resumed his questioning of us. I had heard it said that no officer in our armies kept himself so well informed concerning the enemy as Arnold. I understood, now, why this was so; for he thought of fifty questions to ask in the length of time any other officer would be thinking of one. He pried and pried into our brains, fishing out things we ourselves had forgotten we knew. Above all else, he was possessed to know how many there were of everything: how many Germans with Burgoyne; how many Canadians, how many Indians, how many sutlers, how many women; how many ox carts, how many other carts; how many trees we had felled on Wood Creek; how many bridges we had destroyed.

When he had pumped us dry, he looked at the notes he had made during our talk and tucked them in a slot on his field-desk. "That means hard work," he said. "Hard work. According to present count, General Schuyler tells me, Burgoyne has seven thousand men, and we've got four thousand. Nearly three thousand of those are Continentals. They've got us outnumbered pretty nearly two to one, but if you'll keep close watch on 'em, so they don't surprise us, we'll contrive to lead 'em into a trap somewhere."

Cap, who had been squirming, suddenly bawled: "Tell the general the one about the silver bullets, Stevie."

The general looked at him in surprise; then turned questioningly to Nason, who told him briefly the same tale he had told us.

Arnold glared at us. "By God, I'd like to catch the man that starts such stories!" He banged shut his field-desk, ran a finger around the inside of his black stock, and showed his teeth in a mirthless grin. "Well," he said, "we've got more important things to consider at the moment!"

Nason cleared his throat. "We thought, General, that the stories about General Schuyler are like the ones that Easton and Brown spread about you."

"Of course they are!" Arnold cried. "Of course they are! Do you know what happened about Brown's charges? They spread so far I had to have 'em investigated by the Board of War. The Board found my character had been cruelly and groundlessly aspersed; but a lot of good *that* did me!"

"But these stories about Schuyler——" Nason ventured.

Arnold slapped his table. "They're identical! But you can't stop to resent insults, not with Burgoyne twenty miles away." He looked sourly amused. "Why, see here! I had to resign from this army a week ago, because Congress refused either to give me my proper rank or settle my accounts. They cleared me of Brown's charges, and still they believed 'em! They've let me be twice wounded, and spend the greater part of my savings buying food and supplies for the soldiers they couldn't feed themselves: now they laugh at me: ignore my accounts and tell me to serve under those I commanded a few weeks ago. They disgraced me in my friends' eyes and the army's eyes! They left me no choice! I *had* to resign!"

I felt hot resentment that a patriotic officer could be treated so.

"Well," Arnold said carelessly, "that was before I heard about Ticonderoga. When I heard about that, and General Washington asked Congress to send me up here, I withdrew my request to resign. I'll serve under St. Clair: I'll serve under anyone, I'll do anything—anything!—to make myself useful: to prevent this country from being destroyed by Burgoyne or anyone else!"

He stuck out his under lip and gave us a truculent nod, the nod of a fighter. I am, I hope, not one to be stirred to sudden blazing enthusiasms, like a schoolgirl; and I think today what I thought then: that no more generous and magnanimous act had ever been performed or ever will be performed by any soldier so flouted and insulted.

"General," Nason persisted, "those stories about Schuyler are dangerous. They're spreading all over the place. If they're not stopped, they may do a lot of harm."

"Stopped!" Arnold cried. "They can't be stopped, any more than this damned rain that you get every day can be stopped!"

"General," I said, "we think all these stories come from a woman. We think they're sent into this camp by a woman on the outside."

"What woman?"

"Marie de Sabrevois."

"Oh *that* one!" Arnold said. "Nason's old friend, eh? Where is she?"

"She's with the British. She's with Burgoyne—close to Burgoyne."

"How do you know?"

I had expected this question, and was ready with an answer. "Because of Joseph Phipps," I said, and told him of Joseph's relationship to Marie de Sabrevois. He listened, darting quick glances not only at me but at all of us. His eyes were hard and blue.

"That's all very well," he said, "but what makes you think she's sending out stories about Schuyler?"

Nason spoke up. "Because she once had a hand in sending them out about Natanis."

"What other reason?" Arnold demanded.

"It seems to me," Nason said, "that's reason enough."

Arnold shook his head. "Oh, perhaps it is," Arnold said. "Perhaps this lady *does* propagate lies with the British. No doubt other hired spies do the same. That's to be expected. The harm's done by the jealousy and credulity that make such stories believed—aye, and repeated, with more dirt added to 'em. I've come to believe that jealousy's the motive that accounts for almost everything that's bad and wrong. No human being, I do believe, can achieve any unusual success—display any marked ability—without being attacked by jealous people. Nearly every man, after he passes his thirtieth year, is sour with jealousy. The world's full of nincompoops that want to pull all mankind down to their level. They hate prominence, on general principles. Let them hear a man's name repeated more than a dozen times, and they hate him without knowing why. They magnify his faults out of all recognition; and if he hasn't any, they invent 'em for him. Easton and Brown hated me, and so did Hazen, but they started by being jealous of me. General Schuyler's case can't be much different. There's plenty of men sweating with jealousy of Schuyler's money and position—who think he shouldn't have both; and so they'd like to snatch his position for themselves. Therefore, they circulate absurd stories about him. Jealousy's a terrible power in the world. It's all much simpler than you think."

There was a faint mocking smile on Arnold's lips.

"General," I said, "I don't quite follow you. Was it because of jealousy that information was sent to you that Natanis was a spy? Who would be jealous of Natanis? Was it jealousy that gave rise to the story that the British weren't going to attack by way of Ticonderoga, but would sail to New York from Quebec?"

"Something very like it," Arnold said carelessly.

I saw, then, that there was no way out of it. If he was to be told the full story of Marie de Sabrevois's activities, I could no longer keep silent about Nathaniel. Arnold had sacrificed his private affairs for the general good; and I had no choice but to do the same.

"I'd hoped not to be obliged to mention it," I said, "but I've got to take the risk——"

"I'm glad you've decided to trust me," Arnold said. "I'm glad for several reasons, and the chief of 'em is that I suspect I'm going to learn the truth about your brother."

When I had finished my story, Arnold glanced up at the top of the tent, as if he had hardly heard what I said—as if, in fact, his mind had been on other matters. "I see," he said, "I see. I'll give the matter some thought. Just now I don't see what can be done about your brother or about the lady, either; but it's something to think about: something to think about!"

Without more ado he gave us our orders.

"It'll be no great time now," he said, "before Burgoyne's Indians and light troops break through. God knows why he's been so slow about sending 'em forward; but it's fortunate for us that he has been. You're to take post on the road to the north, well in advance of any pickets that may be sent out from the fort. Build look-out platforms for yourselves in high trees, and keep watch, day and night, of every path from the north. Burgoyne's got to send information through to Howe, in New York. He's got to let Howe know where he is, and what his needs are. Well, those messengers ought to be stopped. But whether they're stopped or not, we want information. This fort's impossible to defend. It's good for nothing but a rallying point—an observation post. But we want to stay here as long as we can. If we go tumbling back down the Hudson before we have to, the country'll go crazy. Some of you'll have to work toward Fort Ann—find out where they are—find out what progress they're making through the felled trees—make good guesses when they'll probably break through. As soon as you find out anything I ought to know, come and tell me. Understand?"

We said we did.

"What's your meeting call, in case I send out others to get in touch with you?"

"A beetle-head plover's whistle," Nason said. "There aren't any hereabouts, so if we hear one, we'll know what it means. And the British won't know but what it's all right. They'll think it's a peabody bird."

Arnold nodded. "I'll leave the rest to your judgment." He got up from his camp chair, and we got up too. I thought he intended to say something more, but he was prevented by Cap Huff, who had our solitary camp kettle with him, and somehow contrived to drop it and fall over it with a clatter. Embarrassed by this mishap, we crowded from the tent with no further formality, and when we were safely out of earshot, Nason spoke sharply to our blundering companion.

"You fool! How long have you got to be in this army before you learn how to behave in front of a major general? Why didn't you keep hold of that camp kettle, the way you ought to have?"

"Listen, Stevie," Cap said. "I dropped that camp kettle a-purpose. Didn't you hear what he said? He said he'd leave the rest to our judgment. Well, Stevie, this section's full of Tories, so I dropped the kettle for fear he'd think of something else to say that would spoil what he said about using our judgment. You let I and Doc use our judgment with a few Tories, and I shouldn't wonder but what pretty soon we had a camp kettle without a hole in it, and maybe a couple of extra shirts, and a little rum to take the taste of Ticonderoga out of our mouths."

. . . To the northward of the fort we made ourselves screens, close to the roadside, out of junipers: dug shelters beneath boulders on hillslopes overlooking the fertile shelf above the river: built little circular platforms, like swollen crows' nests, in tall pines. We slept in the woods, returning to the fort only to report or to get supplies.

Natanis and Joseph Phipps scouted up the Fort Ann road, vanishing in the forest like shadows every evening, and drifting back the next morning with news of the progress that the British made. That progress was wonderful. They reached Fort Ann: the next day they had hacked a way through the fallen trees a mile this side of Fort Ann. Then they were two miles nearer: five miles nearer. How they performed such miracles of speed we could not understand until Natanis discovered that the choppers were not British, but Tories from the back country—Americans like ourselves—who had volunteered to help Burgoyne. Six hundred of them, Natanis learned, chopped and chopped unendingly, to make a passageway through which Burgoyne's troops might reach us.

This discovery enraged Cap. He made a specialty of Tory hunting, prowling from cabin to cabin of those suspected of having Tory sympathies or of being Tories themselves, and searching lofts and cellars on the pretext of having heard of hidden spies. I almost pitied these people, in spite of their enmity to our cause; for although they had little enough to live on, Cap was forever making, as he put it, purchases from them.

"Here," he'd say, when he came across a barrel of cider in a Tory cellar, "I'll buy this. How much is it?" Before the owner could answer, he would add, "Well, put it on the slate. I left my money in my other pants, but I'll pay you when I come back." God knows how much Cap owed the Tories north of Fort Edward by the time he left them; but a cart wouldn't have carried enough money to pay his debts.

When Nason remonstrated with him, Cap had a ready answer. "Listen, Stevie. If these people *ain't* Tories, everything they got is going to be busted and burned, ain't it, when the British break through?" Nason had to admit, of course, that this was the truth. "All right, then," Cap would continue, "and if they *are* Tories, they'll sell everything they own to the British, and won't get nothing in return but counterfeit money; so no matter which way you look at it, ain't I benefiting 'em really? I owe 'em the money, don't I? They got that satisfaction, anyhow; and otherwise they wouldn't have none at all. If I was owed money by a man as good as I am, I'd be all full of nice feelings and pleasure. Ain't it good reasoning to say these Tories ought to feel the same way?"

Cap even contrived to make headway with the Widow McNeil,

though warned by Nason and everyone else not to try it. The Widow McNeil lived a third of a mile north of the fort, at the foot of the high hill on which we had one of our observation posts. She was as large a woman as ever I saw, having legs so vast that she found it difficult to stand on both feet at once, but must stand on one and thrust the other out to one side. Her bust was enormous, so that her arms were held out awkwardly by it; and she had a voice that sounded like shingles being ripped from a roof. She made no secret of being a Tory, claiming that she had a right to her own opinions; and she felt free to state that if any American soldier came near her house, she'd knock off his head with a poker—a hot one, too.

Cap, being diligent in the performance of what he considered his duty, refused to listen to those who warned him against the Widow McNeil. If handled properly, he insisted, she'd be no more dangerous than any other woman. In fact, he proved it. He marched up to her front door and bellowed hoarsely for her. When she waddled out, shaking her fist and screaming at him, he bawled at the top of his lungs, "Who you got hid in the cellar? Got any spies in the cellar?"

There he would stand, bawling and bellowing; and it was surprising how many things were thrown at him by the Widow McNeil. Some were merely rocks she had picked up especially for this purpose; but on several occasions she hurled something usable—once a turnip the size of Cap's head, so that we had a soup out of it, and once a pailful of soft soap, a part of which Cap brought back to us in his hat.

The rest of us watched and listened, listened and watched, all day and all night, shivering in the mists that rose from the Hudson: lighting no fires to dry our sodden garments. For hours on end we lay motionless, looking for the messengers of whom Arnold had spoken, while the mosquitoes and midges drank their fill of us.

We marveled at the inhabitants of the cabins in this fertile country; for they went about their businesses as people do on the slopes of volcanoes in foreign lands, seemingly unconscious of the danger rumbling and boiling almost beneath their feet. We saw, now and then, farmers drifting off singly to the eastward, through the woods, toward Fort Ann, muskets in hand. When we questioned them, they said they were after fresh meat—bear or deer or turkey; but we knew better. They were Tories, going to join the British. What to do about them, we didn't know. They claimed to be hunters: we couldn't kill them in cold blood, nor could we make prisoners of noncombatants.

Those who came past us, moving south, we stopped and questioned. For the most part they were harmless. A few we searched, ignoring their outraged protests; but only once did we have luck.

On the 22nd of July Natanis and Joseph Phipps slipped in at sunrise
to say that the British and Tory axe-men were within two miles of us—
that we must keep a sharp look-out, so not to be surprised. We sent
Cap to the fort to carry this news to Arnold; and on his return he was
bellowing the French song he only sang when well content, or conscious of doing a good deed——

> "Rouli, roulong, ma boule roulong;
> On roulong ma boule roulong;
> On roulong ma boule.

"Hoy!" he said, when he came up with us. "Things look better!"

"Have new troops come in?" Nason asked eagerly. "Have we got as
many as the British yet?"

"New troops!" Cap exclaimed. "Hell, no! They're all deserting or
getting ready to. Two militia regiments ran away yesterday; and it looks
as if the rest might start almost any minute. No! We ain't got no new
troops! The fact is, so many's deserting that the whole damned army's
falling back toward Albany. Yes sir; they're going down river today,
looking for a place where troops won't be so anxious to run away from,
if there is any such. There won't be nobody in the fort tonight, only a
rear guard of a hundred men."

"Good God!" Nason cried. "They're retreating? What for?"

"What for? Why, because the troops ain't got nothing to eat, wear or
sleep under, and because they think Schuyler's going to turn 'em over
to the British. Because they'll all run away if made to stay where they
are! That's what for!"

"And what's to become of us?" I asked.

"We stay right here," Cap said. "Arnold said for us not to move, and
keep our eyes open wider than ever. From the looks of things right
now, I and Schuyler and Arnold and you few fellers have got to fight
the war all by ourselves, so we better get started."

He let out a raucous bellow—"Rouli, roulong, ma boule roulong"—
and made as if to set off for his look-out post.

"What's better about all that?" Doc Means asked. "That don't sound
as if things was a whole lot better—not unless you and me got different
ideas about what 'better' consists of. I s'pose if you got your head blowed
off, you'd say you was better off than you was when you had to lug
that great big empty skull around everywhere."

Cap dropped his hand on Doc's shoulder. "I'll tell you what's better
about it, old Catamount! I kind of paused at the Widder McNeil's cabin
on the way back here. They's a new girl come to stop with her!"
He made caressing motions with his hands, as though he passed them

over the surface of giant pumpkins perched atop each other: then said, "Hoy! Black eyes! Black hair! Name of Jennie McCrae! What some calls a ninf! Guess I better examine the widder's place for spies a leetle oftener!"

Doc moaned weakly. "Ninf!" he whispered. "Ninf!"

"Listen, old Catamount!" Cap said. "When you been in the army as long as I have, you'll know that when it comes to making a war rememberable, a dozen battles ain't to be compared with just one beautiful ninf!"

*   *   *

. . . Late that afternoon Tom Bickford stopped a man leading a cow. In spite of Tom's astuteness, I suspect that if I hadn't happened to come down out of our pine for water when I did, the man might have got away.

When I slid down the tree and started for the spring, I saw Nason, Cap and Tom gathered by the roadside with the stranger and his cow. I went down the hill, filled Doc's water bottle and my own; then, on returning, stopped to see what the others were up to. The stranger was a stocky farmer with the lack-lustre eye common to our backwoods sections. He had a long, tired-looking mustache, and a stubble of black beard.

"What's the matter with him?" I asked.

Tom Bickford said, "It's his cow that's the matter, Cap'n Peter. That cow ain't been feeding in this section. Cows around here are fat, because of the pasturage. From the looks of that cow, she's been eating shavings. She's been traveling, Cap'n Peter. She's come a long way!"

The farmer gruffly said she'd been sick.

"Sick with what?" Nason asked.

"I dunno," the man said. "Jest sick."

"Where you live?" Cap demanded.

The man said he worked for a Tory—a farmer named Jones—up on Lake George. Since the farmer owed him two months' wages, he had helped himself to one of the farmer's cows and now proposed to sell her to the troops: maybe even join the troops himself.

Nason nodded. "That's right," he told Cap. "There's a pile of Joneses around Lake George."

Cap grunted. "There's some a few other places, too! There's enough Joneses to lick everybody in the world except the Smiths." To the stranger he said, "Where'd you come from, brother, before you went to Lake George?"

"Berkshire."

Cap fixed him with a hard eye. "Berkshire, hey? What was it you said you was figgerin' to do when you get to Fort Edward?"

"Join the troops."

"He ain't no Berkshire man!" Cap told us. "Up in Berkshire they don't say 'join.' They say 'jine.' They don't say cow, neither. They say 'caow.'"

"Search him!" Nason said.

In spite of the stranger's complaints, Cap and Tom had him out of his clothes in ten seconds, and few enough of them there were—just breeches, a brown shirt, shoes, stockings, and an old leather hat. Like any Lake George farmer, he had few personal belongings—no documents, no money: only a fishing line, flint and steel, a flask of fermented honey and water. Cap even tore the man's hat to pieces and took apart the soles and heels of his shoes, but still he found nothing.

As the stranger pulled on his clothes, I studied him with increasing suspicion. There was something familiar about him, though I was unable to put my finger on it.

"You say you've never been in the army?" I asked.

"I didn't say," he said, "but I ain't never been, and I ain't never goin' to be after such treatment as this!"

"Ever been to sea?"

He said he hadn't.

"Ever lived in Canada?"

He picked up his ox-goad and gave me a defiant stare. "No! What would I be doing in Canada?"

His face hovered maddeningly on the fringes of my memory. "Got any brothers in Canada?"

"Gosh, mister: I ain't got no idea where my brothers are!"

"He don't use language like he ought to!" Cap protested. "He ought to say 'where his brothers be!'"

Cap was right. The stranger's speech was somehow incorrect. My brain strained sluggishly—and suddenly I had him! I remembered! Mention of Canada had taken my thoughts back to Ellen Phipps and Iberville: to Marie de Sabrevois and the Château de St. Auge; and, like a shadowy figure behind them, I saw again the man who had posed as a doctor and assisted Madame St. Auge to keep me from seeing Marie de Sabrevois.

The stranger with the cow, in spite of the bristly beard and the almost New England speech that now disguised him, was that same man. I was sure of it. Yet there was no proof. Without proof, we might as well let him go free.

Since there was no proof concealed on his body, it occurred to me there might be some on the cow.

"Look here," I said, "I guess we made a mistake. We'll let you go, but we can't let your cow go. We need her for food. What's she worth?"

"Why," the man said, "I thought I'd sell her to the troops. I——"

"We're troops! Troops on scout duty. How much for the cow?"

"Hard money or Continental?"

"You know we haven't got hard money! What's the least you'll take?"

"I'd ought to get four hundred dollars Continental."

That settled the cow. If he was willing to part with it at all, it had no further interest for us.

I studied him. He bore my scrutiny well, seeming to be untroubled. Instead of fumbling with his ox-goad, as anyone under suspicion might well have done, he stood with his arms folded quietly across it. I would hardly have known he had one.

"Let me see that ox-goad," I said.

His eyes shifted. There was a look in them that I found hard to meet. With a sudden heaviness of spirit I realized that in just such a position, save for the unaccountable turning of the wheel of chance, I myself—or Nathaniel—might have stood.

Cap Huff took the ox-goad from him and gave it to me. When I examined it, I found a plug in the end. It plugged a hole that held a spill of paper. I fished out the spill and unrolled it. There was no address on it. It was signed "A Friend of America."

"What's it say, Cap'n Peter?" Tom Bickford asked.

I read it aloud: "My kind friend: Because I have sympathy for your suffering country, I hasten to tell you something important. As you no doubt know, General Schuyler led troops into Canada two years ago. Being a man of unbridled passions, he contracted, at that time, an attachment for an English lady, a papist, by the name of Annabel Brace, and by her had a child. Both mother and child now live at the third house east of Dufresne's wine shop in St. Louis Street, Quebec. Although General Schuyler pretends to have spent his own fortune in the American cause, he has in reality been in league with General Arnold to mulct the public treasury. He has stolen supplies from Canada and sold them at exorbitant prices to your suffering army. He has also privately sold, for his own account, ammunition, shoes and blankets intended for your brave countrymen, so that your army starves and freezes because of his avarice. The proceeds from these transactions have been sent to Annabel Brace in Quebec, and by her transferred to England. After General Schuyler has surrendered your army to the British, he intends to go with this woman to Bristol, in England, and to make his home on a large estate purchased by him on the River Avon.'"

When I finished that bit of venom, Cap's face was fiery red. "Dufresne's wine shop in St. Louis Street!" Cap exclaimed. "By God! We ought to send somebody up there to find out!"

Nason almost burst. "You fool! You blundering damned fool! Can't you see it's all a lie?"

Cap was resentful. "Don't I know it? Of course it's a lie! But my God, Stevie! They wouldn't say just precisely where the woman lives, would they, unless they knew *something* about Schuyler?"

Nason made inarticulate sounds, while I tried to explain to Cap. "It's the story of the silver bullets, almost—the same story, only another version. Now you can understand why the army's retreating: why it's lost faith in Schuyler."

I turned on the stranger. His eyes seemed filled with a baffled wonder, and I saw he was a good actor. "Who were you told to deliver this letter to?"

"I never saw it before," he protested. "I dunno how it got into that ox-goad!"

"Don't you indeed! You gave me a little kind attention at the Château de St. Auge a year ago. You advised me to eat and sleep well, after I'd come over Chambly rapids. You'd had dealings with Marie de Sabrevois."

He shook his head. "No sir! I swear to God I never did! I dunno what you're talking about!"

"You're a liar! You're a spy and a liar! You're as good as a murderer! You *are* a murderer! You're helping wreck the character of the best general we've got, so you can wreck and destroy the rest of us! Who gave you that letter?"

He persisted in his denials. "I never saw that letter before!"

I shook my fist at him. "Marie de Sabrevois gave you that letter! She wrote that letter!"

"No!" he cried. "No! I found this ox-goad laying on the ground up at Jones's farm. I never knowed anything was in it. You're making up lies— making 'em up so you can hang me for not being in the army! I ain't done nothing all my life but work hard chopping wood and harvesting crops, and now you want to kill me for something I ain't done!" He stared at us, his face contorted; and suddenly, distressingly, tears welled from his eyes to cling in irregular silver threads to the black bristles on his cheeks.

"That'll do you no good," I told him. "You've got just one chance. Tell us who that letter was going to, and you may be alive tomorrow. You don't need to tell us who it came from, because I know."

The stranger eyed us wildly.

Cap Huff went to the cow and untied its halter. "What kind of a knot you want?" he asked me. "One that'll break his neck, or one that'll strangle him?"

We silently studied our prisoner.

He cleared his throat. When he spoke, we could hardly hear him. "You wouldn't believe me if I told you."

"If we don't," Cap assured him, "we'll get word to you right away—with a rope."

The stranger cleared his throat again. "The letter wasn't going to anybody in particular. Orders were to leave it where any high-up militia officer would be bound to see it and read it. A colonel maybe; or best of all, a general."

"Oh, here, here!" Cap bawled. "That ain't no kind of answer! Half these militia officers can't read! Come on; where'll we hang him?"

Nason signed to Cap to be quiet. "I shouldn't wonder if that explanation was the truth." To me he said, "If it hadn't been for you, this man would probably have got away. We'll leave the decision to you. What do you want done with him?"

Nathaniel was in my mind; and I know, too, he was in Nason's thoughts, and Cap's and Tom's. I had an inclination to be merciful. "Well," I said, "we ought to hang him, of course, but maybe he'd be more use to us alive than dead."

"Have it your own way," Nason said. "Do you—do you think he could carry back word to—could help your—help your——"

"No!" I said shortly. "The only way we can help the one you're thinking of is to stop the British. I had something else in mind."

Nason nodded. "Go ahead!"

I took the stranger by the front of the shirt and spoke with a confidence I was far from feeling. "Look here! You don't know how lucky you are! You've been closer to death than you'd be if you were down with the black smallpox! We're going to turn you loose so you can go back and tell your friends something! You go back and tell 'em that all the letters and messages they've tried to send haven't done 'em a bit of good! You tell 'em we caught the messengers that tried to spread the stories about the silver bullets—just the way we caught you! You tell 'em we caught the men that tried to carry Burgoyne's messages to Howe—just the way we caught you! Tell 'em they won't get far with a commanding general who spends his nights as yours does. We know all about it! Tell 'em we're letting you go because you know now what's waiting for you if you ever come back again. The same thing's waiting for every Britisher that sets foot on the Hudson. I'll tell you what it is! A grave in the belly of a wolf, four thousand miles from England!"

*　　*　　*

. . . Five days later, on the 27th of July, Burgoyne's Indians broke through to the Hudson. The length of time they spent there, on that day, was measured in a few short minutes; but the results of what they did will never be measured. The echoes of their yells were heard in royal palaces and humble homes. Nay, those echoes lingered for weeks and months; on through the passage of unending years. They toppled kings from their thrones; raised statesmen to power; altered the circumstances of distant peoples. They ruined nations and they saved nations. They set wheels to turning that, for all I know, will continue their crashings and their rumblings when those who read these lines are dust.

We had been warned, the night before, by Natanis and Joseph Phipps. The Indians, they said, were camped with the British light infantry, three miles away, and they were dancing. They had danced all day, showing that something important was afoot; and probably they would dance all night. On the following day they would move. How far they would move, Natanis said, there was no telling; but some were sure to come to the edge of the forest, so to take back to Burgoyne a report of how many American troops were left at Fort Edward.

When Nason heard this news, he scratched his head. "If we could snare a couple to take down to Schuyler and Arnold," he said, "it might be pretty valuable. Let's set a trap."

That was how Doc and I happened to spend the night in a hole beneath a boulder at the foot of our observation tree on the Fort Ann road, while Nason and Cap Huff, with Joseph Phipps and Natanis, kept guard on the low land closer to the river.

Doc and I laid a sapling across the road, a foot from the ground, and in such a position that a man who tripped on it would fall close to our hiding place. If there should be only one man, we knew we'd have him before he knew what hit him. If there were more than one, there'd be a possibility of snaring several.

We spent a wakeful night all for nothing; for the only thing that came near us was a family of skunks. For an hour they disported themselves in our vicinity, digging grubs from the earth and displaying their inquisitive and playful nature by entering our retreat and rambling over us; while we, not daring to move, prayed that nothing would occur to startle them.

When dawn came, I decided we could do no more. "Come on," I said to Doc. "We'll go down and join Nason." Knowing that the Indians were not far from us, I felt uncomfortable in the woods. As anyone who knows Indians can understand, I preferred to be in the open, where we could see what we were doing in case we were cut off.

Doc was all that was mild and harmless. "You go down. I'll take one more look from up in the tree."

"What's the good of that?" I protested. "If only a few come through, we can warn the fort from the bank of the river, just as well as from here. If there should be a lot of 'em—well: in that case a warning wouldn't be much use to anyone—and neither will we."

Doc was obstinate. "I've been thinking Lanaudiere might be with 'em. I got a hankering for a shot at that friend of yours." Apologetically he added, "If I get a crack at him, his head'll be so full of buck-shot that they can use his skull for a sieve. I ain't afraid of those red vermins! If we killed Lanaudiere, you couldn't make 'em travel out in front of the British army no more: not never! Not without you put turpentine on their red tails bright and early every morning!"

There was, I decided, more than a little truth in what he said. I, too, would count it a pleasure to kill Lanaudiere; and more than that, we could do no greater service to the colonies than to wipe out an Indian leader. Such an occurrence frequently awakens entire Indian nations to the obnoxious aspects of war, and starts them slipping off toward home and mother.

"All right," I said. "I'll go with you."

So we dropped double loads of buck-shot in our muskets, slung them over our shoulders, and for the last time climbed to the crow's nest in our tall pine.

The forest to the northward seemed deserted. We watched for Indian signs: for crows flying hurriedly from the direction of the Fort Ann road: for wisps of smoke: listened for the metallic cry with which a bluejay comments on a passer-by. We heard nothing: saw nothing.

The sun came up, a red ball: sign of a hot day. From behind us, borne on light airs from the west, came the odor of wood smoke; the distant rattle of a drum in the fort; the bawing of a cow at Widow McNeil's. It was a mournful bawing, such as a cow makes when over-full of milk. It occurred to me that if the cow was unmilked, the widow, even though a Tory, might have taken precautions against the approach of Indians: might have sought refuge in the fort with her black-haired, black-eyed guest, Jennie McCrae, of whom Cap had spoken with such ardor.

I murmured my suspicions to Doc, but he disagreed with me. "That woman, she's like most fat folks. She's sot in her ways. If fat folks wasn't sot, they wouldn't be so fat. That woman, she's extra fat, and she's sot against us rebels. She's seen us, and she don't like us, so she's sotter against us than she is against Injuns, that she don't know nothin' about. Us thin folks, we got a lot to be——"

His philosophizing came to an abrupt stop. Somewhere behind us there was the sharp whack of a musket-shot, followed by the resonant impact of the sound against the pines on the far side of the river. We listened, rigid. There was another shot, followed by a burst of quavering yowls.

"By Grapes!" Doc whispered. "There they be! They've broke through to the north'ard instead of here!"

Cautiously we advanced our heads over the edge of our crow's nest.

Doc's hand clutched my elbow. Directly beneath us were Indians, running. I saw five; then a sixth and seventh. Then I saw more, hastening along in single file from the direction of Fort Ann.

Except for the slight squelching noise of their feet in the soft soil, they made no sound. They were like shadows, almost: like animals—deer or panthers—and the same color. Now and again one leaped upward to make a violent chopping stroke with his hatchet, but he did it silently.

There were thirty of them, forty, fifty. From where we were they looked misshapen and grotesque: little more than shaven, painted heads balanced on legs and arms that jerked forward and back; forward and back.

At the edge of the forest, instead of showing themselves, they turned to the left, toward the fort, and went slipping and diving through the underbrush. A few stopped and stood quietly, looking down across the cleared land toward the river. We recognized none of them. They looked to me like mixed-blood Indians from around Montreal. There were no British among them that we could see; nor could we find any white man at all—certainly nobody who bore any resemblance to Lanaudiere.

"For God's sake," I breathed to Doc, "don't move! Be careful! We'll get away all right if they don't look up."

Doc said nothing.

There was another burst of musket-shots: then a wailing chorus of jerky howls.

The musket-fire rattled on. It was not far from us—not as far as the fort. I suspected the Indians had caught and surrounded an American picketing party; but I could be sure of nothing except that a few of the red men still remained beneath us, on the edge of the clearing—stationed there, evidently, as a rear guard for the advance party.

The musket-fire stopped as suddenly as it had started. Then there was more yelling—prolonged, quavering, exultant Indian whoops, followed by silence. It was an uncanny silence, unbroken by musket-shot or voice, or by the song of any bird.

Usually the silence of a forest is full of sound: the almost imperceptible noises of insects: movements of small creatures among leaves: the faint murmurings of air currents among the pines. This forest was soundless. The distant Hudson, the fields, the trees, bright in the early morning sun, seemed lifeless and artificial, like a bad painting. The Indians below us were immobile—hardly to be seen against the brown and green carpet on which they crouched. We, too, were no less motionless. We moved only our eyes, and those cautiously.

Life returned to that still landscape at the sound of the clop-clop of a horse's hoofs. The Indians within our vision moved, scratched themselves and spoke excitedly. A bluejay set up a strident squalling. Two muskets barked repeatedly from the bank of the Hudson, and their slow banging gave me a little confidence. They must, I was sure, belong to Nason or Cap or Tom.

The sound of hoofs came nearer. An Indian ran from the underbrush. Under his arm he carried a mirror framed in brown wood. The watchers came around him to peer into it. One tried to take it from him. The man who carried it laughed loudly, an empty cackle, and struck the glass with the butt of his musket. He dropped the frame and, with his fellows, scrambled on the ground for broken bits. Then he picked up the frame and hung it on a bush.

Two more Indians came from the underbrush, carrying an iron kettle. A third had a patchwork quilt draped over his shoulder. Behind them, led by an Indian, was the horse we had heard. Mounted on it was a girl with long hair—long black hair. It hung below her knees, like a black veil. She was unbound, for we saw her push back the hair from her eyes.

Somewhere out of sight we heard a rasping female voice complaining steadily, and knew the voice to be that of the Widow McNeil.

The red men with the kettle and bedquilt, the one leading the horse and the others who had come with them paused beneath our tree: then moved slowly onward, talking and laughing.

More Indians came running up from the direction of the fort. They were empty-handed, except for their muskets. They stopped for a moment at the wreckage of the mirror: then broke away and hurried after those who surrounded the girl on the horse. That girl, we knew, must be Jennie McCrae—the one Cap Huff had described to us with caressing movements of his hands.

"Lie still!" I whispered to Doc. There were so many of them that I was in constant fear they would see us, encircle the tree and shoot us down.

"Lie still yourself," Doc whispered back.

The second group of Indians came up with the girl on horseback. The horse stopped. There they all were, foreshortened figures—actors on a stage—while we lay looking down upon them as though stretched on the uppermost bench of a theatre's highest balcony.

What happened then was unreal, like an unbelievable episode from a blood-and-thunder melodrama. The Indians shouted and waved their arms. Their tones were angry. What they were angry about, God only knows.

So quickly that my first feeling was merely one of surprise, the noisiest Indian slapped the lock of his musket to jolt powder into the pan, jerked the muzzle against Jennie's breast and fired. The horse reared; Jennie fell forward on its neck, her hands thrust stiffly out. Her hair covered her. It tumbled down over her rigid, outstretched arms. It dragged on the ground. I heard myself saying, "Get it out from under his hoofs!"

The Indian who did it snatched at Jennie's hair and pulled her from the horse as though she were a sack of meal. She landed on her face. Another Indian shot her in the back.

The one who had first fired whipped his knife from his breast, where it hung by a string, and slashed the point across the back of Jennie's skull. Then he put his foot against her shoulder and dragged at her hair as one drags up a handful of grass. Again he slashed her two slashes: above each ear; then leaned down, thrust his fingers into the first cut he had made, and pulled. Her whole scalp tore off, like a cap.

I found myself on my knees in our crow's nest, saying over and over, "Here, here! Here, here!" Doc's hand was around the lock of my musket. "Lay down or they'll get us!" he kept whispering. "Lay down or they'll see us!"

Doc's warning came too late. They did see us. In my left shoulder I felt a sensation of intolerable heat and sharpness. From far away the echoing slam of a musket came with singular slowness to my ears.

The tree-top above me described ever-widening arcs.

Doc's persistent voice had its effect at last. "Lay down!" he never ceased saying. "Lay down! Curl yourself around the tree! Cling to it tight! Don't roll over! Cling to it tight!" He tugged at me until he had pulled me into a position that satisfied him.

Below us I could hear the persistent report of muskets. I was conscious, too, that Doc was whistling shrilly—the three mournful minor notes of a beetle-head plover.

"Did you kill any of 'em?" I asked him. "For God's sake, haven't you killed any of 'em?"

"Lay close to the tree!" Doc said. "Just take it easy and lay close to the tree!" I felt him fumbling at my shoulder, and heard him whistling and whistling, whistling and whistling.

In spite of the fire that burned in my entire upper body, I seemed to dip and swoop in a cold darkness; and in that darkness I thought I saw Ellen Phipps, Nathaniel, Marie de Sabrevois, Lanaudiere—everybody I knew—revolving in an orbit from which there was no escape: an orbit whose center was the mangled body of Jennie McCrae.

LXII

I<small>T WAS</small> Nason, Tom and Cap Huff, who, summoned by Doc's whistles, frightened away the Indians and stood guard while Doc lowered me from the tree, half unconscious from the pain of the bullet that had plowed under the muscles of my back and ripped out through the top of my shoulder.

How they got me from the hilltop to the fort, and over the five miles of rutted road that lay between the fort and Moses Kill, to which the army had retreated, I have no recollection. Indeed, I was conscious of next to nothing but a delirium of pain. That night, with my wound dressed and bound up, the pain became a nightmare that continued for days, merging with a maddening frenzy through which I dizzily staggered: the dreadful vertigo of an army in retreat—for the army went back and always back, down the Hudson; across it to the Heights of Saratoga, past Schuyler's big farm house and mills, into the town of Stillwater, closer and closer to Albany.

I remember that road to the south as a river of frightened settlers, awake at last to the consideration they would receive from the British: a torrent of distraught humanity fleeing from the wrath to come, scuttling, trudging, dragging themselves away from Burgoyne and his Indians, through mud and rain, through blinding heat and dank fogs, sleeping huddled together beside the road, crowded around little fires. I seemed to stumble endlessly past sour-faced old women: young mothers carrying children high up against their necks: still older mothers, frantic and harried, calling admonitions to their inattentive broods: past screaming children, snuffling children, children in paroxysms of sobbing: past men and women driving carts, urging forward sway-backed mares, goading cows and oxen, leading pigs by halters; clutching hens to their bosoms. Everything capable of bearing burdens bore them—men, women, carts, cows, children, oxen. They were laden with every conceivable variety of household stores and belongings—pots and pans: bedding and headboards: spinning wheels, scythes, grindstones, mirrors, chairs, milking stools, sleigh seats.

Alongside them straggled disheartened Continentals and the thieving, pocky, ragged, lousy lot that called themselves militia; and if ever

God made travesties of the fighters on whom a nation ought to rely for its safety and its very existence, he must have packed them into those militia regiments. They were dirty, they were furtive, they were draggle-tail, they were out of hand. They limped and shuffled along, paying no attention to their officers; and for that matter, their officers were no better than the men they were supposed to lead. They, too, were shambling and morose; disheveled, unshaven and shifty-eyed. Never a word did those militia officers say when their men snatched food and rum, blankets and kettles, chickens and young pigs from the fleeing settlers.

Cap Huff was in a rage. "By God," he said a score of times—and he bawled it out at the top of his lungs, in the vain hope that a militiaman or militia officer would take offense, "by God, I'll take anything off a Tory, or off a Britisher, or off a dirty, nit-headed, stinking militiaman, or off anybody that's got more'n he knows what to do with; but before I'd take anything off of one of my own people that had just been druv out of his home by a feller I was supposed to keep away, by God, I'd join the militia and suck eggs! I'd join the militia and be a tit-head! Damned if I wouldn't try to get to be a militia officer, so's I could respectfully be called a poop-head by my men, and so's I could run foot-races with 'em to set 'em a good example—yes sir: an example in running away from the British right when I was needed most!"

Cap was wasting his efforts. The truth was that next to no courage or confidence was left in the entire army; and no matter what Cap might have said to the militiamen, they would have gone on stealing from those fleeing settlers the provisions, blankets and kettles their own government was unable to provide.

On every side we heard the lies that had turned the bulk of the army into an apprehensive, dejected, beaten horde: that had been carried to all parts of our eastern country by deserters and by the militia who drifted away like smoke, so that the whole land was smitten with hopelessness and black depression, as by a plague.

Schuyler [the lying whispers ran] Schuyler's to blame! Schuyler's a coward . . . Schuyler's a thief . . . Schuyler's a traitor! Schuyler took the silver bullets. . . . Schuyler stole the bread from the army. . . . Schuyler bought us horse-meat and charged for prime beef. . . . Schuyler's a papist. . . . Schuyler has Negro blood in his veins. . . . Schuyler takes opium and can't be depended on in an emergency. . . . Schuyler's feeding us poison to make us sick. . . . Schuyler's issued flints that won't strike fire. . . . He's put sand in our powder. . . . He's moving us back so he can corner us in a box we'll never get out of. . . . He'll let us be trapped in a place where we can't fight!

How many of those tales originated with the British, I had no way of knowing; but every last one of them was pure invention, and I was certain that one person busy with such inventions and the distribution of them was Marie de Sabrevois. Day after day the men deserted. Day after day militia companies went shambling off, deaf to the curses of Schuyler and Arnold and the few whose courage was unshaken.

I fell into a fevered lethargy, partly due to the condition of my wound. Doc Means clung to me, apparently worrying less about the parlous state of the army than over what might happen if a regular army doctor should get his hands on me. "Why," he said in that quavering voice of his, "they'd put a salve on you that would plug up both ends of the wound, just like plugging putty into the muzzle of a musket. You know what happens when you do that?"

I said the musket was apt to explode.

"Apt to explode!" Doc cried. "Apt to explode! Why she just up and busts wide open!" So he kept me away from the doctors, and I must admit that the cold water he dabbled on my shoulder a score of times a day seemed to keep my hurt from growing worse.

We saw little of Nason, Cap and Tom Bickford. They spent their time somewhere in the rear, coming in to report that all of Burgoyne's troops had arrived at Fort Edward and were waiting there for their artillery: that the Indians were close behind us, striking at everyone within their cunning reach, falling on stragglers from the army, scalping, looting, burning, destroying.

. . . As my shoulder mended, my lethargy passed, and with its passing came a mounting rage at the troops that deserted us. Our numbers were little more than half those of Burgoyne's army. If this continued, nothing—neither Schuyler's optimism nor Arnold's daring—could save us from overwhelming defeat.

I tried to think clearly about Nathaniel. Never, if the British won, could I face my neighbors in Arundel if I owed my home, perhaps my very life, to a brother's attachment to the mistress of a British general. Nor could Nathaniel live again among the people from whom he had sprung. He might think he could, but he couldn't.

Such thoughts as these were troubling me on an August morning at Stillwater when Doc took me to a brook above the Hudson to sop cold water on my still stiff and swollen shoulder. As he sopped, a company of militiamen came slouching out of camp, homeward bound—homeward bound, although the British and the Indians were converging on us from two directions: Burgoyne's army from the north: St. Leger's army from the west.

In the frame of mind I was in, the sight of them was more than I could bear. I got up from beside the brook to watch this straggling company. Doc, protesting at my movements, continued to dab at my shoulder with a cold wet cloth.

If there were officers among the men, there was nothing to distinguish them. They were a slovenly lot, their hair unclubbed and hanging lankly around their ears: their hats tilted on the backs of their heads; their breeches torn and unbuckled; their weskits open over ragged dirty shirts; their coats off and tied over their rumps or around their muskets. The sight of my wound caught their attention, and they looked at me, which was unusual for militia, who, as a rule, loutishly ignore everything near them, barring stealable objects or girls of an age to invite bucolic pleasantries.

"God bless my soul," I said to them, "you're leaving, aren't you?"

One of the men leaped in the air, kicked his heels together and crowed like a rooster. A few laughed. The others stared doltishly.

"Where you boys from?" I asked.

"We're Quoick's milishy from Vanderheiden."

"What do you want to leave now for?"

"Come on! Come on!" they shouted. "To hell with him! Git along!"

"Our time's up," one of the nearer men explained. "Our time was up at six o'clock this morning. We could 'a' left two hours ago."

The men began to drift away.

"Wait," I said, "let me ask you something. What led you to enlist in the militia in the first place?"

"For God's sake," one of them cried, "push him out of the road and come ahead!"

Doc Means ceased his labors on my shoulder. "I don't believe that feller knows what's going on, Cap'n Peter," he said mildly. "I don't believe he ever heard how Jennie McCrae got killed."

The militiamen stopped in their tracks.

"I can tell you about that," I said. "I can tell you how she was killed, because I was up a tree above her when it happened. I'd climbed it to help protect Vanderheiden people from having their skulls split open. I saw her killed. The man that killed her was red, the color of a red fox. He was smaller than any of you. He and his friends got into an argument over her, so he shot her in the breast. He put the muzzle against her and blew the breast right out of her. Another shot her in the back. He shot her in the back when she was lying on the ground. She hadn't done anything to any of 'em. One of the men put his foot on her and pulled off her hair. Tore it off her! Tore it off like a squirrel skin!"

My hands were trembling. My throat was so choked that I could scarcely get my breath. I had never thought of myself as a speaker, yet now words came to me without conscious effort—words that faintly eased my indignation—words that I spoke with all my heart, even though I hardly knew what I said.

"Listen to me," I said. "You owe me that much. I went in the army over a year ago to keep the British away from my people and yours. So far, by God, we've done it! We starved and sweated and sickened: almost drowned and damned near died a hundred times, in Canada; we built the fleet and fought it till the guns split our ears and jarred our eyes loose; we held back the lousy British at Fort Ann; we chopped trees to hold 'em back, till our hands cracked open! For over a year we've fought 'em! You're safe and your homes are standing. This morning your mothers put bread in the oven; your sisters tie ribbons in their hair and sleep sound at night because of what we did: because of what we endured! We went into this war to stop the British! What did *you* go into it for?"

Doc seemed to be waiting for the question. "They went in for twenty dollars."

"Yes, by God!" I said. "I believe he's right! I believe you went in for not one damned thing but a twenty-dollar bounty! I'd never have thought so if I hadn't seen you running home just when the British are getting ready to shoot your mothers in the back and rip off your sisters' scalps, the way they did Jennie McCrae's. She was a nice girl! She hadn't done anything to anybody, any more than your sisters have. Twenty dollars you went in for, by God, and you can't see beyond it! Twenty-dollar soldiers! Twenty-dollar dependables from Vanderheiden, New York! You'll let the British hack everyone to hell and steal a nation away from you because you don't know how to choose between twenty dollars and justice—between twenty dollars and freedom—between twenty dollars and liberty! Between twenty dollars and your own country! Yes, you got your twenty dollars, so you'll get out of the way of the British and let 'em scalp your sisters the way Jennie McCrae was scalped!"

One of the militiamen took a step toward me, gray-faced. "You're a liar!"

Doc Means shook his head sadly. "Pore feller! He wants to fight, but he can't. His time expired at six o'clock this morning!"

"I'm a liar, am I?" I asked the gray-faced man. "How am I a liar? Two weeks ago we had sixteen hundred militia. Where are they, when we need 'em? Gone home! Where are you going? Home! You're leaving us when we're lost if we don't have men! Do you know what'll happen to us if you do what not even a rat would do? Even a rat'll fight for his home! If you and all these other militia regiments run away, the British'll catch us between two fires—between St. Leger and Burgoyne. They'll wipe us out—starve us out—club us to death—rip off our scalps! But don't forget this: when they've got rid of us, then, by God, it'll be *your* turn! They'll hunt you down in the fields and woods! You'll be like woodchucks, chattering under walls! Go home, and you're doomed! Go home, and you're wrecked! Go home, and you've thrown away a nation because you can't see beyond twenty dollars! And you're so thick-witted you call me a liar for telling you the exact truth! God help the nation that has to rely on such judgment as that!"

"Stop talking," Doc said. "You're bleeding again."

I pushed him away and shook my fist at the men before me. The face of the gray man had, strangely, turned a flaming scarlet. I saw, with a faint surprise, that all these militiamen were crimson-faced and breathing heavily. "And let me tell you this," I added—somewhat thickly, since my shoulder was throbbing and burning. "Nothing—nobody, could penetrate one inch into this country if you men would turn out and stay turned out! If our exertions equaled our abilities, this war'd end in a month! You're going home; but if you'd stay here where you belonged, we'd make a human net and a human noose for those that killed Jennie McCrae. There'd never be a red-coat get down the Hudson or back to Canada! They'd die right here! Never a foot of this land would any Britisher ever get! There's no foreign force in the whole damned world strong enough to subdue America unless the corruption and timidity of her own people first force her to her ruin."

I glared at the silent militiamen. Doc caught my arm. "You'll stop your talking," he said bitterly, "or the future of America won't be of no interest to you. None whatever!"

He turned me toward the brook, and as he did, I heard one of the militiamen say, "Come on! Come on out of here!" I looked back at them. A scattered few had set off down the road, toward Albany, but most of them still stood there.

One of them moved slowly in the direction from which they had come so short a time before. Another followed him, and another. The others milled and muttered. Then, one by one, they all shuffled off after the first two—back toward Stillwater.

I watched them go. A tightness went out of my muscles. Doc cleared his throat, cleared it again. As if to apologize for this unprecedented throat-clearing he said faintly, "Kind of irritates my membranes, hearing all them arguments!"

*   *   *

. . . He was working on my shoulder again, when there was a rustling in the brush below the rim of the high bank on which we stood, and an officer came up and looked around. It was young Varick, one of General Schuyler's aides. He seemed almost excited. "By George," he said, "they went back! They went back to camp!"

He eyed me curiously. "Was that you who was talking to 'em?" He didn't wait for an answer. "You certainly talked to 'em! The general wants to speak to you. He's down here. You better come right down."

I got up heavily. "He heard me, did he? I wouldn't have used profanity if I'd known he was down there. What's he want to do? Court-martial me?"

Varick laughed and turned away.

"I'll put on my shirt," I said.

"Come the way you are," Varick told me.

Doc picked up my shirt and coat and we followed Varick down the bank. At its foot was Schuyler and a knot of officers. On the ground near him sat Arnold, working with pencil and ruler on a piece of cartridge paper. Looking over Arnold's shoulder was a man in a light blue uniform. He was about Arnold's height; and, like Arnold, he had a round, swarthy, merry face. I knew him to be Kosciusko, an engineer officer from Poland: a great hand to lay out fortifications and trenches.

When I faced them and saluted, Schuyler seemed annoyed that Doc should still be dabbing at my wound. Arnold opened his mouth at me in a wide and soundless laugh.

"So it was you, was it?" Schuyler asked. "Where did you learn such talk as that?"

"On shipboard, General. If seamen behave the way those militiamen did, it's a sea captain's duty to tell 'em a few things, and take a capstan bar to 'em if they don't like it." Somewhat weakly I added, "Besides, I wasn't feeling good this morning on account of my shoulder."

"Young man," Schuyler said sternly, "don't tell me a sea captain's duty! I was a sea captain when you weren't knee-high to a duck. What I asked you was where you picked up those sentiments—those sentiments about our exertions equaling our abilities, and all the rest of it."

"Sir, I didn't pick 'em up anywhere. I just spoke in anger."

"In anger, eh? Well, now that your anger's passed, can you remember what it was you said?"

"I only recall being a little sharp. I don't recollect the words I used."

"I do," Doc Means said. He pressed his wet cloth against my back and held it there. "I recollect every word, General, and if I hadn't been afraid of inflaming this shoulder of his, I might have told him a few more that wasn't quite so dignified."

"See you don't forget them," Schuyler said. He moved around behind me. Arnold and Kosciusko joined him.

"He's got treat vairy prooty," Kosciusko said. "Thass vairy jonteel: vairy nice wound."

"That certainly is a handsome hole," Doc agreed.

"How is he?" Schuyler asked Doc. "Fit to travel?"

"Well," Doc said, "if he don't overtax himself, and don't go near no doctors, and don't excite himself about militia, he ought to do all right."

I was irritated by their attitude. They might have been examining a shoat. "There's nothing the matter with me," I said. "I can do anything that doesn't require the use of that arm."

I heard Arnold's harsh voice say, "In some cases, General, rest can be more irritating than action, and I believe this is one of 'em."

They moved around in front of me again. "I'm taking you at your word," Schuyler said. "I want you to start south the first thing tomorrow morning. I want you to tell the story of Jennie McCrae to the people that don't seem to understand this war. Varick, where's that map?"

Varick produced a map and held it where Schuyler could see it.

"All right," Schuyler said. "Connecticut's promised us men. They promised 'em three weeks ago. Where are they? Where are the Rhode Island regiments? God knows! We've had our share of Massachusetts men, but they go home!" He ran his finger down the map. "Go there, there and there! Cross over into Massachusetts and work down into Connecticut—Peekskill, Hartford, New Haven, Providence, Taunton— make a circle that ends at Bennington. Talk everywhere to everyone. Talk about Jennie McCrae and our exertions equaling our abilities. Hah! That was good!" He looked almost proudly at Kosciusko; then turned to me. "When you reach Bennington, you can stop talking and come back here.

"You ought to take a month to it. A month's not too long. No: a month's not long enough. Take five weeks. I'll give you a horse. Your friend can go with you, and he can have a horse too. Stop at every settlement. Stop at every village. Call the people together. Tell 'em the story of Jennie McCrae. Tell 'em that if we don't get men, the same thing'll happen to their womenfolks that happened to Jennie McCrae. Tell 'em what you told that militia company."

He put his hands behind his back and seemed to brace himself more firmly. "You've probably heard the stories they're telling about me. They've gone all over the country. You'll have to take those stories into account. You'll have to keep my name out of it. When you ask for men, tell 'em they'll be led by General Arnold. Is that clear?" His voice was as unruffled as though he discussed the prospect of rain. He was a great man—a true patriot, unselfish and generous.

I said everything was clear.

"Travel fast," Schuyler said. "We've got to have men. We've got four thousand: they've got double that. Theirs are old soldiers: ours aren't. Travel fast and get men. If we can have men, they can't get past us. I'll send other men by other routes to do the same thing you'll be doing. If we don't get men—if we don't get men——"

Arnold put in a cheerful word. "Let 'em draw their own conclusions as to what'll happen if we don't get men!"

"Ha, ha!" Kosciusko said. "I theenk that is vairy well! Vairy well hindeed! The pipple who are tol' about thees dead lady will be vairy motch hannoy! I, too, am 'orribly hannoy about thees dead lady. You weel see: they weel come hout, vairy motch hangry."

"It's high time they got angry!" Arnold said. "High time!"

Schuyler turned to Varick. "You'll have to find a uniform for Captain Merrill somewhere. God knows where you'll find such a thing, my boy, but I want it found. You've got to make him look like a soldier somehow. We can't send him on such an errand looking like a scarecrow."

"Let me attend to it, General," Arnold said. "You've got enough on your mind. I think I can find horses and a uniform for Captain Merrill, and I'd like a word with him before he goes."

When Schuyler nodded, Arnold said to me carelessly, "Be at my tent at eight o'clock tonight. Wait there till I come."

Doc and I climbed back to the high land above the river, leaving Schuyler, Arnold and Kosciusko studying the drawings on the cartridge paper.

As we went, Doc was puzzled. "Now what would any feller want to be a general for?" he asked. "It looks to me like it ain't much different from being tied to a runaway horse, except you don't get so much exercise out of it."

Doc's thoughts were of no account to me. I could think of nothing except that on top of all that had happened to me, I was now to be sent ignominiously off for five long weeks on duties that any preacher or wordy lawyer could perform—off to places where I could be of no more help to Nathaniel, if he needed me, than a mouse would be—where Ellen Phipps, now only twenty miles away within the British lines, would be as distant as the stars.

. . . It was ten o'clock before Arnold came back to the log house in which he had his headquarters, and where Doc and I waited on a bench outside. We thought he had forgotten about us, for he stalked into his

cabin without giving us a glance, and we heard him telling his aide to
do this and do that. The aide came hurrying out; and a little later Arnold's Negro servant appeared in the doorway and called us in. We
found the general with his coat off, writing at his little field-desk.

"Here's your orders," he said, and didn't even look up. "Your uniform's
over there in the corner. It's a plain blue one. If it's too small, you can
have it made larger in the first town you come to. My servant's got your
horses. They're in the barn with mine. Sleep there tonight and be on
your way by sun-up tomorrow."

He pushed his field-desk from him and hooked his feet around the
legs of his camp stool. In the light of the two candles before him, his
swarthy face looked lumpy.

He pointed a finger at me. "Look here! When Schuyler ordered you
out to spread the story of Jennie McCrae, this morning, you had your
brother on your mind, didn't you?"

"Yes," I said, "I did."

"I thought so. Well, we've all got something on our minds in addition
to this war. Even a militiaman spends a lot of time worrying for fear his
family'll starve to death if he can't go home. It's hard for him to remember that they'll starve to death just as quick—maybe quicker—if the
British beat us. Most people don't look very far ahead."

"About two inches," Doc said.

I said nothing.

Arnold eyed me morosely. "If you're tempted to start thinking about
your own troubles, you might give a moment's thought to Schuyler. He's
sacrificed everything to hold this army together. Thanks to him we can
stop Burgoyne, if only we can get the men. He's been rewarded by being
called a coward and a traitor. Tonight his officers, even, turned on him."

I couldn't believe my ears. "Turned on him? How *could* they turn on
him?"

"I'll tell you how," Arnold said. "We had word today that St. Leger's
army surrounded Fort Stanwix. If that fort falls, the whole Mohawk
Valley falls. The whole Mohawk Valley'll turn Tory to save itself from
being butchered. If the Mohawk Valley falls, all New York'll turn Tory;
and if that happens, they've got us where they want us! We'd never have
a chance! All our armies would be destroyed! So St. Leger can't be allowed to take Fort Stanwix. He's got to be driven back. He's *got* to be!
You see that, I trust."

"Certainly I see it."

"Our brigadier generals don't see it," Arnold said. "Tonight Schuyler
asked for a brigadier general to lead a relief column against St. Leger.
Not one volunteered. Not one! They sat there like bumps on a log."

"Didn't they have anything to say?"

"Oh yes," Arnold said. "One of 'em, back in a dark corner, said, 'He means to weaken the army.' Schuyler heard him say it. After all Schuyler's done, he heard himself called a traitor by his own officers."

"What did he do?"

"Nothing. He can't let personal affairs interfere with what's got to be done."

"And what about Fort Stanwix?"

"Oh," Arnold said, "I was sent up here to make myself useful, so I volunteered. I'll go to its relief. I'll take a brigade and start tomorrow." His glance was satirical. "We all have our troubles, you see. I just had word from Congress that they'd voted on whether to restore me to my proper rank or not. They voted not to do it. Yes, they saw no reason for doing so. And in spite of all Schuyler's done for their safety, they voted to call him down to Philadelphia to face a court-martial. He'll be relieved of his command, and he'll sit in a hot room in Philadelphia, try ing to prove he *isn't* a traitor—trying to satisfy a lot of politicians that he *hasn't* played the coward."

His words made me sweat. "Who'll take his place?"

Arnold seemed not to hear. "I mention these things because you've got your work cut out for you, and because injustices improve your vocabulary. If you get men for us in New England, you'll have to ignore your personal troubles. You'll have to be in a rage over the injustice and pettiness that's got this country by the throat!" He jumped up suddenly and thrust his swarthy face close to mine. "You'll have to forget everything but our needs! Coax 'em! Shout at 'em! Fight 'em! Hammer 'em! Curse 'em! Get men, and more men, and more men! By God, they've got to come out! They've got to fight! They've got to stand a little part of the things we've stood! They can't stay back there, rotting in their feather beds, chewing and spitting and stuffing themselves with food while we're chased and shot at like rats! God damn it, they can't! They can't!"

He sat down as suddenly as he had risen. My throat was dry; I was shaking all over.

"Can you do that?" Arnold asked quietly. "Can you forget your brother and do that?"

"Yes," I said. The word choked me.

Arnold nodded. "Then there's nothing more to be said, except this: I haven't recommended you for promotion, because if you're promoted you'll have to spend most of your time writing letters asking for things that don't exist and explaining something you didn't do to people who won't believe you, no matter what you write. I want you to stay a captain, like Nason, until we have less need for good scouts. Understand?"

When I said I did, he glowered at me. "You've been a good officer, and don't think I'm not appreciative. Sometime I may be able to show you that I am."

With that, abruptly, he seemed to become impatient and irascible. Complaining bitterly of the letters he must write, he rose and almost pushed us from his cabin, as though he had never wanted to see us in the beginning and hoped never to see us again.

LXIII

God knows how our horses had escaped from the commissaries who supplied us with horse-meat in place of beef; for certainly they were on the verge of death from old age. Nonetheless, they carried us, which was something, even though our legs were sore from kicking them with spurless heels.

We coaxed those reluctant steeds south to Albany and through the neat towns along the Hudson: then crossed the river to the road that carried us across the lower corner of Massachusetts and over the rolling hills of Connecticut. After two days in Hartford, talking and haranguing continually, as we did everywhere, we rode to the eastward into northern Connecticut and Rhode Island, then swung up into Massachusetts and curved to the northward through Attleboro, Framingham, Fitchburg and Northfield.

I found it difficult, at first, to bring myself to speak earnestly to little groups of people. I felt like a pretentious, play-acting fool, mouthing the story of Jennie McCrae a dozen times a day. I grew hoarse, begging silent farmers to come to their country's aid. Every phrase that fell from my lips seemed stale and flat: as unconvincing as an advertisement of a sale of calicoes.

Doc shook his head. "You better get mad. You're thinking about yourself and how you look in that nice blue uniform of yours, and you ain't making no effort to get your dander up! They won't get mad if you ain't mad yourself. Get aggravated at something!"

It occurred to me, then, to fix my attention on the most doltish of those who listened: to lash myself into a fury over his ignorance and unconcern: to have him in mind when I threatened the lot of them with mutilation and death unless they came out against Burgoyne. The first time I did it, a man was waiting for us when we unhitched our horses. It was the dolt, and he had a musket over his shoulder.

When we set off, he followed us. Doc frowned at him. "Where you going?"

"Agin Burgine," the man said.

"We're going east," Doc said. "Burgoyne's over there." He pointed to the westward. The dolt hung his mouth open so a cat-bird might have nested in it. We rode away, and when we looked back, he was plodding off in the opposite direction.

Those to whom I talked had little to say, after the manner of New Englanders, and it was hard to tell how my appeals affected them. The men, at times, seemed uncomfortable, and stared white-eyed at their neighbors. The older women listened with tight-pressed lips and shoulders drawn up. I couldn't be sure whether they disapproved of me, Burgoyne and his Indians, or the whole war. Occasionally, when I told how the Indian had put his foot on Jennie's shoulder and torn off her scalp, a child would squall with fright, and there would be considerable throat-clearing and foot-shuffling among the grown-ups. But on the whole, we seemed to be accomplishing nothing.

Others, we learned, had been sent by Schuyler into various sections of New England to tell the story of Jennie McCrae. I hoped they were making more impression on their audiences than was I. We were wasting our time, I told Doc over and over: wasting time that might have been spent in doing something—though God knew what—for Nathaniel.

But Schuyler had said to take five weeks, and so we spent five weeks riding, talking, riding, talking. And then we had three pieces of news that put a different aspect on things.

The news of Bennington was the first. Burgoyne, still at Fort Edward, had sent a thousand Germans and a few Indians to the eastward, to capture horses and provisions that our people had collected at Bennington. John Stark with militia from New Hampshire and Vermont had surrounded both the slow-moving Germans and the Indians and had either killed or captured every mother's son of them.

The second piece of news had to do with Arnold. He had set out to relieve Fort Stanwix, accompanied by a brigade of Massachusetts troops. By a trick he had led St. Leger's troops and Indians to think his force was enormous; and because of this, St. Leger and all his men had turned and raced precipitately back to Canada. Thus Arnold not only relieved Fort Stanwix, but robbed Burgoyne of one of the weapons with which he had planned to stab us to the heart.

The third piece of news was that Congress had removed General Schuyler from the command of the Northern Army, replacing him by General Gates; and from the jubilation with which this news was received in New England, Schuyler might have been a Nero and Gates a Cæsar. Hearing this jubilation, and knowing what a fumbling fussbudget Gates really was, I wondered whether this monstrous New England lack of understanding could by any chance mean that Nathaniel was right after all, or whether it just meant that all mankind was incurably ignorant.

And then, as the heat of August gave way to the clear days and frosty nights of September, the countryside took on new life. Wherever we went we passed men with muskets on their shoulders, trudging along toward some far destination. They had water-flasks in the pockets of their weskits: blankets over their shoulders: little sacks of corn meal tied to their belts. When we asked them where they were going, they invariably answered, "Agin Burgine." They seemed surprised to be asked, as if everybody ought to know where they were going, and why— ought to be aware that nobody in his right mind was going anywhere except against Burgoyne.

They traveled in groups, or singly, or in twos and threes. Small groups joined larger ones and continued onward together. Once, watching six countrymen straggle past a crossroad farm house, their muskets all skewgee, we saw a boy burst from the farm house carrying a musket twice as long as himself—a boy with enough freckles for ten boys. An old green overcoat was tied around his waist by the arms. A woman stood in the farm house door and watched him go.

He ran along behind the six stragglers, worrying a tin whistle from his pocket. His musket troubled him, but still he contrived to put his whistle to his lips and tootle a jig tune that had a swing to it, and was a master-piece of shrillness. One of the six men took the boy's musket, and the rest got themselves into a sort of line, shouldered their muskets, and went trudging to the westward a little faster, with bucolic guffaws at their sudden military air.

As we went farther west ourselves, the groups became larger. When we rode at night, eager to be back with our friends again, we saw fires in the fields, with men asleep around them. In villages we began to en-counter companies drilling. The groups along the roads, even, were drilling; and we became more and more conscious of the sound of drums: solitary drums at first: then two or three drums together at the head of a company: then drums and fifes.

We began to have the feeling that the whole country was on the move, drifting to the westward, toward the Hudson, "agin Burgine."

When we reached Bennington, Schuyler had said, our work would be done and we could come back; so it was with profound relief, on the thirty-fifth day of our travels, that we rode into that hilly little town.

Our relief was not long-lived; for women were talking in farmyards, standing on doorsteps, hanging from windows, talking and talking, and staring toward the westward.

When we asked the reason for all this talking and staring, they claimed to have heard there had been a battle, though they couldn't give us the source of the rumor. Seemingly it had sprung up in the night, like a toadstool, but vague as it was, it led us to keep right on going.

"It's what I've been afraid of!" I told Doc. "If our troops stop the British and find Nathaniel behind the British lines——" I couldn't go on. "For God's sake, try to get some speed out of that nag of yours."

"Listen," Doc said, "this nag has carried me nigh onto four hundred miles and ain't showed no speed yet. Neither has yours, so what's the use of talking like that? If there's been a battle, it's all over! Half the trouble in this world comes from trying to figure how to change things that can't be changed, on account of having happened."

Fret and fume as I would, we couldn't go faster, and it wasn't until the 22nd of September that we reached the Hudson again and saw once more the rolling fields above Stillwater, and north of them the misty Heights of Saratoga. We crossed the river on a scow into an atmosphere as altered, since we had left Stillwater in August, as the leaves had been altered by September frosts.

In place of the surly, ragged, unshaven men of the previous month, straggling furtively away in little groups and companies, we now saw, moving briskly along the river road, as if bound for a fair, an unbroken stream of men afoot, messengers on horseback, officers in blue uniforms, farmers driving herds of cows, army teamsters bawling angrily at lethargic oxen. Here and there the stream split to flow around ammunition carts and supply wagons.

"Look at that!" Doc said, when we rode up from the ferry and walked our horses into Stillwater. "Look at that! They got shoes! Every last one of 'em's got on shoes with soles!"

It was true. Not a man was barefoot. Their breeches were homespun, but without rents or holes. Their hair was combed and tied. They looked well fed and healthy; and what was most astonishing, there was no weariness or discouragement about them.

Their faces were tanned and cleanly shaven: they were alert, as men in a city are alert. They were friendly, too, as if they owned something in common. It was the same sort of friendliness I had often found among American seamen in foreign ports.

We had an even greater surprise when we reached Bemis's Tavern on the river road. There the road was blocked by entrenchments extending from the cliff to the river, so we turned up the slope to our left and made our way to the heights above Bemis's Tavern. It was on that high land that Doc had washed the wound in my shoulder (a hurt now entirely healed) on the day Schuyler had heard me speak sharply to the militia.

All those heights, since we had left them, had been fortified. They were rimmed with earthworks in which were bastions and redoubts, with cannon in the embrasures. Enclosed by the earthworks was a city of tents and board shelters grouped around a parade ground; and on the parade ground was a regiment of Continentals, white belts crossed on their chests, drilling smartly before militia companies, which were going through evolutions of their own.

Seeing a young officer directing incoming militiamen where to go, I drew rein beside him and asked whether General Arnold was around. He winked at me in high good humor. "*Is* he! Is he *around!*" Words seemed to fail him.

He was a lieutenant, and I gave him a cold look, at which he hastily told me to go straight up the road I was on: then take the road to the north.

"His hut's on the left," he said, "just after you get beyond the fortifications."

We passed through a series of clearings in the forest that covered most of that high land, and located Arnold's headquarters in a log cabin near a larger house—a cabin little larger than a dog-kennel. I gave my horse to Doc to hold, and explained myself to a sentry. The voice that answered my knock, to my surprise, was Varick's. I went in to find him copying letters in a book.

"Good," he said, when he looked up and saw me, "good! I'm glad you're back! Your friends have been pestering the life out of me to know when to expect you."

His use of the word "pester" made me instantly apprehensive. "There's nothing wrong, is there?"

"Wrong?" he asked. "Of course not."

"I didn't know," I said. "We heard there'd been a battle. I hope none of my friends were hurt."

Varick looked at me curiously. "Is that all you've heard? That there's been a battle?"

I said that was all we'd heard.

"You've got a lot to learn." Then he added, "Since General Schuyler was called down, Livingston and I have the honor to be helping General Arnold. Livingston's his aide, and I do what I can." Varick spoke feelingly. "General Arnold has been a true friend to General Schuyler, and it's a privilege to be associated with him."

This was high praise; for like Schuyler, Varick had distinction and breeding, as did Livingston, who later became a justice of the Supreme Court.

When Varick had given me the receipt I requested for our horses, he pushed back his stool, and looked me over appraisingly. "General Arnold's gone out to take a look at the British lines," he said. "He'll want to see you tonight. How did you find things to the eastward? Can we count on more men?"

"They're pouring out," I told him. "They're moving up by the thousands. Who won the battle?"

Varick went to the door and looked out at Doc and the horses. When he came back he said, "Nobody won it, but the British *would* have won it if it hadn't been for General Arnold. Make no mistake about that! As it is, we're just where we were before the battle, except that the place where we fought stinks with dead bodies. It was a hell of a fight! Don't think it wasn't! And if it hadn't been for General Arnold, the British army'd be in Albany right this minute."

His voice sounded bitter—not at all as it should have sounded after such a feat.

"I'm certainly glad to hear it," I said. "Congress can't refuse to give General Arnold his proper rank after he's done a thing like that."

"I wouldn't be too sure of that! They won't have to do anything about it if they don't know he was in the battle."

"I don't believe I get what you mean."

Varick snorted. "I'm not surprised you don't. I'll tell you what happened. Last Friday morning, the 19th, your friend Nason and his scouts came running in to say the British had started for us. General Gates wanted to sit here and wait: sit behind the entrenchments while the British brought up their artillery without hindrance. Why, they'd have blown us to bits!

"General Arnold went to Gates and begged him to send men to attack the British before they could get their cannon out of the woods. Arnold said we could beat 'em in the woods, but not if we waited for them to attack us when and where they pleased. He said we didn't have enough men to fight the British way: we'd got to fight our own way. He kept at Gates for two hours before Gates gave in. Even then Gates wouldn't let Arnold have as many men as he needed and asked for."

Varick's voice rose. "If Gates had given him the men he asked for, we'd have run the British off the top of Freeman's Farm right then and there! We'd have pitchforked 'em into the Hudson River, lock, stock and barrel. That would have been the end of Mr. Burgoyne, Esquire!"

I felt hot under the collar. "Why didn't Gates do it? Why didn't he?"

"Why?" Varick asked. "Because he's an old rat! A timid, scuttling, old gray rat!" He eyed me defiantly. Finding I made no objections to his choice of words, he spoke eagerly. "Look! Arnold took what he could get—Morgan's and Dearborn's riflemen, Learned's brigade and some New York troops: he took 'em through the woods and met the British at Freeman's Farm, a mile from here. He hit the British so hard you could hear it all the way to Albany! Nobody else could have done what he did! He pulled those men of ours along behind him as if he'd been a hurricane! He pulled 'em and drove 'em, lashed 'em and dragged 'em. He slammed 'em against the British till the British had the blind staggers. No troops in the world ever fought better than ours did for Arnold! Why, the British brought up all their reinforcements, trying to get through. Arnold fought 'em for five hours—fought 'em till dark—without getting one damned bit of help from that old rat Gates, and he held the British right where they started from! He damned near had 'em on the run! I tell you there never was a hotter fight than that one!"

"But look here," I said. "What was it you meant by saying they wouldn't have to give Arnold his proper rank if they didn't know he was in the battle!"

"I'll tell you what I meant," Varick said angrily. "Arnold can't get his proper rank unless Congress gives it to him. What Congress learns about the battle, they learn from the report sent to 'em by Gates—by Gates and his aide Wilkinson." He cursed with suprising versatility.

Then he said, "Gates's report to Congress didn't mention Arnold. Without Arnold we couldn't have won, but Gates gave him no credit. According to Gates, there wasn't any Arnold in the battle. According to Gates and Wilkinson, Arnold wasn't on the field! Congress will never know, officially, that Arnold won the battle of Freeman's Farm!"

"That's not possible!" I said. "Men don't do things like that."

"Oh, don't they?" Varick cried. "You don't know Gates and Wilkinson! They're politicians! How do you suppose Gates got himself put in command of this army? He got himself put in command of this army by making Congress believe the troops wouldn't fight under anyone but himself!

"He persuaded Congress to take out Schuyler—damn Gates's pintsized soul to hell! How do you suppose Gates'll hold his command if Arnold wins the battles: if the troops won't fight except for Arnold: if it's Arnold that stops the British: if it's Arnold who saves this country from ruin! Gates can't allow it! He won't have it! He won't let Arnold's name be mentioned in despatches! He won't admit Arnold's alive, even! It's got to be *Gates* that wins battles! *Gates* that thinks of what to do! *Gates*, God damn him!"

"Wait a minute," I said. "Where was Gates during the battle?"

"In his headquarters," Varick said. "He was in his headquarters!"

"He was in his headquarters?" I repeated heavily.

My mind seemed to halt at that picture of Gates, stooped, nearsighted, sly-eyed, squatting in a dark room while Arnold led and lashed and dragged his ragged, hungry troops, smashing the advance of those glittering scarlet columns.

I stared at Varick like a blockhead. I tried to think of something to say, and couldn't. For the thousandth time within the year, I could only have confused thoughts—a baffled wonderment as to why I should remain in such an army when it contained men like Gates and Wilkinson, Easton and Brown, Hazen and Bedel—men who would sacrifice the welfare of their own country—the comfort and the lives of their fellows—to their own warped ambitions. It infuriated me to have to be in mental torture over Nathaniel's fate, when Nathaniel's motives were more worthy than those that filled the incomprehensible minds of our accepted leaders.

I felt a bitter resentment that my fellow-countrymen should so persistently bow to mediocrity: that small men should pursue their devious ways unhindered, and great men be discredited and reviled. I thought, vaguely, that if only I could emerge alive from what lay before us: if only I could find some way to save Nathaniel's reputation, wars and armies and Congresses, for all of me, could go to hell, where they belonged.

Yet, as these things struggled in my mind, I suddenly seemed to catch the faint scent of oak chips and marsh mud: to hear the screaming of mackerel gulls in swift flight above our shipyard in Arundel: to see our workmen, on an autumn evening, stumbling up the slope to drink from our well and then go safely off to their suppers. Strangely, too, there flashed into my mind the freckled boy who had run from the farm house to join that shambling stream that flowed and flowed "agin Burgine": the face of the woman who had come to the farm house door and watched him go. . . .

I felt a faint, unpleasant stirring of something I can only call responsibility, and dimly sensed that no matter what others might be, I was, through no act or wish of my own, a part of the land and the people: an unalterable part of the land and the people. I had an obscure realization that the land and the people were stronger in me than love or hate or fear or aversion to discomfort—that such poor fools as I are doomed to endure war perpetually, just as clouds are perpetually created to shed fertility on a little square of earth, and then perish.

"He was in his quarters!" I murmured again. I couldn't comprehend it. "Why did he stay there? Why didn't he——"

"Oh, God knows!" Varick said. "Why did he act like a blackguard when he took command of this army? When Gates arrived here, General Schuyler, in spite of the mistreatment he'd received, offered him help and hospitality; and do you know what Gates did? He wouldn't even do Schuyler the courtesy to invite him to a Council of War. Why? Why? There's no way of telling! There's no way of accounting for the acts of a man like that!"

He threw up his hands in a gesture of disgust. "It's no use talking about it. Arnold's a true friend to Schuyler, and a great leader. Gates is neither, but he's in command and he can wreck all of us if he sees fit. Talk won't change things!"

I thought best to take this as a hint. "Do you know where my friends are camped?"

He laughed. "I do indeed! They're camped on the slope of the next ravine, where they can be convenient to the British pickets."

I wondered why he laughed.

We left our horses tied to the fence behind Arnold's headquarters and followed the road to the north. The rolling country on both sides of the road was forested with hardwood groves and stands of pine; and as Doc Means said, there were no more signs of British in the neighborhood than of buffaloes. For that matter, once we were out of sight of Arnold's headquarters and a single near-by farm house, there were no signs of anything. There were no tents, no sentries, no pickets, no passing on the road. We couldn't see the Hudson, even; and our own camp with its surrounding fortifications was entirely concealed behind us.

It was when the road dipped into a ravine that we heard something strange. At first it seemed to be the hoarse growling of an animal, followed by the yapping of smaller animals. "By Grapes!" Doc said. "If I was in any civilized section, I'd say that was some kind of a den of bears and foxes; but being off here in the woods this way, I shouldn't wonder if Cap Huff had something to do with it, though that growling certainly don't sound like none of my acquaintances."

We pushed down the ravine. The growling became a human voice struggling with passages from the song *Yankee Doodle*. The accompanying yapping proved to be other humans, demonstrating, from time to time, the proper rendition of that same song. Then we distinguished Cap Huff's stentorian bellow.

"No!" he was saying. "No! How in God's name you ever expect to get to be an American if you keep saying 'Shdug'! It's 'Stuck!' Ess, tee, yew, uck, Stuck! 'Stuck a feather in his cap and called it macaroni!' Come on, now! Get it right this time, or you don't hold Grettle tonight!"

We came into a cleared space on the side of the ravine. A lean-to, made of fir branches, faced the north, and on low bunks within it sat or lay Tom Bickford, Joseph Phipps, and two Indians who seemed almost disguised because of the garish red and white caps they wore—the only means by which our Indians could be distinguished from those who fought with the British. One was Natanis, and the other Lewis Vincent, that friend of Verrieul's who had helped us escape from the Sacs and Foxes.

Before them stood Cap Huff, as red faced and sweaty as ever, in close communion with an odd-looking youth who had yellow hair, broad hips and a habit of standing with such rigidity that he tilted backward. Thus his stomach was thrust forward and he looked fatter than he actually was. He had on the fragments of a pair of once-white breeches, a green coat from which the sleeves and tails had been removed, and the remnants of a pair of dragoon's boots.

When Cap saw us he seized the strange-looking youth by the front of his sleeveless green coat and shook him violently. "Hey!" he bawled deafeningly. "Nix more sing. Veer drink! Brink drink!" He stared anxiously into the young man's eyes. When the young man nodded, Cap sighed with relief and joined the others in greeting us.

"Gosh," Cap cried, "we thought you was going to miss all the fun, Cap'n Peter! You too, old Catamount!" He slapped Doc affectionately, then contorted his face horribly, jerking both thumb and head toward the strange youth, who had gone down on his knees to fumble in one of the bed-places, seemingly hunting for the drink that Cap had ordered.

"What you think of *him*, hey? He's one of them Hessians you've heard about. Name of Konrad! We ain't making no effort to memorize his last name—not till he learns some English so's we can speak his name in a translated form."

"Where'd you get him?"

"Got him in the battle," Cap said. "I thought I captured him, but he claims he deserted to us on account of liking my looks. He says he's going to be an American from now on, just like me, and I guess we ain't going to be able to do nothing to stop him!"

He muttered something about Konrad being more of a responsibility than a sick hound.

"What was the battle like?"

"About the same as all of 'em," Cap said indifferently. "Of course, fighting in the woods don't present the opportunities that city fighting does, but I picked up this Konrad, and four Hessian canteens full of English rum, and a gold gorget. I might 'a' done worse. The truth is, I took this Konrad to carry those canteens. That's what he's doing now: digging up one of the canteens. He tends to our needs, when we got any. He'd be kind of funny if he wasn't such a nuisance to talk to. You have to holler at him so loud it gives you a headache."

Cap might have been a boy with a new puppy, so wrapped up was he in Konrad. "Think up something for him to do," he urged. "He's the helpfullest thing ever you see! Cooks, sews, sings hymns, mends stockings, knits, cleans muskets, makes shoes and waits on table. I dunno what they want to put fellers like that in an army for! You can get soldiers anywhere, but it's a terrible hard thing to get a waiter that won't spill pork drippings down your neck and bring you hoss-meat when you order beef. Now you take those thirty-five hundred Hessians with Burgoyne—there's thirty-five hundred waiters just ruined for no reason at all."

"Where's Nason?" I asked.

"Out with Arnold," Cap said. "Him and Arnold, they go out together all the time, just keeping their ears to the ground. That Arnold, he knows what the English figure on doing before they do themselves. He keeps his ear so close to the ground a mole could lick it."

Konrad brought us a huge wooden canteen and a drinking cup made from a gourd. He gave Cap the cup; filled it with eager care: then stood beaming upon him with idolatrous admiration. Cap drank, exhaled gustily and, with a gracious gesture, indicated to Konrad that he should serve all of us.

"By God," Cap said, as Konrad brought the cup to me, "I dunno what people want to do so much hollering against these Hessians for! I'd ruther have one belong to me than a ox or a steer, any day. I'll bet if people in this country ever get to understanding these Hessians's ways, and how smart and attached they are if you encourage 'em, everybody'd want one or two. In the first place, they learn quicker'n a tame crow, and you can call 'em anything you want to—you can even take and call 'em names you wouldn't like to call a crow, because of course they don't understand you. It's a mighty nice relief, sometimes, to call a man a whole lot of horrible names without having to fight about it. Yes sir, these here Hessians are useful!"

"When'll Nason be back?" I asked him.

"I dunno," he said carelessly. "Prob'ly he won't be back till it's about time for us to go gunning for pickets." He looked up at the heavy sky. "This'll be a nice night for picket-shooting—good'n dark, and not too wet. We ought to get us a picket apiece, a night like this."

I found his reference to pickets puzzling. "How can you——"

Cap laid his hand on my arm. "Listen, I want to tell you what I told all the rest of our people. When we have another battle, keep your eyes open for a she-Hessian. Maybe you'll come across one when we go picket-shooting. If you do, don't let her get hurt: bring her back, so's I can go into the business of breeding 'em when the campaign's over."

I tried to speak, but he crowded closer to me and breathed heavily. "You ought to hear the stuff he's learned. He's *smart!* He speaks pieces for us regular. Soon's we get *Yankee Doodle* taught to him, he'll be as good an American, pretty near, as anyone there is. I dunno but what he's better than a lot of these New York folks, right now. Konrad, he thinks the whole of America's a pretty good place; but a lot of these New Yorkers, they think there ain't no place in America worth a damn, outside of New York."

He turned sharply to Konrad and shouted, "Sprick English!"

Konrad clapped his hands to his side, standing so straight that he leaned backward. In a high, monotonous, unaccented voice he said loudly, "Cheneral Gates iss der greadest cheneral in der vurld." Then he looked at Cap with eager attention. Cap hooked his thumbs in his belt, surveyed Konrad proudly, and strolled away carelessly. Suddenly he turned and raised a forefinger as a signal. Konrad protruded his tongue and forced air noisily around it, making a disgusting sound at which Tom Bickford, Joseph Phipps and Lewis Vincent laughed until they cried.

Cap glowed with pride. "Didn't take over fourteen or fifteen hours to learn him that. Konrad's smart!"

"Look here," I said, "can't you think about anything but Konrad?"

Cap eyed me morosely. "What else would I think about?"

"What else? Why, anything else that's of interest to me! How did Lewis Vincent get here? How is it you can go gunning for British pickets without having your scalps snatched off? Have you heard any news of —any news of my brother?"

Tom Bickford answered for him. "That was the first thing we asked Lewis Vincent, Cap'n Peter, when he got away and joined us. He couldn't get away till after the western Indians went home. That's how it happens we're able to be so free with their pickets."

He spoke more earnestly. "It's lots of fun, Cap'n Peter: honest. There aren't any Indians to bother us, hardly. They went home a week after Jennie McCrae was killed. They felt Burgoyne was being too strict with 'em."

"Listen!" Cap said savagely. "For three years I ain't heard about nothing but war! I've had war for breakfast, war for dinner, war for supper— and damned little else! I've had war morning, noon and night, and some of the nights have been a week long. I've had a bellyful of war, out in these damned dark woods, playing tag with wolves and dead men, and not knowing when some red-coated poop-head'll pop around in back of me and blow off the top of my skull. For God's sake, shut up about the war! Lemme talk to Konrad and forget about it for five minutes, will you?"

Doc scanned him closely. "You're sick."

"I *ain't* sick!" Cap shouted. "I'm tired of this lousy war! I'm tired of folks that tell you to do things they ain't got the gizzard to do themselves! I'm tired of that clay-faced louse Gates and that little antimire Wilkinson, prowling around here and getting the credit for what me and George Washington and Schuyler and Arnold done! For God's sake, ain't it enough to have to fight in a lousy war like this without having to talk about it?"

Cap glared at us, breathing heavily; and for a time nobody spoke. Tom Bickford broke the silence. "We been a little nervous, Cap'n Peter, on account of the rumors we been hearing about General Arnold. We hear General Gates wants to drive him out. We wouldn't feel any too good if we had to fight the British under anyone but General Arnold."

"Nonsense!" I said. "We stopped at his headquarters on the way down, and if there'd been any danger of Arnold leaving, Varick would have said so. You ought to see the way the militia's piling in! There's thousands of 'em on the road, all headed this way!"

"Yes, we heard so," Tom said. "That's another thing we're worried about. If the militia ever starts to run, and Arnold isn't here to stop 'em, they'll get in a panic and run forever. They'll carry everything with 'em —scouts and Continentals and everybody."

"Everybody but Konrad," Cap said bitterly. "That thick-headed Hessian, he'd sit right here waiting for me to come and lead him away by the hand!"

Hard on Cap's words I heard the roar of a heavy gun, straight out in front of us. "What's that?" Doc asked.

"That's their sunset gun," Cap said. "They ain't a mile from us, hardly. If they're that close, how do you s'pose I'll have time to get back here and look out for Konrad in case anything happens?"

It was still light when Nason came down the path carrying a slab of beef which Cap snatched from him. "Raw!" he said contemptuously. "Fresh and raw! That kind of meat's not only tasteless: it's weakening! You'd think you was eating jelly-fish! Why don't you get salt pork, Stevie? There ain't nothing so tasty or nourishing as salt pork." He gave the meat to Konrad, who took it to the fire before the lean-to.

Nason seemed glad to see us, though like most of our Arundel people, he was not one to make a display of emotion. I could tell he was glad because he came up close and looked at us. "I saw Varick and heard you'd got back," he said. "Did you get to Arundel on your travels?"

When I said I hadn't, he said soberly, "I hope we'll be back there before very long."

"You *hope* we will!" Cap shouted. "What the hell's *that* mean! Has anything happened?"

"Nothing to worry over," Nason said.

"My God!" Cap bawled. "Something *has* happened! Something's happened to Arnold! I knew damned well something was going to happen when I saw that little stink-wit Wilkinson in camp! What happened to Arnold? I suppose Gates promoted eighteen or twenty corporals over his head!"

"No," Nason said. "Gates just took Morgan's regiment of riflemen away from Arnold's division, without any explanation."

"Oh, is that so?" Cap asked heavily. "He took Morgan's regiment away from him, did he? Why didn't he take an arm and a leg and a couple of his eyes, too?"

Nason turned to me. "Maybe you didn't know that Washington sent Morgan and his riflemen up to Schuyler before Congress threw Schuyler out of the army. It's the greatest regiment in the world. Every man in it can shoot the head off a humming-bird at thirty paces."

"I never seen 'em shoot humming-birds," Cap remarked sourly, "but I saw 'em working on British officers up at Freeman's Farm. It's God's wonder the British got any officers left! Every time one of 'em came out in the open, where Morgan's men could get a look at him, there'd be about seven bullets hit him. You could hear 'em hit, like a squash pie hitting a barn door."

Nason nodded. "That's right. Arnold used that regiment the way you'd use a whip. He snapped it at 'em, first thing, and it made the British jump and scatter. When he'd rubbed 'em raw with it, he threw his other brigades straight at 'em and busted 'em wide open."

"Why did Gates take it away from him," I asked, "and when did it happen?"

"It just happened," Nason said. "We just heard about it, an hour ago. Wilkinson issued general orders saying Colonel Morgan's corps was to take instructions only from headquarters. As to why it was done, your guess is as good as mine. I'd say it was to aggravate Arnold—make him so mad he'd have to quit."

"Now listen, Stevie," Cap said, exasperated, "he *can't* quit! The British may sail into us again tomorrow, or next day! He *can't* quit!"

Nason looked at him coldly. "What would *you* do," he asked, "if I'd told you to give orders to Natanis and Joe Phipps, and you did; and then I went to 'em and said, 'Don't pay any attention to what that big moose tells you! He doesn't know what he's talking about!' What would you say to that?"

Cap snorted. "What would I say? I dunno as I'd say much, but I'd get me a tent-peg and bust it over that thick head of yours!"

"Well," Nason said, "generals don't bust tent-pegs on each other, especially if one of 'em's the commanding general. If Gates insults Arnold, after what he's done for this army, there's only one thing for Arnold to do."

"Now wait a minute, Stevie," Cap said. "If Arnold goes away, who'll lead us? Gates can't. When there's a battle, he has to stay home to make the beds and empty the pots. Who else is there besides Gates?"

"Lincoln," Nason said. "General Lincoln just came over from New Hampshire."

Cap's voice was incredulous. "Lincoln! I saw him once. He's the fat one, ain't he?"

Nason nodded.

Cap snorted. "How the hell would Lincoln lead us? He's so fat he can't straddle a horse! If he led us, he'd have to be pushed in a wheelbarrow! How would you feel if you was being encouraged to climb that hill at Freeman's Farm by a fat general in a wheelbarrow? My God, Stevie, how'd you like to have to *push* him? *Somebody'd* have to!"

Nason said nothing.

"Stevie," Cap said, "Arnold ain't going to leave us, is he?"

"Yes. He's asked Gates for a pass for himself and his aides, so he can go down and join Washington, where he'll be allowed to make himself useful."

Cap made an ineffectual hissing sound. We sat there, staring at the darkness of the forest across the ravine. I saw from the attitude of these men that in all that Northern Army there was only one leader in whom they had confidence. Without him, I wondered, what would become of all of us?

Konrad lifted the kettle from the fire—a stew of boiled meat and potatoes. We took it from him and ate in silence.

When we were finished, Cap studied his knuckles. "If we ain't responsible to nobody but Arnold," he said to Nason, "and if Arnold's going to leave the army, why don't we take it easy tonight? Why don't we stay right here and get a good night's sleep?"

"We'll do the same as usual," Nason told him. "Those British pickets have to be tended to, no matter what happens to Arnold."

Cap rose and stretched himself. "Well, it's dark enough, ain't it? What are you waiting for?"

"What'll I do?" I asked Nason. "I told Varick I'd see Arnold tonight."

"Keep away from him," Nason said. "You're under my orders. You'll kill pickets with the rest of us."

Tom, Cap, Joseph Phipps and the others gathered up their muskets, powder horns, hatchets and shot-pouches. Konrad, standing stiffly by the small fire before the lean-to, was shivering.

Doc stepped close to him. "Why," he said feebly, "he's crying. He's crying his eyes out!"

Cap came and looked in Konrad's face. "Yes," he admitted, "he certainly is! I wisht I could break him of it. Every time we go out picket-shooting, he cries. Sometimes he cries mornings and afternoons too. What you s'pose is the matter with him, old Catamount?"

"Prob'ly he's homesick," Doc said mildly. "Prob'ly he gets to thinking he won't never see no one he likes, ever again."

Cap sighed gustily. "Well, I s'pose I'll have to let the damned old cry-baby have Grettle. I hate to do it, because every time we let him have Grettle near our bed-places, we all have fleas next morning."

He went to the back of the lean-to and pulled at a chain. A raccoon, malevolent-looking in the firelight, was dragged protestingly from behind the bottom logs of the rear wall. "Here you are, Konrad," Cap said wearily. "Here's this pet flea-farm of yours."

Konrad fell to his knees and gathered the raccoon in his arms. The small animal, a look of incredible craftiness on its masked features, paddled at Konrad's chin with paws like small black hands; then pressed its pointed nose to the man's neck.

As we crossed the ravine behind Nason, we could hear Konrad lavishing noisy kisses on Grettle.

"Listen to that!" Cap said wonderingly. "If I was as homesick as all that, I couldn't get along with nothing so small as a raccoon! I'd want a tame bear, or maybe a moose."

In spite of Cap's pretended intolerance, I suspected that more than one of us had a fellow feeling for Konrad—especially if it was true, as Doc believed, that he feared he might never see anyone he loved, ever again.

LXIV

For two long weeks we were inundated by a flood of doubts, complaints and rumors; and so violent was the flood that there were some who feared the army might be washed away by it, and scattered to every quarter of the country, leaving the road free for Burgoyne to walk through to Albany.

Every night, during those two weeks, we, together with countless other scouting parties, stalked British pickets in the deep woods, pecking perpetually at them so that the army which they guarded might be kept awake and in constant fear of attack.

Each day we asked eagerly for news of Arnold—for Arnold hadn't gone. He was with us still, but under circumstances more strange and outrageous, I truly believe, than ever were endured by any officer in the field. On the first moment when word had flashed through the camp that Gates had wronged Arnold, and that Arnold felt obliged to leave the army, such an uproar arose from all the regiments that their officers were obliged to take notice of it. The men said openly that they wanted Arnold; nor was this surprising, since Arnold had led men in more battles than had any other officer in the army, whereas Gates had never led a man in any battle at all. They applied opprobrious names to Gates, calling him General Back-house, the Old Woman, General Pussyfoot, the Old Gray Mare and others less delicate; and songs began to circulate—rude songs, highly uncomplimentary to Gates.

Cap returned to us, reeking of rum after a visit to the Arundel men in Brewer's regiment, and taught us one of these songs. It was rhymeless and tuneless, but it was easy to learn and the men seemed to like to sit and sing it interminably. One who wished to start it needed only to sing

> "Where was the Old Woman
> When Arnold was fighting—
> Fighting the battle of Quebec!"

On this everybody would bellow

> "She was under the sink
> She was under the sink

She was under the sink
With her fingers in her ears!"

Or they would roar

"She was out in the cow-shed
She was out in the cow-shed
She was out in the cow-shed
Hiding behind a cow."

In countless verses the singers asked how the Old Woman had occupied herself when Arnold was fighting at the Cedars, at Valcour, at Ridgefield, at Fort Stanwix, at Freeman's Farm; and they thought up singular places, none of them creditable, where Gates might have been hidden.

As a result of all this uproar, the higher officers of the army composed a letter to Arnold, begging him to stay. The army needed him, they said: the men wanted him. The letter was signed by all the higher officers, barring only Gates, Wilkinson and the fat Lincoln. Because of this, Arnold stayed. But such was Gates's animosity to him—such was Gates's determination not to permit himself to be dwarfed by Arnold's leadership and popularity—that he deprived Arnold of his command. Arnold stayed with the army; but to no part of it was he allowed to issue orders.

Because I have never ceased to resent the shameful injustices so brazenly inflicted by Gates to further his own selfish designs, I wish to set down what I believe to be the simple truth about him. To my way of thinking no man had fewer redeeming qualities, or came closer to bringing about our overwhelming defeat than Horatio Gates. He was commonplace, vain, sly, jealous, inconsiderate, unfair, unjust. He was slow, incompetent, narrow-minded, ungenerous, unresourceful, petty, boorish and untruthful. He instinctively resented talent, genius and impetuous bravery. He ousted Schuyler and Arnold, and stole the credit for the work they did; he plotted to supersede Washington, as a buzzard might plot to supersede an eagle. All his faults were mirrored in his insufferable satellite James Wilkinson; and while Gates was doing all he could to destroy Arnold, Schuyler, Washington and Daniel Morgan, he was begging Congress to make Wilkinson a general. That was the sort of justice meted out by Gates. He fawned on Congress to obtain a generalcy for the twenty-one-year-old Wilkinson; but for Morgan, who was still a colonel, and had played a giant's part in the battle of Freeman's Farm, he had nothing but contemptuous silence, though Morgan was a thousand times more deserving of being a general than was Gates himself.

Cap Huff's rage at Gates's treatment of Arnold was no greater than Nason's or Tom Bickford's or mine; but it was noisier—possibly because Konrad had been taken from him by Wilkinson's orders and placed with the rest of the prisoners in the rear.

"Listen," he said, his voice venomous. "Arnold transferred us to Morgan, and I'll take orders from Morgan, just the way I'd take 'em from Stevie, but I won't take 'em from no general that's put in Arnold's place. If that gray louse Gates comes out and tries to lead us, instead of Arnold——"

"He won't!" Nason said.

"By God," Cap insisted, "if he does, he better hang a couple stove lids inside his breeches, because from what I hear, there'll be five hundred fellers take a shot at him from behind, and that's a shot they won't miss!"

In the midst of all this excitement and uncertainty we saw nothing of Arnold, as we had been obliged to erect a new lean-to close to Morgan's headquarters, which were in front of the center of the main fortifications on Bemis's Heights.

The militia came in and came in. The camp behind us was full of militia, and the country behind the camp was dotted with the shelters they built for themselves. How large our army had grown by the first week in October, God only knows. None of our officers knew definitely, not even Gates and Wilkinson. On one thing everyone insisted. Our Continental troops alone were nearly equal in number to that of Burgoyne's army. And over and above the Continental troops were the militia, swarming like locusts, and, like locusts, stripping the country of food. There were thousands of them: all day long we could hear their drums as they drilled—a faint, distant rattling, like the dry whirring of the wings of monstrous insects.

And day after day we grew more impatient and more irritable, knowing that Burgoyne, sooner or later, must try once more to break through: wondering why he didn't: wondering, above all, what would happen to us without Arnold.

. . . We had the answer on October 7th.

There had been loud talk, on the morning of that day, from Cap Huff. In his picket-hunting of the night before, he said, he had come across a potato field in which there were potatoes still undug. Since Nason usually required proof of his statements, he had brought it back with him in the shape of a peck of potatoes artfully disposed about his person. Wherever there were potatoes, Cap said, there would soon be British, since many of the British troops were Irish, who have a veritable passion for potatoes. Therefore he proposed that we should steal back to the potato field by daylight. In daylight we wouldn't forever be interrupting a wolf or tripping over a half-buried body, he said, and we could lie there quietly and watch for British to come and dig the potatoes: then, when the potatoes were dug, we could kill two birds with one stone by popping off the diggers and taking the potatoes for ourselves. Since there was more than a little sense to what Cap suggested, Nason had gone to see Morgan about it.

It was around noon-time that I became conscious of scurry and bustle in the camp behind us. I got up and went back to a mound from which I could see the doll-sized farm house in which Gates had his headquarters. Aides and messengers were moving away from it, two or three on horseback and the rest afoot. They were scattering in every direction, and they were hurrying. The horses were galloping, and the feet of the running men raised clouds of dust.

I saw Nason pelting toward me, between the tents of Morgan's corps of riflemen, and as he ran, the ground around those tents suddenly swarmed with men. Morgan's drums began to roll, and farther back, beyond Gates's headquarters, other drums took up the sound.

When I hurried to our lean-to, I found Cap freshening the fire and hanging a kettle above it.

"Don't bother with that," I told him. "Put on a clean shirt. I think we're going to fight."

"I know damned well we are," Cap said, "and I ain't so much interested in a clean shirt as I am in getting those potatoes cooked. For one thing, I ain't got but one shirt, and that's in use. For another thing, if we got to fight, we prob'ly won't get nothing to eat for three or four days—maybe a week. From what I've seen of this army, it always gives you some leeway when it comes to dying. Either you can get shot, or you can starve to death."

Nason, when he came up, put an end to Cap's plans. "Break down this lean-to," he ordered, "and dump your stuff with Morgan's baggage. We're going out with Morgan. Hurry up!"

Cap protested bitterly. "These battles never start when they're supposed to, Stevie! I'll bet there's time enough to cook a whole cow! Lemme cook these potatoes! You go ahead and I'll catch up."

"Bury 'em under the fire," Nason said. "Then you can get 'em tonight."

Cap grumbled and growled. "Tonight! Tonight! Maybe I won't stand in no need of potatoes tonight!"

But he obeyed Nason; then joined Tom Bickford, Joseph Phipps,

Lewis Vincent and Natanis in gathering up personal belongings—and an amazing number of them he unearthed from beneath his bed-place: not only Hessian canteens, but enough loot from the battlefield to have stocked a museum. All these things he wrapped in the skin of a wolf which he claimed to have choked to death one night in mortal combat, though Doc Means insisted the wolf had heard Cap talking to himself in liquor and had dropped dead of shock.

"What's happening?" I asked Nason.

"God knows," he said. "A sergeant came in from the advanced pickets. There's a big column of British moving down on us. They're going to try to break through us along the ridge—as far from the river as they can get."

"How many?"

Nason shook his head. "The sergeant thought fifteen hundred. He said they were bringing up artillery, light troops, Indians, Germans—everything! Over at headquarters they think it's a column to feel us out. If we aren't strong enough to turn it back, they think Burgoyne'll throw his whole army behind it and move right on into Albany."

He hustled us, single file, up to the earthworks and into the camp. Morgan's battalion of riflemen was drawn up in a long double line with Dearborn's light infantry close behind them. Morgan's Virginians were tall men, neatly dressed in fringed hunting shirts and leggins; but tall as they were, their rifles, inlaid on stocks and grips with silver stars, half-moons and eagles, were even taller.

This corps of Morgan's and Dearborn's was only five hundred strong; but never, I truly believe, were there ever any ten regiments as dangerous. For one thing, all the men were woodsmen and hunters, accustomed from boyhood to stalking deer, bears and wild turkeys in the deep woods; and every man had learned through long experience that his health and safety, in the forest, depended on his ability to see his quarry before that quarry saw him, and to stop it in its tracks with a single shot. What was more, they were commanded by two resourceful soldiers who had good cause to use all of their resourcefulness against the British; for both of them, after Arnold's attack on Quebec two years before, had spent the winter freezing in a British prison.

Both Nason and Cap Huff had fought under Morgan at Quebec; and though Virginians, as a rule, have small use for New Englanders, these riflemen, seemingly, had ceased to hold Cap's and Nason's place of birth against them. Indeed, from the way they shouted opprobrious remarks to Cap as he went lumbering past, they had almost an affection for him. "Hey, old rum-scullion, pick me up a extry canteen, if you see one laying around," a rifleman called. Another urged him to stay well in the rear, so not to flush a British general before they could get a crack at him.

The camp was alive with companies and regiments forming. From those rolling fields of Bemis's Heights, beyond which we should have seen the valley of the Hudson, a fog of grayish dust arose to hide the distant hills; and amid the dust men coughed, ran, stumbled, coughed and swore.

What with the rolling of the drums, the shouting and the confusion, I found myself short of breath, and I'm not ashamed to say I was in a nervous sweat, now that the hour was on us that might decide not only my own fate, but Nathaniel's and perhaps that of my country.

I caught Nason looking hard at Doc Means, who wavered along through the dust as though on the verge of dropping. "Doc," Nason said, "how'd you like to look after this baggage for us?"

Doc coughed. "What baggage?"

"This on our backs," Nason said. "Unless it's watched, you never know what's going to happen to it."

"No," Doc said mildly. "No, I didn't come to this war to look out for no baggage. Anybody that's inclined to worry about such trifles ain't got no business going to war or going anywhere else, for that matter. Anyone that wants my baggage can have it. There's a whole half of a blanket in it and one stocking without no heel."

Cap Huff slapped him on the back and they both coughed in unison. "If anybody robs us, old Catamount," Cap shouted, "we'll get ourselves one of Burgoyne's fourteen suits of clothes in place of what we lose!"

When we had dropped our belongings with Morgan's baggage, we hurried back to the long line of waiting riflemen, and attached ourselves to the last company—the one farthest to the right, so that Morgan, who marched always in the rear of his battalion, could use us for messengers if he so desired. We were just in time to see Morgan himself come running out from between the center companies to bawl directions to his troops.

He was a tremendous big man with the voice of an irritated teamster; and when he was in a hurry or in a passion, he was free in his speech, using language that made even Cap Huff emit envious clucks.

"They're on that cleared hill halfway between here and Freeman's Farm," Morgan bellowed. "We're to circle around and take 'em in the flank." He pulled a turkey-call from his pocket and blew into it. At the hurried gobble that emerged, the men laughed uproariously, and a chorus of answering gobbles came from the ranks.

"Turkey-shoot!" the men shouted. "Turkey-shoot!"

"Go ahead!" Morgan roared. He waved his arm like a flail toward the west. Without further orders these tall soldiers turned, shouldered their rifles and went striding off across the front of the camp. In spite of their uniform hunting shirts and their long rifles, there was less of a military air to them than a look of hunters setting off eagerly to stalk game of which they were certain.

Morgan stood where he was, waving his companies on. When the last of us came abreast of him, he fell in behind, growling to us to get along—to hurry. Almost treading on his heels came Dearborn's little column.

We turned into the road to the north, the rutted wagon track down which Doc and I had ridden to leave our horses at Arnold's headquarters. The dusty camp, the ragged rattle of drums, the slowly forming regiments dropped out of sight—became, almost, as though they had never existed.

I had a feeling that this was not what war was supposed to be—this silent battalion of dusty men in their hunting smocks the color of a cat in the dusk, hurrying with irregular steps along a desolate road smelling of dying leaves, cold earth and stink-bush. Then I realized that men had lied so often about war that they thought falsely of it as fine and glorious, whereas it never has been and never can be anything but a monstrous blend of weariness, disappointment, heartache, discomfort, injustice, dishonesty, hatred, fear, waste, stupidity, futility, turmoil, misery, sickness, cruelty and death.

As we drew near the small cabin in which Arnold had his quarters, I craned my neck for a sight of it, wishing I might stop for a word with that man who, through three campaigns, had striven so tirelessly and with so little regard for his own life to bring this war to a favorable conclusion, only to be rewarded with ingratitude and insults. I saw, too, that every head in our long and straggling line was turned in the same direction; and as we came out from behind the trees that screened the clearing in which the cabin stood, there was a murmuring and a muttering in the ranks—a murmuring and muttering like the sound of rising wind in trees.

Morgan lumbered out to one side, where he could see the length of the column. "Silence in the ranks!" he bawled.

Arnold himself was sitting in front of the cabin, his field-desk open before him. When he saw us he got to his feet and went to prowling up and down, up and down, with that peculiar gait of his, his head thrust out and his arms swinging, as though he climbed a steep hill. He stopped and looked at us, then went to prowling again, still eyeing our long column over his shoulder. I wondered what was in his mind.

We went on, across the small ravine on the slope of which Nason, Cap, Tom Bickford and the others had lived before Arnold had been deprived of his command, continued past it for a quarter mile, then turned abruptly west and struck into the deep woods.

❖   ❖   ❖

. . . Those men of Morgan's slipped between the trees like shadows. The fallen leaves through which they passed rustled a little, as dead leaves do when a breeze sets them to whispering dryly. Flankers moved out from the companies ahead to guard us from surprise. Morgan came alongside us again, motioning Nason to send out Natanis and Lewis Vincent on our flanks.

I saw the men ahead of me wedging rifle bullets between the fingers of their left hands, so to have them ready in case of need.

We made a wide circle through the forest. We were on rising ground, cut by gullies—rising ground so heavily forested that the company in advance were half-seen shadows, and the other companies completely lost to sight. We moved up and up, curving continually now, toward the north. I had the same feeling I had known a thousand times before, when circling through timberland to take a deer or a flock of turkeys unaware—a breathless, cautious wonder as to whether my calculations would prove to be correct, or whether, by showing myself in the wrong place, I would lose the results of all my labor.

We hurried on and on, to all appearances a throng without leaders and without discipline—a horde of hunters, our eyes peering constantly into the dark thickets at our right: our mouths half open for greater ease in hearing and breathing: our rifles loosely held against our breasts, as if the game we sought might burst from under foot at every step.

Suddenly and surprisingly, off to our right and on lower ground, we heard a ripping rattle, as of stout cloth sharply torn asunder—the rattle of musketry fire—and hard on its heels the thunder of artillery. We saw the red and white caps of Natanis and Lewis Vincent bobbing among the trees as they came pelting back to us, seeming almost to be running from the gunfire.

"Canadians," Lewis Vincent whispered hoarsely. "Canadians and Indians!"

Other flankers, we saw, were running in, pointing behind them. I heard the gobble of Morgan's turkey-call. He shouted something to Dearborn: then turned to us and swung his arm to the right; and somehow, without further orders, we were all moving to the right ourselves in a long, thin line: moving toward the distant guns—moving cautiously: slipping from tree to tree: craning our necks: watching and listening.

Nason's musket fired past my head. Not a half pistol-shot away a green-clad figure ran crouching from behind a tree, half turned and raised a musket. The whole forest echoed to racketings and bangings. The green-clad figure fell in a heap. I saw an Indian running, and with him two more shadowy figures in green. I snapped at them and had the feeling I had shot too far behind. One of them fell. When I ran forward, he got up and scuttled off, as a turkey does when not hit hard enough.

I stopped to load and found my hands were shaking. Near me Cap and Doc were loading.

"Did you see that, old Catamount?" Cap asked hoarsely. "I got him right under the shoulder."

"He was mine," Doc protested. "I held right on him!"

Cap's voice was bitter. "Like hell you did! I was holding right on him my own self! He showed up big as a horse between my sights!"

"All right," Doc said, and I could tell he was angry, "all right! I bet you don't dast to call your shots after this!"

We caught up with those who hadn't fired. As we passed the dead Canadian, I straightened him out with my boot. His eyes were shot out, there was a bullet through the back of his head, and there were bullet holes in the shoulder and chest of his green buckskin hunting smock.

The firing had stopped. We were near a clearing; for the forest was lighter. The Virginians were at the edge of the wood, where the young growth made a screen. They were strung out in a long line, crouching, kneeling, hiding behind trees, and all intent on what lay before them. Morgan was near their center, making cautioning, silencing motions with his outstretched hands. His men were setting their caps more firmly on their heads, examining the strings of their powder horns for faults, wedging more bullets between their fingers.

We were on a hill. A short way down the slope was a long clearing, a wheat field, pale gold in the slanting rays of the warm October sun. The pale gold was streaked with dark shadows of stumps and girdled trees, for clearings in this Hudson River country are freshly made by settlers only recently arrived.

Stretched across the wheat field were the British in brilliant array—a long line of scarlet and blue and white. They were in three sections, each section on a hillock. Those nearest us were light infantry, in little black leather hats, and scarlet coats and waistcoats above white breeches. Beyond them, holding the center of the line, were German troops, in blue coats and white breeches. On the farthest hillock were British grenadiers in tall bearskin hats. Among the grenadiers were cannon, and from their portion of the line came the roaring and rattling of guns and small arms: from their distant hillock rose clouds of white smoke that curled and drifted into the trees on the far side of the field.

Along the front of the wheat field was a deep ravine that guarded the whole of this gaudy British line; yet on the slope of the farthest hillock, where the guns were thudding and bellowing, little dark figures were coming out of the ravine and flowing up toward the wheat field— creeping and crawling upward toward those roaring guns from which jetted billowing clouds of white.

Nason dumped buck-shot into his musket and laughed exultantly. "By God, who said our men wouldn't stand up to British artillery!"

We heard Morgan shout. He moved from the shelter of the trees and out onto the hillslope, thick with stumps and slashings. We all followed him. It was like moving out into a clearing to shoot at a deer, for we shot as we came out, ran a few steps forward to the shelter of stumps and fallen trees to load and shoot again.

We were fast with our muskets, having learned to throw in powder, thump the butt on the ground, drop in the shot without a wad and slap the lock to prime it, which is a useful method at short range; but fast as we were, the riflemen were almost as fast.

I heard Cap bawling, "The feller with the black sash! The feller with the black sash!" and knew he was calling his shots. I was conscious of the rattle of rifle-fire all around me, and of having to hunt for a rift in the smoke in order to see my targets.

The British light infantrymen were huddled in a mass. I made out officers gesturing to them to change front, so to face our fire instead of letting us rake them; but the men were slow in obeying, because the officers, being clearly distinguishable on account of their swords and sword-sashes, were falling right and left.

They were good soldiers, those British light infantrymen, and I think they might have been successful in changing their front, in spite of the officers we shot down and the men who sprawled in the wheat, kicking and crawling and groaning.

But while they were in a confused mass, half going one way and half another, Dearborn's infantry came bursting from the trees to our right, stopped in a long line, and let off a volley all together. Thus we had those light infantrymen caught between a cross-fire, and such a cross-fire as I hope I may never be called on to endure.

To us it looked as though every scarlet-coated soldier on that hillock had been hit, for all of them were twisting and staggering and tripping, falling over wounded men and over each other. They seemed blasted and withered by the crescent of fire that spat against them, for they fired their muskets into the air; fired them into the ground; stood without firing, staring stupidly at the dead and the wounded lying about them.

I heard Morgan's bellow above the cracking of the rifles. I saw Nason on his feet, Cap Huff beside him: all the Virginians and all of Dearborn's men on their feet. We were all running toward the wheat field—converging toward that milling, tripping mass of scarlet-coated men. The Virginians loaded and fired as they ran.

Those British light infantrymen seemed to burst backward, as though an invisible bomb had exploded before them. Stumbling, leaping over stumps, galloping through the wheat, they fled away from us and into the forest at the back of the wheat field.

All around us were dead and wounded men, every last one of them British. From the wheat rose groans and sharp cries: whimperings of pain: frightened calls for assistance.

We might have helped the wounded if Morgan had not moved us closer to the central mound of the wheat field—the mound which, when we had emerged on the hill, we had seen to be held by Germans. We moved, not as a regiment, but in any way that suited us. Some advanced from stump to stump. Some climbed trees. Some squirmed forward through the wheat. We could see those Germans would be difficult to dislodge. For all we knew, they were impossible to dislodge.

Cap Huff kept up a perpetual argument with Doc Means. "You heard me!" Cap said. "I never fired once but what I called my shot. You heard me, didn't you? And you seen 'em go down, didn't you?"

"I heard you hollering that you'd take the feller in the black sash," Doc said mildly, "but all them officers had black sashes. I must have shot at ten of 'em myself."

"There ain't no pleasing you!" Cap said indignantly. "Even if I let you call my shots for me, you'd find some way of cheating me out of the credit. You'd prob'ly say, 'Get the feller with the red face!' and when I dropped him, you'd claim I'd picked the wrong red face!"

"A bet's a bet," Doc said. "If you're going to claim I owe you money for the ones you kill, you got to prove you killed 'em."

Cap rose suddenly to his feet, staring. From the bottom of the ravine, below the hillock held by the blue-coated Germans, came a babel of shouts and cheers. The ravine was full of men—soldiers in homespun, on their chests the crossed belts of Continental troops. Through the white birches on the far side of the ravine came a brown mare, her neck arched. She tossed her head and stepped daintily on that rough ground, picking up her hind legs gingerly, as though she trod on hot stones. In the saddle was an officer in blue and buff.

"Oh, my God!" Cap said huskily. "Oh, my good God!"

Doc pulled at him. "Lay down! First thing you know, one of them Germans'll call a shot on you and you won't never collect none of your bets!"

Cap just stood there, staring. Then, surprisingly, he bawled, "It's Arnold! Arnold! Come on, Arnold!"

I got up, too, to stare down into the ravine, and so did Nason and Tom Bickford. They shouted hoarse and indistinguishable words; for the man on the brown mare was, as Cap had said, General Arnold.

From the blue-coated ranks on the middle hillock came the rattle of musketry and the roar of heavy guns. Above our heads we heard the clatter of grape shot.

Cap shook his fist at the Germans. "You wait!" he bawled. "You'll roar out of the wrong side of your mouth before we get through with you!"

The brown mare picked her way through the troops crowded among the birches at the bottom of the ravine. Behind those troops we could see other companies pouring down through the birches on the far bank.

The soldiers seemed to caper about the brown mare. They waved their hats and their muskets; and their cheering was shrill, like a squall howling through top-hamper.

The mare leaped up from the ravine to stand on her hind legs and paw the air. Arnold cantered her back and forth before the swarming troops. Then he rose in his stirrups and shook his sword-hilt in their faces. He was shouting at them, we knew; but what he said we could only guess.

The troops, silent now, came pouring out from the birches. Arnold turned the mare and put her at the hillslope. The crest of the slope was ringed with smoke, and from the smoke came the crackling of musketry fire and the thundering of cannon. Long lines of brown-clad Americans poured upward. Across their front, back and forth, rode Arnold, urging them on. We could hear his voice, a high, harsh shouting, between the roaring of guns and above the rippling clatter of musketry.

The brown-clad ranks on the hillslope billowed outward in spots, and in other spots they sagged inward, wavering and uncertain. In spite of Arnold's urging, they slowed to a crawl. From the rear of those ranks, small portions tumbled to the bottom of the slope, like crumbs dropping from gingerbread. In the front of the straggling line, men fell and lay still. Then the whole long line sank downward, as a wavelet slips backward when it can rise no farther on a sandy beach—sank back and back until it reached again the security of the ravine.

Cap Huff, his eyes protuberant, made sounds of exasperation and disbelief.

High up on the slope lay a thin sprinkling of dark figures; and lower, moving always backward and forward before the troops, rode Arnold, shouting to the men and shouting to them, swinging his sword as if to swing them up by main strength. Unendingly, from the ridge above, the smoke of the German guns gushed out with such a thudding and roaring that I expected, every moment, to see Arnold pitch from his horse in a heap.

It was when that long line of men emerged once more from the birches and set off up the slope, after Arnold, that we, led by Morgan, slipped nearer and ever nearer to the blue-coated Germans—so near that we could no longer see Arnold rallying his troops at the bottom of the slope.

We crawled from stump to stump, from girdled tree to girdled tree. Through the smoke we could see the artillery horses: the gun-crews working on the guns. The horses reared and plunged as our bullets reached them. The gun-crews were in confusion.

"Black horse," I heard Cap shout behind me, "I call a black horse!" I heard, too, the quavering voice of Doc Means: "Horses don't count! You can't miss a horse!"

"Get the horses!" Nason said. "They can't move the guns without the horses!"

Two of the horses were down and kicking—three of them—four of them. The gun-crews ran and fell and rose to run again. The whole wheat field was a turmoil of shouts and groans and clattering and cursing—of confused and violent movement—of the screams of horses and the roar of cannon.

Over the crest of the wheat field came Arnold on his bay mare. He seemed to lean out above her head and lift her forward with the reins—lift her forward and hurl her at a gun-crew. He hacked at them with his sword, seeming to throw it rather than swing it. Close behind him, cheering and roaring with excitement, pressed a mass of brown-shirted Continentals.

The gun-crew scuttled from under Arnold's sword. The wheat field was alive with running men—men in blue coats and white breeches. Leaping over stumps and dead horses, diving under guns, stumbling and shouting, open-mouthed with consternation, they ran to the rear, toward the forest, and we ran after them, led on by Arnold and Morgan.

At the back edge of the wheat field was a rail fence. Behind it we could see British infantrymen, their muskets poked through the rails. The fleeing Germans went tumbling over the fence.

Among the infantrymen moved an officer on a gray horse. An aide rode at his elbow, so we knew he was a general. We could see him halting the fleeing Germans: showing them where to take post: stopping here and there to speak to his men. The rattle of musketry came from the rail fence and wisps of smoke rose from it, drifting across the dark wall of forest. We heard the bullets whipping past us, flirting through the trampled wheat.

"Officers!" we heard Morgan roaring in that carter's voice of his. "Get those officers or they'll get you!"

The British general looked suddenly behind him, as though something had gone wrong with his crupper. His hat fell off; and as it fell, he seized it and clapped it back on his head. It fell off again. He bent over in his saddle, putting his hands to his stomach; then pitched forward on his horse's neck. His aide leaped to the ground, held the general in the saddle and led him rapidly off through the trees.

Arnold's bay mare danced impatiently before us; and Arnold himself shouted shrilly at us to come ahead.

We ran after him toward the rail fence. When we got there, there was nobody behind it, only three fallen men in scarlet coats, one of whom was dead.

We stood there stupidly, wondering what to do. "Well," Cap Huff said hoarsely, "that's what I call a good day's work!"

Doc Means seemed disappointed. "Ain't there nothing more to it than that? I ain't hardly got myself warmed up."

I had somewhat the same feeling, and stared wonderingly back at the throng of sweaty, powder-blackened Americans that crowded behind us in half-formed companies—at the militia that still poured up from the ravine by the hundreds; by the thousands.

Three quarters of an hour ago the field on which we stood had been filled with British and Germans in orderly array. Now it was a litter of broken gun-rammers, short German muskets, wrecked ammunition carts, discarded coats and hats, dead men, dead horses, abandoned cannon, knots of prisoners, wounded men who cried out mournfully.

The British light infantry was gone. The British grenadiers who had been under attack when we burst from the forest were gone. The Germans were gone. We had turned them back. In three quarters of an hour we had stopped Burgoyne.

. . . I think it was true, what Cap said. We *had* done a good day's work, though not to Arnold's way of thinking. He sat there on his horse, backed into an angle of the rail fence. He was leaning over, his sword tucked under his left arm, talking to Morgan: clapping Morgan on the shoulder to emphasize his words.

When Morgan nodded, Arnold rose in his stirrups and shook the hilt of his sword at us. His high, harsh voice carried like a bugle, and could be heard, somehow, above any sort of tumult. Cap, in a thunderous bellow, was asking some of Morgan's Virginians where Gates and Lincoln might be, and in the same breath announcing that they were where no bullet would ever reach them; but at Arnold's first word he froze into immobility, his mouth agape.

"You drove 'em!" Arnold shouted. "You drove 'em! They've gone back to their camp! We're less than a mile from it! We're going there! We're going to take that camp! We've got 'em! We'll put an end to all the British and all the Burgoynes right now!"

His voice had a rasping, piercing quality to it that sent shivers down my back. At his words a thousand throats sent up a ragged roar.

"Remember this!" Arnold shouted. "Not all the British and all the Burgoynes in the world can stop you this day! The gun isn't made that can stop us—that can stop you men from Virginia and New England and New York!"

The men before him howled and cheered. Amid their confused shouting I heard the words, "Burgine! Drive 'em! To hell with Burgine! Drive him! Give us a shot at Burgine!"

Arnold opened his mouth as if to say something more. Then he closed it tight, whirled his horse, made a half circle, set it at the fence and cleared it. Cheering and laughing, Morgan's men tore down the rails and went pelting into the forest after Arnold.

. . . I have heard it said that Arnold was drunk that cold October afternoon—that he was mad with blood-lust—crazed by the injustices heaped on him by Congress and by Gates, and so was able to perform prodigies.

The folk who say such things reveal their ignorance of battle; their unacquaintance with the effects of liquor; their total incomprehension of the clarity of brain and the sureness of hand and eye required of a leader who acts as Arnold did.

A seaman, befuddled with drink, wrecks his ship in a crisis: an intoxicated soldier gives the wrong orders when able to give them at all: a drunken horseman, attempting such a race with death as Arnold rode, would tumble in the dust before he had more than started.

The truth is this: all his life Arnold was a performer of prodigies—a man who saw how to do, and freely risked his life to do, what other men said could not be done; and to small and common minds a performer of prodigies must always seem a little mad or more than a little drunk. But if ever a man had all his senses, and had them in the highest degree, it was Arnold in that second Battle of Saratoga—the one some call the Battle of Bemis's Heights, and others the Battle of Still-water.

There was a cutting through the forest—a road along which the British had brought their troops and guns when marching to the wheat field. We hurried down it after Arnold—a human river, dun-colored in the gathering gloom that had come with a threatening sky and the lateness of the day. It was a river that flowed with the noises of a turbulent stream—with the jouncing of powder horns and cartridge boxes: the screaking of belts and chafing of musket straps: the thudding and rustling of hurrying bodies. Like a storm-fed torrent it murmured and rattled, thumped and clattered, clanked and grunted, roared and rushed.

We came out of the woods into a long and shallow valley. It was a cleared valley, blocked by two low hills; one fairly close at hand: the other a quarter mile beyond the first. Up the slope of the nearer hill climbed small figures, some scarlet and white: others blue and white. They were the remnants of the proud detachment we had blasted from the wheat field.

Ahead of us the road wound through the stumps of the cleared land: then turned and vanished between the two low hills. On the summit of each of the two hills were breastworks, stockades, trenches: on the nearer hill, trees had been felled to make an abatis.

We came into the valley helter skelter—men from Learned's brigade of Continentals running alongside Morgan's and Dearborn's men: men from Poor's brigade of Continentals scuttling here and there, looking for their own companies and not finding them. There were no companies: there seemed to be no captains: no order: no rallying point—nothing but a confusion of shouting and running.

Nason caught me by the arm. "There's Morgan." Morgan was ahead of us, his face scarlet, bawling words nobody could hear. Nason pulled at me. "Come on! For God's sake, come on!"

Out in front of us Arnold, too, was shouting, his voice shrill and rasping. With his sword he made sweeping, scythe-like motions. His horse pranced and caracoled with excitement. Men hurried toward him, shouting unintelligibly. They were mostly Continentals and militia, among them a few of Morgan's men.

"They're going with Arnold," I shouted at Nason.

"We're with Morgan, you damned fool!" he said.

Cap Huff, his mouth wide open and his face dripping perspiration, couldn't take his eyes off Arnold.

Nason kicked him violently. "Get down the road where you belong! Follow Morgan!"

Cap and Doc turned and ran. I called to Joseph Phipps and we hurried with Nason after Cap. We caught up with a ragged drift of Morgan's riflemen, some of Dearborn's among them, a group of bewildered-looking Continentals and a few wild-eyed militia.

I looked back. Arnold was reining his prancing, curveting mare off the road, toward the nearer of the two fortified hills, and after him poured a yelling mob, waving their muskets above them.

Arnold whirled the mare. She bucked and kicked; then set off at a canter toward that silent nearer hill. Behind him raced his motley assemblage of soldiers.

Out from the forest poured more militia and more Continentals; more militia and still more militia. Some followed us down the road, but mostly they spread out, fan-wise, to scramble after Arnold.

The sight of those frantic, joyous soldiers, howling and running through the fields behind that speeding officer in blue and buff, made me feel I had somehow lost the chance to do great things.

That feeling lessened when the top of the hill toward which Arnold was charging erupted in smoke, flashes and thunderings. The whole valley shook with the crashing din. Momentarily I expected the mob following Arnold to falter, to throw themselves down, to go tumbling back whence they came.

They did nothing of the sort. They ran on and on, behind the galloping Arnold: ran to the base of the hill and started running up it.

All this I saw as I went hurrying toward the silent farther hill, pushed on by Nason, who ran at my elbow. I wondered whether that hill, too, contained within itself companion thunderings to those that crashed and rolled unendingly from the hilltop toward which Arnold and his mob were pressing. I wondered how far beyond that hill, and where, Nathaniel was—Nathaniel and Ellen Phipps.

* * *

. . . Nason shook me. He had been speaking to me, and I, in my absorption, had heard nothing. "I asked you," he said, "whether you ever scouted out as far as this?"

When I said I hadn't, he said that the two hills were the British right flank: that he and Natanis had often worked close to them at night.

I had forgotten Natanis. I looked around for him, and saw his red and white cap, and Lewis Vincent's, close behind, as though they kept watch on us.

"It's not the main camp," Nason said, looking at me curiously. "Their main camp's off to our right, closer to the river. It's in the main camp that they have their hospitals and stores and—and camp followers."

I knew why he said what he did. He wanted to warn me not to expect to find Nathaniel easily.

Cap Huff twisted his upper body, as he ran, and gazed eagerly into Nason's face. "All we got to do," he said hopefully, "is to throw 'em off those hills, ain't it? If we throw 'em off those hills, they ain't got no right flank, have they? If they ain't got no right flank, we can run right around 'em, can't we?"

"We certainly can!" Nason said.

"Yes, by God," Cap said, "and if we do, we can get what's left of those hundred and twenty-five thousand gallons of rum! I bet they ain't got more'n ten thousand gallons left—not hardly enough to make your breath smell!"

I heard Doc Means muttering as he wavered along beside Cap. "I don't scarcely ever touch rum, on account of it distressing me; but feeling the way I do, I dunno but what I could drink quite a lot of those ten thousand gallons—maybe a thousand of 'em."

"Like hell you could!" Cap said. "I'm going to drink all ten thousand of 'em myself!"

*   *   *

. . . We weren't long left in doubt as to what we'd receive from the hill we approached. The stockade at its top opened on us with musketry at two hundred yards. The rattling and clattering of those muskets seemed to me mild and harmless by comparison with the turbulent roaring still echoing from that other hill where Arnold was.

Nonetheless, I was glad to crouch, with Nason and Cap and the motley throng with whom we had run, behind a shelf at the foot of the hill—a shelf made by the gnawing of a brook. It was a God-sent breastwork, almost shoulder-high, behind which we could stand and fire up the slope at the stockade above us. So far as I could see, we were wasting our bullets on the stockade; for it was a stout one, made of fence-rails packed lengthwise between ten-foot posts. It was defended, Nason said, by Hessians.

How we'd ever have scaled that hill and taken the Hessian stockade, except for what happened, I have no way of knowing, nor do I know what otherwise would have befallen those of us that tried. I only know our chances of living through the scaling would have been smaller than I liked.

It was a gentle hillslope, without cover, and it seemed to me that those behind the stockade could no more miss a man who set foot on it than a housewife could fail to sweep a crumb from a table.

What happened was this, and we could see it as though it took place on the palms of our hands:

The British breastworks on that other hilltop, a quarter mile away, were protected on one side by an abatis of trees, felled so their tops, pointing down the hill toward Arnold, were interlaced. Arnold had chosen this slope for his attack, even though it was protected by the abatis, because it was the gentlest slope and also the one nearest him.

Dragged and driven onward by Arnold, that horde of Continentals and militia went swarming upward, and crawled into the abatis like ants crawling beneath a wall. They crawled in and crawled in, vanishing from our sight.

Arnold plunged into it, horse and all; probably he found a sally-port through which British pickets had come and gone. We lost sight of him and his horse, but it seemed to us that he and his men were snared and held in that web of tree tops.

Then Arnold broke through. That hill was shallower than ours, and even from the base of ours we were on ground high enough to let us see the tossing head of his horse, the familiar figure in the saddle and the flashing bright sword as he came out into the cleared space between the abatis and the British breastworks.

In my imagination I heard that high, harsh voice of his, calling the men forward: calling them out of the abatis. We saw their hats and heads and shoulders, and the glint of bayonets. We saw them duck for cover and knew they were crawling on the ground: lying behind rocks and stumps, singly and in groups. And yet that single figure on the horse had no cover, and marvelously did not fall, though the breastworks thundered and covered themselves with clouds.

Arnold rode his mare up and down, as if to be sure his men were planted as he wished them. Then he wheeled her and, passing between the breastworks and the abatis, set off toward us, galloping across the whole British front—between two hedges of smoke and spurting flashes. He passed, we knew, through a waist-high hail of bullets that should have tumbled him from his horse at every step he took, ripped open in a score of places. That it did not was some sort of miracle, as when a partridge, once in a thousand times, flies unhit through a charge of shot, even though such a thing can be proved to be impossible.

There was something more than exciting in the ride of that lonely figure between the lines and down the hill to the rolling stump-filled valley between. The day had turned grayer and more gloomy, and dusk was close upon us. It almost seemed that Arnold rode not only a race with death, but a race with some dark force that strove to reach us first. He rode hunched over, as if to lift his galloping mare over the stumps she sometimes had to jump; and the mare, grotesquely elongated by her straining, outstretched head, had the appearance of fleeing from an awful threat.

Those around me fired perfunctorily at the stockade above us; then fumbled with their powder horns and ramrods, clumsy for once in their reloading, because of the intensity with which they watched Arnold's mare. They watched and breathed noisily: made slow play with their ramrods: shot hurriedly at the stockade: turned again to watch intently. "The damned fool!" they muttered. "Where's he going? What's he think he's doing? What's he want?"

Other American troops, we saw, had entered the valley and were marching toward us on the road we ourselves had followed. They were coming fast, and they were Continentals, for we could see white belts crossed on their chests. Arnold spurred toward them. We could hear his voice, now; his high-pitched, strident voice. We caught the rasping tones in which he was calling, even though the words were indistinguishable.

There were quick movements among those oncoming troops. They moved like dry leaves, caught by a sudden breeze. They eddied and spread out. From them came a confused shouting.

We saw Arnold gallop to a point abreast of their center and pull his horse to an abrupt stop. The column of men billowed toward him, running. His horse wheeled and went straight away from them, heading for the shallow valley that divided the hill at whose foot we stood from that other hill on which cannon still boomed and musketry rattled.

So busy had we been with our own stockaded hill, and with our efforts to pick off the Germans behind the stockade, that we had paid no attention to this shallow valley, except to note that it contained two log cabins, seemingly deserted. Now we saw they were not deserted, for from their windows and between their logs came jets of flame. Men in suits of green-fringed buckskin ran from the doors to kneel behind near-by bushes and fire at the charging troops.

"Now how in Tophet did he know them Canadians was there?" Doc Means demanded. "Guess we'd 'a' knowed it ourselves if them cabins had been close enough to us! We'd 'a' got a cross-fire from 'em before this—but they been laying so low I'd 'a' needed a dowsing rod to find 'em!"

"Arnold smelt 'em!" Cap roared. He seized Nason by the shoulder. Doubled over, he jumped clumsily with elephantine exultation. "He smelt 'em, Stevie! By God, he smelt 'em! He smelt 'em, and there they go!"

He emitted an ear-splitting bellow. On both sides of us the Virginians had ceased to fire on the stockade. They crouched in strange attitudes in the shelter of our overhanging bank, staring open-mouthed at Arnold and the running Continentals. They made gentle hissing and clucking sounds, and whispered softly to themselves, as if with a faint regret, such words as "Sho!" "By gravy!" "Look thar!" "Gawsh!"

"There they go!" Cap howled again. He meant the Canadians. They were tumbling from the windows and doors of the cabins and racing off up the valley into the uncut timber, to escape Arnold and the on-rushing Continentals.

As for Arnold, he seemed to bounce away from in front of the troops. His mare made a sharp turn and scrambled in our direction. We heard the pelting of her hoofs, louder and louder, on the heavy soil. She splashed through the water of the little brook beneath whose welcome bank we stood; she clawed up the bank like a cat, and then, above us on the slope, went into a run. Nason and Cap and Doc, Tom Bickford and Joseph Phipps, all the Virginians, Natanis and Lewis Vincent, and scattered militiamen from God knows where that had tumbled among us—every last one of us howled like madmen as Arnold went by.

He turned, circling, and was back in a matter of seconds. It was close onto sundown. The light was dim and fast getting dimmer. I thought I felt a spit of rain.

Arnold pulled off his hat and wiped his face on the sleeve of his sword-arm. All along the stockade above us, musket-fire crackled.

"We've got half an hour of daylight left—half an hour to take this hill!" he shouted. "Half an hour: no more! If we can take this hill, we'll get everything!" He looked over his shoulder at the stockade and the puffs of smoke that jetted from it. "There's no use wasting time here! There's a sally-port round behind 'em, on the other side of the hill!"

A howl went up from those who pressed around him. "We'll take it!" we bawled. "Go ahead!" "Sally-port!" "Take it!"

Arnold shook his sword at us. "I'll lead you there! Let nothing stop you!" His voice ruffled the hair on the back of my neck. His brown mare reared and plunged, then pranced ahead, playful still in spite of the sweat and lather on her. We climbed from the gully and scrambled after her as fast as we could run. I felt a terrible exasperation at the dripping, pop-eyed faces of those around me: at their meaningless and frantic yells: at this sudden hurry—this sudden demand that everything be done in half an hour: at the British, for building stockades that had to be taken in half an hour; at the ever-growing darkness; at the stabbing pains that pierced my head after these hours of noise and confusion and shouting and running. My tongue was swollen: my throat dry: my eyes ached. I wished to God, as I ran, that the half hour lay behind and not before us.

Cap had me by the arm. "Remember," he panted hoarsely, and because he loped like a moose, the words came jolting from his mouth, "remember about getting me one of them she-Hessians! She ought to be a young one, without no blemishes!"

I pushed him away; heard him jerkily blurting his needs to Doc and Tom Bickford. We turned the shoulder of the hill, puffing and blowing.

Arnold spurred his horse higher on the slope. His rasping voice lifted us on—that warning, penetrating voice that made the heart leap. "Here!" he shouted. "Here! Come up! Come up!"

We streamed upward and saw the gap in the stockade. The whole camp of the Germans was open before us. We saw tents, carts, huts, baggage, running women, officers beating at their men with swords to make them face us. We felt the breath of the place, redolent of damp and dirty wool, of sweat and gunpowder and charred wood; of stale food, horse-manure, sourness. Everything, in the falling dusk, was a turmoil of shouting, of musket-flashing.

Arnold stood in his stirrups, and hurled us into it. "Get in here! Get in here! Throw 'em out! Push 'em out! Blow 'em out!"

Virginians crawled to the shelter of carts and began to fire. Groups of Hessians, on the far side of the camp, shot wildly at us: then broke and ran, their officers cursing and striking at them. A German general faced running Hessians, swinging his sabre against their heads and breasts, beating them to the ground as they tried to pass him. One of them pushed his musket against the general's stomach and fired. The general's sabre flew from his hand and he sat slowly down.

Morgan lumbered past us, bellowing. I saw Dearborn run in with a handful of his men, almost as though he had his shoulder against them, forcing them in by main strength. There were Americans everywhere, loading, firing, howling, swinging clubbed muskets at fleeing figures.

Arnold kept on shouting, "Get in here! Get in here! It's ours!"

A dozen running Germans turned, faced us and raised their muskets. I heard Nason shout, "Load with buck-shot!" We shot at the Germans. Four sprawled to the ground. The others fired and ran.

Behind me there was a breathless scrambling and commotion, a rattling thumping. I looked around. Arnold's mare was on her back on the ground, her legs waving. Arnold was caught under her. I ran to him. It seemed, almost, that everyone did the same. His free leg, still across the belly of the fallen horse, was bent at a queer angle. Soaking through the white buckskin of his breeches was a splotch of blood the size of my head.

Cap Huff struck the straining mare a terrible blow behind the ear and threw his whole weight across her neck. She lay still. A score of hands caught at her legs; at her bridle. Voices spoke hurriedly, as if half stifled. "Here! Here! Get him up! Look out for her legs! What's the matter with him! Where's he hit?"

"Pull her off, God damn it!" Cap shouted. "She's dead!"

Nason seized the mare by a front leg and swung her clear of her fallen rider.

Arnold lay there, staring down at the widening stain on his breeches.

Dearborn had him by the shoulders, holding his head from the ground. "Where'd it hit you?" Dearborn asked.

"Same leg," Arnold said. "Same leg." He made a little straining noise. "I wish it had been my heart."

He looked up at us suddenly. "Don't stand here, boys! Go to work! It's almost dark!"

I heard Morgan's booming voice. "They're gone! Breymann's killed. Some surrendered, and the rest ran. It's all over!"

"Then we've turned their flank!" Arnold cried. He made that straining sound again. "We've turned Burgoyne's flank! We've got him! Send for reinforcements! This place has got to be held! Don't let him get it back!" He groaned and twisted in Dearborn's arms. "I could take his whole damned army tomorrow, if it wasn't for this leg!"

What he said, I know now, was the truth; and even at that time I knew that although without Arnold we might have held back Burgoyne on that 7th of October, we never in God's world, without him, would have driven the Hessians from their great redoubt, turned Burgoyne's right flank and obtained the advantage that brought about the ruin of the British.

Arnold closed his eyes. His face was drenched with perspiration.

We heard a horse clattering up the hill. The Virginians picked up their rifles. When the horse came in at the sally-port, we saw the rider was Major Armstrong, one of Gates's aides.

He shot a quick glance at the German camp, at the Americans hustling here and there to make the place secure against counterattacks, then asked, "Where's General Arnold?"

Nobody answered. He saw Dearborn then, and whom he was holding. He swung himself from the saddle and pushed between us to stand looking down at the two men.

"General Gates presents his compliments to General Arnold," he said, extremely formal and military, "and requests that he return at once to his quarters."

"What for?" Arnold breathed. "What for?"

Armstrong coughed. "He was afraid you might do something rash."

Colonel Morgan laughed hoarsely, then asked politely, "Did you just leave General Gates?"

"No," Armstrong said. "No, General Gates sent me out from headquarters two hours ago. I just now caught up with General Arnold. Nobody seemed to know where he was."

Arnold nodded and turned an ironic eye toward Colonel Morgan. "Under those circumstances you'd better send me back. I wouldn't want to worry General Gates." He pointed at Nason. "Let him take me. He'll get me there somehow."

Cap disappeared, floundering and stumbling, and was back in no time with blankets and a pair of gun-rammers, from which we made a litter.

It was dark when we got Arnold on it. Rain had begun to fall. We contrived to keep pine-knots alight, and there were fires along the route at intervals to guide the wounded, who were limping and crawling back to camp, through the darkness and the rain, like a groaning procession of the damned. We found more fires blazing in the wheat field where we had first fought; and by their light we saw women—American camp followers—stripping the dead men of their clothes. In the far distance wolves yelled and howled, like innumerable mournful dogs.

Arnold must have fallen into a stupor, for he said nothing, not even when Doc renewed the wet rags on his wounded thigh, which he did whenever we crossed a brook. He just lay there in the sagging blanket, muttering a little now and then, and the rest of the time puffing weakly as a child puffs to extinguish a candle.

LXV

THE next morning, in a drenching downpour, Burgoyne's retreat commenced—a retreat that carried him only ten miles and left him stranded on the Heights of Saratoga, surrounded by an ever-tightening ring of Continentals and militia that picked unceasingly at his hungry, wearied, harried Britishers and Germans. Even then, thanks to Gates's slowness in pursuit, Burgoyne might have safely drawn the remnants of his army off to Ticonderoga and so to Canada. But slow as Gates was, Burgoyne was slower; and Providence, which had so stubbornly refused to come to the aid of the American cause during our invasion of Canada, at Valcour, and in the retreat from Ticonderoga, now strangely and with a furious energy worked in our interests both day and night—and God knows we needed everything Providence could spare us.

"You know how I'm situated," I had told Nason, the night of the battle, after we had taken Arnold to the hospital in the camp and made ourselves a fire in front of a deserted lean-to, so to snatch a little sleep before daylight came. "If you're going back to join Morgan, I want you to give me separate orders of my own."

"Orders to do what?" Nason asked.

"I don't know," I said. "Orders to watch the roads to the north. Orders to make a scout to Ticonderoga. Any kind of orders that'll give me a free hand to hunt for Nathaniel. Let me take Doc and Joseph Phipps. I'll guarantee we'll be as useful, off by ourselves, as we'd be if we went back to Morgan with you."

Nason scratched his chin and stared at me. On this, Cap Huff put in his oar. "Stevie, that aide of Arnold's won't make no bones about giving us scouting orders if you ask for 'em. There's some things we know that Morgan nor nobody else don't know; and the most important of those things is that there's a lady somewheres inside those British lines whose case ought to be attended to. Maybe you're forgetting about her; but I ain't, and Peter Merrill ain't. She raised a good deal of hell with you, once, and with me, too; and she raised all the hell she was able to with Schuyler and Arnold, and with God knows how many other people, including Peter Merrill's brother, didn't she?"

"Yes, she did," Nason admitted.

"Yes," Cap said, "and come to think of it, we persuaded that boy to enlist as a scout, and we took him up into Canada where that hellcat could get her fingers on him"—he coughed affectedly and hastily added, "though that's something we ain't got to take into consideration."

"Not in the least," I said.

"Don't try to confuse the issue!" Nason told Huff severely.

"Why, Stevie!" Cap exclaimed. "I wouldn't do no such thing, whatever you mean by it. And here's somep'n else, Stevie: If we go back to Morgan, we'll just sit on our tails for as much as two whole days, on account there ain't been any food issued for two days, and it'll take another two days to issue it and get it cooked. We might as well be off killing a few more Britishers on our own account and picking up our own food while we go."

Seeing that Nason still regarded him coldly, Cap coughed virtuously and added, "I dunno as I told you, but while I was hunting those blankets for Arnold, I got into a little argument with some kind of a officer over a bottle of rum that somebody'd left in one of the tents, and I had to hit him over the head with the flat of my hatchet."

"An argument with one of Morgan's officers?" Nason asked quickly.

"I dunno," Cap said. "All I know is he was an American, because he said, 'Here, gimme that bottle!' I ain't anxious to go right back there, not till things quiet down a little."

"Where's the bottle?" Nason asked.

"Right here," Cap said wistfully. "It's mostly only bottle." He produced it from the rear of his garments, and all of us had a drink of the remnant.

"All this that you're telling me," Nason said to Cap, "merely means that you want to go with Peter Merrill if he goes looking for his brother."

Cap's reply was melancholy. "There you go, twisting a man's words every which way! Anything to make him out selfish! Listen, ain't I got your best interests at heart, Stevie, same as always?"

Nason snorted.

"Captain Nason," Tom Bickford said, "I'd like to go with Cap'n Peter. I'd like to do what I can to help Nathaniel."

Nason stared into the fire for a moment: then, without another word, left us. In half an hour he came back with a written order signed by Varick, authorizing Steven Nason and his command to scout wherever necessary in behalf of General Arnold, on the lookout for certain individuals of interest to the Continental Army.

This order would, I knew, take us wherever we wanted to go, for in view of Arnold's part in the battle we had just fought, no officer but Gates or Wilkinson would presume to question his orders, even though he had been deprived of his division. More than that, it was an order that even relieved us of the necessity of answering questions, since every officer worth his salt knew that Arnold was forever sending out scouts for the obtaining of information that no other general seemed able to get.

In the morning, as daylight broke, we crossed the Hudson to the eastern bank, and moved up to high land from which we could look over to the artillery park, the hospital tents, the piles of supplies, and the British troops moving slowly northward.

Wherever we moved, on that eastern bank, we found American militia—more militia than we ever dreamed existed; and surrounded by these noisy, turbulent, undisciplined farmer-soldiers we stalked the British during the earlier days of that week as a setter stalks a wounded bird.

We watched them straggle off, leaving their hospital tents, full of their sick and wounded. We watched their fires at night; and during the day we peered at them through rain squalls so violent that the heavens seemed dissolved in tears at the wretched plight of that stricken army.

It was when, staring across the river, we saw British bateaux set off upstream that my hopes rose high. Not only were they piled with stores and ammunition, but they carried women camp followers as well. Any one of the draggled women, perched so disconsolately in the clumsy boats, might, I knew, be Ellen; and with her might be Nathaniel. Indeed, every woman I saw, huddled in a boat on the far side of the Hudson, seemed, at first glance, to look like Ellen.

Nason and Cap and the others shared my excitement. "Pick out the boat you want, Cap'n Peter," Tom Bickford said. "We'll get it somehow."

I settled on a bateau that bore three women and a man, in addition to a heap of stores and two bateau-men. We followed along the bank as it poled slowly up river; and at a shallow spot, Tom and Joseph Phipps and Lewis Vincent dashed in with leveled muskets and ordered it ashore while the rest of us, stepping into view at the water's edge, threatened its passengers with death if they resisted.

It came ashore fast enough. The women were Irish slatterns who wept and squalled. The man was a sutler.

Militiamen, quick to profit by our example, splashed into the river and captured all the rest, so that we quickly abandoned the one we had taken and raced from boat to boat, looking for Ellen and Nathaniel.

All our efforts were unavailing: we might have been searching for a needle in a haystack—for one particular grasshopper out of a meadow-ful. All the women in all the bateaux were haggard, frightened harridans: the men were a cowed and red-eyed lot, glad enough to be captured: to be freed at last of the burden of sleepless nights and constant fear of death that had weighed on them for weeks.

We questioned some of the women concerning the whereabouts of Ellen Phipps, but they either didn't know or wouldn't answer. Before we let them go to add to the burdens of the British, the militia had stolen not only the stores from the bateaux, but even the thwarts and thole pins. Given a little more time, they'd have pried out all the nails.

Cap Huff shook his head over the behavior of those militiamen. "Stealing's like killing," I heard him tell Doc. "There's times when you can kill a feller in spite of the Bible, and nobody'll think any the worse of you for it, except maybe the feller that gets killed don't take no liking to you for it. Then, again, there's times when it's kind of a public duty to steal a little here and a little there; but you got to use judgment about it, same as about killing and kissing and everything else. There's some of these soldiers, not Continentals, that ain't got no judgment about nothing—not about nothing whatever! They'd steal anything from anybody, even from each other; and I wouldn't trust 'em to use a mite of judgment about who they kiss and who they kill."

It was true that the militia had no social graces whatever; but they were there to plague Burgoyne: not to display their breeding and gentility; and plague him they did.

Harrassed by unending musketry fire, and by the pounding of artillery which by now had come up the eastern bank to make life more hideous for the hard-pressed invaders, the retreat became chaotic. We saw those hounded Britons abandon wagons that had stuck in the quagmires to which the river road had been turned by the incessant rain. They burned baggage, camp equipage, wagons, carts. They destroyed their bridges behind them. We watched them stumble at last up the low hills of Saratoga, burning Schuyler's fine house and buildings as they did so; and there on those heights, with their cattle and horses dying among them for lack of forage, they stayed day after day.

Even the greatest chowder-head among the militia, by this time, knew Burgoyne had to surrender. But beaten and helpless though the British were, they were under discipline as strict, within their camp, as though they planned to fight at any moment. Not only did we find it impossible to approach them; but from none of the many British deserters or prisoners could our party on the eastern bank find out anything about Nathaniel or Ellen.

So I, of all the thousands of Americans ringed around Burgoyne, was in despair. If the British surrendered, Nathaniel, of course, would be with them, and so, too, would Ellen. In such a case, I could see but two eventualities. Either Nathaniel would have the protection of the British and so would be imprisoned with them, or he would be taken from them as a deserter, perhaps hanged, and certainly disgraced. As for Ellen, she would go into captivity with the other camp followers; and what would happen to her, God only knew.

Cap Huff had his great idea the very day Burgoyne signed the Convention which made prisoners of every Britisher, every Hessian, every Canadian, every Indian and every camp follower remaining in the proud army that had set out from Canada against our rabble four long months ago. The news of the surrender, in some mysterious way, seemed to reach, in a moment's time, not only the American regiments gathered around the Heights, but the scattered militia companies that wandered on the outskirts of the army, making nuisances of themselves. Even the countryfolk in all the scattered farm houses, cabins and settlements on both sides of the river within a score of miles knew, as if by magic, that Burgoyne had signed the Convention, and that all his army was to be marched at once to Boston and there embarked for England, never more to fight against Americans. What they couldn't know was that Congress would refuse to abide by the Convention, and that this wretched army was doomed to wander for four long years among the hills of Virginia, starved, penniless, ragged, despised, and hating from the bottom of their hearts a Congress and a people so regardless of justice and honor.

No sooner had the news reached us than Cap Huff smote his thigh a resounding thwack. "Look here!" he said. "If these Britishers and their camp followers are marched to Boston, they'll march together, won't they, and they won't have no guns nor nothing, will they?"

We agreed that this would unquestionably be the case.

"Well, then," Cap said, "our problem ain't nothing but a military one, kind of, like the way I got that keg of wine up at St. Mary's, or like you'd get chickens out of a henhouse without nobody thinking about it."

We stared at him.

"Listen, Stevie!" Cap said. "You remember St. Mary's, don't you? I started a fight out in front of a tavern, and when everybody run out of the tavern to see what was happening, I slipped around to the back door, all quiet and peaceable, and helped myself to the keg, didn't I? You'd ought to know! You must 'a' drunk about three gallons out of it!"

"What's St. Mary's got to do with Nathaniel Merrill?" Nason asked.

Cap made sounds of exasperation. "This here! All we got to do is keep watch on the British camp followers till we find Nathaniel Mer-

rill. When we find him, I'll start a fight; and when everybody runs to
look at it, the way everybody always does when a fight starts, you can
grab Nathaniel and anyone else you want. Then when the fight's over,
Nathaniel won't be there. He'll be gone, with you. Nobody won't know
nothing about him, and nobody won't be able to stop and inquire, on
account of having business down east in Boston."

"That's not a bad idea," Nason said.

"Not a bad one! Not a bad one, hell!" Cap cried. "Ain't my brains
never going to get their simple due?"

I was able to think of a few objections; but I kept them to myself.

That was how it happened that, having re-crossed the river, we
waited, on that 17th of October, amid a strangely silent throng of countryfolk on the river road, to the southward of the low hills of the Heights
of Saratoga. North of us the whole American army was drawn up in long
lines on both sides of the road, waiting; and in a meadow even farther
north, where there were no American eyes to witness their shame, the
British laid down their arms.

It was one of those warm, sunny, still October mornings, when fox-
sparrows scamper in the dead leaves beside the road as noisily as turkeys. We strained our ears and eyes for sound or sight of our conquered
enemies, and I was sure I could hear far-off strains of music from a
British band—the strains of the tune to which Nathaniel and I had
listened in the rotunda at Ranelagh. I could almost hear Nathaniel's
voice, softly singing its frivolous words:

> "What happy golden days were those
> When I was in my prime!
> The lasses took delight in me,
> I was so neat and fine;
> I moved about from fair to fair,
> Likewise from town to town,
> Until I married me a wife
> And the world turned upside down."

I thought how Marie de Sabrevois had come into my life to the music
of that very song, bringing unhappiness and evil with her, and something of good, too, since except for her I would never have known Ellen
Phipps; and my heart pounded heavily in time to the distant music;
for I had the feeling that perhaps it might be drawing our lives together
—my own life, and Nathaniel's, and Ellen's, and that of Marie de
Sabrevois—and drawing them to a tragic climax.

The music died away. From the endless double line of soldiers to
the northward came a faded calling of small and lonely voices—the

voices of officers. The lines wavered a little; then grew rigid. The bayonets of their grounded muskets took on the look of hedges of polished
steel, built with the precision of a master craftsman and guarding a lane
that vanished over a distant rise, but might, for all we knew, go on and
on forever.

Over the valley of the Hudson hung a breathless stillness, and in
that stillness scarlet figures appeared at the northernmost end of the
lane. They moved toward us, between the hedges of bayonets, and
other scarlet figures rose to flow along behind them. They flowed on
and on, until the lane was filled. They flowed with as little sound as a
stream of blood would make.

They filled the lane completely and began to come out of it near us,
passing between the silent fringes of countryfolk among whom we
stood.

The officers who led them were colonels: handsomely dressed men
whose white breeches were soggy and spotted from the crossing of a
stream. They affected an utter indifference to their own circumstances
and to the countryfolk on either side; but the younger officers who
followed them displayed less reserve. Some muttered indignantly to
brother officers; others, doubtless considering themselves irrevocably
disgraced and ruined by their defeat at the hands of a rude and untrained rabble, wept openly. As for the long line of unarmed red-coats,
their faces were bitter and resentful, and the glances they darted at us
were truculent. They moved in a singularly oppressive silence—a silence
somehow made more profound by the scuffing of their feet on the
soft dirt, the faint screaking of their belts, the rubbing of cloth on cloth.

It was a silence that was soon broken; for although the long lines of
American troops had no word to say to any of the thousands of British
who passed them, the farmers all around us had a-plenty, especially
when the British infantrymen, having come out from their bayonet-
hedged lane, sullenly eyed the doltish-looking yokels who stared at
them with mouths half open and began to curse them for a pack of
lousy rebels.

On this there was so much retaliatory cursing from the farmers that
Cap moved quickly from his coign of vantage to stand farther back,
out of temptation, as he put it. Even more loudly did the farmers curse
the Germans, when they came lumbering along behind the British regiments. They were a disheveled-looking lot, their uniforms dirty and in
tatters from hard usage. With them marched their women, more slat-
ternly, even, in appearance, than the camp followers of the New York
regiments who stripped the dead after the battle we fought in the

wheat field. With them, too, they had their pets—their squirrels, their weasels, their raccoons, their bear cubs, their tame ducks in cages of woven twigs: even a tame deer; and Doc Means swore that he saw one peer into a canteen and whistle at a tame fish.

My heart was in my boots as the camp followers, women, officers' servants and rag-tag and bobtail passed us, for nowhere in the whole column had I seen Nathaniel. I even stared hard at the little group of Canadians and Indians that brought up the rear of the prisoners, striving to preserve an imperturbable aspect in the face of the howls of execration with which they were greeted; but all to no avail. Not only could I see no one who resembled Nathaniel, but I could find no trace of Ellen Phipps: none of Marie de Sabrevois. Even Lanaudiere wasn't there.

My disappointment was so bitter that I refused to admit I had seen correctly. "We missed 'em," I said, after Nason, Cap, Doc, Joseph Phipps, Tom Bickford, Lewis Vincent, and Natanis had made the same report.

Nason shook his head. "If they'd been here," he said, "I'd have seen 'em. I'd know your brother, even back-to and in a British uniform; and as for that other one——"

"You mean Ellen?"

"No," he said, "the other one."

Cap winked at me. "He means the hellcat."

"She wasn't there," Nason maintained. "She couldn't have put on any disguise thick enough for me not to know her."

Cap grunted cryptically.

"You're wrong!" I insisted. "You're all wrong! They've *got* to be there! If Nathaniel's feelings had altered, since I talked to him at Button-mould Bay—if he'd decided to leave that woman—he'd have found some way to tell me. He's there, and we've got to find him! Go the whole length of that column again, all of you. Run ahead, all the way to the front of the line, and work back to the rear again. If we can only find one of them, we can find all the others."

They did what I asked; and I, of course, did what they did, but without result. Neither Nathaniel, Ellen, Marie de Sabrevois nor Lanaudiere was with the British.

"If you want to know what I think," Cap said, "I think that hellcat sneaked back to Canada long ago and took your brother with her." He smacked his lips. "If I didn't have to do so much fighting, damned if I wouldn't kind of like to get on friendly terms with that hellcat and let her take *me* back to Canada with her!"

"He never went back to Canada with her," I said. "Never! That would have made him out a traitor, and he'll never be that. What he's done, he's done because he thinks all of us will be helped by it."

Joseph Phipps nodded. "My sister never go back to Canada. She American now, same as me: same as you."

Cap was exasperated. "All right, if they ain't here, and ain't gone back to Canada, point 'em out! I got some nice jewelry off that slick lady once, but I heard afterwards there was some left! Where'd you say she was?"

An outburst of angry yelling distracted us. A mob of farmers and American camp followers were pressed close around the little unarmed group of Indians and squaws who marched in the rear of the long line of British prisoners. Some of the farmers were beating on tin pans, and we heard them shouting, "Burn 'em! Scalp 'em! Slaughter 'em!"

Nason ran toward them, with Cap close behind. They went plunging into the close-packed mob of farmers, pulling them aside, climbing over them, until they reached the Indians and their squaws. As we clubbed and shoved our way through, following Cap and Nason, we saw Cap snatch a tin camp kettle from an angry farmer, cram it down over the farmer's ears, and hit the kettle a discouraging blow with his fist. The farmer sank to a sitting position. Cap seized two other farmers by the necks and cracked their heads together. They fell on the one whose head was still jammed in the kettle.

"Who the hell *are* all you fellers?" Cap bellowed, making play with his ham-like fists. "You got ugly faces, but they ain't familiar. I don't remember of seeing none of you at Freeman's Farm or Bemis's Heights! These here's *our* prisoners. Let 'em alone! If you want prisoners to play with, enlist and pick up a few! If you fellers are so damned excited over these here Injuns, why ain't you in the army, anyhow? Or don't you fight nobody but folks that ain't got no guns and can't hit back?"

He dealt the kettle-bottom another fearful whack, and rammed his blackened fist against the nearest jaw. The farmers fell back before our threatening musket-butts, and we hustled the Indians along, out of danger.

They were a stolid-looking crew, apparently without gratitude for the good turn we had done them; and I suspected, as I watched their expressionless faces, that they had taken it for granted they were to be killed: had even resigned themselves to such a fate, as they might have resigned themselves to going without food for a day. They were, I saw, returning terse and haughty answers to the questions Natanis and Lewis Vincent were putting to them.

"Who are they?" I asked Joseph Phipps. "Where are they from? Why don't you ask them about Lanaudiere?"

"They know nothing," Joseph said. "They Montagnais—dirty Indians from way down St. Lawrence. They get here just before battle: find all other Indians gone home. I think they go themselves, only battle start too quick. I think they very cross Indians."

He stared indifferently at the sky; then said to me, in a weary, lackadaisical voice, "You look that squaw behind man with blue shirt hanging over leggins. What you think about that squaw?"

I looked at her. At first glance she was like any other Indian squaw of a certain age—square-bodied, heavy-featured, somewhat bow-legged and extremely pigeon-toed. Then I recognized her.

"For God's sake! She's the one that was in the tent at Buttonmould Bay! The one that kept watch over Ellen!"

"I think yes," Joseph said.

He spoke sharply to the woman. She moved nearer, obedient and uninterested. I called to Nason, and when he looked around at me, he hurried back, bringing Natanis and Lewis Vincent.

When Natanis had questioned the squaw, Nason turned a speculative eye upon me.

"What is it?" I whispered. "Where's Ellen? Does she know where Ellen is?"

"In the hospital," Nason said.

"Hospital!" I cried. "Hospital! What hospital? What happened?"

"Wait a minute," Nason told me. "She's not sick. She went there with somebody."

"Nathaniel!" I said. "She went there with Nathaniel! What's wrong with him? For God's sake, why doesn't he ask her what's wrong with him?"

"He did," Nason said, "but we don't know it was your brother she went with. Anyway, whoever she went with was hurt. He'd been shot."

"It was Nathaniel!" I said heavily. "She said he was shot?"

"Yes," Nason said, "he was shot."

"In a battle? Was he shot in the battle we just fought?"

"No; before that."

I stared at him. Nathaniel was shot. Nathaniel was shot before the battle.

Nason spoke reassuringly. "We can't depend on anything this squaw says. She's like all Indian squaws: she'll give us the answers she thinks we want to hear. We won't bother with her any longer. We'll go to the hospital. It's in Albany. The British sick and wounded have been sent there. We'll go to Albany. Our orders permit us to go there."

"Albany!" I exclaimed. "That's thirty miles! It'll take forever!"

"No it won't!" Nason said. "We'll run most of the way." He put his hand on my shoulder. "Don't worry. You can run hard enough to stop worrying, can't you?"

LXVI

THE chief surgeon for the British in Albany, John McNamara Hayes, seemed to be in a perpetual state of indignation—indignation at the inadequacies of the church allotted to him as a hospital for his four hundred sick and wounded; indignation because of the high price of food and drink, the climate of America, the savagery of Americans, the outrageous distances between cities in this barbarous country of ours; and above all he was indignant because we dared to burst into his hospital at such an early hour and ask to see one of his patients.

He came to us in the vestry, which had been cut into two rooms by a rough partition. The outer room, where we were, had no cots and was apparently part laboratory, part receiving room. The very sight of our weather-stained garments, wrinkled and ripped from nights of scouting through Hudson Valley fogs, seemed to irritate Dr. Hayes almost beyond endurance.

"I've been obliged to issue an order," he complained. "The place is full of curiosity seekers! You Americans would come for miles, I do believe, just to stand and stare at an Englishman! I can't permit people coming here and disturbing my patients merely out of idle curiosity. It's an invasion of their privacy as well as mine, and I'll not allow it! Now then: have you an order from your headquarters, permitting you to see one of the inmates of this hospital, or have you not?"

"Doctor," I said, "I'm not here on army business, but to see my brother."

"Your brother, eh?" he exclaimed. "It makes no difference! You'll have to have an order from your headquarters."

"But that's in Saratoga, thirty miles away, doctor!" I protested. "I started from there yesterday and walked all night to get here. Don't make me walk another sixty miles to Saratoga and back again, just because curiosity-seekers have made nuisances of themselves. It's not curiosity that brings me here, sir: it's concern for my own flesh and blood: my young brother."

"If we make an exception in your case, we'll have to make a thousand exceptions!" he protested. "It's impossible! Ah—what's your brother's name?"

"Nathaniel Merrill," I said.

His irascibility changed suddenly to a haughty coldness. "Indeed! Mr. Merrill, your brother sees no one! Your brother, sir, was shot while attempting to desert from the British camp to the American lines at a critical moment in our army's existence. When he has sufficiently recovered, he'll be tried by a British court-martial on the charge of desertion, and if guilty will be fittingly punished."

"Shot in the act of deserting!" I exclaimed. "Deserting from what? He wasn't in the British army, was he? After you've bamboozled him for a year, and lied to him, and then shot him, you can't try him for desertion on top of all that!"

Dr. Hayes's voice was icy. "Good morning, sir. This interview is terminated!"

"Wait," I said. "Wait! I spoke hastily. I withdraw what I said. I apologize. My brother—it's my brother, you understand."

Hayes just stood there, waiting for me to go.

"Look here, doctor," I persisted, "if you won't let me see my brother, you'll surely let me see Ellen Phipps. I've got to see Ellen. I know she's here with him. You know who Ellen is, don't you? Where is she?"

Hayes shook his head. "I've already said 'Good morning.' Under the circumstances, I can do nothing for you unless you have an order—an order from your own headquarters."

Joseph Phipps spoke up suddenly. "She my sister. Not need no order to see sister!"

Hayes eyed him curiously, seemed puzzled by Joseph's manner of speaking: then shook his head contemptuously. "It's too transparent! You could claim to be anyone's brother, and I'd never know the difference."

"Let's get at this another way," I said. "Do you know Marie de Sabrevois?"

Hayes looked vacant and murmured, "I beg your pardon?"

"Marie de Sabrevois," I repeated. "She wasn't with the army when it marched out of camp, so she must be here, too. I think as things are, even she'd tell you that we're what we claim to be. She's here, isn't she?"

Hayes stared. "Never heard of her."

Joseph Phipps turned from us and went to the inner door. "I go find Ellen. She my sister."

Hayes came suddenly to life.

"I'll conduct this hospital without your assistance," he said brusquely, and with that he pushed past Joseph Phipps and left us.

I have no doubt that during the moments that followed, my companions spoke to me. It may be, even, that I answered them; but what they said, and what I replied, I don't know now, and I think I didn't know then.

I know, though, that I stood there, swallowing, breathing heavily, and that all at once, into the soggy darkness that clouded my very soul, there strangely seemed to come, with a queer kind of brightness about it, the figure of Ellen Phipps.

The door opened and she stood there before me, no different than she had been at Iberville, or at Crown Point, or at Skenesboro—no different, except that her long, straight look at me carried the words to me as clearly as if her silver-clear voice had spoken them, "Yes, I am here. You knew, of course, I'd take care of your brother for you, didn't you?"

She stepped forward and touched my arm with such a small and child-like hand that I wondered stupidly how it could be of use in a soldiers' hospital.

"You mustn't let Nathaniel stay here any longer. He'll get well if you can take him away."

The chief surgeon spoke sharply. "You can't take away a deserter, Miss Phipps. You've proved yourself a good nurse, but that doesn't give you the right to talk nonsense. I gave you permission to step out here and speak to your brother. Kindly do that and nothing else."

Ellen ignored him and spoke to me. "If you don't take Nathaniel away, I'm afraid he won't get well."

"Upon my word!" Hayes cried. "I never heard such nonsense! The ball merely passed from the sub-clavicular region around into the deltoid muscle, leaving a slight intercostal inflammation on the left side. Except that, the fellow's as healthy as I am!"

Ellen shook her head. "It's true the wound in his body isn't a bad one, but the one in his mind is. In his mind? Ah, in his heart, poor boy! In his heart!"

"Yes," I said bitterly. "Heart, reputation and body too: he has wounds enough! Where is she who put them there, Ellen?"

Ellen's voice was as bitter as mine. "Where she'll not help him or us. Lanaudiere went back to Canada long ago; and before the last battle he sent for her, and she went. I heard her talking with your brother, that night when she was going—I heard him speaking hoarsely; heard her tell him he was tiresome and had tired her a long time. After that he understood what had happened to him, and why it was, and so he didn't want to live. He tried to cross to the American lines, and the British sentries shot him. I've been with him ever since, trying to make him want to live, but I can't. You'll have to do that, if you can."

In spite of the tragic pictures that came into my mind at Ellen's words, I felt a little thrill of pride in Nathaniel. At least he had tried to come back to us. Whatever might happen to him now, I said to myself, his wound was an honorable one.

"So she told him he was tiresome."

Ellen nodded. "She called him *gauche*. His innocence, she said, was painful to her. It was no longer refreshing to deceive him."

It seemed strange to me that as she spoke, my mind, instead of being filled with the two people dearest to me in the world, and now close to me after a long absence, should be filled with a picture of the woman I hated—Marie de Sabrevois. I say "hated," and yet I think that word doesn't express the feeling I had for her, which was a curious, bitter, poisoned kind of admiration. She'd been too much for us all—too much, years ago, for Nason: too much now for Ellen, for me, and alas and alas, for Nathaniel. One might even say she'd been too much for Arnold and Schuyler. She had helped do them infinite harm. She'd harmed us all: damaged everything she'd touched; and yet she went scatheless. I seemed to see her, perfumed and elegant, in Quebec—nay, in London again, and Paris, always evil, always plotting mischief, disaster, tragedy for helpless victims.

My thoughts turned to the last time I had seen her, in the tent at Buttonmould Bay, blue-eyed, golden haired, contemptuous, but for the moment silent and wary because of dangerous information I pretended to possess.

"I think," I said to Ellen, "that we can still call on Marie de Sabrevois to help Nathaniel and help us, too, in spite of where she's gone. I think she'll make it possible for us to take Nathaniel away—and immediately."

"You're insane, all of you!" Hayes said. "Miss Phipps, go back into the hospital at once."

"No, Ellen," I said, "don't do it! Stay where you are."

"Go back into the hospital," Hayes repeated. "Miss Phipps, you're a part of the British army still. You're subject to its discipline."

"That's not the truth," Ellen said. "I was held with your army by my aunt. At no time was I a part of it, no more than poor Nathaniel. It's true I ate your food, but I've paid for it by working in this hospital, nursing your soldiers. I won't be subject to your discipline."

"She's going with us," I told Hayes. "So's my brother. Have him brought out here."

Hayes laughed disagreeably.

"Doctor," I said, "if I've learned anything in my life, I've learned that arguments over war are as useless as those over politics and love. A man engaged in an unjust war, or pledged to the cause of a worthless politician, or infatuated with the lightest of women, holds to his opinions and dies for them. So I won't argue with you. I'll say this, though: if my brother's guilty of anything, he's not answerable to you for it: he's answerable to his own people, and that's who he's going to answer to."

"Not while I'm in charge of this hospital," Hayes said. "Miss Phipps, did you understand me to say you're needed inside?"

"Before you go, Ellen," I said, "I want you to tell Doctor Hayes something."

She raised her eyes to mine.

"Last year, Ellen, you carried letters from a certain lady to certain other people."

She nodded. "I carried letters from my aunt, Marie de Sabrevois, to people here, in Albany."

"If necessary, could you prove that?"

"Oh yes, because Joseph is here, and Joseph was with me. He saw the letters. He saw the answers, too, and read them."

"The answers, as I recall it," I said, "were written in a peculiar manner, and referred to other persons in Albany."

"They were written in onion juice. To read them, we had to heat them. In them we found the names of two hundred persons."

I turned to Dr. Hayes, and it seemed to me, as he glanced sharply into my face, a quiver of apprehension mingled with his sharpness. I have no doubt the face before him was dark and harsh; I meant to have Nathaniel, and felt no scruples as to how I did it.

"Doctor," I said, "the names in those letters were the names of two hundred British sympathizers, obtained by Marie de Sabrevois to help in the defeat of these colonies. Now, doctor, that's information possessed only by Marie de Sabrevois, by the headquarters staff of your army, and by those in this room. I'll tell you what I'll do: I'll trade you those two hundred Tories for Nathaniel. That's a generous offer."

He looked staggered. "Trade them? Trade them?"

"Yes, trade them. Ordinarily, Tories in Albany who might come to your support would have little interest for me. That's particularly true now. Burgoyne's captured. The campaign's over. You'll never threaten us from the north again. It doesn't matter to me whether people in this section are Tories or not; but I think the Patriots who live here would be glad to know the names of those friends of England. They'll lose property, liberty—even their lives if the Patriots happen to be in a hanging mood. You're a humane man, doctor, I take it. Now then: either you release my brother, or I'll make public the names of those two hundred Tories, and their blood'll be on your head."

Hayes eyed me uncertainly. "I have no authority," he began. "You're asking me to surrender a prisoner——"

At that I interrupted him by laughing, and not politely. "Prisoner! Let's not be quite that ridiculous! You're a prisoner yourself, and I'm an officer of the army that holds you. My prisoner refuses to give up his prisoner to the captor of both of them. Make an end of it, doctor! I want my brother, and you ought to be humane and not ridiculous. If that's not enough for you, I'll take other measures."

"Dear me!" he said. "Yankee Doodle!"

But his derision was feeble, so that I knew he was beaten. He said no more, but drooped his shoulders and went to the door. Ellen gave me one swift look, stepped after him, and the two of them left us, closing the flimsy door behind them. Even Cap Huff was silent while we waited.

When the door opened again, Hayes wasn't there. Nathaniel stood waveringly before us, his arm across Ellen's shoulders. He gave us a quick glance; then stared at the floor.

Ellen guided him in and knelt beside him so that he could lower himself to a bench. He looked ghastly.

I went and sat beside him and put my hand on his knee. His lips moved.

"I'm sorry to see you like this," I said.

"Not badly hurt," he said shakily. He sighed, a faint, ironic sigh. "Hit in the back!"

"Nathaniel," I said, "we're going to take you away. We're going to look out for you."

"Thanks." He drew a quivering breath. "Glad to get away from the British. They don't like us. Very hard people to live with."

I began to feel choked, but did my best to speak naturally. "We've been trying to find you for weeks, Nathaniel, all of us. Don't worry. We understood how it was. We understood how everything was, Nathaniel."

"No—I don't think anyone can do that. What's happened to me—and what I've done—it's been strange. I don't think—it could be understood."

Nason cleared his throat. "Yes—it could be," he said gravely. "Strange things happen to a good many people: we think things are strange because they happen to us—but they happen to other people too. We're your friends, Nathaniel. We'll help you all we can, and by that I mean you must count on us for everything that human beings can do."

Nathaniel's head was sunk on his breast. "Thanks," he whispered.

"We'll take you to see Arnold," Nason said. "He's in the American hospital, and it's not far from here. We'll go to Arnold."

LXVII

T<small>HE</small> military hospital for the Northern Army stood on a hill looking down on Albany and on the silvery ribbon of river that curved around the town, and I thought for a time that our long drive was to be in vain; for the attendants who came out to meet us insisted on regarding us as patients—perhaps because Ellen sat beside Nathaniel, her arm around him to support him against the bumping of the cart—and were determined to send our cart away and back to the town again, with the address of a private house where we could receive medical treatment from army doctors.

"Not another bed!" a distracted young man kept telling us, slapping the horse's rump to start him off. "Not another bed in the place! We've sent away eleven other carts this morning! Not another bed to be had! The place is full of our own men, and prisoners too—British, Germans, Canadians. Just keep going right back into town."

At this repeated rump-slapping, the horse backed and filled, joggling us so that our protests were jounced from our mouths, until Cap Huff leaped from the cart in a rage, shouting, "Keep your hands off that horse's tail if you don't want something serious to happen to your own!"

When we got it into the attendant's thick skull that we wanted to see General Arnold, he became as dubious as he had been officious. "I dunno about that! He's been raising Ned, General Arnold has. Anybody that goes near him gets his head snapped off!"

"Why *wouldn't* they get their heads snapped off," Cap demanded, "if they stand around slapping horses' tails and not listening to what's said to 'em! Go on, now: go tell General Arnold his scouts want to see him!"

"Who, me?" the attendant asked. "*Me* tell him?"

Cap made a contemptuous sound. "What you afraid of! Here, I'll go with you. I and Arnold, we been through three campaigns together. He won't say nothing to *me!*"

He took the attendant by the arm and set off: then seemed to change his mind; for he hesitated and came back to us. "I was just thinking," he said to Nason. "Maybe you better go. I ought to stay here in case a provision cart drives up or something."

"Provision carts don't drive up here," the attendant explained. "They drive up at the back."

"I'll go around back," Cap said immediately.

"You'll stay right where you are!" Nason told him. He climbed from the cart and went with the attendant along the veranda that extended across the front of the hospital. We saw Nason enter the western wing, and almost immediately appear and beckon to us. We lifted Nathaniel from the cart and helped him up the steps and to where Nason waited.

We could hear Arnold's voice within—a venomous, rasping voice. "Charlatans!" he railed. "Empirics! Not a doctor among you that knows what he's doing or why he does it! Why don't you learn your trade, so you won't have to spend your life guessing, guessing, guessing! A set of charlatans and empirics: that's what you are!"

"Hm!" Doc Means said. "I guess one of those doctors must have done something pretty interesting to get himself called names like that!"

"What do those names mean?" Cap asked. "What's a empiric?"

"Well," Doc said, glancing apologetically at Ellen, "I don't like to say right here."

A man whom we took to be a doctor, since he carried a black bag, threw open the door at the end of the veranda. He was red-faced and indignant, and stalked past us, muttering.

"Wait," I said to Nason. "Arnold's angry. We'd better come back later."

"No," Ellen said. "No!" She smiled at Nathaniel. "It's better to face a man when he's angry, you understand, because his anger can't last forever; and as it grows less, he becomes kind. Remember this while you're with him, Nathaniel!"

He nodded heavily. She raised her eyes to mine, and at that, suddenly ashamed of my timidity, I pressed Nathaniel toward the door. Cap, Doc, Tom, Natanis and Lewis Vincent waited on the veranda, and the rest of us went into Arnold's room.

It was a small and barren cell, smelling of medicines, soap and pine planking. Arnold lay on a narrow cot, his bandaged leg looking like a bolster beneath the coverlet, and the collar of a flannel nightgown buttoned high around his throat. He thrust out his lower lip as he watched us come in, so that his face appeared to be compressed and choleric. His pale blue eyes looked cold as ice. It seemed to me I had never seen a man look so angry, and yet so lonely and forgotten.

I thought of Gates, back at Saratoga, entertaining gaudy British officers in his tent and receiving the admiration and acclaim of all the countryside; while this man, who had won the battles for which Gates was being honored, lay shattered here alone. To pass the time he could,

I saw, stare through a dust-streaked window at the town he had saved, but I doubted that he'd much entertain himself in that way.

At the sight of Ellen, he pulled the neck of his flannel nightgown still higher and made a sort of grimace, so that I knew every movement pained him. "Well," he said, "this is an unexpected pleasure! I remember having the honor once before—at Crown Point, wasn't it?"

"Yes," Ellen said. "At Crown Point. Ah, General Arnold, in those days I thought you were a terrible man—a dreadful person, who killed women and little children; who stole communion cups from churches. You see, I was with a lady then—a lady whom I loved and trusted. Her name was Marie de Sabrevois, General."

"I see," Arnold said. "I see."

Ellen turned to Nathaniel, then back to Arnold again. "I know it's not customary for a soldier to sit down in the presence of a general, but poor Nathaniel has a wound. He was shot trying to get back to fight with you, General. Will you let him sit down, please?"

"By all means!" Arnold said. "By all means! And you, too, ma'am!"

I was filled with amazement at the manner in which Ellen, as innocent and harmless-looking as a small brown wren, had in two sentences disarmed an old soldier.

He lay there staring at her as we helped to let Nathaniel down easily into a chair. Then the cold blue eyes swung sharply to my brother. "That's how you got shot, was it? Decided to come back—at last—did you?"

Nathaniel's hopeless eyes didn't meet the cold blue fire that glinted from Arnold's, nor did he speak; but Ellen, leaning toward him, touched him gently upon the arm; then she turned to the bed.

"Will you let me tell you, General? It was early in October that the lady I spoke of received a letter from Monsieur Lanaudiere. I think you know of him, General. He went with that lady to London, two years ago, to see Lord Germain. So now, when Lanaudiere thought Burgoyne was lost, she went away with the Indians Lanaudiere sent to bring her back to him. General, others have understood what happened to our friend here—our friend who'd have served you better except for that lady, but who tried to come back to serve you. You say 'At last,' General, but I think you are a man who understands a great deal without much being said. I've been with our poor friend, and I've a little mind —not a great one like yours—but I understand him, and I think it was a splendid thing he tried to do—to come back to you, even 'at last.' I wanted to stop him, because I thought it was certain death; but he said No. He knew the truth now, he said, and must go to his own people and fight for them; not wait another hour. So he tried to get by the pickets even before it was dark. It was a man with a broken heart who tried to come back to you, General. Most people, when their hearts break, won't try to do anything. But he did. He tried to come back, and follow you, and fight in your cause, General Arnold."

Arnold looked at her fixedly. "How do you get around the fact that although Nathaniel Merrill was not a prisoner, he nevertheless remained within the British lines during an entire campaign? What's your excuse for that?"

But upon this all of us except Nathaniel had an excuse to offer, for Ellen and Nason and I burst into speech at the same time, so that the general glared at us and slapped the counterpane of his bed: then winced and pushed out his lower lip and lay staring up at the ceiling, his forehead glistening with perspiration. Ellen went quickly to his side, wiped his brow with her kerchief and stood looking down at him.

Arnold relaxed. "Very sorry, ma'am. Ah—let's see: oh yes! What's the excuse?"

"You hear no excuse from Nathaniel himself. He's the only one who makes none. But we know what was in his mind. He believed what was told him by the woman he loved, who wasn't a fool. She believed it herself, and so did every experienced officer and old soldier in the British army. Why shouldn't Nathaniel believe it? They made him believe it! They all believed the cause of the colonies was lost, and all who fought in that cause were doomed—that there was no hope left for the American army or for the American people; and so the sooner the American people knew it and stopped fighting, the better it would be for them. Nathaniel was helpless except to stay where he was—and ah, that was where the woman he loved was, too, General—but he thought that if he stayed, he might help his mother, his sisters, his father, his brother, and all his own people at home, when the war was at an end. Ah, but I believe you understand this, General. I do believe you do."

Arnold frowned. "Oh, understand it! Understand it!" he said harshly. "Anybody can understand a man's behaving as Merrill has, since he believed what you say he did. The trouble is to understand his believing such nonsense, even though he heard it from a handsome woman!" He laughed angrily and added, "Yes, and from experienced British officers! Good God!"

He breathed heavily, glaring from one to the other of us. Then, irascibly, he said to Nathaniel, "Well, what was it they told you? What were their reasons for thinking the cause of the colonies was lost?"

We looked expectantly at Nathaniel. He sighed and said nothing. Ellen sank to her knees beside him and seized his hand. "Nathaniel!" she whispered. "Nathaniel! Didn't you hear? We're waiting for you to

speak! We came here with you! We're helping you, and you're not helping us! They're all waiting! Your mother! Your sisters!"

Nathaniel looked at Arnold. "They had a thousand reasons. All the
old reasons."

His eyes were fixed on the floor.

"Well, let's have 'em," Arnold said. Once more Ellen seized Nathaniel's hand.

"Money, army, officers, men, French," Nathaniel muttered. Then he
raised his eyes to Arnold's and spoke clearly. "The chief thing was our
militia system. They said half-trained troops couldn't fight. They had
figures showing how many times our militia had run away in battle.
They said militia would always run away, as soon as the fighting
reached open country. They said our officers weren't competent to plan
battles. They said two-thirds of the people in America didn't want to
fight England, and those people were the best and ablest. They said the
Loyalist regiments outnumbered Washington's regiments and fought
ten times better. They said our money was almost worthless, and becoming more worthless every day, so that no food or clothes or ammunition could be bought for the army. They said we had no government
worth the name. They said we had no chance whatever to win unless
we could get help from the French, and they said we'd never be such
fools as to do that—never!"

"They did, did they? Did they give their reasons for thinking we
wouldn't be such fools as to do that?"

"Yes. They said France never yet did anything except to serve her
own interests, and never would. They said that if we let France help us,
she'd own us, body and soul—that we'd be out of the frying pan into the
fire—that worthless as our Congress was, it couldn't be so idiotic as to
exchange English rule for French."

Arnold's pale eye fixed itself expressionlessly on mine. I knew he was
recalling Dr. Price's book on Civil Liberty: the one he had read the
night before we fought the Battle of Valcour Island. I remembered, too,
what Price had said: that a Parliament or Congress which subjected itself to any sort of foreign influence would, by that act, forfeit its authority: that a state which submitted to such a breach of trust in its
rulers thereby lost its liberty and was enslaved.

Arnold's eyes went back to Nathaniel. "And you believed all this?"

"Yes sir."

Arnold snapped his fingers sharply. "And you left them before the
second Battle of Saratoga! You came back to us before that battle! Then
you must have come back to us still believing what they'd told you—
still believing we couldn't win!"

Nathaniel looked helplessly at me.

"Speak up!" Arnold said. "You still thought we couldn't win, didn't you?"

Nathaniel's voice was desperate. "I'd stopped thinking! I wanted to be with my own people—with my brother. If he's beaten, I want to be beaten too! Whatever the British are for, I'm against! I've done too much thinking! If you're going to fight, you mustn't think!"

Arnold stared angrily from me to Nason. "What is it you want? You bring this boy here, and then you stand around saying nothing! For God's sake, either say what you've come here to say, or get along back to the army."

"General," I said, "Nathaniel's been gone from his command for a year. He's made a mistake—a terrible mistake: such a mistake that it's almost killing him. It's a mistake he'd do anything to wipe out. I want him to have a chance to do just that. If he's given a chance, he'll prove himself as valuable a man as you can find anywhere—valuable to you and valuable to the American cause."

"That's what you think, is it?"

"I *know* it! I never was surer of anything in my life."

Arnold looked at Nason. "What do you think?"

"It ought to make him dependable. I'll give him a try. He ought to be a good man."

Arnold frowned at Nathaniel. "You hear what they say. Do you think I could count on you?"

Nathaniel's hands were clenched on his knees. He made a gasping sound: then nodded abruptly.

"This damned leg!" Arnold groaned, as if just aware of it. "Here, give me that field-desk, somebody! Nason, get that field-desk! Open it and hold it so I can use it."

He glared at us; then shot a quick glance across the desk at Ellen. "I had the impression, ma'am, that you were in love with Nathaniel Merrill, but I see I was mistaken."

Ellen put her hand on Nathaniel's shoulder. "I care for him very much. I care very much for him—and for his brother."

Arnold spoke sternly. "His brother? Perhaps he has more than one? Which of his brothers do you mean? Not this one here, I trust. I'm sure you could never mean Captain Peter Merrill! That's impossible, of course. Impossible!"

Ellen's color was high, but she was brave. "No! There's nothing impossible about it. But if I didn't care for him—that, General, would be impossible."

"So!" Arnold cried, and gave me a glance of disgust. "A lady's man after all!"

I couldn't have been more uncomfortable; I knew I was turkey-red and, as people say, I'd have been glad to drop through the floor—except that if I had, I couldn't have seen the proud, sweet look that Ellen gave me then. She did a strange thing—a thing that would have touched any man's heart and made him feel ashamed that he wasn't more deserving; for she burst out and spoke in praise of me to General Arnold. She said many things, all nonsense, but she said them beautifully; and she held herself with a high spirit as she spoke, so that in my pride in her and my own embarrassment, I think I could have cried if I had been alone with her.

"Dear me! Dear me!" Arnold said, when she seemed to have finished. "Captain Nason, have you ever remarked any of these attributes in Captain Peter Merrill? Nay, have you ever seen one single thing to warrant the young lady's enthusiasm?"

Nason shook his head soberly. "Captain Peter Merrill's a fairly good soldier, but the lady puzzles me, General. I admit she puzzles me."

"Puzzles you!" Arnold said. "Why no: delirium's a simple matter. The young lady's been through a great deal; but with rest and quiet she'll be herself again some day."

Still with a stern expression on his face he took up his pen and began to write; and I thanked God that Cap Huff had not been present during this interview.

Arnold frowned as he wrote, and when he had finished he folded the paper, motioned for the desk to be taken away, closed his eyes and lay back on his pillow, pain upon his forehead. He seemed to have forgotten the paper that he held loosely between his fingers on the coverlet.

"Nason," he said, "you and my other scouts have been waiting for orders from me, I know. Well, I have no command, but they'll let you go on my recommendation. Get south: get south and report to General Washington."

He opened his eyes. "Every man in this army that can walk ought to be on his way to join General Washington by tomorrow night. Yes, tomorrow night; but Gates, that humpbacked old dressmaker, won't stir a regiment out of here for a month! The greatest day in Gates's life will be when he sees Washington treated as Schuyler was—thrown out neck and crop and replaced by Horatio Gates, Esquire, Midwife-in-Chief!"

He made a hissing sound; then said, "There. That's all. I haven't an army to send to General Washington, though I can send him my scouts. Tell him I sent you, and be off with you. That's all."

Nason spoke hesitantly. "General, you haven't said—but am I to understand that Nathaniel Merrill's to go with us?"

"No!" Arnold's eyes grew bright, and he spoke to me, though he looked at Ellen. "Captain Merrill, take your brother home and stay with him till he's in health again, body and soul." He put out his hand to Ellen; she took it, and, bending low, touched it lightly with her forehead.

"Tut, tut!" he said, and remembered the paper he'd written, which was beneath his other hand upon the coverlet. He gave it to her. "There. That's for your brother, ma'am—I mean the brother of the gentleman of whom you've formed so singular an opinion. I told him once I'd try to do something for him if I had the chance. I'm sorry it isn't more, but it seems to be what he wants."

"General Arnold," Ellen said breathlessly, and tears were quick in her eyes, "will you let us thank you—will you let us try to express our gratitude—will you——"

Instantly he seemed incensed. "Be off with you!" he cried angrily. "My leg's playing the devil with me! Do you think all this talking's improving it, or my temper, or the state of the country? Be off with you, all of you! Be off with you, confound you! Good-bye, confound you! And send my damned orderly in to me as you go! Off with you! Good-bye! Good-bye!"

On the veranda outside we stood and heard him storming at the orderly. Ellen unfolded the paper the general had given her, and she and Nathaniel and I, standing close, read it together, though I think that perhaps the eyes of both Ellen and Nathaniel were too blurred to read it as quickly as I did.

It was dated "Valcour Island, October 11th, 1776"—the date on which our little fleet had first gone into action—and it read, "Nathaniel Merrill, scout, Captain Nason's company of scouts, is ordered on detached duty until this order is rescinded. B. Arnold, Brig. Gen., Commander of the Fleet."

Diagonally across the original order was written: "Order rescinded October 18th, 1777. B. Arnold, Maj. Gen."

LXVIII

I⊤ ʜᴀꜱ not been my purpose, in this book, to tell the story of Benedict Arnold. My purpose has been to make clear what happened to my brother Nathaniel, and to tell truthfully what I saw and thought and felt during the two tumultuous campaigns through which we struggled to turn back Burgoyne. But Arnold was an inseparable part of those campaigns: without him our labors and our sacrifices would have been in vain: he was as much a part of my experience as were the British themselves. Therefore I must have my say on the subject of Arnold.

People tell fantastic tales about him, just as they did about Schuyler. They call him a horse-jockey, though he was a gentleman. They say he was arrogant and a braggart, but he was not. They call him a pirate for owning shares in privateers, but they sometimes fail to remember that Washington and Knox, too, owned shares in privateers. They tell how his soldiers hated him, even though no general, aside from Washington, was so admired by the soldiers of the whole army.

His generosity to friends and relatives was extraordinary. Joseph Warren was a great man and Arnold's friend. When he was killed at Bunker Hill, he left four motherless children. Arnold eventually persuaded Congress to pay for their education; but while Congress quibbled and wrangled and tried to evade its responsibilities, Arnold gave the money—though he himself had received no pay for four years. He is falsely said to have been sordid and avaricious—to have descended so low that he stole from his soldiers. I have heard a maudlin tale of how he robbed a poor old sergeant of five thousand dollars. The truth is that wealthy men in our colonies were rich in land and goods: not in specie. A man with five thousand dollars in hard money was a Crœsus and possibly a general of militia: never a sergeant. If any sergeant had such a sum, it was struck off on the printing press of Congress, would buy next to nothing, and wasn't worth stealing. Yet witless folk repeat that tale, and always find stupid people to believe it: they insist, too, that Arnold must have been dishonest since Congress refused to settle his accounts. It is true that Congress *did* refuse, up to the very end, to reimburse him for the sums he so lavishly spent in the service of his country. If such a refusal is a mark of dishonesty, then every man of the many who have advanced money to America and looked to Congress for reimbursement has been dishonest; for never has Congress repaid a private loan during the lifetime of the man who made it, and never will it do so, since no votes are to be gained by paying debts of honor.

Now nothing, it seems to me, is so valuable to a nation as the truth. All of a nation's woes, and all the woes of those who dwell within that nation, have their rise in men's inability to recognize the truth, or their unwillingness to tell the truth—the truth as to why wars are fought, and how they are bungled and protracted, while those who fight them lose their lives and fortunes; the truth as to why taxes are levied, and how politicians misspend them; the truth as to the pettiness and ineptitude of those who, by flattery and misrepresentation, rise to high places. Only by being told the truth can man be saved from his own follies, and from repeating in the future the insanities that in the past have brought disaster.

That is why patriotic speeches by politicians set me all a-sweat; for I saw how frequently, even in the darkest days of our rebellion, politicians placed their own small interests ahead of the truth, ahead of the army, ahead of their country—just as they always have and just as I fear they always will. That is why my gorge rises when village wiseacres deliver profound judgments on men and measures of which they know next to nothing. And that is why I find it agonizing to hear some little antimire of a man, without knowledge of how battles were fought or how our country was governed, or how America tottered for a decade on the brink of destruction, talk mighty condescending and contemptuous about Arnold; mouthing that his treachery cannot be extenuated.

Knowing Arnold, and the sort of man he was, and the battles he planned, and his hold on the hearts of those who fought under him and beside him, I have this to say, and I say it gladly. Benedict Arnold was a great leader: a great general: a great mariner: the most brilliant soldier of the Revolution. He was the bravest man I have ever known. Patriotism burned in him like an unquenchable flame. But of all his brave and patriotic deeds, the one he was surest would, in the end, be most useful to this country, was, I truly believe, the tragic step that branded him forever with the name of traitor.

I have learned this about a man whose works command attention. Whatever he does follows a certain pattern; and there is an unmistakable similarity in all his acts. The artist so wields his brush that his canvas needs no signature. An author has a style that sets it apart from other writings. Given two statesmen, a man of judgment knows that each must act differently toward a given problem, and according to the established workings of his brain. A thief, in his robberies, displays a similarity that in the end betrays him. Even seamen have styles of sailing that distinguish one from another. Because of this I say that Arnold's act, which we call treason, was inspired by his patriotism.

Above all else, Arnold despised the traits that forever threatened to nullify the labors and sufferings of brave and patriotic men. Those traits were pettiness, timidity, inefficiency, futility and hesitation; and it was exactly those traits that were the principal assets of the American Congress in the days when we fought England. Eventually the inefficiency and the cowardice of Congress came to be a more dangerous enemy than England; and Arnold had cause to know it better than any of us.

That fumbling, muddle-headed Congress was our only government. There was no President to assist it: no Senate to control it: no Supreme Court to guard and direct it: no Cabinet to inform it. It grew daily weaker and more witless. Each year it was composed of men of smaller calibre—pettifogging lawyers from benighted homes: blatherskites in fustian, whispering knowingly in corners; exchanging fears that the army, in righteous rage, might turn and rend them for their shortcomings: dwarf-brained creatures, shallow, bigoted, opinionated, contrary, unreasonable, hidebound, time-serving: strong only in their unyielding ignorance: in their determined avoidance of intellectual integrity. They forced Schuyler from the army. They demanded the resignation of Knox and Sullivan and Greene for questioning Congress's appointment of a Frenchman, DuCoudray, over their heads. They would have banished Washington to Virginia if he had not eternally deferred to them with the endless patience of a saint. By their persistence in wasting bounties on the militia, they wrecked our finances. They were pigmies whose every act was contrary to common sense, to courage and to the welfare of the nation.

This wretched Congress had no power to tax—no control, in short, over the different states, which did as they pleased most of the time. Yet it exercised control over our army, and so it was our government, even though the states would not admit its authority. Since it could raise no money from the states, and since the currency which it printed had no value, it was obliged to turn somewhere for money, and so it turned to France; and by so doing it put a sort of desperation into the hearts of those of us who knew France and the French.

Congress was insane on the subject of the French. Any French officer who came to Congress, demanding a commission, received it at once, no matter how little his ability and experience. The follies of that nature perpetrated by this unspeakable Congress of ours were beyond belief. It would have made DuCoudray a major general in command of our artillery, except for the protests of Greene and Sullivan and Knox. In

July of 1777 it gave to the nineteen-year-old Lafayette a major general's commission, for no reason on God's earth save that he was a wealthy, amiable boy of influential family. At the same moment it still withheld from Arnold the major general's rank his brilliant efforts had so amply earned.

I say this, not to detract from Lafayette or from the many brave Frenchmen who eventually fought for us, but to show why those of us in the Continental Army were filled with a hatred of this vacillating, blundering, wrong-minded Congress—a hatred that grew and grew with each passing month, until it turned into something worse than hatred. We knew at last that in spite of all our strivings and sacrifices to be free, those muddle-headed men, by piling blunder on blunder, were forcing us closer and closer to chaos and to the eager arms of France—closer and closer to the grip of a nation whose rule would be more tyrannical and infinitely more oppressive than that of England.

Our desperation and distrust were shown to be justified at the end of the war, when public and private credit collapsed because of the lack of confidence in Congress. Parts of the army mutinied. The states, yielding to the temptation to issue paper money, became bankrupt. The farmers of western Massachusetts revolted. Tennessee was in insurrection against North Carolina. Vermont, led by that blustering demagogue Ethan Allen, dickered with the Governor of Canada, preparatory to becoming a separate principality under England. Every state, hating its neighbor, was on the verge of raising tariff walls against every other state; and at last Congress, headless, spineless, impotent, utterly baffled and at sea, collapsed.

The French minister reported to the watchful French Government that there was now, in America, no general government—neither Congress, nor President, nor head of any one administrative department. So far as could be seen, the Union of States was dissolved, and our eight years of war had gone for nothing. We were defeated—not by England, but by Congress.

It was by a series of accidents that our stubborn, feeble states, three years later, agreed to a convention for the framing of a constitution that might again bind them together. By the grace of God the delegates, after months of squabbling, miraculously compromised on the form of government advocated by the Connecticut delegates; and by that compromise was created a Senate not elected, as was Congress, by the votes of the people—a Senate that therefore might, God willing, act forever as a brake on the dreadful and criminal follies always perpetrated by legislators whose positions depend on the votes of the masses. Twelve years after we had saved America from the British at Valcour Island, our new constitution took effect, and the states were again united. We elected General Washington President; the Supreme Court, the Senate and the House of Representatives came into existence; we had a government at last.

The danger of being wrecked by an uncontrolled Congress had been foreseen by many men—by Washington, by Franklin, by Arnold, by Silas Deane and scores of other Americans, as well as by Englishmen and Frenchmen. Repeatedly we had been on the verge of military destruction; and that, too, had been admitted by Washington and Deane and Franklin and others. But where so many leaders anticipated defeat and chaos, and the ultimate tyranny of the French, yet felt themselves unable to avert that end, Arnold, on becoming convinced of it, laid plans to avert it, that being his nature.

He had been the first to insist upon the value of Ticonderoga, Crown Point and St. John's in 1775, and to plan their capture. He was the first to foresee the possibility of taking Quebec, and it was by his planning that the heroic march was made. It was he who foresaw the need of a fleet to stop the British; and he who planned the fleet and the battle that it fought. It was he who comprehended the need of a stronger American navy and the way in which it might be obtained, though his proposals were ignored. It was he who planned the sudden march that turned St. Leger back to Canada: he who with Kosciusko chose the battleground on which to make a stand against Burgoyne; he whose leadership dealt the blows that wrecked the schemes of England. Every military move he made was planned with masterly skill.

Knowing all this, I say it was impossible for Arnold, the brilliant soldier, the planner of campaigns, to formulate a sudden angry plan that might have boiled from the addled brain of any spleeny child or shrewish woman—a plan inspired, as the ignorant believe, only by revenge, and with no object save to betray. If he sought to give everything to England until we had regained our strength, it was done to fight a greater threat than England.

Scores of officers who fought with him and thousands who fought under him know in their hearts that Benedict Arnold was a rare and solitary genius—one who, foreseeing the inevitable that was miraculously averted, had the courage to attempt what no other man dared. Other leaders said, "We're beaten: let it be so; let Congress wreck us: let all our states dissolve in Civil War; let France come in to snatch us up again." Arnold said, "No! This imbecile, coward Congress can *not* destroy the freedom *we* have fought to gain!"

I know, when I lie in my cabin with the screaking of the rudder and the gurgle of water in my ears to keep my mind on an even keel, that man's understanding being what it is, Arnold is forever doomed to be cursed by the mass of those who still benefit from his bravery and fore-sight. Fortunately, since neither France nor England rules over us, it is a free country, and I am free to speak my mind. Those who wish may curse Arnold; but I shall never do it. I'll curse the Congress that so nearly wrecked us: the human shrimps like Gates and Wilkinson, Easton and Brown, Hazen and Bedel, whose vision moved perpetually in a fog: the militiamen who ran off home and left us to fight at Saratoga. I'll curse the quarter million men of military age who skulked behind while a pitiful twenty thousand of us anguished and sickened, starved and froze and fought. I'll curse the merchants who trafficked and dick-ered and grew rich out of our wartime needs; but never, though I myself be damned for not doing it, will I curse Benedict Arnold.

There: that's my say for him. I owe him much, and so, I believe, does this country; but there's an ancient saying that republics are ungrateful —meaning, I suppose, that all nations, whatever their government, are ungrateful; and that is but a step from saying that they may be vindic-tive. School children, for generations, will be taught to abhor the name of Benedict Arnold, nor will that be changed by any words that I can write here, or by anything that anyone anywhere can do. His mistake was tragic—most tragic of all in that it blackens his memory and makes his name the very name of dishonor. But I am an individual, and not privileged, as a country is, to be ungrateful. I followed him in war, loved him, and saw his figure as the leaping bright sword of America—ah, when America's swords were few! I cannot think of him without remem-bering how Ellen and Nathaniel and I stood clinging together on the hospital veranda outside his room that day when we had read the paper that gave my brother back to life and honor once more.

Then, still clinging together, we went back slowly to where the cart waited for us. I had heard Benedict Arnold's voice for the last time.

LXIX

The Arundel Company of Colonel Brewer's Twelfth Massachusetts regiment went home by way of Bennington, Portsmouth, York and Wells, and we went with them, Ellen sitting by Nathaniel in a tumble-down chaise, gray with age, while I plodded along beside them to give our ancient mare the necessary attention when she showed signs of stopping, which she did too often to suit a man who is eager for his home.

When we set off through the Berkshires, the main road on which we traveled was populous with homeward-bound militia, drinking and brawling in the neighborhood of taverns, hurroaring and hurrooing around fires at night, beating on drums and tootling on fifes, as martial and swaggering as though they longed for a chance to meet all the armies of Europe in mortal combat. Then they began to drift away in twos and threes. They slipped off down side roads, bawling farewells to those who still went onward. We saw them moving around to the back doors of farm houses, where friendly dogs fawned on them and barked ecstatically, and children ran adoringly beside them. They drifted away and drifted away, and we went on and on to the eastward, over roads on which there were fewer and fewer to keep us company. Only Brewer's regiment, then, was left; and that thinned out and thinned out, until the Kittery company turned off up the Piscataqua, and we went on alone—on down the road that skirts the long marshes and the tumbled sand dunes to the westward of Arundel.

Luke Hitchcock, the captain, came back to me when we had our first glimpse of the breakers that lie like lace along the far-off inlet of Wells River. "We'll take 'em in together, Cap'n Peter," he said. "It's been a long time since you been home. Come on up and march alongside me."

"No," I said. "No. You take 'em in alone. I'll stay back here with Nathaniel."

Hitchcock halted his straggling, talkative soldiers on the windswept plains that guard the Upper Village, and sent his lieutenant, young Joshua Nason, to bring up the provision carts so the men might be rid of their encumbrances—the unsightly camp kettles that clinked and bumped on their hips, the three wives that trudged in the ranks, the tame bear cub that rocked and snuffled by the side of young Nathaniel Davis, who was only fifteen years old, but had killed his first Britisher at Bunker Hill and been in the army ever since. The bear sat heavily on his worn pincushion of a tail, moving his upper lip nervously at the thought of leaving his master.

"He ain't no harm, Cap'n," young Davis protested. "He minds real well."

"Leave him have his b'ar, Luke," Thomas Dorman said. "We ought to have *somep'n* to show we been at Bemis's Heights."

"If you're going to keep that b'ar, Davis," Captain Hitchcock said severely, "go on back in the rear rank where he won't be underfoot. It ain't fitten, now we're getting close to home, for soldiers to be put all out of step on account of having to stop and kick a b'ar. We're heroes of Saratoga, and we got to try to look it."

The men snorted. A few tittered dryly. I noticed, however, that all of them pawed at their accouterments, straightening them: set their hats at a better angle: pulled up their stockings. A sergeant emerged from a clump of trees with a bundle of spruce tips. He went from man to man, thrusting a sprig of spruce into the barrel of each musket. It was an old trick to make the men hold up their muskets, so the sprigs wouldn't fall out. Captain Hitchcock walked the length of the company, scrutinizing their nondescript, mud-splashed garments with a tolerant eye.

They made a good appearance. They were lean and hard. Their hair was clubbed and tied. Their muskets were spotless. A bayonet scabbard hung at every hip. Their cartridge boxes had a comfortable, swollen look. Across their chests were the crossed belts of Continental troops. It's true they wore homespun coats of various shades; and the breeches of some were leather and others cloth; but across every right shoulder was a brown blanket, every blanket rolled and slung as correct and shipshape as it could be slung by the best trooper in the world.

Some just stood there, staring across the brown marshes to the long, irregular sand dunes rising like toy mountains against the cold, gray ribbon of November ocean. Their eyes were remote, as if they brooded on a far-off battle; but they were, I knew, watching with a speculative eye the flights of ducks drifting across the marsh in long black streamers. The ducks were flying low, stirred by the rising southwest wind. Every man in the company, I suspected, would be up at dawn the next day to shoot himself a mess.

Hitchcock formed them in a column of twos while the drummer braced his drum and the fifer slatted moisture from his fife. The drum rattled and thumped: the fife shrilled into the rollicking strains I had last heard beside the Hudson on that still morning when Burgoyne's regiments laid down their arms:

What happy golden days were those
When I was in my prime!
The lasses took delight in me,
I was so neat and fine;
I roved about frcm fair to fair,
Likewise from town to town,
Until I married me a wife
And the world turned upside down.

Remembering where and under what circumstances Nathaniel and I had listened to that tune, I tried to look unconscious of it, but I might have spared myself the trouble.

"Listen to that, Peter!" Nathaniel said. "That's what they played at Ranelagh the night we nearly saw the King!" I glanced at him apprehensively, but he laughed and added, "Another world, Peter: another planet: another era—almost another language!"

Nathaniel, I saw, with a choked feeling of thankfulness, was himself again.

The men picked up the tune delightedly, whistling it, and went swinging off, all the muskets canted at the same slant; left arms moving machine-like, out and in, at a sharp angle to their bodies, so to keep from interfering with their cartridge boxes. They were worth looking at; and I, watching them, found it hard to believe they were the same wild-eyed maniacs who had stormed up the hill and into the abatis behind Arnold, to help us turn the British right flank at Bemis's Heights.

I felt Ellen's eyes upon me. "We're almost home," I told her, and I fear my voice wasn't as calm as it should have been. She smiled and shook her head, as if she realized it was hard to speak naturally when you're almost home.

When the road turned down the hill to the bridge across the river, we saw we had caught the townsfolk unaware, for there was no one in sight when we came round the bend: no one but Sammy Hill, the village idiot. He, despite his idiocy, possessed some strange power that enabled him to be always at the spot where anything occurred, and at the precise moment of its occurrence. Sammy had been dumb from birth, able to make only inarticulate sounds, but when he saw us, he opened his mouth wide, and from it came a hoarse and jubilant shout. The fife and drum struck up again; and when we crossed the bridge, heads appeared in doorways, stared wild-eyed, and precipitately vanished, doubtless to summon others.

Boys ran and dogs barked. Then, in a moment's time, the street was full of people.

To my surprise, when we came up to them and they opened to let us through, I saw that many were crying—a sight not often seen in our Province of Maine, where folk content themselves with looking bleak when deeply moved. They hurried along beside us, boys leaping and shouting; the dogs in a frenzy of apprehension and anger at young Nathaniel Davis's bear; the men eyeing us a little blankly, while tears of which they seemed unconscious trickled ludicrously down their cheeks and into their mouths; the women, young and old, stumbling and weeping and laughing, as if the sight of us had freed them of a dreadful dark oppression.

I was glad to hear Captain Hitchcock refusing their offers of hospitality. "Can't stop," he said a thousand times. "Can't stop. We got to get home." The men, bent on making a good appearance, kept their eyes to the front; and the drum, echoing beneath the elms that arched above us, took on a resonance that seemed to draw us on more rapidly, as narrowing banks speed on an idling stream.

We left the village and came out into the meadows that lie above the river. There is a peculiar sweetness to this section of the world—some singular quality to the atmosphere, like that which gives the leaves their added brilliance in the autumn. The very grass has a perfume of its own, and the land is redolent of sea and pines; of strength and freshness.

"We're almost there," I told Ellen. "Look—around the bend—the red one! The red house! There's someone at the gate!" I coughed, to show my coolness.

The drum made a triple flourish and the fife squealed *Yankee Doodle*, over and over. There were people shouting from the gateways and the paths—people who had known us from the days when we robbed cherry trees and ran yelling home from school. I would have liked to look at them and smile, but dared not, and so looked straight ahead.

The horse, of its own accord, stopped at our front gate, and I heard my mother's voice. "Nathaniel!" she cried. "Father! It's Nathaniel! It's Nathaniel and Peter!"

I lifted Ellen from the chaise and set her before my mother and the girls. My mother fumbled uncertainly with the white collar of her dress; then spoke quickly to Jane and Susanah. "Don't stand there staring! The yellow room! She'll have the yellow room!"

She touched Ellen's brown curls, a poignant reminder of how I had longed to touch them, just so, when first I had seen her, two long years before. Ellen's arms went around my mother's shoulders, and I turned away, with dimmed eyes and a brimming heart, to watch Hitchcock's company swinging down the straight road that leads to the sea. Some of the men looked back and waved. They were a fine lot. Rabble, the English had called them. The spruce tips in the musket barrels were as straight and even as the top of a spruce wind-break. The fife and the drum seemed to repeat the word "Rabble" with derisive chuckles.

My father came to stand silently beside me. Neither of us, evidently, felt the need of words.

The southwest wind brought us the soft aroma of the pines, the dry odor of dead leaves, the scent of the marsh and of the gray mud, washed by the tides. It seemed to me the most beautiful country in the world—more beautiful, in spite of the November chill and the dull autumn twilight, than the mountains of Spain or the parks of England—than the broad rivers, the prairies, the lakes, the towering cliffs of the west. There was something about it that caught at my throat—that filled me with a sense of exultation: of freedom. It was my country. In it there was something mysterious and unseen that could never be taken from me. Others might call it theirs: might drive me from it: might burn down the house: might fell the gnarled apple tree beside the kitchen door; but the river would be there still, winding in S's through the marsh. The sea and the pines and the rounded ledges would be there always, waiting. There would always be ducks, contentedly peering beneath the banks for the strange things ducks eat: always a green heron to flop from the marsh in a frenzy of fear: always the fragrance of mallow and lilacs in the spring, the sweet breath of the sea, the web of song from the bobolinks and robins. Whatever happened, it would be my country still.

In the travail and the turmoil, in the sweat and the pain and the blood that lay behind me—that probably lay before me—a nation was being born. Those crowded ranks in the dead pits of Isle aux Noix had labored and died to form that nation. They had been a part of it. In the dark waters beneath the cliffs of Valcour lay others who had been a part of it. Those whose gnawed bones were scattered in the thickets of Freeman's Farm had been a part of it. We, living, were part of it. Millions yet to be born were part of it; and other millions that would come from foreign lands would be part of it. Whatever we did with it, or made of it, one thing was certain: the suffering and the labor had been ours, and so must the fulfillment be ours.